"I SPEAK OF A WO
EARTH. . . ."

"Another world?" D

"Yes," the stranger

"But you are human, surely."

"You fear I am an alien?" he asked.

"Yes," she whispered.

"In one sense it is true, I am an alien. I have come from a different planet. But my ancestors came from Earth. Have no fear. I am every bit as human as you are. And that is why I am so dangerous to you—because I understand you. . . ."

"And this world of which you speak. Is it—"

"Yes?" he said.

"Is it a world where women such as I," Doreen asked, "are bought and sold as slaves?"

"Yes."

"What are you going to do with me?" she asked, hardly able to speak for the sudden fear that gripped her.

"Can you not guess?"

DANCER OF GOR

JOHN NORMAN
Books available from DAW;

The GOR Series:

HUNTERS OF GOR
MARAUDERS OF GOR
TRIBESMEN OF GOR
SLAVE GIRL OF GOR
BEASTS OF GOR
EXPLORERS OF GOR
FIGHTING SLAVE OF GOR
ROGUE OF GOR
GUARDSMAN OF GOR
SAVAGES OF GOR
BLOOD BROTHERS OF GOR
KAJIRA OF GOR
PLAYERS OF GOR
MERCENARIES OF GOR
DANCER OF GOR
RENEGADES OF GOR (available March 1986)

Other Titles:

TIME SLAVE
IMAGINATIVE SEX
GHOST DANCE

DANCER of GOR

John Norman

DAW BOOKS, INC.
DONALD A. WOLLHEIM, PUBLISHER

1633 Broadway, New York, NY 10019

Cover art by Ken W. Kelly.

DAW Collectors Book No. 651

First Printing, November 1985

1 2 3 4 5 6 7 8 9

PRINTED IN THE U. S. A.

Contents

1 / A Bit of Silk

I knew that I did not conform to the cultural stereotypes prescribed to me. I had known this for a long time. The dark secrets which lay hidden within me I had been forced to conceal for several years. I do not know from whence the secrets arose. They were directly contrary to everything that had been taught to me. Their origins, it seemed, were deep within me, and, I feared, as I lay awake at night afraid, sweating and distraught, native to my very nature. But such a nature, I wept, could not be, and if it were, so subtle, so insistent, so persistent, so unrelenting, so tenacious, it must never be admitted, never, never! Yes, I fought them, these secrets, these covert knowledges, these anticipations, these dreams. Yes I struggled, in accord with the demands of my culture, my training and education, these things telling me how I must be, how I must be as I was told to be, to drive them from me. I repudiated them, again and again, but to no avail. They returned, ever again, mercilessly, horrifying me, taunting and mocking me, stripping me in the darkness of my bed of my pretences and lies. I squirmed and thrashed in my bed, twisting and weeping, pounding it with my fists, crying out, "No! No!" Then I would put my head fearfully on my pillow, dampened with meaningless, rebellious tears. Could I be so weak and terrible? Could I be truly so different from others? Surely there could be no one in the world so degraded, so shameful and terrible as myself. Then one night I rose from bed and went to the vanity and lit the small candle there. I had bought this candle weeks before, probably because deep within me, within my deepest self, in my anguished mind, in my tortured breast and heart, I knew this night would come. I lit the small candle. I stood there in the flickering light, for some minutes, looking at myself. I wore a white nightgown, anklelength. I have dark hair and eyes. At that time my hair was cut at shoulder length. Then, not looking back to the mirror, I crept in the candlelight and shadows to the dresser and there, from beneath several layers of garments, where I had concealed it, I drew forth a small bit of scarlet cloth, tiny and silken, with shoulder straps, a garment I had myself sewn weeks ago, one in which, save for fittings, often done by feel, with my eyes closed, I never even dared to look upon myself. This, in a sense, was the third such garment I had attempted. The material for the first, not yet even touched by needle and thread, or scissors, I had suddenly discarded in terror, months ago. I had actually begun work on the second garment, some two months ago, but, in touching it to my body, for it was the sort of garment which touches the body directly, with no intervening investiture, I had suddenly, comprehending its meaning and nature, begun to shake with terror and, scarcely knowing what I was doing, I feverishly cut and tore it to pieces, and threw it away! But even as I had destroyed it I knew, weeping and distraught, terrified, I would make another. I took the third garment from the drawer. Suddenly I thrust it back in the drawer, again under the other garments, thrusting shut the drawer. Then, after a moment, breathing heavily, trembling, I opened the drawer again, and removed it, once more, from its place. I went back to the vanity not looking in the mirror. I dropped the bit of scarlet silk near my feet on the rug. I was trembling. It seemed I could scarcely get my breath. I lifted my eyes then again to the figure in the mirror. She was not large, but I thought she might be pretty. But it is hard to be objective about such things. I supposed there could be criteria, of one sort or another, in some place or another, of a somewhat ascertainable, quantitative sort, perhaps what men might be willing to pay for you, but even then they would probably be paying for a spectrum of desirabilities, of which prettiness, *per se,* might be only one, and perhaps not even the most important. I did not know. I suppose even more important would be what a woman looked like to a given man and what he thought he could do with her, or, seeing her, knew he could do with her. I looked at the figure in the mirror. Her nightgown, anklelength, was of white cotton. It seemed rather demure, or timid, I supposed, but there was little doubt that there was a female, and perhaps a rather attractive one, though, to be sure, that would be a judgment for men to more properly make, within it. There were the stains of tears on the cheeks of the girl facing me in the mirror, I noted. She trembled. Her lips moved. Why was she afraid? At what she saw in the mirror? It was herself, surely. Why should she fear that? I saw she wore a nightgown. I liked that. I did not like pajamas. To be sure, she was perhaps too feminine for a woman in these times, but then there are such women, in spite of all. They are real, and their needs are real. I looked at her. Yes, I thought, she was objectively pretty. There was no doubt about it. To be sure, she might not seem so to a crocodile or a tree but she should seem such to a male of her species, and that was what counted. Yes, that was what counted, objectively. To be sure, he would doubtless wish to see if the rest of her matched her face. Men were like that. They were like traders of horses and breeders of dogs, interested in the whole female. I again regarded the girl in the mirror. Yes, I thought, she was too feminine, at least for these times. This was not the sort of woman wanted in our times. She was like something beautiful stranded on a foreign beach. Surely she belonged in another time or place. She seemed in her hormones and beauty, in her needs, like a stranger flung out of time. There she stood in a world alien to her deepest nature, not a man, and not wanting to be one, a victim of time and heredity, of her genetic depths, of biology and history. How lonely and unbefriended, how frustrated, unfulfilled and doleful she was. How tragic is she indeed, I thought, whom the lies of one's time fail to nourish. I looked again at the girl in the mirror. Surely she might better have cooked meat in the light of a cave fire, the thongs on her left wrist perhaps marking whose woman she was, or with sistrum and hymns, under the orders of priests, welcomed the grand, redemptive, sluggish flows of the Nile; better she had run barefoot on a lonely Aegean beach, her himation gathered to her knees, a fillet of white wool in her hair, watching for oared ships; better she had spun wool in Crete or cast nets, her robes tied to her waist, off the coast of Asia Minor; better she had broken her dolls and put them in the temple of Vesta; better she had been a silken girl breathless behind the wooden screens of the seraglio or a ragged slut on her knees desperately licking and kissing for coins in the sunlit, dusty streets below; better she had been bartered for a thousand horses in Scythia or led to Jerusalem tied by the hair to a Crusader's stirrup; better to have been a high-born Spanish lady forced to beg to be the bride of a pirate; better to have been an Irish prostitute, her face slashed by Puritans for following the troops of Charles; better to have been a delicate lady of the Regency carried into Turkish slavery; better to have been a Colonial dame spinning in Ohio, looking up to see her first red master. I put down my head, and shook it. Such thoughts must be put from my mind, I told myself. But the girl stood there, still stood there, in the mirror. She had not left, or fled. How bold she was, or how deep were her needs! I shuddered. How many times I had awakened from sleep, moving against the coarse. narrow cords which had held me down, above and below my breasts and crossed between them, leaving their cruel marks on my body! How many times had I awakened, seeming still to feel the tight bite of cruel shackles on my wrists and ankles. How many times had I, bound at their mercy, looked up at them? How many times had I recoiled from the blows of their whips, only to crawl then to their feet, piteous and contrite, begging to please them? I was a female. Not looking in the mirror I drew off the nightgown and held it clenched in my hand. I then crouched down and put it gently on the rug, beside the bit of silk. I hesitated. Then I picked up the bit of silk and, standing, not looking in the mirror, I drew it on. It was on me! I closed my eyes. I felt on my skin its silken presence, almost nothing, little more than a whisper or a mockery. I drew it at the hem down more against my body, perhaps defensively, that I might feel it on me the more, that I might assure myself, I told myself, the more of its presence, that I was truly garmented, but this, too, of course, merely confirmed upon me not uncertainly the insidious disturbing subtlety of its slightness, the so undeniable, so insistent, scandalous feel of it, its shameful, mocking silken caress, and, too, as I drew it down, it clung more closely about me; it seemed that it would then, almost as though scornfully, imperiously, in amusement, given its nature, respond to my efforts at modesty only by producing a further and yet greater revelation and betrayal of my beauty. I stood there, the garment on. I turned then to the mirror, and opened my eyes. Suddenly I gasped and was giddy. For a moment it seemed blackness swam about me, and I fought for breath. My knees almost buckled. I struggled to retain consciousness. I looked in the mirror. Never had I seen myself thusly. I was terrified. In the mirror there was a different woman than the world knew of me, one they had never seen, one they had never suspected. What was that thing she wore? What sort of garment could that be, so delicious and brief, so excruciatingly and uncompromisingly feminine? Surely no real woman, hostile, unloving, demanding, shrill and frustrated, zealous in her conformance to stereotypes, attempting desperately to find satisfaction in such things, would wear such a garment. It was too female, too feminine. How could she be identical to a male in such a garment? It would show her simply that she was not. How could she keep her dignity and respect in such a garment? She could not. It would show that she was beautifully, and utterly and profoundly different from a man. It was the sort of garment a man might throw to a woman to wear, amused to see her in it. What sort of woman, of her own free will, would put on such a garment? Surely no real woman. It was too feminine. Surely only a terrible woman, a low woman, a shameful, wicked, worthless woman, a reproach to her entire sex, one with depths and needs antedating her century, one with needs not indexed to political orthodoxies, one with needs older and deeper, and more real and profound, more ancient and marvelous than those dictated to her by intellectual aberrations antithetical to biology, truth, history and time. I put my hand before my mouth, frightened. I stood there, regarding myself, then, shamed, and humbled and thrilled. I knew then it was I in the mirror, and none other. Perhaps what I saw was not a real woman in some invented, artificial, contemptible, grotesque modern sense, but I thought she was a woman nonetheless and one in some even more profound sense, so small, so soft and curved, and desiring, and vulnerable, and helpless and needful, a sense not indexed to criteria of economics and politics, not to the demands of platforms and parties, not to the likings of frustrates and freaks, but to something more profound, something deeper, to ancient, precious, biological womanhood, and its fundamental nature. If what faced me in the mirror was not a real woman in some contemporary, transient, idiosyncratic political sense, it was at least something biologically far deeper, and a thousand times more real, a true woman. And standing there I was suddenly very frightened, for I realized suddenly, the thought never before having struck me in just the same way, and with the same suddenly significant force, that that there were two sexes, and that they were quite different. I regarded myself in the mirror, and trembled, wondering what this might mean, fully. I feared to consider the matter. What did it mean, that we were not the same as men, that we were so different? Was this really totally meaningless, a unique accident in the history of a world, a random paragraph written in the oceans, in the records of steaming swamps, in the journals of primeval forests, in the annals of the grasslands and deserts, of vacillating glaciers and damp, flowering valleys, of the basins of broad rivers and of the treks of nomads, wagons and armies, or were there biological proprieties, destinies and natures to be fulfilled? I did not know. But I knew how I felt. I lowered my hand and turned, slowly, before the mirror. I considered myself, and was, truly, not displeased. I was not a man, and did not want to be one. I was a female. I choked back a sob. I wondered what it might mean, that men, until we had managed to turn them against themselves, until we had managed to tie and cripple them, were so much stronger, so much more powerful, than we. There was no nether closure, by intent, in the tiny garment I had fashioned. It was open at the bottom. This had seemed to me necessary, somehow, when I had made it. That had seemed to me interesting at the time, but I thought that now I might more fully understand its meaning. It was the garment, particularly in its brevity, of a woman who, whether she willed it or not, was to be kept open to the touch of a man. It was, in its way, a convenience for the male, indeed, even an invitation to his predation; too, similarly, it was, to her, to the so-dressed female, a mnemonic device, and a symbol of her vulnerability, and nature, reminding her of what she was, and her meaning. I wondered if anywhere there might be true men, men capable of answering the scream of need in a woman, capable of taking us in hand and treating us, and handling us, as what we were, females. Alas, I did not think so. Before the mirror I sobbed. Then I thought that somewhere, surely, there must be such men. But where? Surely, somewhere in nature, there must be such men! Surely somewhere in nature there must be an explanation for my needs. I had not invented them. I was their captive! Surely somewhere in nature there must be an accounting for them, as there was an accounting for the dances of bees and the fragrance of flowers, for the fleetness of the antelope and the teeth of the tiger, for the migrations of fish and birds, for the swarming of insects, for the turning of turtles to the sea. Somehow there must be a reason for the way I felt, something beyond all the denials, denunciations and rationalizations. Such needs bespoke something deep within me, but I dared not consider what it might be. I was lonely and miserable! I wondered if somewhere in nature there might lie not only an explanation for these needs, so seemingly mysterious and inexplicable, given my environment, my education, my training, my conditioning, so different from them, but also some dark complement to them, some response to them, or answer to them. Did they not belong in some organic whole, in some natural relationship, selected for throughout time and history? The bee's dances betokened the direction and distance of nectar; the fragrance of the flower, seemingly such a meaningless thing of beauty, called forth, luring the bee to its pollen; the swiftness of the antelope paid tribute to the ferocity and agility of the carnivore, the fangs of the carnivore to the elusiveness of his quarry; at the ends of migrations lay the spawning waters and nesting grounds of species; swarmings brought sexes into proximity; and meaning was given to the trek of the turtle, as it led at last to the sea. I considered what might be the answer, the response, in nature, to the needs I felt, if there was one, what might be the nature of the startling organic whole, if it existed, the natural relationship, if there should be such, in which they figured. I wondered what might possibly be the complement in nature to these overwhelming, undeniable, persistent things within me, which had so distressed and troubled me, which now so obsessed me, which caused me such anguish, these irresistible calls and cries within me, the agonizing needs I felt, and I shuddered. I looked in the mirror. How brazen she was to see herself in such a garment! I wondered how she might look, so clad, or perhaps in less, to a man. Suddenly she seemed small, and beautiful, and so vulnerable, and inutterably desirable. I sensed then what might be the nature of the complement in nature to my needs, what might be their flower, their sea, their carnivore, and I stood there terrified, sensing the imperiousness of that complement, its power, its uncompromising ferocity, what it might be to be its object, and knowing that if it existed it would have its way and be absolutely served.

How pleased I was, then, that surely no such complement could exist, that I was safe. I had nothing to fear.

I continued to look at the girl in the mirror. She was exquisite, I thought. She is beautiful, I thought, standing there in the brief silk, in the candlelight, so softly revealed. I had not realized she was so beautiful. I had never seen her before, it seemed, thusly. I had not guessed how marvelous she might be. Yes, it is fortunate that men such as those in my dreams do not exist, I thought, for what then, beauty, would be your fate at their hands? I considered what I might look like, with a chain on my neck. Such men, I thought, would take few chances of losing you, Doreen. Doubtless you would be kept in superb custody, if even the least sort of escape were remotely conceivable. I wonder if you would learn quickly to serve them well, according to their tiniest caprices. Yes, I thought, I would learn quickly and well. It would not be pleasant to feel their whips. I wept then, again, wondering if perhaps I had not been born elsewhere, perhaps time and time again, in other times, if I had not lived in Egypt or Sumer, or Chaldea, in rocky Hellas, or verdant Sybaris or bustling Miletus, if I had not been kept in the great palace in Persepolis, if I might not have seen Alexander, kneeling to him as a Persian slave, if I might not, a barbarian girl, have entered Rome in chains, herded before the chariot of a general, gracing with others his triumph, if I might not, as a Moslem girl, have served Crusaders in some remote fortress, or, as a Christian slave, found myself shamelessly exhibited and sold in an Arab market, thence to be taught to dance for masters.

Then I put such thoughts from my head. I did not think the

explanation for my needs, the mysterious things within me, which were so different from what I had been taught, could be so complex, or simple, as racial memories, or the memories of individuals whom I might have been in other places and times. They were rather, I suspected, though I could not know, a simple heritage of my sex, but there was this to be said, had I lived in another place or time I might perhaps have found female fulfillments which, categorically, it seemed, were to be denied to me in my present world, the neuteristic, anonymous world, so inimical to individuality and love, in which I found myself a prisoner of time and circumstance.

I looked into the mirror, and smiled. To be sure, I thought, perhaps you were once an Irish girl tied between the benches of a Viking ship, bound for Iceland, or a pale, prim English lady carried to Barbary, in 1802, who will be taught to feel, and serve dark masters in helpless ecstasy, but perhaps, too, you were not. That was she, and not really you. But who are you? Is there a ship somewhere that will come for you? Are the chains forged that will bind your limbs? Is there an iron, somewhere, waiting to be heated, which will mark your body? Is there a collar, somewhere, unknown to you, that you will someday know well, because it has been locked on your neck? I wonder. You are beautiful. I do not think men would be patient with you. They would want superb service, with no hesitation or compromise. You are that beautiful. Be pleased that men do not exist such as in your dreams, Doreen, for in their power, and in their arms, you would be raped, humiliated and unspeakably degraded. You do not know, responding helplessly to them, what they might make you, what you might become. You would be owned, like a pig or dog. What you might become, I laughed, scornfully. What you might become? How pretentious you are! Do you think I do not know you, who you are, and what you are? Perhaps what you are is hidden from all the world, but it is not hidden from me! I know you, and what you are! Speak honestly or be beaten! What you might become, indeed! What you might become, I retorted, you already know in your heart, and know it fully well, you petty, lovely hypocrite, you already are!

The girl in the mirror looked startled, and then pouting, and angry.

"Is it not true?" I challenged her.

"Yes!" she sobbed. "It is true!"

"Are you not rather burdensomely garbed?" I asked.

She drew off the tiny bit of silk. I watched her in the mirror.

"You may dance," I told her.

She looked at me, defiantly.

"You want to dance," I told her. "Dance."

I then, in the candlelight, on the rug, before the mirror, silently, to no music but what was in my own heart, danced. I danced my need, my anguish, my frustration, my misery, my loneliness.

"Now," I said, "dance, if you dare, as what you are!"

I then, startled, saw her, myself, in the mirror. "Who are you?" I asked. "Who taught you to move like that? Where did you come from? Can you be truly Doreen? You are not Doreen as I have seen her before. Are you I? Are we the same? Surely that cannot be I! No one showed you such a dance! Has there been such a dance lurking in you all this time? Can we be the same? Surely that cannot be! Surely I must stop! You are the Doreen I must conceal, the Doreen whom I must, whatever be the cost or anguish, never permit to be seen, or even suspected! You are the Doreen I must deny. You are the Doreen I must hide! Yet you are my true self. I know that! It is my true self then that I must deny, and hide!"

I watched her.

"You bitch!" I chided her. "You brazen bitch! You meaningless, brazen little bitch!"

I watched. How shameless, how meaningless, how terrible, how worthless she was, that girl in the mirror, that writhing, astounding, uncontrollably sensuous little bitch!

She continued to dance.

I saw that she was worthless indeed, worth less than the dirt beneath the feet of gods, but that, too, in her way, she possessed incredible riches and power, in her beauty and femaleness, and in her dance. In the sense in which a free person was priceless, she was worthless, but, too, in her way, I could see that she would have value, value as a pair of boots might have value or a dog. She was the sort of person who would have a finite, measurable value. She was the sort of woman on whom a fair price could be put.

I collapsed to the rug, naked. I felt its coarse nap on my thigh and side. I clutched my arms about myself. I drew my legs up. I was terrified. I wept. I could not understand what I had done, and seen. The girl in the mirror was now gone. We were now one. I trembled.

I lay there for better than an hour, I think, in the flickering shadows, naked, on the rug. I listened to the sounds from outside, mostly those of traffic. Eventually the tiny candle burned out.

After a time I rose to my knees. I knelt there on the rug with my head down. It was a submissive posture. I then raised my head, miserably. "My masters," I whispered to the darkness, "I am here! Where are you?"

I then rose to my feet and crept to my bed. I lay there for a time and then, later, fell asleep.

2 / The Dictionary

"The book is here," I said, "on the bottom shelf."

"Get it," he said.

Never again, of course, had I dared to don the tiny silken garment. I would have been too terrified to have done so. It brought out things too deep and marvelous, too shameful and terrible, too precious and beautiful in me. But it remained with my things, in the dresser. Nonetheless my life had changed, somehow, in perspective or understanding, if not greatly in overt deed or obvious fact, that night when I had seen myself as I was, or might be, in the mirror, when I had come to incontrovertibly learn my true nature, a nature which must be forever denied, thwarted and frustrated, a nature that had no place in my world.

"Yes?" I had asked, looking up from behind the reference desk. My heart had almost stopped beating. He was large, and supple. His hands and arms, long arms, seemed powerful. He was dressed in a dark business suit, with a tie. There seemed, however, something subtly awry with this vesture. He did not seem at ease somehow in this garment. There seemed something alien about him, something foreign. What startled me most about him at first, I think, was his eyes, and how they looked at me. I was not certain I could fathom such a look, but it had terrified me. It was almost, I had inexplicably felt, as though his eyes could see through my clothing. Perhaps, I thought, such a man has looked on many women, and would have little difficulty in conjecturing the general nature of my most intimate lineaments. In that instant I had felt, in effect, naked before him. And then he had lifted his head and was glancing about the room, as though he might understand my apprehension at being beneath a gaze such as his. "Yes?" I repeated, as pleasantly as I could, catching my breath. He looked back at me, swiftly, fiercely. He was not interested in my pretenses, my games. I quickly lowered my head, unable, somehow, to meet that gaze. It is difficult to explain this, but if you meet such a man, you will know it. Before such a man a female can suddenly feel herself nothing. Then I sensed him turning again to one side. Mercifully I knew he had freed me of his gaze. I lifted my eyes a little, but not so much as to risk, should he turn, encountering his.

"Have you *Harper's Dictionary of Classical Literature and Antiquities*?" he asked.

"Of course," I said, in relief. Suddenly our relationship became explicable, and modular. "Its number is in the card catalog," I said.

I sensed him looking at me.

"You can find the number for it in the card catalog," I told him.

He did not move toward the card catalog.

"Can you recognize it?" I asked.

He was silent. I sensed he might be becoming angry. Did he think I was going to wait on him?

"If you can recognize it," I said, "I can tell you where it is. It is down that aisle, and on the left, toward the end, on the bottom shelf."

"Show me," he said.

"I'm busy," I said.

"No, you are not," he said. To be sure, he was right. I was not really busy. Perhaps he had determined that before he had come to the desk. I had a distinct, uneasy sense, then, that he might be remembering, and keeping an account in some way, of my petty delays.

I rose from behind the desk. He stood back. I would precede him. That was appropriate, of course, as it was I who knew where the book was. To be sure, it made me uneasy to walk before him. No one, or hardly anyone, as far as I knew, incidentally, ever used that book or showed any interest in it. We learn of it, of course, in library science. It is a standard reference work in its area. I knew where it was, from shelf reading. Too, of course, I knew the general range of numbers within which it fell. Indeed, I had had to memorize such things for examinations. I preceded the fellow to the aisle, and down it. It seemed, somehow, now, that the shelves were close on both sides. The space between them seemed somehow narrower, and more wall-like, than usual. The library is well lit. I was very conscious of him behind me. I did not think he was a classics scholar. "Perhaps you want to look up something for a crossword puzzle," I said, lightly. Then I was afraid, again, doubtless foolishly, that he might be keeping an account of such things as my remark. Perhaps it had not pleased him. But what did it matter whether he was pleased or not?

"You are wearing a skirt," he said.

I stopped, frightened. I turned and looked at him, briefly. He was a quite large man anyway, but here, in this enclosed space, the shelves on each side, he seemed gigantic. I felt tiny before him. His bulk, somehow seemingly ungainly in that suit and tie, seemed to fill the space between the shelves. "Is the book here?" he asked. "No," I said. But I felt suddenly, and the thought frightened me, that he knew where the book was, that he knew very well where the book was. I then turned and continued down the aisle. In a moment I had reached its vicinity. I could see it there now, on the bottom shelf.

"It's there," I said, "on the bottom shelf, that large book. You can see the title."

"Are you a female intellectual?" he asked.

"No," I said, hastily.

"But you are a librarian," he said.

"I am only a simple librarian," I said.

"You have probably read a great deal," he said.

"I have read a little," I said, uncertainly, uneasily.

"Perhaps you are the sort of woman who has read more than she has lived," he said.

"The book is on the bottom shelf," I said.

"But soon perhaps," he said, "books will be behind you."

"It is down there," I said, "on the shelf, on the bottom."

"Are you a modern woman?" he asked.

"Of course," I said. I did not know what else to say. In one sense, of course, I supposed this was terribly false.

"Yes," he said, "I can see that it is true. You are tight, and prissy."

I made as though to leave, but his eyes held me where I was, immobile. It was almost as though I was held in place, standing there, before him, by a fixed collar, mounted on a horizontal rod, exending from a wall.

"Are you one of the modern women who are intent upon destroying men?" he asked.

I regarded him, startled.

"Are you guilty of such crimes?" he asked.

"I do not know what you are talking about," I said, frightened.

He smiled. "Are you familiar with the book on the bottom shelf?" he asked.

"Not really," I said. It was a standard reference source, but in a limited area. I had never used it.

"There are several such books," he said, "but it is surely one of the finest."

"I am sure it is a valuable, excellent reference work," I said.

"It tells of a world very different from that in which you live," he said, "a world very much simpler, and more basic, a world more fundamental, and less hypocritical, and far fresher and cleaner, in its way, and more alive and wild than yours."

"Than mine?" I said. His voice, now that he spoke at length, seemed to have some trace of an accent. But I could not begin to place it.

"It was a world in which men and women stood closer to the fires of life," he said. "It was a world of tides and gods, of spears and Caesars, of games, and wreathes of laurel, of the clash, detectable for miles, of phalanxes, of the marchings of legions, in measured stride, of the long roads and the fortified camps, of the coming and going of the oared ships, of the pourings of offerings, wine and salt, and oil, into the sea."

I said nothing.

"And in such a world women such as you were bought and sold as slaves," he said.

"That world is gone," I said.

"There is another, not unlike it, which exists," he said.

"That is absurd," I said.

"I have seen it," he said.

"The book is here," I said, "on the bottom shelf." I was trembling. I was terribly frightened.

"Get it," he said.

I lowered myself to my knees. I drew out the book. I looked up at him. I was on my knees before him.

"Open it," he said.

I did so. Within it was a sheet of folded paper.

I opened the sheet of folded paper. On it was writing.

"Read it," he said.

" 'I am a slave,' " I read. Then I looked up. He had left. I leaned over, on my knees, bending far over, clutching the paper. I was giddy and faint. Then I looked up once more after him. The aisle was empty. I wondered if he would come back for me. Then I felt suddenly frightened, and ill, and hurried to the ladies' room.

3 / The Library

I put the bells about my ankle.

It was dark now in the library, and it was past ten thirty. We had closed more than an hour ago.

The incident in the reference section, that in connection with *Harper's Dictionary of Classical Literature and Antiquities*, that in which I had been so frightened, had occurred more than three months ago. In that incident it seemed that I had found myself at the feet of a man. To be sure, it was merely that I was kneeling to draw forth a book. I was a librarian. I was only being helpful, surely. Too, it had seemed that I had, before him, aloud, confessed that I was a slave. But that was an absurd interpretation, surely, of what had occurred. I was only reading the paper I had found in the book. That was all. I had taken the paper home. The next day, after a troubled, restless night, and after hours of anxiety, misery and hesitation, I had suddenly, feverishly, burned it. Thus I had hoped to put it from me, but I knew the thing had happened, that the words had been said, and had had their meaning, that which they had had at the time, and not necessarily that which I might now fervently desire to ascribe to them, and to such a man. That the paper might be burned could not undo what was now transcribed in the reality of the world. The incident, as you might well imagine, had much disturbed me. For days it dominated my consciousness, obsessing me. Then, later, mercifully, when I gradually began to understand how foolish my fears were, I was able to return my attention to the important routines of my life, my duties in the library, my reading, my shopping, and so on. Once in a while, of course, the terrors and alarms of that incident, suddenly, unexpectedly, would rise up, flooding back upon me, but on the whole, I had, it seemed, forgotten about it. I rationally dismissed it, which was the healthy thing to do. The whole thing had been silly. Sometimes I wondered if it had even happened. I would recall sometimes the eyes of the man. The thing that had perhaps most impressed me about him, aside from his size, his seeming vigor and formidableness, was his eyes. They had not seemed like the eyes of the men I knew. In them there had seemed an incredible intelligence, a savagery, an uncompromising ferocity. In those eyes, in that fierce gaze, I had been unable to detect reservations, inhibitions, hesitancies or guilt. He seemed to be the sort of man, and the only one of this sort I had ever met, who would do much what he pleased, and take what he wanted. He seemed to carry with him the right of power and lions. I had no doubt that he was totally my superior. There had been, however, I think, one explicit consequence, or residue, of that incident. I think it served, somehow, in some way, to trigger a resolve on my part to do something which for me, if not for other women, required great courage. It brought me to my lessons. For months before, I had toyed with the idea, or the fancy, or fantasy, the idea first having emerged after I had seen myself in the mirror on that incredible night in my room, of taking lessons in dance. I had almost died on the phone, making inquiries about these things, and more than once, suddenly blushing crimson, or, from the feel of it, I suppose so, had hung up the phone without identifying myself. I was not interested, of course, in such forms of dance as ballet or tap. I was interested in a form of dancing which was more basic, more fundamental, more female. The form of dance I was interested in, of course, and this doubtless accounted for my timidity, my hesitation and fear, was ethnic dance, or, if you prefer, to speak perhaps more straightforwardly, "belly dancing." Happily it was always women who answered the phone. I do not think I could have dared to speak to a man of this sort of thing. Like most modern women I was concerned to conceal my sexual needs. To reveal them would have been just too excruciatingly embarrassing. What woman would dare to reveal to a man that she wants to move, would dare to move, before those of his sex in so beautiful and exciting a manner, in a way which proves that she is vital, and alive, and female, that she is astonishingly beautiful and inutterably desirable, in a way that will drive them mad with the wanting of her, in a way that shows them that she, too, has powerful sexual needs, and in her dance, as she presents and displays herself, striving to please them, that she wants them satisfied? Surely no virtuous woman. Surely only a despicable, sensuous slut, the helpless prisoner of her undignified and unworthy passions. In the end I called up the first woman, again, on whom I had, some days ago, hung up. "Have you done belly dancing before?" she asked. "Not really," I said. "You are a beginner?" she asked. "Yes," I said. I had not really thought much about it before, but it seemed there must then be various levels of this form of dance. I found that intriguing. "I understand it is good exercise," I said. "Yes," she said. "New classes begin Monday, in the afternoon and evening. Are you interested?" "Yes," I said. I had said, "Yes." That affirmation, I think, did me a great deal of good. I had publicly admitted my interest in this sort of thing. Somehow that made things seem much simpler, much easier. If I had lost status in this admission, it had now been lost, and it was now no longer to be worried about. But the woman did not seem surprised, or offended or scandalized. "What is your name?" she asked. I gave her my name. I was committed. I had taken these lessons now for almost three months, and in more than one course of instruction. I kept my new form of exercise, or my new hobby, if you like, secret from those at the library, and those I knew. It would not do at all for them to know that I was studying ethnic dance. Let them think of me merely as Doreen, their co-worker or friend, the quiet reference librarian. It was not necessary for them to know that sometimes, when we utilized costumes, other than our leotards and scarves, that that quiet Doreen, barefoot, in anklets and bracelets, with whirling necklaces, with her midriff bared, sometimes with her thighs stripped, swirled in fringed halter and shimmering skirt, with tantalizing veils, to barbaric music. I think I was the best in my classes. My teacher, she also with whom I had spoken on the phone, proved to be an incredibly lovely woman. She seemed incredibly pleased with my progress. Often she would give me extra instruction. I was her star pupil. Often, too, she would call to my attention offers or engagements, at parties and clubs, and such. It was natural that she would be contacted with regard to such matters. I always refused to go, of course. "But you would be beautiful, and marvelous," she would encourage me. "No," I would laugh. "No! No! I would be terrible!" One or another of the other girls, then, would be contacted, and they would go. Several, I thought, were wonderful. Women are so beautiful, thusly. Never would I, however, have had the courage to dance publicly. Too, suppose someone had seen me, *like that*. To be sure my dance, whatever might have been its motivations, conscious or subconscious, did have various lovely accompanying effects. I found myself slimmer and trimmer than before, and more vital than before. Too, I think the dance served some purpose within me, though I am not sure what it was. Perhaps it helped me get more in touch with my womanhood. To be sure, sometimes it made me sad, as if in someway it seemed incomplete, as though it were only part of a whole, a lovely part of a whole that was not fully available to me. "It would help, of course" my teacher said to me, "if you would perform. It is meant to be seen. You do not know what it is truly like until you have performed." "I would be afraid to perform," I said. "Why?" she asked. I put down my head, not wanting to speak. "Because there are men there?" she asked. I looked up, "Yes," I said. "Do you think these dances are for women?" she asked. I did not respond. "They are made to be seen by men," she said. "That is their purpose." "Please," I protested. "And there would not be one man there, one real man," she said, "who, seeing you half naked in your jewelry and veils, would not want to put a chain on you, and own you." I looked at her, startled. "I see that such thoughts are not new to you," she smiled. "I thought not." How could she have known that I had had such thoughts? Could it be that she, too, had them, as she was a woman? I will recount one further anecdote from my lessons. It occurred yesterday evening. We were in class. We were dancing, twenty of us, in leotards, and shawls or scarves, to the music on the tape recorder. Then suddenly she said to us, scornfully, "What is wrong? You are dancing tonight like free women. You must improve that. You must dance like slaves."

"Like slaves!" I said.

"Yes," she said. "Keep dancing, all of you!" In a moment, she said, "That's better. That's much better." She walked about, among us. Then she was before me. I was in the front row. "Keep dancing, Doreen," she said, warningly. I was then, for the moment, afraid of her. I kept dancing. "Imagine now," she said to me, "what it would be to do that before a man, Doreen. Suppose, now, there is a man present. He is a strong man. You are before him. Dance! Ah! Good! Good!" I gather I must have danced well. "Good," she said. "Very good. That is very good. Now you are dancing like a slave."

"I am not a slave," I protested.

"We are all slaves," she said, and walked away.

I smiled, hooking the scarlet halter before my belly and then turning it and putting my arms through the straps, pulling it up, adjusting it snugly into place. I am, like most women, amply, but medium-breasted. I ran my thumbs about the interior of my belt, adjusting the drape of the skirt. I have a narrow waist with, I think, sweetly wide hips. My legs were short but shapely, excellent I think for a dancer, or at least a dancer of the sort I was, an ethnic dancer. I put on armlets, bracelets and, opposite the bells on my left ankle, a goldenlike anklet on my right ankle. I put my necklaces about my neck, the five of them. With such an abundance of splendor I thought might strong men bedeck their women. I examined myself in the mirror in the ladies' room at the library. How amusing, and absurd, I thought, that my teacher had said that we were slaves. I was ready.

I turned off the light in the ladies' room and emerged into the hall-like way between the interior wall, that enclosing the wash-rooms and part of the children's section, and the openings between the shelves on the western side of the library. One of the doors to the children's section was on the left. The information desk was to the right. I sometimes worked there. I stood for a moment in the hall-like way. It was dark in the library, quite dark. Then I went right, making my way along the hall-like way toward the open, central section of the library, where the information desk was, and there went left, toward the reference section. On my right were the card catalogs and then, later, the xerox machines. On one of the tables in the reference section I had left my small tape recorder. With it were some tapes which I had purchased. They were tapes of a sort suitable for ethnic dance. I used them often for my private practice. Also, from time to time, I sometimes told myself it was because of the smallness of my apartment, I was in the habit of coming to the library, after hours, of course, to dance. I would let myself in through the staff entrance. This was on the lower level, near the parking lot. I enjoyed dancing here. I do not think, really, that this was all simply a matter of space. Perhaps it amused me to dance here, where I worked, I do not know. Perhaps I enjoyed the contrast, known only to me, between quiet Doreen, the librarian, and Doreen, the secret Doreen of my heart, the dancer, or far worse. Too, there seemed something meaningful, something rich and almost symbolic, perhaps even defiant, about dancing here, in this place where I worked, with its whispers, its sedateness, its cerebral pretensions, to dance here, in this place, in such a place, *as a woman*. No, I do not think it was really all a matter of space. How startled my co-workers would have been if they could have seen me, Doreen, barefoot, half naked, belled and bangled, dancing, and such dancing, dancing almost as though she might be a slave! And so it was here, in this private, perfect place, that I presented, in effect, my secret performances, performances which I had, of course, determined to keep wholly to myself, performances which I would never permit anyone to see, here where no one would ever know, where no one would even suspect, here where I was absolutely alone, where I was perfectly secure and safe.

I moved, warming up, preparing my muscles. I was intent,

and careful. A dancer, of course, does not simply begin to dance. That can be dangerous. She warms up. It is like an athlete warming up, I suppose. As I warmed up, I could hear the jewelry on me, the tiny sounds of the skirt. Bells, too, marked these movements. I was belled. These I had fastened, in three lines, they fastened on a single thong, about my left ankle. Men, I sensed, somehow, would relish an ornamented woman, perhaps even one who was shamefully belled.

I went to the table where rested the small recorder. I was excited, as I always was, somehow, before I danced. I picked up one tape, put it aside, and selected another. It was to that that I should dance.

Men had always, it seemed, at least since puberty, been more disturbing, and interesting and attractive to me than they should have been to a modern woman, or a real woman. They had always seemed far more important to me than they were really supposed to be. They were only men, I had been taught. But even so, they were men, even if that were all they were. I could never bring myself to think of them, really, as *persons*. To me they always seemed more meaningful, and virile, than that, even the men I knew. To me, in spite of their cowardice and weakness, they still seemed, in a way, men, or at least the promise of men. Beyond this, after that night, long ago, in my bedroom, that night in which I had admitted to myself my real nature, though I had denied it often enough since, my interest in men had been considerably deepened. After my confession to myself, kneeling before my vanity in the darkness of my room, they had suddenly become a thousand times more real and frightening to me. And this interest in them, and my sensitivity to them, and my awareness of them, had been deepened further, I think, in my experience with dance. I do not think this was simply a matter of a modest reduction in my weight and, connected with this, and the exercise, a noticeable improvement in my figure, helping me to a more felicitous and reassuring self-image, that of a female in clear, lovely contrast to a male, or of the dance's prosaic improvement of such things as my circulation, my body tone, and general health, though, to be sure, it is difficult for a woman to be healthy, truly healthy, and not be interested in men, but what was really important, rather, or especially important, I think, was the nature of the dance itself, the kind of dance it was. In this form of dance a woman becomes aware of the marvelous, profound complementaries of sexuality, that she, clearly, is the female, beautiful and desirable, and that they, watching her, being pleased, their eyes alit, strong and mighty, are different from her, that they are men, and that, in the order of nature, she, the female of their species, belongs to them. It is thus impossible for her, in this form of dance, not to become alertly, deeply, keenly aware of the opposite sex.

Do we truly belong to men, I asked myself. No, I laughed. No, of course not! How silly that is!

I inserted the tape in the recorder.

My finger hesitated over the button. But perhaps it is true, really, I thought. I shrugged. It seemed that men did not want us, or that men of the sort I knew did not want us. If they did want us why did they not take us, and make us theirs? I wondered, then, if there were a different sort of men, somewhere, the sort of men who might want us, truly, and take us, and make us theirs. Surely not. Men did not do what they wanted with women, never. Surely not! Nowhere! Nowhere! But I knew, of course, that men had, and commonly had, in thousands of places, for thousands of years, treated us, or some women, at least, perhaps luckless, unfortunate ones, exactly as they had pleased, holding them and keeping them, as no more than dogs and chattels. How horrifying, I thought. But surely men such as that no longer existed, and my recurrent longing for them, a needful, desperate longing, as I sometimes admitted to myself, must be no more than some pathetic, vestigial residue of a foregone era. Perhaps it was an odd, anachronistic inherited trait, a genetic relic, tragically perhaps, in my case, no longer congruent with its creature's environment. I wondered if I had been born out of my time. Surely a woman such as I, I thought, might better have thrived in Thebes, or Rome, or Damascus. But I was real, and was as I was, *in this time*. Did this not suggest then that somewhere, somehow, there might be something answering to my yearnings, my hungers and cries? How was it that I should cry out in the darkness, if, truly, there were no one, anywhere, to hear? Be pleased there isn't, little fool, I snapped to myself. Of course there wasn't, I reassured myself. How terrifying it would be if there were. I decided I would now dance. I recalled that the man in the aisle, he in the incident which had taken place some three months ago, that in connection with *Harper's Dictionary of Classical Literature and Antiquities*, had spoken of a world like one long past, a world in which, as he had said, women such as myself were bought and sold as slaves. I dismissed the thought immediately from my mind. But I knew there was another reason I had come to the library to dance, one I had seldom admitted to myself. It was here, in this place, over there to my left, where I had found myself kneeling before a man, where I had found myself saying aloud, "I am a slave." I would now dance. I decided, as a pleasant fancy, that I would pretend something naughty, as I occasionally did, that I was truly a slave, on such a world, and that I was dancing before masters. Oh, I would dance well! The masters, as I dreamed of them, of course, and as they figured in my fancies, were not the men of Earth, or, at least, not men like most of those of Earth. No, they would be different. They would be quite different. They would be such as before whom a girl could quite properly, and, indeed, perhaps even in fear of her life, realistically dance, and dance desperately, hoping to be found pleasing, or acceptable. They would be true men. They would be her masters.

I pressed the button on the tape recorder and there, in the darkness, in the library, my bare feet feeling the coarse piling of the thin, stained carpet, to the soft sound of bells, those tied on my ankle, I danced. I danced for some time, lost in my delights, and I danced, or tried to, as would have, as I had planned, a mere slave, needful and fearful, before those who held over her the power of life and death, before her masters.

I cried out, suddenly, startled. I stopped, with a jangle of bells, and a swirl of skirt. I shrank back, my hand flung before my mouth. "Who are you!" I cried, to the figure standing in the shadows, some feet away, but I knew. I backed away, my hand at my breast. I was suddenly conscious, terribly, of my bare feet, of the bells on one ankle, the anklets on the other, of the nakedness of my legs within the swirling, veil-like skirt, of the bareness of my midriff, of my bared arms and shoulders, of the jewelry upon me. My breasts heaved, as I struggled for breath, within the scarlet halter which confined them. I put my hand out, as though to fend him away, backing yet further away. "Who are you!" I cried.

"Do you think to play games with me?" he inquired.

"What are you doing here!" I cried.

"Can you not guess?" he asked.

"You have no business here," I said. "Go away!"

"My business brings me here," he said.

I looked wildly about me, and was going to turn, and flee, when I cried out, again. To my right there was another man. I spun about. Behind me, a few feet, and to my left, there was another!

The man who was to my right turned off the tape recorder.

I stood there, in swirling skirt, and bells. Then suddenly I fled between the man before me and he on my right, running between the tables and toward the shelves. The fellow on the right, I think, came after me. I fled, with a jangle of bells, down the stairs, to the lower level. I yanked wildly on the heavy door there. I was terrified, I would run out into the night, even as I was. It did not budge. The handle seemed warm. The bolt area, too, was warm. I gasped. It was rippled. It had apparently been exposed to great heat, in a small area, and it had melted there, and then hardened. The door would not open. In effect, somehow it seemed welded shut. Hearing the man, or one of them behind me, I then fled to the other stairs, and thence upward again, to the main level of the library. I hurried toward the front entrance. The fellow whom I had first seen was now standing there, before the door. He looked at me. He slipped a small object into his pocket. That door, too, I thought, wildly, is now sealed! Thusly they could close a door. Similarly, doubtless, with heat, they could as easily open one! There was a technology here which frightened me. I turned and fled back, again, toward the area where I had originally been surprised. The return desk was on my left, the information desk ahead and to my right. I turned suddenly to the left and fled down the hall-like way between shelves and the washrooms. At the end of this I saw another man, I think he who had originally followed me. I turned to the left, to lock myself in the ladies' room, but the door hung awry on one hinge. I had not heard breakage. It must have been done, again, with heat. The door was useless! I could not hide there! I cried out in misery. But then, too, I realized, suddenly, if I had hidden there I would have been trapped. They could open that door, surely, as easily as they opened and closed others. Why then had they set the door awry? With a sinking feeling I realized perhaps it had amused them, that it must have been merely to inform me that there was no place, really, to hide! Too, there seemed something symbolic in this. In my culture men could not enter the ladies' room. Its precincts were not permitted to them. It was a place where women could go, and be safe. But now, it seemed, that I had not even this symbolic security, this pathetic figment of a convention, to protect me. There was no place to hide! There was no place to be safe! These men, I feared, came from a place where perhaps no woman, or no woman of certain sorts, was fully safe. They came, I feared, from a place where they might follow a woman, or such a woman, anywhere, where they might pursue her anywhere, where they might go after her anywhere. I fled back down the hall-like way toward the information desk, stopping suddenly, with a jangle of bells, near the end of the hall-like way. I looked wildly about. I was fearful of precipitously flinging myself into the arms of a man. I threw a wild look over my shoulder. The fellow was approaching. I turned wildly right, toward the main doors again. Perhaps the first man, he I had first seen, he whom I knew, no longer blocked them! But he was still there! I cried out in misery and darted across the open space, past the information desk and the office, past the periodicals and into the reading area, toward the main-level porch, overlooking the lake. That door, too, was sealed. I tried to pick up one of the small armchairs, to smash through, and perhaps squeeze through, one of the high, narrow windows, but it was too heavy for me, and the man was now close behind me. Even if I could have lifted the chair he would have been upon me before I could have reached the glass. I darted back again toward the main section of the library. They were in no hurry, it seemed, to close in on me. They were letting me run, letting me learn perhaps, learn as a female, what it was to run. I fleetly crossed the open space of the central section of the library and ran up the iron, iron-and-wood-banistered stairs to the upper level, where we keep biographies and fiction. My bare feet sounded strange to me, striking on the surface of the stairs. I wondered if anyone had ever ascended them barefoot before, here, in this place. I suspected not. The corrugated surface of the stairs, too, felt strange on my feet. My soles stung at the top. Then I was again on carpeting. I fled down the aisle. I heard a man coming up, behind me, slowly. I hid between two of the shelves perpendicular to the main aisle. My ankle moved, slightly. There was the tiny sound of bells. They would know where I was! Again I must run! I leapt up, crying out, and fled again, irrationally, terrified, wildly, miserably, weeping, my every step again betrayed by bells, this time about the far end of the tiny side aisle between the shelves, away from the main aisle, away from where I thought the man would be. Then I hid again, between two shelves, and fumbled feverishly in the darkness with the tie on my bells. I could do nothing with it in the darkness. I had belled myself well, I thought bitterly. I had belled myself as might have a slave, who knows that her bells must be on her tightly, firstly for psychological reasons, that she knows herself belled, and is conscious of all the erotic and humiliating richness of this, she, a belled animal, and secondly and thirdly, of course, for mechanical reasons, that they be responsive to her slightest movements, as in the slowest, subtlest portions of her dance, and will not slip, or come loose, in the more rapid portions of her dance, despite her swiftest gyrations. I wept. I could not free the bells. Even as I tried they would make their tiny sounds. I tried to remain absolutely still. I held them with both hands, trying to keep my ankle absolutely still. But I was breathing heavily. I could not help myself. Tears ran down my cheeks. Surely my breathing, if nothing else, would betray me. Too, in the tiny movements of my body, even in breathing, the bells would sometimes make a tiny sound. I looked up. There, at the opening to my side aisle, in the main aisle, tall in the darkness, looking down at me, loomed a man, one of the three whom I had seen, he, I think, who had followed me about so quietly and tenaciously, originally to the lower level, up again by the other stairs, down the hall-like way, across the open space, toward the porch area, back again across the open space, and now up the stairs. I leaped up and fled away from him, utilizing the narrow space at the edge of the porchlike upper level, between the safety bannister and the shelves, to the second stairs, on the east side of the upper level, leading down to the main floor. No one was there. I hurried down the stairs. I darted between tables, toward the first-floor shelves on the east side of the building, where we keep most of our reference materials. I heard him coming down the iron stairs behind me. I hurried into one of the aisles, between the reference shelves. I crouched down there, at the far end. I looked behind me. He had entered the aisle. With a cry of misery I leapt up and fled about the end of the shelving area turning wildly with a swirl of skirt and a jangle of bells into the adjacent aisle and was caught! He had apparently been waiting in this place. His hands were on my upper arms. I was held as helplessly as a child. I had literally, running, unable to stop, stumbling, with a cry of misery, struck against him. I had flung myself, it seemed, into his arms. He had thrust me back a bit, and now held me, helplessly, by the upper arms, his hands like iron on my arms, but inches from him. It was he whom I had encountered some three months ago in the library, he, of course, of the incident in the aisle, this very aisle, even, and in this very place in this aisle, that puzzling, frightening incident involving *Harper's Dictionary of Classical Literature and Antiquities*. Minutes ago, in terror, before running, I had recognized him. I had recognized him even before he had spoken. I had known him unmistakably in my woman's heart, even in the darkness. I feared him terribly. Now I was in his grasp. He lifted me up a little, easily before him, so easily that I might have been a child. I squirmed, helpless. Only my toes, their very tips, could touch the carpet. He looked at me, peering into my eyes, his hands so tight on my arms. I began to tremble, and could not look at him, and was terrified and weak. He let me down, so that I might stand, but I could not do so. It was only his hands which kept me on my feet. The other man was now behind me. He then released my arms and I, weak and frightened, unable to help myself, sank to my knees before him.

"Look up," he said.

I did so.

"You know where you are, of course," he said.

"Yes," I said. I looked to my right. There, in the darkness, where I could reach out and touch it, on the bottom shelf, in its place, was *Harper's Dictionary of Classical Literature and Antiquities*. Probably it had not been moved since it had been replaced, months ago. I then looked up at him, again. I was in the same place where, months before, I had, in a very different reality, found myself on my knees before this man. Then, of course, I had been a helpful librarian, obedient, dutifully, to the instructions of an imperious patron. It had been a bright afternoon. I had been fully and modestly, clothed. I had worn simple, quiet, unostentatious, dignified garments. I had worn a long-sleeved blouse, a dark sweater, a plain skirt, dark stockings and low-heeled shoes. Indeed, in the dress code of the library, it was posted in the employees' room, where our lockers lined one wall, such garments were prescribed for us. But things were now much different. It was no longer a bright afternoon. It was now late at night. Others were not about. We were now alone, absolutely and frighteningly alone. I did not now kneel before him in a blouse, sweater and skirt. I now knelt before him, semi-nude, in jewelry and silk.

"Do you remember *Harper's Dictionary of Classical Literature and Antiquities?*" he asked.

"Yes," I said.

"Do you remember the paper that was in the book?" he asked.

"Yes," I said.

"What did it say?" he asked.

"It said," I said, " 'I am a slave.' "

"Say the words," he said.

"I am a slave," I said.

He then reached down and took me by one arm, the left arm, and drew me to my feet and then pulled me beside him, down the aisle, toward the open part of the library, the northern part of it, near the reference desk. When we were there, he released me. "Kneel," he said.

I then knelt there on the carpet. Without really thinking I smoothed the veil-like skirt about me, so that it was in an attractive, circular pattern.

He smiled.

I looked down.

The third man was in this area, near one of the tables. On the table he had opened an attaché case.

"Did you see me dance?" I asked.

"Look up," he said.

I did so.

"Yes," he said.

I looked down, miserable. It had been meant that no one would see me dance, especially as I had danced this night!

"But you stopped, and before the end of your dance, and without permission," he said. "Thus, you shall dance again."

I looked up at him, again, startled.

"And," he said, "this will be the first time you will dance knowingly before men."

"How could you know that I have never danced before men?" I asked.

"Do you think you have not been under surveillance," he asked, "that we do not know a great deal about you?"

"I cannot dance before men," I said.

He smiled.

"I will not!" I said.

"Get on your feet," he said.

I rose to my feet. The man near the table ran the tape back on the tape recorder.

"You will begin at the beginning," he said. "You will perform the entire dance, from beginning to end, for us."

"Please, no," I said. I could not stand the thought, the terrifying thought, of putting myself, in the beauty of dance, before men such as these. I could not even dream of letting such men see me dance. It was utterly unthinkable. I had not even dared to show myself thusly to common men, to banal, safe, inoffensive, trivial, conquered men, men of the sort with whom I associated, men of the sort I knew. Who knew what they might think, how they might be tempted to act, what they might be prompted to do?

The man pushed the button of the tape recorder, and I danced.

The tape played for eleven minutes and seventeen seconds, its playing time. The piece was excellent, in its melodic lines, its moods, and shifts. It was one of my favorites. But never before had I danced to it in terror. Never before had I danced to it before men. Then it finished in a swirl and I spun and sank to my knees before them, my head down, my hands on my thighs, in a common ending position for such a dance. Never before, however, I think, had I been so suddenly and deeply struck with the meaning of this ending position, it following the beauty of the dance, its presentation of the dancer in a posture of submission.

"You were frightened," he said.

"Yes," I said.

He drew forth from his pocket a tiny, soft piece of cloth. He threw it to me, and I picked it up.

"Do you recognize it?" he asked.

"Yes," I said, in fear. It was a tiny garment which I had made for myself long ago, that which I had dared to wear only once, in the candlelit secrecy of my bedroom.

"Take off your clothes, and put it on," he said. "Leave the bells on your ankles. They help us keep track of you."

I looked at him, in protest.

"You may, of course, avail yourself of the privacy of your washroom," he said.

I then walked between two men, the second and third man, to the ladies' room, and brushed aside the loose door. They waited outside, almost as though they might have some respect for my privacy. I turned on the light. I removed the jewelry, the anklets and necklaces, and such, I had worn. Then I reached behind my back and unhooked the scarlet halter, and slipped it from me. I looked at my breasts. In the tiny bit of scarlet silk they had given me to wear, their form, and loveliness, if they were lovely, would be in little doubt. I then slipped from the tights and skirt. I was naked, save for a leather thong on my left ankle, and bells. I felt strange, standing there in the ladies' room in the library, naked. Then I drew the small bit of silk over my head. They had obviously searched my room, perhaps ransacking it, and found it. They seemed to know a great deal about me. Perhaps they had thought it their business to learn about me. Perhaps there was little about me that they did not know. They knew even about that bit of silk, now on my body, one of my most closely guarded secrets.

I then turned off the light in the ladies' room and, to the small sound of the bells on my ankle, returned to the central area.

"Stand there," said the man. I did. "Now, turn slowly before us," he said.

I obeyed.

"Good," he said.

I looked at him.

"Kneel," he said.

I knelt.

"In your dance," he said, "you were frightened."

"Yes," I said.

"Still," he said, "it is clear that you are not without talent, indeed, perhaps even considerable talent."

I was silent.

"But it is also clear that you were holding back, that as a typical female of Earth, you would cheat men, that you would not give them all that you had to give. That sort of thing is now no longer permitted to you."

"—of Earth?" I said.

"Women look well in garments such as that you are wearing," he said. "They are appropriate for them."

Again I was silent. It was dark in the library, but not absolutely dark, of course. It was mostly a matter of shadows, and darker shadows, and lighter places, of darker and lighter areas. Here where we were light came through the high, narrow windows to my left, from the moon, and from a street lamp, about a hundred feet away. It was near the western edge of the parking lot, by the sidewalk, fixed there, mainly, I suppose, to illuminate the street running at the side of the library. The front entrance is reached by a drive. It was spring. At that time I did not realize the significance of the time. The building was warm.

"Are you a 'modern woman'?" he asked.

"Yes," I said. Again I did not know what else to say. He had asked me that question long ago, months ago, in the aisle, in our first encounter. I supposed it was true, in some sense.

"It is easy enough to take that from a woman," he said.

I looked at him, puzzled.

"Are you a female intellectual?" he asked.

"No," I said, as I had responded before, when he had asked the question long ago, in our first encounter.

"Yet in your personal library, that in your quarters, there are such books as Rostovtzeff's *History of the Ancient World* and Mommsen's *History of Rome*," he said. "Have you read them?"

"Yes," I said.

"They are now both out of print," he said.

"I bought them in a secondhand bookstore," I said. He had spoken of my "quarters," and not, say, of my "rooms" or my "apartment." To me that seemed odd. Too, as he spoke now, at greater length, his accent, as it had once been before, was detectable. Still, however, I could not place it. I was sure his native tongue was not English. I did not know what his background might be. I had never encountered a man like him. I had not known they existed.

"Women such as you," he said, "use such books as cosmetics and ornaments, as mere intellectual adornments. They mean no more to you than your lipstick and eye shadow, than the baubles in your jewelry boxes. I despise women such as you."

I regarded him, frightened. I did not understand his hostility. He seemed to bear me some hatred, or some kind of woman he thought I was, some hatred. I was afraid he did not wish to understand me. He seemed unwilling to recognize that there might be some delicacy and authenticity in my interest in these things, for their own value and beauty. To be sure, perhaps a bit of my motivation in their acquisition had been from vanity, but, yet, I was sure that there had been something genuine there, too. There must have been!

"Did you learn anything from the books?" he asked.

"I think so," I said.

"Did you learn the worlds of which they speak?" he asked.

"A little about them," I said.

"Perhaps it will do you some good," he mused.

"I do not understand," I said.

"But such books," he said, "are now behind you."

"I do not understand," I said.

"You will no longer need them where you are going," he said.

"I do not understand," I said.

"Such things will no longer be a part of your life," he said. "Your life is now going to be quite different."

"I do not understand," I said, frightened. "What are you talking about?"

"You are doubtless the sort of female who has intellectual pretensions," he said.

I was silent.

"Do you think you are intelligent?" he asked.

"Yes," I said.

"You are not," he said.

I was silent.

"But you do, doubtless, have some form of intelligence," he said, "in your small, nasty way."

I looked up at him, angrily.

"And you will need every bit of it, I assure you," he said, "just to stay alive."

I looked at him, frightened.

"Hateful slut," he said.

I squirmed under his epithet. I was conscious of the light silk on my body. The bells on my ankle jangled.

"Yes," he said, regarding me, "you are a modern woman,

one with intellectual pretensions, I see it now, certainly, one of those modern women who desire to destroy men."

"I don't know what you're talking about," I said.

"But there are ways of treating, and handling, women such as you," he said, "ways of rendering them not only absolutely harmless, but, better still, exquisitely useful and delicious."

"I don't know what you're talking about!" I protested.

"Do not lie to me," he snarled.

I put down my head, miserable. The bells on my ankle moved.

"Your garment is an interesting one," he said. "It well reveals you."

I looked up at him, frightened.

"To be sure," he said, "it is a bit more ample than is necessary, not as snug as it might be, not cut as high at the thighs as it might be, not cut as deeply at the neck as it might be, and, surely, as I determined earlier, it is insufficiently diaphanous."

I looked up at him.

"Take it off," he said.

Numbly I pulled the tiny garment over my head and put it beside me on the carpet.

"It may be a long time" he said, "before you are again permitted a garment."

I trembled, naked.

The third man went to the table, that on which rested the attaché case. He removed an object from the case. I gasped in terror. He handed it to the man in front of me. It was a whip. It had a single, stout, coiled lash.

"What do you think your name was?" he asked.

"Doreen," I said. "Doreen Williamson!" That had seemed a strange way to inquire my name, surely. Too, they knew so much about me. They must have known my name. What did he mean then, "What did I *think* my name was"?

"Well, Doreen," he said, "do you still remember *Harper's Dictionary of Classical Literature and Antiquities?*"

"Yes," I said. The way he had said my name somehow alarmed me. It was almost as though that name might not be mine, really. It was almost as though he had simply, perhaps primarily as a convenience for himself, decided to call me that, if only for the time.

"Fetch it," he said.

I looked at the whip. I leapt to my feet, in a jangle of bells, and hurried to the place where the book was. In a moment I had it and had returned, and, holding the book, knelt again before him.

"Kiss it," he said.

I did so.

"Put it down," he said, "to the side."

I did so.

He then held the whip before me. "Kiss the whip," he said.

I did so.

"Kiss my feet," he said. I put my head down, frightened, the palms of my hands on the carpet, and kissed his feet. I then straightened up, and knelt back on my heels.

"Put your hands, palms down, on your thighs," he said.

I obeyed.

"Apparently you do have some intelligence," he said. "Now put your knees apart."

"Please, no!" I said.

"Perhaps I was wrong," he mused.

Swiftly I put my knees apart.

"Perhaps you will survive," he mused.

He then nodded to the fellow on his left. To my horror the fellow went again to the attaché case and this time brought out coils of chain. I could not see well in the half darkness what it was. Then he was behind me. To my horror I felt a metal collar locked about my neck. It was a very sturdy metal collar. It had, apparently, an attachment, or ring, of some sort, I supposed, in the back, and to this attachment, or ring, the long chain was attached. The fellow behind me must have held it mostly coiled in his hand. The collar encircled my neck closely. I touched it, frightened. I put my finger inside the rim of the implacable encirclement. There was only a half inch or so between its metal and my throat. I could not think of slipping it. I heard the chain behind me. I felt its weight on the attachment, or ring. I was leashed. I wore a chain leash. I was terrified. Perhaps no one can conjecture my feelings, truly, who has not been, too, the helpless prisoner of such a device.

"Slut," he said.

"Yes," I said.

"Are you a virgin?" he asked.

"I see," I said. "I am to be raped."

"Perhaps," he said.

"Your question is personal," I said. Then I felt the metal chain at the back of the collar jerk upward, savagely. The collar cut at the back of my neck, and was tight under my chin. I held my head as far down against the collar as I could, in spite of the additional tightening this effected under my chin, that I might relieve the pressure of its lower rim against my throat. This also forced me to lower my head, submissively. I was half choked. I was unable to speak. I was terrified. I no longer knelt on my heels. I had now been jerked up, off them. Then the collar was suddenly, angrily, turned on my throat, relieving the pressure on my carotid artery, and jerked downward. My head and neck followed it. The long chain was then thrown back between my legs and I felt my ankles crossed and a proximate part of the chain wrapped about them. I was thus held, bent over, my head low, my neck in the collar, kneeling. I strained to look up, lifting my eyes. To my terror I saw the man before me uncoil the whip. "I am a virgin," I whispered. "I am a virgin!" He made a sign and the chain was unwrapped from my ankles and the collar turned again on my neck. I was then jerked backward, half choked, but with the pressure substantially high on my neck, under the chin, doubtless by intent, and then lay before them on the low-piled, coarse carpet, so muchly trodden by our library patrons.

"Split your legs," he said.

I did so, obediently.

In spite of my terror, I felt incredibly alive doing this, obeying him.

He crouched near me. He put the whip on the rug.

"You are a virgin?" he asked.

"Yes!" I said.

"Are you lying?" he asked.

"No!" I said.

"If you are lying," he said, "you will be whipped."

I looked at him, from my back. I could not begin to understand a man who was so strong. How absurd it seemed! Did he not know that women could do anything with impunity, that no matter what we did, even if it were to bring about the destruction of a man's manhood and the ruination of his life, we were never punished? And yet this man seemed ready to punish me for so little as a lie, or perhaps for something as insignificant as simply not being fully pleasing to him! What sort of man was this? It was almost as though he were not a man of Earth! How had he managed to escape his weakening? Had he, somehow, not been suitably trained and conditioned? How different he seemed from a man of Earth! Was he one of the rare men of Earth, I wondered, who had seen through the debilitating and demeaning hoaxes of his society, who had cast forth from him, like poisons from his body, the unnatural and pathological conditioning programs to which he had been subjected?

"Do you understand?" he asked.

"Yes," I said.

"I wonder if you really do," he said.

My lip trembled.

"You might perhaps think of lying now to a man," he said, "but I assure you, my dear, the time will come when you would be terrified to even think of lying to a man."

I was silent.

"Hold still," he said.

I tensed.

"This will only take a moment," he said. "I will be extremely gentle."

I pulled back a bit.

But he was gentle, extremely gentle.

"Is she a virgin?" asked one of the men standing nearby, the third man, he near the table on which rested the attaché case.

"Yes," said the man beside me.

I blushed, hotly.

The fellow near the attaché case then turned to it, and seemed to sort through some objects within it. Then he found one and placed it on the table. I do not know if I could have told what it was, in the shadows, had I been standing. Lying as I was, of course, I probably could not, from my position, have seen what it was even had the room been as light as it had been long ago, some three months ago, on that bright afternoon when I had for the first time to my knowledge found myself under the eyes of my current captor. Whatever it was, it did not seem large. It made a metal sound when placed on the table.

"Are you going to rape me now?" I whispered.

"No," he said.

"No?" I asked.

"No," he said.

"Why not?" I asked.

"You are a virgin," he said.

"I don't understand," I said.

He smiled.

"But if you are not going to rape me," I said, "what is this about?"

"Get on your knees," he said, standing up.

I rose again to my knees, with a small sound of bells, the chain leash on my neck.

He seemed a bit angry. The other two men, too, he near the

attaché case, and he who held my leash, his fist now close to the back of my neck, seemed somewhat angry. I gather they had not been particularly pleased to learn that I was a virgin. Had it not been for that I gathered they would have seen to it that I pleased them muchly.

"If I am not to be raped," I said, "I do not understand what is going on. What is this all about?"

"Have no fear," said the man, "eventually, in your new life, you will be well and frequently raped. Indeed, your life, in effect, will be one of rape."

"My new life?" I said. "I do not understand what is going on."

"She is stupid," said the man behind me, he controlling my leash, allowing me so little tether on it.

"No," said the man before me. "She has her tiny spark of intelligence, nasty, petty and small though it might be, which, hopefully, may perhaps facilitate her survival. It is just that these things, now, are beyond her ken."

"I do not understand," I said.

"Can you not guess, cuddly beauty?" he asked.

"No!" I said.

"Remember, long ago," he said, "when we first met, and we spoke of an ancient, beautiful world?"

"Yes," I said.

"A world in which women such as you," he said, "were bought and sold as slaves?"

"Yes," I said, uneasily.

"Perhaps you remember saying that that world was gone," he said.

"Yes," I said.

"And perhaps, too," he said, "you may remember me remarking that there was another, not unlike it, which exists."

"Yes," I said.

"You said that that was absurd, as I recall," he said.

"Yes," I said. "And it is absurd!"

I felt the man's hand tighten a little in the chain. This made me more conscious of the collar on my neck.

"Do you recall what I said then?" he asked.

"Yes," I said. I shuddered.

"What?" he asked.

"That you had seen it," I said.

"It is true," he said.

"You are mad!" I said.

"And you, too, will see it, my dear," he said.

"That is absurd!" I said. "You are mad! You are all mad!"

He reached down and picked up the whip.

"You must learn deference to males," he said, "absolute deference to males."

I shrank back. But he was coiling the whip. Then with a butt clip and a blade clip, he put it on his belt. I almost fainted.

"There is no such place!" I said.

"I was born there," he said, "as were my fellows."

"There is no such place on Earth!" I said.

"That is true," he said.

"What are you saying?" I gasped. "Who are you?"

"I am Teibar," he said. "My colleagues are Hercon, to your right, and Taurog, behind you, who holds your chain."

"I do not understand such names," I said. They did not even sound like the names of men of Earth!

"I suppose they are unfamiliar to you," he said. "They are not found here, or at least, I suppose, not frequently."

"Here?" I asked.

"Yes," he said, "on Earth."

"I don't understand," I said.

"I speak of a world which is not Earth," he said.

"Another world?" I asked.

"Yes," he said.

"Another planet?" I asked.

"Yes," he said.

"But you are human, surely," I said, "some sort of human, though perhaps of a different sort from those to whom I am accustomed."

"You fear that I am an alien?" he asked.

"Yes," I whispered.

"In one sense it is true that I, from your point of view, am an alien," he said, "the sense in which I have come from a different world. In another sense, however, I am not an alien, as I am identically a member of your own species."

I looked at him.

"My ancestors came from Earth," he said, "rather as yours came from Europe. Have no fear. I am every bit as human as you."

"I see," I said.

"And that is why I am so dangerous to you," he said, "because I am a member of your own species, because I understand you, because I know how you think, because I am familiar with your nasty little mind and emotions, your slynesses, your pettinesses, your selfishness, your stupid little tricks, everything about you, and what you are."

"And this world of which you speak," I whispered, "supposing it exists, it is like, in some ways, the other world, the vanished world, of which we spoke?"

"Yes," he said.

"Is it like it in one way in particular," I asked.

"It is like it in many ways," he said, seemingly amused. "Do you have anything particular in mind?"

"Is it a world—" I asked.

"Yes?" he said.

"Is it a world in which women such as I," I asked, "are bought and sold as slaves?"

"Yes," he said.

"What are you going to do with me?" I asked.

"Can you not guess?" he asked.

I leaped upward but, cruelly, instantly, with an expert turn and throw of the leash, I was thrown twisting, gasping and choking, to my belly on the rug. I was startled with how excellently, how easily, how smoothly, and with such little thought this had apparently been done. I had been utterly helpless, like something of no account in Taurog's control. I felt his heel on my back. It pressed me cruelly down on the rug. The collar was on my abraded neck. Some links of its chain lay beside my throat. I lifted my head as I could.

The fellow before me made a sign and Taurog removed his heel from my back. I could still feel its print there. I was frightened. I could feel the rough, flattened coarseness of the carpet beneath me. I noted the difference between the feel of it, from lying upon it on my back, before, and as I did now, on my stomach. It had seemed plain, hard and scratchy to my back, a suitable surface, I supposed, on which a girl's virginity might be tested, but as I lay on my stomach, to my softness, to my breasts and belly, to my thighs, it seemed oddly different. I was now much more conscious of it, the irregularities of its surface, the subtle unevenness of texture, the flat, stained spots, the sudden, tiny, abrupt roughnesses, where a shoe might have moved the pile. I had walked upon that carpet thousands of times. Never before, however, had I lain on it, on my stomach, naked.

"Kneel," said my captor.

I struggled to my knees. My body was still sensitive to the feel of the rug. Taurog had not been gentle with me. I could still feel the print of his heel on my back. I gathered that I was not the sort of thing to which gentleness need be shown.

I looked at my captor.

"It might interest you to know that you have been on our list for some time," he said.

"List?" I said.

"Yes," he said, "lists, actually. You have been on our scouting list for a year, on our consideration list for six months, and on our active list for some three months."

"I am not a slave!" I cried.

Slowly the man approached me and I shrank back. Then he took me by the upper arms and pulled me up, from my knees, before him, until I was half standing. "On the contrary," he said, "my hateful little charmer, you are. I assure you of it. There is not the least doubt about the matter. We know our work. To a practiced eye, a discerning eye, one which is trained to look for, and recognize, such things, you are obviously a slave. The suitable condition for a woman such as you is perfectly clear, deny it and squirm though you might."

"No, no," I whimpered, turning my head away from him.

"Do you think I cannot recognize slaves?" he asked. "It is my business."

I moaned.

He shook me, and my head snapped back, and I cried out with misery.

"Look at me," he said.

I did so, terrified.

"I, like many others," he said, "can recognize slaves, and, have no fear, I have recognized you as one."

"No," I whimpered, not wanting to look at him.

"Look at me," he said.

Again I looked at him, terrified.

"It is in your eyes," he said.

"No," I wept.

"Even months ago," he said, "when I looked into your eyes, when you sat in those silly garments, behind that foolish desk, I saw that you, beneath all that cotton and wool, were a naked slave."

"No," I wept.

"And I look into them again now," he said, "and see that it is true."

"No, no, no!" I wept, turning my head away. I dared not meet those fierce eyes which so frightened me, which seemed somehow to look through me, burning through me like fire, bringing unwelcome, frightening torches to my secret darkness, penetrating to my deepest and most closely guarded secrets, to what lay in the most secret belly and heart of me.

"Shall I have you dance again, before men?" he asked.

"No," I said. "No!"

"Do not fear," he said, "you will dance again before them, and dance as you have never dreamed a woman could dance before men!"

"No!" I wept. "No, no!"

He released me, and I subsided weakly to my knees before him. It seems that one could do little but kneel before such a man. Then, angrily, he thrust silk in my mouth, my own, that which he had made me take off earlier. I was silenced.

"On all fours," he said.

I went to all fours before him. A loop of the chain leash hung down by my neck, to the right, a foot or so, and then looped up to its attachment. I could feel its weight. It turned the collar a little to the right.

The men then spoke for a few moments among themselves. I could not understand the language. It seemed expressive, and highly inflected.

The leader turned to me. I saw him remove the whip from his belt. I put my head down. I bit into the silk, holding it in my mouth. I knew I could not remove it without their permission. He had put it in there. I saw the blade of the whip shaken free. I began to tremble. I whimpered, the silk in my mouth. I whimpered that I not be beaten.

"You understand the whip, don't you, slut?" he asked.

I whimpered, plaintively, pleadingly.

"That is one of the few things a little animal like you clearly understands," he mused.

I whimpered.

"Look at her," said Teibar, my captor, to his man, Taurog, he holding my leash, "she has never felt it, but she senses what it might be like to feel it, what it could do to her."

"Yes," said Taurog.

"But then," said Teibar, "I suppose that all females understand the whip, or if they are stupid, and do not, they may be brought swiftly enough to its proper understanding."

"Yes," said Taurog.

I then felt the blade of the whip move lightly upon my back. I shuddered. I wanted to scream, but I could only whimper, plaintively. The whip, it seemed to me, strangely enough, somehow, was not a stranger to me. I seemed to know it. I wondered, wildly, if I had felt it in former lives. Something about it seemed almost a terrifying memory. Could I be remembering it, I wondered, from a sunlit shelf in Memphis, from a patio in Athens, from a post in Rome or a ring, cords on my wrists, in a women's quarters in Bokara, Basra, Samarkand or Bagdad? Had I felt it before, somewhere, or in many places, and never, even through a succession of lives, forgotten it? No, I told myself, that would be quite unlikely. On the other hand, I had little doubt that many women in the past, in such places, and in thousands of others, had had their behavior corrected with perfection by just such instruments and their kin, such as the switch, the strap, the bastinado. There was something in me, however, which seemed to know the whip, and terribly feared it. I suppose that this might have been an effect only of the startling alarms of my imagination, they informing me with some vividness as to what it might be to feel its stroke, but I suspect, really, that there was more involved. I suspect that there was a kinship of sorts between myself and the whip, that we were perhaps, in some sense, made for one another, that even if I never felt it I recognized it as having something authoritative, and intimate and important, to do with me, and what, in my heart, I secretly was.

I felt the lash brushing my back, twice more. It seemed to do so thoughtfully, meditatively. I whimpered, biting on the wet silk. Tears fell from my eyes to the carpet. I whimpered, tiny, begging sounds, pleading for mercy. It did not matter to him, I was sure, that I was a modern woman in the Twentieth Century. I might as well have been, as far as he cared, only a curvaceous, beautiful barbarian servant in Epidaurus, or, in the keeping of Crusaders, or in the tents of Mongols, a Persian dancing girl. He was literally considering beating me. What we all had in common was that we were women. Similarly I had not the least doubt that if he wished to beat me, he would do so. He was fully capable, I sensed, of doing whatever he might wish to me, and with perfection.

"No, little slut," he said, removing the whip and replacing it on his belt, "it will be better later."

I shook with relief. I sobbed with relief. I was not to be beaten! I was not to be beaten! Then suddenly I shuddered. I wondered what he might possibly have meant, "that it would be better later."

I looked up at him.

"You delicious, meaningless, sly, vicious, hateful thing," he snarled.

I could not understand his animosity, his seeming hatred of me.

"Take her out of my sight," he said to Taurog, "lest I be tempted to kill her."

"Come, little slut," said Taurog. He moved beside me, and then ahead of me, and I felt the pressure of the interior of the collar at the back of my neck, on the left, and the tug of the chain. The collar had now, in response to his movements, shifted on my neck. It was apparently not a ring where the chain was attached but, it now seemed, some sort of fixed-position, heavy, welded-in metal staple. This device, to which the chain was attached, where it now exerted its force, was now under my jaw, to my right. I followed Taurog now, on all fours, the silk stuffed in my mouth. He pulled me back behind the xerox machines, where the sight of me would not offend Teibar. There, with his foot, first against my arms and hands, then against my knees and thighs, brushing them outward, toward my extremities in both cases, he let me know his will with respect to my limbs. I went first to my elbows, and then to my belly. I do not think Taurog spoke much English. He had, however, conveyed his intent to me. I realized, lying there on the cool surface, it is a composition surface in that area, on my belly, naked, among the machines, that it is not always necessary to understand a man's language to obey him, or for him to command you. I heard Teibar speaking to Hercon, and then Hercon left for somewhere, as I later found out to gather up my things from the ladies' room. Teibar himself whom I thought of as my personal, and most meaningful, captor, stayed in the vicinity of the table, that on which the attaché case rested. I thought I heard him moving some things about there.

In a short while Hercon returned to the vicinity of the table. A moment later, Teibar said something, apparently to Taurog.

Taurog jerked the chain upward, twice, gently. It was little more than a sound of links, and only the slightest of pressures, twice, on the attachment. It was a signal to me.

Taurog made a sound of approval as I rose immediately to all fours. He then led me back to the table on which the attaché case rested, where Teibar, whom I feared mostly, my chief captor, waited.

I saw a pile of my things there on the carpet, the dancer's costume, my purse, my clothes, those I had worn to the library, and such, near the table. That had been I supposed a result of Hercon's brief absence. He was now back. Taurog said something to Teibar.

"Taurog," said Teibar, looking down at me, "is pleased with

you. He thinks you may have an instinctive understanding of chain signals."

I could not speak, the wet silk in my mouth. I could only look up at him.

"It is possible," he said. "You are a woman."

I looked up at him, angrily.

He then removed a small object from his pocket. I think I had seen it before, near the front doors of the library, when I had seen him there, and had fled back, away from him. He pointed it at the pile of clothing, and diverse articles. A line of light, causing me to pull back, crying out, half blinded, burned forth from the object. When I could see, I saw that the rug was gone there, and that, about, there were only ashes.

"There is this other thing," said Hercon, lifting the tape recorder. Doubtless the tapes were near it.

"Leave it, and its musics," said Teibar. "Let those who come upon it ponder its meaning."

Hercon replaced the recorder on its table.

I was trembling. I had seen what had become of the clothing, and such, on the floor. I was not familiar with the technology these men had at their disposal. It seemed, however, powerful, and sophisticated. Oddly enough, it did not seem congenial to the type of world of which he had spoken. Could it be that on that world such devices were not permitted? I saw the small object pointed at me. I shook my head, wildly, whimpering, biting on the silk, tears in my eyes. I knew its burning line, that intense beam or blade, could divide me, fluids hissing, boiling, in an instant. "You understand what we could do, if we wished, don't you?" he asked. I nodded vigorously, affirmatively, tears in my eyes. Then he returned it to his pocket. I collapsed to the rug, unable even to bear my own weight.

"Put her on the table," he said.

Taurog reached down and picked me up, lightly, and put me on my back, on the table, near the attaché case. The men pushed chairs back, so that they might stand about the table.

I looked up at Teibar, terrified. He drew the silk from my mouth.

"Please," I wept.

"Were you given permission to speak?" he asked.

"No," I whispered.

"Perhaps I do not wish to hear you speak," he said. He was opening, and then smoothing out, and folding the bit of wet silk I had had thrust in my mouth. It was then in a soft, damp, layered, folded form some six or seven inches square. He put it beside me, beside my left hip.

"May I speak?" I asked. I then realized that no gag was needed to silence me. It could be done to me as simply and effectively by the will, or mere whim, of men such as these. By such men I could be silenced by a mere word, or a gesture or glance.

"Remove her bells," he said to Hercon. "Anklet her. The virgin anklet."

"Please," I said.

"Very well," he said.

"What is this all about?" I begged. "What are you going to do with me, really?"

I felt Hercon's strong fingers working with the thong on my left ankle. I heard the rustle of bells.

"Who are you!" I demanded.

"Teibar," he said.

I moved my head in frustration. The collar, so close, and heavy, and confining, was on my neck. I heard the movement of the chain, behind me, where it dangled over the edge of the table.

"But what are you?" I begged.

"Human," he said, "as are you, in your petty, nasty way."

"Why do you hate me?" I asked.

"Because of what you are, and what you would do to men," he said.

"What?" I asked.

"Destroy them," he said.

"I am not going to destroy men!" I said.

"I know," he said, "now."

"I don't understand!" I wept.

Then I felt the bells removed from my ankle. Hercon handed them to Teibar, who placed them, on their thong, on the soft, damp silk beside me.

"Why are you doing this?" I asked. "What are you, really!"

"I am a businessman," he said.

"What is your business?" I asked, plaintively.

"I am an exporter," he said.

I then felt a sturdy metal anklet closed about my left ankle, where the bells had been. It snapped shut. I had no doubt it locked. I gathered there might be different sorts of such anklets. This one, I had gathered, was a "virgin anklet."

"What do you export?" I asked.

"Women," he said.

I reared up on the table, but, by the hair, with a rattle of the chain on my collar, was pulled back onto it, on my back.

"Lie still," he said.

I saw Hercon lift up, and shake out, a large, folded leather sack. It was heavy, dark, long, and narrow. It had straps, and a lock, at one end.

"I have prepared the mask, and solution," he said to Hercon.

I strained to see the sack. Hercon was now folding it three times, and placing it on the table.

"You will be placed in that, head first, gagged, and bound, hand and foot," said Teibar, "but, even if you were not bound, it would be very difficult for you, because of the tightness and narrowness of the sack, to do more than wiggle a little."

I tried to rise up but a conical, stiff, rubberized mask was thrust over my nose and mouth, and, by means of it, I was pushed back on the table. Taurog held my wrists, pinning me back on the table's surface. Hercon held my ankles. I struggled. My eyes must have been wild over the mask. Teibar poured some fluid from a small bottle into an opening, or through a porous mesh, at the apex of the mask. He held it firmly over my nose and mouth.

"Steady, steady, little slut," said Teibar, soothingly. "There is no use to struggle. Your struggles will avail you not in the least."

I tried to fight the mask but I could not. I was held. I was held, helplessly. My strength, that of a woman, was nothing to theirs, that of men. I wondered what might be the meaning of that, in a natural world.

"Breathe deeply," said Teibar.

I tried to move my head, but, because of the tightness of the mask, over my nose and mouth, and how he held it on me, pressing it down upon me, I could not. I tried to hold my breath. I felt a drop of liquid, and then a trickle of liquid, run on the bridge of my nose, and then take its way down my right cheek.

"Breathe deeply," said Teibar, soothingly.

I fought to hold my breath.

Hercon said something.

"Come now," said Teibar, to me, "you are disappointing Hercon."

I looked up at him, wildly.

"Breathe deeply," he said. "You do not wish to disappoint Hercon. Taurog, too, was so proud of you, You would not wish to disappoint him, too, would you? Not after you did so well, in the matter of the chain. The time will come, I assure you, when you will be extremely concerned that you not disappoint men in any way, in the least."

I suddenly coughed, half choking, in the mask. I gasped for air, plaintively, eagerly, desperately, in those tiny, hot confines. There was a closeness, an oppressiveness within them.

"Good," said Teibar. "Now, breathe slowly, regularly, deeply."

I looked up at him over the tight rubber rim of the mask.

"Surely you understand that resistance is useless," he said.

I sobbed. My eyes wee bright with tears. I breathed in, deeply.

"Good," said Teibar. "Good."

It seemed there was a kind of heaviness inside the mask. It was not a strangling sensation and then, with my first gasp for air, an obliteration of consciousness, almost like a blow. This was quite different. It was patient, slow and gentle. I breathed in and out, deeply, slowly, regularly, in misery. Too, of course, it would be relentless, and implacable.

"Good," said Teibar.

Hercon released my ankles. I sluggishly, groggily, moved my feet. I felt the anklet with my right foot, and tried weakly to push it from my ankle, but, of course, it was useless. It only hurt the side of my right foot a little, and the inside of my left ankle. It was on me. I could not remove it. It was there, on me, until someone else, not me, might want it off. I was "ankleted," whatever that meant.

"Breathe deeply," said Teibar. "Good. Good."

Taurog released my wrists. He put my hands at my sides. I could not lift them.

"Deeply, deeply," said Teibar, soothingly.

I felt a key thrust into the lock on the collar I wore. It was then removed from me. I was dimly conscious of Taurog coiling the chain and replacing it in the attaché case.

"Struggle now, if you wish," said Teïbar, "slut."

But I could scarcely move. I could not raise my arms. I could not even bring my hands to the mask, and had I been able to do so, I would have been too weak to push it away. About the peripheries of my vision it seemed dark. It was hot under the tight mask. I felt another drop of liquid within the mask.

"You are ours now, 'modern woman,' " said Teibar.

But I scarcely heard him, or understood him. I supposed, in some sense, I was a "modern woman." I remembered, vaguely, that Teibar had said, earlier, that that could be taken away from me. I did not doubt it. Then I lost consciousness.

4 / The Whip

I screamed suddenly under it awakening under it startled not believing it not expecting it the suddeness it was like lightning the cracking sound like the sky breaking the snap like fire my body wrenching I pulling upwards the chain on my neck I fell to my side I pulled at the chain then the snap again no no please no so sharp so loud the fire the pain I screamed I was naked the chain cut my neck "Kneel," he said, "head to the floor," I obeyed then the snap the cracking sound again the lightning I fell to my stomach "Kneel," he snarled, "head to the floor," I sobbing obeyed.

"So," said he, "the modern woman under the whip."

I trembled, kneeling, my head down, the palms of my hands on the floor.

"Now, slut," said he, "your power is gone, all of it, that mistakenly given to you by foolish men."

I moaned, bent over, small before him, in a position of obeisance to his manhood, in pain.

"You are no longer on your world," he said. "You are now on my world."

I trembled.

"Look up," he said. "Kneel, kneel straightly. Put your hands on your thighs. Head up. Split your knees. More widely, slut!"

I obeyed.

I was then kneeling before him, straightly, my head up, my hands on my thighs, my knees widely spread, the chain from my collar dangling down before me, between my breasts, I could feel it on my body, and going back, between my knees, to a ring. I was terrified. I thought I must be mad. My body was in pain. There seemed something different here. The air was different, a thousand times, it seemed, cleaner and fresher. I had never known such air existed to be breathed. It made me feel somehow charged, and alive. The whip seemed still, hot and terrible, to burn on my body. And something else was different, too, something subtle, something I supposed I might quickly become accustomed to, but that now frightened me, terribly, in its implications. Literally the world had a different feel. Its gravity, preposterously enough, seemed less than that with which I was familiar. I dismissed this from my mind as some sort of confusion, or illusion. But I knew that I was in pain, sharp, miserable pain, fiery, burning pain, put on me by a man, and that that was real. Too, I knew I knelt before a man. That, too, was real. I was an educated, civilized woman, a modern woman, I supposed, in some sense, but I found myself kneeling before a man! Too, this startling me, this strangely affecting me, it seemed that this was somehow appropriate for me, that it was rightful for me, that it was where I belonged. I felt incredibly alive, and rightful there. Too, he had whipped me awake. What did that mean? What must be my nature here, then, I wondered, or my condition or status, in this place, that I could be so awakened? Though I was an educated, refined, civilized woman, a contemporary woman, a modern woman, I supposed, in some sense, I had been awakened by a whip! I had felt the lash!

"Where am I?" I begged.

"On my world," he said, simply.

"Please do not lie to me," I begged.

"Interesting," he said. "Are you accusing a man of lying to you?" He shook out the whip's coil.

"No," I said. "No!" I understood then that sexuality was important in this place, wherever it was, and that we were not of the same sex.

"Ah, I see," he said. "Of course. You are merely still simple, and naive. Yes, I suppose it would be hard for you to believe, very hard, particularly with your banal, sly, limited intelligence, my delicious, nasty, little animal." To my relief he recoiled the whip.

"Your world?" I said.

"Your life is going to be different now," he said, "quite different, dramatically different in a number of ways."

"Your world?" I begged.

"Yes," he said.

"Another *planet*?" I asked.

"Yes," he said.

"You do not seriously ask me to believe that, do you?" I asked.

He shrugged.

"Really!" I said.

"Can you not detect a difference in the atmosphere?" he asked. "Is it so difficult to detect? Too, can you not, really, at least now, more importantly, sense differences in the gravitational field?"

I shuddered.

"I see that you can," he said.

"I am now truly on another planet?" I asked.

"Yes," he said.

I felt faint. For a moment everything seemed to go dark. I wavered. In my heart I knew that what he was saying, incredible though it might seem, despite the startling enormity of it, was true.

"You have many adjustments to make, my pretty little animal," he said.

I looked at him.

"And there is no escape for you," he said, "from this world. You are here to stay. It is now your world, as well as mine. You are going to be here, and live on its terms, and exactly so, my modern woman, my hateful little charmer, for the rest of your life."

"Please, no!" I said.

"Put your hands, clasped, behind the back of your head, and put your head back," he said.

I did so.

"Farther back," he said.

I put my head farther back.

"Please," I said. "Please!"

He walked about me. "It is here that sluts such as you belong," he said.

I shuddered, feeling the coils of the whip move on my stomach.

"Yes," he said, coming around in front of me again, "I think you will do very nicely."

"Do?" I said.

"You may resume your original position," he said.

I returned then to my former position, with my hands on my thighs.

I knelt before Teibar, who had captured me on Earth, making me his prisoner after hours in the very library where I had worked. He was clad now in a tunic. I did not understand this, but it seemed to fit in well with the plain room in which I was confined. That garment, so simple, so physically freeing, so attractive, I supposed, might be congenial to this world, as it had been to several of the worlds of Earth. I suspected it was not untypical of this world. He had strong arms, and strong legs. I was even uneasy looking at him in such a garment. I knew that I had found him physically disturbing, and deeply and profoundly so, even on Earth, and had felt helpless and weak before him, but now those feelings, now that I saw him as he was on his own world, so splendid and powerful, so uncompromising, so fierce, so vital, so masculine, masculine like no man I had ever seen, or had known could exist, seemed multiplied a thousand times. It was like a lion before me, a lion whose teeth could rend me, whose paw, with a blow, could break my neck. And I was chained within his reach!

He was regarding me.

I dared not meet his eyes directly. I saw the whip in his hand. Men on this world, I suspected, were not patient with women, or at least women such as I.

"What is to be done with me, on this world?" I asked.

"You are not wearing clothes," he said, as though he might be just noticing this.

"No," I said.

"You are chained by the neck," he said.

"Yes," I said.

"I think it must be obvious," he said.

I shuddered. I wondered what it might be like, to be a female on a world like this, or the sort of female I was, on a world like this, where, unlike Earth, men had not been weakened.

"You are afraid, aren't you, slut?" he asked.

"Yes," I said.

"Good," he said. "That is as it should be. And you have every right to be afraid, I assure you, even, indeed, far more afraid than you can even begin to understand now."

I shuddered.

"It is amusing," he said, "to consider how the nature of your life is going to change."

"Were many women brought here?" I asked.

"In your shipment," he said, "one hundred. You were the hundredth."

"That seems a great many," I whispered.

"I do not gather them all, of course," he said. "There are others engaged in these enterprises, as well. The captures are brought together from various places, one from here, one from there, this attracting little attention."

"From various countries?" I asked. "America, England, France, Germany, Denmark, China, Japan?"

"Yes," he said. "But your shipment was largely regional."

"Is it difficult to 'gather' these girls?" I asked.

"No," he said, "they are trapped more easily than the small animals you call rabbits. Consider your own case."

"Do your people do this sort of thing regularly?" I asked.

"We have our schedules," he said.

"Are there other groups engaged in this sort of thing?" I asked.

"I think so," he said. "But I know little about them."

"I was the hundredth?" I asked.

"Yes," he said.

"I was saved for last?" I asked.

"Yes," he said.

"That was your doing?" I asked.

"Yes," he said.

"Why?" I asked.

"I have asked for a transfer to other duties," he said, musingly, regarding me. "It is thus possible that you may be the last female I will bring here from your world. To be sure, I will doubtless capture other women from time to time, here on my world, women native to my world, and perhaps, from time to time, Earth girls who have been brought here earlier."

"But you chose me for your last catch," I said.

"Yes," he said.

"Why?" I asked.

He smiled, fingering the coils of the whip.

"Surely you could have taken others," I said.

"Yes," he said.

"But you did not," I said.

"No," he said.

"Why?" I asked.

He did not respond.

"There is something different or special about me, somehow, from your point of view, isn't there?" I said. I had sensed this from the first.

"I did wish to make my last catch a particularly delicious one," he said.

"I do not understand," I said.

"Do not underestimate yourself, and your desirability as a female animal," he said.

"I am too short," I said. "I am too meaty. I am not tall, spare and willowy."

"Do not be stupid," he said.

"Am I attractive?" I asked.

"Certainly," he said. "You are a superbly cuddly slut. Do you think I would get my pay if I did not bring in first-class females?" I then realized that the tastes of men here might run more to the natural female, sweet and cuddly, and marvelous, than the stereotypes of beauty on my own world. In a sense I was moved with pleasure to learn this. In another sense I was terrified. Here I then understood I might find myself the object of powerful lusts and desires. Here I might find myself desired, and sought, and hunted, perhaps even as an animal, exquisitely delectable female quarry.

"But even so," I said, "perhaps you found something, or thought there was something, different or special about me?"

"I find you personally," he said, "quite desirable, even excruciatingly attractive."

I shrank back in the chain. How could he speak so openly of sexual matters? Too, I was afraid, as a female, found of interest, before him.

"But, yes," he said, "beyond such things you are special to me."

"In what way?" I asked.

"In your capture there is something symbolic," he said. "It is thus fitting that you be what might be my last capture of a female from your world."

"You seem to hate me," I said.

"Yes," he said. "I do."

"Why?" I asked.

"You are a modern woman," he said, "and, as such, you represent a perversion of humanity, a pernicious and wanton perversion, one maliciously deleterious to the centralities of human sexuality, both of the male and female, and thus one literally inimical not only to the quality but, ultimately, to the very future of the human species."

I looked at him, startled.

"You are a modern woman," he said, "and would destroy men."

"No!" I said.

"But you will not, I assure you," he said, "destroy men here, Modern Woman. Here, rather, you will serve them fully, and fearfully, and delectably, and to the utmost of your abilities."

"I am not a modern woman," I said. "I have never, in my heart, been a modern woman. In my heart I am a primitive woman, one who has been bred upon from the time of caves, an ancient woman, a Medieval woman, a Nineteenth-century woman, a natural woman, a needful, loving woman! I was as alien, and sorrowful, and lost, and miserable, in my world as you were!"

"Liar!" he cried. He snapped the whip in fury, and I shrank back, startled by its sound and threat, before him. "You are so clever, you lying slut!" he hissed. "You are so quick, so cunning, so dangerous!"

"Please," I said.

"But I see through your tiny tricks!"

"Why do you think I am a modern woman, in some sense you despise," I asked, "because I can speak clearly, because I can think, because I have read a book? Do you not think that true women, loving, needful women, can do these things? Do you not think that what you can love, they, too, can love?"

"They demean such things," he said, "using them as baubles and adornments."

I wept.

"Perhaps those little adornments, those little vanity devices," he said, "will make you more amusing, and interesting, in your collar."

"My collar?" I asked, aghast.

"Have you not seen what is being done to men on your world?" he asked.

I was silent.

"If you are not active in such matters," he said, "what have you done to reverse them?"

I was silent.

"You are thus, at the least, an abettor, or accomplice, in such crimes," he said.

"No!" I said.

"Thus, if only by tacit consent, you, too, are guilty of them," he said.

"No!" I protested.

"What do you think of the men of your world?" he asked.

"I despise them! They are weaklings!" I cried, suddenly. "They deserve to have us take their world from them, to be thrust aside with words and writs, to be superseded by contrived legalities, to be relegated by statutes and slogans to the peripheries of power, to become trammeled, and crippled, and incapable of action, like tied sheep, bleating contentedly, as they are advised, as they are castrated, to become nothing, to be deprived of their pride and strength, and thus even of the potentiality of their unused manhood, to take our orders, to obey us!"

"Your position, I take it," he said, "is motivated by your hatred, jealousy and envy of men?"

"I do not think so," I said. "I do not want to be a man. I want to be a woman. My anger, my frustration, is motivated, I think, not by their manhood, and that I am not a man, as seems to be the case almost universally with the women you despise, if we can believe physicians in the matter, but rather by their lack of manhood, which denies me as well as them, which keeps me from being a full woman."

"You are a clever slut, in your small way," he said. "I never doubted it. How cunningly you would turn things! But I am not deceived by your petty tricks. You envy men, and not being one, would try to destroy them."

"No!" I said.

"Yes," he said, "you are a modern woman, and would, like others, if you could, destroy men. I find you, and others like you, guilty, and grievously guilty, guilty of crimes against the very future of the human race on your world. Here you will discover, however, that men, the men of my world, are not inclined to find this sort of thing acceptable. You will learn here, I fear, that they do not see fit to tolerate such intentions and attempts."

I trembled.

"Here," he said, "my young, lovely, charming pretentious slut, you are going to learn what it is to be a woman, truly. Here, too, by my intent, I having brought you here, it pleasing me, you will in a lifetime of beauty, degradation and service pay for your crimes. Here, modern woman, your being a modern woman will be taken from you. You will henceforth be another sort of woman."

I looked up at him, frightened.

"We will revenge the men of Earth," he said.

I put down my head, terrified. I supposed, in some senses, I had been a modern woman, and that I was, in some sense, guilty of crimes. I had little doubt I would be punished. Men would doubtless have their vengeances upon me.

I looked up at my captor.

He had brought me to this place, at least in part, it seemed, out of just such a sense of fittingness, out of just such a sense of rightfulness, and justice.

"Good morning, Miss Williamson," he said.

"Good morning," I whispered. As he had used my name I was not at all sure it was really mine. It had sounded different, somehow. I suddenly feared that I might have any name, almost like a dog.

How incredibly attractive he was to me! How weak he made me feel!

I thought that I was, as human beings went, quite intelligent, but before this man, before such a man, I sensed that my intelligence was as nothing. I sensed, as I had long before, in the library, that he, in his power, intelligence and maleness, was totally my superior, indeed, that I could at best be little more than an animal at his feet.

"Hold still," he said. He crouched before me, the whip in his hand.

"What are you going to do?" I asked.

"Position," said he. I readjusted my position, improving it, kneeling, back on my heels, my back straight, my hands on my thighs, my knees spread.

"What are you going to do?" I asked. My body could still feel, dimly, the hot marks of the lash.

"Put your head back," he said. "Farther back."

I was then looking, in effect, at the beams and plaster of the ceiling.

"This is a test," he said.

"Ai!" I cried, suddenly, recoiling, jerking back, falling to my side, in a rattle of chain. I was then at the end of the chain, away from him, it taut from the ring, it holding my head forward. I could withdraw no further. I put my knees together, tightly. I put my hands over them. I looked at him in horror.

"Good," he said. "It is as I thought."

I could not believe what he had done.

"You are alive," he said, coiling the blade back against the staff. "I had thought you would be. Your body, its curves, suggests a rich abundance of female hormones. Such will put you, of course, more at the mercy of men."

The touch had been totally unexpected.

"Beast!" I said. "Beast!"

The touch had been gentle, but it had been purposeful. Apparently it had told him what he wanted to know.

"Beast!" I wept.

I had not realized what he was going to do. I had not had an opportunity to prepare myself for the touch, to perhaps steel myself into inertness. I was then suddenly fearful. What if such men simply did not permit a woman to steel herself into inertness, what if it were literally incumbent upon her to feel, and irreservedly, perhaps even under the threat of discipline, of fierce punishment, or worse, in all her hot, sweet, vulnerable openness? As it was, taken unawares, I had been forced to show myself, and before this beast, this lion of a man, responsive. I blushed red, hotly.

He stood up. "Return here, and kneel," he said, "and as you were before." He indicated the spot, gesturing with the whip, near the ring, where I had knelt.

He shook out the blade of the whip.

I hurried, crawling, to the spot, and knelt there, as I had been before.

He looked down at me.

"Make me pay," I whispered.

"What?" he said.

"I am ready," I whispered.

He smiled.

"I am naked before you," I said. "I am on a chain. You have aroused me. You have made me show myself responsive. You have taken all pride from me. You despise me. You hate me. I gather that I am to be made to pay for my crimes, that men here will make me pay for them, for being a modern woman. I am ready to pay. Make me pay."

"On your back," he said. "Throw your legs apart." Tears in my eyes, I obeyed.

"The modern woman," he smiled, "on her back."

"Where I belong!" I said.

"Or on your stomach," he smiled, "or kneeling, bent over, or in any one of a thousand postures of submission and service."

I shuddered, understanding the sorts of things that might be required of me, and even routinely, on this world.

I closed my eyes. I feared I might swoon at his least touch. I had never met anyone who remotely compared with him. I had not even known such men could exist. To such a man I knew that I, even with all my refinement, education and intelligence, could never be more than a dog, a panting bitch, at his feet. He had even spoken of a "collar." What could he have meant?

I opened my eyes.

"Do you beg?" he asked.

"Would you make me beg?" I cried.

"Yes," he said.

"Very well," I wept. "I beg!"

"The modern woman begs," he smiled.

"I beg," I said. "I am no longer a modern woman."

"Oh, yes," he smiled, "you are still a modern woman, as of now. But, in time, you will no longer be one. In time, that will be taken from you."

"I beg!" I said. "I beg!"

"Surely you have forgotten something," he said.

"What?" I asked, in misery.

"You are a virgin," he said.

I looked at him, wildly, tears in my eyes.

"Kneel, as you were before, slut," he said.

"Beast!" I wept. "Beast!" But I crept to my knees, and knelt before him, as I had been commanded. I was shaking. Tears fell from my eyes. He had had no intention of having me. My virginity, somehow, seemed a factor in this. I wondered what this, really, could have to do with anything. Had it not been for that I think I would, even in the library, by such a man, have been put to lengthy uses. Muchly I suspected would I have been forced to pleasure him, and doubtless Taurog and Hercon, as well.

"Beast!" I wept.

"I am leaving," he said.

I looked up, frightened.

"It was only that I wished to see you before I left, and how you might look, here, a chain on your neck, hateful, charming slut, in a waiting room."

"A waiting room?" I asked.

"Yes," he said. "They will be coming for you shortly. You will have a busy morning. Others are already being processed."

"Processed?" I asked.

"Yes," he said. He then turned away from me.

"Wait!" I cried.

He turned about, again to regard me.

I thought desperately. I wanted to keep him with me. "Are all women awakened here," I asked, "by the whip?" My body was still sore from the blows.

"No," he said, "of course not. It was merely that I thought it might be informative and salubrious for you to be awakened thusly, that you might then, from the beginning, obtain an inkling as to what, for you, was to be the nature of your new world."

I regarded him, aghast.

"Have no fear," he said. "Such a thing, if ever, is rarely done. As you may well imagine, it tends to interfere with a woman's sleep."

"With her beauty sleep?" I said, ironically.

"In a way, that is quite true," he said. "Good rest is important to her, for her loveliness, her alertness and service. It is the same with other domestic animals."

I looked at him, angrily.

"Most of your beatings will occur, at any rate, I assure you, when you are fully awake."

"Beatings?" I asked.

"A hazard of what is to be your condition," he said.

"An occupational hazard?" I inquired.

"The condition is not an occupation," he said. "An occupation is not something you are, but something you do. Too, you might change an occupation. Your condition, on the other hand, in the sense I have in mind, is not what you do, but what you are. Similarly, you will be totally unable to change your condition. You will be absolutely powerless to alter, influence or change it in any way whatsoever. Once it is imposed upon you it will then be something which you, quite simply, and categorically, are. To be sure, susceptibility to the beatings of which I spoke, similarly to an occupational hazard, in its way, is an inevitable concomitant of what will be your condition. The frequency and nature of these beatings, of course, will probably depend much on you. If you are not pleasing. you will doubtless be beaten, and well. If you are pleasing, and perfectly so, you may or may not be beaten."

I looked at him, trying to understand what was being said to me. I did know, of course, I could be beaten. I had already felt the lash. I was not eager to feel it again.

"What is wrong?" he asked.

"I do not understand what you are saying," I said.

"Oh?" he asked.

I put my hands on the chain that attached me by the neck to the ring in the floor. "I do not understand what I am doing here," I said. "What is going to be done with me?"

"You mean, immediately?" he asked.

"Yes," I said.

"You're going to be branded," he said, "and put in a collar."

I regarded him with disbelief.

"But so, too, will the other girls," he said. "You will all have your brands and collars."

I could not speak.

"Such things are prescribed by merchant law," he said.

"This," I whsipered, frightened, "is then truly a world such as that of which you spoke, a world on which women such as I are bought and sold as slaves?"

"Position," he said.

Immediately I released the chain and knelt as I had before, back straight, back on my heels, my hands on my thighs, my knees spread.

"Yes," he said.

"And that is the fate you have decided for me," I said, "that I be a slave."

"Yes," he said.

I was silent.

"It will be amusing, from time to time, to think of you in exacting and perfect bondage, where you belong, so right for you, striving desperately to please masters, for fear of your very life, my delectable, hateful slut."

"That is why you did not take my virginity," I said, "because you had this fate in store for me."

"Yes," he said.

"My virginity could affect my price?" I said.

"Yes," he said.

"It is as if I were an animal," I said.

"Soon," he said, "you will be an animal, in full legality."

"You captured me," I said, poutingly. "My virginity belongs to you. It is yours, truly."

"I do not want it," he said.

I looked at him, startled.

"I give it to whoever buys you, and welcome," he said.

I bit my lip, to keep from crying out in anger.

"Against my will I find you extremely attractive," he said, "even infuriatingly so. Indeed, I must put you from my mind. Soon I will forget you. Soon you will be only another number, another entry in my records. But it is you I find attractive, and not some meaningless part of you. What is the virginity of a hateful modern woman, a despicable slut like yourself, really worth? Nothing. It is worthless. Oh, it might be amusing, as an act of imperious arrogance, to take it from you, to rend it, to be the first to force you apart, to be the first to open you for the uses of men, but it is even more amusing to show you my disdain for that worthless bit of fragile, temporary tissue by which you set such grand and unnatural store, and leave its fate to the lotteries of markets, and to whoever makes the successful bid on you. Let it go to him, whoever he is, who first buys you."

I clenched my fists on my thighs. I sobbed. I wept.

"It is thus," he said, "I show my contempt for you."

I looked up at him.

"Charming," he said.

I sobbed.

"But it is not I, but others," he said, "who will put your charms to use."

"Don't leave me," I begged.

But he had gone.

I lay down on the floor. I pulled my legs up. After a time I heard the voices of men outside the door. I did not understand their language. They were coming for me.

5 / Training

"Eat!" said the man. My face was thrust down, into the trough, half into the moist gruel. His hand was in my hair. I feared for a moment I might suffocate. I pressed my face down into the gruel. I opened my mouth. With my teeth and lips, and tongue, desperately scraping, scooping, pulling, licking, biting, pushing down, moving my head, I tried to get as much into my mouth as I could. My head was then pulled up, and held back, by the hair. I swallowed what I had in my mouth. It was not easy to swallow it. I knelt before a wooden feeding trough, with other girls. The man crouched beside me. My eyes were closed. Gruel was upon my face and in my hair. He then threw my head forward again, over the wooden rim of the trough, and pushed my face down again, deeply, submerging it, to the ears, in the gruel. Again I struggled to get as much as I could into my mouth. Then his hand had left my hair and I lifted my head from the moist substance. I blinked, gruel upon my face, its particles like wet, unmelting snow on my eye lashes. He had gone further down the line. I struggled to swallow what I had in my mouth. I pulled a little, weakly, at the light, lovely manacles which confined my wrists behind my back. I looked at the other girls, to my right. They, too, were similarly manacled. We were not yet permitted to use our hands in feeding. I looked to my left, and made certain that the man was not watching. I then bent down and tried to wipe my closed eyes and face on the wooden edge of the trough. He was not treating everyone as he had treated me. I had received special attentions in the matter. That had to do with something which had happened earlier. I looked to the girl to my right, a blonde. She put her head down, again, to the trough, her wrists linked behind her, like mine, in those lovely feminine confinements, little more than two lock rings and a tiny span of gleaming chain. We were all naked. It was easy to tell, however, which of us were virgins, for the virgins, like myself, wore the "iron belt." Its horizontal portion, like an iron oval, would close about my waist, and the vertical portion, like a "U," hinged in front to the horizontal portion, flattened, shaped and slotted at its center, would swing up between my legs and there its flattened, laterally slotted end, like a hasp, would be placed over the staple on the left side of the oval ring, the other side of the oval ring, the right side, already over this staple, and secured there, behind my back, with a heavy, dangling padlock. There was little danger I would be penetrated while wearing this device. The girl to my right did not wear it. She had already been "opened for the uses of men," as it is said here. She was thus free, of course, for the uses of the guards, who did not fail to avail themselves of their privileges. Once she had been dragged forth from her kennel, down several from mine, to the right, and they, so eager were they, such men, to have her, that they had not even seen fit to wait until they had pulled her on her leash to their own quarters. I pretended not to watch. But later, after they were finished, and had returned her to her own kennel, and I was alone, I wept, so aroused I was. I did not know if she were from Earth, and if so, from what part of it, or if she were of this world. We are almost never permitted to speak to one another, and we are never, at all, permitted to speak during the feeding period. When she had been used before my kennel she had been under "gag law," as is common when the guards use a girl, forbidden speech, save for moans and whimpers. I had understood many of the commands given to her, of course. I had begun to learn this language. I looked at her. It was possible she was of this world. Men here, I had learned, were every bit as ready, and as prompt, to put their own females to their purposes as the females of Earth. Our origins made no difference in these matters. What was important was what we had in common, our sex, simply that we were females. To be sure, the girls here from this world regarded themselves as immeasurably superior to us, those of Earth, and perhaps the men did, too, in some sense, but, as far as I could tell, that made their chains no lighter, nor the blows they received any the less severe. Some men, of course, many men even, seemed to find women of Earth of special interest, and treated them with particular harshness. Teibar, who had captured me, I think, was such a man. Others, however, seemed to prefer visiting these abuses on the women of their own world. Others, which made sense to me, seemed to think in terms of the individual woman. I think it would be true, however, to say that generally, aside from people's opinions as to the proper sort of treatment for us, we did not have the same "standing" as the women of this world. More often than they, for example, we would be put in earrings, which here is regarded, interestingly enough, as an almost consummate degradation of a woman. Similarly, another indication of our status here is that, occasionally, one of our names, an Earth-girl name, would be bestowed on a girl of this world, as a punishment, usually a temporary one, indicating that she was now to be regarded as one of the lowest of the low. I had now been branded, a small, graceful mark burned into my left thigh, high, under the hip. It had a vertical bar, a rather strict one, with two curling, frondlike extensions, rather near its base, as though in submission to it. It looked a little like a "K." That was mine. There were variations on this theme. Some of the other girls had similar brands, but, in one respect or another, somewhat different. There were other sorts of brands, too, but the "K-type" brand was the most common. Most of these brands, of whatever sort, were on the left thigh, as mine was, near the hip. On my neck, also, there was now a flat, narrow steel collar. It was close-fitting. I could not remove it. It was locked there. It was not uncomfortable. I seldom even thought about it, but it was there.

I looked to my left. The fellow who had thrust my face into the gruel was looking in my direction. Quickly I put my face back into the trough, thrusting it into the moist gruel. Feeding time was almost over. I did not care for the gruel much, as it was tasteless and flat. I ate it, however, as it was incumbent upon me to do so. Too, I was hungry, and it was undeniably nourishing. It, like other aspects of our diet, the fruits and vegetables, and the cylindrical pellets we were given, seemed intended to slim our bodies and bring us to a peak state of health. The gruel was appropriate enough for us, I supposed. It was clearly a form of animal feed.

I sneaked a look to my left, and, frightened, saw that the man was coming in my direction. Swiftly I thrust my face back into the trough and addressed myself to the gruel. I sensed he would now be behind me. I ate quickly, and well. I then heard the gong sound, which signified the end of the feeding period. Immediately I withdrew my head from the trough and knelt back on my heels, my back straight, looking straightly ahead. When the gong sounds the girl stops eating immediately, and assumes this position. Obedience is to be instantaneous.

I heard the man moving away. Yes, he had been behind me. I breathed more easily.

I was now eating quite well. They did not have any more trouble with me on that score, not now.

A week ago I had, not because I wanted to starve, or die, as some of the Earth girls in my group had proclaimed hysterically in their own cases, and not even because I was trying to be difficult, really, I had refused to eat. I had done this, I think, as an experiment, as much as anything else. I had wondered what they would do. Too, I think I was trying to find out the limitations within which I was functioning, what I might be able to do, and might not be able to do. I wanted to know the nature and extent, and the existence or nonexistence, of the discipline to which I might be liable. I wanted to know something about the boundaries of my world. I was trying to find out where the fences were, the location of the walls. I found out. There had been seven of us involved in this matter. Our leader was a short, plump blonde who had been a political columnist for a small suburban newspaper on the northeast coast of the United States. She had been a political-science major in college. We were taken immediately in hand, all seven of us. Three of us, our leader and her two chief cohorts, were immediately kenneled, publicly, in the feeding area. The rest of us were tied on low "perches," also in the feeding area, at one wall, platforms fitted with "T" beams, a ring in the back of the "T" beam. Such things are often found in such houses, like rings and posts, commonly being used for purposes of display and discipline. Our ankles were put in leather shackles, behind the vertical post. Our arms were hooked over the horizontal post and fastened in front of us with straps and leather manacles, which buckled shut. Our heads were then pulled back and, by our hair tied about the ring behind the post, held painfully in this position. Narrow tubes were then brought, with plungers. These, to our dismay and discomfort, and horror, were thrust down our throat to our stomach. These tubes were inserted through heavy leather balls put in our mouths. We could not close our mouths or bite on the tubes because of these obstructions. Food was then forced into our stomachs. The tubes were then withdrawn. We could not rid ourselves of the food, even had we wished to do so. Our hands were secured. We looked at one another. Some of the girls had tears of helpless frustration in their eyes. If the men chose not to permit it, they could not even starve themselves. In my eyes, however, I think, was something less like helpless rage and defeat than reassurance, wonder and respect. I was pleased to learn, terrible though it may sound, how strong these men were, and how, with them, I was totally helpless. None of us requested a second demonstration of their power. We went quickly enough to the trough after that. The other three who had been kenneled were not fed. Soon the two cohorts were begging to be fed. It seems that, truly, they had no wish to die. Too, it was clear the men would simply permit them to do so, if they wished. After some two days the two cohorts, piteous and pleading, were drawn forth and permitted, when it was the feeding period, and not before, to feed. The leader, then, too, the blonde, begged to be fed. They kept her in starvation three more days. Then they put her in a tiny cage, where she could not exercise, and could scarcely move, and, heavily, abundantly, every two hours, using the tube and ball, and the cruel plunger, using rich foods and creams, which she could not taste because of the tube, forced-fed her. Soon her corpulence became pathetic. She was then removed from our midst. Some men, we were told, like such women. She was being readied for the "Tahari trade," we were told. This seemed to amuse the girls from this world who were amongst us. The Earth girls, like myself, however, did not understand the allusion.

The gong sounded again and we rose up, and turned toward the door.

When I came to the door a whip was lowered in front of me. In that moment the line paused. Swiftly I moved to the side, and knelt, my back straight, my knees wide. The line continued on its way. I had been removed from it by the whip. The padlock behind the small of my back made a tiny sound as, dangling, it moved against the "U"-shaped bar, fastened up, between my legs. I adjusted my position, carefully. I knelt before a man. The whip was held toward me, and I kissed it, deferentially, and then drew back my head.

"Your lessons have proceeded well, Doreen," he said.

That was now my name, "Doreen," only that, simply "Doreen," nothing more.

I looked up at him.

"Quite well," he said.

I could understand him. To be sure, my grasp of this language still left much to be desired. There were still many words, even common words, I did not know, and sometimes I could not follow even elementary constructions. I think, however, all things considered, that it could not be gainsaid that my progress in it had been remarkable. I was the quickest of my Earth sisters in this respect. All of us, however, I thought, were doing extremely well. This was not simply because of the frequency and intensiveness of our lessons, and our finding ourselves in an environment where this language, it seemed, was simply, or primarily, spoken, but because of our motivation. We strove to learn it. We were desperately eager to learn it. We had learned that not only the quality and nature of our life on this world, but perhaps our very survival, could be contingent on our success in understanding and speaking this language. Too, we were often accorded private instructresses. These girls, though collared, and doubtless branded, as we were, wore brief tunics, which put them immeasurably above us. How we envied them! Too, they carried long, supple leather quirts. These they used on us when not satisfied with our responses, or progress. I had been quirted, but not often. My usual instructress was "Tina," the name which she had been given on this world. I do not know what her original name had been. She had once been from Pittsburgh. I think she was a good instructress, and she had helped me much. A part of my success, I am sure, was due to her. She was supposed to be one of the best of the instructresses. They had assigned her to me. She was exacting. More than once I had felt her quirt. The instructresses, of course, had their own report lines. If their charges did not do well they, themselves, were held responsible. I recalled seeing one of the instructresses stripped and whipped because the skill levels of her charge were judged insufficient. After that, for better than a week, she was permitted only a half tunic. She began, then, to use two hands on her quirt. Almost immediately her pupil improved her performances considerably. When the instructress had been stripped I had seen that she, like the rest of us, was branded. Her brand, too, was one of the "K-type" brands. It was somewhat different from mine, but it was clearly of the same sort. I do not know what the nature of Tina's brand was, as I never saw it, but I am sure it was there, probably high on the left thigh, like mine, beneath that brief skirt. There was no difficulty, of course, in seeing the collar on her neck. That was visible to anyone. It was probably one of the "K-type" brands. They seemed to be the most common brand, at least of those I had seen. The lessons of which the man had spoken were not all linguistic, of course. I had also received lessons in the proper performance of domestic servilities, such as cooking, sewing, laundering, cleaning, and such. Other lessons were almost lessons in customs, manners and decorum. For example, we were taught how to serve at a table, deferentially, skillfully, unobtrusively and, for the most part, silently, and how to move and walk, and kneel and rise, gracefully, and even such tiny, interesting things, as how to pick up a fallen object, by crouching down, retrieving it, rather than bending over. We were being taught, it seemed, to be graceful and beautiful. Too, of course, we were taught our place, and proper relations to men. A significant portion of our training was intimate and erotic, or sexual and sensual, in nature, ranging from such things as make-up, body ornamentation, cosmetics and perfumes, to techniques, psychological and physical, generally a combination of both, of pleasing men. In the latter range of our studies some of the girls were even instructed in the rudiments of what, perhaps for lack of a better word, might be described, using the Earth expression, as "ethnic dance." It did not surprise me that the men of this world, who seemed to have such a lust for, and such a relish for, and appreciation of, females, would command such dance of them. I gathered this form of dance was quite common here and that it might be required of any female, or any female of our sort. Interestingly enough I had had only two days of this sort of instruction before I was stopped, and sent from the room, to be applied to other lessons. I was told that my skills in these matters, as they had now ascertained, and confirming reports on my "papers," or "records," were already far beyond the rudiments that I would obtain in such a class. I was simply dismissed from the class, to address myself to other lessons; I had, so to speak, "validated that requirement."

I put my head down, gratefully. I was pleased that he was pleased. Girls such as I are eager to please such men. It makes us happy to do so. It satisfies something warm, and deep and marvelous, in the very bottom of our bellies to do so. If we do not, of course, they simply see to it that we do. Our behavior is then quickly, and often painfully, corrected.

"It is hard to believe that you are a virgin," he said.

I did not lift my head. I moved a little in the iron belt. It was not as well fitted to me as it might have been. They just take belts they have at hand, and, finding one of the proper size, or approximately so, they put it on her. The "U-shaped" vertical bar on this belt was, at the center, hammered flat, shaped and slotted. It chafed the upper interior of my thighs a little. I had diffidently called this to the attention of a fitter some two weeks ago but, after he had checked it, and had determined to his satisfaction that the matter was not serious enough to have warranted my complaint, he had simply cuffed me, and sent me, blood in my mouth, back to my lessons. I had not complained afterwards. That I was a virgin had undoubtedly been included by Teibar in my papers, or records. On the other hand, when I had begun my lessons, and given the apparent alacrity with which I took to them, they had, to make sure, removed the belt, and checked the matter. The report had been correct. The belt was then replaced on me. I had, for most practical purposes, worn it since, even sleeping in it, in my kennel. I gathered they did not entirely trust the discipline of the guards. To these men, and to men such as these, I gathered, I was attractive, perhaps even extremely so. This undoubtedly had something to do with the sexual tastes of such men, seeming to run more toward the normal, natural female than toward the current commercial paradigms of feminine beauty in my culture, but I think, too, I was pretty, really pretty, genuinely pretty, and very desirable to them, and very attractive to them, aside from such general considerations. Too, of course, these were extremely vigorous and virile men. Probably very few females, of any sort, would have been really safe in their vicinity.

"And you have become beautiful," he said to me, "and even more beautiful."

I kept my head down.

In the flattened, shaped part of the metal under my belly, about a quarter of an inch from my body, there was a curved slot about three inches in length and three-eighths of an inch in width. The interior edges of this slot, heavy and iron, were serrated, jagged, like the teeth of a saw. The belt, accordingly, equipped with this device, and locked so closely upon me, so fixedly upon me, would be likely, I thought, to frustrate or discourage a male, unless, of course, he had its key, or a tool to remove it.

I felt the hand of the man in my hair. He was not being cruel to me. He was shaking my head, good-naturedly. I looked up at him, gratefully. We are grateful for such small signs of recognition, even as dogs are. This man was pleased with me. He did not hate me, even though I was a woman of Earth. I was only another charge, or student, or pupil, to him. He did not bear me anything like the ill will, the hostility, that Teibar, who had been my captor, had. Indeed, very few of the men I had met here seemed hostile toward me, as he had been. There might have been a very simple reason for that, of course. Teibar had been to Earth, and had seen what was being done to men on that world. These men, I supposed, might be ignorant of that. Indeed, they might even be incredulous that such a thing could occur. It was perhaps the sort of thing they would not have believed, unless they had seen it with their own eyes. Accordingly, it seems it did not even occur to them to see me, as Teibar had, in terms of guilt, crime and villainy, nor, in hatred, to make me some sort of helpless proxy, something fit to be punished for the wrongs which had been visited upon the men of my world.

The man put his hand down by my face, touching it, gently, and I kissed and licked it, looking up at him. I was naked before him, and branded, and collared. He smiled down at me. He was fond of me, as men might be fond of a lovely, sleek little animal. His name was Ulrick. I would not use his name to him, directly, of course, but I might use it to others, in reference to him.

"I have news for you, Doreen," he said.

I looked up at him.

"We have done about as much with you here as we have the inclination to do, given our schedules," he said. "Too, you and two of the other girls, have come along very well."

I looked up at him, puzzled.

"You have learned a great deal here," he said. "But you have really only begun your education here. It will soon become apparent to you, outside, how little you know. It is my recommendation that you continue to apply yourself, and be diligent. Strive constantly to improve your skills, and value."

I could not understand, exactly, what he was saying. I think this was not so much a matter of the words, as of their seeming import.

"We have an order to be filled," he said, "from a wholesaler, for three Earth females."

I shuddered.

"Remember," he said, "eventually, on the block, when you are retailed, presumably in different markets, do not tighten. Be fresh and supple. Breathe deeply. Be beautiful. Be only so afraid that you are superb, not so afraid that you are awkward, or clumsy."

I shuddered.

"It is a good time of year," he said. "It will soon be the peak season."

I was terrified. I gathered then that it may not have been an accident that I had been captured by Teibar when I had. He had "gathered" me, as he might have put it, so simple and unpretentious a verb, suggesting the casualness of his efforts, at a certain time of year pertinent to his own world, at a time when I would have enough time to be delivered here, trained, at least to some extent, and then, at an optimum moment, it seemed, brought to market.

"You are going to be sold," he said.

I looked up at him, terrified.

"Do you understand?" he asked.

"Yes, Master," I said.

6 / Transportation

It is all part of the hood, the leather ball, the strap attached at the front of it, and the belt, with its double loop, on the outside, held in place by the hood's belt loops, at its opening. Some hoods are little more than sacks, of canvas or leather, with drawstrings. The leather ball was thrust, by a thumb, into my mouth. I then felt its strap, attached at its front, drawn back between my teeth, and buckled behind the back of my neck. The hood itself was then placed over my head and some tucks were taken in it. It was then, by the double loop of the belt, passed twice about my neck, drawn shut. The hood was now closed about my neck. It was snug under my chin, held by the belt. The belt was then buckled shut behind the back of my neck, as the gag strap, inside the hood, had been. A small padlock, passed through two rings, the buckle ring and one of the small rings, sewn in the belt, now adjacent to it, secured the arrangement on me. I was locked in the hood.

I, and apparently the other two Earth girls, Clarissa and Gloria, had been found acceptable by the wholesaler's agent. They were already kneeling in their hoods, naked, their knees spread, in the neck chain. I then felt the chain put on my own neck. Seven other girls, too, similarly hooded and in postures of submission, were on the same chain, but I did not think they were from Earth. Our hands, too, those of all of us, were secured, braceleted behind our backs. We all, too, had new collars on our necks, probably transport collars. They had metal tags attached to them. There had been two lots, it seemed, one of seven girls from this world and one of three from Earth. We had not actually been paid for, as I understood it, except for a deposit, and were merely being sent on consignment to the wholesaler, who, similarly, for deposits, filling his own orders, would deliver us to various retailers. Our sales would then, presumably, take place in various places, and the moneys, except for the retailer's profit, would return to the wholesaler, for his profit, and eventually to Ulrick's people, for theirs.

I knelt in the hood.

I was a slave girl.

This was a world called "Gor."

On Earth Teibar had told me that there was a world such as this, though he had not told me its name, a world on which women such as I were "bought and sold." I had not believed him, of course. But I had now learned that he had spoken the truth. I had now learned that there was such a world, and that its chains were real. I wore them.

A command was spoken and we rose. Another command was uttered and we stepped forth, beginning with our left foot.

I thought, somewhat bitterly, how amused Teibar would have been to see me, chained and hooded, in coffle, the "hateful slut," the "modern woman," he had so despised, now in her place, now, at last, getting her due. How he had hated me! I still could not understand the full extent of his animosity. I took measured, graceful steps. We must be beautiful in coffle. We can be whipped if we are not. Doubtless he would have relished the thought of a lifetime of degradations and vengeances to be visited upon me. I should have rejoiced, I suppose, that he had gone his way, he who was so fierce and had hated me so keenly, doubtless never to lay eyes on me again, content doubtless now to merely ponder, upon occasion, with amusement, the fate to which he had consigned me, but, to be honest, I would not have minded being seen by him again, or kneeling at his feet, or trying to show him what I had learned, or even trying to please him, and as what he had seen fit that I had now been made. I suppose I should have hated him, for what he had done to me. But I think I cared for him. When I thought of him, I often wept. Like a cuffed, kicked bitch I would have crawled back to him, if I had had the chance. But he had not kept me, as I supposed he could have, and as Ulrick, questioned earnestly by me on this matter, had confirmed. It would have simply been a matter of paying a good price for me, but one discounted within the house, one well within his means. But he had not wanted me. He had spurned me and sent me, his despised "modern woman," doubtless in disdain and amusement, to the chains of others. I would have liked to have seen him again, perhaps to try to convince him, humbly, that I had learned my lessons, that I had profited from his instruction, and what he had done to me, that there was, even now, this soon, very little of the "modern woman" left in me. And, eventually, I supposed, there would be none of it left in me. He had said that it could be taken from me, and I now had little doubt not only that it could be, but that it would be, and totally. Indeed, I wanted, myself, to rid myself of its narrownesses, its contaminations, its uglinesses, as quickly as I could. I supposed I was a wicked, worthless woman and, far worse, only a despicable natural slave, but something deep in me, fundamental in me, profound and ancient in me, loved men, and I did not want to make them small, and nothing, but I wanted, rather, to please them, to obey them, to serve them, to give my all to them, to make them strong and proud, grand and glorious, to make them happy. But here, among the virile men of Gor, I had little choice in such matters. Such things, regardless of whether or not I might wish to bestow them of my own free will, would be simply commanded of me. Even did I hate men I would have no choice here but to deliver perfections to them. Here among masters and slaves were literally instituted the practices and relationships, and required of me, under the threat of terrible punishments, and even death, which in my heart I would have longed to bestow of my own free will on men, or at least men so free and proud, so much the natural masters of a woman.

I was now outside, probably in a walled court. I could feel the air on my body. My feet were bare. I realized, with a shock, I loved what was being done to me.

I heard the creak of wagon wheels, the shuffling of some sort of beast.

"This way," said a man.

We moved, but only a few feet. Tugs on the neck chain guided me. It was warm in the hood. The extension on the neck chain of the first girl, who was also hooded, serves as a leash for her, guiding her, and her chain guides the second girl, and the second girl's guides the third, and so on. I was last in the coffle. I did not know if this were significant or not at this time. Sometimes the most exciting girl is put first on the coffle, and sometimes last. Sometimes beauties and lesser beauties are mixed. Sometimes the coffle is simply arranged in order of descending height.

I suddenly jerked, and almost fell, uttering, startled, a stifled sound, my head moving, the gag straps pulling at the back of my neck, the girl in front of me almost off balance, the snap of the lash, too, had startled me, the lash had stung my calves, sharply, cruelly.

"Stand straight," said a voice.

I improved my posture immediately.

We sometimes have a tendency, I am afraid, to be a little slothful or lax when not directly under the eyes of men. Some say we are all lazy, and must be kept constantly in line by the whip. I do not know. Perhaps, on the other hand, it is simply that we are human, so very, very human. In the hood, of course, it is hard to know if a man is looking at you or not. It is best to assume, naturally, that one is always doing so. I had been lax. I had been careless. I had been foolish.

I felt a man's hand on my arm. "This way," he said.

That is one of the disadvantages of being last in the coffle, incidentally. It is easiest to strike one in that position. Too, as I, locked in my hood, had foolishly permitted to slip my mind, there is often a guard there, towards its end.

"Stand here," said a man.

I should have kept myself beautiful, particularly here, in the open, where there were men about.

The back of my calves still stung.

I hoped I would not be struck again. I was trying to stand well.

I then felt myself lifted up, lightly, in the hood, the chain still on my neck, in a man's arms, his hands thusly supporting me, one beneath the back of my knees and the other behind my back, and was handed up to another man, who then put me down, kneeling, on a higher, metal surface. I heard the snorting of some beast. I did not know what it was. I did not think it was a horse or ox. It was perhaps some draft animal native of this world. It frightened me. The surface seemed to move a bit under me. There was a girl on my right, linked to me by her neck chain, she who had preceded me on the coffle. No girl was on my left. I was the last on the coffle. I heard a body, doubtless that of the fellow to whom I been handed, descend from the surface. I then, a moment later, heard the closing, heavy and metallic, of a door, or gate. I even felt the vibration of this through the metal flooring, on my knees and toes. I then heard a rattle of chain, the thrusting home of a heavy bolt and the closure of what sounded like a heavy, dangling padlock, one with a bolt perhaps a half-inch thick. I had seen many such in the house. Several of our kennels, where our blankets and pans of water were kept, had been closed with similar devices. My own kennel, on the other hand, had been closed with two locks intrinsic to the door itself. I could still feel the air on my body so I thought we were not in a solid-sided enclosure, but, probably, a cage. I put back my head. I could then feel the bars. They were heavy, about an inch or an inch-and-a-half thick, I would have supposed, and about three inches apart. This cage, I gathered, from the height of the surface, and its movement, was mounted on a wagon.

I tried to move the leather ball around a bit in my mouth, with my tongue. I managed to adjust it a little, so it was a bit more comfortable.

I then heard the sliding of canvas, and its being pulled down and adjusted, and the sound of various buckles. The cage was being covered.

In a moment then there was a cry to some animal and the shaking of a harness.

There was also the snapping of a whip. That sound frightened me. I had learned to know it better than I cared to.

I was thrown off balance a little to my left as the vehicle began to move.

It seemed to me we were being held in a great deal of security. We were gagged and hooded; we were stripped, our brands thusly bared; our wrists were menacled behind our backs; and we were attached to one another, in coffle, by neck chains. Beyond this we were caged, and the cage, too, was covered. That may have been, of course, that we not attract too much attention, naked slaves being transported through streets. I wondered if there were any free women on this world. I had never seen one. To be sure, slave girls on this world were often held in great security. One of the most significant securities, of course, was their collars, marking them unmistakably as slaves, and, usually, identifying their masters. It seemed to please these men, so proud, so strong, so uncompromising, so imperious, to keep us in bonds, chains and such. Our strongest bond, of course, that which would hold us if none other, that which we could never hope to break, was our condition itself, that we were slaves. Still, beyond these things it seemed to me that there might be something a little mysterious, if not excessive, in the careful way we were being treated, handled and moved. I had gathered that it was not really unusual, particularly in certain places, though in others it was apparently regarded as being tactless or vulgar, for slaves to be marched naked, in coffle, through the streets, for example, for their own edification or instruction, that they be helped to understand that they are truly slaves, as a form of advertising for their owner's house, or merely, as the case might be, as a matter of simple convenience. Certainly they were often kept this way, I had been given to understand, on highway and road treks, if only to protect their tunics from sweat and dust. And there seemed little objection anywhere to marching them through the streets in tunics or camisks, a narrow, poncholike garment. To be sure, they were generally transported naked, in closed wagons, their ankles chained to a central bar. But they were presumably not then gagged and hooded, or confined as closely as we. I did not understand these things. I did not question the will of masters, of course, for the will of masters, quite simply, is not to be questioned, but I was curious, or puzzled, to know why it was being done this way. Too, more interestingly, I did not even know where I was. I did not know where the house in which I had been trained was located. I did not even know the name of that house. I did not even know the name of its master. Now I was being taken from it, toward some equally unknown destination. None of the girls, too, as far as I could tell, were any the better informed than I. But whatever the explanation might be for these anomalies, if anomalies they were, there was no doubt that I was now a slave. Teibar, who had been my captor, had seen to that.

To be sure, interestingly, I did not really object to these various things, neither to the anomalies, if anomalies they were, nor to what might be the more typical or standard subjugations, rigors and strictures, fierce and terrible though they might be, to which I was subjected. Though I would scarcely admit this to myself, I was thrilled to be branded and collared. I was thrilled to have been stripped, and gagged and hooded, and manacled, and put in neck coffle, by the will of men. I was pleased that they had taken me in hand and, wishing to do so, had made me their slave. I was inutterably thrilled to be now absolutely and categorically subject, in the order of nature, to their uncompromising domination. It was for this sort of thing that I had longed all my life. It was for this reason, I thought, that I had so despised the males of Earth, because they had permitted themselves to be deprived of the birthright of their manhood, because they would not see to it that I was put in, and kept in, my rightful place in nature, where I wanted in my heart to be. My beauty, I felt, belonged to them, if they were strong enough to take it, and put it where it belonged, at their feet. I had wanted to kneel before them, lovingly and worshipfully, and yield them my total submission. They had not been strong enough, however. I had been almost consumed with anguish, and filled with contempt for them, and tortured and torn by loneliness, hatred and misery. Then, to my amazement, I had found myself brought to this world. Here men had no such weakness. Here I found myself, in all my helpless womanhood, whether I was pleased about it or not, whether I wished it or, whether I willed it or not, at the feet of masters. No, I did not object to the collars and brands. They put my womanhood on me. I did not object to the will of men, and to their bonds. Such told me that I was theirs. I did not object to being kept in ignorance, as this was their will, and gave me further evidence that I was only their animal, and slave, as I wanted to be, and to such men, so marvelous and mighty, could be nothing else. Did we, on Earth, take our dogs and cats into our confidence? Similarly, though I did not want to feel their whips, and dreaded them terribly, the knowledge that I was subject to them, and that these men, such men, were fully ready to use them on me, and would, if I were not pleasing, was deeply moving, reassuring me of their mastery over me.

I knelt back on my heels. I moved a bit with the motion of the wagon. The chain moved a bit on my neck, looping up to the throat of the girl on my right. It was hard to tell in the hood but I thought I detected the smell of salt air. We had now been in the wagon perhaps an hour.

It sounded now, judging from the sound of the metal-rimmed wheels, and felt, judging from the vibrations, like we were moving over cobblestones.

The back of my calves, where I had been struck, now felt better. That had really been foolish of me, standing in a slovenly manner in the coffle, when there might have been men about, and, indeed, had been one, and with a whip. That I had been lashed, however, showed me that I was, in a way, important, and that men cared about me. I was a female. I made some sort of difference to them. They were genuinely interested in females, and liked them, and were concerned with them. They wanted us to be as charming and beautiful as we could be, and would, frankly, hold us accountable for such things. How many times, I wondered, had a man on Earth, irritated with an Earth woman, or girl, been tempted to seize her and, say, pull gum from her mouth, or straighten her hair, or adjust her halter, or tell her to straighten her body or to change her posture, or to sit or kneel in a certain way, but, of course, had not done so? Here, however, men, I gathered, at least with women such as I, felt few reservations, inhibitions or compunctions about taking immediate and often direct action in such matters. They tended to view us with a certain proprietary interest, even, in certain cases, with a certain possessive zeal and zest, and seemed determined to see to it that we were as marvelous as we could be. We were, after all, the females of their species.

I was now more sure than ever that I could smell salt air. We continued on our way. Once I heard a sort of sudden bellowing snort and hiss, it seemed, from the closeness, and the associated jerk on the traces and movement of the vehicle, from the beast drawing the wagon. It frightened me. I wondered what its nature might be. Hooded, of course, I had not seen it. I knew really very little about the world to which I had been brought. I listened to sounds from outside the wagon. There were more of them now. The wagon seemed, now, to be generally descending.

I pulled a bit at the light manacles which fastened my hands behind my back. They were light, but they were, I was sure, a thousand times strong enough to hold me, and perfectly. I thought about them. They seemed obviously made for women. That was interesting. It told me something, I supposed, about the culture. It was a culture in which there was apparently a call for such articles. It was a culture in which they had their role, and utilities.

I heard men calling out, or shouting, here and there, now and then, as we continued on our way, usually descending.

I also heard, once, it startling me, a woman's voice, raised, shrill, angry, screaming, scolding. I shuddered. I would not have dared to do that. I would have been whipped. I could not make out what she was saying. I do not think it had anything to do with us or the passage of the wagon. I doubted that any woman who could be like that wore a collar or knelt before men. I then began to suspect, with some certainty, and trepidation, that not all women on this world were as I. That thought, justifiably, as I would learn, filled me with alarm. There would be doubtless a kind of war between women like that and women such as myself, I thought, a war in which women such as I, in effect, would be unarmed, and, perhaps despised and hated by them, fully at their mercy, totally helpless before them.

I smelled something cooking.

I heard another woman's voice, this one hawking fish, and then the voice of another woman, that one hawking suls. The sul is a large, thick-skinned, starchy, yellow-fleshed root vegetable. It is very common on this world. There are a thousand ways in which it is prepared. It is fed even to slaves. I had had some at the house, narrow, cooked slices smeared with butter, sprinkled with salt, fed to me by hand. We had loved them, simple as they were. I, on my knees, my hands manacled behind me, had begged prettily for them. Sometimes they were simply thrown to us, on the floor, and we squirmed for them on our bellies, competing with one another for them. Then the insistent cries of these two women, proclaiming the excellence of their respective offerings, were left behind. We were different from such women, I feared, quite different.

Then I was suddenly startled as I heard a man's hand slap loudly, good-naturedly, against the side of the wagon, within which was our cage. He yelled something raucous and ribald. It had to do with "tastas" or "stick candies." These are not candies, incidentally, like sticks, as, for example, licorice or peppermint sticks, but soft, rounded, succulent candies, usually covered with a coating of syrup or fudge, rather in the nature of the caramel apple, but much smaller, and, like a caramel apple, mounted on sticks. The candy is prepared and then the stick, from the bottom, is thrust up, deeply, into it. It is then ready to be eaten. As the candy is held neatly in place there is very little mess in this arrangement. Similarly, as the candy is held in its fixed position, it may, in spite of its nature, be eaten, or bitten, or licked or sucked, as swiftly, or slowly, and as much at one's leisure as one might please. These candies are usually sold at such places as parks, beaches, and promenades, at carnivals, expositions and fairs, and at various types of popular events, such as plays, song dramas, races, games, and kaissa matches. They are popular even with children. I had learned of these things from Ulrick, back in the house. I had wondered why he had sometimes summoned us to our duties and lessons, with the call, "Come, tastas!" The expression was occasionally used by men for women such as we. To be sure, there seemed to be a great number of such expressions for us, such as "morsels," "puddings," and "candies." When there was the sound of the slap of the man's hand on the wagon side, it so unexpected, and sounding so loud, and his sudden shout, several of the girls had moved, stirring suddenly, in their chains. I, too, frightened, startled, had moved in mine. We had had no doubt that outside was a strong, virile man, much more powerful than we, and that we were slaves.

I then heard, it startling me, too, and frightening me, too, and even more than before, a stick beating savagely on the side of the wagon. I heard, too, the shrill screaming of a woman's voice. It had a very ugly sound. I could not make out all she was saying but its import was surely uncomplimentary. Among other things she called us "she-sleen" and "she-urts." I did not know what a sleen might be, but I did know what an urt was. When we had begun our training, shortly after we had been branded and collared, we had been kept in a lower level of the house, in a dank, dark, cold, musty area, seeming to consist largely of narrow corridors and cells, an area of damp, cold stone walls, of shadows and pools of water, chained in a large, common cell. In this cell we bedded on damp straw, cast over the stone. Our food, in the temporary light of lamps or lanterns, was thrown from pails to us, garbage perhaps, from the meals of others, and we could not, under penalties of the whip, use our hands to retrieve it. Too, as we soon discovered, we were not the only denizens of that place. Often the urts, those tiny, swift, sleek, furtive rodents, bold in their familiarity with, and seemingly assumed privileges in, the place, would rush to food before we could reach it and, almost at our cheek, snatch it up and scurry away to their holes, through the narrowly spaced bars and small crevices. They would come at night, too. It was hard to sleep, for one might suddenly, unexpectedly, scamper over one's body. Too, one would be awakened by other girls, screaming, or crying out hysterically, at the sounds, or movements, or touches in the darkness of the tiny beasts. Some girls were bitten. We strove mightily in our lessons, to be found worthy of being raised to a higher level. This seemed almost symbolic, and was doubtless intended to be. None of us, of course, were permitted to ascend to the next level until all of us had attained at least its minimum requirements. This put great pressure on us all to excel. One girl was determined to be refractory. She was fiercely disciplined that night, as though by merciless, raging cats, by her chain mates. In the morning she considerably improved her performances. It seemed that she had only wanted that excuse, really, that sop to her pride, to eagerly serve men with perfection. She soon became one of the best of us. Indeed, as she wheedled with the guards, and would sometimes even receive a candy, many of us became quite jealous of her. Gradually, with our class less than a week, we were all on a higher level. Then, a week or so later, we had our own tiny kennels, small and cramped, but dry, and above the level of the urts. These things helped us to understand, first, how much we were at the mercy of one another, and, secondly, how much we were all, fundamentally, ultimately, both collectively and individually, at the mercy of men. We were then, in a minute or two, beyond the screaming of the woman and the intense, cruel beating of her stick. As that sort of thing was going on, we had scarcely dared move. I think all of us were terribly frightened, and perhaps the Gorean girls more than the Earth girls, for they surely must have known more of what was going on, or was involved, than we naive Earth women, so new to our collars and chains. Yet even we, I am sure, sensed the terrible, frightening hostility, the hysteria, the fury, of the woman outside. I am sure none of us would have cared to meet her, or find ourselves within the range of her wrath. Teibar, I thought to myself, must, of course, have known there were such women in this place. I wondered if the thought of this, too, amused him, that he had brought me, his despised "modern woman," as a helpless slave, to this place, this place where I might find myself defenseless within the ambit of such fury.

I could hear various folks outside the wagon, as the wagon now moved slowly. It seemed, now, too, to be moving on a level, on a wooden, planked surface. It sounded hollow beneath the wheels.

I realized, suddenly, that my knees were pressed closely together. That had occurred during, and I had kept them that way afterwards, the beating on the wagon of the woman, and her screaming. It had been a defensive gesture, bringing my knees together, tightly, because I was afraid. Perhaps, too, I supposed, just as a male might find the spreading of a female's knees appropriate, deferential or placatory, so, too, such a woman might prefer their closure, finding it respectful, or placatory. Perhaps she might be mollified to some extent by such an apparent modesty. I did not know. Still, looking down at me, I did not think she would be likely to be fooled by it. I did not think she would be stupid. She would probably know what I was, really. It was probably not hard to tell. Perhaps we were just different sorts of women. I did not know. I did realize that such women, in all their frustration and anger, would probably want me to be like them. That thought horrified me. I found it terrifying. It would be like going back to the sterilities, the barrenesses, the pathologies, of Earth. Tears formed in my eyes, in the hood. What was I to do? I recalled that Ulrick had told me that certain kinds of slaves, house slaves, "tower slaves," and such, whatever they were, might kneel with their knees together, but I had also been informed that I, and the other girls, were not such slaves. We were some other sort of slave, it seemed, though exactly what sort I was not perfectly clear. "Masters will teach you," had laughed Ulrick. For us, at any rate, for whatever sort of slave we were, the open-kneed position was commanded. Too, I felt that it was the one which was right for me, at least before men. I then decided that my best mode of action would be to pretend to be unsexual, and modest, before women such as she who had beaten on the side of the wagon but, when with men, and as they would undoubtedly require, kneel as I had been taught, placing myself shamelessly, vulnerably, deliciously, delightfully, happily, at their feet. I felt the knee of the girl next to me touch my knee. She, too, I supposed, had been considering these matters. Doubtless I was not alone in my fears, or concerns. She, too, was an Earth girl, Gloria. She was from Fort Worth, Texas. She had been put on the coffle before me.

She had now spread her knees, the shameless slut! I then moved a bit to my left, toward the gate of the cage, and spread my own knees, doubtlessly just as shamelessly. It gave me great pleasure to do this. It was like an act of rebellion, or defiance, in my heart, to the woman who had beaten on the wagon. To be sure, she, with her stick, could not see me. I would not have been so brave, doubtless, if she had been about. But I was now pleased to be again so kneeling. It was the way I was supposed to kneel, and it was the way I would kneel, I decided, even before free women, if a man were present, unless he ordered me to kneel differently. It was to men that I belonged, not women. Let them rant! Let them cry out with rage. I was proud to belong to men, to men such as those of this world! I would thus, rightfully, and joyously, kneel before them as what I was, a woman, and their slave. What was the problem of women such as she who had beaten on the wagon? Did she wish, in her heart, I wondered, that she, too, could kneel thusly, owned? Then I dismissed that thought as foolish, doubtlessly foolish. Not such a woman! Never such a woman! But then why was she so hostile? Did she think that our service and beauty, our yielding to our hearts, lessened or demeaned her in some way? What a puzzling inference! What an absurd conclusion! What a grotesque mockery of thought that would be! Must all women be alike? Could there be legitimately only a single type of female, and that the grotesque projection of her own feminine insufficiencies, her misery and hatred? If anything, it seemed that our abjectness might have made her own status, presumably different from ours, seem even finer and more exalted. Perhaps she hated men and it was thus an insidious, half-understood way of attacking them, by attempting to spoil and ruin us, by trying to make us inert and like herself. The issues seemed complex. At any rate there seemed no objective justification for her trying to make us like her. What was so marvelous or desirable, really, about her unhappiness and hardness, her cruelty and frustration, that we, lesser women, should find it preferable to love? Why did she so hate us? Did our nature, and softness, contradict her views, showing them false? Perhaps that was it, that she in some strange, almost incomprehensible way felt refuted by us, and our feelings, or threatened by us. Was it importam for her, perhaps in a war with men, perhaps in her graspings for power, I wondered, to maintain that she, in her hatred, ambition, envy and narrowness, stood for an entire sex? How ridiculous! But, if so, it was easier to understand how she might hate us so, for our very existence, and that of women like us, natural, loving women, subservient in the order of nature to masters, undermined her lies. How fearful it would be, I thought, if such a female, or such females, in all their hatred and frustration, should manage by lies, propaganda, misrepresentation, manipulation, distortion, chicanery and law, swiftly or gradually, perhaps almost unnoticeably, to bring about the ruination of the natural relationships between the sexes, to subvert the biotruths of an entire species, to impose their grotesque perversions, for their own purposes, on an entire world. Then I realized how little I knew, really, about that particular woman, doubtless a native of this world. My reflections were colored, in effect, by the pathologies of a far-off world. Her anger might have been motivated by so small a thing, but so natural a thing, as the interest that some man took in a woman such as we, and perhaps not in her. Who knew? It might be easier, then, I supposed, to be cruel to us than to him. Perhaps he would have simply turned his back on her, walking away from her, ignoring her. Perhaps he would have cuffed her to silence. Who knew? I pulled a bit at the manacles which held my hands behind my back. My wrists were well locked in them. I had considered earlier how they were made for women, and that this seemed significant in this culture. In this culture it seemed that slavery, bondage such as mine, at least, was an essential ingredient, that it was unquestioned, or, if it had been questioned, that the questions had been resolved long ago, and in favor of the collar, that it was a matter of tradition, perhaps a tradition of thousands of years, a tradition institutionalized in its social customs and fixed permanently and ineradicably in its legal structures. Too, in this culture, where there were such men, I did not think there was any real danger of susceptibility to the debilitating, antibiological pathologies of Earth. I shuddered. In this culture, at least, women such as I had nothing to fear, having everything to fear.

I then tried to dismiss the woman from my mind.

Whatever might be the case with her, she was, it seemed, quite different from me.

Suddenly I was afraid. I had had, for a time, my knees clenched closely together! I did not think there was a man in with us. The fellow who had been lifting us into the cage, taking us from the fellow below, had, I was sure, descended from the wagon. I did not know for certain, of course, because of my hooding, whether or not there might have been a man in the cage with us, a guard, perhaps, or even, say, an unhooded female slave, one of the instructresses, for example, perhaps charged to observe our deportment. But I did not think so. Too, I was sure the cage had been covered, as I had heard the drawings-down, and tightening, of canvas, and its bucklings, but, to be sure, there might have been a flap, or peephole, or something, perhaps behind the wagon box, from which, from time to time, we might have been observed. I began to sweat. I had been lashed earlier, across the back of the calves, for an imperfect posture or carriage. I hoped I would not, now, be punished, after the wagon stopped, for some similar breach of beauty or decorum. I pulled at the manacles. I moaned softly in the hood. I now kept my knees widely separated, determinedly so. I tried to kneel straightly, too, beautifully, in the neck chain. I did not know if there were men to see or not.

Then, suddenly, the wagon stopped. I could sense the movements of other girls, by the chain on my neck, the sounds, the vibrations, those tiny physical transmissions, indicative of their stirrings, through the flooring of the metal cage. They were all frightened, I think, as I was. We had arrived, somewhere. They were adjusting their postures. I, too, tried to improve mine, even further.

We heard voices. The driver seemed to descend from the wagon box. We waited. There was very little sound now. We were very quiet. There was occasionally the tiny sound of the stirring of links of chain, from the chain on our necks. I moved a little, to feel the tiny metal tag, slung on its tiny closed chain, the chain closed about my collar, move delicately, lightly, on my skin, just below my neck. It had something to do with my transportation, or disposition. We all had such tags, now, on our collars.

We heard some canvas being thrust up, near the gate. "Sit, or lie, as you will, sluts," said a man's voice. He was a fellow from the house. I recognized the voice. The canvas was then pulled down, again. We would be here for a while, it seemed. We adjusted our positions, as we could. I lay down on my side. My knees were sore from the metal flooring, and the movements of the vehicle. The smell of salt air was strong here.

We waited, doubtless in various postures of ease. The others, I would suppose, were as grateful as I to break position. It seemed nothing was happening. Doubtless outside the wagon, though, something was happening, if only an inquiry into a delay, a tallying or accounting, a certification of papers, a checking of arrangements, something. Inside the wagon, we waited.

I thought again of the woman who had cried out, beating on the side of the wagon.

I moved the leather ball about a bit in my mouth, it held in my mouth by its strap, pulled back between my teeth, buckled behind the back of my neck. I felt it behind my lips and teeth, over my tongue, obstructing my oral orifice. I could not speak. Indeed, I could make very little noise at all. I pressed up on it with my tongue. I moved my lips and teeth about it. I could not begin to dislodge it. It is a secure, effective device. It does its job well, as it is designed to do. My head, in its hood, now rested on the metal flooring. I could feel the flooring through the leather.

I was afraid, remembering the woman who had beaten on the wagon. I thought that probably I, and women like me, would have much to fear from such women. I did not think she was, really, as I might have hoped, an isolated aberration. Who could protect me then from such as she, only men, surely. She, too, thus, in her way, regardless of her intentions, would be putting me all the more at the mercy of my masters, men. I feared her, and such as she. How shrill and ugly she had sounded! I did not know, of course, but I suspected she might have been coarse-featured, or homely. She had even sounded ugly. I was pretty. That made me even more afraid of her, and her kind. I thought they might resent me, and hate me, for being pretty. Too, I was apparently a type of woman, short, with shapely legs, and nicely breasted, which men on this world often found attractive. That, too, might be held against me. Such things, of course, are not that unusual. For example, if one is not strong, one might tend to disparage strength, or claim that it is not important. Indeed, one might, grotesquely enough, even resent it so in others, as to come to hate those who are strong. Similarly, if one is not beautiful, or attractive, one might tend to disparage beauty, or attractiveness, or claim that it is not important. Similarly, one might, grotesquely enough, resent such things so in others as, sooner or later, to come to hate those who are beautiful or attractive. On Earth those who espoused such eccentric and paradoxical perspectives might, on the whole, unless they became politically powerful, be ignored or avoided. Here, however, I feared, the beautiful, and attractive, might find themselves at their mercy. The terrors of this situation were further impressed upon me by the understanding that it was most likely the beautiful, and the attractive, who would be sought out for impressment into helpless bondage. They would be the prizes. I myself, I knew, in some sense, was such a prize. Teibar had told me that he was paid, in effect, for bringing in "first-class females." I was thus, it seemed, at least from the perspective of this world, a "first-class female." I recalled he had used such expressions to me as "little charmer" and "cuddly slut." These expressions, though probably intended to humiliate me, and demean me, and put me in my place, as a female, nonetheless seemed to attest to his finding me of genuine sexual interest. To be sure, he had not seen fit to keep me. Ulrick, though, had assured me, and I think truthfully, of my attractiveness, and had even done me the kindness of speculating somewhat skeptically on the soundness of Teibar's judgment in the matter. He, at any rate, had regarded me as being pretty enough to wear Teibar's collar. Too, more than once one of the guards at the house had angrily tested the security of the iron belt on me, and then, finding it secure, had thrust me from him, then taking another girl in hand, one not in such a belt, for the satisfaction of his fierce needs.

I heard voices outside, but, it seemed, nothing was being done with us. We must wait.

I was truly afraid of women such as she who had beaten on the wagon. I did not even have a cloth to put on my body before her. I would be naked to her stick or switch. And even the instructresses I had seen had been barefoot and worn only brief tunics. Women such as I, I feared, thus, even if clothed, would be clothed in distinctive manners, manners which would be particular to us, manners which would mark us out, and make us prominent and visible, manners which would leave no doubt as to our condition, and status, and generally, I suspected, scantily, and revealingly, as the instructresses had been, for the pleasures of men.

We waited gagged, stripped, hooded and chained.

Perhaps the woman who had beaten on the wagon was really not so different from us, I thought. Perhaps it was only that she had not been taken in hand, imperiously, and branded and put in a collar. Perhaps, on some level, in some way, she was jealous of us and wanted to be like us, a woman whom men might conceivably find of interest. Perhaps somewhere in her there was even a true woman. Perhaps somewhere in her there was, too, a slave, who yearned to serve at the feet of masters. I did not even think it mattered whether or not she might be homely or plain. Men are sometimes fools, I think, putting too much store, at least at first, by such superficialities. One need not be beautiful, I was sure, to be a loving, slave treasure.

But regardless of what the truth in these matters might have been, I was certainly not eager, now, to make the acquaintance of such women. After they were stripped and in chains, and crouching fearfully, with branded thighs, their necks in collars, fearing the whips of men, that would be soon enough for me, if ever! We were, at least as of now, regardless of what might be the fundamental and ultimate truth in these matters, quite different sorts of women. Social chasms separated us, social chasms unbridgeable except by the brand and collar.

We waited.

I wondered why we had been hooded, and had had heavy ball gags thrust in our mouths, and buckled back, in place. I did not think our hooding was to conceal our beauty from the casual glances of men. Men such as these, I had gathered, were seldom reluctant to show off the beauty of the baubles on the "slaver's necklace." Too, we were stripped, and, even so, I was sure, were being kept in a covered cage. I supposed the motivation of the hooding, in part, might have been to remind us that we were slaves, and men could do these things to us, but, too, I suspected, it was to keep us in "slave ignorance," a condition often deemed appropriate for women in bondage. At any rate none of us knew where we were, or where we had been. We did not even know the name of the house where we had been trained, or the name of its master. In this sense, we did not even know who owned us. The Gorean girls had tried to read one another's collars, but the markings on them had apparently been in coded symbols, incomprehensible even to them. That seemed strange to me. Though I was learning to speak Gorean, incidentally, I could not read it. Neither I, nor any of the other Earth girls in my group, had, as far as I knew, in spite of the intensity and frequency of our lessons, received any instruction whatsoever in reading it, even in an elementary way. We were illiterate. I suspected we would be kept that way. Still, the degree of "slave ignorance" in which we were being kept, not even knowing the name of our master, for example, seemed extreme, if not absurd. It was connected, then, I reasoned, with some sort of measures of security. This might explain, too, the gags, which were perhaps not simply a way of men telling us that we are subject to them, and may be gagged, as we might be blindfolded, chained, tied or beaten, at their pleasure, but rather to keep us from speaking with one another, particularly the Gorean girls, perhaps exchanging information or speculations, or, more likely, daring to call out to others, perhaps passers-by in the vicinity of the wagon, teasing them, bantering with them, begging prettily, perhaps, for tiny bits of information.

I adjusted my position a little. The metal flooring was hard on my shoulder and thigh. I wished I had had my blanket, which had been in my kennel, with my pan of water. It had much eased the harshness of the kennel's cement flooring.

I went to my back. I felt the flooring on my shoulder blades. I pulled my wrists up, in their linked rings, taking advantage of the space at the small of my back.

We waited, caged, in your hoods and chains.

I thought again of the woman who had frightened me so, she who had beaten on the side of the wagon.

Certainly, as of now, at any rate, we were quite different sorts of women.

I wondered at what the nature of the delay might be. I wondered what it might be that we were waiting for.

We were not passengers, of course, who might inquire, perhaps impatiently, into the nature of delays, perhaps even demanding explanations; we were only animals, being shipped; we were cargo.

I moved again to my side.

I pulled again, a little, at those lovely, stern impediments of steel, linked together by a small sturdy chain, which held my wrists behind my back. How well they confined me! The chain, too, was on my neck, keeping me with others. Too, with others, I was caged, I had heard the door, or gate, being locked. The cage, too, I conjectured, judging from the metal flooring, from the weighty, efficient sounds of the closing and locking of the gate, from the feel of the stout bars behind me, was quite sturdy. It would probably hold men, and with perfection, let alone females.

I struggled to sit up. I managed it. My shoulder hurt. My thigh was sore. I then put my back against the bars.

I had gathered that female slaves in transit, in general, must look forward to bonds or confinements. But the usual arrangement in these particulars, I had gathered, was a simple coffle chain, most commonly a neck coffle, but sometimes a wrist or ankle coffle; a slave cage, mounted on a wagon, in which the girls were free; or a slave wagon, within which, stripped, their ankles were chained about a movable, central bar, it fixed in place, locked, during transit. Surely it was not typical that they were treated to the attentions which we enjoyed, being gagged, hooded, neck chained, manacled and caged. This, too, I supposed, might represent some sort of security measure, but, if so, it seemed to me, of a depth and degree which must be unusual. Perhaps, on the other hand, it had to do, simply, with our being new slaves. New slaves are often treated with great harshness. It helps them learn quickly that they are slaves. Later, when the girl is well trained and her services become perfections she may be treated more leniently, even lovingly, like a dog. To be sure, if she should become in the least bit lax, the original strictures, or worse, will be instantly reimposed, or instituted.

The ten of us had been in the wagon now, even after it had stopped, at least an hour, perhaps two.

I thought of Teibar.

He, and men like him, were inutterably superior to me. I had not known such men could exist. I had only dreamed of them. Before such men, I, a refined, educated, highly intelligent woman of Earth, knew myself nothing. I could be, in effect, no more than a dog at their feet.

I pressed back against the bars.

And, interestingly enough, I was not discontented. I could have wished, I suppose, for lesser men but I did not really want lesser men. I wanted the mightiest men, the most powerful men, the most glorious men, the most ferocious, grandest men. I did not want men who were like me, I wanted men who were like men, men in whose arms, ravished, loving, crying out, overwhelmed, mastered, I could be myself, and find myself. I wanted such men, and knew in my heart that I belonged to them. I wanted a man who was greater than I, and incomparably so, one whom I must, in the order of nature, obey, one to whom I must look up. And I did not care I if it was from my knees, black with dust, a collar on my neck, naked, that I looked up to his glory. I wished, tears in my eyes, that Teibar had kept me, his "modern woman," as a pet, as his bitch. I would have tried to serve him well. I would have been overjoyed to have been to him the only thing I could really be to men such as he, the lowly bitch of such men. I would have brought his sandals to him in my teeth. I would have begged to clean his feet with my tongue. I would strive to show him that the "modern woman" was gone, and that in her place was now his bitch, his legal property, his woman, his woman in all ways, helpless and loving beyond loving.

I lay down again on the metal flooring.

I thought again of the woman who had beaten on the side of the wagon. How afraid she had made me! How different she seemed from us, from the ten of us, chained in this cage. She was, I was sure, free. She must have been free, to have been permitted to scream like that, and carry on like that. There seemed to be no other possible explanation. The thought made me shudder. She was then, even if stupid and ugly, worlds above and beyond us. She would be priceless. Our value, even if we were desirable and beautiful, on the other hand, would be finite, a function quite simply of fluctuations in the market, and what men were willing to pay for us. We were properties. She, I supposed, was not. That would seem to be the major difference between us. We could be bought and sold. She, I supposed, could not, unless, of course, men saw fit to reduce her, too, to bondage, and then, of course, she would be no different from us, and our competitions would be reduced to the same common denominator, that of mere females. I lay there, hooded, a new slave, trying to understand, down in my belly, what it was, truly, to be a property. I could thus come into the ownership of anyone who had the wherewithal to buy me, male or female. Too, I had little doubt that not all the men on this world could be of the nature of Teibars and Ulricks, and the guards in the house where I had been trained. Doubtless there were men here, too, if not as on Earth, men who might be fretful, petty and weak, men the very sight and smell of which I might find offensive, men whose appearance and least touch I might find literally sickening, men I might find inutterably disgusting, men who were unclean, who were cruel, and loathsome and gross, who might be hideous and frightful, men I might find myself shrinking from, almost vomiting in disgust and terror, but they would own me, as much as any other, and I would be obliged, as a slave, to bring myself warmly and unquestioningly into their arms, and bring my lips obediently and hotly to theirs, to submit wholly to them, to give myself wholly to them, to surrender wholly to them, holding back nothing, to please them, fully, and intimately. These things were simple attachments of my condition, consequences of what I was. I could not change them. They were simply part of what it meant to be what I was, a slave. We do not choose our masters nor is it up to us, whether or not we will please them, or to what degree. We must strive to be perfection all ways, for anyone. That is part of what is to be a slave. In reconciling myself to bondage I had, also, to reconcile myself to this condition. It is a part of bondage. It is something which the slave must accept. Without it there can be no true slavery. I had accepted this condition, at least theoretically, verbally acknowledging its incumbency on me, in my training. Somehow, interestingly, this acceptance, too, seemed liberating to me. It made my bondage much more real to me. Too, interestingly, in its way, it also made it seem much more precious to me.

Still, I supposed one could not truly understand what being a property was until one had been sold, and had come into the keeping of masters. Doubtless Teibar's "modern woman," his arrogant, pretentious Earth female, as he had thought, his despised catch, would come to understand what that was. How amused he would be from time to time, I supposed, thinking of what he had done to me, the fate into which he had brought me. I tried to hate him, but could not. I wanted rather to kiss his feet. But then perhaps he did not even remember me. Perhaps he had forgotten me! Perhaps I was now alone, totally alone, on this world, having been brought here for a price and then, having earned my coins for others, discarded, cast into the markets, set adrift uncertain weathers, on trackless seas, to vanish from sight, to disappear tracelessly, with no one noticing or caring, at the mercy of whatever course winds and currents, and fortune, and the will and interests of men, might take me. But I would never forget Teibar. I would remember him, always, even as I moaned in my dreams.

I jerked suddenly, frightened, in the manacles. I could belong to anyone, to anyone who could pay for me! Surely that was wrong for a woman of Earth! How could it have come about that I was now only a lowly slave? I had been a woman of Earth! Of Earth! How could it have come about then that I was now, on this world, only a collared animal, stripped and chained, at the mercy of masters? Could it truly be I here, in this cage, in chains? Had I gone mad? Could I be dreaming? But I pushed up with my tongue, straining my tongue, against the bottom of the leather ball in my mouth, fixed there so mercilessly, so effectively. I moved my lips and teeth about it. I could feel its shape and size. But I could not dislodge it. I shook my head a little, moving the chain on my neck. It was on me. I hurt my wrists, pulling against the manacles that confined them. But I could not relieve their stern clasp in the least, nor extend by an iota the tiny span their links allotted me. I moved my shoulder and thigh on the metal flooring. My shoulder was sore, and my thigh was sensitive, and perhaps red. The flooring gave us a very obdurate surface. It was very solid. It was plated, and heavy. I supposed it might be of iron. The plates, I conjectured, judging from the apparent weight and solidity of them, must be an inch thick, at least. No, I was not dreaming. It was I, here, truly, in this place, now a slave. Then again I was content. How had Teibar, and others, I wondered, have known that I was a slave? It had not been hard to tell, I had gathered. I was frightened, but, too, I knew I was where I belonged, in bondage.

We waited.

No more concern was being taken for us, it seemed, than for crates, bales or boxes.

I heard Gloria, next to me, moan. She, too, doubtless, was feeling the hardness of the flooring. I felt the chain on my neck move, as she changed her position. On the other side of her was Clarissa, who was from Wilmington, Delaware. She had even received, more than once, a candy from a guard. No longer was she refractory. She, too, had learned herself slave. The first seven girls on the chain were Gorean girls. Clarissa had not been a virgin, or at least for long, in the house. I had seen two of the Gorean girls, and Clarissa, rather regularly put to the uses of the guards. I had noted, with interest, that although they were from different worlds, they, in the throes of their instimate employments, at first submitting to and enduring, then accepting, then reveling in, and, at last, kneeling and licking, mutely begging and pleading for their ravishments, in their whimpers and moans, and clutchings, denied speech, obedient under "gag law," had sounded the same. I supposed under certain conditions we all sounded the same. We were all women. That was what was important. I do not think, really, even from the point of view of men, that there is anything to choose from, between a Gorean girl and an Earth girl, assuming both have well learned their collars. It is doubtless, really, all a matter of the individual woman. What we all have in common, of course, is that we are all females.

We might have been animals kept waiting, horses, or pigs or dogs! Then I recollected that that was what we were, animals, slaves.

We waited.

We were chained.

There was little danger, I thought, that we would escape. Too, on such a world, where would one run? And even if one could get one's collar off, one was branded, marked. I was not interested in running away. I had learned the penalties for such things. I did not wish to be whipped, or hamstrung, or have my feet cut off, or be fed to sleen. Here men were not tolerant of attempted escapes. They did not have the patience for them. Here, for women such as I, escape was not an option; here, for all practical purposes, it was simply impossible. At best, we might hope, against all hopes, at great personal risk, even mortal risk, it seemed, to escape from the chains of one master into those of another, in which case, of course, we would be a "caught slave," a modality that would be almost certain to assure us of the cruelest of treatments and the harshest of confinements, followed, perhaps, if our captor pleased, by a return to our original master.

I suddenly sat, half up, on the metal floor. Then I lay on it, on my back, shuddering, pulling my wrists up, behind the small of my back. I raised my knees.

As properties we had value, like other properties! Suddenly I realized, this thought frightening me, as I contemplated myself the object of such considerations, there might be a further point in chaining and confining us. It need not be simply construed in terms of such things as keeping us in a given place, or together, say, for purposes of custodial neatness, or rendering escape impossible, or discouraging thoughts of it, as if such thoughts needed discouraging, or reminding us that we were slaves, or disciplining or punishing us, or pleasing men, who delighted to see us so helplessly their captives, but for another reason, too, obvious now that I thought of it. We were properties! We were valuables, like money, or dogs or horses. Indeed, by some men, we might even be regarded as treasures. We might then, like other animals or goods, be subject to theft! We might be stolen! Thus it made sense that, if for no other reason, we might occasionally find ourselves kept, in effect, under lock and key. I did know that it was not unusual for slaves to be confined at night. In the house we had been locked in our kennels. Too, I had heard that at night it was not unusual for beautiful female slaves to be chained at the foot of their master's couch, fastened there to a slave ring, the chain usually running to a manacle on their left ankle or a collar on their neck.

The fact that I now realized I was subject to theft frightened me, but it, too, like many other things, seemed an attachment of my condition, a simple consequence of what I was. I recalled hearing now, in the house, of "capture rights," respected in law. I had originally thought these rights referred to the acquisition of free women but I had later realized they must pertain, more generally, to the acquisition of properties in general, including slaves. I had not thought much about such things, in a real, or practical, sense, until now, now that I was outside of the house. I tried to recall my lessons. Theft, or capture, if you prefer, conferred rights over me. I would belong to, and must fully serve, anyone into whose effective possession I came, even if it had been by theft. The original master, of course, has the right to try to recover his property, which remains technically his for a period of one week. If I were to flee the thief, however, after he has consolidated his hold on me, for example, kept me for even a night, I could, actually in Gorean law, be counted as a runaway slave, *from him*, even though he did not technically own me yet, and punished accordingly. Analogies are that it is not permitted to animals to challenge the tethers on their necks, or flee the posts within which they find themselves penned, that money must retain its value, and buying power, regardless of who has it in hand, and so on. Strictures of this sort, of course, do not apply to free persons, such as free women. A free woman is entitled to try to escape a captor as best she can, and without penalty, even after her first night in his bonds, if she still chooses to do so. If she is enslaved, of course, then she is subject to, and covered by, the same customs, practices and laws as any other slave. The point of these statutes, it seems, is to keep the slave in perfect custody, at all times, and to encourage boldness on the part of males. After the slave has been in the possession of the thief, or captor, for one week she counts as being legally his. To be sure, the original master may attempt to steal her back. A popular sport with young men is trying "chain luck." This refers to the capture of women, either free or bond, viewed as a sport. In war, of course, women on this world, slave and free, like silver and gold, rank high as booty.

Then, suddenly, startling me, I heard canvas being unbuckled and pulled away. My body suddenly felt hot sunlight fall upon it. It was warmer in the hood. I was afraid, in the hood. I struggled to my knees. I heard, too, the movements of chain, from our necks, and the small sounds of the chains linking manacles, and the stirring, and scrambling, the movement of naked bodies on the iron flooring, of the other girls. I heard a key being thrust in a heavy lock, and the lock being opened, it seemed loudly, abruptly. I heard the rattle of chain at the gate, and the opening of the heavy gate. I assumed the standard open-kneed position, back straight, stomach in, shoulders back, head up, immediately. I assume the other girls did, too. We did not even hear a man snap, "Position." It had not been necessary. We were, to some extent, at least, trained girls.

I heard a body ascend to our level. I felt strong rough hands on me. "This way," said a man's voice. "Move this way." But he was talking, it seemed, to the other girls, for I felt myself literally lifted up and lifted back toward the gate, the chain pulling against the left side of my neck as it was pulled away from the right side, dragging Gloria, doubtless on her knees, or half crouching, after me. I was handed down to the level. My feet were on warm boards. Gloria was then handed down, after me, and then the others. I heard the hootings, whistles, sucking and clicking noises, and sex calls of men, gathered about. It seemed there must be a great many of them, a small crowd, even. They had probably wandered over here, as we were being disembarked from the wagon. I felt a man's hand in the chain on my neck and he pulled me stumbling where he wanted me. For a moment it seemed I was the head of the coffle. Then I was turned about, and was standing alone, confused. I did not know where I was, or even in what direction I faced. I think, then, the lead girl was drawn around, and forward, properly orienting the coffle, and that I, though I was not sure of it, was again at its end. Gloria, judging from the chain, was somewhere to my right. She should have been, though, either in front of me, or behind me. I did not know where I was, even with respect to the coffle. I heard more of the hootings and noises, the sex calls, closer now. I began to tremble. I then jerked and almost fell. The snap had been so loud, so frightening, and the leather burned me so terribly! I had thrown my head back, gasping, sobbing out, wildly, fighting the ball in my mouth, in the hood. Then I uttered a tiny, frightened, anguished, protesting, stifled sound. "Stand straight, sluts!" we heard. "You are in the presence of men!" I then, jerking, in fear, reacting, but the lash was not on me, heard it strike twice more amongst us. This time the lash had been not on my calves, but fully on my back. I stood as straight, and beautifully, as I could. My back stung. It was as though a narrow path had been cut into it, and left raw, and burning, on it. I heard an increase in the hootings, the noises, and sex calls. Some of the men were now, apparently, crowded closely about. I had difficulty holding my position. I felt a man's hand on my left breast. I felt a man's hand squeezing my right thigh. "Do not touch the merchandise," laughed a guard. It was a voice I knew from the house. It may have been the fellow who had struck me, and the others. "Unless you want to buy," he added, chuckling. "Does she have a face to match this luscious form?" asked a man. "Yes," said the guard. "She is marvelously beautiful." I was grateful to him. I wondered if it could be true, that I might count as being marvelously beautiful, to men such as these. And if so, what might that mean? Did it suggest, I wondered, that I in my helplessness might then expect to be the object of persistent and unusual predations? "They are all superb slave meat," said the guard. "From what house do they come?" asked a man. But the guard did not respond to him.

I heard chains. I felt myself literally turned about. I was now, I conjectured, behind Gloria again.

"Move," called a man.

The chain pulled at the back of my neck, so I was drawn forward.

The boards beneath my feet seemed thick and hot. They were

splintery. At one point I thought I stepped in warm tar. The smell of the salt air was very strong here.

The coffle slowed.

A man's hand on my arm stopped me.

"Ahead now," I heard a man say. "Step carefully. The board is narrow. Climb. Do not be afraid. We will steady you." I then heard the chain move again, uncertainly. In a moment or two, I felt myself guided forward by a man's hand on my arm. I felt frightened. "Here, now," he said, "lovely naked lady, step up a little." His hand was on my arm, almost as though escorting me, as though, indeed, I might be a lady! "At least she is not face-stripped!" called a man. There was laughter. How it must have amused them, these jokes, as though ladies might be publicly naked! How they mocked me! I was no "lady." I was branded. They well knew, all of them, I was branded! They needed only look. It was visible to all, as I was, on my left thigh, unmistakable and prominent, burned into my body. "There," he said. But I was grateful for his help, as a female, in this predicament, even an enslaved one. I felt an ascendant board beneath my feet. Too, on it, as I discovered, twice stepping on them, there were crosspieces. When one man's hands left my arm, a moment later, another's hand reached out, steadying me, from the side, by the wrist, and then another's reached down to me, and, again by the arm, helped me up. Once the board I was climbing shifted a little. This was unexpected. I was frightened. But I was steadied by the second man. It was as though the upper end of it had moved slightly. I was then lifted up, and down, onto another wooden surface, this one as smooth as a floor. I had moved some seven or eight feet, maybe ten feet, at an angle of perhaps twenty degrees. I was then guided a bit to my right and forward, and turned, and knelt there. I felt a movement on the chain. Gloria must be to my left. They knelt us closely together. My left shoulder touched her right shoulder. I felt the floor move beneath my knees. I then felt a chain put about my neck, and locked there. A moment later I felt its other end move, and heard sounds as though it were being twined about metal. I then heard the sound of another lock, a heavy one. Something similar had been done, I supposed, at the other end of the coffle, utilizing the first girl's lead chain. The coffle was now, I supposed, secured on both ends. There was again the movement beneath my knees. There was no mistaking the movement. We were on a floating surface.

"Which of these are white silk?" asked a man.

I heard the sound of a long, heavy board, being drawn over wood. It was then, it seemed, placed somewhere to my right.

"Check their tags," said another man.

"Here is one," said a man, lifting my tag. There was a cry of good-natured protest from a fellow somewhere to my left and in front of me.

"Here is another," said another man, to my left.

"We will need three," said another man, somewhere. I felt my tag being lifted a second time. "Wouldn't you know it," grumbled a man. He then let the tag drop back against my flesh, under the collar.

I heard the sound of ropes being drawn aboard, and a noise like that of wood pushing on wood. We moved. We seemed to be swinging to my left.

I heard some metal apparatus put down on wood, near me.

I heard the men calling out to one another. I heard the creaking of wood. I then heard what sounded like a number of poles thrust through wood.

"Kneel up," said a man. "Higher, up, off your heels. Keep those pretty knees wide. Hold still."

I felt then the encircling clasp of metal closed about my waist, and then, swinging up between my legs, another piece of metal. These things were fastened in place, the right side, and the lower portion, hasplike, over the staple on the left side of the apparatus. The whole was then secured behind my back with a padlock. Once again I wore an iron belt.

I then heard the dropping and unfurling of canvas from above me. A moment or two later, it briefly snapping and flapping, it was under control. I then felt it in the very boards beneath me, it exciting me with the pressing weight and smoothness of it, its strength, its directness and awesome power, the force of the wind filling and shaping, and thrusting against, this large, extended, exposed canvas surface, transmitting its power through the yard, the ropes and the mast which must hold it in place. I was indescribably thrilled. I wanted so much to see. I wished I had not been in the hood.

I then heard a sound like the beating of a mallet on a wooden surface, slowly, regularly, every few seconds. With its stroke oars, it seemed, entered the water. There must then be several oarsmen. I supposed they would be strong, virile men, to draw oars. I squirmed a little, uneasily, in the hood, in the iron belt.

I heard a bell from somewhere. It was perhaps on a buoy, marking a channel in a harbor.

We were being taken somewhere, the Gorean girls and the Earth girls. None of us, I am sure, knew where.

"You may kneel back on your heels," said a man.

I did so, immediately.

He was probably the fellow who had put the belt on me.

"Would you like to be out of the hood?" he asked.

I whimpered.

"Whimper once for 'Yes,' twice for 'No,' " he said.

I whimpered once.

"We will soon be clear the harbor," he said. "Are you pretty?" he asked.

I did not respond, immediately. I did not wish to sound vain, nor was I sure, really, that I was pretty enough to count as being "pretty," so to speak. Much surely depended, too, on the opinions of men. Was it not really up to them, to decide whether I was pretty or not? A girl who might bc attractive to one man might not be so to another, I knew. I supposed I should whimper twice, for a negative response, but then, I feared, what if he, or someone, should unhood me, as doubtless someone would, sooner or later, if only to feed and water me. I might then, if I had responded in the negative, be punished for lying. I recalled Ulrick has thought me pretty, and others had, too. Also, only a few minutes ago, the guard had said to someone that I was "marvelously beautiful." Whereas that might have been an exaggeration, even an absurd one, it seemed that on the basis of it, I might be legitimately entitled to view myself as at least "pretty." Too, I recalled that Teibar, apparently unwillingly, apparently in spite of himself, apparently to his fury and disgust, considering what he took to be my nature, had seemed to find me attractive, even extremely so, maddeningly so. To be sure, he had not kept me. Too, I considered the sexual tastes of these men, tastes according to which, this sometimes terrifying me, I apparently counted as being unusually desirable or attractive. Indeed, on this world, rightly or wrongly, I did count, it seemed, really, or at least to many men, as being "beautiful," perhaps even, as the guard had said, "marvelously beautiful." To be sure, I was alarmed to consider what might be the consequences of being beautiful, and a slave, on a world such as this, among men such as these.

I whimpered once. I tensed, fearing I might be struck for vanity. But I was not struck.

"Later, in an Ahn, or so," he said, "we will remove your gags and hoods. Things will then be more pleasant for you."

I whimpered once, signifying my pleasure, my gratitude, hoping to encourage him.

"Do you know when we will do this?" he asked.

I whimpered twice.

"When we are out of the sight of land," he said, "totally out of the sight of land."

I lifted my head in the hood, to the sound of his voice.

"Do you understand?" he asked.

I whimpered once.

7 / Brundisium

"This is Brundisium!" said one of the girls, peeping out of the wagon. "I am sure of it!"

"I want to be sold here," said another.

"It will depend on the conditions of the market," said another.

"I think we are already past its street of brands," said another.

"We are still within its walls," said another.

"It is one of the greatest ports," said another.

"It is here that the Cosian fleet landed," said another.

We were naked in a slave wagon, our ankles chained to a central bar. The high, squarish framework of the wagon was covered with blue and yellow silk, under which was common canvas. The silk is often removed during bad weather. We had thrust up the canvas and silk, an inch or two, at the top edge of the wagon bed, and, turned and kneeling, some half sitting, half lying, eager, curious, our ankle chains twisted, were peeping out.

"There are still soldiers and sailors of Cos about," said one of the girls.

"There is one," said another girl.

"He is handsome," said another. "I would not mind being owned by him."

That remark I suddenly found disturbing, and frightening. I had accepted that we could be owned, and, indeed, were, but it still frightened me, to hear it spoken of so openly, owned, and by a private master!

"There are the banners of Cos, too, as well as those of Brundisium," said another.

"Yes," said another.

"We must have come from Cos," said one of the girls.

"Perhaps Telnus," said another.

"Yes," agreed the first.

We had apparently come into the keeping of our wholesaler outside the walls of this city, at a temporary slave camp. Gorean girls with us had learned, or claimed to have learned, that this avoided the taxes levied on commercial transactions within Brundisium. Similarly, of course, such camps presumably had other values, as well. Space outside of a city's walls is usually cheaper to rent than space within its walls. Too, such camps may be moved about, making them more versatile commercially. For example, they may be shifted to areas where women, perhaps because of large-scale raids or the falls of cities, may suddenly be abundant and cheap, and to areas, too, where there may be an unusual increase in retail demand. It also made them, I suppose, more difficult to trace, if anyone were interested in doing that sort of thing. A disadvantage of such camps is that they are more vulnerable to attack than if they were located in, say, housings or courts within a city's walls. On the other hand, they are usually located quite near cities, usually within the sight of their walls, and this tends to reduce to some extent the likelihood of such attacks. In any such camp, of course, and there had been in this one, there are usually several merchants. These are generally both wholesalers and retailers, but primarily wholesalers, for retailers are usually indigenous to given cities. These wholesalers usually distribute to retailers, in their individual cities, or, often, also, in well-known slaving centers, of which there are many, for example, Ar, Ko-ro-ba, Venna, Vonda, Victoria, on the Vosk, Market of Semris, Besnit, Esalinus, Harfax, Corcyrus, Argentum, Torcadino, and others. Most of the wholesalers, I suppose, do have permanent headquarters, somewhere, but they, or their agents, often frequent these camps, as well, availing themselves of the considerable advantages accruing to their trade in such places. The group with which I now was contained, as had the original coffle, ten girls. Three, however, were new girls, all Goreans, and we now had only seven of the original ten in the wagon. Gloria and Clarissa, as well as myself, interestingly, all the Earth girls, were still with this group. We did not know who the wholesaler was who had handled us. As soon as land had first been sighted, we had again, the original coffle of us, been subjected to our original securities, our hands back-manacled, our mouths gagged, our heads covered with heavy, opaque, buckled, locked hoods. These manacles, gags and hoods, and our neck chain, had been removed only in the cages in the slave tents. This morning we had been put, rather as normal slaves, subjected apparently to only ordinary securities, in the wagon. I think we were all pleased at this new lenience, effective as it still was, in the manner of our keeping. I know I was. We were now, apparently, as nearly as I could tell, being delivered to one or more retail outlets.

"Look!" said one of the girls. "There are so many burned buildings here!"

We saw that what she had said was true, peeping out. It seemed, here, that an entire district, or streets, at least, of buildings, had been burned in this area. It did not seem that the fires had been of recent origin. They may have happened weeks, or months, ago. Indeed, in various places, sometimes between gutted, blackened shells of buildings, there were cleared areas. Here it seemed that burned structures must have been razed, and debris carted away. Here and there, too, supporting this idea, were great heaps of charred timber and rubble, presumably awaiting some disposition. In many places tents and temporary buildings, sometimes little more than shacks, had been erected. Too, here and there, permanent structures, with basements and foundations, and stone walls, seemed clearly to be in the process of construction.

"I am sure this is Brundisium," said the girl who had first spoken. "There was a great fire in Brundisium five months ago."

"Call out to someone," suggested another girl. "Ask."

"Not me," said the first girl. "You call out."

"Clarissa," said one of the Gorean girls. "You ask." She did not mind risking Clarissa. Clarissa had been very popular with the guards. We were all, or those of us who had been with her in the former house, somewhat jealous, I suppose, of her attractiveness to them. We probably all wished we could have been that desirable. She had even received candies. I thought, however, that perhaps if I had not been forced to wear the iron belt, I, too, might have been similarly popular. I, too, might have received a candy or two. I was sure that I, if I had set my mind to it, could have pleased a man, and myself, as well as she! To be sure, I reassured myself, quickly, assuaging a shred of the dignity of the frigid Earth female, still left in me at the time, I would have had no choice in the matter. I would have been whipped, or punished terribly, or perhaps even killed, if I had not. And, certainly, too, guards had been interested in me. More than once, they had investigated, and tested, and seemingly to their anger and disappointment, the obduracy and effectiveness of the metal device in which I had been fastened.

"Gloria," suggested the Gorean girl.

"No!" said Gloria.

"Doreen, then," said the Gorean girl, Ila.

"No, no," I said. I did not want the driver or guard to hear me call out to anyone. I was not interested in being whipped tonight.

"Earth she-urts," said the Gorean girl.

"You do it," said Gloria. I was pleased Gloria spoke up. She was a larger girl. She could stand up to the Gorean girl, who was also a large girl. I was smaller, and afraid of her.

The Gorean girl, Ila, however, did not call out to anyone, either. She, too, was afraid. She, too, as we, belonged to those brutes, men. She, too, no more than we, cared to be placed beneath their imperious, disciplinary lash.

I delighted to look out through the crack between the wood and the canvas and silk. This was a beautiful world, and I reveled in it. I found almost everything I saw different, and interesting, the men and women, the children, the clothes, their accouterments, the streets, the buildings, the tents, the stalls, the trees, the flowers, everything. It seemed so open, and beautiful, and free, though, to be sure, I within it was a slave. I was startled, and a little frightened, even, by the strange, scaled, long-necked, placid, lizardlike quadruped that drew the wagon. These might be human beings, here, but I was not on Earth.

"Oh, no," said one of the Gorean girls, angrily, in frustration. "We are coming to the gate! We are going to be leaving the city!"

Three or four of the other girls, too, Goreans, all moaned in protest.

"I want to be sold here!" said one of them.

"What difference does it make?" asked Gloria, peeping out.

"Earth fool," said one of them, "you know nothing! You can wear your collar in a small town, in a camp, in a peasant village, if you want! I want to wear mine in a great city!"

"Let Gloria pull a plow, let her hoe weeds, let her carry water on a great farm," said one of the girls.

"She is too pretty," said another Gorean girl. "No peasant could afford her."

I hoped that I, too, might be too pretty for a peasant to afford.

"One has a much easier life, almost always, in a city," said one of the Gorean girls.

"It depends on your master," said another.

"Yes," agreed another.

I supposed that was true. The most important thing was not whether you were in a city or not, but your master. He would surely be the most important single element in your life. You would belong to him, literally. However, I thought, it might be nice, other things being equal, to live in one of these lovely cities. Also doubtless the labors of a slave in such a city would be easier on the whole than those of one, say, on a farm.

"Pull the canvas down, quickly," said one of the girls. "We are coming to the gate!"

We pulled the canvas and silk down, as best we could, and then, very quietly, turned about and sat in the wagon. We heard papers being checked. Then we heard a man's voice. "Stay as you are. Don't kneel." The canvas at the front of the wagon was opened, and a man, from the floor space before the wagon box, looked in upon us. We sat quietly, not meeting his eyes, naked, the chains on our ankles about the central bar. "Ten kajirae," he said. This word was the plural of 'kajira' which was one of the words, the most common one, for what we were. It means 'slave girl', 'slave woman', 'she-slave', that sort of thing. The brand on my left thigh was a cursive 'kef', the first letter in the word 'kajira'. The best translation is doubtless 'slave girl'. Then he closed the canvas again. Then, in a bit, we had trundled through the gate. Apparently we had only cut through this city, which might be Brundisium, enroute to somewhere else. We had saved time, it seemed, taking this route, rather than driving about its walls. It was, I gathered, a large city.

"So, where are we going?" asked one of the Gorean girls, of another.

"Samnium, doubtless Samnium," was the response.

8 / The Platform; The Annex To The Sales Barn

I sat on the long, heavy, wooden platform, raised about a foot above the dirt, one of several in this exposition area, in this annex to the sales barn, naked, my feet tucked back, near my left thigh, my ankles crossed, my left hand on my left ankle, my weight muchly on the palm of my right hand, on the platform. A chain was on my neck, an individual chain. It was about five feet long. It ran from a ring set in the platform to my collar.

We were not in Samnium, but in Market of Semris. This is a much smaller town, south, and somewhat to the east, of Samnium. It is best known, interestingly enough, ironically enough, as an important livestock market. In particular, it is famed for its sales of tarsks. Too, of course, there are markets here for slaves.

"This is not Samnium!" had cried Ila, when the canvas and silk had been pulled aside, and the central bar unlocked from its socket.

"No," said the fellow handling us. "It is Market of Semris."

"Those are tarsk cages!" had cried Ila, when we had been unshackled.

We had been lifted down from the wagon and placed on our feet in a high-walled courtyard. The shackles usually stay with the wagon, particularly when the wagon does not belong to the dealer to whom delivery is being made. The cages to which she referred were to the left, a few feet away, against the wall of the courtyard. There was, too, very strong, the smell of animals in this place.

"Yes," said the fellow. "But tonight tarsks are not being sold, not four-legged tarsks, at any rate."

"I will not be sold here!" cried Ila.

He indicated the cages to our left. We stood there, barefoot, closely together, in the dirt. Too, was straw scattered about. It was muchly broken and trampled. In the dirt there were numerous tracks and prints, many of them of small hoofs, marking perhaps the place of passage of small groups of some sort of animal. Too, there were the tracks of wagon wheels there, and of sandals and boots, and of small, high-arched bare feet, doubtless those of girls. The cages were long, low and narrow, such as may be stacked and tied on long, flatbed wagons. They had stout frames of metal, were floored with sheet metal, and roofed, sided and gated with heavy meshes of a chain-link-type metal, the links passed through, and clinched in, apertures in the frame. As the mesh was formed its openings were about two-inches square.

"I will never get in such a thing!" cried Ila. "Never!"

Then the lash, from behind her, fell upon her, and she sank crying out, reaching behind her, sobbing, to her knees, and then, with the next blow, was flung by its force to her belly in the dirt before the man. Thrice there in the dirt was she struck, writhing and sobbing, begging forgiveness. Then, on her hands and knees, swiftly, at a gesture, she crawled, poked by sharp sticks, hastened by the cry "Quickly, she-tarsk!" to the first of the low, narrow cages and scrambled, weeping, within it. She was a large girl, and formidable to us, except perhaps to Gloria, but, compared to the men, she was only another female, no different from us. Compared to them, her size and strength, really only that of a woman, was, like ours, when all was said and done, simply negligible. Compared to them she was, like us, simply small and weak. Before them, and to them, she could never be any more than we, only another female, small, lovely and helpless, a mere female, totally at their mercy. We looked swiftly, wildly at one another and, in these swiftly exchanged glances, I think, honestly, there was pleasure as well as fear. We were pleased that the insolent Ila, often so pretentious and lofty with us, had been put immediately and sternly, to her instruction and anguish, in her place, that of a female slave, like us. We were glad the men had taken the action they had. We had been reassured by it. In it we had had a demonstration of their firmness and power, of the meaningfulness and reality of their mastery. It had served, too, to remind us all, graphically, of what we all were, women, and slaves, and that we were subject, as such, to them. The insolence of Ila, too, was an embarrassment to us, and, in its way, a reflection on us, and our sex. To be sure, we were also afraid. We did not wish her behavior to draw down the wrath of the men on us all. We were not eager to share the lash with her. We now saw Ila in the cage, her fingers hooked in the mesh, looking out. Her eyes were frightened. In them, too, there was grievous pain. She was a lashed slave. The rest of us then, quickly, at gestures, hurried to the cages, dropped to all fours, and entered them. Two cages sufficed for us all.

I sat on the long, heavy, wooden platform, raised about a foot from the dirt, one of several in this exposition area, in this annex to the sales barn, naked, my feet tucked back, near my left thigh, my ankles crossed, my left hand on my left ankle, my weight muchly on the palm of my right hand, on the bench. A chain was on my neck, an individual chain. It was about five feet long. It ran from a ring set in the platform to my collar. On the upper portion of my left breast something was written, inscribed there with a grease pencil. I had heard that it was the number "89." I could not read it. It was my lot number.

"Out, out, hurry!" had said the man this morning, pounding with his pointed stick on the linked, metal mesh of the cage's roof. We had mostly backed out, for the cages were narrow, and then remained there, in the dirt, in the gray light of the early morning, on all fours. During the morning and afternoon of the day before, when we had first arrived in Market of Semris, after we were caged, other wagons had arrived, and unloaded their own fair occupants, they, too, in short order, to be caged. Still later that afternoon some groups of small, fat, grunting, bristly, brindled, shaggy-maned, hoofed, flat-snouted, rooting animals had been herded in, also with pointed sticks, and they, too, had been guided into identical cages. We had looked out of our cage, our fingers hooked in the mesh, to other cages, some of them with girls in them, some with the fat, flat-snouted, grunting, short-legged, brindled quadrupeds.

"Those are tarsks," said one of the Gorean girls.

I nodded.

They were not to be sold that night, however, I had gathered. We had learned that that night tarsks were not to be sold, not "four-legged" tarsks, at any rate. I recalled the other footprints we had seen in the dirt, left over, probably, from the day before, those smaller, lovelier, daintier, high-arched prints, doubtless those of girls. I did not know where they were. I would later learn that they were in the exposition area, on the platforms, where we, the next day, would find ourselves. The day in the cage had been warm, and the night, too, had not been unpleasant, but, toward morning, it had turned cool. Happily it had not rained. I shivered. I was glad to be out of the cage, moving now, on my hands and knees, in the dirt, across the courtyard. I had not yet been given clothing on this planet. We had had, however, in the house where I had been trained, blankets in our kennels.

"Stop," had said our herder, he with the stick. "Wait."

We had come to a long, narrow, wooden, calked, semicircular tanklike container, about two feet wide and ten feet long, half buried in the dirt, its forward edge reached by a low ramp. It was filled with a dark fluid. Here we had to wait while a group of fifteen tarsks, one by one, herded up the ramp, plunged into the fluid and swam to the other side where, scrambling out of the container, they shook themselves, and hastened down the descent ramp.

"Now you two-legged tarsks," said the man, waving toward the container with his stick.

We shuddered. None of us, I am sure, cared to enter that dark fluid.

"Do not swallow the fluid," he said.

We looked at one another, from our hands and knees. We would be sure not to do so. We needed no encouragement in the matter. Clearly it would not be simple water.

"You, first, two-legged tarsk," he said to Ila.

"Yes, Master!" she said, hastening to obey, hurrying up the ramp on all fours and plunging into the dark fluid. In an instant she was in the center of the container. A little past that point, one of the men, reaching over the side of the structure, thrust her head under the fluid. Then, in a moment, she was scrambling out of the container.

"Stay on your feet," she was told.

"Yes, Master," she said, now at the foot of the descent ramp, shivering, holding her arms about herself. Ila, we noted, to our satisfaction, was now properly deferential. Too, she was quick to obey. It seemed she had learned her lesson yesterday, that she was, like us, a woman and a slave. As she had been the first into the first cage yesterday, and we had had, for the most part, to back out of the narrow enclosures, it was natural that she had been at the head of our group this morning. I, for what it was worth, whether it was meaningful or not, whether it was a tribute to my beauty, or an indication of my assumed esthetic inferiority to the others, or a matter of accident, of simple happenstance or original positioning, with no significance, or height or whatever, was again at the end of the group. To be sure, I was neither the tallest nor the shortest of the group. One of the Gorean girls, Tutina, was smaller than I. It was, thus, I think, only an accident in its way, at least with respect to what was going on this morning, that Ila had been chosen to be the first to enter the fluid. The man had not even seemed to remember that she had been refractory, or resistant, the day before. He was thus kindly, I think, letting her begin again.

I plunged from the incline of the ramp, from my hands and knees, into the dark liquid, on my belly, as had the others before me, and the tarsks before them. I was suddenly almost totally immersed. I cried out, sputtering, raising my head. It was shockingly cold. It seemed foul. My head went under again and again I desperately raised it. I then had my feet under me, and stood up, the fluid about my waist. I was then, by a man's hand in my hair, pulled from my feet forward, and again into the liquid. It was stinging my eyes and nose. My eyes were filled with tears. I could barely see. I thrashed forward and then, wildly, reaching about, seized the side. I pulled myself, then, clinging to the side, the fluid swirling about my neck, toward the other end. Apparently they wanted us well immersed. At the center point a man seized me by the hair and, to my acute distress, forced my head under the fluid. He held me there, under that terrible, foul, stinging, cold fluid, for a terrible second or two, and then released me. I then, moving forward, getting my feet under me, climbed stumbling, falling, splashing, up the end of the container, and pulled myself, at last, gratefully, onto the descent ramp. In a moment I was standing with the others, in the dirt, in the open courtyard, near the foot of the descent ramp. I was freezing. My teeth were chattering. I held my hands about myself, trembling with cold.

"This way," said the man.

Hurriedly we followed him. I looked about. I wondered if the others could possibly be as miserable as I was. I am extremely sensitive to cold, and to feelings of almost all sorts. I wondered if one of the criteria for selecting a woman for slavery might be her tactile sensitivity. I myself, I know, am extremely sensitive to such things as textures, for example, the feel of silk or leather, or a manacle, on my body. It is sometimes almost as though my entire skin was a single, extensive, sheetlike, marvelous tactile organ. Too, I reacted to the feel of a man's hands on me, even in handling me in so simple a manner as to put me in a cage. These types of skin sensitivity, of course, make us much more alive to our environment. Indeed, part of our training was to increase our awareness of subtle sensations. These features and capacities, too, of course, made us more sensitive to both pain and pleasure. Thus, they put us all the more, it seemed, at the mercy of masters. I looked about. Surely none of the girls could be as miserable as I! But I saw them, in their misery, in their cruel discomfort, regard me as well. I wondered if they were thinking the same thoughts as I. We were all terribly miserable. We were all such, it seemed, as to be helplessly at the mercy of our sensitivities, tactile and otherwise, of our helpless responsiveness, and our feelings.

"This way," said the man.

We were very pleased to follow him into a large, wooden building.

"This is the annex to the sales barn," he said. "The exposition spaces are here."

I hardly heard him, so eager I was to get within the building. Within, in the center of the building, in the center of its dirt floor, was a fire pit, in which blazed a cheerful fire. His stick, held out, prevented us from running toward it. Then, amused, he lowered the stick, and we ran to stand near the fire, crowding about it. Blankets, too, rough and brown, were there, in piles, and, permitted, at a gesture of the stick, we seized them up and clutched them gratefully about us, drying our bodies, and our hair.

There seemed five exits from the lofty, raftered room. We had entered through one, coming in from the courtyard; another led through double doors to our right, and another, also with double doors, now barred, lay at one end of the room. It seemed to lead to another yard. There were also two smaller doors, giving access perhaps to offices or corridors. In this large room there were also a large number of low, sturdy platforms, raised about a foot above the dirt flooring. Some of these platforms were flush with the walls, but others, by far the larger number, were arranged at regular intervals, about four feet apart, in rows, the effect being that of providing aisles between and about them. I did not know about the platforms next to the wall, but it seemed that the platforms in the open part of the room, though formidable, and heavy, would be movable. They could thus be brought out, and arranged, or removed, or dismantled, and taken away, it seemed, according to desire. In this fashion it seemed the room might be capable of serving various purposes.

"Comb your hair," said a man, bringing out a box of wooden combs, "and then you will be fed."

We took the combs and knelt, letting the blankets fall about our waist, and combed our hair. I think it pleased the men to see us do this. Gorean men relish women, and enjoy watching them, even in the performance of such simple, homely acts as combing their hair. To be sure, we were bare-breasted, and slaves, and obeying. We had not been asked to form a combing circle, probably because they were willing to permit us to remain in the vicinity of the fire. There were too few of us to circumscribe the fire. We would have had to withdraw from the fire, or most of us. In the combing circle we kneel in a circle, each girl combing the hair of the girl in front of her. Making us comb our hair before we were fed, incidentally is typical of the manner in which Gorean men treat female slaves. The woman is to be presentable and beautiful, before she is permitted food. How much darker, I noted, did my hair, and that of the other brunets look, when it was wet. The combs were of yellow wood, and had long teeth. The entire comb, including the teeth, was about five inches square. There are various hairdos in which such combs are worn in the hair. Usually, however, the hair of slaves is worn long, and loose, or confined only in some simple way, as with a ribbon or woolen fillet. Some masters like the ponytail hairdo on a slave, which, on Gor, is usually spoken of as the "leash," or "hair leash," for, by it, a girl may be conveniently seized and controlled. Upswept hairdos are usually reserved for free women, or high slaves. They are a mark of status. To be sure, one of the reasons for permitting a hairdo of that sort to a slave is the master's pleasure in undoing it, in loosening it, thus reminding even the high slave that in his arms, ultimately, she, the high slave, is yet a slave, and as much or more than the lowest girl in the most remote village. The loosening of a woman's hair on Gor in an extremely sensuous, meaningful act. "Who loosens her hair?" is a way of asking, in effect, who owns her.

"When is Teibar coming to inspect these women?" asked a man.

I suddenly almost fainted. Teibar! He had not abandoned me, I thought wildly. I gasped. I looked about, wildly. Some of the other girls looked at me, strangely, unable to understand my sudden agitation. My heart palpitated madly. Surely everyone must hear it. My breast heaved. I fought for breath. The other girls perhaps thought me mad. I did not care! It made no difference! Teibar owned me! I was his! Teibar! He was here! He had not forgotten me! He wanted me! He had come for me! It was I he had picked out, even on Earth! I would love and serve him forever, forever and forever, no more than a dog at his feet, but living in the light of his presence, a loving, panting bitch, loving him forever, loving him forever with a love beyond love!

"What is wrong?" whispered Gloria.

"Nothing!" I whispered. "Nothing! Nothing!"

"They are bringing food," said a girl.
"It smells good," said little Tutina.
"Yes, yes!" I said.

I sat on the long, low wooden platform, in the annex to the sales barn, in the exposition area, naked, my feet tucked back, near my left thigh, my ankles crossed, my left hand on my left ankle, my right hand supporting most of my weight, the chain on my neck dropping down to the wood, to my right, then lifting, running back over my thighs, then keeping its rendezvous with its ring, behind me and to my left. On my left breast, on its upper portion, inscribed there with a grease pencil, in Gorean, was a number. I had been told it was "89," and that it was my lot number.

After we had eaten this morning, though I, so excited, had scarcely touched food, we were knelt in a line, facing one of the small doors.

I had strained to hear the smallest scraps of conversation among our keepers. I had learned that this place was an appurtenance of the house of Teibar, who was a well-known slaver in Market of Semris. He owned this complex and dealt also in the sales of livestock, in particular those of tarsks. This particular complex was, it seemed, one of the best-known areas in Market of Semris for the sales of tarsks. Indeed, in the very area where I now was, the platforms cleared away and pens put forth, projected sales lots of tarsks were commonly displayed, often prize lots, to be bid upon later in the sales barn itself. To be sure, the platforms made it obvious that this area, too, could, and did, serve another purpose, as well, the vending of yet another form of livestock, the female slave. To be sure, most of his sales, those of women, apparently took place at another facility, one more precisely adapted to their display and merchandising. How like Teibar I had thought, to deal in both tarsks and women. I had smiled. He well knew how to keep us in our place, did he not? And what a rich joke, I had thought, this was doubtless supposed to be, that I would find myself here, his "modern woman," in a place where really, more appropriately, and usually, not women, but tarsks, were sold! It was this place, I had surmised, thinking I had penetrated his joke, where he had planned to reclaim me, I suddenly finding myself again in his power, that of the house of Teibar, and in a very complex of his, "where women such as I might be bought and sold." Surely he had planned this coup, this joyful, lovely trick, his master's jest, so rich and delicious, even from the time of the library on Earth, even from the time the conical, stiff, rubberized mask had been placed over my nose and mouth.

We were kneeling, facing one of the small doors.

"Heads to the dirt!" called a man.

Swiftly we assumed a common form of slave obeisance, kneeling, the palms of our hands on the ground, our heads to the ground. Many masters, though it tends to be rather associated, usually, with given cities, require this position of their girls, usually when they first enter his presence, or find themselves, as in a room which he has entered, in his presence. She is then, usually, when given permission, permitted to lift her head, but is to remain kneeling before him, beautifully, in a standard position, her knees closed if she is a house or tower slave, her knees open, if she was the sort of slave I was, whatever sort of slave that was supposed to be. It is almost universal, as far as I know, that a slave kneels in one fashion or another when entering her master's presence, or if she should find herself in his presence. She also commonly kneels when spoken to by any free person. This is simply a matter of respect. To be sure, she can be slain, if she does not do so. The kneeling position, of course, which the master's, or free person's, permission, either tacit or explicit, is usually required to break, is commonly an initial position. For example, after its deferential assumption, she may be dismissed from it, to other duties, such as cleaning, shopping or cooking.

I heard the small door open. I heard some men, one or two of them talking, entering the large, dirt-floored room. I did not hear Teibar speaking. I was sure, though, he must be there. Perhaps he did not wish to alert me to his presence, yet. He preferred to keep me in suspense. Perhaps he would announce his presence to me only when he pulled me to my feet and crushed my small, helpless, maked enslaved body to him, bruising it against his leather.

I began to tremble, violently. I could not lift my head and look, of course. At the end of our line I sensed men.

"I think you will find these a good lot," someone said. That pleased me. I wanted our lot, or our group, to be a good one, and I wanted, if possible, to be the best in it! I wanted that, if only for Teibar. But I heard no response to the man's remark.

"Lift your head," I heard a man say to someone, at the end of the line. It had to be Ila.

"Excellent," said someone. Ila, I conjectured, was now being scrutinized. She was doubtless kneeling very beautifully.

"What do you think, Teibar?" I heard.

I again almost fainted that Teibar, my master, he who had come to reclaim me, was near.

Then I feared, terribly, that he might more desire Ila than me. A wave of sudden terrible hatred swept over me. I wanted suddenly to leap up, screaming, and run at her, like a raging cat, to scratch out her eyes, to tear every last strand of that long, silky blond hair out of her head! Then I was frightened. I remained exactly in place. I did not move. I could be terribly punished, perhaps even tortured and killed, if I, a mere property, seriously injured, or diminished the value of, another property. Short of such things, though, we could do much what we wanted to one another, and Ila was larger and stronger than I! I felt helpless.

But there had been no response to the man's question.

I reassured myself that it was not Ila he had wanted. He could have had her at the house of our training, or bought her there, and for a discount, if he had wanted! He hadn't! To be sure, she was a larger woman than I, and meatier. Did that make her better? I did not know. Perhaps she was more beautiful. I did not know. But it was I whom Teibar had desired, not she! Perhaps I was more beautiful. I did not know. I did know that I was beautiful, and even if I were not as beautiful as she, I was desperately needful, willing and loving. Surely such things should count for something! Too, it seemed, undeniably, that he had found me desirable. I thought, and hoped, that perhaps I might be special to him, somehow, in some way, more so than others, as he was to me, he who was the loved, dreaded master of my heart.

"Stand," said a man to Ila. She stood. Something then, it seemed, was done to her. "Kneel," she was told. She knelt.

I kept my head down, kneeling. I trembled. I awaited the approach of my master.

"Look up," had said the man, then, and then "Stand," and then, after a moment, "Kneel," to one of the women, after another, approaching me, down the line. "Look up," he said to the woman next to me, Gloria. She was a large girl, with swirling red hair. To be sure, before the men, she could be, like Ila, only another female slave.

"Stand," was said to Gloria. She stood. Something was done to her. "Kneel," she was told. She knelt.

I kept my head down. They were then before me! I trembled. I awaited the command to lift my head, to view my master, to greet him with joy, to prove to him that I was no longer a hated "modern woman," no longer a spoiled, pampered woman of a sick, antibiological world, that I was now only his, a female slave, vulnerable and exposed in the fullness of her womanhood, belonging to him, totally, fully on his own terms, on his own world.

"This, Teibar," said a man, "is the last of the lot."

I had been saved for last. My master had saved me for last!

"Look up," said a man.

"What is wrong with her?" asked a man.

"What is wrong with you?" asked another.

"Speak," said another.

I looked wildly, sick, from one face to another. I was shaking. I tried, wildly, irrationally, to shut from my mind what I saw. I tried, in my mind, to change what I saw. I tried, wildly, irrationally, to force myself to see another, among those faces, one who must be there.

"Where is Teibar?" I asked.

"I am Teibar," said one of the men.

I began to shake, uncontrollably.

"Stand," said a man.

But I was so weak I could not stand.

One of the men went behind me and lifted me up, by the arms, holding me.

I almost lost consciousness.

I felt a pressure on the upper portion of my left breast. It seemed to be being drawn upon, or marked, by a cylindrical object with a soft, smooth, rounded point. It traversed my skin easily, with little friction, though I was clearly aware of its downward pressure. In the wake of the object there appeared a bright, thick, red line, moving about and circling, completing a course, a configuration, on me, which perhaps to some who looked upon it, but not to me, was significant. And then, in a moment, the object was withdrawn, the marking fixed upon me. I looked down upon it, what was written on me.

"You have it?" asked the man with the cylindrical marking device, some sort of grease pencil, to another, who held a clipboard, with attached papers.

"Yes," said the fellow with the board, making a notation on the papers.

"Kneel," said the fellow with the pencil, putting it back in one of the compartments of an open, triple-sheath attached to his belt.

The man who was supporting me, holding me from behind, let me sink to my knees. I could not stand by myself.

I looked down at my breast, at what was written there, so boldly and brightly.

"Can you read?" asked a man, he who had said he was Teibar.

"No, Master," I whispered.

"You are an Earth female, are you not?" he asked.

"Yes, Master," I whispered.

"Perhaps, as an Earth female," he said, "you are not used to having your body written upon, for the convenience of men."

"No, Master," I said.

"But here you will grow used to it," he said. "Too, here, you are no longer, really, an Earth female. You are now no longer of Earth. You now belong to this world, ours."

"Yes, Master," I said. It was true. I now belonged to this world.

"Would you like to know what it says?" he asked.

"Yes, Master," I said.

"It is the number '89,' " he said. "It is the number of your individual sales lot."

"Yes, Master," I said.

"What is wrong?" he asked.

I looked up at him, tears in my eyes.

"I am Teibar," he said.

"Yes, Master," I said.

"Ah," he said, softly, "it is then some other Teibar you were thinking of."

"Yes, Master," I whispered.

" 'Teibar,' " he said, "is a common name."

"Yes, Master," I said.

"It is a very common name," he said.

"Yes, Master," I said.

"Hold her," I thought I heard someone say. Then I must have lost consciousness.

I sat, waiting, on the long, heavy, wooden platform, raised a foot or so above the dirt floor of the exposition area, it located in the annex to Teibar's sales barn, he of Market of Semris, a dealer in tarsks, as they said, four-legged and two-legged. The platform was one of several, arranged in orderly rows. The platform I was on was near the center of the room. I sat there, waiting, small, helpless, naked, my feet tucked back, near my left thigh, my ankles crossed, as though they might be held together by a small chain, my left hand on my left ankle, my weight muchly on the palm of my right hand, a chain on my neck, running to its ring in the platform. I do not know how long I had been unconscious. I had awakened here, on the platform, feeling its heavy, sturdy, smooth wooden surface beneath my body. I had also become aware of the chain on my neck. A little later I learned what space and movement it would permit me. I could stand comfortably in it. This was intentional on the part of the masters, being connected with a concept of latitudes suitable for the appropriate display of merchandise. We were a ten-lot originally, it seemed, but, as though in anticipation of a projected decision, we had been given different lot numbers. It seems they had not been fully decided, at least at one point, whether to sell us as a unit, a given ten-lot, or to break the ten-lot and sell us individually. They had now decided, it seemed, to sell us individually. I suppose it was a sound commercial decision, given the conditions current in their area. I do not really know. At any rate, they would do what they wanted, the same as with any other sort of merchandise. We were not the only ten-lot now in the room. There were girls, now, on most of the platforms, usually three girls to a platform. These others, I gathered, had been brought in during the day by wagons, or had perhaps been marched over from some other facility. Such things were the concerns of masters, not mine. My head was down. There was a number on my left breast. I was alone. Teibar, my Teibar, who had so easily and imperiously captured me on Earth, and who had brought me here, seeing to it that I was suitably impressed into helpless bondage, had not wanted me. My hopes had been absurd. How naive I had been. What a fool I had been. I should have known better. I could cry no more. It was now early in the evening. Somewhat before noon we had been watered, doubtless that we would be freshened and our bellies pleasantly rounded. The men, customers, natives of the locality, agents, dealers and others, were then admitted, to examine us, and, if interested, take notes on our lot numbers. On the platforms, I, and others, had endured the most intimate scrutinies. They had moved about us, circulating here and there, going from one platform to another. They usually did this, it seemed, in a precise pattern, beginning at one point or another, thus making certain that the contents of every platform came within their purview, that they did not miss even one of the displayed wares. We, of course, perforce, must respond to their instructions. We found ourselves often standing, or sitting or kneeling, or moving or assuming attitudes, or pursing our lips, and so on, according to their commands. In these times we were often handled quite objectively, the firmness of our breasts and thighs being tested, and so on. But then animals are often handled on such a basis, slapped on the flanks, and such. Sometimes they would even put us bodily in desired attitudes. They wanted to form some ideas, it seemed, as to our condition and soundness, and what it might be for them, or their clients, to own us. We were even, occasionally, touched intimately. Under such attentions I could not help squirming. This seemed to amuse them. I gathered from some of their remarks, somewhat indelicate remarks, scarcely fit for the ears of an Earth woman, or one who had once been from Earth, that under true male attentions I might prove to be utterly helpless. I found this dubious. I assumed that it was false. I would learn later that it was not. Still I was so distraught, so much numbed, so much in shock, so despondent, so much in despair, so miserable over my rejection by Teibar, that I was not even remotely as responsive as I would normally have been. And this had to do not simply with feelings. Sometimes I was hardly aware of, or caring of, what was being done to me. Sometimes I knelt, and moved, and posed, almost without understanding or thinking about what was being done to me. To these men, I am sure, I must have appeared, though perhaps beautiful, inert. They were now gone. The exposition area was now closed to the public. It was in the early evening. I supposed that we would be watered again, later, that we might again appear fresh, our skin with excellent tone, glistening and smooth, our bellies sweetly rounded. After a large breakfast this morning, we had been fed very lightly, however, only a handful of dry gruel put in our mouths after the closing of the exposition area. To be sure, I supposed it was enough for us. We need far less food than men. It is cheaper to feed us than male slaves. There were other reasons, of course, why we had been fed so lightly today. Tonight they did not want us to be lethargic or sluggish. Too, they did not wish, particularly in the case of new girls, their stomachs turning and wrenching in misery, and terror, to risk disgusting accidents.

"Position!" we heard.

Immediately every girl on every platform assumed position. I looked about, as I could. Every girl that I saw had assumed, as I had, the open-kneed position. It was required of them, I gathered, as it was required of me. They were all attractive. I wondered what sort of slaves we were, that we must kneel in this fashion.

In a few moments we were lined up, according to our separate lots, I at the end of mine, facing not the large, closed double doors which led to the area outside, those doors through which the customers had entered, but the other large, closed double doors, those which, apparently, led somewhere else. Gloria was in front of me, as usual. Her hands were manacled behind her back. My hands, too, were identically secured. On her neck, as on mine, was a buckled, two-ringed, leather collar. It was the sort of collar which may be easily put on, and removed from, a girl. The girl, of course, if manacled as we were, is helpless in it. The rings are located at 180 degrees from one another. This permits girls to be fastened, the collar oriented appropriately, either side by side, in ranks, or behind one another, in files. A leather strap, with snaps at both ends, joins the rings, usually the ring at the back of one collar to the ring at the front of another. Glorida, being ahead of me, was thus leashed to the ring at the back of the girl's collar ahead of her, and I was leashed to the ring at the back of Gloria's collar. As I was at the end of the line, the ring at the back of my collar hung free, against the leather, not utilized.

The double doors before us were opened.

I could see a long corridor, dimly lit with lamps. It was, like the exposition area, floored with dirt. That made sense, as doubtless tarsks, those of the four-footed variety, those bristly, squat, grunting animals, as opposed to the two-footed variety, those soft, smooth, shapely animals, were often conducted through it.

I looked down the long, dark, dirt-floored corridor.

Our group, it seemed, would be neither the first, nor, given our position, the last to enter that corridor.

I looked down at the writing on my left breast. It was, I had been told, an "89," my lot number.

We had been fed very lightly today.

There was a reason for that. Tonight we were going on the block.

9 / The Sales Barn; The Block; The Cage

Our group would be the next into the shoot. We could see it on the other side of the barred gate, the narrow, wooden ramp, with the low, wooden walls, open at the top, with the two gates, one for the shoot itself, to control the number of animals entering it, the other, slanting, behind which men might stand, which, when closed, given its diagonal, served to guide animals into the shoot, the shoot's gate, for such a purpose, then being held back, or, if it were desired to admit several animals, hooked back, open.

Gloria, ahead of me, was squatting over the bowl.

We were still in line, but we were no longer in the two-ringed, leather collars, or leashed, or manacled. Bars were in front of us, and behind us. This was one of several holding areas, and the last before the shoot. Two holding areas back we had been given water, ordered to drink plentifully. That water, of course, as of yet, had not had time to pass through our system.

A man slid the bowl back to me. "Relieve yourself," he said.

I squatted shamed, over the bowl.

"How do you feel?" asked a man. I looked up. It was Teibar, he of Market of Semris. His voice was kindly. He seemed not unconcerned. The last time he had seen me, I supposed, might have been when I had collapsed, unconscious, overcome, before him, and the others, in the exposition area, shortly after my lot number had been written on my breast.

"Very well, Master," I said. "Thank you, Master."

He then turned away. Like most Gorean men, and unlike Teibar, the Teibar who had captured me, he seemed to bear me no ill will, or hostility, on the grounds that I might be from Earth. Perhaps he no more than most others, knew what was going on there. To him I was doubtless no more than another pretty girl, another charming female, correctly imbonded.

I was still squatting over the bowl.

I looked up and met the eyes of the other fellow, he who had slid the bowl back to me, he who had ordered me to relieve myself. They were stern. "Yes, Master!" I said. Quickly then I relieved myself. I thought to myself with bitter amusement how Teibar, my Teibar, might have smiled, to see me squatting here, his "modern woman," now a frightened slave, on his world, relieving herself at a man's command. Doubtless he had known full well, he, a native of this world, that such things would be required of me. The bowl, incidentally, is not an improper precaution. It is often used before sales. Though there is usually a liberal sprinkling of sawdust on the block it is usually there less, I think, for practical purposes than for symbolic ones, for example, making clear the animal nature of what is vended there, and for the sake of tradition. Goreans have an unusual reverence for tradition. Still it could serve. The bowl, however, is better.

I stepped away from the bowl. The man pushed it with his foot to the side. I looked toward the front of the holding area. I was startled. Ila, and at least three of the other girls, had already entered the shoot. They were on all fours, crawling up the wooden ramp. Two men along the edge of the shoot, standing outside it, with pointed sticks, spaced them, and informed them, one at a time, when to move ahead. Then two other girls were sent through the barred gate to the end of the shoot. There, at its opening, on the wood, they were ordered to all fours. I suppose this amused the men. Too, it was appropriate, given the dimensions of the shoot. It was really made, like this facility, as a whole, it seemed, for the vending of four-footed animals, primarily, I supposed, tarsks. I then saw little Tutina taken through the gate and put in the shoot. She was tiny, but dainty, lovely thighed, and very prettily curved. I thought she might bring a high price. I wondered what I would sell for. I was not even aware, really, of the monetary system here, or its units, or their worth. Too, I would not know what the other girls sold for, I supposed. Perhaps I could find out from my master, whether the price I had gone for was a good one or not. I hoped he would not whip me for such curiosity. I had been told that "curiosity was not becoming in a kajira." On the other hand I suspected that the very existence of such a saying witnessed in its way the widespread nature of exactly such a charming feature, or weakness. Doubtless females were as curious here, as elsewhere. I hoped that I would not be sold to a brothel or tavern. I saw Clarissa put in the shoot. That startled me. How could that be? She was from Earth! How could that be done to her? She was different! But she was not different. She was only another female. Gloria was in front of me, standing at the gate. She, too was from Earth. We were Earth girls. Surely this could not be happening to us! I was guided by the arm toward the barred gate. I saw Clarissa hastened in the shoot by the jab of a pointed stick. The shoot's gate was held shut behind her. She moved in the shoot, I noted, like the other girls, the Gorean girls, no differently. Gloria was thrust through the barred gate to the shoot gate. I recalled how Clarissa had, one evening at the house where we had been trained, early in our training, been, or pretended to have been, refractory, and how the other girls had disciplined her. She had then, the meaninglessness and absurdity of her little rebellion, or pretended rebellion, demonstrated to her, accepted, and then rejoiced in, her bondage. She had now learned that she was a slave, totally, and only, that. I was sure she would prove a marvelous purchase for a man. Even the guards, not easy to please, had given her candies. I thought she would be marvelous, lovely Clarissa, in a man's domicile, and in his arms. Then I wondered how I could even think such things. She was from Earth! Then I realized that such considerations were quite beside the point, quite inconsequential. Clarissa was no longer a free woman, and of Earth; she was now something quite different; she was now only a slave girl, and only of Gor.

Gloria was thrust through the barred gate, and I was drawn to it.

Tarsks were sold in this place, I thought. I observed the long, narrow, low-walled wooden conduit, leading up and forward. I could not see where it led. Tarsks were herded through it, with pointed sticks. It was a tarsk shoot. Tarsks were sold in this place.

Lovely Gloria, then, with her lovely red hair, was in the shoot, on her hands and knees. She, too, like Clarissa was from Earth. I was thrust forward, before the shoot gate. It had been shut behind Gloria. I might not yet go forward. It was in front of me. It was about waist high to me. I looked at the slanting wooden ramp, beyond it. I looked at Gloria, crawling now in the shoot. She was a large girl. She had been able to stand up even to Ila. To be sure such things were important only in our small interpersonal relationships, in the wagons, in the cages. I saw her hurried up the ramp, with the poking of a man's stick.

The gate was opened in front of me. It swung back, against the inside of the shoot. A man controlled it, standing behind the shoot wall, in back of the other gate, the long diagonal gate which closed the corridor beside the shoot, sloping toward the shoot. At the gesture of one of the pointed sticks I went to all fours on the wooden ramp. I cried out, protesting, at the poke of a stick. I moved forward. I heard the gate shut behind me. I was in the shoot. I felt another jab from one of the sticks. Head down, I began the ascent of the shoot. Then I felt another jab. I must move faster. I did so. In a few moments I was several yards along the shoot, and approaching a level. There, leaning over the shoot, his arms on it, was another man. In his right hand, it resting on the top of the shoot wall to his left, he held a stick. He straightened up and tapped on the inside wall of the shoot. I hurried ahead to that point. There he put the stick in front of me, as a barrier, and I stopped. "Belly," he said. I went to my belly there, in the shoot. I law there on the wood. Beyond this point the shoot seemed to be level, at least for a way. On the ascent portion of the shoot, and where I lay, toward the end of that section, there were, every two feet or so, small crosspieces, these, I suppose, to aid tarsks in the climb. One was beneath the palms of my hands and my right cheek. Another was at my belly, and another was below my knees. I could smell tarsk in the shoot. I knew the smell from the courtyard, and the narrow cages. The wood, too, was indented in innumerable places with the marks of their hoofs. I supposed many tarsks had climbed this shoot, and many women. I remembered the library, the reference desk, the shelves, the card catalogs, the doors, the upper level, the carpeting, the periodicals, the return desk, the xerox machines. Too, I remembered my fellow workers there. I wondered if they ever wondered what had become of me. My true fate, I conjectured, could not even begin to enter their speculations. It would simply be incomprehensible to them. It could not enter their ken. What ever became of Doreen? They would not guess for an instant that someone had seen values in her that they had not seen, or suspected, that Doreen, quiet, lovely, timid, shy Doreen, their reliable, unobtrusive co-worker, whom they had so much taken for granted, had come to the attention of men quite different from those to whom they were accustomed, or knew existed, and that now she, quiet, lovely dark-haired Doreen, lovely, shy Doreen, no longer wore her blouse and dark skirt, her dark stockings, and low-heeled shoes, but rather lay naked in the keeping of men, a branded slave, theirs, on a far-off planet, on a world they did not even know existed.

"Up," said the man, looking down the shoot.

I rose to my hands and knees.

"All right," he said. "Proceed."

I again addressed myself to this journey on the wooden surface. He tapped me twice, rather smartly, but not cruelly, not to hurt me, with the side of the stick, swinging it to his right, as I passed him. It had been done with a good-natured, if perhaps somewhat vulgar, familiarity. It was like the good-natured, possessive slap below the small of the back with which men sometimes speed slave girls about their business. In his way he was complimenting me. I must endure such touches, of course. Men owned me, and could do what they wanted with me. I belonged to them. Actually, of course, I was pleased that he had done so. In its way it was a kindly act. Indeed, it may have been intended to hearten and reassure me. Slave girls seldom object to such treatment, vulgar though it might seem to free women, and even free women, I think, in spite of the scandal they profess to feel in its wake, do not really mind it. It is a way in which women are informed that they are of sexual interest.

I continued to crawl along the shoot. Here and there there was a man with a stick. I hoped they would not strike me or jab me with their sticks. I kept my head down and did not dally. I was frightened as I passed them, one by one, almost cringing, almost recoiling, from the fear of blows that might alight upon my body, knowing myself so much exposed, so much at their mercy, at their whim or caprice. Then I was past them. I was grateful to them for not having beaten me. There was little left in me now of Teibar's "modern woman," I feared.

Then I was at the end of the shoot, at another gate.

I looked through the wooden slats of the gate.

I could see to my left what looked like a part of a muchly trodden circular dirt area, within a solid wooden railing. Behind this railing, standing, crowded about, there seemed to be many men. Directly before me, and to my right, there was a low, wooden wall, about four feet high. This prevented me from seeing much ahead or to my right, and would prevent most of the men, assuming they were crowded about an extension of the circular railing to my right, from seeing me. The interest of the men who could see me, however, as nearly as I could determine, was on something to my left, and raised above the dirt surface.

A man opened the gate and motioned me out, still on all fours, onto a small wooden platform. I could smell sweat, and hear voices, excited voices. One voice seemed predominant among them.

He knelt me back and put manacles on my wrists, joined by about a foot of chain.

I knelt there, the chain across my thighs.

The gate was closed behind me. I saw another girl. I did not know her, now behind the gate. She must wait.

Suddenly the nature of the calls and responses from the crowd became clear to me. There were calls for bids, and there were bids, literally bids, and something was being sold.

I inched forward, to see better. I could see the forward edge of a large, rounded block, about five feet high, set back on the dirt, a few feet within the railing. A double chain seemed to be extending upward, toward it, on a pulley system. I moved forward on my knees, nearer the wooden wall in front of me. I saw Gloria there, on that rounded, raised surface, standing, her wrists over her head, in manacles much like mine. The chain on her manacles extended upward in an inverted "V." It had been placed over the lower hook of a two-hooked, short chain. It was about two feet in length. The higher hook on the chain had been placed over one strand of the double chain overhead. About Gloria a man walked, with a whip.

I looked back, trembling, at the girl still on all fours in the shoot. Her face was frightened, behind the slats of the gate.

The man who was near me took a short length of chain. It had a hook at each end. It was about two feet in length. He put one end about the chain on my manacles, and held the other.

I suddenly almost cried out with fear. From my left, from the rounded, wooden surface, there had come the snap of a whip. I heard the movement of a chain overhead. I saw Gloria being drawn from the surface by the manacles, doubtless, by means of them, to be lowered to the ground on the other side.

The man then slung his end of my short chain, that whose lower hook was about the chain on my manacles, over the chain extending upwards.

Gloria had been sold!

The chain moved a little, and my wrists were pulled upward.

"No!" I cried, in English. "No, please!"

Then I felt the manacles drawn upward and my arms extended. I was pulled to my left and then, suddenly, my feet were off the platform and I was swinging inches over the dirt. The sides of the manacles cut into my wrists. I was then being lifted up, toward the surface of the block. The gate beneath me, and behind me, was opened. The other girl was now doubtless being brought to the platform, behind the low wall, out of the sight of most of the crowd, and another was moving to the gate. I saw, now, being lifted, that there were tiers behind the standing area, extending back and toward the back of the building. On them, though I could not see them well, there seemed to be many men, sitting. I could not see any females. The only females in the building, I supposed, might be females such as myself, naked females, up for vending. There must have been some four or five hundred men in the building, in the tiers alone, not counting those crowded by the low railing. As I was lifted I could see the semicircular nature of the dirt flooring. Doubtless, the large platform removed, tarsks would be sold there. It was a lofty, raftered building. I put my head up. I saw the chain moving. I saw more rafters, too, high above me, almost lost in the darkness under the roof. It was a barnlike building. My wrists hurt. I was then suspended above the platform. The men were looking at me. It was a sales barn. Then the chain slackened a little and my feet touched the surface of the platform. I stood, it seemed, in a half inch or so of sawdust. My wrists were still held high over my head. I heard the crack of the whip and I jerked, frightened, in the manacles. Some of the men laughed. The whip had not touched me. My response though, I think, aside from being startled, had informed the men that I was not totally unfamiliar with the whip. Indeed, though I had felt it very seldom, I had felt it. Indeed, the first sensation that I had been aware of on this world had been the stroke of Teibar's whip, awakening his "modern woman" to her new reality. He had struck me three times. I had never forgotten the feel of those informative, salutatory blows bidding me welcome to my bondage.

The fellow put his left hand on my breast, holding it still, reading it. Then he nodded to another fellow, behind me and to my left, on the platform.

"Lot 89," called that fellow.

Various men at the rail and in the tiers rustled papers, or glanced at notes, held in their hands. I gathered that many of them might be the sort of men who would buy more than one woman. That frightened me.

I listened to the fellow behind us, scarcely understanding him. It was called to the attention of the buyers that I was another Earth female. I was characterized as being intelligent, and as having, for my time on Gor, attained some skill in comprehending the language. I would be capable, I heard, of understanding most simple commands put to me. I myself thought my grasp of Gorean far exceeded such a minimal level but perhaps they wished to be conservative in their claims on my behalf, if only to protect themselves against the possible complaints of dissatisfied customers. Too, they probably weren't certain, really, how good my Gorean was. I had been here only since yesterday morning. I then heard my height and weight, given in Gorean measurements, thirty and a quarter Gorean stone and fifty-one horts, or approximately, in Earth measurements, one hundred and twenty-one pounds and five foot three and three quarters inches, and a large number of my other measurements being similarly recounted. These would be my "block measurements," those which were mine as of now, on the date of my sale. Some masters will hold a girl to her block measurements, by the whip, if necessary. Others will insist on their improvement, under the penalties of a similar discipline, in one direction or another, depending on their own preferences. Other masters are quite lenient, or tolerant, at least within certain limits, pertaining to such measurements. Clothing sizes were not given, as there is little concern on Gor with a slave's exact sizes in such matters. Most Gorean garments for female slaves are either loosely fitting, and drape, or they are pulled tight, sometimes strapped or tied about her, to reveal her. If it is of interest, however, and we are speaking of fixed-ring sizes, I would take a number-two wrist ring and a number-two ankle ring. My collar size is eleven horts. These are average sizes. Gloria, for example would have taken larger sizes. Men's sizes, those of male slaves, incidentally, though the numbers are similar, are on a different scale. The buyers were also informed that I was "glana," or a virgin. The correlated term is 'metaglana', used to designate the state to which the glana state looks forward, or that which it is regarded as anticipating. Though the word was not used of me I was also 'profalarina', which term designates the state preceding, and anticipating, that of "falarina," the state Goreans seem to think of as that of being a full woman, or, at least, as those of Earth might think of it, one who certainly is no longer a virgin. In both terms, 'glana' and 'profalarina', incidentally, it seems that the states they designate are regarded as immature or transitory, states to be succeeded by more fully developed, superior states, those of "metaglana" or "falarina." Among slaves, not free women, these things are sometimes spoken of along the lines as to whether or not a girl has been "opened" for the uses of men. Other common terms, used generally of slaves, are 'white silk' and 'red silk', for girls who have not yet been opened, or have been opened, for the uses of men, respectively.

I suddenly wondered, wildly, my hands high, held fast in the manacles, if Teibar, my Teibar, might be out there somewhere among those men, perhaps high in the tiers, in the darkness, waiting to bid on me! Then I realized how foolish that would be. He could have bought me at the house, at a discount, if he had wanted me, not waiting, not following me for great distances, not almost certainly paying more in an open market, not risking losing me to a higher bidder in a place such as Market of Semris. No, Teibar would not be here. It was I who was here, alone.

I heard myself characterized as being "semitrained." Was that all my training in the house counted for, I wondered, rising so early, retiring so late, the busy days, the long lessons, their frequency, variety and intensiveness, administered to us morning, noon and night? I then wondered if this, like the claims made with respect to my Gorean, were intended to be precautionary, or conservative, perhaps to avoid possible subsequent difficulties with disappointed buyers. But this time I did not think so. I had some inkling, by now, given my training in the house, of the sorts of things which could be involved in "training," many of which we had not even had time to touch upon. I was sure that given the possibilities of slave service I was still very naive and backward, still muchly uninformed. Indeed, I suspected that there would always be more to learn about service and love, that such things were fathomless and limitless, and, thus, in a sense, the notion of being "fully trained," or knowing all there was to know, was in actuality less of a practical goal than a lovely ideal, one which might perhaps be approached ever more closely, but would never be, and perhaps should never be, fully attained. Let the girl revel in her growth, and not fear that one day there will be no more to learn, nowhere else to go. There are no summits on the heights of love. Ulrick, however, had assured me in the house, once, that I had talent. I hoped so. Such, among the imperious masters of this world, might improve my chances for survival. I did have a live body, some understanding of my womanhood, and a desire to please men. I looked down into some of the faces below me, behind the railing, across the dirt, across the tarsk run. I had better be pleasing to such men, I thought, shuddering. Then I moaned to myself. Teibar was not here. I was alone. What was I doing here? Why was I brought here, to this world? My wrists hurt, held up so high in the steel. Were the men not being cruel to me? Could they not see I was naked, and helpless?

"Category," I heard, "—Pleasure Slave."

When I heard this categorization, so matter-of-factly given, concluding the fellow's recounting of attributes and features, measurements, and such, I was suddenly, inordinately, startled. I had known, of course, I was not a house slave, or a tower slave, for I was not permitted to kneel in fashions appropriate to those varieties of slave. Too, I had understood, of course, that many of the things I was taught seemed to have direct application to the pleasing of masters, and even profoundly sensuously so, but I had not, until now, heard that exact simple, direct expression. We had never been told, in so many words, that that was the sort of slave we were. Perhaps the Gorean girls had understood it, clearly enough, but I do not think we girls of Earth had, at least not in so direct a way, not in the way, certainly, which seemed to be summarized so clearly and succinctly by that one expression. Ulrick had not even told me the sort of slave I was. He had laughed, and informed me that I would learn from masters. Now, it seemed, on the sales block, I had done so. I threw back my head, and moaned. The chain overhead tightened and I was pulled up a little more, so that only my toes were on the block.

The auctioneer lifted his whip, cracked it, and called for the first bid.

My wrists hurt. He was calling for a bid on an illiterate barbarian. I realized, suddenly, that that was I.

I was an educated, civilized, refined woman on my own world. Here I was an illiterate barbarian!

I heard someone call out from the floor. I realized, suddenly, I had been bid upon. I was being sold! Too, he was not bidding on part of me, say, on my body. He was bidding in the Gorean fashion on all of me, on the whole slave. The bid had been for twenty copper tarsks. In a moment I had heard twenty-two, and twenty-seven.

On my own world I was a modern woman, of sorts, independent, and free, and with political power, particularly with fearful, cringing men. But here men were not fearful and cringing. But then I had been taken from Earth, and my power, to be brought here to be utterly powerless, to be a slave, to be a pleasure slave! How reductive, I thought, to be a pleasure slave! Then I knew that that was what, on a proper, natural world, I would be, that that, on such world, was right for me. "No, no!" I wept, in English.

I heard more bids.

The auctioneer walked about me. He touched me, here and there, with his whip. He turned me on the chain, I on my toes, exhibiting me.

Then I again faced the men. There were more bids.

I thought how amused Teibar might have been, to have thought of me, his hated "modern woman," as he thought, being sold, and being sold in this place, a place fit for her, a sales barn, where tarsks, four-legged, and two-legged, like herself, were sold. I wondered if Teibar knew I would be sold in this place. He was doubtless privy to the records of the house. But he may have left their service before I was consigned to the wholesaler outside Brundisium. But it could be this was a common clearing point for their slaves. It could be, too, he had retained contacts with the house. He might very well know I was here. He may have even, for his amusement, arranged that it would be here, or in a similar outlet, that I was sold, influencing the orders in some fashion. Perhaps that I was here, naked in a sales barn, my wrists in manacles over my head, being bid upon by strangers, was part of his vengeance on me. At the least he would have known that this, or something similar, would be done to me! How amused he must be, when he thought of such things, his haughty, pretentious "modern woman," as he thought, she whom he held in such contempt, to her dismay and terror, and misery, now being sold naked from a slave block, into absolute bondage!

Then I became aware of someone, or one or two men, actually, calling up from the floor. It was not bids they were calling. I tried to understand them. In my misery and distress it was hard to even begin to understand them. I did not know if it were their accents, or I simply, in my confusion, my misery and distress, had suddenly lost almost all my command of Gorean. I could not really understand them.

The chain slackened above me and my arms fell, somewhat. The auctioneer put his whip on his belt, held me by the left arm in his right hand, and, with his left hand, reaching up, lifted the chain between my manacles off the lower hook of the short chain, that attached to the strand of the double chain overhead. His hand on my arm kept me from collapsing to the sawdust. My hands were down, the chain on the manacles now against my thighs. He said something to me, but I did not understand it. Then he reached in front of me and gathered the chain between my manacles into his hands and lifted my wrists up, bending my arms back. He put my wrists back, behind my head, and then released the chain on the manacles, letting it drop behind my neck. "Clasp your hands behind the back of your head," he said. I understood him now. "Bend back," he said. "Display yourself." I obeyed, of course. Too, the whip was now again in his hand. "Flex your knees," he said. "Now, turn," he said. "Do not forget our friends to the right," he said. I then displayed myself, again, identically, at the right side of the block. I did not think the other girls had been removed from the chain, or not many of them, given the speed with which the line had moved. Why should I be favored in this respect? The bidding had been interrupted at eighty-eight tarsks, whatever that meant. I did know that there was apparently something about me, perhaps unfortunately, which many Gorean men found of interest. I do not think this was simply a matter of figure and face, though I think these appealed to a Gorean taste, but perhaps something else, something deeper, which they seemed to sense about me, some sort of possibility, or potentiality, or something, which I myself did not fully understand, or yet understand. Sometimes he touched me with the whip, calling attention to a curve or a flank. Teibar's "modern woman," I thought, is now displaying herself naked to Gorean buyers. He then had me kneel and bent me back, painfully, my hair back to the sawdust, to the center, and then the left, and then the right, before the buyers. He then had me straighten up and unclasp my hands from behind my head. He then lifted the chain forward, over my head. It then hung, between my wrists, a little below my neck. He let me lower my hands. My hands then, and the chain, were again on my thighs. My hands chained as they were, I could not both keep them on my thighs and maintain a full, open-kneed position. I looked up at him, from the sawdust.

Men were calling out, from behind the railing, and some from the tiers. To my surprise the auctioneer removed a key from his belt and removed the manacles from me. I rubbed my wrists. There were marks on them where the manacles had cut into me, when I was lifted to the block.

The auctioneer cracked his whip.

I looked up at him, from the sawdust. I was to be put through slave paces.

I tried to put from me what was being done to me.

I wanted to go back to the library.

The sawdust was in my hair, and its particles clung to my sweating body.

"Yes," I thought, "I can find that book."

I was on my belly, naked, in the sawdust.

"Yes," I thought, "there was quiet, shy Doreen in the library, going quietly about her duties, there, walking about, returning to the reference desk, over that flat carpet, from the information desk, past the xerox machines." I rolled in the sawdust.

Yes, there she was, there, in that simple sweater, that plain blouse and dark skirt, the dark stockings, the low-heeled black shoes. Surely no man could find her of interest. Then she became aware of a man at the reference desk, looking down at her, one bright afternoon, a man whose look penetrated into her deepest heart and belly, and stripped her, and saw the slave there. And he had caught her in her dancer's costume, that in which no man had ever seen her before, and she had then, in swirling skirt and scarlet halter, and bells, danced in the darkened library, danced before him and his men. I was vaguely aware of a cry of pleasure from the crowd. I had performed the transition between two of the moves in the slave paces with the startling, sensuous agility of a dancer. It then seemed that it was the dancer in the sawdust, on the block, she who had worn the skirt and halter, and bells. How beautiful they seemed to find her! How she moved! She heard the exclamations of praise. The auctioneer stood back, the whip lowered, startled. "No!" I cried. Then again I was awkward and fearful, and only an Earth girl, miserable, confused and terrified, cringing in the sawdust of a slave block on an alien world.

"What is wrong?" asked the auctioneer.

"Nothing, Master," I whispered, cringing before him on all fours.

A gesture of his whip informed me I should lie upon my back. Then I was supine before him. He turned about. He stood partly over my body. He faced the crowd. He had one of his legs between mine.

"Two," was called to him from the floor. "Two!"

"Two!" repeated the auctioneer, holding up two fingers. "Two!"

The auctioneer did not sound angry at this bid. I myself was startled. The bids had been in the eighties before. Now, it seemed, they were reduced to only two.

I was on my back, gasping, lying there.

The auctioneer stepped a little away from me, and turned to face me.

It was now as though I could hardly move. I was terrified. I hoped he would not beat me, because the bids were now down to two.

He looked down at me, puzzled.

I think I must then have seemed to him quite otherwise than I had but moments ago. I do not think he understood this. It was almost, I suppose, as though there were not one, but two women on the block, almost as though he had two different women to sell.

I rose up on my elbows but he, with the heel of his bootlike sandal, thrust me back to the sawdust. He then, with his bootlike sandal, turned me to my stomach. "Kneel," he said. I knelt. He then replaced the manacles on my wrists. He turned me so that I knelt facing the crowd. He pulled down the short chain from the horizontal chain. "Stand," he said. I obeyed. "What is wrong with her?" called a man. The chain between my manacles was looped over the lower hook on the short chain. I could hardly stand. I was terrified. I looked out on the men. Any one of them, I realized, could own me. I was a slave! I could be owned! I could belong to them! They could do with me what they might please, anything. They would have over me total power. But I was a woman of Earth! This could not be happening to me! Then, as the higher chain, the strand of the double chain, took up its slack, my wrists were again pulled up, high, over my head. Again I could touch the block only with my toes. I had not been as Ulrick had wanted, not at the end. I had been too much afraid. I had not been fresh and supple. I had not controlled my breath well. I feared I had not been beautiful. I had been too afraid, too afraid to be truly beautiful. I had been awkward and clumsy. I had not done well! Oddly enough I had not wanted to disappoint Ulrick, who, I think, had liked me. Too, I didn't want to be punished for not having done well. Surely they had wanted to make more money on me than "two," two of whatever it was.

I looked down into the faces. They were masters, and I was a slave. My eyes met those of one fellow, a large, corpulent man, stripped to the waist, very hairy, with crossed belts running across his chest. He had a drooping mustache. He had a long scar at the left side of his face. He was one of the grossest, most frighteningly ugly men I had ever seen. He looked up at me, and grinned. On the right side of his mouth a tooth was missing. I looked up, away from him, at the manacles on my wrists. They again hurt my wrists, my body stretched, and pulled up, as it was, on my toes. My toes hurt, and the back of my legs. I looked above the manacles, to the chain. Chains are so strong. We cannot break them.

The auctioneer was now behind me and to my left. "Is there a further bid?" he asked.

I think the ambiguities in my performance, if that is what they were, may have puzzled several in the crowd, as well as the auctioneer.

The house was quiet.

I looked down again. Again my eyes met those of the large, corpulent fellow. He grinned. He did not seem puzzled. I feared he might be a perceptive master, in spite of his grossness, his ugliness, from whom a girl could not keep secrets. I looked hastily away, again, from him.

"Am I bid only two," inquired the auctioneer, "for this luscious merchandise?"

I felt the whip touch my flank and waist, on the left.

He then stepped a bit before me, to my left. He turned and touched me twice with the whip. "Consider this flank, and belly," he said.

I tried to hold myself perfectly still. The light touches of the whip, though, had made me terribly uneasy.

He again moved behind me, and to the left.

"I have been bid two," he said, "for this lovely barbarian pleasure slave. Do I hear more? To be sure, she is only semitrained, and perhaps not yet fully broken to the collar. That I would not gainsay. But surely she has some promise. Yes, I think so. Some of you, I am sure, suspect that she has promise."

I did not know what he meant by that.

"Is there a higher bid?" he asked. "Shall I close my hand?"

A wave of anger suddenly swept over me. I, a pleasure slave! Absurd! How reductive! How degrading! I wanted suddenly to prove to them that I was no pleasure slave. I was an educated, refined, civilized woman of Earth! I was a modern woman, at least of sorts! I was no pleasure slave! But I knew, looking down at those faces, that if any of them owned me, I would have to be fully pleasing to them. I would have to bend all of my efforts, and all of my beauty, my charm, my grace, my knowledge, my intelligence, my tact, everything that I was, and could hope to be, to that end. I would have to be to them, and perfectly, a pleasure slave. And what horrified me most, I think, was that I wanted this. I wanted to serve men, and give them pleasure, to be precious to them, to be loved and appreciated, to make them happy. What a terrible woman I was, to want to make men happy. Then, again, I strove to be cold and hard, to be cruel like stone and leather. I must not allow myself to feel! But what, I asked myself, if I were not allowed to be my own mistress? What if men simply did things to me, forcing me to feel, as it pleased them, forcing me to yield, and melt, against my will, forcing me to feel, and experience, things which on Earth I had never even dreamed of, forcing me to be what I most feared, permitting me nothing else, a woman in the order of nature? Then I steeled myself again. I was no pleasure slave. There was no pleasure slave in me! I was above such things. I was my own mistress. No man could change that!

"Aii!" I cried, suddenly, startled, squirming wildly, leaping in the manacles, twisting, with a movement of chain, then my weight on them, the chain taut, my knees lifted, almost to my belly, my eyes shut, my teeth gritted.

There was much laughter from the house.

When I opened my eyes again, my body now again stretched

out, standing on its toes, my wrists high over my head in the manacles, I looked down, across the dirt area, over the railing. The large, hideous, gross, corpulent fellow was there, looking up at me, grinning. I blushed hotly. I looked away from him.

I had not expected the touch.

There was more laughter.

My body was crimson with shame.

It had been revealed to the men that I had a vital, living body.

I held my ankles, and knees, and legs as closely together as I could. I was terrified. I was suddenly aware then, dimly, of what men might do to me, how they might take me out of myself, subjecting me to incredible sensations as they, not I, might wish, or choose. Too, if I had so reacted to so small and simple a thing, it was difficult to conjecture how I might behave if subjected to more detailed, subtle or prolonged attentions. I suddenly felt terribly helpless, and yet, too, in a way, eager. Too, what if, horrifyingly enough, I was not permitted resistance but must, under the sanction of terrible penalties, under the command of masters, open myself fully to feeling, if I were forced to yield, and fully, and was forced, thusly, to collaborate in my own conquest? There was one thing which perhaps, in a way, was in my favor. My entire skin, and body, tonight, was much less responsive than it would normally have been. I could tell that, even from this morning. I had known it, too, from my responses on the platform in the exposition area of the sales barn, at the other end of the long corridor. This had to do with my disappointment in the matter of Teibar, that I was still not within his grasp, that he had not brought me here, in some master's jest, to reclaim me. I had then understood that, despite all my hopes, I was really, in the end, nothing to him, only another pretty Earth girl, to be brought here merely in the line of his business, to wear the collar and lick the whip. My sense of abandonment had been acute. How alone I had suddenly realized I was here, on this strange, beautiful world. I had been almost in shock, and without feeling. Too, tonight, I had been, particularly in the last few minutes, almost numbed with misery, and terror, understanding myself being sold. I had been frightened, constricted and tight. I had been, I feared, not beautiful. I had been just the opposite, I feared, of what Ulrick would have wanted. Thus, even though I had been taken unawares by the sudden movement of the auctioneer's whip, and had moved suddenly, inadvertently, in a manner which might have suggested to some that I was a pleasure slave, I knew that the fullness of what I conjectured would be my typical response to such a touch had not even been hinted at. The full range of my responsiveness, thusly, I congratulated myself, still lay concealed. None could suspect it. I shuddered, though, to think of what it, so delicate and deep, might be under a master's hands. I could suspect, even from the simple touch I had received, how helpless I might be.

"Two!" called a fellow from behind the rail, raising his hand. "Two and fifty!"

"Two and fifty!" called the auctioneer, pleased. "Two and fifty! Do I hear more?"

The house was quiet.

I looked down. The fellow who had just made the bid, whatever was its amount, was the large, gross, corpulent fellow, he who was so ugly, so frightening.

"Shall I close my hand?" asked the auctioneer. His hand was open, held out to the side.

I looked down at the man.

I twisted in the manacles. I could not free myself. I was a slave!

I looked down at him.

I would wear a collar. I was branded.

I looked down at him.

I knew that in time my body would regain its sensitivity levels, that inexorably its awareness, and helplessness, would return. It would be inevitable, like the rising of water in a well. I could do nothing about it.

I looked down at him.

He looked up at me, and grinned.

"The barbarian is yours!" said the auctioneer, closing his hand.

I heard a movement of chain above me and I was then, by the manacles and chain, over the hook on the short chain, drawn across the block and, suspended, lowered to the other side. Another girl, then, would be brought to the surface of the block. In a moment, my knees giving way, I was on another platform, much like the one on the other side of the block. Here, however, the low wooden wall was to my left and front. The manacles were removed from me, and I was thrust toward another gate, and shoot. In a moment I was again crawling on the wood. I strove to maintain consciousness. I was glad, now, we were to crawl. I do not think I could have walked. I heard the auctioneer behind me, calling for a bid on a new girl. It would be she who had come to the gate behind me. I recalled seeing her face behind the slats of the gate. I did not know her. I passed a man with a pointed stick. He did not hurt me. I could not throw up. I had not been fed enough. I could not soil myself, or the wood. They had prevented that. Too, the greatest danger of those things is during the early moments, or the final moments, of a sale. I moved down the shoot. My lot number was still on my left breast. I wondered if I would be picked up tonight. I supposed not, as it was late. I came to the end of the shoot. There was an opened tarsk cage there. I crawled into it. I was the first one in this particular cage. I crawled to the end of it. There would probably be five girls in this cage before it was locked. In other cages, which had been removed, I supposed, from the shoot's exit, I could see other girls. I saw Clarissa and Gloria in the cage to my right. They had preceded me in the coffle. They looked frightened. I supposed I did, too. We had been sold. Gloria had her fingers hooked in the heavy mesh of the cage side. Ah, Teibar, I thought, you have your vengeance on your "modern woman" now, indeed! She has been sold like a tarsk, in a sales barn! Too, you would doubtless much approve of the master into whose hands she has now come! Did they think, I wondered, angrily, that I existed only to give pleasure to men? But then I thought, wryly, ruefully, that that was exactly for what Teibar's "modern woman" now existed. That was now the whole purpose of her existence, that, and only that. It was that for which she must now live, only that. I considered my fate. Teibar had known it was to be mine. Indeed, he had chosen me for it. How amused he must be, then, from time to time, I thought, if he ever saw fit, perhaps in an idle moment, when freed of more pressing concerns, to recollect me. To what a delicious and amusingly appropriate fate he had consigned me! But no longer, now, really, was I a "modern woman." I was now only a vended slave girl. I thought of my master, and trembled. I put my fingers in the mesh of the tarsk cage. I wept, for a time. Then I lay down in the cage, naked, the number on my breast. I pulled my legs up. Then I lost consciousness.

10 / The Kitchen

My head was down, my hair over his feet. I was naked, frightened. I had been summoned into his presence, and had performed obeisance at the end of the long carpet, leading to the dais. I had then, when permitted, approached the dais, head down, on all fours. I had climbed, on all fours, up the broad, carpeted steps of the dais, and now lay, on my belly, half on its surface, the lower part of my body, my right knee flexed, across the final two steps before its height.

"You lick and kiss well," he said.

"Thank you, Master," I said.

"Like the other females of Earth," he said.

"Yes, Master," I said. I gathered I was not the first Earth female who had come this way.

"You may continue," he said.

"Thank you, Master," I said.

"It is not unpleasant," he said.

"A slave is grateful if her master is not displeased with her," I said.

"You are very pretty," he said.

"Thank you, Master," I said.

"You wear a collar," he said.

"Yes, Master," I said.

"Whose collar is it?" he asked.

"Yours, Master," I said.

"And whose is that?" he asked.

"The collar of my master, Hendow, of Brundisium, master of the tavern of Hendow, on Dock Street, in Brundisium," I said.

There was a slave whip across his knees.

His feet and ankles were large, and the sandals had heavy straps on them. His calves and thighs, too, were sturdy and powerful. His forearms and arms, too, were frighteningly thick, and sturdy, like the trunks of small trees. They were inches greater in dimension than my own small limbs. He was of broad girth. His shoulders, too, were broad, like the beams of a house.

I could not begin to conjecture the strength of such a man. He could have handled me like a doll. I felt helpless. It was like a flower before a mace of iron.

I was terrified. He was my master. I was eager to please him.

His hand, reaching down, prevented me from licking higher than midway upon his calves.

"You already know something of what it is to be a slave, don't you?" he asked.

"Yes, Master," I said.

"Desist," he said.

I desisted in my ministrations.

"You are a virgin, aren't you?" he asked.

"Yes, Master," I said. He knew that, of course. It had been in my sales information. Too, it had been checked by his man the morning following my sale, before I had been prepared for shipment here.

"Would you risk your virginity here, in this place, at this time?" he asked.

"My virginity," I said, "belongs to my master. He may do what he wishes with it."

"I have plans for it," he said.

I was silent. It would be as he willed. He was Master.

"How do your lessons proceed?" he asked.

"I think well, Master," I said. It seemed to me in my best interests to be conservative in my estimations. Doubtless he had better information at his disposal than I could give him, from his dancing slaves, and his whip master.

"You are a dancer," he said, "and have in you the makings of a superb pleasure slave."

"Thank you, Master," I said.

"It is interesting that you are from Earth," he said. "One might have thought that you were Gorean."

"I am a woman," I whispered.

"Yes," he said. "That is probably the important thing. In the end it is probably all pretty much the same. There are men, and there are women."

"Yes, Master," I said.

"Did you know that many times Earth women turn out to be superb pleasure slaves?" he asked.

"We are women," I whispered, shrugging. I saw no reason why we, properly controlled and disciplined, should not be as perfect for a man as a Gorean woman. Indeed, considering the social and political deserts in which we were sexually starved, it would not have surprised me in the least, if we, once it became clear to us, to our joy, that we now had no culturally prescribed alternatives to being women, that we were now no longer subjected to social pressures to be something else, our womanhood being denied, or demeaned and despised, to coming home to our sex, and nature, proved to be every bit as good, if not in some ways better, than our Gorean sisters, or at least some of them, unaware of such deprivations. But in the end, I suppose, it all depends on the individual female. In the end, we were all women.

"Look up," he said.

I rose to my knees, and lifted my head.

"You have a beautiful face," he said.

"Thank you, Master," I said.

"And you have a luscious form," he said.

"Thank you, Master," I said.

"Kiss the whip," he said.

I did so, quickly, that I might not seem to dally, or he draw it from me, but then, as he held it in place, permitting me to continue, more slowly, more lingeringly. Then he drew it back, and I knelt back, before him.

"Are you going to be any good?" he asked.

I looked up at him, startled, frightened. He had said I had a beautiful face, and a luscious form. What more could anyone want? Then I swallowed hard, understanding him. Of course, of course, I thought. Such things would be only a beginning, perhaps only a small beginning, and doubtless not even a necessary beginning, of what men would expect of me. "It is my hope that I will be pleasing," I said.

"I have high hopes for you," he said.

I was silent.

"I think," he said, "that you will be *very good*."

"It is my hope that I will be pleasing to my master," I said.

"And to any to whom, in your master's service," he said, "you are explicitly, or implicitly, consigned."

"Yes, Master," I said.

"And to men, in general," he said.

"Yes, Master, of course, Master," I said. I was a female slave. I existed now for the pleasure of men. It was what I was for.

"Sometimes," he said, "one encounters an Earth female who believes, at first, for a short time, that she may be resistant, in some respect, either secretly or overtly, to masters. Are you such a female?"

"No, Master," I said.

"In any way?" he asked.

"No, Master!" I said.

"Such recalcitrance is detectable," he said. "It is betrayed by subtle body cues, uncontrollable, and unmistakable."

"Yes, Master," I said, looking down.

"There are drugs, too," he said, "which are pertinent to such matters."

"Yes, Master," I said. I had not known that. I had known about the other sorts of things. They had been graphically illustrated to us in the house of my training. Some had to do with skin blotching and nipple erection. One simple test had been with five of us, one of us, not known to Ulrick, to take a ring and hide it. By holding her hands and looking into her eyes he had almost immediately determined the "guilty girl." He had then, merely by holding her arm, had her guide him, involuntarily, to where she had hidden the ring. These things were done primarily by acute observation and differential muscle tensions, indexed to the girl's knowledge and inward states. The meaning of the lessons, however, had been clear. If our slavery did not go through us, so to speak, if it was not complete, we could not conceal that from the masters. Our choice then, in effect, was to be complete slaves, whole slaves, total slaves, or die. I, and, I think, my entire class, interestingly, had rejoiced in this knowledge. We knew we were slaves in our hearts, as we had learned in our training, and we wanted to be slaves. The knowledge then that we would be unable to conceal any inauthenticity in our slavery from the masters, even if we wished to do so, was a liberating insight. It imposed a welcome, healthful psychological consistency upon us. It deprived us of even the last excuse which our pride or vanity might have left to us not to be perfect in our bondage. To be sure, sometimes a master encourages open defiance or rebellion on the part of a girl, he then enjoying forcing her to serve, and perfectly, so obviously, so visibly, against her will. Too, sometimes, he is amused to indulge a girl's "secret" recalcitrance, well aware of her games, her transparent reservations, her supposedly so carefully guarded and secret resistance, letting her think it is unknown, even unsuspected. When he tires of this sport, however, he reveals to her, to her horror, that she has been all this time as open to him as a book. She can then make the decision of the slave girl, to be a true slave, a full slave, or die.

"Look into my eyes," he said.

I did so. It was not easy.

"Yes," he said, "you are a slave."

"Yes, Master," I said.

"Even though you might regret your bondage, or rage against it, from time to time," he said, "yet, in your heart, you know you are a slave."

"Yes, Master," I said, frightened.

"You were a slave even on Earth," he said.

"But a secret slave," I whispered.

"Here," he said, "your slavery is patent."

"Yes, Master," I said.

"What was wrong with you, at the end of your sale?" he asked. "You seemed suddenly so awkward, so clumsy, almost as though you were paralyzed."

"I do not know," I said. "Perhaps I realized, suddenly, what was being done with me, that I was being sold."

"But a slave must expect to be sold," he said.

"Yes, Master," I said.

He looked down at me.

"I was frightened, Master," I said.

"Are you frightened now?" he asked.

"Yes, Master," I said. This was the first time I had been in his presence, to my knowledge, since my sale in Market of Semris. I kept my eyes from meeting his. I could see the vast, hairy chest, crossed by the two belts. The large, drooping mustache suggested a casual, almost indolent power. The scar at the side of his face had been wrought, I supposed, by some primitive device or weapon, perhaps even, though it seemed hard to believe for a female of Earth, in combat. From my point of view, he seemed clearly a barbarian. He would think nothing of owning women. To be sure, from his point of view, it was I, though a refined female of Earth, who, on this world, counted as being the "barbarian." He had been coming back from some place called Torcadino, or near Torcadino, where he had gone, either there, or in its vicinity, to purchase cheap girls for his tavern. I gathered that women, for some reason, were cheap in that vicinity. He had stopped at Market of Semris on his way back to Brundisium, boarding his girls overnight at the house of Teibar. He had stopped in that evening at the sales barn. There he had purchased me. He had not, as far as I knew, made any other purchases there.

"Good," he said. "It is well for a slave to fear her master."

"Yes, Master," I said. I kept my head down. What he said was true, of course. It was indeed well for a slave to fear her master. The master can do what he wishes to her. He has absolute and total power over her.

I watched his fingers move idly on the butt of the whip and on its single, thick blade, coiled back, twice, against the butt.

I suppose I would have feared any Gorean master, they are so strict with us. But I was sure, too, I feared this one more than I might have most. He was so large, and so beastlike, a complex man, I sensed, but one of simplicity in the sense of undividedness or singleness of purpose. To be sure, this lack of self-division, of self-conflict, tends to be characteristic of Gorean males. Their culture does not try to control them by setting them against themselves when they are too young to understand what is being done to them, in some cases, by half tearing them apart. To some extent, I suppose, it satisfies them, and keeps them content, rather as one might throw meat to lions, by throwing a certain sort of woman in their way, the slave. The man who owned me might indeed be, as I had first perceived him, in Market of Semris, he free, looking up at the slave block where I, a naked slave, displayed in high manacles, was being vended, too corpulent, too broad of girth, too gross, too scarred, too loathsome, too hideous, but now that I was his, and within reach of his whip, these initial perceptions were surely expanded or altered by other more pertinent, more trenchant ones. I was now aware not so much of these first-glimpsed things, things which might occur to a stranger looking casually upon him for the first time, from a distance, as other things, things which became much clearer with closeness, closeness such as when one might be kneeling naked before him, so close he could reach out and touch you, a sense of intelligence, and power, and perception, such that one felt he could look through you, and see what was within you, anything, and uncompromising mastery, and perhaps mercilessness. The most obvious thing about him, of course, now, from my point of view, was that he owned me, that he was my master.

"But you are not so frightened now," he said.

"No," I said.

"Why?" he asked.

"The sale is over," I said. "I know that I am now a sold slave. That is behind me. I have been summoned into the presence of my master. In this he has honored me, for he has many girls. He has been kind enough to express his satisfaction with trivialities of his slave, that she has a beautiful face and form, and his belief that I may perhaps prove to be pleasing in more significant manners. Too, he has informed me that my tongue work upon his feet has not been entirely displeasing."

"For a slave new to her collar," he said.

"Yes, Master," I said. "Of course, Master. Thank you, Master."

"I think you were not too pleased to have been purchased by me," he said.

I was silent.

"Perhaps you find me gross," he said, "even hideous?"

I was silent.

"Some women do," he said.

I did not speak.

"It is amusing then to me, sometimes," he said, "to abuse them, and make them, despite their will, cry out for my touch."

"Yes, Master," I said.

"It pleases me to have them crawling to me on their belly, begging piteously to be used."

"Yes, Master," I whispered.

"Perhaps you find me gross and loathsome," he speculated.

I trembled, head down.

"But it doesn't matter," he said. "You are my slave."

"Yes, Master," I said.

"And at so much as the snapping of my fingers, you will bring yourself running to me, obediently and warmly, desperate to please me."

"Yes, Master," I said.

"But there is time enough for such things," he said.

I was silent.

"I was not displeased that your performance on the block was as ambiguous as it was, toward the end of your sale," he said.

"Master?" I asked.

"A kajira is occasionally entitled to terror," he said.

"Thank you, Master," I said, hesitantly.

"And it perhaps confused certain buyers," he said, "inhibiting them from submitting higher bids. I turned it thus to my profit."

I kept my eyes down.

"Come closer," he said.

I did so, on my knees. "Ohh," I said, touched by him. I leaned forward, tears in my eyes, pressing myself toward him, gross as he might be, my hands on the sides of the great chair in which he sat. I put my head down on his left knee.

"I thought so," he said. "Look up. Look in my eyes."

I did so, frightened.

"Yes," he said, looking into my eyes. "You are a slave. That is all you are."

"Yes, Master," I whispered.

"Kneel back," he said.

I knelt back then, tears in my eyes.

"Keep your knees open," he said.

"Oh, please, Master!" I begged.

His eyes were stern.

Immediately I opened my knees, widely, as was appropriate for the type of slave I was, a pleasure slave.

"One might think almost," he said, musingly, "that you were not a virgin. It is interesting to speculate what you will be like when you have been adequately opened and regularly utilized."

I kept my head down.

"It will probably not even be necessary to encourage you with the whip," he said.

I did not dare to speak.

"But the whip will be always there, should you require refreshening on your status, or become to any degree less than perfectly pleasing," he said.

"Yes, Master," I said.

"You may have fooled others in your terror," he said, "but you did not fool me."

"Master?" I asked.

"Beneath the terror," he said, "I saw the beauty, and the slave."

I did not speak.

"I saw, too," he said, "the dancer, particularly in your transitions between the attitudes commanded of you in the slave paces. I knew then you were either a dancer, or had the makings of a dancer. Too, of course, your response to the slaver's caress, later, was indicative. That, of course, would have been obvious even to a tharlarion."

"Yes, Master," I whispered, head down.

"But it was, of course," he said, "for you, a very poor, or limited, response, certainly one far below what might ordinarily have been expected from one with your sensitivity levels."

I looked up at him, startled. How could he have known that?

"To a discerning eye," he smiled, "it was evident, in your subsequent movements, and certain tiny, fleeting expressions, though these were subtle things, as you were inwardly relieved, pleased at how well hidden, you thought, remained the real depth and urgency of your needs."

I regarded him with horror.

"We are not going to have any secrets between us, are we?" he asked.

"No, Master!" I said, frightened. Before him I realized that it might be not only my body which was naked, but my mind and heart as well. I felt utterly exposed before this man, as only a slave can feel exposed to her master.

"Do not be frightened," he said.

I trembled, uncontrollably. Too, I remembered his touch.

"In a man's arms," he said, "you are the sort of woman who is so much alive, that you will be splendidly, utterly helpless."

I sobbed, shuddering naked, in my collar before him.

"Do you think you will like Brundisium?" he asked.

"I think so, Master," I whispered. I understood that Brundisium was one of the largest and busiest ports of this world. It was a commercial metropolis of sorts. I remembered in the slave wagon that several of the girls had hoped, desperately, not to be taken from this place. They had hoped fervently, it seemed, to wear their collars here. Ironically, it had been I, purchased in Market of Semris, a barbarian, who had been brought back to Brundisium. Many of my chain sisters, surely, would have envied me my good fortune. I was pleased enough to be here, from what I knew. Too, the city had seemed colorful and exciting to me, in my glimpses from the slave wagon. To be sure, at least one district through which we had passed in the wagon was still black with the residues of a great fire, one which had reportedly taken place in Se'Kara, some months ago. If I were never permitted outside the precincts of the tavern, of course, as I had not yet been, I did not think I would much enjoy the city. I had hopes, however, that I might, as several of the girls were now, eventually be granted such a lovely liberty. In such a matter, of course, the masters take little, if any, risk. The girls are collared and branded so there is never any doubt about what they are or where they belong. Too, in Brundisium, as with most Gorean cities, kajirae are not allowed outside the city gates unless in the keeping of a free person. In these peregrinations about the city, of course, the girls were sometimes expected to wear their master's advertising on their tunics.

"Did you enjoy the trip here?" he asked.

"Master was kind," I said, "to provide us with blankets."

We had spent the night of our sale in the cages located in the exit corridor. The next morning, at dawn, the cages had been opened, and we had been ordered forth, each to our own disposition. My hands had then been manacled behind my back, by my master's man. He had then given me a handful of slave gruel, putting it in my mouth as I knelt before him, my wrists chained behind me. We were not fed by the house of Teibar, of Market of Semris, that morning, as we were no longer its responsibility. I was then gagged and hooded, utilizing the devices of the ball-gag, the straps, the leather covering, the buckles and lock, as I had been when first leaving the house of my training. There were very good reasons for this, as I later learned. I was to be transported by tarn basket. When a girl cannot see and cannot communicate, it is much easier to manage her. I was taken out into the courtyard, gagged, hooded, and manacled. Then I was put on my belly in the dirt. I knew nothing about what was going on. Then I heard a succession of wild, startling sounds, like the snapping of great sheets, and it seemed I was in the midst of a whirlwind, mad, choking dust swirling up and about me. I tried to rise, but a man's foot pressed me back to the dirt. I also heard a sudden, shrill, terrifying, piercing scream. It was not a human noise, but the cry of something terribly large and fierce. It could only be, I conjectured, some sort of giant bird. I lay trembling in the dirt, helpless, the man's foot on my back. I would learn it was indeed a large bird, one called a "tarn." And, I would later learn, it was not even a warrior's mount, bred for swiftness and aggressiveness, a war tarn, but a mere draft tarn. I had been gagged, and hooded and manacled, and put on my belly, because the first sight of such a beast, at close hand, I was told, not unoften, in its size and ferocity, and terribleness, produces a miasma of terror in a female, and she is unwilling even to approach it, whips being often necessary. Happily I was unaware of the full terror within whose orbit I lay. I was pulled to my feet by an arm and walked for a few feet and then put down, on my back, on a blanket, on the ground. This blanket was wrapped about me, closely. It was then secured on my body apparently by ropes, above and below my breasts, about my waist and below my knees. I was then lifted in it and set down, sitting, on what seemed to be a heavy wicker surface. A leather collarlike arrangement was then put about my neck and my head was pulled back, apparently, as I could tell, pressing back through the hood, against a vertical wicker surface. This held me in place. I was then pushed back, further, against the vertical wicker surface. A broad belt then, perhaps some five or six inches in width, was put about my waist, drawn snug, and buckled shut. This, too, held me in place. My knees were up slightly. My ankles were then roped together, and fastened down, in place. This was done, apparently, by the rope being threaded once or twice through the wicker flooring and then being resecured about my ankles. I then heard again, it startling me, terrifying me, that sudden, loud, shrill, piercing scream, this time, it seemed, from terribly close, surely no more than a few feet away. I squirmed helplessly in the tight blanket, in the manacles, in the straps and ropes. I knew almost nothing of what was going on. We are so helpless when we are gagged and hooded. I then was conscious of other weights being placed in the area where I was, and being cinched in place. I was conscious of their movements, and squirmings, through the wicker. Then, in a few moments, it seemed a side gate was shut, near me, and roped shut. I heard the rattle of harness, sensed the attachment of ropes, the tying of knots, the drawing of them tight, their testing. Then, in a bit, I heard a cry and the jerking of harness, and that wild scream again, so piercing, hurting my ears, making me again leap and squirm, terrified, miserable, in my bonds. I heard great snapping sounds. There was a sudden swirling of air. I felt the pitting of dust against the hood and my feet. I heard the striking of small pebbles against the outside of the wicker. Then, to my astonishment, the object in which I had been placed began to slide rapidly along the ground and then, in a moment, it taking my breath away for an instant, it swung free, and was rising. I was off the ground! We were climbing. After a few minutes we were moving in a level manner. I could feel, even with the blanket, the wind whistling through the wicker walls. I hoped the object in which I was confined was strong. I sat very still. I did not want to risk weakening its structure in any way. I had no idea as to how high we were. It was cold. After a few hours, from the warmth in the hood, on my right, I conjectured we might be flying west, and perhaps to the north. My wrists were sore. Earlier, in my fear, I had fought too much with the manacles. My ankles, too, felt cut and raw. Too much in my earlier terror I had fought against the close loops, the coarse, narrow, bristly bands that confined them. My struggles had been futile, of course. Gorean slave girls are tied by men who know what they are doing in such ways that they cannot even think of escaping or freeing themselves. My struggles, I now realized, had been foolish, but at the time I had not seemed able to help myself. They had been the reflexive, or almost reflexive, struggles of a bound girl finding herself absolutely helpless in a terrifying reality. I hoped I had not marked or cut myself in such a way that scar tissue might form, for I might be beaten for that. Too, I did not want such marks, or scars, to detract from my appearance. I supposed I had a slave girl's vanity. Things had then seemed calm. It seemed the ropes suspending this object would hold, that the surface on which I was confined was not likely to suddenly give way. I was then mainly grateful, in the cold, that we had been given blankets. Then, as my composure grew, I became eager and curious to know more about my surroundings.

I did not know in what sort of device I was located. I did not know how high I was. I wondered what the countryside below might look like. Were there fields down there? Rivers? Forests? Would I be able to see the shadow of our passage, fleet and rippling, on the terrain below? What was the nature of the beast, or bird, that drew this carriage so swiftly through the sky? I wished I could see. That, however, was not now possible. That liberty had been denied to me by my master.

"It was nothing," he said.

I lowered my head humbly before him, my master. It had not been nothing, of course. At the height, and in the wind, and the cold, we might have half frozen, had it not been for the comfort of those blankets. I had not been unhooded, and ungagged, incidentally, until I had been inside the tavern, in a slave receiving room. My manacles had not been removed until I had been taken downstairs to the basement, and was standing before the gate of a kennel. I had then been put to my hands and knees, and thrust into the kennel, which had then been locked behind me. I had, when the man had left, turned about in the kennel and looked out, through the bars. I could kneel in the kennel, but I could not stand upright in it. I held the bars, and looked out. It was a dim basement. To my left and right, though I could not see them well, there were additional kennels. Several girls might be kept in such places. As nearly as I could tell they were empty at that time. I supposed there might be other holding areas, too. There was straw in the kennel, and a part of a blanket, a pan of water, and a pail for wastes. The next morning I was fed, pellets and gruel, in a pan thrust under the kennel gate and then, later, when I had relieved myself, brought forth for the first of my lessons in dance.

"Master," I whispered.

"Yes?" he said.

"May I speak?" I asked.

"Yes," he said.

"I understand that you are satisfied with the price for which you purchased me," I whispered.

"Yes," he said.

"That it seemed a fine buy to you," I said. It seemed strange to me, then, that I, the former Doreen Williamson, the timid, shy reference librarian, from Earth, should now be inquiring into matters such as my price. As a free woman I had been priceless, and thus, in a sense, without value, or worthless. As a slave, on the other hand, I did have a value, a specific value, depending on what men were willing to pay for me.

"It was," he said.

"What did you pay for me?" I asked.

"Surely you recall," he said.

"It was two and fifty," I said, "but I do not know, really, what that means."

"Two silver tarsks," he said, "and fifty copper tarsks, not tarsk bits, but tarsks, whole tarsks."

I looked up at him.

"Ah," he said, "you vain little she-tarsk, you want to know if that is much money, don't you? You want to know how much you brought, really, on the block, as a stripped slave. You want to form an estimate as to your value. You want to know what you are worth. You are curious to know what you might bring in an open market."

"Yes, Master," I whispered.

"Curiosity is not becoming in a kajira," he said.

"Forgive me, Master," I said. I quickly put down my head.

"First," he said, "you must understand that women are cheap. It has to do with the wars. Because of the many dislocations, and the famine in parts of the country, many women have had to sell themselves into slavery. Too, thousands of females from Torcadino alone, over the recent months, in virtue of one coup or another, have been put into the market. Too, mercenaries and raiders abound. Slavers grow more bold, even in larger cities. Crowding, and the influx of refugees, too, in such cities as Ar, refugees who are often beautiful and defenseless, and easily taken, have contributed to the depression of the market."

"I see, Master," I said.

"But you would still be curious as to your comparative value," he speculated.

"Yes, Master," I said looking up.

"Even under normal conditions," he said, "a silver tarsk would be a very high price to pay for a semitrained girl."

"Ah," I said softly, mostly to myself. I was very pleased. I, semitrained, and a barbarian, had gone for more than twice that price!

I did have value!

"Let me put it in another way," he said, "in one that may be even more meaningful to you."

"Yes, Master?" I said.

"That was the highest price paid for a female that night," he said.

"More than was paid for Gloria or Clarissa?" I asked.

"Who are they?" he asked.

"The two girls who were sold before me, just before me," I said.

"Earth sluts, like yourself," he said.

"Yes, Master," I said.

"Each went for a silver tarsk ten," he said. "Both were superb. I was tempted to bid on them myself."

I was stunned that I had sold for more than Gloria and Clarissa. I had regarded them both as far superior to myself.

"You are a virgin, of course," he said.

"Oh," I said.

"That is of value to me," he said, "for I am a tavern owner. After you have performed the virgin dance, I will raffle off your virginity."

"Yes, Master," I said. I did not really understand what he was saying. I did realize, of course, and had realized this shortly after the beginning of my training, that my value might depend not simply on what I was, in myself, but even on the sort of woman I was, say, that I was a barbarian, and the relative abundance or scarcity of that commodity in the markets. Similar considerations apparently pertained to such matters as hair colors and body types. If these things were so, then I supposed that it was natural that my virginity, or lack of it, might also, at least in some cases, affect my price. My master, I noted, did not seem to be personally interested in my virginity, only in what it might mean to him in terms of its possible commercial value.

"But even if it were not for that," he said, "it is probable that you would have brought more than your lovely terrestrial compatriots."

I looked at him.

"Most Gorean men," he said, "would regard you, exhibited on the block, knowing only that much about you, as superior slave meat."

I shuddered.

"I think," he said, "in that market, that night, even if you had not been a virgin, you would have brought more than your friends. I would have thought you might have brought something in the neighborhood of a tarsk eighty or a tarsk seventy."

"But there was a bid of two for me," I said, "before your bid."

"That seems a high bid," he said. "Perhaps it was the bid of someone new to the markets, perhaps one who had not seen many women vended, who did not realize how beautiful any woman is when she is put through merciless slave paces."

I blushed, naked before him, in his collar.

"You bid two and fifty," I whispered.

"That is because I saw in you what others, at the time, did not," he said. "I saw in you the dancer, one I can use in the tavern. I saw in you, too, the helpless pleasure slave, who could be made the prisoner of her own passions, becoming an obedient, eager, grateful, spasmodic animal in her master's arms."

I blushed crimson.

"I think," he said, "that in time you might become a five-tarsk girl, perhaps even a ten-tarsk girl."

I looked up at him, frightened.

"You want to cover your breasts with your hands, don't you?" he asked. "You want to clench your knees tightly together."

"Yes, Master!" I begged.

"Remain kneeling exactly as you are, pleasure slave," he said.

"Yes, Master," I said.

"And so," he said, "although the price I paid for you might have seemed high it was, from my point of view, in virtue of what you are, and will become, a splendid bargain."

"Yes, Master," I whispered.

"Are you pleased," he asked, "aside from questions of the price I paid for you, or my reasons for it, to learn that you are valuable, that you might well bring a price in the neighborhood of two silver tarsks in an open market?"

I did not know, precisely, how to respond to this question. It seemed that I was, as I had hitherto suspected, of genuine interest to Gorean men, or at least to many of them. Should I find pleasure in this, or a cause for alarm? Gorean men are generally such as to know how to handle women. They know what to do with them. Yet I did not think I would really want to be in the arms of other sorts of men.

"You have been asked a question," my master reminded me.

"Forgive me, Master," I whispered. I looked up at him, shyly. "Yes," I whispered, "I am pleased. I am extremely pleased."

"Vain she-tarsk," he said.

"Yes, Master," I smiled. I was delighted to learn that I had brought a good price, even if he thought it such a bargain. I was delighted, too, to learn that I might have, even had he not been there, brought as much as two silver tarsks. One fellow had bid that much! Too, perhaps most importantly, most significantly, no other girl had sold for so much that night as I! I had brought the highest price in the whole market that night! This astonished and delighted me. To be sure, it was doubtless an isolated market, and we were probably all only semitrained girls, or less, girls being sold that night as little more than "slave meat," as my master had put it, so frightening me. But still, even as "slave meat," it was I who had brought the highest price! I wished Teibar could have known that, that his catch from the library on Earth had brought the highest price in the market, and on her first sale, too! But I supposed that he, the monster, the beast, would have merely congratulated himself on his taste in selecting captures, turning it all to his own credit! The buyers would have known very little about me, of course. They had seen me the way most other Gorean men would see me, at first, or until they learned more about me, I supposed, as no more than another pretty girl in bondage, as, in effect, in a sense, no more than mere "slave meat." I was proud, however, to have been regarded as an attractive slave, or, if you like, as promising slave meat. How strange it then seemed to me that I, the former Doreen Williamson, of Earth, a shy librarian, should now be elated that she had some simple, independent value as a female, if only as slave meat! Then I realized how superficial was my view of this matter, even in so simple a business as vending a girl from a block. Gloria was larger than I and, in this sense, would surely have been expected to have brought more if we were really being considered as "mere slave meat." But she had not brought more. They had considered us, and, for one reason or another, properly or improperly, wisely or not, at that particular time, at least, had bid more for me. The men call us "slave meat," and such, and perhaps this amuses them, and helps to keep us in our place, at their feet, but only a woman who is a fool believes them. They want, and own, the whole slave. Even Gorean law makes it clear that it is the entire slave who is owned, not merely a part of her. To be sure, Gorean men do not play the games of some fools of Earth, pretending that the bodies of women are not of interest to them, but only their minds, or such, or whatever the currently prescribed cultural values recommend. They relish our bodies and see that they derive from them, exploiting us, if you will, every last ounce of pleasure that they can yield to them, but even in these merciless predations, showing us so little concern, it is the whole woman, the whole of their property, which they tease, and torment, and relish, and make yield to them.

"But there is good discipline kept in this house," he said, lifting the whip.

"Yes, Master!" I said, quickly. Here, in this house, I then

understood, though I might have some value in a commercial sense, I was only a slave.

"Crawl back down the steps, facing me," he said, "and then kneel at the foot of the dais."

I obeyed. I now felt very small before him, kneeling there, a slave, he, my master, so high above me in that great chair.

From a small sack at his side, walletlike, attached at his belt, he drew forth a tiny object, made of cloth. He crumpled it easily in the palm of his hand. It was clearly very compressible. I did not know what it was.

He threw it to me. It struck my body and fell before me, to the rug, at the foot of the dais. I looked down at it. I looked up at him.

"Put it on," he said.

Quickly I reached down and picked up the object, its folds tucked in among themselves. I opened it, and shook it out. It was a brief slave tunic, slit deeply at the hips, with narrow shoulder straps, little more than strings. I looked up at him, gratefully. It was the first garment of my own I had been given on this world. To be sure, I had been, upon occasion, given blankets or sheets to hold about myself, usually for warmth, and I had been, in my training, put in various costumes, mostly, I suppose, for my masters to see what I looked like in them, such as the common and Turian camisk, and the scandalous garb prescribed for Tuchuk slave girls. Too, I had been taught the wearing of, and arrangement of, simple, typical slave garments, such as tunics of various sorts, and ta-teeras, or slave rags. I had even been taught the tying of slave girdles, in such a way as to emphasize, and sometimes more than subtly, my figure. And, indeed, part of my training had not been only how to wear, and move in such garments, but also how to remove them provocatively, and gracefully. Even the blankets and sheets we had been given, presumably mostly for warmth, we had to remove in certain fashions that clearly, from a man's point of view, would have counted as an extremely sensuous disrobing. Then, recollecting that I had been ordered to put it on, I pulled it over my head and put my arms through the straps. In a moment I had drawn it down about me.

"Stand," he said.

Happily I stood, pulling the garment down more, hastily, modestly, about my thighs. Then I realized, blushing, that doing this must have as its consequence the greater accentuation of my figure.

"Turn," he said. "Walk about. Then return and stand before me."

Happily I moved about in the garment.

"Do you not know how to walk?" he asked.

"Forgive me, Master," I said.

I then walked as a slave, proudly, my shoulders back, gracefully and beautifully, as a woman owned by men. As an Earth female I would never have dared to walk in such a way. Such movements are probably indexed, like physical distances between individuals, to the culture. In Gorean culture, generally, it seemed to me that people stood closer to one another than I was accustomed to on Earth. In this way it was natural for men here, for example, to stand much closer to the scantily clad slave than the average man of, say, northern Europe, on Earth, would be likely to, to a woman of his area. Indeed, he usually stands so close to her that it would be easy for him to put his hands on her, and draw her to him, taking her in his arms. The dynamic consequences of these proximities are minimized considerably, of course, by the fact that the slave often kneels in the presence of the free male. It is customary in the kneeling position to remain back a few feet from the male. The kneeling position, itself, expresses the servitude of the slave, and her submission. The distance serves three major purposes. It symbolizes in the distance, as well as in the differential in height, the social inferiority of the slave to the master. It puts the slave in a position where all of her, for the master's delight, can be seen. A kneeling woman is incredibly beautiful. It also puts enough space between the slave and the free male so that the releasing of his rapacity is then likely to require a decision, and is less likely to be simply, reflexively, triggered. This is regarded as being particularly important when the slave is in the presence of a male who is not her master. The kneeling position, thus, interestingly, can occasionally provide a measure of security, if a somewhat tenuous one, for the slave, tending to reduce to some extent the frequency with which, in a culture with such interpersonal proximities, she might otherwise be subjected to unauthorized rape. This same tiny measure of protection, of course, puts her in much greater danger from her real master, for he, observing her, seeing her kneeling beautifully before him, can also delay in his considerations as to her suitable exploitations. How shall he use her? What shall he have her do, and so on. To be sure, sometimes he simply takes her and when he wants her, and almost by reflexive whim. She is his. The main reason why a slave kneels, of course, aside from such subtle and complex considerations, is simply that she is a slave, and that that position, accordingly, is appropriate for her.

I loved the tiny garment! It was the first that I had had since I had come to Gor. In it much of me was still bared, my legs, my hips to the waist, my shoulders, and so on, and it left little doubt about the lineaments of my form, but I loved it. No longer was I absolutely and starkly naked, save for a metal collar. I adjusted the strap on my right shoulder. The small, soft, rounded shoulders of a woman, incidentally, like the rest of a female, Gorean men tend to find very provocative. They seem to relish, and respond to, perhaps to a much greater extent than many of the men of Earth, the entire woman. They are likely to find exciting even such small details of a woman as her delicate ear lobes. That perhaps explains, at least in part, the momentousness of ear piercing to Goreans, which those of Earth take so much for granted. To the Gorean, the piercing of the woman's ear, with its analog of penetration, and the fixing in it of earrings, chosen by the master, ornamenting her for his pleasure, is an act of power and claimancy scarcely less significant than her branding and collaring. Free women, incidentally, seldom, if ever, bare their shoulders. Doing so is almost like offering themselves for the collar. "If you would be stripped as a slave, then be a slave," it is said. Similarly free women on Gor seldom, if ever, wear earrings, either of the natural or of any other variety, such as the clip variety. Earrings are regarded as being fit, rather, for slaves, and usually the lowest of slaves. Nose rings, interestingly, are not regarded in the same light. They are worn even by some free women, I understand, in the far south, the women of the Wagon Peoples there, as well as, generally, by the female slaves of such peoples. In short, Gorean men seem to find the whole woman exciting. To be sure, the shoulders, for example, lead to the delicious curvatures of the breasts, those, too, the property of the master, and thence to the waist and belly, and thighs, and the slave's helpless, delicate intimacies. The ear lobes, too, lead to the throat, and thence, beneath the collar, to the shoulders, and so on. Similarly, the foot leads to the ankle, and that to the lusciously rounded calf, and that upward to the thighs, and those, again, in their lovely softness, to the girl's exposed, hot, open, helpless, delicate intimacies. It is not unusual for a Gorean male, in his zest for females, to cover her entire body, bit by bit, with kisses and caresses, moving toward her helplessness. It is not easy to prevent these attentions, either, as you may well imagine, when you have been simply chained down for his pleasure. Sometimes you scream for him to hasten, begging him with every bit of your female helplessness to do so, but he, of course, will do as he pleases, for you belong to him or he has your use, and he is a free male, the master.

I returned then to the foot of the dais, to stand there before Hendow, of the tavern of Hendow, on Dock Street, in Brundisium.

"You are very beautiful," he said.

"Thank you, Master," I said. I was elated that he had seen fit to give me a garment. Too, he had said that I was beautiful! I wondered if he liked me. I wondered if I could use that, and possibly manipulate him in some way. I decided I had better not try. He was not a man of Earth. He was a Gorean male.

"Yes," he said, "you are very beautiful."

I felt radiant. I did not think he would hurt me now. I did not know, though. The garment I wore, incidentally, was more modest, in its way, than the garment of red silk I had made for myself on Earth, that which Teibar had thrust in my mouth in the library, showing me that I was forbidden to speak. He had withdrawn it from my mouth only on the library table, when I had lain there before him on my back, before he had put the conical rubberized mask over my face, introducing the chemicals into it which had forced me to lose consciousness, a consciousness I had regained only on Gor, awakening to the blows of his whip.

"Do you like the garment?" he asked.

"Yes, Master!" I said. "Yes, Master!"

"Take it off," he said.

"Yes, Master," I said, tears in my eyes. I stood then before him again, absolutely and starkly naked, except for a metal collar. I clutched the tiny garment in my hand. He could give me such a garment. He could take it away. I must put it on at his command. I must remove it at his command. I was his.

Hendow, of the Tavern of Hendow, on Dock Street, in Brundisium, rose from the great chair. He stood on the dais, looming above me. In his hand he held the whip. I looked at the instrument of discipline, frightened.

He then descended from the dais, and stood near me. I looked straight ahead, clutching the tiny garment. He was huge, next to me. I felt very tiny. He put the coils of the whip under my chin, and pressed up a little. I held my chin up. The nearness of his presence, and his virile, brutish masculinity made me terribly uneasy.

"What is your name," he asked.

"Whatever Master pleases," I said, quickly.

I had not yet been named in this house. The words 'slut' or

'slave' served well enough to summon me. I trembled. I realized I might, in a moment, be named. Then that would be who I would be, as simply as that, like any animal.

"Come here," he said, "and lie down, on your back, on this step."

He had indicated the second step leading to the height of the dais. I complied.

"Place your left foot on the first step," he said, "and put your right foot here, on the third step."

I did so. This opened my legs.

"Now," he said, "put your arms back, over your head."

"Yes, Master," I said.

"That exposes your armpits," he said.

"Yes, Master," I said, puzzled.

He looked down at me. "What were you called in the house of your training?" he asked.

"Doreen," I said.

"Very well," he said, "you are Doreen."

"Thank you, Master," I said, named. This had been my name on Earth. I wore it now, of course, only as a slave name. It could have been anything.

"Doreen," he said.

"Yes, Master," I said, responding to my name.

"You are now to lie as you are," he said, "until you receive permission to change your position. You are to lie in this position, and very quietly. If you do not, it will be extremely dangerous for you. In particular, make no sudden moves."

"Yes, Master," I said, puzzled.

He then went to the side of the room, where there dangled three or four cords. I lifted my head a little to watch him. He drew on one of these cords. I saw a panel lift in the wall. It exposed a low opening, only about a yard in height. It was dark within this portal, but I saw, it stretching backwards, what appeared to be a low, dark tunnel. He then came back, and crouched down, near me, above me, on the third step.

He put his whip aside, near him. He put his hand gently on my collar.

"Master?" I asked.

"Be quiet," he said.

I lay there, quietly. Then, suddenly, I felt hair on the back of my neck rising.

"Master!" I said.

"Lie quietly," he said.

I could now hear, from some distance down the tunnel, the

sound of something approaching. It was coming rapidly. I heard snuffling noises. I heard panting. I could hear claws on the floor of the tunnel.

"Lie quietly," cautioned my master, literally holding me in place, his hand gripping my collar.

Then something burst into the room.

Half choking, my head was forced back down, by the collar.

"If you want, keep your eyes closed," he said.

Whatever it was had apparently stopped just within the room.

"It will take a moment for its eyes to adjust to the light," he said. "But it is done very quickly."

The room was not brightly lit.

"I think you will like Borko," he said.

"What is it?" I whispered. My head was held down, back on the second step.

"Keep your legs apart," he said. "It is a gray sleen. I raised it from a whelp. Ah, greetings, Borko! How are you, old fellow!"

I would have screamed and reared up, but I was thrust back, helpless, half strangled, scarcely able to utter a sound, to the step. So our masters can control us by our collars. To my terror, then, pushing over my body, to thrust its great jaws and head, so large I could scarcely have put my arms about them, into the hands and arms of my master, was an incredible beast. It had an extremely agile, active, sinuous body, as thick as a drum, and perhaps fourteen or fifteen feet long. It might have weighed a thousand pounds. Its broad head was triangular, almost viperlike, but it was furred. This thing was a mammal, or mammalian. Its eyes now had pupils like slits, like those of a cat in sunlight. So quickly then might its adaptive mechanisms have functioned. About its muzzle were gray hairs, grayer than the silvered gray of its fur. It had six legs.

"Good lad!" said my master, roughly fondling that great, fierce head.

"We have been through much together, Borko and I," said my master. "He has even, twice, saved my life. Once when I was struck, unexpectedly, by one foolishly thought to be a friend, the origin of this scar," he said, indicating good-humoredly the hideous, jagged tissue at the left side of his face, "I told Borko to hunt. The fellow did not escape. Borko brought part of him back to me, in his jaws."

I watched in terror as my master, over my body, scratched and pulled, and shoved, at that great head. Clearly he was inordinately fond of that terrible beast, and perhaps it of him. I saw his eyes. He lavished affection upon it. He cared more for it than his girls, I was certain. Perhaps it was the only thing he trusted, other than himself, the only thing he knew that he could rely upon, other than himself, the only thing, of all creatures he knew, who had proved its love and loyalty to him. If this were so, then perhaps it was not incredible that he might bestow upon it a fondness, or love, which he, betrayed perhaps by men, might withhold from others, from men, and slaves.

"Do you know what you and Borko have in common?" he asked me.

"We are both your animals, Master," I said.

"Yes!" he said. "And do you know who is most valuable?"

"No, Master," I said.

"Borko," he said, "is a seasoned hunting sleen. Even to strangers he would bring a hundred times what you would bring in the market."

I was silent. I was frightened with those huge jaws, the two rings of fangs, the long, dark tongue, over me.

"But I would not sell him for anything," he said. "He is worth more to me than ten thousand such as you."

"Yes, Master," I whispered.

"Borko!" he said, sternly. "Borko."

The beast pulled back its head, observing him.

"Learn slave," he said. "Learn slave."

I then began to whimper. "Hold still," said my master.

The beast then began to push its nose and muzzle about me, thrusting it here and there, about me. I now understood why I had been spread as I had, on the steps.

"The sleen," he said, "and especially the gray sleen, is Gor's finest tracker. It is a relentless, tenacious tracker. It can follow a scent that is weeks old, for a thousand pasangs."

I whimpered, the beast's snout thrust between my thighs, sniffing.

"Please, Master," I whimpered.

I felt it nuzzling then at my waist and breasts. It was learning me.

"Do you know what the sleen hunts?" he asked.

"No, Master," I said.

"In the wild it commonly hunts tabuk and wild tarsk," he said, "but it is an intelligent beast, and it can be trained to hunt anything."

"Yes, Master," I whimpered.

He held back my right arm, further, exposing more the armpit.

"Do you know what Borko is trained to hunt?" he asked.

"No, Master," I said.

I felt the snout of the beast then poking about my throat, and under my chin, to the side, and then at the side of my neck. My master then held my left arm back further, exposing the armpit to the beast.

"It is trained to hunt men, and slaves," he said.

"No!" I wept.

I squirmed, but my master held me steady, by the collar and my left wrist, held back. The beast thrust its snout against me, there, in the armpit, and then sniffed along the interior of my left arm, and then along the left side of my body.

I whimpered in terror.

"Try not to be afraid," he said. "That might excite Borko."

"Yes, Master," I whimpered.

Then the beast drew back its head.

"Doreen," said my master to the beast, slowly, clearly. "Doreen. Doreen."

The beast again sniffed me.

"Doreen," said my master, grinning, to the beast. "Doreen."

I shuddered.

The beast then drew back its head again.

"Back, Borko," said my master, and the beast inched back, its eyes on me.

I was shuddering. I dared not move.

"Borko is trained to respond to a variety of signals," he said.

"Yes, Master," I whispered.

"He now knows you," he said.

"Yes, Master," I said.

"Whose are you?" he asked.

"I am yours, Master!" I said, quickly.

"Do not try to escape," he said.

"No, Master!" I said. "I will not try to escape!"

"Borko, go back to your kennel," he said. "Go, now!"

The beast then backed off a few feet, and turned. In a moment, it had withdrawn through the low portal. My master went then to the cord which controlled the panel, and closed it. I was shuddering on the step. I did not move. I was almost too afraid to do so. Too, I had not been given permission to break position.

"Kneel at the foot of the dais," he said. Swiftly I did so. I found I was still clutching the tiny garment I had been given. It had been clutched in the palm of my right hand, all the time. It was now wet with sweat. The prints of my nails were deep in it.

He retrieved the whip and ascended to the height of the dais, where he took his place in the great chair.

He looked down at me, the whip across his knees.

"Perhaps now, Earth woman," he said, "you understand more clearly what your situation is on this world."

I shuddered.

"Do you understand, girl?" he asked.

"Yes, Master," I said.

"Stand," he said.

I stood.

"You may put on your garment," he said.

Quickly I donned the tiny garment, and drew it down, as I could, about me.

I stood there.

"Yes," he said, "you are beautiful."

"Thank you, Master," I said. I flushed with pleasure. I was valuable. Doubtless I would be a high slave.

He stood. "Mirus!" he called. Mirus was one of his men. I knew him from the house. He had brought me to this chamber. In a moment, Mirus appeared through the door, that at the end of the carpet, that leading into this chamber. He approached, and took up a position a bit behind me and to my left.

"She is lovely, isn't she?" my master asked Mirus.

"Yes," he said.

"Do you like your garment?" my master asked me.

"Yes, Master," I said. I recalled the last time he had asked this I had been shortly thereafter ordered to remove it. He could do that again, and I would again be forced to disrobe, and instantly. Too, this time it would also be before Mirus. It is one thing to come naked before a man, and another to strip yourself, or be stripped, before him. Too, it is something else again, to do this, or have it done to you, before others. Mirus was not my master, but only my master's man. To be sure, I was a slave, and would have to obey. Coming nude before men, and stripping herself, or being stripped, before them are things such as a slave girl must expect. After all, what else could she expect? She is, after all, a slave. Indeed, sometimes girls are stripped in public, even in the squares, because masters are so pleased to show them off. Sometimes this occurs in heated discussions of the relative merits of different masters' girls, and the girls are ordered to disrobe on the spot, sometimes then being put through slave paces, there, on the very tiles of the squares and plazas, the matter being left to the acclamations or votes of the spectators, and woe to the girl who comes out second best in such a contest! Too, it is not uncommon, as a discipline, to send a girl out naked on errands. In such a case she is often locked in an iron belt. Too, it is not unusual, in taverns, particularly lower taverns, as I would learn, for girls to be publicly naked. I was diffident, though, at this time, to remove my clothing before Mirus. I would have been embarrassed, or humiliated, to do so. I was not yet a brazen slave. I had not yet even been on the floor of the tavern. My attitude, of course, as I understood, was undoubtedly a bit irrational. Mirus, after all, had seen me naked. Indeed, he had never, really, seen me clothed. He was the one, incidentally, who had unhooded and ungagged me in this house. He had been pleased with my face. He had then unroped the blanket which had been tied about me, and opened it, folding it back, almost as though I might have been a present. "Superb," he had said, this pleasing me. "Are you white silk?" he had asked. "Yes, Master," I had said, shrinking back from him in the manacles. He had then taken me down to the basement, removed the manacles, put me on my hands and knees, and thrust me into my kennel, locking it behind me. Why, then, was I embarrassed, or humiliated, at the thought that I might now be ordered to disrobe in his presence? I was not sure. I supposed it was because I was not yet fully adjusted to my slavery. I was not yet a brazen slave. I had not yet, at that time, even been put out on the floor of the tavern. Perhaps I still thought, at that time, that the fullness of my beauty was, particularly, for my master, and not for others. I did not really stop to think, at that time, however, that Hendow was a tavern owner, and that, thus, the fullness of my beauty was not only for him, but, as he saw fit, or as it might please him, also for his customers.

"She looks lovely in the garment, doesn't she?" asked Hendow. I gathered he was proud of me.

"Yes," said Mirus.

I again felt the suffusion of pleasure in my body. I looked down, shyly, smiling. My master, I was sure, liked me. I did not think, now, he would order me to remove the garment before Mirus. I recalled that he had paid the highest price for me of any girl at the market. I was valuable. I would be a high slave!

"Do you know, Doreen," asked my master, "what sort of tunic it is?"

"No, Master," I said.

"It is a kitchen tunic," he said.

I looked at him, startled.

"Take her to the kitchen," he said to Mirus. "Teach her to clean pots and pans."

"Yes, Hendow," said Mirus. Then he turned about. "Come, slave," he said.

Quickly I fell to my knees before Hendow, he in the great

chair on the dais, and put my head to the carpet, the palms of my hands, too, on the carpet, beside my head, performing slave obeisance. I then leaped up, turned, and hurried after Mirus, who, now, at the end of the carpet, was near the exit.

"Mirus," called Hendow.

Mirus looked back to the dais.

"See that her dance lessons continue," he said.

"It will be so, Hendow," said Mirus.

"And double them," said Hendow.

"Yes, Hendow," said Mirus. He then turned about and left. I fell again to my knees at the far end of the carpet, and again performed slave obeisance. I then leaped up, again, and hurried after Mirus.

He would take me to the kitchen, where I would be put to work.

11 / The Raffle; The Alcove; The Kennel

I waited, frightened, within the threshold, clutching the sheet about me. I leaned back against the wall, my eyes closed for a moment. Beyond the threshold I could hear the conversation of men, sitting, cross-legged, at the low tables.

The library seemed faraway now.

There was a beaded curtain hung in the threshold.

I listened to the sounds of the men.

Sometimes, I had heard, before nights such as this, a girl is kept in close chains, sitting or lying, scarcely able to move. Too, sometimes, for days before a night like this she wears the sirik. I had very seldom been in sirik, though I had worn one in my training once or twice, so that I might be instructed in the strict limitations it would impose on me, and how I might, nonetheless, move in it, if it were set to suitable widths, in a way pleasing to masters. The full sirik consists of a collar and three chains. One of these chains, a long, vertical chain, attached to the collar, dangles downward. To it are fastened two horizontal chains, one, from its attachment point near the lower belly, terminating in slave bracelets, wrist-rings, or manacles, and the other, from its attachment point at the end of the dangling chain, usually lying on the floor, or ground, terminating in shackles or ankle-rings. Parts of this arrangement may function separately, of course, for example, the long chain as a leash, the horizontal attachments as, say, slave bracelets or ankle shackles. Too, in many siriks, the chain widths are adjustable. In that way the latitudes of movement accorded to the slave may be enlarged or reduced, as the master pleases. They are, as many other things in the slave's life, under his exact governance. In the harshest adjustments of the sirik the girl, in effect, is in close chains; in the freer adjustments, she may move with considerable grace and beauty; indeed, in some siriks, it is possible for her to dance. In the sirik adjustments often prescribed for a girl before a night like this she can scarcely walk, the vertical chain's lower attachment point being drawn up between her ankles, which are then separated by as little as three or four inches, and her wrists, too, before her body, are even more closely confined. My master, however, had not seen fit to exercise such precautions in my case. He knew, and I knew, they were unnecessary. I leaned back more against the wall, my eyes closed. I clutched the sheet more closely about me. There was nowhere to run, nowhere to go. I was branded and collared. I would be naked or scantily clad. There was no one to rescue me, or free me. I would be bond, and a property, to any who might come upon me, like a dog or horse. The entire legal resources of this world would be marshaled toward returning me to my master. Too, I thought, shuddering, as if such things were not enough, my body, and its odors, with my name, such that it might be included with appropriate triggering signals, had been imprinted on the dark, eager brain of a massive hunting sleen. No, I would not run away. When my master came for me, to take me by the arm and lead me to the floor, I would be here, in the only way I could be here, waiting, and docile.

I listened again to the murmur of the men outside, the small sounds of their goblets and plates.

I considered again the sleen. "I think you will like Borko," had said my master, before I had seen the beast, when I had only heard him in the tunnel, and then entering the room. I recalled the huge head, the two rows of fangs, the dark tongue, the widely set eyes, the thrusting, prowling snout, the claws. It had been trained, I had learned, to hunt men, and slaves. Obediently it had withdrawn to its kennel at the word of my master. But just as swiftly, I was sure, it could be summoned forth again, and set about its master's bidding, implacably, unquestioningly, innocently, mercilessly, eagerly. I shuddered. That beast, I thought, if nothing else, would serve to keep good order among the women of Hendow, a taverner on Dock Street, in Brundisium. I smiled to myself. Sometimes women, either free or slave, are called "she-sleen." I had not known, until a few days ago, what a sleen was. I now knew. I might be a "she-urt," or a "she-tarsk," I thought, but I certainly was not a "she-sleen," even figuratively. To be sure, at that time, I did not know about the miniature, silken sleen that are sometimes kept as sinuous pets. Perhaps it is that sort of she-sleen, which, if not properly controlled, tends to be sly, nasty and dangerous, that men have in mind when they sometimes apply that expression to a woman. I do not know. To be sure, as the men say, it seems that even the woman who is a "she-sleen" needs only a strong master, one who brings her swiftly to her knees and teaches her that she is a female. The husk of the she-sleen, as it is said, can be torn away, never to grow again, leaving behind only the soft flesh of another slave.

I opened my eyes. I heard bells outside the threshold, from the floor.

I inched to my right, and turned, looking out through the beaded curtain. I could see the men there, at the tables. It was a broad, low-ceilinged room, with pillars. It was dimly lit, mostly with tharlarion-oil lamps, hung on chains from the ceiling. There were some fifty tables in the room, tables at which, if not placed adjacently to one another, generally four men might sit. Some men, too, were sitting about the walls, leaning against them. There was a crowd in the tavern tonight. I had heard the eighteenth bar struck some time ago. It would soon be the height of the evening, the time for the special entertainment, an entertainment in which I had a prominent role. There had even been some handbills distributed by boys about the city, and others, I had heard, had been tacked up on public boards. There had been signs painted too, I gathered, here and there among similar signs, usually on poorer streets, or in alleys, where magistrates, less inclined to object, were also less prone to patrol. To be sure, most of my master's clientele came from such areas.

I looked out. The bells I had heard were apparently on Tupita.

I wondered how many of the men out there had come for the special entertainment this evening. Some, I was sure.

I did not care much for Tupita, and she did not care much for me. I saw her kneeling beside a man, pouring him paga. She was naked, like the other girls on the floor. Hendow liked his women, or at least his paga slaves, on the floor, that way. Too, in the lower paga taverns it is not uncommon. Tupita knelt back from him. I think she was afraid of him. I hoped he would take her to an alcove and put her through her paces! I heard the sound of a blow, probably with the back of a hand, and a cry of pain and saw, to one side, to the right, Ilene, struck back to her left thigh, looking up, frightened, at one of the men, now on his feet. He took her by the arm, pulling her to her feet, conducting her then, she stumbling, hurried, to one of the alcoves. Perhaps she would be further punished there. Though "Ilene" is an Earth-girl name, Ilene was Gorean. Such names are sometimes given to Gorean girls, sometimes to inform them, to their horror, that they are now to be as low and succulent, and helpless, and luscious, as Earth females in Gorean bondage. I was, incidentally, the only Earth girl in the house. I drew back my head and leaned back again, breathing deeply, against the wall, to the left of the threshold, as one would enter it. I was afraid of such men!

I again closed my eyes.

I could hardly stand. Tonight I was to dance before men, such men! I felt ill. I had danced hitherto only before Teibar, and his men, at the library, and once or twice before the men in the house of my training, and, of course, here, in my lessons, before some men, in particular, the musicians, and some men from the house, who, from time to time, would pause to watch me. But I had never danced in the open, so to speak, before a crowd, before strangers, so to speak. I had never even danced before Hendow, my own master. Mirus had seen me several times, though, and he, I am sure, had conveyed reports to my master. Mirus, when I had knelt before him at the end of my lessons, seemed generally, on the whole, and particularly lately, quite pleased with my progress. I received such intelligences with extreme relief, kneeling before him, for I did not wish to be whipped. Sometimes, in my lessons, as I danced, I could see Mirus, and other men of the house, watching me, their eyes alight. Sometimes they licked their lips, almost as though I might be food. Yesterday, at the conclusion of my last lesson, when in a swirl of music, I had lowered myself to the floor, in a dancer's posture of abject submission before men, I had heard several of them cry out with approval, and strike their left shoulders repeatedly, fiercely, with the palms of their hands. They had then crowded about me. On my knees, rising, I had been conscious of their legs, and whips, about me. What whips I could I seized to me and kissed, hastily, in fear. I had been afraid they would beat me. But "Marvelous!" and "Superb!" I heard. Mirus was then, almost by force, pushing them away from me, and ordering them to return to their duties. Grumbling they disbanded, leaving the room. When we were alone, after even the musicians had left, and I was still at his feet, I looked up at him. It was he, first among these men, second only to Hendow, my master, whom I must most strive to please. "Master?" I asked. "You have talent," he said, drily. "Thank you, Master," I said. I put down my head and kissed his feet, delicately, in deference and gratitude. He then turned away from me, rather suddenly I thought.

"Master!" I called to him.

He stopped, and looked back.

"Yes?" he said.

"May I speak?" I asked.

"Yes," he said.

"When am I to be put forth upon the floor?" I asked.

"You have not been told?" he asked.

"No, Master," I said.

"Tomorrow night," he said. He then left.

I remained kneeling there for a long time, in the practice room. Tomorrow night I would go forth upon the floor. I trembled. Surely I was not yet ready! Yet that judgment, one as to my readiness, was not mine to make. It lay rather in the province of masters. They had judged me "ready." To be sure, I would be ready only as a "new girl" is ready. I would be ready, in effect, simply to begin, to begin to become a female slave. Could I truly be ready to begin, I wondered. I recalled the faces of the men from a few minutes ago. Yes, I thought, perhaps the masters are right. Perhaps I am ready for that beginning. I trembled, looking down at the floor. How they had looked at me, so eagerly, so excitedly, relishing me, reveling in what they saw, and knowing that I, the dancer, was collared, that I could be owned. Mirus, I recalled, had almost had to drive them away from me, almost as one might force lions from meat. Mirus, too, I recalled, had himself turned away from me, at the end, when we were alone, with a sudden abruptness. I now thought that I understood that. He, too, I suspected, like the others, had found me not without interest. Indeed, the first question he had addressed to me in this house, when he had unroped the blanket from about me, and I was before him, naked, my wrists manacled behind my back, was whether or not I was "white silk." Had I not been I think he might then, even as I was, manacled and on the blanket, have put me to his purposes. Now, this evening, he had abruptly turned from me, with surprising abruptness I had thought. I smiled, looking down at the boards of the floor. I do not think he trusted himself to be alone with me. I sensed then that I had great power over men, and that there was much I could do to them, simply by being a female, and myself, and beautiful. And I had this power even in my collar, and perhaps especially in my collar, for this seemed to make me a thousand times more beautiful to them. But then I realized that, ultimately, I had no power, for I was a slave. I could be brought to my knees at a word, and to my back at a gesture. I was afraid to go on the floor. I was afraid to begin the life of the slave. I hoped I would be found pleasing. I hoped I would not be too much beaten.

I opened my eyes, standing there, leaning back against the wall, within the threshold leading out to the floor.

Someone was approaching.

I knelt.

"Are you all right?" asked Mirus.

"Yes, Master," I said. "Thank you, Master."

"It looks like a good house tonight," he said, looking out through the curtain.

I was silent.

"It is nearly the Nineteenth Ahn," he said.

"Yes, Master," I said.

"We will not begin precisely at the Nineteenth Ahn," he said. "We will let them grow a bit restless."

"Yes, Master," I whispered, holding the sheet about me looking up at him, I a slave in the presence of a free man. He then left. I did not rise to my feet. I did not even know if I could stand.

Outside there were men, Gorean men. I was to dance this night before them. I did not even know if I could get to my feet.

I heard the approach of slave bells, coming from the outer room. I wanted to rise but the strings of the beaded curtain were too quickly flung aside.

"Ah," said Sita, "that is where you belong, Earth slut, on your knees."

"Yes, Mistress," I said to her. I must address all the female slaves in the house of Hendow as "Mistress." That order would be in effect until it was explicitly rescinded, probably, depending on my behavior and progress, in a few weeks. This is sometimes done with new girls. It helps to keep discipline among us. I would then, when the order was rescinded, be able to call the girls, with the exception of the "first girl," by their own names. I would be one of them. Tupita was "first girl." We must all call her "Mistress." I was pleased it had not been Tupita who had come through the curtain and discovered me on my knees, though, to be sure, had she done so, I would have had to kneel before her. Sita did not like me either. She was an ally of Tupita, and often informed on the other girls.

"You will learn tonight what it is to be a slave, Earth slut," hissed Sita.

"Yes, Mistress," I said. Sita then, with a sound of bells, went down a corridor, toward the kitchen.

I looked after her, angrily, from my knees. She, too, was only a slave! I hoped that tonight some man would not be satisfied with her and would whip her well. Last night, a customer had put Tupita at a whipping ring and expressed his displeasure with her attitudes. She had then begged to please him in an alcove. He had left her only this morning. Mirus had unchained her later, sometime around noon.

I inched over and, on my knees, looked out through the curtain. There were more men in the tavern now. It must be near the Nineteenth Ahn! Again I hid back, frightened, and sick, behind the wall, away from the curtain. Out there, among the tables, I had seen the dancing floor. It was there I would be placed. The space for the musicians was to the left, as I had looked out. The form of dance to which I had been drawn on Earth, for whatever reason or reasons, whether because of some sort of feared innate, ungovernable sensuousness, or extreme deep-seated feminine dispositions or needs, or perhaps even, simply, a sense of what was appropriate for me, whether I wished it or not, considering the realities of my ultimate nature, I had preferred to think of as "ethnic dance." I had been secretly thrilled, of course, but had scarcely dared, even to myself, to think of it as "belly dance," or, as the French have it, "*danse du ventre*," a term popular with some, with some perhaps as a euphemism, and with others as a sensuous way of expressing the matter, one with the same objective meaning as "belly dancing" but which, for them, perhaps, has rich and special connotations. To be sure, both terms are in a sense reductive misnomers, for in this form of dance, as in other forms of dance, the dancer dances with her entire body and beauty. I had never cared too much for the term "exotic dance" as that term seems to me too broad, in that it covers not only "ethnic dance," if, indeed, it really covers that, but many other forms of dance as well, which seem to have little in common other than their capacity to be sexually stimulatory. But then, to a discerning eye, most, or all, dance, and certainly ballet, for example, is sexually stimulatory. Those who fear and hate sex have, I think, understood these things better than many others, for example, low-drive individuals and the sexually inert. On Gor, dance of the sort in which I was expected to perform, is called, simply, "slave dance." That is presumably because it is a form of dance which, for the most part, is thought to be fit only for slaves, and would be performed only by slaves. The thought crossed my mind that the lovely woman who had been my teacher on Earth had once remarked to me, "We are all slaves." I think that is true. Certainly, however, not all women are *legal* slaves. Many women are free, *legally*, whether it is in their best interest or not. Such dances, then, "slave dances," at least on Gor, are *not* for such women. If a "free woman," that is, one *legally* free, were to publicly perform such a dance on Gor she would probably find herself in a master's chains by morning. Her "legal freedom," we may speculate, would prove quite fleeting. It would soon be replaced, we may suppose, with a new and more appropriate status, that of being a slave *legally*, a status fixed on her then with all the clarity and obduracy of Gorean law, and fixed on her for all the world to see, fixed on her as plainly as the collar on her neck and the mark on her thigh. "Slave dance," on Gor, incidentally, is a very rich and varied dance form. It covers a great deal more than simple "ethnic dance." For example, it includes dances such as hunt dances, capture dances, submission dances, chain dances, whip dances, and such. Perhaps what is done in slave dance on Gor would count as "exotic dance" on Earth, but, if we are thinking of the actual kinds of dances performed, then there is much in slave dance, for example, story dances, which are seldom, if ever, included in "exotic dance" on Earth, and there are forms of dance in "exotic dance" which, for one reason or another, are seldom, if ever, seen on Gor, for example, certain forms of carnival dancing, such as bubble dancing or fan dancing. Perhaps the reason such dances are seldom, if ever, seen on Gor, is that Goreans would not be likely to regard them as being "real dance." They would be regarded, I think, as little more than culturally idiosyncratic forms of commedic teasing. They are, at any rate, not the sort of dance, or the "*danse-du-ventre*" sort, so pleasing to strong men, which a slave on Gor, fearing the whip, must often learn to perform.

I heard bells coming, from down the corridor, from within. I was still on my knees. Sita hove into sight, returning to the floor. She paused, looking down at me, kneeling there, clutching the sheet about me, frightened. She was naked, except for her collar, and some beads, colorful, cheap wooden beads, slave beads, and her bells, on her left ankle. She regarded me, at her feet, contemptuously. I looked up at her, angrily. Why should she regard me so contemptuously? I was clothed. I had a sheet about me! She wore only her collar, and a few beads, and slave bells! "You're naked!" I said to her, angrily.

Swiftly she crouched down before me, and, with two hands, angrily, there in the hall, near the curtain, tore the sheet back, away from me, thrusting it back, and down, over my calves. "So, too, are you!" she hissed. About my neck had been slung several strands of beads, large, colorful wooden beads, slave beads, of different lengths. To some extent they concealed me, but they, other than my collar, were all I wore.

Then, it startling us both, we heard the ringing of the nineteenth bar.

She smiled at me.

Hastily I pulled the sheet up and put it about me as closely as I could, holding it even, in my two fists, high, about my neck.

I looked at her, frightened.

"In a bit," she said, "Tupita and I will put the leash cuffs on you."

She then rose up, quickly. Perhaps she had been away from the floor too long. She hurried through the beaded curtain.

I heard a man outside strike on the table with his goblet. "The nineteenth bar! The nineteenth bar!" he called. "The nineteenth bar has struck!"

"Bring forth the slave!" called another.

"Bring her forth!" called another.

Another man or two added to this din, by pounding their goblets on the tables.

I knelt back, out of sight, near the curtain, frightened, clutching the sheet about me. I was not to be brought forth immediately at the Nineteenth Ahn, Mirus had told me. It seemed that it was their intention that the men should wait, at least for a time. They wanted them, apparently, to be kept in suspense, to become eager and restless, perhaps even impatient. I was certainly in no hurry to be conducted onto the floor. On the other hand, I was frightened, too, if the men were too long kept waiting. Perhaps then they would expect too much. What if they were disappointed? I was a new slave, really. How could I please them, truly? I moaned softly to myself. I did not want to feel the lash.

The men seemed now to be fairly quiet outside. Perhaps most of them did not expect me, really, to be brought out on the stroke of the nineteenth bar. Perhaps those who had smote their goblets on the tables and called for me, had, as much as anything, been voicing a natural disgruntlement at the unwritten customs which seemed to govern such affairs, at the institution of a time to be set aside for the whetting of appetites. I supposed that there would have to be a judicious sense of timing involved in such matters, that the time must be long enough to bring the audience to a point of eager readiness, perhaps even impatience, without, on the other hand, dallying so long that they became unruly or hostile. I assumed that the house must know what it was doing in these matters. Doubtless I was not the first girl to be conducted out onto that floor, and probably not even the first Earth girl.

"How are you, Doreen?" asked small Ina, crouching down, solicitously, beside me.

I looked at her, gratefully. "All right, Mistress," I whispered.

"Good," she smiled, reassuringly.

Ina did not care in the least, really, I was sure, whether I called her "Mistress" or not, but we had both agreed, two weeks ago, when we had become friends, both of us in the kitchen, that it would be better for me to do so, as I was the newest girl. We were both afraid that if I called her by her name, and someone heard, I, and Ina, too, if she had not imposed discipline, would have been punished. For example, we would not have wanted to let either Tupita or Sita catch us in such a negligence.

"Have you had your slave wine?" asked Ina.

"Yes," I said. This is not really a wine, or an alcoholic beverage. It is called "slave wine," I think, for the amusement of the masters. It is extremely bitter. One draught of the substance is reputed to last until the administration of an appropriate "releaser." In spite of this belief, however, or perhaps in deference to tradition, lingering from earlier times, in which, it seems, less reliable "slave wines" were available, doses of this foul stuff are usually administered to female slaves at regular intervals, usually once or twice a year. Some girls, rather cynical ones, I suspect, speculate that the masters give it to them more often than necessary just because they enjoy watching them down the terrible stuff. This is unlikely, however. There are cheaper and more easily available ingredients for such a mode of discipline than slave wine.

"Good," said Ina. "There is then nothing to worry about."

I looked at her. It had not occurred to me, really, that I had "nothing to worry about."

"The time to worry," said Ina, "is if they decide to make you a breeding slave."

I nodded.

"You must then drink the releaser," she said.

I nodded numbly.

"I have been told it is quite good," she said.

I looked at her, with horror.

"Really," she said.

"I am sure it is," I said, weakly.

Slave wine makes sense in a slave-holding culture, such as Gor. The breeding of slaves, like any sort of domestic animals, and particularly valuable ones, is carefully controlled. As a slave, of course, I could be bred, or crossed, when, and however, my master might see fit. It is the same as with other animals.

I lifted my head a little.

Outside the men were becoming impatient. I could hear the striking of goblets more often now on tables. I heard some shouting.

When the girl is taken to the breeding cell or breeding stall, she is normally hooded. Her selected mate is also hooded. In this fashion personal attachments are precluded. She is not there to know in whose arms she lies, or piteously, and in misery, to fall in love, but to be impregnated. And in accord with the prescribed anonymity of the breeding, as would be expected, the slaves do not speak to one another. They may be slain if they do. Their coupling is public, of course, in the sense that the master, or usually, masters, and sometimes others, whether in an official capacity or not, are present, to make any pertinent payments or determinations.

The men outside, it now seemed to me, were becoming unruly.

"Don't be afraid," said Ina.

"What are men like?" I asked Ina.

"They are glorious, and our masters," said Ina.

"That is not what I mean," I protested.

"What do you mean?" she asked.

"What will it be like?" I asked. "Will they hurt me?"

"I suppose some of them may hurt you," she said. "And I suppose any of them would hurt you sometimes. But you must expect that. You are only a slave."

"I do not mean that," I said. I knew, after all, I was a slave. I knew that I must strive to be pleasing to masters, and perfectly so. I knew that I was subject to discipline. I knew I might be, and would be likely to be, punished for the least infraction in my discipline, the least imperfection in my service and the least failure in my pleasingness. Indeed, I knew that, as a slave, my master did not even need a reason for punishing me. He could punish me for no reason at all, unless perhaps it might simply be that it pleased him to do so then, or, say, it occurred to him to do so then.

"What do you mean?" she asked.

"Bring out the virgin!" cried a man.

"Get the white-silker out here," called another. "Let us see her!"

"I mean will they hurt me!" I moaned.

"You mean when they open you?" she asked.

"Yes!" I said.

"Probably not," she said. "But you may be sore."

"I see," I said.

"Oh," smiled Ina. "You really mean, in general, don't you? What it's like?"

I put down my head.

"You silly virgin," said Ina. "You really don't know, do you?"

"No," I said.

"Tonight," she said, "will doubtless be hard. Do not worry about tonight. It is the first time. Just try to survive. Tonight it will doubtless be like when a city falls, or one is used for a sex feast."

I looked at her, not even understanding her.

"But wait, slave," she laughed. "Later it will be quite different."

I looked at her.

"Later, Doreen," said Ina, smiling, "you will beg and scratch for it."

I heard the men shouting outside now. They seemed angry. Then I saw Tupita and Sita coming through the beaded curtain. They carried certain objects.

"Put your wrists out," said Tupita.

The sheet fell a little. Tupita fastened a leather cuff on my right wrist. It was not a lock cuff. It buckled shut. It did have a snap ring on it. Sita fastened a similar cuff on my left wrist. Both of them carried long leather leashes. Tupita, with the snap ring on the leash, fastened the leash to my right cuff, and Sita fastened the other leash on my left cuff. The snap rings on the cuffs themselves, of course, make it possible, if one wishes, for the cuffs to be linked together.

I saw the legs of a man. I looked up, and then, swiftly, the palms of my hands on the floor, the cuffs on my wrists, put my head to the floor before him. Tupita and Sita, similarly, rendered immediate, fearful obeisance.

"Stand," said the man, "all of you." We then stood before Hendow, our master. Behind him was Mirus. Mirus had a canvas sack slung at his belt. Two of Hendow's girls, Aynur and Tula, were behind Mirus. Each of them carried a deep copper bowl. Aynur's bowl was empty. Tula's was filled with oval, narrowly slotted ostraka.

"Hold the sheet closely about you," said Tupita.

I needed no urging to comply with this request.

Hendow regarded me, possessively. He owned me. Tonight, too, he planned on making money on me.

"You have pretty feet, and ankles, and calves, Doreen," he said.

"Thank you, Master," I said.

The sheet I clutched about me so desperately, came a little below my knees. It was of white silk.

My master stood near me. I trembled.

Tupita and Sita, holding the leashes to my cuffs, stood nearby. Ina, too, was there.

My master took the edges of the sheet I held about myself and pulled it a little to the side, and down, revealing my shoulders. He took from his wallet a ribbon. It was about a foot long, and an inch and a half in width. He looped it about my collar, and jerked it down, snug. The ribbon, like the sheet, was of white silk.

I heard the men clamoring outside.

"Do not be afraid," he said.

"No, Master," I said.

He nodded to Mirus.

Mirus, followed by Aynur and Tula, made his way through the beaded curtain. In a moment I heard him quieting the crowd, which was becoming unruly.

The musicians, now, five of them, came from down the corridor. They waited within the curtain.

"Sight unseen," called Mirus to the crowd, "who will try the luck of the first ostrakon? Only a tarsk bit each! Who is first? Who is for the first ostrakon? You, sir! Yes! And you the second! The third! Yes. And you! And you!"

I listened to him selling the ostraka.

"Some men," said Hendow, "think the first ostraka are luckiest."

"You!" called Mirus. "Yes! And you, yes! Yes!"

In a little bit the first flurry of sales had lessened.

"Now," said Hendow, "we come to the more cautious buyers, those who would like to purchase early ostraka, but would appreciate a bit of reassurance. Too, we have now done, presumably, with the fellows who would buy a chance on anything, as long as it is a chance, and, too, those fellows to whom a virginity in itself, regardless of whose it is, is of great interest. They would take a chance on the virginity of a tharlarion."

"Yes, Master," I whispered.

"We have not seen this slave," said a man. "Is she any good?"

"Tell us of her," called another man.

"She is described in the handbills," said Mirus.

"Is she any good?" called the first man, again.

"Tell us of her," called the second man, again.

"Her hair and eye coloring, and complexion, and height and weight, are as mentioned in the handbills," said Mirus. "Other pertinent measurements, too, as you may recall, are specified in the same bills."

I blushed, looking down.

"Is she any good?" repeated the first fellow, insistently.

"She has a lovely face and form," said Mirus.

"But is she any good!" laughed the man.

"That you may determine promptly and firsthand, if you win," called Mirus.

There was laughter.

"Seriously," said Mirus, "understand that this is only a virgin slave. In that sense, she will not be much good, probably not for a few weeks. Remember it is only her virginity we are raffling off tonight."

"Yes, yes," agreed several fellows.

"True," called the first man.

"But she is beautiful, and unusually desirable," said Mirus. "Surely it would be a triumph to open her."

I clutched the sheet more closely about me.

"She is a treasure," said Mirus, "and, in time, we expect her to become exceptionally good."

"She is an Earth slut," called a man. "It says so on the handbills. They are all frigid."

"But you know as well as I," called Mirus, "that they do not stay that way."

"True," laughed the fellow.

There was general laughter.

I clutched the sheet more closely about my neck.

"We know you, Mirus," said a man. "What do you think of her?"

"She was purchased by my employer, your host, master of this tavern, Hendow," said Mirus. "I think you know well his taste and expertise in selecting women."

This point seemed to have its effect with the crowd.

"What of you, Mirus?" pressed the fellow who had asked the original question. "What do you think of her?"

"I would purchase an ostrakon, myself, or several," said Mirus, "but if I, an employee of the tavern, were to win, you would all, would you not, every one of you, suspect collusion and duplicity?"

"Yes," said a fellow. There was laughter.

So, I thought to myself, it was not my imagination. Mirus did desire me. That, doubtless, was why he had so suddenly turned away from me last night.

"And so," said Mirus, "I can wait."

I shuddered. I had not thought of it much, but it was true. After tonight, I would be only another of Hendow's girls. I would not only have been "opened" for his customers, but I would be available as well, as a matter of course, to his men. The use of a tavern's girls is one of the perquisites of employment in such a place. After tonight, I would have to serve Mirus, and the others, as they might want me. I recalled that in the house of my training the "opened" girls had been available to the guards. The kitchen master, too, I knew had had his eye on me. Usually, laboring there, on our knees, bending over the low, steaming tubs, our arms immersed in the suds to our elbows, cleaning pots and pans, he had had Ina and I remove our kitchen tunics. He had used Ina several times. I swallowed hard. Doubtless I would be put back in the kitchen from time to time. He was probably waiting for me.

"I will take an ostrakon!" called a fellow, he, I think, who had asked Mirus his opinion of me.

"And I!" said another. "And I," called several others.

"Yes, astute sirs," said Mirus. "Come, sluts," said he, doubtless to Aynur and Tula, carrying their bowls.

In a bit, then, these sales had been made.

Hendow gestured with his head to the musicians, and they made their way, one by one, through the beaded curtain. There were five of them, a czehar player, two kalika players, a flautist and a drummer. In a moment or two, as Mirus solicited further interest among the customers, I heard the sounds of the instruments, the czehar and kalikas being tuned, the flautist trying passages, the drummer's fingers light on the taut skin of his instrument, the kaska, then adjusting it, then trying it again, then tapping lightly, then more vigorously, with swift, brief rhythms, limbering his wrists, fingers and hands. The music of Gor, or much of it, is very melodious and sensuous. Much of it seems made for the display of slaves before free men, but then, I suppose, that is exactly what it is made for.

Then the musicians were silent.

"Let us see her," called a man.

"Bring her out!" called another.

"Bring her out!" called yet another.

I heard the pounding of goblets on the tables.

"Bring her out!" called another man. "Bring her out!" called another. "Bring her forth!" cried another.

"Bring her forth! Bring her forth!" they cried.

"Are you ready?" asked Hendow.

"Yes, Master," I said.

I felt his massive hand moving the sheet as it closed itself, like a vise, about my upper left arm. I was almost lifted from my feet. It was like being a doll in his grasp. I looked up at him. I was absolutely helpless. My fists still clutched the sheet high about my neck. The leashes on the cuffs went behind me, slack, on each side, and then looped up to the keeping of Tupita and Sita, Tupita on my right, Sita on the left. Hendow drew me beside him through the beaded curtain. Tupita and Sita followed, and, too, small Ina. These, slaves themselves, would present me, a new slave, to the men. But it was in the grip of my master, this perhaps symbolizing his ownership of me, and his authority over me, that I would be brought to the floor.

"Aii!" said a man.

"Ah!" said a man. "Superb!" said another. I heard the intake of breaths.

"What did I tell you?" asked Mirus.

I heard sounds of relish, and anticipation. I began to tremble. I looked up at my master. He was proud of me! Too, there were conventionalized sounds, indicative of interest and approval, the intake of breath through saliva, certain sounds made with the tongue and lips, certain clickings and smackings, and such, of the sort that might cause a free woman to swoon with dismay, but are addressed appropriately enough, and usually to her pleasure, to slaves. Too, I heard whistles and sex calls. Some men, by such noises, summon a girl, running, to their feet. If she is close enough, of course, noises of the preceding sort may also be used for this purpose.

"Please, please, sirs," said Mirus, in mock protest. "Desist! This is a virgin! You will embarrass her!"

There was much laughter. This was a splendid joke, I gathered. Who, after all, cares for the feelings of a slave?

"No woman like that," said a man, "with a collar on her neck, is a virgin!"

There was more laughter.

I gathered that that was supposed to be a compliment. I glanced up at Hendow. How pleased he seemed to be to own me. How proud he seemed to be! I was afraid, but I was pleased, too, and grateful, that he was pleased with me. I wanted to be pleasing to him. He was my master.

"But she is a virgin!" laughed Mirus.

"Who cares?" called a man.

There was more laughter.

"Among our guests this evening," said Mirus, gesturing, "is one well known to you all, Tamirus." He indicated a good-natured-looking fellow, sitting to one side in green robes. This fellow lifted his hand, in good humor, to the crowd. "Later," said Mirus, "when our lovely chain-daughters in attendance, Tupita, Sita and Ina, whom some of you well know, and intimately, and whom I recommend to you all, as I also do my lovely assistants, Aynur and Tula, have presented to you another chain-daughter, this lovely slut, their sister in bondage, we shall call upon Tamirus for his attestation."

There was a good-humored cheer, acknowledging which Tamirus, grinning, once more lifted his hand. The attestation, I gathered, was little more than a formality, but, I supposed, some of the fellows would want it.

I stood toward the center and about a third forward from the rear of the floor, my arm still in the grip of Hendow, my master.

"I will buy another ostrakon!" called a man. I saw Aynur and Tula glance at one another. Aynur's bowl was no longer empty. Tula's now held less.

"We shall reopen the sale of ostraka presently," called Mirus.

The musicians were on my left.

"Hendow," called Mirus, dramatically, "my employer, and dear friend, Hendow, are you not the master of this tavern?"

"I am," grinned Hendow.

There was laughter.

I was afraid my arm would be bruised where Hendow held it. His grip was like iron.

"And you own many women?"

"Yes," said Hendow.

"We see you have a slave in hand."

"Yes," said Hendow.

"Do you own her, as well?" asked Mirus.

"Yes," said Hendow.

"And is it your intention to keep her all for yourself?" asked Mirus.

"No," said Hendow, grinning.

There was a cheer.

"She is then to have the same status as your other women, and to be available to your customers, and such?" asked Mirus.

"Yes," said Hendow.

There was another cheer.

"She is then to be not a private slave, but a public slave?" inquired Mirus.

"Yes!" said Hendow.

This announcement was greeted with another cheer.

"If she is a treasured private slave, noble Hendow," said Mirus, "take her swiftly to your chambers. If she is not, but is as your other women, then, noble friend, we pray you, step back from her, leaving her upon the floor before us."

I felt Hendow's hand release my arm. He stepped back. There was a cheer. I did not know where he was. I supposed he might be somewhere behind me, and to my left. I felt very much alone. To be sure, the other girls were still near me. But we were all slaves, before men.

"Come forward, come forward," said Mirus, coaxingly, beckoning to me.

I came forward, in the cuffs and leashes, clutching the sheet, the girls with me. I now stood back about a third from the front edge of the dancing floor. The men could see me very well now. The musicians were now back, and to the left.

"I will buy an ostrakon!" called a man.

"And I!" called another.

"And I!" said another.

I watched Mirus take tarsk bits from these men. He dropped the coins into the sack at his belt. From the distention and apparent weight of the sack I gathered he had already taken in several tarsk bits. I supposed that I should feel flattered. I clutched the sheet up higher about my neck. I wondered where Hendow was, somewhere behind me, I thought. When a fellow had paid his tarsk bit Mirus would reach into the copper bowl carried by Tula and draw forth from it one of the small, about three inches long and an inch wide, thin, flat, brittle, glazed, baked-clay ostraka. They were oval and, along the long axis, slotted. The ostraka are lovely and fragile. A number, the same number, was written at the bottom and top of each item. I winced as Mirus snapped one of the ostraka in two, giving half to the purchaser and throwing the other half into Aynur's bowl. "Good luck!" he said.

"What is her name?" called a man.

" 'Doreen'," said Mirus. "At least that is the name by which she is known to Borko."

I shuddered, and the men laughed, seeing my fear. I did not think the nature of Hendow's Borko, that massive hunting sleen, was unknown to them.

I heard the snappings of ostraka.

"Bring her over here, so we can see her better," said a man.

"And over here," said another, on the other side.

"Come, frightened urt," said Tupita. She guided me to the right, where I must stand at the edge of the floor, there, and then further to the right, and back. I then saw Hendow, my master. He was standing back, near the wall at the back of the tavern, near the threshold with the beaded curtain, that through which I had entered.

I was then moved further to the right, in a circular pattern, and I then stood at the back, right corner of the dancing floor, as one would see it from the front. I was then a moment later conducted again to my right, and I now stood in the vicinity of what would be the front, right corner of the floor, as one would see it from the front. I was near the edge. Tupita apparently wanted me to be close to the men, that my proximity, I suppose, might stimulate them.

I heard the snappings of more ostraka.

"Oh!" I cried. I was frightened. I could not pull away. "Stand as you are," said Tupita. "Yes, Mistress," I said. A man, sitting near the edge of the floor, had put out his hand and held my left ankle. He then, with his thumb, rubbed slowly below and behind the anklebone, and then, with his fingers, up, just below the calf. I shuddered at his touch. I went up an inch or two on the toes of my foot.

"Look at that," called a man.

"That is no virgin," said another.

"She is a virgin," averred Mirus, snapping another ostrakon, not even looking about. "You will shortly have the attestation," he said.

"I will take another ostrakon," said the fellow who had touched me.

"I, too," said another.

My ankle released, Tupita, aided by Sita, again put me toward the center of the floor, near the front, much where I had stood before.

I was trembling. I could not help how I had moved under his touch.

The men looked at me. I heard laughter. I blushed.

There was more laughter.

"In time, however," said Mirus, continuing his transactions, "we expect her to feel at least some minimal slave heat."

There was laughter.

I must have turned red, all of me that was not covered by the sheet, my face and neck, and my calves, ankles and feet. There was then more laughter. Suddenly I wished I was one of those women like leather who hated men. But then in a moment I did not really want to be like that either. I was too soft, too lovely, and too feminine for that. I was not that sort of woman. I was a different sort. I was afraid then, very afraid. I sensed vaguely, in my virgin's belly, the thought terrifying me, what men, such men, might do to me. These intimations, however, did not serve to prepare me even for what, as a matter of course, in even a few weeks, I could be forced to feel, or for what it would be to be made the helpless victim of "slave needs."

"Five!" called a man. "Five!"

"Two here!" said another.

I looked about, from face to face, and then I looked away, not daring to meet such eyes, those of masters.

How faraway seemed the library.

Incredibly, here, on this world, I was owned.

"She is lovely," said a man.

"Yes," said another.

There were sexual noises, and calls. I could not object to these. I was a slave.

How powerful seemed these men. I think any of them could have broken me in pieces, like the lovely ostraka. And how fierce they seemed. How they would make a woman obey them! And how they looked upon me, with such eagerness and interest, seeing me as what I was, a slave!

I clenched my fists on the sheet. Beneath it, save for a steel collar and some beads, I was naked.

"Let us have the drawing," urged a fellow.

I felt inordinately helpless, so small and weak, and desired, among such men.

I heard the snappings of the ostraka.

How absurd then, and artificial, and unreal, suddenly, seemed

Earth, with all its preposterous political myths, its subversion of nature, its insidious conditioning programs, its pretendings to deny the simple, obvious truths of aristocracy, its contrived trammelings of right and power, its desperate attempts to destroy the natural relationships between men and women, to level and mediocratize the diversity and glory of nature, its corrupt machineries of falsification and repression. Men can do with us as they wish, I thought, and Gorean men, at least if the woman is a slave, will. I was not on Earth. I was on a different world. I stood now on a dancing floor in a tavern, in a complex, beautiful civilization, one quite different from my own, one in which strong, proud men had refused to relinquish their natural sovereignty. I did not stand before them as a primitive. Their civilization had a history as long and complex as my own. I did stand before them, however, in a collar, and in the order of nature.

I felt tension in the leashes attached to the rings on the cuffs I wore. Tupita and Sita, on my right and left, respectively, stood near to me. They had muchly coiled the leashes and their two hands, each on their own leash, and turned in the leash, and gripping it tightly, were about a foot from the rings on the cuffs. I sensed Ina behind me. She took hold of the sheet, at the shoulders, from behind, that it might be lifted gracefully from me.

Earlier Hendow had brought me to the floor, helpless, like a doll, in his grip. He had then, in response to the ritualistic petition of Mirus, removed his hand from my arm, stepped back from me and left me there. The symbolic meaning of this was clear. He was not reserving me for himself. I was also for his customers. I was a new girl in his tavern. I was a public slave.

I felt tension through the cuffs, I heard the tiny noises of the joined rings, those on the cuffs and leashes, I felt the pulling of the leash rings against the rings on the cuffs. My wrists were slowly being drawn to the sides. The men leaned forward. I could not keep my hands on the sheet without opening the sheet myself. Tears in my eyes I released the sheet. Ina then, gracefully, drew the sheet away and, carrying it, withdrew from the floor.

I stood there, my wrists at my shoulders. I could not draw my hands together to cover myself. The cuffs I wore, buckled tightly on me, and the taut leashes attached to them, in the keeping of Tupita and Sita, saw to it. I stood there, then, in collar and beads, displayed, a tavern slave, a paga slave, a public slave, naked on a Gorean dancing floor.

The hands of men smote repeatedly on their left shoulders.

"Yes!" cried several. "Yes! Yes!" "Marvelous!" breathed some. "Superb!" cried others, pounding with their goblets on the tables. I gathered that Teibar, who had picked me for the collar, had known his business.

There was then slackness in the leashes. My arms went to my sides.

There was a white ribbon looped on my collar, and drawn down about it, snugly.

"You are naked before men," whispered Tupita. "Obeisance!"

I quickly knelt before the men and put my head to the floor, the palms of my hands, too, on the floor. I heard several of the beads touch the wood.

I was then jerked up to my feet by the leashes, and drawn about the floor, being shown to the men on all sides.

Men swarmed about Mirus, who was hard put to satisfy their demands for ostraka.

I was then knelt near the center of the floor, and a little toward its front. I knelt as I had been taught, and as the sort of slave I was, the sort of slave I had first learned I was in Market of Semris, a pleasure slave. My hands, my wrists buckled in the leather cuffs, were on my thighs. Tupita and Sita stood near me, and a little behind me. The leashes were slack.

"Alas, generous sirs!" cried Mirus. "The ostraka grow few in number!"

I saw men rise hurriedly to move toward him.

"I shall take ten," said a man.

"No!" cried another.

"Let us have the attestation!" cried Mirus, forcing the two fellows apart.

Tamirus approached me. He wore green robes. I did not know at that time but this indicated he was of the caste of physicians. That is a high caste. If I had known he was of high caste I might have been a great deal more frightened than I was. Most Goreans take caste very seriously. It is apparently one of the socially stabilizing forces on Gor. It tends to reduce the dislocations, disappointments and tragedies inherent in more mobile structures, in which men are taught that they are failures if they do not manage to make large amounts of money or excel in one of a small number of prestigious professions. The system also helps to keep men of energy and high intelligence in a wide variety of occupations, this preventing the drain of such men into a small number of often artificially desiderated occupations, this tending then to leave lesser men, or frustrated men, to practice other hundreds of arts the survival and maintenance of which are important to a superior civilization. Provisions for changing caste exist on Gor, but they are seldom utilized. Most Goreans are proud of their castes and the skills appropriate to them. Such skills, too, tend to be appreciated by other Goreans, and are not looked down on. My virginity had been checked at various times. Teibar had done it on Earth, in the library; it had been done in the house of my training, shortly after I had arrived there; it had been done outside Brundisium, by the wholesaler there, and in Market of Semris twice, once when I had arrived there, by the men of Teibar of Market of Semris, and once before I had left, by Hendow's man. It had also been checked when I had arrived here, and again, this afternoon, before I had been bedecked in these beads I wore, slave beads.

"How are you, my dear?" asked Tamirus.

"Very good, Master," I said. "Thank you, Master."

"On your back, idiot," said Tupita.

I looked at her, angrily.

By the leashes, pulling up and twisting, to my surprise, handling me quite easily, with surprising expertness, she and Sita pulled me up, half on my feet, and then brought me back, gasping, off balance, and lowered me to my back. I had not realized their skill, nor how easily I could be controlled by the two leashes. There are many tricks, of course, with leashes, in the management of slaves. Tupita held down my right wrist, and Sita my left wrist. "Throw your legs apart or we will do this differently," said Tupita. I obeyed, on my back, on the dancing floor. There are various attitudes in which the virginity of a girl may be checked. The least embarrassing to her is probably this one.

Tamirus was careful with me, and gentle. He checked twice, delicately.

"Thank you, Master," I said to him, gratefully.

He stood up. "It is as certified by the house of Hendow," he said. "The slave is a virgin."

"Not for long!" called a fellow.

"Thank you for your public confirmation in this matter," called Mirus.

Tamirus lifted his hand good-humoredly, graciously, to Mirus, and then, too, to the others in the tavern, and returned to his table. There, waiting for him, was a goblet of paga, doubtless a gratuity for the loan of his expertise. Too, he would doubtless have his choice of Hendow's women this night, with the probable exception of myself, for we went with the paga. Indeed, I thought he might already have made his choice. Near his table, but back a bit from it, discretely, at slave's distance, knelt luscious Inger, blond and voluptuous, from the north, from Skjern, who had come to Brundisium in the heavy shackles of Torvaldslanders. It was she who had brought his paga. It would doubtless be she who would serve him this night, with the fullness of the Gorean slave. With pen dipped into an inkhorn at his belt Tamirus was signing a paper. He replaced the pen in the inkhorn, which closed the horn, shook the paper a bit and held it up. A fellow near him handed it obligingly to Mirus. I saw Inger inch a little closer to Tamirus, on her knees. Doubtless she had served him before. Perhaps she wished him to purchase her.

"Here is the signed attestation," said Mirus, handing it to one of the fellows near the floor. They began to pass it about.

"Only seven ostraka are left," called Mirus. "Who would like them? Only one, regretfully, I fear, may be now allowed to a customer."

I watched the attestation being handed about the tables.

Men crowded about Mirus.

I no longer had the sheet of white silk about me. It had been taken from me.

"Alas," then cried Mirus. "The ostraka are gone!"

There were cries of anger.

"Do not be dismayed, noble patrons of the tavern of Hendow," he called, "for the number of ostraka was determined in advance. If too many were sold, the chances of any particular one winning would be too few. Surely those of you who have already purchased one or more ostraka can appreciate the weight of this consideration."

Several men seemed to offer assent to this.

"And do not forget, noble patrons," he continued, "that although only one may be the first to open this lovely slave, she is now one of Hendow's women. Accordingly you may all return, time and time again, over the next weeks, and months, to sip her pleasures at your leisure."

"True," said a man.

"And I think I can guarantee," said Mirus, "by all the whips in the house of Hendow, that she will do her best to please you."

There was laughter.

I shuddered. Of course I would do my best to please them. I would have no choice. I was a slave. Too, these were not the men of Earth, so tolerant, so understanding, so considerate, so forgiving, so easily put off, so weak. These were Gorean men. If I was not perfect for them, and whenever, and however, they wished, they would make me pay, and well. On Gor there are many sayings about masters and slaves. One is in the form of a question and an answer. The question is, "What does a slave owe a Master?" The answer is, "Everything, and then a thousand times more."

"Some of you have apparently found this slave of some interest," said Mirus, "for although she has not yet even danced, already are the ostraka gone."

"True," said a fellow.

Many girls, I had gathered, do not dance before their virginity, in such contests, is disposed of. Not all girls are skillful dancers, particularly at first, before they have had slave sexual experience. I was to be danced, however, I had gathered, not only because I could, at least to some extent, dance, but also as a form of advertising, Hendow taking this occasion to introduce me to his patrons. He had hopes for me, I had gathered, as a dancer. He hoped, I think, through me, to bring new and additional business to his tavern. I hoped he would not be disappointed in me, as I did not want to be punished.

"May I have the attestation paper?" asked Mirus. He retrieved it from a fellow over to the right. "Thank you," he said. He then waved the paper over his head. "Here is the signed attestation of the noble Tamirus," he said. "She is a virgin!" He then rolled the paper and pointed to me with it. I looked at him. "Behold her," he said, "kneeling there before you, a beautiful slave awaiting her first use master."

I put my head down, trembling. I knelt there, my knees wide, awaiting my first use master.

"Dispense more ostraka!" called a man.

"No!" cried others.

"Which of you hold the winning ostrakon?" inquired Mirus. "Is it you, sir? You? Or, you?"

"I hope it is me," called a fellow.

There was laughter.

"Doreen," said Mirus.

"Yes, Master," I said, looking up, startled. I had not expected him to speak to me.

"Who will win, Doreen?" he asked.

"I do not know, Master," I said, weakly.

"Speak up, Slave," said he.

"I do not know, Master," I cried, in misery.

"Nor will you," he said.

I looked at him, in consternation.

There was laughter. I did not understand this.

"Do you beg now to dance before your first use master?" asked Mirus.

"Yes, Master," I said.

"And before the guests of Hendow?" he asked.

"Yes, Master," I said.

"And before all present?" he inquired.

"Yes, Master!" I said.

"Adorn her," said Mirus.

"Ina," called Tupita. "Sit," she said then to me, "with your hands on the floor beside you, leaning forward, your right leg advanced."

Ina came forward, from the back, through the beaded curtain, with a flat, shallow box. Tupita and Sita removed the leather cuffs from my wrists.

There are some three senses of the expression "virgin dance" on Gor. There is a sense in which it is a kind of dance, rather than a particular dance, which is deemed appropriate for virgins. In that sense I was not expected to perform a "virgin dance." One would seldom see such dances in taverns. The second sense is the obvious one in which it is a dance danced by a virgin, and usually just prior to the loss of her virginity. In that sense it could be almost any dance which serves the purpose of displaying the girl before her initial ravishing. The third sense of the term is that of a specific dance, or type of dance, most often, interestingly, not even danced by a virgin, but usually by an experienced slave. It is not exactly a story dance, but more of an emotional or attitudinal piece, more in the nature of a "role dance," a dance in which the slave dances as though she might be a virgin, but knows she is to be ravished, and that she is expected to be pleasing. The dance I was expected to perform was, I suppose, a "virgin dance" in both the second and third senses of the term. Mirus, paradoxically, speaking obviously in the third sense of the term, had told me that I would do better at this sort of dance when I was no longer a virgin.

I felt metal anklets being thrust on my ankles by Tupita and Sita. They put several on each ankle. They then, similarly, placed narrow bracelets on both my wrists, several on each wrist. A long belt of cord, to which were attached numerous metal disks, suspended and shimmering, was then looped twice about me, the first loop secured high, and tight, at my waist, and the second loop, a larger loop, a framing loop, was secured in such a way, in the back, that it would hang quite low on my belly, well below my navel. The purpose of this belt was to call attention to, and enhance, by sound and sight, the movements of the hips and abdomen. With the slave beads I already wore I felt inutterably displayed, and barbaric. I could not move now without the sounds of the beads, the anklets and bracelets, the shimmering belt with its two loops.

"Stand," said Tupita.

I did.

The men gasped with pleasure. I was frightened.

"Prepare to dance, slave," said Tupita.

"Good," said a man.

I stood before them with my hands lifted over my head, the backs of my hands facing one another, my knees flexed. It is a common beginning position in slave dance.

The musicians readied themselves.

I looked out on the men. These were not men of Earth, defeated and tamed by propaganda and lies. These were Gorean men, men like lions. I stood before them, weak and helpless, a woman from Earth, now a collared slave who must dance for their pleasure.

The czehar player, sitting cross-legged, now had his instrument across his lap. He was the leader of the musicians. He had his horn pick in hand.

I stood barefoot, naked, save for collar and adornments, on the dancing floor of a low-ceilinged Gorean tavern. I must prepare to please masters. I wondered what the men who had worked at the library would think if they could see me now, their so-much-taken-for-granted Doreen, her beauty now at the disposal of masters, men who could break them in pieces. I wondered if they would lament my plight, deploring it with typical, whining, hypocritical cant, or if they, too, would sit there, at those low tables, their blood racing, their eyes alight, becoming men.

Aynur and Tula were now behind me, kneeling at the back of the floor, with their bowls. Tula's was empty. Aynur's held the house's halves of the divided ostraka. One of them would prove to be the "lucky ostrakon." Ina, the flat, shallow box of adornments beside her, was back with them. So, too, with the cuffs and leashes, were Tupita and Sita. Mirus, too, had now withdrawn to the back.

If I did not dance well I did not doubt but what I would be whipped.

I looked out on the men.

One of them would be my first use master. In a special sense my "virgin dance" must be dedicated to him. But, in general, I must dance, too, before the guests of Hendow's tavern, and, too, before all who were present. This included Mirus, who, I think, had often wanted me. Too, I could see others of Hendow's men about, come to see the dance, and now, too, to one side, the kitchen master. After tonight, at the tubs, I would doubtless be no safer from him than Ina.

Perhaps if I danced poorly? But I did not want to be whipped!

Then I knew I did not want to dance poorly. Out there there were men, real men, many of whom excited and stirred me, even in my virgin's belly. I could scarcely imagine what it might be to be helpless in their arms, and at their power, as a slave. I was desperately eager to please such men. I wanted to be marvelously exciting and beautiful before them. I wanted them to desire me. I wanted them to want me! Too, I knew many of the girls despised me as a woman of Earth. I wanted to show them, too, women such as Tupita and Sita, what a woman of Earth could do to their Gorean masters, how, she, too, could excite them, and twist them with torments of desire, and make them gasp and scream with pleasure! Too, in my anger at having been abandoned by Teibar, who had been my capture master on Earth, I wanted to dance well. He had let me go! But I had sold for two and a half silver tarsks, on my first sale! I had been purchased by Hendow, of Brundisium, who, I had gathered, was noted in this city for having an excellent eye for the selection of slave meat! Certainly the girls in his tavern, Inger, and Tupita, and Ina, and the others, were superb! Perhaps, I, too, then, was attractive! I saw the men, even now, looking at me! I could sense the heat and desire in them. They would not compromise with a woman like me. They would want her too much. They would throw her to their feet. They would dominate and master me, mercilessly! I was a female. In the arms of no other sort of man could I be fulfilled! Too, let Teibar cry out with anguish if he could find out how desired I would be, and what an excellent slut, what superb slave meat, I, his despised "modern woman," proved to be! I would become a high slave! I would cost a great deal of money! He would not even be able to afford me! Let him scream with the wanting of me, but it would be at the feet of others, in their collars, that I would kneel!

"Are you ready?" asked the leader of the musicians, the czehar player.

"Yes, Master!" I said, eagerly.

"Aii!" cried a fellow, pleased, as I began to dance.

The music was rich about me.

"I told you that was no virgin," said a man.

"Who cares?" asked another.

In the dance I had power. In the dance I was beautiful. I saw delight in the eyes of men. I heard gasps of admiration. To be sure I was of a body type, that of the natural woman, short-legged and well-curved, that tends to be attractive to Gorean men, and I think my face, which some had told me was delicate and sensitive, and lovely and intelligent, which so easily betrayed my emotions, may have been pleasing to them, but I think there was more to it than these things. Had it been merely a matter of face and figure I do not think the effect would have been the same. Many things were doubtless involved. One, of course, was that it was a slave who danced. The dancing of a slave is a thousand times more sensuous than that of a free woman because of the incredible meanings involved, the additional richness which this furnishes, the explosive significance of this comprehension, that she who dances is owned, and, theoretically, could be owned by you. Too, she is naked, or scantily clad, and is bedecked in a barbaric manner. This speaks of reality and savagery, of ferocity, and beauty and barbarism, and of the fundamental meaningfulness of the male/female relationship, that of power and ferocity to beauty, of dominator to dominated, of master to slave. The dancing of the female before the male, that she be found pleasing and he be pleased, is one of the most profound lessons in all of human biology. Others are when she kneels before him, when she kisses his feet, when she performs obeisance, when she know herself subject, truly, to his whip. Another is when she is seized in his arms, imperiously, and crushed to him. Too, I think in this dance I was also as successful as I was because of the sort of woman I was, one who possessed deep female needs, and profound passions. I was ready, even at that time, as I now realize, to have the relentless torches of men set to the tinder in my belly, that slave fires might be lit there, thence by service, submission and love, my condition as slave, and the commands and touches of men, to be fanned, whether I willed it or not, to my dismay and joy, into open conflagrations. But I think, too, more simply, that there are skills involved, and that I was an excellent dancer, even at that time.

I danced, as the slave I was.

"Here, slut, here!" called more than one man.

I teased them, dancing close to them, swaying, my belly alive for them, with the jangling metal pieces, the anklets clashing on my ankles, the bracelets sliding and ringing on my wrists, and then, as they attempted to seize me, drew back, backing away, or whirled, with a swirl of beads, away from them. I picked one man after another out of the audience, seeming to dance my beauty most meaningfully to him. Perhaps he would be my use master. I did not know.

Several began to keep the time with their hands, clapping them together.

"She is not a virgin," said a man.

"No," said another.

I came about then to the back of the dancing floor. Tupita, and the others were there. "You are good," said Tupita to me, grudgingly.

"I am superb," I said to her, angrily. Then I added, hastily, "Mistress!"

I looked to the back of the tavern, where, near the beaded curtain, stood Hendow, my Master, his arms folded. I swayed before him. I wanted to convince him that he had not made a mistake in purchasing me. I saw in his eyes that I had much to learn. I moved a little to my left, dancing before Mirus, who crouched there at the back of the floor, the sack of tarsk bits heavy at his belt.

"Do not change anything," he said to me, "but I would have thought you would dance rather more like a virgin."

I whirled away from him, to my right. Yes, I thought to myself, what are you doing, Doreen? What has gotten into you? Why are you doing this? Why is your belly so alive? Why are you so excited? Why is your body so hot? Why is it moving like this? You are dancing more like a purchasable slut, a common girl from a market, a girl who has been well taught by men and the whip the meaning of her collar, one who has already learned to whimper behind the bars of her kennel and scratch at its walls, than a virgin, fearing, but curious about, her first taking.

"Look," said a man.

"Superb," said another.

I did not think Mirus would mind if I changed my performance in this fashion, particularly, as I would, later, return to the taunting, sensate splendors of the aroused woman, and then, at the end, to the helpless pleading of the begging female, she who knows herself, ultimately, at the mercy of masters.

Actresses need only be actresses. They need not be dancers. But she who is a dancer must be more than a dancer. She must be an actress, as well.

"Ah, yes," said a man.

Suddenly in my dance it seemed I was a vigin, reluctant and fearful, terrified in the reality in which she found herself, but knowing she must respond to the music, to those heady, sensuous rhythms, to the wild cries of the flute, to the beating of the drum. I then danced timidity, and reluctance and inhibition, but yet reflecting, as one would, in such a situation, the commands of the music. I examined in dismay the beads about my neck, the cords at my waist, my barbarically adorned ankles and wrists. I touched my thighs, and lifted my arms, looking at them, and put my hands upon my body, as though I could not believe that it was unclothed. I pretended to shrink down within myself, to desire to crouch down, and conceal and cover my nudity, but then I straightened up, fearfully, as though I had heard commands to desist in such absurdities, and then I extended my hands to the sides, to various sides, as though pleading for mercy, to be released from the imperatives of the music, but then reacted, drawing back, as though I had seen the sight of whips or weapons. The kaska player, alert to this, reduced the volume of his drumming, and then, five times, smote hard upon the taut skin, almost like the cracking of a whip, to which I reacted, turning to one side and another, as though such a disciplinary device had been sounded menacingly, on all sides, in my vicinity, and then I continued to dance, helpless before the will of masters. Then, as the dance continued, I signified by expression and movement my curiosity and fascination with what I was being forced to do, and the responses of my body, reconciled now to its reality, helplessly obedient now to the music.

I am a basically shy person. But now I was dancing such things as shyness, and timidity, and fear, and curiosity, and fascination, as roles. Like many shy persons I can find myself in roles, and blossom forth in them.

I suddenly by expression and movement, an almost involuntary contortion of my belly, seemingly startling me, and frightening me, appeared to suddenly sense, or glimpse, my sexuality.

"Ah," said a man, appreciatively.

I approached him in the dance, and then others, my belly seeming to register, with its jangling accouterments, their presence. Each time I would draw back from them, but my belly, my hips, would seem to propel me again toward them, or toward yet another. I then felt my hips, and thighs, and breasts, and belly, as these seemed to come alive in the music. And then, throwing my head back, I danced unabashedly as an acknowledged, aroused slave, much as I had before, taunting them, teasing them, delighting in my power, but then, suddenly, as though I sensed my ultimate helplessness, my ultimate inability to achieve total fulfillment without the wholeness of sexuality, without the master and the yielding, which gave meaning to the incipient passions within me, I danced the aroused slave who is the property of the master and begs his touch.

"Good," said a fellow.

"The slut is excellent," said another.

Then I realized suddenly that I was actually aroused. The interior of my thighs were hot. My belly, hot and burning, seemed to beg to be touched. I do not know, really, whether I had done this to myself in the dance, which is possible, or if my arousal had merely came upon me in the course of the dance, but I was aroused. I was a helpless, aroused slave! This now was no role. It was what I was.

I returned to the back of the dancing floor, piteously, that I might sway before my master, he in the back, by the beaded curtain, gross, loathsome Hendow. He, I felt, of all those in the tavern, would understand what was now within me. I felt I could keep no secrets from him. It seemed he had a way of looking through me, and seeing whatever was within me, no matter how I might try to hide it. But I did not want to hide this from him. Rather I wanted his understanding. I wanted him to offer me comfort, or perhaps even rescue me from the floor. In my fears it was natural that I should seek him out, gross and loathsome though he might be. He was the one who owned me. He was my master.

Hendow nodded to me, almost imperceptibly. Then, pointing to me, and lifting his finger twice, he indicated I should turn away, and return to my dance, in the center of the floor, facing the crowd.

I knew the music was approaching its climax, and the dance must be concluded.

I then, in the coda of my performance, danced helplessness and beauty, and submission, surrendering myself as I, in my collar, must, into the hands and mercies of masters.

As the music concluded I performed floor movements, and the eyes of the men blazed, and fists pounded on the tables, and then the music was done and I lay before them on my back, my breasts rising and falling as I fought for breath, my body sheened with sweat, my hands beside me, palms up, my knees lifted slightly, my right knee highest, a slave before masters. I heard roars of triumph, shouts of pleasure. I was frightened. The men were on their feet. There was a thunder of applause, the striking of the shoulders in the Gorean fashion, and, too, the crashing of goblets on the tables. I crept to my knees in the bedlam. I became aware of Hendow standing near me now, and Mirus was to one side. "Back," called Hendow. "Back!" I felt small among the legs of the men. Mirus and Hendow, gently, were forcing men back, away from the floor. Then I was kneeling there, small, between them.

Mirus looked down upon me. Swiftly I pressed my lips fervently, placatingly, to his sandals. "Look up," said he. I looked up, frightened. Would I be punished for altering the dance?

"I did not think you could do better," he said. "I was wrong."

I regarded him, frightened. Would he then be angry? Would I be cuffed, or kicked?

"You did well," he said. "I am pleased."

I almost fainted with relief, and, gratefully, pressed my lips to his sandals. But then a girl is seldom punished for improving her service. Indeed, as I would later learn, girls are encouraged to be rich and creative in such matters.

I looked up from my knees at my master. "Is your belly still hot?" he asked.

I looked down, blushing. He had known, of course. "Not now, Master," I said.

"Well," he said, "you had better start heating it up again."

I turned crimson, my head down, kneeling there, scarcely able to believe what I had heard. To be sure, he was the proprietor of the tavern, and I was his.

I felt my head pulled up by the hair, a double handful of it grasped in Hendow's fist. I was almost pulled up, from my knees. "Did you like her?" he called to the crowd. Most of the men were still standing. There were no women in that crowd other than slaves. Women are on the whole not permitted in paga taverns, unless, of course, they wear collars.

"Yes! Yes!" cried several of the men.

"She will be a dancer in my tavern," said Hendow.

This intelligence was greeted with raucous enthusiasm, shouts, and the pounding of shoulders.

I shuddered.

"Come, see her often!" invited Hendow.

"Have no fear," called a fellow. There was laughter.

"But she is only one of several lovely dancers," said Hendow, "any one of whom is her superior or equal!"

I doubted that that was true.

"All of whom have been chosen to please your senses!"

I would grant the beast, my master, that.

"Come often to the tavern of Hendow," said Hendow, "for the finest paga in Brundisium, and the most beautiful paga slaves, wenches chosen for their luscious beauty and steaming bellies!"

I trembled. Not all paga slaves are tavern dancers, but all tavern dancers are paga slaves.

There was another round of cheering.

"The drawing!" called a man. "Let us have the drawing!"

Hendow nodded to Mirus, and Mirus summoned Aynur to the center of the floor, and near the front, with her copper bowl, laden with the halves of broken ostraka.

"Return to your seats!" called Hendow.

As the men sought their places Tupita, Sita and Ina came forward. Ina brought with her not only the flat, shallow box but a large towel as well. "Sit as you were before," ordered Tupita. I did so, leaning forward, my hands on the floor, my knees up, my right leg advanced. Sita removed the belt from me, with its double loop. Tupita began to take the anklets and bracelets from me, putting them in the box. "Treasure your silly virginity," said Tupita, "for you will not have it long." "Red-silk slut!" I said to her, angrily, adding, "Mistress." "By tomorrow," said Tupita, "you, too, will be only a red-silk slut."

"You were beautiful tonight," said Ina.

"Thank you," I said, "Mistress."

With a jangle and shimmering of metal pieces the cord belt, in its length, was dropped by Sita into the box.

Aynur shook the bowl of ostraka. She stirred the contents with her two hands. Delving deeply into the bowl she lifted up handfuls of ostraka again and again, each time letting them fall like showers back into the bowl.

Mirus and Hendow observed her doing this.

The last bracelet was deposited in the box. Sita was lifting the strands of slave beads from my neck, placing them, too, in the box.

"That is enough," said Hendow.

"Yes, Master," said Aynur, desisting mixing ostraka.

I trembled, for the moment of the drawihg drew near. Sita lifted the last strand of slave beads from about my neck and put it in the box. Ina, then, began to dry my body, from the sweat of the dance.

I felt very naked then, without even the beads to cover me. "Will I not be given the white sheet again?" I asked Ina.

"No," she said, "the time of the white sheet for you is over."

"Let me keep a strand of beads," I begged.

"No," said Ina. "Your use master, in handling you, might break them."

"Oh," I said, frightened.

"Too," she said, "we would not want anything to stand between you and your use master when he presses you in his arms."

"No," I whispered, frightened.

"Now you are as nude as any slut," said Tupita, jerking down on the ribbon on my collar, ascertaining that its fixture there was suitably snug.

I saw Mirus, near the front of the floor, draw a red ribbon from his wallet. It was identical in size and shape to the white ribbon I wore on my collar. My use master, I gathered, when he was finished with me, would change the ribbons. This would be significatory of the alteration in my status, informing anyone who might look upon it that I had now been "opened." He also had in one hand the attestation paper. There was a place at the bottom of the paper where a streak of blood, mine, might be smeared.

"Who shall choose the lucky ostrakon?" called Hendow.

"The slave!" cried a man.

"The slave! The slave!" cried others.

"Very well!" said Hendow.

I moaned.

Hendow approached me.

"Please, Master," I begged him.

But I saw him draw forth from his belt a half hood. This covers the head to the upper lip.

It was put over my head and drawn back, tightly, and buckled shut. I then heard a lock snapped through rings. It was locked on me, in place. I could not see under the device, at all. In this respect it differed from imperfect blindfolds and resembled the full slave hood. Similarly, although it is usually regarded as inferior to the full slave hood in its security, it tends to be more secure than many blindfolds, particularly makeshift ones, seized up from materials at hand. For example, unlike many blindfolds, it, and in this respect it is similar to the full slave hood, is not likely to become dislodged or loose, even if the girl is handled with great roughness. It does, however, of course, possess certain of the rich and attractive advantages of the blindfold, such as allowing its fair captive to speak, to use her tongue, to lick, to kiss, and so on.

"Please, Master," I begged. "Do not make me choose!"

"Do you question me?" he inquired.

"No, Master!" I said, hastily, I moaned. I must choose my own rapist.

I felt myself drawn to my feet, and, by the upper left arm,

pulled forward, half dragged, to the copper bowl. There I was knelt, and my hands were placed on the ostraka.

"Mix them further, slut," said Hendow.

Obediently, doubtless as the men watched intently, I stirred them about. I felt them in my hands. They had numbers on them, I knew.

"Dig about," said Hendow. "Sift through them. Pick some up, then let them fall through your fingers."

I obeyed.

"Now," said he, "choose one."

I lifted my head in the half hood to him, piteously, my lip trembling.

I heard nothing, no reprieve, no rescue. This was not such a world. Here I was a slave, ineradicably, and truly.

I held my head level, although I could see nothing. I thrust my hand into the ostraka, and closed my fingers on one. I lifted it before me. I felt someone, doubtless Hendow, pull it from my hand.

"One hundred and seventy-seven!" he called.

There were cries of good-natured protest, sounds of disappointment. "No!" cried more than one man.

"One hundred and seventy-seven," he repeated.

"There!" called Mirus. "There!"

Someone must have been getting up.

"Hold up the ostrakon!" called Mirus. "Let us all see it!"

"He has it, all right!" called a man, from somewhere out there in the front. There were groans of mock anguish in the house, and laughter, and applause.

"Come forward, Sir," invited Mirus. "Claim your prize."

"Take her well, for me!" called a fellow several yards away.

"Make her jump, for me!" laughed another, closer.

I sensed someone coming forward, others perhaps about him, slapping him about the shoulders and back.

There was applause.

"Here, Sir," said Mirus, at my side, "is your prize."

In the hood I could see nothing. I was frightened.

I then gasped, surprised. I felt myself being lifted to the shoulder of a man. He was very strong.

"Use the Ubar's alcove," said Mirus. "I will bring the attestation and ribbon."

I was helpless on his shoulder.

"Lucky sleen!" called a man.

The Ubar's alcove, I knew, was well fitted with a variety of chains and whips.

I felt myself being carried toward it.

"Make her squeak and yell!" called a man.

I was being carried as a slave is often carried, my head to the rear.

"There is only one who is first," called Hendow, "but we will draw forth fourteen more ostraka!"

There was a cheer.

I did not understand this. I was helpless on the man's shoulder.

"Then there will be a free round of paga for all!" he said.

This generosity was greeted with another cheer.

I felt the man step up, over the high threshold of the alcove. He then put me down on soft furs, on my back, within the alcove.

"Here is the paper, and the ribbon," said Mirus.

I heard the movement of paper. Then Mirus, I gathered, withdrew. I heard a paper being put to one side. I then heard the leather curtains of the alcove being drawn closed, and buckled shut. Within the alcove I supposed there would be some light, probably from the small tharlarion-oil lamp on its bracketed shelf, on the wall to the left, as one enters. I did not know, of course. In the hood, I could see nothing. I heard his garment being cast aside. I supposed the lamp would be lit, that there would be light for him. Men usually like to have some light in such a place, that in its soft glow they may see how beautiful are the slaves. Such alcoves, incidentally, are quite comfortable. They are not close, or stuffy. In them there is a subtle but efficient circulation of air. Air, for example, can enter at the threshold, in the vicinity of the curtain, rise, and exit through various inconspicuous vent holes, generally high in the walls. I wondered, if there were light, if I looked pleasing to him, lying on the furs. I gasped, as he knelt across my body. I had never had a man do this before. I could not move. I felt my hands pulled up and snapped into manacles, apart, at the sides of my head. His knees were on either side of my body. I pulled a little at the manacles and chains. I was chained! I felt terrified, and trapped, as indeed I was. I had been chained before, many times, of course, in my training. But this was not training! Then to my surprise he drew back from me, crouching then, or kneeling, I think, beside me. He was on my right. I shuddered. I had felt his body. I turned to my left side, away from him, as I could, and drew my knees up, as closely as I could, to my belly. I whimpered, as I understood that this, too, exposed me as a slave to him, but I did not know what to do! It seemed, suddenly, that all my training had fled from me, that it had gone from me, that I could remember nothing. I felt his hands take my ankles, one in each hand, and, by means of them, not gently, he turned me again to my back, and then flung apart my legs. I lay there then, in this attitude before him, helpless in the chains, and the darkness of the hood. He had not spoken to me, nor I to him. I did not realize this at the time but he would not do so either, nor would the others, unsuspected by me at this time, who would follow him this night. By custom my initial ravishings as a paga slave in Brundisium would be performed in anonymity. This custom is dictated by considerations similar to those involved in the hooding of mating slaves, considerations having to do with the preclusion of interpersonal complications. I heard a whip being removed from the wall. I lay there, trembling. I grasped the chains, above the manacles. I did not want to be lashed! But the whip was thrust to my lips. Eagerly, lifting my head, I licked and kissed the whip. I did not want it used on me. My ardor in this matter, and this explicit expression of my understanding of what I was, a slave, may, I suspect, have mollified him to some extent. For he then, delicately, gently, tested me. He grunted, surprised.

"Yes, Master," I said. "I am a virgin!"

He then seemed to have drawn back for a time, perhaps kneeling there, thinking. I do not think, now, he had believed that I was really a virgin, in spite of the attestation, and such, and I do not think either that my virginity had really been of great interest to him, whether or not it was actual. He had been angry, I now think, that I had been behaving in a timid, or virginal, fashion with him, perhaps to secure some gentleness of treatment, when I was not really a virgin at all. Perhaps mollified then to some extent by my placatory behavior in kissing the whip he had decided to take the time to make test of my virginity rather than simply and with terrible force utilizing me, moving aside whatever obstacle, if any, might have attempted to impede the progression of his mastery.

"Master?" I asked.

To my surprise, then, I felt a shackle put on my left ankle. He then removed the manacles which had been on my wrists. I heard the whip cast to the side.

"Master?" I asked. I knelt, rubbing my wrists.

He then, apparently crouching near me, took me with extreme gentleness into his arms. I began to tremble. I felt his lips at the left side of my neck, above the steel collar locked there. "I am afraid, Master," I whispered.

He soothed me with a kiss on the shoulder. I was grateful, but, too, I could feel the heat of his breath there, it making me uneasy, and disturbing me, and I could sense the strength of his arms.

"Oh, master," I sobbed. "Master!"

One of his hands was behind my back. With the other hand he indicated I should rise up a bit, and I did so, and he placed that hand then behind my knees. He then, lifting me, and gently inclining me backwards, supporting me with his hand behind my back, lowered me gently to the furs. I then lay there, on my back, in the hood, before him.

I felt his hands lift up my right ankle, that which did not wear the shackle. I felt his lips on my ankle. His hands were very strong. I tried to pull back a bit, uneasily, but could not do so. He continued to hold my ankle, and kiss my leg. I moved my left ankle, in its shackle. I heard the tiny sounds of the links of the chain, running between the shackle and its ring. I pulled back my left ankle, and lifted it, frightened, alarmed by the sensations I was beginning to feel, and learned what limitations had been placed on its movements, imposed by the metal impedimenta whose prisoner it was. I could not leave the alcove of course, but I had been permitted slack, enough to kick, it seems, as in the throes of passion or, helplessly, as though to hold on for dear life, to clench my legs about a master's legs or, if I were pulled down, closer to the ring, his body. His touches and kisses were now disturbing me, but he was very gentle.

"Oh, Master!" I said.

The flesh behind the knee and above it is very sensitive.

He was patient.

"Thank you, Master," I said, gratefully.

Over the next quarter of an hour or so he also addressed his attentions to my other leg, but desisted in his ministrations when he had come midway up the interior of my thighs.

"Master!" I breathed.

Then he was kissing my hands, their backs, and kissing and licking in the palms, and then moving up the interiors of the wrists, and forearms. In another quarter of an hour or so, he had come again to my neck, near the collar, where he had first kissed me, and then, slowly, kissed my shoulders. I lay there, frightened, wanting to respond. I senses his lips near mine, by the feel of his breath. I lifted my head a little, and kissed him, timidly, gratefully. Then I felt his head, and hair, below my chin. "Ohh," I said. Then he kissed, and licked, and caressed me about the sides, and back. "Ah," he said, appreciatively. I was not really responding to him, or at least in no overt way I was really aware of, but I think he did not really mind this, or, at the time, expect anything much different. I think he did find me beautiful. And I think he took pride in the simple handling of such a slave.

Then he was kissing me about my hips and belly, and then, much lower, above the midpoint of the interior of my thighs.

"Master," I said.

"Oh!" I said. "Oh!"

His hands, and his tongue, and his kisses, were unbelievable!

Suddenly I lifted my hips to him. "Master!" I begged. "Master!"

His large hands were on me, gripping me, holding me an inch or two above the furs. I felt his thumbs. They pressed deeply into me, at the sides of my belly, but did not hurt me. They only held me fixed in place. I could feel the strength of him. I could not even think of escaping that grip.

"Master!" I begged.

I knew then that I belonged in a collar, and so, too doubtless, did he.

"Oh!" he said, frightened. I was tense, waiting. "Oh," I said, softly, frightened.

He was so strong!

"Oh!" I said, softly.

He kissed me, gently, holding me.

"It's done," I whispered. "It's done!"

He kissed me again.

What a fool I am, I thought to myself, and what a fool he must think me. Of course, it has been done!

I had sensed the parting of that tissue, its giving way, but it had not hurt. I had expected it to hurt. It had not hurt!

"I am no longer special," I said. "I am now only another girl."

He laughed.

What a small thing it had been! There had been nothing to it! What an absurdity to be concerned over so small a thing, so trivial a thing, I thought. I knew that in some women, of course, the matter was not so simple. I was pleased, and relieved, accordingly, that in my case it had all happened so quickly, so simply, so painlessly.

He kissed me again.

I had been opened, I thought. I was now "red silk"!

I was still, of course, locked in his arms. I felt his power and surgency.

He then began to make use of me.

"Master!" I gasped.

Perhaps his patience was then at an end, or perhaps he felt he had waited long enough, or perhaps he found me, suddenly, too beautiful to resist, I did not know, but he then began, with apparently little regard for me, to content himself.

I clung to him, startled.

It may be, of course, that this was merely another kindness on his part, that I be now reminded of my status, that I wore a collar, that I was naught but a slave, I do not know.

"Yes, Master!" I whispered.

I suspect I was not the first girl he had opened. He realized, I think, as I did not, at that time, that at this time there would be severe limitations on my capacity to respond to him, limitations attendant on my opening, and on being a new girl, not yet finding herself the victim of helpless slave needs.

"Master!" I cried.

I clung to him. I jerked my legs. I felt the chain on my left ankle. What can we be but vessels of pleasure to such brutes, I thought. To be sure, the slave must sometimes expect to be used with complete unilaterality. This feature is attendant on her condition. She is, after all, only a slave. Most slaves, incidentally, welcome this, for they treasure their bondage, many of them more dearly than their life, and they know that without it, and such things, they cannot be true slaves. Even such a service, perhaps paradoxically, they find exciting and fulfilling. Too, after one has been a slave for a time, it is difficult to be touched by a man without becoming responsive, and extremely so. Thus a girl is often grateful for her master's touch, and weeps with pleasure in her usage, even when he is not concerned in the least with her. This is a part of her helplessness, and having been made the prisoner of her slave needs.

"Ah," he said, as though interested.

Could I actually be responding to him, this brute who had opened me in a Gorean tavern, this monster who had but a moment ago red-silked me!

"Oh, Master!" I whispered, startled.

Oh, he had been patient, he had been kind, I knew. He could have cuffed me and torn me open in an instant but he had not done so. I was grateful. But now what was he doing to me? What were the sorts of things I was beginning to feel? To be sure, as I would later understand, these were, in their depth, only incipient sensations, little more than the hints of sensations, but even so I did not know now, how to cope with them. Something here seemed to be different now from the simple, intimate, unbelievable, unspeakable deliciousness of his earlier attentions. Something within me that I now sensed, something deep in my belly but which seemed to radiate out through my whole body, now hinted obscurely of something different, of sensations and feelings, of yieldings and submissions such that I hastily attempted to drive even the thought of them from my mind.

"Ah!" he said again.

I could not help how my body had moved, or how it had gripped him!

We are the submitted and the conquered, I thought. Otherwise we cannot be ourselves!

I tried to push him away, sobbing. But he pressed me the more closely to him.

My hips moved.

He laughed.

I hated him!

"What are men going to do to me?" I asked. "What are they going to make me?"

He tapped with his finger on my collar. He put his hand on my left thigh. I realized, suddenly, that was where my brand was.

"I am already a slave," I sobbed, "totally a slave!"

He laughed, softly. I shuddered. I gathered I had not yet begun to learn my slavery.

Then he began again, having granted me this respite, to make use of me.

"Oh," I said, softly. "Oh!"

It is difficult to make clear the wholeness of this experience, even within its limitations, for as I now understand, and I am sure he understood at the time, it provided me with little more than an inchoate intimation of how I might be subdued and owned in the arms of men. But even so, even at that time, the experience was a startling, astonishing whole. That is something I think many men do not grasp, the wholeness of the sexual experience for the woman, its enhancement and deepening by the beautiful and intricate context, that it is not simply a matter of skillfull epidermic stimulations. If it were, for example, I would never have been drawn to the beauties of ethnic dance. Here, of course, in a Gorean alcove, and given our conditions, he free, I a collared slave, who must submit and obey, there was just such a totalistic context. Indeed, the situation of bondage itself is such a context.

"Oh!" I cried, softly. And then I could not believe, suddenly, how tightly I was held. How helpless we are! "Oh," I said, then, and for the first time felt the imperious casting forth within me, seeming to fill my helplessly held body, of a man's triumph. How precious suddenly seemed such stuff to me. We could not make it. We could get it only from men. I had little doubt that in the arms of such a man, had I not had "slave wine," I would have been impregnated. How could my body have resisted such floods of seed? But I knew I had little to fear, or hope for, in such matters. My breeding was not under my own will. It was under the will of masters. It would be controlled, and supervised, and regulated, as carefully as that of any other domestic animal. I needed not fear pregnancy until the matter had been decided otherwise by masters.

I clung to my use master. I did not want him to let me go, not yet.

Then I was afraid and angry. With what insolence, with what arrogance, he had cast his seed within me! And I must endure such things, as it pleased him! How he had held me, and then loosed himself within me! What arrogance, what insolence! He had not asked my permission. He had simply taken me, as a slave might be taken! Did he not know I was from Earth? Did he think I was only another Gorean girl? But I realized, then, that here I was perhaps even less than a Gorean girl, and, at best, only another slut in a collar.

"Please do not let me go, Master," I begged. "Hold me, please."

He then for a time kept me in his arms.

I was not displeased to be a woman.

It was what I wanted to be, if there were such men.

I clung to him. He kissed me. "Thank you, Master," I whispered. It was lonely and dark inside the hood, but his body was warm. In a way I was pleased to be hooded. Otherwise I might have fallen in love with him. As it was, and this was according to the will of masters, I could not relate to him as a woman to a man, but only as a woman to any man, or men.

I heard sounds in the tavern outside.

I knew I was now a red-silk paga slave. I heard slave bells outside, the sort sometimes fastened on slaves, on their ankles, their wrists, their collars. Perhaps those I heard were bound on Tupita's or Sita's well-turned ankle.

I clung yet more closely to him.

I was troubled.

He had made me begin to feel sensations, though doubtless I was now ready for them, which had alarmed me, sensations which spoke to me of female helplessnesses, and of female helplessnesses beyond them, and perhaps even beyond them, intriguing, fascinating helplessnesses, helplessnesses dimly sensed and terribly feared, yet somehow desperately longed for, of which I could scarcely conjecture.

He then thrust me away.

I lay there, in the darkness of the hood. I felt a coolness on my left thigh, like a thread. I had not noticed it before. I knew what it must be. I did not touch it.

I heard him dress.

He came back and, I think, crouched beside me. I felt his thumb rubbing on the interior of my left thigh. I then heard him pick up a sheet of paper and, seemingly, clean his thumb on the paper. He then rubbed his fingers on my thigh and lifted them gently to my mouth. "Yes, Master," I said. Obediently I licked his fingers, finding on them, sweet with sweat and oil, the dampness of my virgin blood. I thus, being granted the permission of my use master, tasted the fruits of my own first ravishing. The paper on which he had smeared blood was doubtless the attestation paper, the blood being presumably put at the bottom, in the place for it.

I sensed him stand.

I knelt before my use master. I put out my hand to him.

He had been kind to me. He had been patient with me. He had been gentle, even in the rupturing of that fragile tissue, my virgin's defense, that mockery of a wall made for a man's sundering. I sought his legs, and, finding them, groping, put down my head, kissing his feet. "Thank you, Master," I said.

I heard a slave girl crying out with pleasure outside. I shuddered. She must be being used so simply as having been flung across one of the tables, perhaps her hair and back in spilled paga.

I lifted my head, in its hood, to him. "Do not leave me," I begged. "Stay with me!"

He said nothing. This was in accordance, of course, with the custom in Brundisium, and in certain other cities, that in the light of which I had been given my first ravishing.

I then heard the snap of a slave whip outside the leather curtain, rather close to it, and a girl's cry of pain. "We are going to the alcove, slave!" I heard. "Yes, Master!" she cried. It was Sita. I heard her then, probably, judging by the jangling of slave bells, being conducted, stumbling, to an alcove. Probably he had her head at his hip, held by the hair. "Yes, Master!" she was weeping, her voice fading. "Yes, Master!"

"Please," I begged, frightened. "Please!"

He was silent.

"Please, Master," I wheedled.

He had been kind. It seemed possible to me then, that he might be weak, like the men of Earth, that perhaps I could manipulate him. What a fool I was! Did I not understand he was a Gorean male?

"Please, Master!" I begged, prettily.

His only answer was a cuff that threw me to one side, startled, where I crouched, disbelievingly, at the end of the chain. Then he took me and thrust me to my back on the furs and, as he had before, when we had first come to the alcove, manacled my hands at the sides of my head. He then removed the shackle from my left ankle.

My lip had been cut by his blow. I could taste blood there. "Master?" I asked.

Then I felt him, and I could not have stopped him, had I wished to do so, as I was chained, remove the white-silk ribbon from my collar. In a moment he had fastened something else there, in its place, doubtless another ribbon, doubtless the red-silk ribbon which had been given to him earlier by Mirus. He jerked it down on the collar, snugly.

He was then, I think, crouching near me. I pulled at the manacles. I was helpless. There was another trickle of blood on my leg. He put his thumb in this and scrawled a 'Kef' on my belly, the first letter of 'Kajira'. Then I felt the whip thrown beside me. "Master!" I wept. "Forgive me, if I have been displeasing, Master! Please, forgive me!" I recoiled, whimpering, from a kick, from the side of his foot. Then I heard him unbuckling the leather curtain, and leaving. I was helpless in the alcove. "Master!" I called after him, "Master!" I tried to rise but, by the chains, was prevented from doing so. I sank back, miserable, on the furs. He had been kind to me, and the first thing I had tried to do was to take advantage of him, to bend him to my will. I had then been cuffed. Then he had chained me. Too, he had thrown the whip against me, and had kicked me, showing me his contempt for me, a caught, would-be manipulative slave. Then he had left. I moaned. What a fool I had been! He was Gorean! Had I not understood that it was I who was the slave, and he the master? Perhaps the whip had been flung against me to remind me of my subjectability to it. Or perhaps he had flung it there that my master, or his man, might understand, when he came to unchain me, that at the least failure in my pleasingness I was due for a whipping. Yet he himself had not used it on me. That was perhaps yet another evidence of his kindness, or of his understanding and patience with me, his recognition that I was still naught but an ignorant and naïve novice with respect to the rigors of my bondage. Had I irritated him further, however, I do not doubt but what he himself would have used it on me. As it was, he had not been pleased when he had left me. If he were to use me again, in the future, I feared he would be merciless with me, treating me as the foolish and errant Earth woman I had been.

"Master?" I asked. I had heard the curtains being parted. "Master!" I said, elatedly. "Master?"

But then I felt my ankles flung apart.

"Oh!" I said, suddenly and smoothly penetrated, deeply.

I lay there, absolutely still.

This was not the same man!

I did not dare to move, so penetrated.

He made an animal noise.

"Master?" I asked.

I was very alive to him, so much so that I was unwilling to move.

"Dance," said Tupita, apparently from the opening of the alcove. There was laughter there, too, mostly that of men. The curtain I realized had not been drawn!

"He wants you to dance, slave," laughed Tupita. "You are a dancer. Go ahead, dance."

I moaned.

"Did you see the "Kef" on her belly?" asked Tupita.

"Yes," said a man.

"It belongs there," she said.

"Yes," agreed another fellow.

"There is now a red-silk ribbon on your collar, Doreen," said Tupita. "What is the meaning of that?"

"That I have been red-silked, Mistress," I said.

"Yes," said Tupita.

"Close the curtan, Mistress!" I begged.

"Why?" asked Tupita. "Are you modest?"

"No, Mistress," I sobbed. Slaves are not permitted modesty.

"You are now only a red-silk slut, Doreen," she said, "no different from the rest of us!"

"No, Mistress," I said.

"And do not forget it," she said.

"No, Mistress," I said.

There was laughter.

"Do you hear pounding?" asked Tupita.

"She has already been pounded," said a man.

There was laughter.

"Listen," said Tupita.

I could then hear pounding. It was far off, somewhere perhaps in the front of the tavern.

"Do you hear it?" she asked.

"Yes, Mistress," I said.

"Do you know what it is?" she asked.

"No, Mistress," I said.

"It is your attestation paper, together with your white ribbon, being nailed to the wall in the vestibule of the tavern," she said. "It is there now with mine, and Sita's, and those of some of the other girls."

I did not respond.

"But not with Inger's," said a fellow.

"No," laughed Tupita.

Several of the fellows laughed. Inger, from distant Skjern, had been taken by Torvaldslanders. She was voluptuous. Too, Torvaldslanders seldom deliver virgins to the slave markets.

"You are fortunate that I am not a man," laughed Tupita.

"Mistress?" I asked, puzzled.

"In the case of a man, the repetition of a command is commonly a cause for discipline."

"A command, Mistress?" I asked, frightened.

"Yes," she said.

I knew that Tupita was having her sport with me, but, too, I knew that she might beat me tomorrow, in the slave area. As first girl she had that privilege. I did not want her to whip me, or switch me, or have the other girls put my ankles over the low bar and tie them there, and then have her spank the soles of my bare feet with the springy, flat board. It is very painful, and it is hard to walk after it.

"What command?" I asked, frightened.

" 'Dance,' " laughed Tupita.

"Mistress, I am chained!" I said. "I am held!"

"Dance," said a man, from the entryway of the alcove.

Immediately I did what I could.

There was laughter from the entryway, and a grunt of pleasure from him in whose arms I lay slave captive.

I had been commanded by a man. I obeyed immediately, or did my best to obey. If a command needs to be repeated, as the saying goes, the girl needs to be punished. If the girl thinks, however, that the command may have been, say, an inadvertence, or mistake, or that the master might relent, or something along these lines, she might, say, beg or inquire. She is reassured of the intent and seriousness of the command if, for example, she is asked if the command need be repeated, which eventuality she will presumably be anxious to avoid. If she has, sincerely, and not as a girl's trick, not understood the command, or has not heard it, or fears she may not have heard it correctly, she may also inquire into the matter, of course, and normally without penalty. In such cases the repetition of a command is not regarded as cause for discipline. A girl is seldom punished for trying to be pleasing, at least at first. If her efforts continue to fail, however, that is a different matter. The whip is an absolutely marvelous instructional device for improving female conduct.

I had not even wanted to move, him so within me!

But I was a slave. I must obey.

"You wriggle well, Doreen," called Tupita.

I cried out with misery.

"Come, see the slave dance!" called a man from the entryway.

"Do not stop, slut," warned Tupita.

I moaned.

I had not even wanted to move, him so within me! But now, choicelessly, I moved. He was mostly quiet within me. It was I, the slave, who must move! I twisted and writhed. I then became aware, to my horror, that I was being forced to arouse myself upon him.

I whimpered in protest.

"Come, look," called a fellow. "She is getting hot!"

I sensed men crowding about the entryway.

"No!" I sobbed. I was a woman of Earth. I must remain frigid! I must not be "hot"! But then I realized I was no longer a woman of Earth. I was now only a Gorean slave.

"Please him," said Tupita.

"Yes, Mistress!" I sobbed. "Yes, Mistress!"

"Ai!" growled the brute who held me like chains.

The techniques of ethnic dance, as is perhaps no well-kept secret, because of the movements of the hips, the control of the muscles of the abdomen, and such, have delicious applications in the making of love. It is no wonder that this form of dance, for centuries, was commanded by emirs, pashas and caliphs of their concubines and slaves. Too, of course, it is initially arousing to the woman, for she understands that she is dressed as a slave, is displayed as a slave and must dance as a slave. And later, of course, if she is truly a slave, she must satisfy, and with dividends, the passions she has aroused in her dance. If a woman could be a dream of pleasure to men, let her learn this form of dance.

"Ai, Ai!" said the fellow.

I then began to feel incredible sensations, sensations I did not fully understand.

But then he gripped my hips so I could scarcely move, and pulled me tight to him, and was eager, surgent and eruptive within me! Then he withdrew, with something like a snarl and a smacking of his lips. I feared I had been bruised. "Master?" I asked. Would he leave me, so soon?

"I am next!" said a fellow.

I then again felt my ankles flung apart. I heard Tupita laughing.

"Oh!" I said, forcibly entered.

"Dance," called Tupita.

I recalled, suddenly, what I had heard, from back on the floor, behind us, when I was being carried on the shoulder of my first use master to the alcove, that fourteen more ostraka would be chosen!

"Dance!" laughed Tupita.

Again I danced.

It must have been near morning. I lay alone now in the alcove, now on my belly, my hands manacled apart, at the sides of my head. One of the men, earlier, when I was on my back, had put me in left-ankle shackle, had freed me of the manacles, had tied my hands behind my back, and had then had me please him, astride him. He had then, afterwards, left me lying on my side in the alcove. The next fellow had freed my hands of the thongs, put me on my stomach, and chained my wrists apart, at the sides of my head, much as I had been before, for much of the evening, but now turned, now on my stomach, and had then freed me of the ankle shackle.

I had lost count of the men, but there had doubtless been, counting my first use master, the full fifteen who had purchased winning ostraka.

It was quiet outside in the tavern.

I did not remember if the curtain had been drawn shut by my last use visitor, when he had left, or if he had left it open.

I lay there alone, on my belly, chained.

The former Doreen Williamson's virginity had been raffled off. And so, too, had her first uses. I supposed that Teibar, who had been my capture master, who had caught me on Earth, and brought me here to be a slave, would have found that amusing, his "modern woman" being taught her sex on Gor.

I rubbed my belly a little on the furs. I held the chains above the manacles closed about my wrists.

Yes, I thought, I had been taught something about my sex tonight.

I supposed I stank of the uses of men.

Outside, near the front of the tavern, indeed, in its vestibule, I gathered, nailed to a wall there, with other such objects, was my attestation paper, with its smear of my virginal blood upon it, and the white ribbon which had been on my collar.

There was now another ribbon, I gathered, tied on my collar, one of red silk.

I was now, at any rate, "red silk."

I wondered what the men who had worked at the library would have thought. I wondered if they, too, would have crawled to me, and put me to their purposes.

It would be their right, of course. I was now a slave.

I lay there, troubled.

I wanted to cope with my feelings. I was confused. The first fellow had been, on the whole, very gentle and understanding with me. I thought I would always be grateful to him for that. He could have been quite otherwise, for I was only a collar-slut whose virginity he had won in a raffle. After he had removed my virginity he had treated me with much less courtesy and patience. In his arms, after my virginity had been taken, I had had the first genuine intimations of what it might be to be a slave in the arms of a man. In the arms of the second fellow I had begun to feel incredible sensations but he had then, eager in his own pleasures, seized me helplessly to him, and, as I was held, startled, the helpless vessel of his pleasure, used me, and left. In such a usage, and public as it was, before Tupita, and others, I was well reminded that there was a steel collar on my neck. But I was then, too, to my transitory shame, until I recalled I was a slave, and such feelings were required of me, more than ready for the next man, and then, more eagerly than I perhaps now cared to recall, I "danced" for him. Helpless, and in chains, hooded, almost alone with my sensations, I was discovering my sexuality, the root sexuality of the used female. To be sure, as I would later discover, I was only doing something like beginning to respond to them. When the fourth man had entered the alcove, and he seemed to be just standing there, not yet touching me, I had actually lifted my belly to him, begging. He had laughed. I had then sunk back in a paroxysm of humiliation and embarrassment on the furs, overcome with shame, from my grotesque anti-sexual Earth conditioning, in which female merit is regarded as being threatened or diminished by any sign of truly deep sexual needs, or any evidence of intense, genuine interest in the opposite sex. But if I wanted their touch why should I not ask for it, or beg for it? As a slave what else could I do? Too, even if my needs and my interests, and the incredible depth and intensity of my desires proved that I was "worthless" and without "merit," I did not care! Of course I was worthless, though, to be sure, men would pay hard cash for me! I was worthless because I was only a property! I was worthless because I was bond! I was worthless because I was the sort of woman who could be put upon a slave block and be sold! I was worthless because I was only an owned animal! Of course I did not have "merit"! I was beyond "worth" and "merit," of those sorts. I was only a slave! But thus I could be as free, and piteous, and begging, and lewd, and loving, and sexual as I wished! I had nothing to conceal, nothing to keep secret. I belonged to my master, all of me, my thoughts, my love, my body, everything I was and could be! I lay there for a moment moaning in shame. But then he had crouched near me and, with a few deft, unbelievable touches, had me, in spite of myself, leaping and squirming before him. Then I realized he had laughed at me not so much to humiliate me, though perhaps he had enjoyed doing so, as I was an Earth woman, but because he was amused at my obvious readiness, unusual in so new a slave. I gathered that this vitality, or responsiveness, coming from so new a branded slut, must be surprising. Then he entered me, and I think I pleased him.

I lay there, trying to cope with my feelings.

To some extent, doubtless, the conditioning to which I had been subjected on Earth was attempting to war with the liberties of my bondage. Indeed, some women try to carry the frigidities of their freedom into their bondage, but these are soon whipped out of them. They are swiftly taught that they are now a different sort of woman. Then, choicelessly, gratefully, they yield eagerly to their slavery. You see, some of the "liberties of bondage" are also, in a sense, "necessities of bondage." For example, not only is a woman free then to open herself fully to the ravishings of masters, to be participatory, to feel as deeply, and profoundly and excitingly as she can, to be as responsive and orgasmic as possible, but she *must* do so. Such things are commanded of her. Similarly the authenticity of her responses can be recognized and tested. And failure to obey, and be pleasing, can be cause not only for grievous punishment, but death. Accordingly, my Earth conditioning could do little more now than attempt to war with my needs and urges. In each hour on Gor it seemed to be becoming less and less effective. My needs, and my reality, were now revealing its lack of soundness, its historical eccentricity, indexed to outmoded ideologies and conditions, its idiosyncrasy, its absurdity, making it obsolete, and overthrowing it. In a natural world it was, without its constant reinforcements, crumbling. Too, as a slave, I must, whether I wished to or not, ignore it. To be sure, I think, in the final analysis, it was being primarily undermined by so simple and profound a thing as my own womanhood. Its poverty, vacuity and falsity I think I had recognized long ago, even on Earth.

I lay there on the furs, wondering about my feelings and responses. I wondered almost who the girl was, who lay there. She seemed very different from the former Doreen Williamson, who had worked in the library, so long ago, now, it seemed. To be sure, she still had the name 'Doreen', but that now was her only name, and she had it only as a slave name, a name given to her as an animal is given a name, a name put on her, like a collar, by the will of a master, a name to which she must then, like any other named animal, respond, and in all ways.

I was still hooded.

I lay there, and thought about the feelings I had experienced. Putting aside occasional episodes of chagrin or shame, understandably contingent on my Earth conditioning, as I was faced with various indisputable evidences of my vitality and responsiveness, I had found myself subjected to an astonishing variety of mixed emotions and feelings. Sometimes I had been confused by the unfamiliarity of these feelings, and sometimes delighted, and intrigued. Too, sometimes I had felt a desperate longing for them to continue, and had been eager for them, and others, some charming, and subtle, and some almost overpowering, making me feel weak, and held, to surface in me, like wonders, some bursting up, some rising slowly, in my depths. Too, sometimes I had felt genuine fear, as I seemed to sense, far off, feelings and emotions so incredible and overwhelming that I knew I would be helpless in their grasp, feelings that would be as commanding and irresistible to me as the movements of the earth and the tides of the sea. In short, I was on the brink of learning my femaleness. To be sure, nothing had been done to me at that time that would make me scream my submission, and beg helplessly with all the tears and beauty in my body for more. Too, at that time, I had not realized something of great importance, namely, how my body and nervous system could change under its uses, how my helplessness and needs could deepen, increase and intensify, how they could grow upon me and make me their prisoner. Although I was now almost ready, as Ina had put it, shocking me at the time, "to beg and scratch for it," I still had no clear idea as to the extent to which my belly and body could be gripped by "slave need." I still had no clear understanding as to how it was that a girl could bruise herself against the bars of her cage, trying to touch a guard, or crawl naked on her belly to a hated master, if only to feel the blow of his hand or foot. In short, though I had come a thousand miles from the naive girl in the library, I still had no understanding, really, of slave sex. I had not yet experienced even a small slave orgasm. But in the context of these reflections, seemingly focused primarily on simple feelings and sensations, let me reemphasize the wholeness of the context. It is in the slave's life as a whole that these things, so overwhelmingly, find their place. The life of the slave is an entire modality of being, and this modality of being enhances the feelings and sensations just as, in turn, the feelings and sensations enhance and enrich the modality of being. The life of the female slave is a consistent, totalistic and indissoluble whole.

I heard someone part the curtains.

I was frightened.

Someone was there.

I pressed down into the furs, on my belly. Then, it frightening me, and embarrassing me at the time, I felt an involuntary movement, the subtle lifting, just a tiny bit, of my behind, in the furs. Then, swiftly I lay even lower, more frightened, more closely, in the furs. I had once at a zoo, I recalled, seen a female animal, a female baboon, actually, frightened at the stalking, menacing, meaningful approach of a stern, dominant male, turn about and timidly offer herself to him. I had seen the same sort of behavior among chimpanzees. It is a form of placatory, female-submission behavior. It is familiar to ethologists. It is common among primates. I realized, reddening, that I had, in my fear, engaged in exactly such behavior.

A man knelt or crouched near me. He felt my flanks. He had very strong hands. Again my body lifted itself, but this time, not so much in fear as in response to his touch.

"Interesting," said Hendow, my master.

I whimpered and tried to hide lower in the furs.

"Do not be upset, slave," he said. "It is for just such things that I bought you."

I felt the key thrust into the locks on the manacles, and they were removed from me. I was then turned to my back. The only bond I wore now was the half hood.

"Are you sore?" he asked.

"A little," I said.

"Inside," he said.

"A little," I said.

My body, otherwise, though I would not feel it so much for a few hours, would be stiff here and there, and sore in places. I would discover, too, I had some bruises. Some of the men had treated me with great roughness. That was permissible. I was a slave.

I felt a chain belt put about my waist and padlocked shut at my navel. At the back of the belt, attached to it, was a pair of light manacles of the sort suitable for females, which I would learn are called "slave bracelets."

"Master?" I asked.

I did not understand why I was being braceleted, now.

"You will wear these at night," he said, "for three nights."

"Yes, Master," I said.

"You will not be put out on the floor again," he said, "for three days."

"Thank you, Master," I said. I supposed that was what I should be saying.

"That will give you a chance to heal, if you need it, and, too, it will give you a chance to gather your thoughts together and to reflect upon your experiences."

"Yes, Master," I said, puzzled.

"You will spend your time during the day," he said, "as before, in the kitchen."

"Yes, Master," I said, apprehensively.

"Do not be afraid," he said. "You will be in the iron belt."

"Now?" I asked. I was now, after all, red silk.

"Yes," he said.

"Yes, Master," I said.

"Too," he said, "in the iron belt, and braceleted at night, and working in the kitchen, you will have a chance to simmer."

"To simmer, Master?" I asked.

"Yes," he said.

I did not understand him.

Then he picked me up, very gently, and carried me downstairs, to the basement, and my kennel. There, before my kennel, he put me in the iron belt. He then removed my hood. It seemed light there, even in the dimness of the basement. I saw that there was now a whole blanket, not just a part of one, in my kennel.

"Thank you for the blanket, Master," I said.

"Crawl into the kennel," he said. "And lie down."

I did so, and he covered me with the blanket, rather gently, I thought. "Good night, Doreen," he said.

"Good night, Master," I said.

He then closed and locked the kennel door. I watched him through the bars as he went across the room, and blew out the small tharlarion-oil lamp there. He then went upstairs. Again I wore an iron belt. I did not understand why until I had slept and, well before dawn, awakened in the darkness. I squirmed. Then I pulled at the bracelets, futilely. I realized then, suddenly, feeling helpless, I would have to wait three days for a man's touch.

12 / The Floor

I knelt at the feet of the handsome fellow and kissed and licked about his ankles. I looked up at him. He was large and strong. "I would be pleased," I whispered, "if master would see fit to take me to an alcove."

"I am here," said Tupita, squirming on her knees, nearby. "Go away!"

He looked down at me.

"My use is included already, in the price of master's drink," I said. "I cost nothing more."

"Go away," said Tupita.

"You are Doreen, who dances, aren't you?" he said.

"Yes, Master," I said.

"Go away!" said Tupita.

"Be silent," said the man to her.

"Yes, Master," she said. "Forgive me, Master."

"But you do not dance tonight?" he asked.

"No, Master," I said. "Tonight I am only a paga slave."

The red-silk ribbon was no longer on my collar. The girl wears it for only a week.

"I have seen you dance," he said. "You are quite good."

"Thank you, Master," I said.

"Quite good, indeed," he mused.

"Let me dance for you, alone, in the alcove," I whispered.

He smiled. I saw that this thought intrigued him, to have a private performance by a dancing slave, that she would dance her beauty for him alone.

"Please, Master," I begged.

"You want to go to the alcove, don't you?" he asked.

"Yes, Master," I said.

"And you would dance and beg for it?" he asked.

"I love to dance, Master," I said, "but even if I did not, yes, I would dance and beg for it!"

"Are you any good at bringing the whip to a man in your teeth?" he asked.

"Yes, Master," I said.

"But are you not a woman of Earth " he asked.

"Once I was a woman of Earth," I said. "Now I am only a Gorean slave."

"In the baths," he said, "I have seen the names of slaves and taverns scrawled on the walls."

"Oh?" I said, uneasily.

"And sometimes they are ranked in order of someone's opinion as to their desirability," he said.

"I see," I said.

"May I speak, Master?" asked Tupita, with an almost catlike movement of her body. I thought I must learn to do that.

"Yes," he said.

"Were slaves in the tavern of Hendow so ranked?" she asked.

"Yes," he smiled.

"And did the name of Tupita not head the list?" she asked, glancing meaningfully at me.

"No," he said.

"Who was first?" she asked.

"Inger," he said.

"My name then was second," she said.

"No," said he, "it was third."

"And who was second?" she asked, angrily.

"Doreen," he smiled.

"The fellow who wrote the names up was surely mistaken," she said, angrily.

"I can give you my opinion on that," he said, "at some later date. I have used you before. You're quite good. Even excellent. There is no doubt about it. But tonight I shall try something different. I shall try the dancer, Doreen."

"Thank you, Master!" I breathed, happily. Tonight I had searched hard for a use master. It was the middle of the week, when business is slower. Many men receive their hiring fees at the end of the week. Too, tonight, it seemed that many of the men had come to the tavern only to drink and talk, and some, too, near the walls, where it was quieter, to play kaissa, a Gorean board game. I did not care for kaissa. Men grew so absorbed in it, it seemed, that they could be totally oblivious even of a beautiful slave whimpering on her belly near them. Because of kaissa we had to sometimes wait hours for attentions! Too, I had come to the floor late, Tupita having assigned me cleaning duties in the slave area. This had happened before.

"To be sure, Tupita," he said, giving her head a shake, "such estimations are often quite subjective. It is wise not to take them seriously. The woman who is one's man pudding may, for one reason or another, having sometimes little to do with her, be only another man's porridge."

This I had learned was true. Slaves, and even some whom I regarded as objectively quite beautiful, even marvelous, were sometimes rated very differently by different men. Why, for example, does one man bid gold for a girl that another man would not buy with copper? Perhaps because one man sees that the girl is worth gold, and the other does not. Who knows?

"But I have been waiting for you this evening!" said Tupita.

"Belly to another tonight," he said, "slave."

"Yes, Master," she said, angrily, and rose up, and, with an angry look at me, hurried away, in a jangle of bells.

I looked up at him, gratefully. He was very strong and handsome, and I was a slave. I wanted his touch.

"She is angry," he said, looking after Tupita.

"Yes, Master," I said.

"Shall I call her back to be whipped?" he asked.

"Please, no, Master," I said. "It is only that she desired you."

"She is first girl, is she not?" he asked.

"Yes, Master," I said.

"Are you not afraid?" he asked.

I shrugged. "Many times," I said, "particularly in my first weeks here, she took men from me."

He looked down at me. "I do not think she can do that so easily any more," he said.

I looked down. "Perhaps not, Master," I said. "I do not know." To be sure, this was not the first man I had taken from Tupita. Normally, however, to be perfectly honest, she still took them from me. It is not unknown, of course, for slaves to compete for the attentions of masters.

"Are you not afraid?" he asked.

"No," I said, "not really. If she hurts me too much, or makes it so I cannot dance, or go out on the floor, our master would not be pleased."

"I see," he said.

Too, though I did not think it would have been appropriate to say so, I thought that I was becoming more popular with the customers. Too, I knew I was popular with several of my master's men, such as Mirus, and I thought, too, sometimes, that even my master might like me, a little. That, of course, frightened me, for he was large, and gross and loathsome. These things, I thought, would give Tupita at least a bit of pause when she might be tempted to use the switch or bastinado on me.

"But you must be apprehensive," he said. "She is first girl."

"Yes, Master," I said. "I am a little afraid."

"Why then have you approached me?" he asked. "Why have you undertaken these risks? Why have you rendered obeisance? Why have you rendered slave ministrations, with your lips and tongue, to my feet and ankles? Why have you knelt here? Why do you look up at me, as you do? Why do you tremble?"

"Because I want your touch," I said.

He looked down at me.

"I cannot help myself," I said.

"Why?" he asked.

"Because I am a woman, and a slave," I whispered.

"Precede me to the alcove," he said.

"Yes, Master," I said eagerly, gratefully. I then rose up and preceded him to the alcove, hurrying, the slave bells jangling on my ankle.

13 / The Passageway; Intrigues

I hurried back, elatedly, through the beaded curtain, fleeing, laughing, from the dancing floor. I had scrambled on my knees for the coins flung to the floor, seizing them, thrusting them hastily, so many of them, with one hand, into the lifted, bunched portion, held by my other hand, of the dancing skirt, a lovely, swirling skirt, scarlet, open on the right, of diaphanous dancing silk. I had been permitted a scarlet halter of the same material. My midriff, like my right thigh, was bared. The skirt was low on my hips. I wore a double belt of threaded, jangling coins, one strand high, one low, as with the corded belt of metal pieces I had worn in my virgin dance, weeks ago. I also wore a triple necklace of coins, together with necklaces of slave beads, of both glass and wood. These coins, all of them, would be counted by Mirus when I disrobed. On my left ankle were bound slave bells. My right ankle wore several anklets. I was barefoot. On my wrists were bracelets. On my upper left arm was a coiled armlet. A ruby, held by a chain, was at my forehead. Wound in and about my hair were strands of pearls.

"It is a good house tonight," said Mirus, who was waiting for me.

"Yes, Master!" I said, happily. I could hear the men still calling out and pounding at their shoulders with appreciation. I looked at Mirus. Should I hurry back through the curtain?

"No," said he. "Stay here."

"Yes, Master," I said.

"Here," he said, holding open the sack. I emptied the coins from the dancing silk into the sack, and smoothed the skirt.

"You dance well," he said.

"Thank you, Master!" I said, happily. On Earth I had never dreamed that I would dance as a slave before masters.

"You have done much for the tavern of Hendow," he said.

"I am pleased, if I have been found pleasing," I said. I gave the ruby on its chain, from my forehead, to Mirus. He put it in his wallet. I then began to unwind the strands of pearls from my hair.

"Receipts are up twenty percent from a month ago," he said.

"I am pleased," I said. I handed the pearls to Mirus, who put them, as he had the chain and ruby, in his wallet.

"You are finding yourself now as a dancer," he said.

"I have been in the arms of men," I laughed, "men such as you, Master, who know how to turn a girl into a woman, and a woman into a slave."

"I think," he said, "you may be one of the finest dancers in Brundisium."

This startled me.

"You are really quite good," he said.

"Thank you, Master," I said.

"Hendow's investment in you was a sound one," he said. "You are paying off well for him."

"I am pleased to hear that," I said. I was also relieved to hear it. I did not know what would have been done to me, had it been otherwise. I supposed I might have been muchly whipped.

"But you still have many things to learn," he said.

"It is my hope that master will consent to teach me some of them," I said.

"Sassy she-tarsk," he said.

I laughed, but I was not altogether joking. Mirus was one of those men of a sort to whom, when my needs were enough on me, I could crawl, pleading. And he knew that, the brute. Certainly I had crawled to him enough! And, when my needs were enough upon me, of course, I was ready to crawl to any man, pleading, perhaps even to one of Earth, but they, probably, to my frustration, disappointment, and agony, would not know what to do with a slave. I was pleased to be on Gor, where men well understood the handling of imbonded females. I lifted the necklaces from my neck. I gave that of coins to Mirus, which he put on top of the coins in the sack, and I put the others in the box which was on the floor, just within the curtain.

"You are coming along well in your slavery, Doreen," he said.

"Thank you, Master," I said. I looked at him. He made me feel hot between the thighs. I was only a slave.

"You were beautiful tonight, Doreen," said Ina, hurrying by in slave bells.

"Thank you," I said.

Too, Ina wore a snatch of diaphanous yellow silk. The girls in Hendow's tavern now often went silked on the floor, not naked, as before. "We are becoming quite fashionable," had said Sita, reaching eagerly for her tiny bit of silk. Tupita had, however, only cast me a glance of hatred. To be sure, she did not refuse her own bit of silk. In most paga taverns, of course, the girls are silked. Usually it is only in the meanest, the cheapest and lowest of taverns that the girls serve naked, much as would the females of a conquered city at the victory feast of their conquerors, now, or soon to be, their masters. Slave silk, and certainly that sort which is commonly worn in paga taverns and upon occasion in brothels, when the girls are permitted clothing there, is generally diaphanous. It leaves little doubt as to the beauty of the slave. Some girls claim they would rather be naked, claiming that such silk makes them "more naked than naked," but most girls, and I think, even those, too, who speak in such a way, are grateful for even the wisp of gossamer shielding it provides against the imperious appraisals of masters, even though it must be pulled away or discarded instantly at a man's whim. Too, I think most girls know that they are very beautiful in such silk, and this, I suspect, is why they love it, and treasure it so. Free women, on Gor, it seems, are frightened even to look upon such material, apparently finding it scandalously offensive, or somehow profoundly disturbing to them, let alone let it touch their body. Some free women, captured, when such stuff is thrown to them, profess to prefer death to putting it on, but when this choice is that which is actually offered to them they put it on quickly enough. Too, such women, it is said, make excellent slaves. But Goreans believe, of course, that any woman, properly handled, becomes an excellent slave. I think this may be true. It is true, at any rate, in my case. There are a large number of ways in which slave silk is worn. It can be worn, for example, on the shoulder or off the shoulder, with high necklines or plunging necklines, in open or closed garments, tightly or flowingly, and in various lengths. Sometimes it is put on the girl only in halters and G-strings, or mere G-strings. Sometimes it is done, too, in strips wound about her body. The tying of slave girdles, with such silk, and otherwise, to emphasize the girl's figure and make clear her bondage, is an art in itself. Often, too, and as usually in paga taverns, it is worn in brief tunics. Most of these are partable or wraparound tunics. Such may be removed gracefully. Some tunics, however, like some regular slave tunics, have a disrobing loop, usually at the left shoulder, where it may easily be reached by both a right-handed master and a right-handed slave. A tug on the disrobing loop drops the tunic to the girl's ankles, also gracefully.

I sat down on the tiles there within the hall, near the beaded curtain, at the feet of Mirus, easily, as a slave girl, thinking nothing of it, sits at the feet of a man, and slipped the anklets from my right ankles, putting them in the box to my left.

Mirus was looking down at me, and I glanced up at him, and then looked down again, shyly.

I decided to pretend not to notice how he was looking at me.

I felt briefly like a pet at his feet, and then I supposed that in a sense I was a pet, and that all we girls were, at least in a sense, pets, slave pets.

But we were a thousand times more than mere pets, we were slaves, total slaves.

I put my bracelets in the box, and then the armlet from my upper left arm.

I tried to undo the thong on the bells on my left ankle. The knots were tight, drawn by a man's hand. I fought with them. My fingers were small and weak.

"Let me help you," said Mirus, and crouched down, near me. He had put the bells on me. It is often men who put slave bells on their girls. Such bells are indicative of bondage. Accordingly I suppose it makes sense that they might enjoy putting them on us, like brands and collars. Some men even dress their girls, and, always, the girl's choices of such things as garb, cosmetics, perfume, jewelry, and such, and, indeed, her entire ensemble, are subject to the master's approval. Indeed, most often, whether in only a simple tunic, before she hurries forth to shop, or in luscious slave silk and exciting adornments, before she is to welcome and serve her master's guests, displaying herself as one of his treasures, she is expected to present herself before him, for his inspection. She is owned.

He held my ankle. His hands were very strong. I put down my head, so that he might not see my eyes.

He then, in a moment or two, had the thong loose, and, its loops unwound, five of them, dropped it, with its strung bells, in the box.

But his hands then were on my ankles.

I looked at him.

"Are you naked beneath the silk?" he asked.

"Yes, Master," I smiled. He knew that. Indeed, as the silk was diaphanous, he could, for most practical purposes, see that.

"Slave naked?" he asked.

"Yes, Master," I said. This, somehow, is a far more disturbing, or meaningful, admission than the first. Somehow the nakedness of a slave seems far more naked than the nakedness of a free woman. Doubtless this has to do with her being a property, and owned. Too, 'slave naked' suggests being naked naked, so to speak, being helplessly naked, as a slave is helplessly naked. It has, sometimes, too, the connotation of being vulnerably, and arousably, naked, as a slave is helplessly, vulnerably, and arousably naked.

He looked at me.

"Yes, Master," I whispered. "Beneath the silk that is the way I am naked, slave naked."

I felt slave arousal. I could not help myself. Long ago, now, weeks ago, men had lit slave fires in my belly.

I was aroused, and as a slave.

To be sure, I had no understanding, at that time, of what could become the fuller impact of these things. I was still, at that time, in effect, a new slave.

Then he removed his hands from my ankles.

"Master?" I asked.

"Stand," he said. We both stood. "Belt," he said.

I reached behind me to undo the double belt of coins, with its two loops, one high one low. The coins on the belt, as well as those on the necklace, would be counted by Mirus.

"You look well with your hands behind your back," he said.

I looked up.

"Your hands are now bound behind your back," he said.

"Yes, Master," I said. I must now keep my hands or wrists in contact with one another, and behind my back. I was now "bound by the master's will." I could not separate my hands or wrists from one another now without permission. There are many ways, of course, of "binding by the master's will." The behind-the-back position is one of the simplest and loveliest. This exposes the girl, frames the beauty of her breasts and makes her helpless. That the bond is a "will bond," too, makes clear to her the power of the master over her. Another common bond of this sort is when the girl must kneel, grasping her ankles. Another is when she is forced to sit and reach forward between her legs, passing the right arm from inside the right thigh to outside and beneath the right calf, to grasp the right ankle from the outside, and the left arm from inside the left thigh to outside and beneath the left calf, to grasp the left ankle in the same way. In this position she is helpless and cannot rise. Too, after a time, it becomes apparent to her that she also cannot close her legs. A girl may be kept in such bonds for hours. Too, of course, she may be tied in such positions. There are also, of course, different ways of decreeing such bonds. For example, with the behind-the-back-hands-tied bond in which I had been placed I could have been informed, but had not been, that my shoulders were pulled tightly back, which, of course, forces the breasts forward for the pleasure, or attentions, of the master.

"I think I shall find it difficult to remove the belt," I smiled, "bound as I am."

He stood close to me, and put his arms about me. "I shall remove it," he said.

Tupita came then through the beaded curtain. She glanced at me. She was not pleased to see me in the arms of Mirus, who was a desirable male, and first among my master's men. She looked at me in hatred. She did not think twice about the position of my hands. She could see I had been "bound by the master's will." It could have been done as easily to her, at a word.

She came close to Mirus. She licked at his shoulder. "Will you call for me tonight?" she asked.

"No," he said. "Return to the floor."

"Yes, Master," she said, and, with a look of fury, cast at me, slipped back through the curtain.

"You are good for Tupita," he told me. "Because of you she is becoming more attentive and more desperate to please."

"I am attentive and desperate to please," I said.

"Yes," he said, "but not because of her."

"No, Master," I said.

"Because you are a slave," he said.

"Yes, Master," I said. How I loved his arms about me!

"You are a splendid natural slave," he said.

"I knew it even on Earth," I whispered to him. Indeed, I had even wondered, strangely, at times, I supposed, if I might not have been a slave in former lives, in other eras, perhaps in the Ancient World or in the Medieval Middle East, in times more in tune with the true natures of human beings, natures as they really were, in themselves, and not as they might be when denied, thwarted, twisted and perverted by ideological insanities. And, at times, recollecting, or seeming to recollect, such times and places, and their naturalness, and rightness, and their fulfillments and ecstasies, I, lonely and yearning, seemingly an exile in the sexual deserts of my own world and time, had wept. But regardless of the truth or falsity of such things, and regardless of the explanations or reasons for the things which lay so deep within me, whether they were recollective or merely the irrepressible fruits of genetic truths, so anomalous in my own time, so uncharacteristic of everything I had been taught, I had known they had lain within me. That was incontrovertible. I knew that I, who was then Doreen Williamson, had been born for the collar. I had never expected then, however, to wear it. I had never even suspected there was such a world as Gor where, as my capture master, Teibar, had put it, "women such as I were bought and sold."

"Of course," he said.

"Yes, Master," I said.

"What was your master like on Earth?" he asked.

"I did not have a master on Earth," I said.

"You, a woman like you, so obviously a natural slave, did not have a master?" he asked, interested.

"No, Master," I said.

"You were not a legal slave on Earth?" he asked.

"No, Master," I smiled. "I did not become a legal slave until I was brought to Gor."

"Surely the men of Earth are somewhat imperceptive," he said.

"Some of them, perhaps, Master," I smiled.

"Here," he said, "we have made good their oversight."

"That is true," I smiled.

He looked down, into my eyes. "You should have been a legal slave on Earth," he said.

"Yes, Master," I said. I supposed that was true. But then, too, I supposed that many women on Earth should be made slaves. Certainly I had known many women who might have profited, and considerably, in one way or another, from bondage. Certainly I had sometimes speculated what one or another of them might have looked like, as a slave. Also, of course, I had often considered what I myself might have looked like, as a slave. It was for such a reason, I suppose, at least in part, as well as for the stimulation and truth, and fittingness, of it, that I had made the tiny garment of red silk I had had on Earth.

"But doubtless," he said, "even if you somehow managed to escape the collar on your own world, to be caught and rightfully wear it here, women such as you are almost universally held in bondage on Earth."

"No, Master," I said.

"Why not?" he asked.

"I do not know, Master," I said.

"Certainly they should be," he said.

"Yes, Master," I said, humbly. It was true.

"Here," he said, "they would wear their collars."

"Yes, Master," I said. I did not doubt that that was true. Here, on Gor, women such as I, surely, would be swiftly sorted out, taken in hand, prepared for sale, and sold.

"But, at least, you wear a collar now, as you should," he said.

"Yes, Master," I said.

"You are now, at last, a legal slave."

"Yes, Master," I said, frightened. I was now, truly, here on this world, as I might have been in Ur, or Sumer, or Babylon, or Assyria, or Chaldea, or Egypt, or Greece, or Rome, or Persia, or Barbary, a legal slave, a slave held in full legality.

"Does it frighten you," he asked, "to find that you are a legal slave?"

"Sometimes," I said.

"Does it terrify you?" he asked.

"Sometimes," I said.

"That makes no difference, of course," he said.

"I know," I said.

"You are a slave," he said, "whether you like it or not. That is simply what you are, that and only that. You are absolutely helpless to alter or change your condition in any way, as much as a vulo or a tarsk."

"I know," I said.

I felt his hands on my hips.

Sometimes I was terrified by the collar on my neck, knowing its meaning, knowing that it, like my brand, marked me slave, knowing how it put me at the mercy of masters, knowing that anything could be done to me.

His grip was bold. He was a master, I a slave.

I tried to press my belly against him. His hands prevented this.

"You belong in a collar," he said.

"I know, I know!" I whispered.

"You are a superb collar-slut," he whispered.

"Tupita is your favorite," I whispered, frightened.

"No," he said.

"Who then?" I gasped, his grip tight on me, but holding me from him.

"Doreen," he whispered.

"No!" I whispered.

"Are you so afraid of Tupita?" he asked. "She is only a slave."

"I, too, am only a slave," I said, "and she is first girl!"

"She is losing her grip on the girls," he said. "She may not be first girl for long."

"Oh?" I asked. That interested me, that Tupita might be reduced in rank, to being then only one slut among others, she herself then having to kneel to another girl, be subject to her disciplines, and addres her as "Mistress."

"Who would be first girl?" I asked.

"It would not be you," he said. "You are from Earth."

"I do not want to be first girl," I said.

"Too," he said, "you are not the sort of woman who should be giving orders, but taking them."

"I am ready to take your orders now," I said.

"Are you no longer afraid of Tupita?" he asked.

"I am a slave," I said, lightly. "I must obey."

"I think it would probably be Aynur," he said, "who would be the new first girl."

"Not Sita?" I asked.

"She has been too closely allied with Tupita," he said. "Do you think Aynur would make a good first girl?" he asked.

"I think so," I said. "She would be strict, but, I think, she would be fair."

"That, too, is the estimation of Hendow," he said.

"I think it is true," I said.

"You have great respect, it seems," he said, "for the judgment of Hendow."

"He is my master," I said, guardedly. I did, in fact, have great respect for the judgment and intelligence of Hendow. Gross and loathsome as he might be, I had never, after our first interview, doubted his probity and acumen, nor, more significantly, from my point of view, his insight and native shrewdness. My most secret thoughts seemed to be open to him. He could read me like a book, or a naked, frightened slave.

"And he purchased you," said Mirus.

"Yes!" I laughed.

I felt his thumbs at the sides of my belly.

"I like these rounded bellies on women," he said. "In them a man may lose himself with pleasure. I do not like those firm, flat bellies on women."

I said nothing I felt his thumbs,. They were not hurting me. I was pleased, of course, that Mirus, such a man, and such a master, found my sort of woman, one running more to the statistical norms of the human female, pleasing, as I wanted him to find me pleasing. Firm, flat bellies are less popular in women with Gorean men than among the men of Earth. Perhaps the Goreans find such bellies rather too much like those of boys, or young men. I do not know. Before her sale a girl is sometimes even forced to drink a liter or so of water, to round her belly more. I had had to do this in Market of Semris. Similarly, and perhaps for similar reasons, Gorean men tend, on the whole, it seems, to prefer normal-sized, lovely breasted, sweetly thighed women, with broad love cradles, as opposed to unusually tall, breastless, narrow-thighed women with narrow hips. Accordingly, such women, regarding themselves as unusually desirable by Earth standards, probably have little to fear from the slaver's noose, unless they can compensate in other ways, as by an unusual beauty of features or an extremely high intelligence. A woman who regards herself as a beauty on Earth might, accordingly, find herself laboring in the public kitchens or laundries on Gor. She would then have to learn, from the beginning, so to speak, and perhaps lengthily and painfully, how to please men as best she can, within her imposed physical limitations. And some of these girls, I understand, eventually, in spite of these limitations, become jewels and treasures to their masters. The most important criteria for slave selection, however, I suspect, are such things as having extremely strong female urges and incredibly profound emotional depths.

"Perhaps Master desires to remove the belt from me," I said. "As I am bound, I cannot do so."

"Do you know that you are beautiful?" he asked.

"Some men have been kind enough to tell me so," I said. "I do not know, of course, if they are correct or not."

"They are correct," he said.

"Thank you, Master," I said. It pleased me if Mirus should find me beautiful. He was a strong and handsome master. I wanted to serve him.

"Are you familiar with the ratings posted in the baths?" he asked.

"I have heard of such things," I said, reddening.

"In several of them," said he, "you now hold highest ranking in the tavern of Hendow."

"Higher than Inger?" I asked. "Than Aynur, than Tupita?"

"Yes," said he. "In some of them, at least."

"I am not better than them, really," I said. "I am sure of that."

"That is for men to decide," he said.

"Yes, Master," I said, frightened.

"But," said he, grinning, "you are probably right. You are all, doubtless, ultimately, very similar. You are all marvelous slaves. Such ratings are notoriously subjective. Some women will appeal more to one man, and some to another. Too, you are newer, and thus fresher to the tastes, and this perhaps accounts at least in part for your position in the rankings. When your popularity has crested you will perhaps subside to being merely another luscious and marvelous slave."

I looked at him.

"Too, you are a dancer," he said, "and this has undoubtedly improved your position. Many dancers, even plainer ones, hold high rankings."

"Yes, Master," I said.

"But one thing is certain," he said, "such rankings, even granting their subjectivity, and their silliness, and all the nonsense and absurdity associated with them, point to something, and that is your beauty and desirability."

I looked at him, frightened.

"You are one of the most beautiful and desirable slaves in Brundisium," he said.

"I am in your grasp," I whispered.

I would have pressed my belly against him but I could not do so. He held me from him. I would have reached forth to touch him, but I could not do so. My hands had been bound behind my back, by his will.

"Hendow has received several offers for you," he said, "excellent ones, but he has not sold you."

I was startled. So simply I could change masters!

"Do you wish to know their nature?" he asked.

"Curiosity," I said, humbly, "is not becoming in a kajira."

"Very well," he said.

"Please! Please!" I begged.

"Two of them were from other tavern owners," he said. "But several have been from private individuals."

I wondered what it would be like to have a private master. I would surely try to serve such a one well. Almost all girls hope, someday, to have a private master.

"What were the amounts?" I asked, eagerly.

"You are a slave, aren't you?" he asked.

"Yes!" I said.

"One was for seven tarsks," he said.

"Seven!" I cried. "I am not worth so much."

"True," he said. "I myself only offered five."

"Five!" I cried.

"Yes," he admitted.

"You made an offer on me?" I asked, delighted.

"Yes," he said.

I wondered what it would be like to be owned by Mirus. Slaves often wonder what it would be to be owned by this man, or that. I found him extremely attractive. If he purchased me, I would certainly try to serve him well. Of course, too, any man who purchased me I would have to serve well, and, indeed, as I was a Gorean slave girl, in so far as I could, perfectly.

"I am not worth five tarsks," I laughed.

"True," he said.

"Why, then, did you offer so much?" I asked.

"I was drunk," he said.

"Tonight," I said, "I am not scheduled to return to the floor."

"I know," he said.

"Master prepared the schedules," I laughed.

"Yes," he said.

"Summon me to your quarters," I whsipered. "I will show you that maybe I am worth five tarsks after all!"

"Perhaps I will summon Tupita," he said.

"No, Doreen," I said.

"Did you know that Hendow is thinking of placing restrictions on your use?" he asked.

"Why would he do that?" I asked.

"I think he is fond of you," he said.

"I am pleased, if my master finds me pleasing," I said.

"Has he never ordered you to him?" asked Mirus.

"No," I said.

"Interesting," said Mirus. "Normally he disciplines new girls well."

I shuddered. I had no doubt that Hendow, my master, could discipline a woman well. He seemed remote, and mighty. He was the master of the entire tavern, and of all the girls. There were twenty-seven of us. I was terrified of him.

"But I do not think he will really put restrictions on your use," he said.

"Why not?" I asked.

"I do not think it would be good for your discipline," he said.

"I understand," I said. In relationships between men and women, it is a common observation that the relationship tends to be improved considerably when the woman is subject to his usage. When she knows that that a fellow may, if he wishes, simply hurl her to his feet and put her to woman uses, she is likely to behave rather differently toward him than toward one who does not have this power over her.

"You have not displeased him lately, have you?" asked Mirus.

"Not to my knowledge," I said. "I hope not."

"Something is going to be done to you," he said.

"What?" I asked, apprehensively.

"But if you have not displeased him lately," he said, "I gather that it is not being inflicted as a punishment."

"What?" I asked.

"You haven't heard?" he asked.

"No," I said.

"A leather worker is coming to the tavern tomorrow, with his kit," he said.

"Why?" I asked.

"I'm sorry," he said. "I thought someone would have told you."

"What?" I asked.

"It is nothing to fear," he said.

"What?" I asked.

"It is done to many slaves," he said.

I looked at him, frightened.

"You have not displeased Hendow?" he asked.

"I do not think so," I said.

"That is what I thought," he said. "Then it is being done merely to improve you, to make you even more desirable."

"Please, Master," I said, "I am a helpless slave. What is to be done to me?"

"Hendow is going to have your ears pierced," he said.

I looked at him, disbelievingly.

"It is true," he said, gravely.

I tried not to laugh.

"What is wrong?" he asked.

I laughed, out loud in his grasp.

"I do not understand," he said.

"That is all?" I asked.

"All?" he asked. "Do you not understand the gravity of this?"

"I always wanted to have my ears pierced," I said. "Only I never had the courage."

"You wanted it?" he asked, startled.

"Yes," I said.

"What a slave!" he breathed.

"Oh?" I asked. To be sure, I was a slave, in my heart, as well as now, on this world, whether I wished it or not, and helplessly, in all public legality.

"Surely you know that if such a thing were done to you," he said, "no man thereafter could look upon you except as a slave."

I laughed. "I am a slave," I said.

"It is so barbaric," he said.

"Perhaps," I said.

"How exciting you will be with your ears pierced," he said.

I smiled.

"You do not mind?" he asked.

"No," I said.

"Interestingly enough," he said, "once it is done, afterwards, few girls mind. Indeed, many are thrilled with what has then been done to them, and are eager to display themselves to men in their new condition, and delight and revel in the new ornaments which they may then wear, so excitingly enhancing their appearance."

"I can understand that," I said.

"You see," he said, "it makes available to them a diverse and fantastic array of new adornments."

"Yes, Master," I said.

"How beautiful you will be in such adornments!"

"It is my hope I will be pleasing to Masters," I said.

"You must understand, of course," he said, "that there are dangers inherent in having your ears pierced."

"What dangers, Master?" I asked.

"Those attendant on having been made additionally desirable to strong men," he said.

"I understand," I said. I had recognized, of course, that such things as my garb, or lack of it, my brand, burned into my body, my collar, which I could not remove, placed on me by men, and such, and, above all, my condition, that of slave, had made me far more sexually stimulatory to men than I would otherwise have been but I had never, along the same lines, given much thought, or at least in detail, to the idea that, in this culture, similar effects might be consequent on things which, from the point of view of a girl from Earth, were as simple and familiar as having pierced ears or wearing earrings. To be sure, pierced ears, and wearing earrings, were stimulatory, too, I was sure, even to men of Earth, or, at least, to those who were capable of responding to such things, the piercings of the woman's flesh, with its allegory of penetration, of her appropriate submission to the mastery, and the use of these piercings, marking and recollecting them, to mount upon her beautiful adornments. I had sensed the barbaric and sexual connotations of these sorts of things on Earth, and, perhaps because of them, had always feared to have my ears pierced there. Here, of course, it was going to be done to me, whether I wished it or not. I was not discontented. I was, indeed, extremely pleased.

"I am eager to see you in such ornaments," he whispered.

"Kiss me," I whispered.

My hands were together behind my back. I could not part them without permission.

"Perhaps if your ears were pierced," he said, "I should find your request irresistible."

"Then I hope, Master," I said, "that they shall soon be pierced."

"They will be," he said.

I trembled, then, a bit, understanding then, a little more than before, what it might be, on this world, to have pierced ears.

He took his hands from my hips and put them further about me, to remove from my waist the double belt of coins.

I pressed my body against his.

"Were you given permission to approach me?" he asked.

"No, Master," I said. "Forgive me, Master." Swiftly I drew

back, so that our bodies were not touching. But my breasts were but an inch from his broad, strong chest. And they were bound, and covered, in only tissues of slave silk. I felt much alive, and frustrated, and hot, and charged, and helpless. I was under his control, totally. I was even "bound by his will." My midriff was bared. This too, excited me, its exposure, and its nearness to him. I wanted to thrust my belly, in its low-hanging drape of delicate silk, against him.

I felt his hands behind me, beneath mine, where I had them together, bound by his will.

"Please!" I begged.

I felt him disengage the large clasp at the back of the belt, to which both strands of coins, on each side, were fastened.

"Please," I said.

He took the belt and dropped it into the nearby sack, with the coined necklace and the coins I had picked up and brought back from the dancing floor, weighty in my lifted silk.

He looked down at me. My head came only to his shoulders.

"Do you beg?" he asked.

"Yes!" I said.

"Who begs?" he asked.

"Doreen begs!" I said.

"Doreen what?" he asked.

"Doreen, the slave, begs!" I said.

"To my lips, slave," he said.

Gratefully, eagerly, I pressed forward, rising on my toes, he half lifting me, his hands under my arms, holding me.

I melted to him.

"Unbind me!" I begged. I wanted to put my arms about him.

"Do you wish to be beaten?" he asked.

"No, Master!" I said.

We kissed, so together, the two of us, as to be almost one thing, and I almost swooned in his power. I fought, seemingly only half conscious for a moment, to keep my hands together behind my back. Then he put me down and back a little. "I am still bound!" I moaned.

"And you may stay that way," he said, huskily.

"As Master pleases!" I said, sensing the urgency in him.

He then held me from him, by the arms.

"You have the ruby on its chain, which was on my forehead, and the pearls which were in my hair," I said. "You have the coins cast by masters on the dancing floor, which I gathered for you. You have the necklace, the belt! The other things, the ornaments, the slave beads, the bells, are in the box. Surely now, you wish to store my silk!"

He smiled.

"Tear off my silk," I begged. "Take me here, on the tiles, in the passageway! I am ready! I beg it!"

"Coin check," he said.

"Of course, Master!" I wept. How well he reminded me I was a slave!

"Open your mouth," he said. I felt his finger run about within my mouth.

Mirus was efficient. He would not forget to subject me to coin check.

"Hold still," he said.

"Yes, Master," I said.

He was thorough.

Some girls, I had been told, sometimes try to swallow small coins but this is foolish. The coin can be produced swiftly enough in such cases by emetics and laxatives. Similarly, her wastes may be subjected to unscheduled examinations. Too, even if she is successful in recovering the coin herself, there is usually little she can do with it. There are few places to conceal such objects in a cell or kennel. Similarly, she is often under surveillance, of one sort or another, by other slaves or free persons. Also, if she should be found to be in possession of a coin or coins, for example, by a tradesman, guardsman, or any free person, she will be expected to have an excellent explanation for this anomaly, which is then likely to be checked with her master. In most cities, even the touching of money, unless in an authorized situation, is prohibited to slaves. They cannot, of course, own money, any more than any other form of animal.

I looked at Mirus, tears in my eyes.

"What is going on here?" asked Hendow, who had approached down the passageway.

Swiftly I knelt, and put my head to the floor before my master. My hands were still held behind me, as I had been bound by a man's will.

"She has danced," said Mirus. "We have just completed coin check."

"Lift your head," said Hendow.

Immediately I did so, and then knelt there, in the dancing silk, my knees wide, my hands behind my back, a woman before men, a slave before masters.

"I trust all the coins are accounted for," he said.

"I have not yet counted," said Mirus.

"Should she not be back on the floor by now?" asked Hendow.

"She does not return to the floor tonight," said Mirus, "unless you wish to send her forth there."

"It is so on the schedule?" asked Hendow.

"Yes," said Mirus.

"Very well," said Hendow, and then continued on his way, through the curtain, out to the public area.

I looked up at Mirus.

"Stand," he said.

I did so. Then I was before him, again. My hands were still behind my back.

He looked at me.

I lifted my rib cage a little. I pulled my arms back a bit, further accentuating my figure.

"Please," I whispered.

"You should be returned to the slave area," he said, "or put in your kennel, where you belong."

"I do not belong in my kennel now," I pouted.

"Where do you belong now?" he asked.

"In your arms," I said.

"I do not think Hendow is pleased that I should hold you," he said.

"I am free to all his men," I said, "and you are one of his men."

"True," he said.

"Will you not summon me to your quarters tonight?" I asked, plaintively.

"It is perhaps better that I not do so," he mused.

"As Master pleases," I said, indifferently, shrugging. I did not dare, of course, take my hands from behind my back.

He looked at me, and I tossed my head, haughtily, and looked away from him. I had not been dismissed yet, of course. I could not see his eyes, but I supposed he was considering whether or not I should be whipped. It could be done to me as simply as by his whim.

"Do you think you are a free woman?" he asked.

"No, Master," I said.

"I thought you might," he said.

"No, Master," I said. "I am under no delusions on that score."

He must have been looking at me. I had the feeling I was being looked at, as a slave.

"Am I dismissed?" I asked.

"Beware," he said.

"Perhaps I have concealed a coin in my halter," I said, "or in a fold of my slave silk."

"Have you?" he asked, amused.

"You will not know, will you," I asked, "unless you have checked?"

"You look well in slave silk," he said.

"Thank you, Master," I said.

"You would look better without it," he said.

"Yes, Master," I said. He then unknotted the silk of the halter, from about my neck, and behind my back, and drew it away from me. I stood as close to him as I could, without actually daring to touch him.

I saw him lean forward and, his eyes briefly closed, revel in the scent of my perfume. It was perfume of a sort not worn by free women on Gor. It was slave perfume. Such perfume says to men, in effect, "This is a slave. Use her as you will."

He then drew away the dancing silk and I, in the passageway, barefoot on the tiles, was naked before him.

"Are you haughty now?" he asked.

"No," I said.

"There are tears in your eyes," he said.

"My need is on me," I said, "and I am helpless."

He dropped the silk to the floor, beside us.

"You may kneel," he said.

Swiftly I knelt, and then looked up at him.

"Speak," he said.

"I, Doreen, the slave, beg use," I said.

He looked down upon me.

I squirmed on my knees before him, in misery and frustration, my hands behind my back.

"You are ready, aren't you?" he asked.

"Yes, Master!" I said.

"Please touch me!" I wept.

"You beg it?" he said.

"Yes, Master!" I wept. "I beg it!"

"Since first I saw you, when I had unroped the shipping blanket, and put its folds to the sides, revealing you, helplessly manacled, when you first came to the house from Market of Semris," he said, "I dreamed that you would one day be so hot and needful before me, and would beg me for my touch."

I was astonished and delighted to hear this, that so mighty a man as this Gorean master, second in this house to Hendow, my master, might have found me attractive, and from so long ago. But this did not, of course, relieve in the least the desperate need

I felt. It did not reduce my tensions. It did not diminish or assuage my sufferings. I still knelt helpless before him.

"It is interesting," he said, "what can be done with a woman."

"Please, Master!" I wept. I who had once been Doreen Williamson, a shy, lovely librarian on Earth, had now begun to feel slave needs. To be sure, at that time, kneeling before Mirus, I had no idea how acute such things could become.

He looked down at me, amused.

"Mock me as a needful slave," I said, "but I beg of you, touch me!"

He was silent.

"I am a naked slave," I said. "I kneel before you! I beg use!"

He savored my desperation. I wished for a foolish moment that I might be again like a woman of Earth, one without needs, or with such low need levels as to be for most practical purposes inert, or with need so rigidly and effectively suppressed as to provide a functional surrogate for such inertness, or, perhaps, even one who might, with some convincingness, pretend to such inertness, but then, again in a moment, I did not wish for such things. To have no needs, if, indeed, there were women truly without them, would be a tragedy, and if one had any need at all, then it would be only a matter of time until under Gorean tutelage they were revealed, deepened and enlarged; until they were imperiously summoned forth into the open for inspection and encouragement; they would then be cultivated; they would be forced to grow, in both size and intensity; they would soon become such that they would begin to surface periodically and irresistibly within her, like forces of nature, she as powerless to alter or effect them as she would be to alter or effect the tides, the rotation of the earth, the risings and settings of the sun. Too, they would always be with her, ready and meaningful, never far beneath the surface. This would constitute a condition of her existence. She would come to realize that, as the Goreans say, "slave fires had been lit in her belly." She would learn, too, that these fires, even when they seemed most inert, could be suddenly fanned into raging, consuming flames by as little as a command, a glance or touch. Such things the girl must learn to cope with. It does not matter, of course, for she is only a slave. I myself, of course, do not object to such things. I have learned on this world that the insensitivity of tissue is not an indication of virtue but of physiological inferiority.

I looked up at Mirus, tears in my eyes. I was now without pride. I was now only a naked, needful slave. I squirmed before him. I could not attempt to relieve my own tensions, as my hands, by his will, had been bound behind me. Yet for all my anguish I would not have wanted to be other than I was. I had not known such needs, such feelings, such emotions could exist. I was a thousand times more alive than I had ever been on Earth. And complementary, of course, to the pain of such deep needs, the other side of the coin, so to speak, are the incredible fulfillments of having them satisfied, fulfillments in the light of which the anguish of the needs, terrible though it was, then seems negligible. We may be totally at the mercy of masters, and as mere animals, and even to our lives, but just as it is within the power of these uncompromising brutes who own us to do as they wish with us, so, too, it is within their power, when it pleases them, to grant us transport to ineffable raptures, to fling us ecstasies of which the free woman can not begin to conceive.

"The woman of Earth begs use?" he said.

"Yes!" I said. "She begs use!"

"That is not typical for a woman of Earth, is it?" he asked.

"Doubtless those who have been taught bondage do," I said. "I do not know!" I could certainly imagine myself kneeling before a Greek or Roman master, or a harnessmaker in Damascus, his Christian slave, in the 14th Century, or a Barbary prince, a captured, harem-silked English lady who had now had time to learn something of the touch of men, in the 19th, and doing so. Indeed, I had wondered sometime if, in a former life, or lives, I might not have done so. The thought of this sort of thing, oddly enough, did not seem unfamiliar to me. To be sure, I have deep and urgent female needs, and had had them, even on Earth. To be sure, they had not been ignited on Earth as they were ignited now, and, too, at this time, of course, I did not have any idea as to how deep and urgent, and progressively overwhelming, they could become later. I was still only, in effect, a new slave, and new to the rigors of my condition. I had not yet begun to learn my collar.

He looked at me.

"Surely I am not the first woman from Earth whom you have had at your feet, begging," I said.

"No," he admitted.

"What?" I asked.

"No," he repeated.

"More than one?" I asked.

"Of course," he said.

"Oh," I said. Immediately I felt a wave of jealousy for those other girls.

"We learn quickly enough to beg on Gor, do we not?" I asked.

"Yes," he said.

"I am here," I said. "I am at your feet. I am naked, collared and owned. I beg use. I can do nothing more." I looked up at him. I must now wait. He would do with me as he saw fit.

"Perhaps I should send you out on the floor," he said.

"Not tonight," I begged. "Use me yourself!"

"The schedules could be rearranged," he mused.

"As Master wills," I said, bitterly. I was, of course, at the mercy of his schedules.

"Perhaps I could warm you for Hendow's customers," he speculated.

" 'Warm me'?" I laughed, bitterly. "I am already flaming!"

"If I sent you forth on the floor in your present condition," he said, "you would probably belly to the first male whose sandals you saw."

"Perhaps, Master," I said, bitterly. If he was so cruel as to deny me his touch, of course, I would, driven by my needs, have to make do elsewhere. It was Mirus, of course, who had now lit these flames in my belly. It was for him that they burned. The particular man is terribly important to the woman. He is a part of the whole that enflames her. To be sure, the slave is so needful and alive that it is not hard for her to see the beauty in any man. If I were sent forth upon the floor, however, in my condition, as it was, I do not think I would have bellied to the first man I saw. I would still have been able to look about, and select one out, one suitably incendiary to the wholeness of my need, and then prostrate myself before him. No, I was not so desperate that I would have bellied to the first man I saw. At that time, I did not even realize I could ever be so desperate as to do that. I would learn later, however, that I was wrong.

"But if you were to do that," he said, "it might not fit in as well as one might wish with the new image of the tavern, as we have now upgraded our decor, slave silk for the girls, and such, and service."

"Oh?" I asked.

"We would not want them thinking the paga slaves of the tavern of Hendow were too easy," he said.

"Of course not," I said, puzzled.

"They must play hard to get," he said.

"A slave?" I asked. I could imagine being punished terribly for such a thing. We must run to a man eagerly, at his least summons. We could be "gotten" as easily as by a snapping of the fingers.

"Some fellows would like to think that the girls had at least taken a look at him before they flung themselves to their belly at his feet."

"I understand," I said.

"Of course he may simply pick out one that pleases his fancy, and summon her to his table, and command her."

"Of course, Master," I said.

"You seem puzzled," he said.

"How, really," I asked, "are we to play hard to get?"

"You must make certain he has paid for his drink first," he said.

"Ah, I see," I smiled. "Master sports with the slave." I had thought that perhaps he had been referring to something I had heard about in training, the dangerous "pretended disinterest" sometimes commanded by masters of their girls, usually with respect to supper guests to whom he intends to lend her for the night. She must then, even if her belly is raging for the touch of the guest, attempt to pretend to disinterest in him, and even loathing, if the master wishes, though she must, of course, serve him with perfection. She then, gradually, permits herself to let her true feelings appear, thus attempting to give the impression of having been seduced by him, and then, later, after a suitable time, she is honestly piteous, kneeling beside him, licking and kissing. He then sends her to his room, that she may prepare it, and herself, for him. Most masters, however, do not do this sort of thing for it is meretricious, and, at best, a joke. Too, it can be dangerous for the girl, as she is usually under the obligation, at least by the seventh Ahn, if he has not penetrated to the heart of the matter by then, which is usually the case to inform the use master of her master's jest, which intelligence he might or might not appreciate. Many girls have been whipped for such things, which are not really their fault. They are only obeying, as they must. But then a girl must sometimes expect the whip, I suppose. She is, after all, a slave. On the other hand, few men will whip a girl for having pretended not to be attracted to him, if she is actually attracted to him, particularly if she has done so under her master's orders. Such devices, of course, but without the authenticity and the ultimate surrender, are often resorted to by "lure girls," slaves who serve as bait for captains who need crewmen, masters of work gangs, and such. Such work can be very dangerous, given the astuteness of many Gorean masters. Such a pretense, however, can be maintained with many men for at least a few minutes, and with some men for an hour or so, which is generally more than enough time for the purposes of the master, and the master's men, unobtrusively, are usually near at hand. It is not unknown, of course, for a girl who serves at such a supper, and is genuinely disinterested, or repulsed, by a given guest, to be given to him for the night. Such things can amuse the master and the guest. Too, they tend to be good for the girl's discipline.

I looked up at him.

"Yes?" he said.

"We are to remain, then, full paga slaves," I said.

"Yes, though now, at least occasionally, silked," he said.

"I understand, Master," I said.

"The only difference," he said, "is that such silk may now be pulled away by the master, or discarded instantly, upon command, by the slave."

"Yes, Master," I smiled. We were still to be hot, and ready, paga slaves, eager to serve, and fully, the silk no more than an invitation to its removal. This was not much different, incidentally, than what was the case in even the most prestigious paga taverns. In such places free women were generally not permitted. In them, usually, the only women to be found would be collared slaves, generally belonging either to the tavern keeper or the guests, who may have brought them in, to avail themselves of the facilities of the alcoves. In such places, the mastery was practiced. Such places, regardless of their cost, their location, their appointments, the excellence of their food and drink, the beauty of their slaves, the quality of their music, existed, as did the tavern of Hendow, for the pleasures of men. That was the purpose of such places, whether they were within lofty towers, reached by graceful bridges, or near the wharves, close enough to hear the tide lapping at the pilings, whether they had a dozen musicians or only a single, dissolute czehar player, alone with his music, whether the girls were richly silked or stark naked, save for brands and collars, whether there were chains of gold and luxurious furs in the alcoves or only wire and straw mats. They were paga taverns.

"But perhaps we should make an exception in your case," he said.

"Master?" I asked.

"Perhaps it is better if we do not let them know that Doreen, the dancer, is such a hot slave."

I looked at him, frightened.

"If she seems more prideful, colder, more haughty and aloof, perhaps it will be better for the tavern, as the fellows may look forward then to commanding her in an alcove, melting her defenses, and then, she now abjectly tamed, turning her into only another squeaking, writhing paga slut."

"It will be done with me as Masters please," I said. "But am I commanded to attempt to conceal my passion?"

"No," he said, "You are not that kind of dancer. You are too beautiful, and needful. You must be as you are, vulnerable, hot and marvelous."

"Thank you, Master," I said. "Once more you sport with a slave."

"Do you mind?" he asked.

"No, Master," I said. As if it mattered what a slave might mind!

He smiled.

"It is only another way in which you toy with me," I said.

"Are you still hot?" he asked.

"Yes!" I said.

"Do you still beg?" he inquired.

"Yes, yes, yes!" I said.

"Then," said he, "I think we may now send you to your kennel, in a belly chain, its lock at your navel, your hands braceleted closely behind you, to the chain."

"Please, no, Master!" I wept.

But he was then crouching before me, and had swept me into his arms. My head was back, my eyes closed. His strength was overwhelming. I felt my softness lost somehow within that embrace. "Unbind me," I begged. "Let me hold you!"

"No," he muttered, his voice thick with the wanting of me.

I must try to keep my hands together behind my back!

Then he put me to my back, and not gently, on the tiles in the passageway, near the beaded curtain. My body leapt to him and closed gratefully about him. I was joyful, held. I was collared. Tomorrow my back would be bruised from the tiles. I cried out, knowing the bliss of bondage.

"It is time you were taught submission," he said.

"I submit!" I said. "I submit!"

"You are unbound," he said.

Swiftly I pulled my hands free and grasped him.

"You are an incredible pleasure slave," he said.

"Master!" I wept.

"You needed only this world, and the collar to bring it out," he said.

"Yes," I whispered to him. "Please, please."

I was enraptured, as a female, and a slave.

"Master!" I cried, softly.

"So the female of Earth now calls men Master," he said.

"Yes, Master! Yes, Master!" I said.

Of course, I would call men "Master"! They were my masters, and not only in the order of nature, but here, too, in the order of law.

I felt overwhelmed in his arms, and could not believe the feelings I felt.

I uttered a tiny, plaintive cry, asking for a little respite, for a moment of mercy.

It was granted to me.

I looked at Mirus. I had always wanted, even on Earth, though I had feared it, too, to be at the mercy of men so powerful, so magnificent and commanding, that in relation to them I could, in all right, justice and propriety, be only a slave. Then I had been brought to Gor, where I had found such men, and, too, had found myself in a collar, theirs.

I moaned softly. Then I said, "Oh," startled.

"Perhaps you are ready, Earth woman," he said, "for a slave orgasm."

"Master?" I asked.

"You have a responsive body," he said. "Thus, even though you have not been a slave long, it is possible you are ready for such an orgasm."

"Yes, Master," I said.

I was trying, wildly, to recollect that feeling, that hint of feeling, which I had just felt.

How could he have done that to me? How could anyone have done that to me?

"Are you listening?" he asked.

"Yes, Master!" I said. I tried to pry myself loose from my sensations, but it was not easy, locked as I was in his arms.

"I think you might be ready for your first slave orgasm," he said.

"I do not understand, Master," I said.

"It is time, I think, that you made a beginning in such things."

"Yes, Master" I whispered. "Ai!" I suddenly said. "Oh!".

It had been done again to me.

I looked at him, wildly.

"No," he said. "You will not be shown mercy."

I moaned.

"It is pleasant to hold you in my arms," he said.

"Find me pleasing," I begged. "Please, find me pleasing!" I did not want him to stop, for anything.

"You are not without interest," he said.

I cried out, softly. I began to whimper.

"Is anything wrong?" he asked.

"No, no!" I said.

"Do you want me to stop?" he asked.

"No!" I said.

"No, what?" he inquired, politely.

"No, Master, Master, Master!" I sobbed. "Forgive me, Master!"

I cried out, startled. I began to make soft, helpless noises.

As I had noted before, as early as the house of my training, women of diverse backgrounds, for example, those of Earth and Gor, made much the same noises while being ravished. These noises are to be distinguished from conventionalized exclamations, which do tend to be culture bound. I had discovered, too, that I made such noises.

"Oh!" I said, softly.

Suddenly I clutched him. I had again felt the sensation. Then I was afraid.

"Master!" I said.

"Do not be afraid," he said. "Your body is being honed, and trained."

I clutched him again, and gasped.

"Yes," he said, "you will give masters much pleasure."

Masters, I thought! Does he not know what he is doing to me! Can he be ignorant of the things I myself was feeling?

"You will do well," he said. "You are a deliciously servile little beast."

"It is my hope that I will be pleasing to masters," I said. Did he not know what he was making me feel!

"I think you are now ready for the first of your slave orgasms," he said.

"Master?" I asked.

"Inducing them in a slave is one of the pleasures of the mastery," he said.

"Forgive me, Master," I said. "You are giving me great pleasure. But I do not even know what you are talking about."

"At first," he said, "you will be capable of only small ones, but do not fear, you will grow in such things."

"I do not understand," I said.

"You are very beautiful, and soft, and are in my arms," he said.

"Yes, Master," I said. I was grateful that he should speak in so kindly a fashion to me.

"And you are naked, and collared, and owned," he said.

"Yes, Master," I whispered.

"What are you?" he asked.

"I am a slave, Master," I said, puzzled.

"And do you surrender wholly to your masters, and yield totally to them?" he asked.

"Yes, Master," I whispered. I knew that I could not lie in things of this sort. Gorean masters, or many of them, were skilled in reading women. My Master, Hendow, was frighteningly adept at this. Too, I did not think that I could fool Mirus either in such matters. When a girl's most secret thoughts can be read as easily as slave numbers written on her breast her only viable option is total honesty, and as complete submission was required of Gorean slave girls her only practical recourse under such stringent circumstances is either to choose death or become in true reality a full slave, in her heart, in her mind and in her behavior. In short, as deception is impossible, the girl must either choose death or the reality of true bondage.

"You will now prepare to yield," he said.

"Yes, Master," I said, suddenly, startled, then beginning to understand the orgasm in the natural matrix of male dominance, and intensified by the fixing, enhancement and intensification of this within the institution of total female slavery. When I yielded it would be not only as a female to a male, but as slave to a master!

No longer then could I even hear the noises of the tavern beyond the curtain. There was now only myself and Mirus.

"Let me yield!" I begged.

"Wait," he said.

I was collared!

"Please!" I wept.

I was naked, and in the arms of a man whose sandals I was not fit to lick.

"Master!" I begged.

Must not what might remain in me of the proud Earth woman attempt to resist this?

"Master!" I cried.

"No," he said, sternly.

But what might remain in me of the Earth woman was utterly powerless!

"Please, please!" I whispered.

"No," he said.

Then what might have remained in me of the Earth woman was gone and in her place there was now only a terrified Gorean slave on the brink of she knew not what.

I was not simply going to be fondled or kissed, with attentions appropriate to the bland etiquettes of Earth. I was to be conquered!

"Please!" I wept.

"No," he said.

I would not be permitted to retain a shred of dignity or pride. My yielding would not be of the sort of yieldings approved of on Earth, those mild, meaningless ripples of sensation, indicative of acceptable congenialities, the most that many of Earth, it seems, could manage, but would be rather the result of his will and power, of his enforcements and determination, the exercise over me of his strength, making me helpless, having me as he wanted me, owning me. It would not be a compromised act. It would be a complete act, a fulfillment, for him and also for me. It would manifest his power, and my weakness, his triumph and my shattering, and overwhelming. It would be an act of his uncompromising power, imposed upon me, which I, the female could not resist.

"Let me yield!" I begged.

"Wait," he said.

I moaned. I did not want polite love. I wanted to know that I was in the hands of a man who was capable of being excited, and whom I excited, who found me truly marvelous, to whose fury of power I appeared whose fierce and voracious appetites I triggered. I wanted to be in the arms of a true man. I did not want to be possibly mistaken about whether I had been had or not. I did not want to be touched as though I might break. I did not wish to be in danger of drowsing off during the making of love. I wanted him to own and master me, and whip me if I was not pleasing.

"I am ready!" I said. "I beg to submit, and as a slave!"

"Not yet," he said.

I began to weep with wanting to yield.

He was not simply going to enjoy me, or pleasure himself with me. He was asserting the mastery upon me. I was not merely to be used even used as a mere slave, as it sometimes amuses Gorean masters to do with us. I was going to yield, and fully. I was not simply having love made to me. The experience was far more meaningful and devastating than simply that. I was being dominated, and mastered. I was to yield, and I had to, as a slave, totally!

"Please!" I wept.

"No," he said.

I was to be vanquished, utterly.

"Please!" I said.

"Will it be necessary to gag you?" he asked.

"No, Master," I said.

"Are you ready?" he asked.

"Yes, yes, Master!" I wept.

"You may then yield," he said, "—as a slave."

I then yielded to him, and wholly, and without compromises, as slave girl to a master.

I then looked up at him, wildly, disbelievingly.

"Master," I whispered, acknowledging that it was right that I belonged to men. I then lay in his arms, an incredulous, frightened slave girl. The experience had been a whole, the context conditioned by my abject surrender, by our relationship, that of master and slave.

Gently he kissed me.

I had not known on Earth that such men could exist. I had only dreamed of them, men to whom I could be rightfully only on abject slave. But now on Gor I was subject to such men. And now, naked and collared, I lay in the arms of one.

"What was it?" I begged. "What was it you did to me?"

"Nothing," he said.

"Master!" I protested.

"It was a slave orgasm," he said.

I trembled in his arms.

"Surely such would be appropriate enough for you," he said.

"Yes, Master!" I said.

I have had a slave orgasm, I thought, wonderingly.

"It was a small one," he said, "to be sure."

" 'Small'!" I said. "Take pity, I beg you, Master, on a poor slave. Do not mock her so."

I had never experienced anything of that power, of that nature, before. I was still shaken from it. In its grip I had been overwhelmed, utterly helpless.

"You will grow in such things," he said. "They are small in the beginning."

"There can be more?" I asked.

"You are only at the beginning of what men can make you feel, Doreen, slave girl," he said.

I shuddered. I had never hitherto guessed that the power of men over me could be so great.

"Do you wish to feel such things again, and more?" he asked.

"Yes!" I whispered. "Yes!" How much we were at their mercy! They held over us not only the power of pain but also that of pleasure. They had now, in the person of Mirus, let me have a taste of incredible pleasure, perhaps that I might then have some inkling as to what such things could be. Now they could either grant me such pleasures, or withhold them from me, as they wished. I would obey with perfection, trying to please them!

"What is it that you would wish to have again?" he asked.

"Please do not make me say it, Master," I begged.

"What is going on here?" asked a voice.

Swiftly Mirus and I drew apart. I knelt, my head to the tiles. He stood.

"You took her here, in the passageway?" asked Hendow, my master.

"Yes," said Mirus.

I could not see the face of Hendow, but I sensed that he was not pleased. Mirus seemed uneasy before him. I was frightened.

"You are training her?" asked Hendow.

"Yes," said Mirus.

"Here?" asked Hendow.

"I also enjoyed her," said Mirus, angrily.

"How is she?" asked Hendow.

I reddened.

"She is good, for a new slave," said Mirus.

The performance, responses, and such, of slaves, may be discussed openly, as those of other animals.

"Did she yield?" asked Hendow.

"Yes," said Mirus.

"Wholly?" he asked.

"Yes," said Mirus.

"To you," said Hendow.

"Yes," said Mirus, angrily.

"Look up, slave," said Hendow.

I obeyed, instantly.

"Did you yield?" asked Hendow.

"Yes, Master," I said.

"Wholly?" asked Hendow.

"Yes, Master," I whispered.

"To him?" he asked.

"Yes, Master," I said, frightened.

"Did she attain slave orgasm?" asked Hendow.

"Yes," said Mirus.

"Slave?" he asked.

"Yes, Master," I said.

"That is your first, is it not?" asked Hendow.

"Yes, Master," I whispered.

"Perhaps you would have preferred to have brought her to this point yourself," said Mirus. "If so, I did not know. In such a case, had you made your wishes known to me, I would surely have respected them."

"What difference does it make," asked Hendow, "who induces the first slave orgasm in a slave?"

"No difference, of course," said Mirus. He shrugged.

"Did you like it, slave?" asked Hendow. I had never seen him like this.

"Yes, Master," I whispered.

"Is that all?" he asked.

"I loved it," I whispered, terrified.

"What was it you loved?" asked Hendow, angrily.

I looked at him, aghast. I was bashful, and shy. I was timid. I was from Earth. I did not want to say such words.

"She is a new slave," said Mirus. "Perhaps—"

"Be silent!" said Hendow.

Mirus stiffened, as though he had been slapped. I was startled. How could Hendow have spoken to a free person in this fashion? Never had I seen him as he was.

"With your leave," said Mirus, coldly.

"Stay," said Hendow.

"I did not know the slave was of interest to you," said Mirus.

"She is meaningless, as is any other slave," said Hendow.

"Of course," said Mirus.

Then Hendow looked at me, again. His eyes were fierce. I must answer. It was painful for me. On Earth I had even been reluctant even to describe the liberating sort of dance I loved so much by such an expression as 'belly dance'. I quailed before that gaze. It was the gaze of my master.

"My slave orgasm," I whispered.

"Speak up, slave," said Hendow.

"My slave orgasm," I said. I shuddered to hear such words coming from me.

"And you want more of them, don't you?" he asked.

"Yes, Master," I said, my eyes suddenly filling with tears. How helpless I was before such men.

"And desperately so?" he said.

"Yes, Master!" I wept.

"You perhaps understand now," he said, "that there is more to slavery than collars and chains."

"Yes, Master," I said.

"You are more thoroughly imbonded now than ever before," he said.

"Yes, Master," I said. It was true. I wanted such incredible sensations. I would do anything for them. To be granted them I would strive to be a perfect slave. I suddenly put my head in my hands, weeping.

"Hendow," protested Mirus.

"Have you counted the coins?" asked Hendow.

"Not yet," said Mirus, angrily.

"Perhaps you should consider doing so, when you can find the time," said Hendow.

"Of course," said Mirus, angrily. "Do you want the slave sent out on the floor, or to your quarters?"

"It was my understanding that in the schedules she was not to go on the floor this evening."

"Yes," said Mirus. "I shall have her cleaned and sent to your quarters."

"No," said Hendow. "She is to be put in her kennel, belly chained and braceleted, hands behind her back."

"I will see to it," said Mirus.

"Tupita will see to it," said Hendow.

"Of course," said Mirus.

Hendow then turned about, and left. I put my head quickly to the tiles, as he left, and then raised it. I looked, then, at Mirus.

"I do not understand," said Mirus, looking after Hendow. "I do not understand."

"Master?" I asked.

"Hendow is my friend," said Mirus. "We would die for one another."

"Master," I said, lifting my hand to Mirus.

"No," he said, angrily. He stepped back. I gasped. His attitude was now so different than it had been. He looked at me. "But you are beautiful, aren't you, Doreen?" he said.

"I do not know, Master," I whispered.

"It is true enough," he said, bitterly. "Perhaps you are even too beautiful."

I put my head down.

"But you are only a slave," he said.

"Yes, Master," I said.

He then turned away from me, and went through the curtain. "Tupita!" I heard him call. "Tupita!"

But it was not Tupita, at first, who came into the passageway.

It was Sita, in her silk. She knelt down beside me. "What is wrong?" she whispered to me.

"I do not know," I said.

"Is there trouble with Mirus?" she asked.

"Hendow is angry, I think," I said.

"It has to do with you," she said.

"I think so," I said.

"You may have favor with Hendow," she whispered.

"I do not think so," I said.

"There are rumors about," whispered Sita. "Have you heard them, that there may be a new first girl?"

"I have heard something about it," I said. "I do not know if it is true."

"Speak well for Sita," she whispered.

"But you are the friend of Tupita," I said.

"Tupita has no friends," she said.

I looked at Sita, puzzled.

"Speak well for Sita, with the masters," she said. "If I am first girl, you will be second."

"It is thought that Tupita is losing her control of the girls," I said. There were twenty-seven of us.

"She is," said Sita. "I have seen to it. Who do you think has undermined her?"

"To how many of us have you offered the post of second girl?" I asked.

"Only to you," she said.

I smiled.

"It is true," she whispered. "With the others I needed only rely on Tupita's unpopularity, her arbitrariness, her favoritisms, and, naturally, the promise of an easier time under me."

"Why am I special?" I asked.

"Because of Hendow," she whispered.

"I do not understand," I said.

"He likes you," she whispered. "I am sure of it."

"No," I said. "I am only a meaningless slave to him."

"Men kill for slaves," said Sita.

I shuddered.

"Speak well for Sita," she whispered.

The beaded curtain parted and Tupita entered the passageway.

Sita sprang to her feet. "You are a stupid slave," she cried to me. "You must learn to better please men!"

"Yes, Mistress," I said.

"What is wrong with Mirus?" asked Tupita. "I have never seen him so angry."

"It has to do with Hendow," said Sita. "He is angry with Mirus."

"It has to do with this slave?" asked Tupita.

"Yes," said Sita. "I have made her confess. Look at her. You can see she has recently been used."

"Here?" said Tupita.

"Apparently," said Sita.

"Return to the floor," she said.

"Tupita!" protested Sita.

"There is a fellow at table fifteen. He is depressed. He is having problems with his companion at home. Belly to him. Console him."

"Yes, Mistress," said Sita, and went back to the floor.

"So there is trouble between Mirus and Hendow?" she asked.

"Perhaps, Mistress," I said. "I do not know."

"And it is over you?"

"Perhaps, Mistress," I said. "I do not know."

"I wonder how that could be," she said. Then she walked about me, looking at me. "Yes," she said, "I suppose it is possible." She stopped in front of me. "Do you know what is to be done with you?"

"I am to be kenneled, belly chained and back-braceleted," I said.

"So you were used here?" she said, looking about.

"Yes, Mistress," I said.

"That is my impetuous Mirus," she said.

I was silent.

"Did you yield well to him?" she asked.

"Yes, Mistress," I whispered.

"He teaches us our slavery well, doesn't he?" she asked.

"Yes, Mistress," I whispered. "Please do not whip me, Mistress."

"Why would I do that?" she asked, lightly.

"I thought you might be angry," I said, "about Mirus."

"We are all free to the men of the house," she said. "And you are pretty."

"You are not angry with me?" I asked.

"Of course not," she said. "What were you to do? You are only a slave."

"Thank you, Mistress," I said.

"Follow me to the kennels," she said. "I will chain and bracelet you there. Too, I will not make the belly chain any tighter than is necessary."

"Thank you, Mistress," I said.

"And I will bring you a pastry later from the kitchen," she said, "and put it on the floor of your kennel. Though you will not be able to use your hands I expect that you will enjoy it, just the same."

"Thank you, Mistress," I said.

"Speak well of me to Hendow," she said.

"Yes, Mistress," I said.

"If I am kept on as first girl," she said, "I will make you third girl, second only to myself and Sita."

"Thank you, Mistress," I said.

I then rose to my feet and followed her down the passageway, to the stairs leading to the basement, where most of the kennels were. She was as good as her word, and did not make the belly chain tighter than necessary, and, too, she brought me a pastry later from the kitchen.

"Speak well of me to Hendow," she said.

"Yes, Mistress," I said.

I then, lying on my side, and turning my head, ate the pastry. Afterwards, as I could, with my teeth, I pulled the blanket up about me. I then lay there in the darkness, in the kennel. I pulled a little at the slave bracelets. They were not too tight, but they were on me snugly and well. They would hold me, perfectly. I remembered what a man had done to me, and how much of a slave he had made me. Hendow had told me later that I was never so thoroughly imbonded as now. I remembered the sensations. It was true. I did not know whether to weep with the power of men over me, or cry out with joy. I did know I was a slave, and, in spite of its vulnerabilities and terrors, loved it. I would try to serve well.

I was frightened by the intrigues of the slaves, Tupita and Sita, and the other girls. I did not really want to be involved in them.

I lay there then and loved the men of Gor. I had not really, in spite of strong feelings and intuitions on Earth, begun to understand my sex until I was imbonded, until I found myself in my place in nature, subservient to men. I now loved my sex. I now loved being a woman. It was marvelous, and wonderful!

14 / Punishment

I knelt on the rug at the foot of the dais, that surmounted by the curule chair of my master, Hendow, of Brundisium. My head was to the rug, the palms of my hands on the floor. I had been summoned into his presence.

I trembled, kneeling before him, my head down.

I was afraid in this room. I had been here before. It was the receiving chamber of my master, Hendow. Too, to one side was the panel which, opened, admitted the gray hunting sleen, Borko. Somewhere in the dark, simple, terrible brain of that beast my name and scent had been imprinted. It could now be commanded with respect to me, even in my absence.

I trembled.

I did not know why I had been summoned into the presence of my master.

"Lift your head," said Hendow, of Brundisium, "stand."

I obeyed.

"Approach me," he said, "and kneel here, before the chair."

I climbed the broad, carpeted steps of the dais, and knelt before him. He leaned forward. "Turn your head to the left," he said. "Now, turn it to the right."

"Good," he said.

My ears had been pierced. It had been done yesterday morning. The metal worker had put tiny, circular training pins in them, to keep the wounds from closing.

I was relieved. It seemed my master had only wished to inspect the results of the metal worker's work. Too, I was pleased to note that he seemed pleased with the work.

"You may now return to the foot of the dais, and stand," he said.

I backed down, my head down, to the foot of the dais, and then stood there, erect and graceful before my master, as would be expected of a female slave.

I expected to be dismissed.

But I was not dismissed.

I became afraid, again. "May I kneel, Master?" I asked.

I would feel more comfortable kneeling in the presence of Hendow, such a man. Too, as I was frightened, it would be easier, in a kneeling position, not to falter, or fall.

"No," he said.

I remained standing. I trembled. Standing as I was, and at the foot of the dais, I feared he would have little difficulty in reading my body. My slightest tremor, or the slightest weakness in my legs would be visible to him.

"The metal worker did his work well," he said. "Your ears are excellently pierced."

"Yes, Master," I said. "Thank you, Master." I was pleased, too, of course, that the work had been well done. Indeed, I was eager to adorn myself with such devices, that I might be rendered even more attractive to men. Too, I had some understanding of the meaning of earrings to Gorean males, and the effects upon them of such things.

"Remove your garment," he said.

I reached to the disrobing loop at the left shoulder of the brief silken tunic I wore. It was opaque silk, for it was morning, and not the diaphanous silk we customarily wore in the evening, when on the floor, when serving our master's customers. Silk such as this we might even wear outside the tavern. To be sure, it was silk such as would be worn only by a pleasure slave. We are dressed according to the preferences of men. I had never, incidentally, been allowed outside the tavern grounds. I did have the liberty, at certain times, of walking in, and exercising in, a small, enclosed back court of the tavern.

Then I was naked before him, the garment at my feet.

He regarded me.

I was now more sure than ever that he wanted to read my body. I trembled. Sometimes it seemed to me that he could look upon me, and know my most secret thoughts. I caught myself, my knees weak. I regained my balance.

"Are you afraid?" he asked.

"Yes, Master," I said.

"Why?" he asked.

"I am in the presence of my master," I said.

He continued to look upon me.

I then breathed more confidently. It seemed to me then that perhaps he only wished, really, to look upon my beauty, if beauty it were. Such things are not unusual with Gorean masters. It is not uncommon with them to have their girls strip, and turn before them, and assume attitudes and poses, and move in certain ways, and such. Gorean men, like lusty males generally, have an incredible appreciation of female beauty. Too, in the case of the slave, they own the girl. Thus they may command her, and have her perform, and precisely, as it pleases them, and she must, of course, obey with perfection. She is their slave. I suppose this is in part, at least, the result of an understandable desire to appreciate and take pleasure in one's possessions, or what one might regard as one's precious objects, or treasures. For example, we would not think it strange if a fellow of Earth, once in a while, drew forth his coin or stamp collection and spent some time lovingly pouring over it, scrutinizing and inspecting its items, and such. He is very fond of them. Similarly, if it seems understandable that, say, a high magistrate, a general, a Ubar, or such, might enjoy sitting in his pleasure gardens and inspecting his women, having them before him naked, or clothed according to his preferences, it is just as understandable that a less rich or well-fixed person might, similarly, on a more modest level, enjoy the sight of his girl, or girls. Indeed, the fewer he has, perhaps the more he will relish the one, or ones, he has. If one is a male, and has, occasionally, perhaps on the street, or, say, on a bus or in a subway, seen a woman whom one found attractive, perhaps one has considered, with pleasure, what might be within the power of a master, an owner of the female in question, what it might be to be able to say, simply, perhaps giving her a name that pleases you, "Remove your garments, and perform." Those to whom such considerations are not incomprehensible will presumably understand something of what I am attempting to convey. Those to whom such considerations are incomprehensible, because they have low-level sexual drives will not be able to make much sense of it. When one has ordered the girl stripped, and perhaps required performances of her, and such, it is then not unusual that one would make use of her. On the other hand, it is not always done. Sometimes the master, having relished her beauty, merely has her reclothe herself and return to her labors. To be sure, he may recollect her later in the day, or evening. This sort of thing, needless to say, can be arousing, and frustrating, to the female slave. It is hard to remove your clothing before a man, and perhaps be forced to perform before him, naked, and not be sensible of the keenly disturbing stirrings of one's own needs.

"It is interesting," he said.

"Master?" I asked.

"You are quite beautiful," he said.

"Thank you, Master," I said.

"But surely there are many women as beautiful," he said.

"Master?" I asked, puzzled.

"What, then, is different about you?" he asked.

"I do not understand, Master," I said.

"Are you an Earth woman?" he asked.

"In a sense, Master," I said, "the sense in which I am a woman from Earth. In another sense I am not an Earth woman. I am now only a Gorean slave girl."

"What have you learned on Gor?" he asked.

"I have learned to call men 'Master,' " I said.

"Is that well put?" he asked.

"Master?" I asked.

"Why do you call men 'Master'?" he asked.

"I understand, Master," I said. "Forgive me, Master. I spoke imprecisely. I should have expressed myself more clearly."

He regarded me.

"I have learned on Gor that men are my masters," I said. It was true.

"It is then suitable that you call them 'Master,' " he said.

"Yes, Master," I said.

"I have had your ears pierced," he said.

"As it pleased you, Master," I said.

"You are now only a pierced-ear girl," he said.

"Yes, Master," I said, puzzled.

"Do you know what that means?" he asked.

"I am not sure," I said.

"Never hope, now, to be out of a collar," he said.

"Yes, Master," I said. I had gathered that he had, for some reason, or reasons, perhaps to make me more exciting to his customers, and men, in general, had my ears pierced. Too, in some way, I gathered, this had confirmed my slavery upon me, and made it a much more profound thing. But I did not care. I was a slave!

"Do you know why I had your ears pierced?" he asked.

"No, Master," I said.

"There are various reasons for doing such a thing to a female slave," he said.

"Master?" I asked.

"It improves her as a slave," he said. "It makes her more stimulatory, and more seductive. Too, it makes her more arousable, more excitable."

"Yes, Master," I said, blushing from head to toe.

"In this, too, there is an economic consideration. Such things improve her price."

"Of course, Master," I said.

"There are many reasons," he said. "Those are just a few."

"I understand, Master," I said.

"Too," he said, "in your case, I thought it particularly fitting."

"Master?" I asked.

"You are a pierced-ear girl," he said, "and were, even before your ears were pierced."

"Yes, Master," I said, puzzled.

"I despise you," he said.

I put my head down. I did not doubt but what he might despise me. But, too, I suspected his feelings toward me were more complicated. I was sure they exceeded a simple contempt for a bond wench.

"And so," he said, "I have had your ears pierced."

"Yes, Master," I said.

"You belong in a collar," he said. "Now it has been seen to that you will remain in it."

"Yes, Master," I said.

"Are you not distressed, ashamed?" he asked.

"No, Master," I said.

"What a brazen, shameless slave," he said.

"Yes, Master," I said.

"You like being a slave," he said.

"I am a slave," I said. "Thus I must acknowledge what is in my secret heart, confessing it openly, then finding my happiness and fulfillment in it."

"You slut," he said. "You like being a slave."

"Yes, Master," I said. I supposed that I needed not tell him that I loved it!

"We are thinking of appointing a new first girl," he said.

"I have heard rumors to that effect," I admitted.

"What do you think of Tupita?" he asked.

"I speak for her," I said.

He smiled. I supposed he knew how cruel Tupita had been to me, how we were enemies. On the other hand, I had told Tupita I would speak for her. Too, she had not belly chained and braceleted me as tightly as she might have, the night before last.

"Did she offer you the position of second girl for your support?" he asked.

"Third girl," I said.

"Who would be second girl?" he asked.

"Sita," I said.

He smiled.

"Doubtless Tupita believes Sita to be her ally," he said.

"Yes, Master," I said.

"What do you think of Sita, for first girl?" he asked.

"She would not decline the post," I said.

"Would you speak for her?" he asked.

"Yes," I said. "I speak also for Sita." I kept my head down. I did not really want to be involved in these intrigues.

"What did she promise you?" he asked.

"The position of second girl," I said.

"Clearly, then," he said, "you would wish to support Sita over Tupita."

"No, Master," I said.

"You favor Tupita then," he said.

"I speak in support of both," I said.

"There can be only one first girl," he said.

"Yes, Master," I said.

"Whom do you favor?" he asked.

"Of the two, Tupita," I said.

"Why?" he asked.

"Sita is disloyal to Tupita," I said. "She betrays her. She pretends to be her friend, but is not."

"Do you think that Tupita, were their positions exchanged, would behave differently?" he asked.

"I do not know, Master," I said.

"And not because Tupita gave you a pastry?" he asked.

I looked at him, startled.

"I have had her whipped for it," he said. "She must want the position of first girl very badly, to risk stealing a pastry. To be sure, she doubtless did not expect to be found out."

"Master?" I asked.

"The missing pastry was noted by the kitchen master," he said. "Only Tupita, first girl, other than staff, and assigned kitchen slaves, had had access to the area before it had been seen to be missing. Her fingers, licked, had sugar on them. Crumbs were found the next morning in your kennel."

"I see," I said.

"She was given only five lashes," he said.

"Master is generous," I said. It could have been a thousand, or she could have been slain. She was only a slave.

"What do you think of Aynur?" he asked.

"I think she would be a good first girl," I said.

"Can you think of a better?" he asked.

"No, Master," I said.

"Apparently both Tupita and Sita wished to enlist your support in their cause," he said.

"I think each tried to speak to several of the girls," I said.

"To some extent," he said, "but not as much as you might think."

"Oh?" I asked. That surprised me.

"Both apparently thought you might have influence with me," he said. "Do you think that you have influence with me?" he asked.

"No, Master," I said hastily. I had hardly even seen Hendow, except here and there in the tavern. He had never even put me to intimate uses, suitable for slaves. Indeed, this had puzzled me a little, and made me wonder about my attractiveness, at least to him. Surely he made use often enough of other girls. Indeed, it seemed they muchly feared the call to his chamber, because of his ugliness and grossness. Too, I gathered, he was not gentle with them, and, in spite of their distress, misery and loathing, forced them to serve with uncompromising perfection. Indeed, in the slave areas, it seemed that most of them envied me my apparent immunity from his attentions. Interestingly enough, and perhaps paradoxically, I did not regard him with the same repulsion as many of my chain sisters. I feared him as my master, of course, but I also had a considerable respect for him, for the strength, the shrewdness, and intelligence I sensed in him. Also, I sometimes felt sorry for him. I thought that his life must have been very hard. He had once been betrayed, it seemed, and left for dead, by his best friend. Borko had avenged him. Had I been summoned to his chamber I would have tried to serve him as well as I could. Too, though I was not eager to serve him, I was not really afraid to do so. Indeed, I had been sometimes curious about him, wondering what it might be like to serve him. Men are so different, one from another. Perhaps it was my willingness to be summoned to his chamber which had, paradoxically, effectuated my security in this matter. I did not know. Perhaps for some reason, known only to himself, he took delight in forcing frightened, unwilling women to his pleasure, and, if I am not mistaken, particularly women who found him dismaying or sickening, who might even loathe him. He would take such a woman, and then turn her inside out, with yielding to him. To be sure, when they returned, bruised and shuddering, scarcely able to walk, to the slave quarters, they had little doubt as to their femaleness or the power of their master. I did not think, however, that I had been summoned here for typical slave purposes. Surely nothing had suggested that to me. Too, he usually had women sent to him in the evening. I was not exactly sure why I had been summoned here. Perhaps it had been simply to inspect the piercing of my ears. He had done that. Perhaps, too, he had wanted to look upon me, naked, as his property. He had done that. Perhaps, too, he had wanted to sound me out about various girls, for it seemed that, truly, he was thinking about a change in "first girl." He had done that, too.

I stood before him, at the foot of the carpeted dais, naked, in my collar.

He looked down upon me. He seemed heavy in the chair, almost somnolent. Yet I knew he was a creature of great energy, and vitality.

"Why are you frightened?" he asked.

"I am in the presence of my master," I said.

I was apprehensive. I had not been dismissed. I had not been permitted to kneel.

He scrutinized me, not speaking.

I was very conscious of my brand and collar.

I regarded my master.

I was conscious, too, now, perhaps oddly, of the tiny, circular training pins put in my ears by the metal worker yesterday morning. I stood before my master. I was now a pierced-ear girl. To an Earth girl, on Earth, at least, this might not seem to be a matter of great import, but I was not on Earth, and here, I knew, such things, somehow, rationally or not, had great import. In some way, they confirmed my slavery upon me, perhaps even more, here, than the brand and collar.

"You are an excellent and valuable slave," he said.

"Thank you, Master," I said, relieved. Perhaps I had been brought here to be praised.

"You are a superb dancer," he said, "perhaps one of the best in Brundisium."

"Thank you, Master," I said.

"Your name is written high in the lists at the baths," he said.

"Thank you, Master," I said.

"The business of the tavern has increased considerably since your acquisition," he said.

"I am pleased if I have been of value to my master," I said.

"Did Mirus tell you things of this sort two nights ago?" he asked.

"To some extent, yes, Master," I said. I had not seen Mirus since the day before yesterday.

"They are true," he said.

"Then I am pleased, Master," I said.

"Do you think you are a high slave?" he asked.

"No, Master," I said.

"Do you grow proud?" he asked.

"I do not think so, Master," I said. "I hope not, Master."

"To your right," he said, "against the wall, there is a box. Open it, and bring me its contents."

I turned about and went to the side of the room. There, against the wall, as he had said, there was a box, a heavy coffer, with iron bands, with a curved lid. I knelt before the box. I lifted the lid. In the box there was but one object, a slave whip.

I removed the whip from the box and rose to my feet, and returned to the dais, where I climbed the stairs and knelt before Hendow. I kissed the whip, and holding it with both hands, my arms extended, my head down, between my arms, proffered it to him. I then rose to my feet and withdrew to the foot of the dais, where I stood.

I looked up at Hendow.

My bit of silk, on the rug, was at my feet, on the right.

He stood up. He was a very large man. On the dais, standing, he loomed over me. In his right hand was the whip. He shook out the coils. I was naked. I was small, and weak. I was collared.

"When you were first in this room, several weeks ago," he said, "you may remember that I said you were beautiful."

"Yes, Master," I said, warily.

I saw the blade of the whip swing a bit, almost indolently.

I regarded the instrument of discipline, frightened.

He suddenly cracked the whip in the air. It made a report like a rifle shot. I could not help but move, and cry out with misery.

"Think carefully," he said. "When I said that you were very beautiful, several weeks ago, the first time that I said it, you considered whether or not that might indicate an interest, or weakness, on my part, and whether or not you might be able to exploit it."

"No, Master!" I cried, frightened. "No, Master!"

Then I saw him approaching me suddenly, descending the steps, swiftly for so large a man, his arm drawn back.

"Please, no, Master!" I wept. Then I felt the lash. I stumbled back in agony, turned about, and fell to the carpet. There the leather once more informed me of the displeasure of my master. I screamed, miserable. Then another blow like lightning was on my back and I sobbed at his feet, on my belly on the rug. "Yes, Master!" I wept. "Yes, Master, I thought such a thing, but I could not help it. I am only human. I am only a female! Do not punish me for what I could not help! I put the thought from me!"

I lay there on my belly at his feet. I did not care for the whip. I did not want it. I feared it, terribly. It hurt so. It is a quite effective instrument of discipline for females. It is no wonder the masters use it on us. It, and numerous other disciplines and devices, we so helpless, serve to keep us well in line.

"You have not been struck for that," he said.

"I do not understand, Master," I sobbed.

"I have not chosen to beat you for what you cannot help," he said. "It was clear to me that you had thought the better of your girlish vagary."

"Why, then?" I asked.

"Do I need a reason?" he asked.

"No, Master!" I cried. "No, Master!" The girl belongs to the master. He can do what he wishes with her.

"You do not know why you were struck?" he asked.

"No, Master," I said.

"Perhaps you are stupid," he mused.

"Perhaps, Master," I said.

"You were struck," he said, "because you lied."

"Yes, Master," I said. I lay there, startled, terrified now. How perceptive was this man! Earlier, weeks ago, once, and only briefly, I had considered, swiftly in fear putting the thought from me, that I might be able to use his interest in my favor, perhaps manipulating him, or, in virtue of it, somehow improving my lot. He had, it seems, sensed, or understood, this transitory, swiftly rejected consideration, probably from some fleeting expression, or movement of my body, one I had scarcely been aware of. He had not chosen to punish me for that, a thing I could hardly help. For that I was grateful. To be sure, had I continued to consider such matters, I supposed he might have instructed me, sooner or later, with the whip or some other means, as to the unacceptability of such considerations. What he had whipped me for was something else, for now, just now, having lied to him.

He then gave me another blow and I scratched at the carpet in agony.

"Despicable slut!" he said.

"Yes, Master!" I wept.

He then struck me again, and tears burst from my eyes anew. I lay helpless before him, a punished slave.

"Kneel," he said, "swiftly, facing away from me."

I obeyed, in terror, almost frenziedly. I now faced the door.

"To all fours," he commanded.

I obeyed, trembling.

Twice more then he struck me, and the second blow, as I cried out with misery, sobbing, flung me again to the carpet on my belly.

"Kneel, as you were before," he said.

I obeyed.

"All fours," he said.

I went again to all fours.

He then, crouching near me, reaching about me, put the whip to my lips. I kissed it, frightened, again and again.

"Kneel now, in the following fashion," he said. "Do not waste time."

He then had me kneel with my head to the floor, my hands clasped tightly behind the back of my neck. I cried out, grasped, fixedly held, put to his fierce, disciplinary purposes.

He then drew back from me.

I was now on my belly on the rug, gasping in disbelief. I understood more of my slavery then than I had before.

I think he may then have ascended the dais, and perhaps resumed his place in the curule chair. I did not really know. I did not dare look back.

I lay there, disciplined, punished, half shattered. I had never doubted that he would be strong, but I had never expected such power. I had not understood that he was such a man. I could hardly believe what he had done to me, and the force and peremptoriness with which it had been done.

"Report to the kitchen," he said.

"Yes, Master," I sobbed.

His voice, indeed, had come from above and behind me. He was on the dais then, certainly. I did not know if he were seated or not.

I reached for the silk beside me.

"No," he said.

I drew back my hand.

"You are denied clothing until further notice," he said.

"Yes, Master," I said.

"And have the kitchen master put you at the tubs," he said.

"Yes, Master," I said.

I struggled to my feet. I think I understood, then, how it was that girls came back to the slave quarters scarely able to move.

"May I speak, Master?" I asked.

"Yes," he said.

"Am I to be put in the iron belt?" I asked.

"No," he said.

Before, when at the tubs, kneeling there, working beside Ina, our arms immersed to the elbows in the hot water and suds, I had been protected by my virginity. Now, however, I would be as exposed and helpless there as Ina.

I made my way down the long rug, toward the door.

I was under no delusion now that I might be in the favor of my master. I was under no delusion now that there might be something special about me, that I might even be a preferred slave or a high slave. I knew now, and knew it well, that I was only another girl, no different from any other in the house.

"Slave," said he.

"Yes, Master?" I said. I, addressed, knelt, but I did not turn about. I did not know whether it would please him or not. If he wanted me to turn about, I would doubtless be informed of that fact.

"Do you recall one named Mirus," he asked.

"Yes, Master," I said.

"He is no longer in my employ," he said.

"Yes, Master," I said.

"You are dismissed," he said.

"Yes, Master," I said. "Thank you, Master."

I then rose to my feet, and withdrew from the presence of my master, Hendow, of Brundisium.

15 / The Hood and Leash

"Hist," I heard, "hist," a tiny, soft noise.

"Who is there?" I asked, frightened. I pulled the blanket up, about me, inside my kennel, in the basement of the tavern of Hendow. It was dark.

"It is I, first girl, Tupita," I heard, a whisper.

"Mistress?" I asked. I quickly knelt in the small kennel, in the darkness. It was the voice of Tupita, of that I was certain. I clutched the blanket about me. She struck no light.

I heard a key fitted into the two locks, one after the other, on the gate of the kennel, and the gate was opened.

"Mistress?" I asked.

"We are on secret business for our Master," she said. "You are to come with me."

"I do not understand," I whispered.

"Do you question me?" she asked.

"No, Mistress," I said.

"Come out," she said. "Be silent. Few must know of this."

I crawled from the kennel. The blanket remains behind. I was naked. I had been naked for several days, ever since I had been punished in the chamber of my master, for having lied to him. Beyond such things, however, it was not at all unusual that I should be naked. Girls are often kept naked in their kennels. Too, even if not caged or kenneled, they often sleep naked, that they may be the more accessible to the master. At the least they sleep scantily clad or in garments that may be swiftly drawn aside, revealing them. Some men, to be sure, enjoy having at least a bit of cloth or a slave rag on their girl, so that she will understand, even if she is awakened rudely, that there is some veil which is being removed from her.

"What is going on?" I asked.

"You will soon learn," she said. "Kneel."

I knelt. I felt my hands being drawn behind me. I then felt steel touch my wrists, and heard the tiny sounds of the ratchets and pawls. I was braceleted.

"What are we going to do?" I asked.

"We are going into the city," she said.

"I do not understand," I said. Then I was leashed.

"Do you want to spend longer in the kitchen?" she asked.

"No," I whispered. "No."

"You are going to be cloaked, and hooded," she whispered.

"I am not allowed out of the house," I said.

"Tonight is different," she said.

I felt a warm, long cloak put about me. When I stood, it might come even to my ankles. She tied it under my chin.

"Please tell me what is going on," I said.

"I am first girl," said Tupita. "Do you question me?"

"No!" I whispered, swiftly.

"I told you that we are on the secret business of our master," she said. "Shall I inform him that you are recalcitrant?"

"No, Mistress!" I said. "Forgive me, Mistress!"

"I am acting under the orders of Hendow," she said. "Trust me."

"Yes, Mistress," I said. How bold she was, I thought, to have used our master's name in that fashion, speaking it unnecessarily, not referring to him in terms such as "the master" or "our master."

"Open your mouth," she said.

I did so, and felt a heavy, rolled-leather wadding thrust back, behind my teeth, over my tongue, so that I could scarcely move my tongue. This device would be secured in place by a broad, mouth-covering strap, with three smaller straps attached to it, one to secure the broad strap at the upper lip, another to secure it across the mouth, pulling it back between the teeth, and one to secure it at the chin. These straps were then pulled back tightly, and fastened, to the top strap above my ears, behind the back of my head, and the two lower straps behind the back of my neck. The roll in my mouth then loosened a little, as I could not help struggling with it, and this, by design, caused it to expand and, secured in place, pack my entire oral orifice.

"Are you well gagged?" she asked.

I made a very tiny, pathetic, affirmative whimper. I could do little more.

She then pulled the hood of the cloak up and put it about my head, and pulled it down before me, fully over my head, and tied it, as she had the strings, earlier, about my neck. I was now effectively hooded, as well as gagged.

"Come along, my dear," she said.

She then drew me to my feet by the leash, which was now doubtless coiled. She apparently held it only a few inches from my neck. In this fashion she could help me up the stairs.

16 / Thieves

"Let us see her," said a voice.

I was on my back on a wooden table. My feet had been tied down, and apart. The cloak, in so far as it continued to conceal me, was thrown back.

"Excellent," said a man's voice.

The strings to the cloak, which were still fastened about my neck, were then undone. I then felt hands working at the second set of strings, those by means of which the cloak's hood, it still enveloping my entire head was tied about my neck. In a moment they, too, were undone. I felt the hood brushed back.

"Superb," said a man.

I blinked against the torchlight.

"Common kajira brand," commented a man.

"Yes," said one of the fellows.

"It is Doreen, Hendow's slut, all right," said a man. "I have seen her dance."

I half sat up, wildly, startled, but, by a hand in my hair, from behind, was drawn down again to my back. My hands were still braceleted behind me. In the moment I had sat up I had seen there were five men in the room, and Tupita, to one side, smiling, modestly cloaked.

"You are pleased?" she asked the men.

"Yes," said a fellow. "We are pleased."

In the instant, too, I had been up I had seen there had been two rings, at the bottom of the table, one on each side. A single narrow strand of coarse rope ran between these two rings. By means of this single strand of rope, and two simpe knots, my left ankle had been tied just inside the left ring and my right ankle just inside the right ring.

"She is beautiful," said a man.

"Yes," said a man. "And see those delicious slave curves."

I squirmed, frightened.

"Do not be afraid, my lovely, curvy, brunet kajira," said a fellow, leaning over me.

"Her ears are pierced, too," said a man.

"Superb," said another.

"I wonder if she is vital," said a man.

"Her ears are pierced," a fellow reminded him.

"We shall see," said another.

I writhed, whimpering, squirming. My ankles jerked, burned, in their rope loops. There was a sudden metallic sound as the linkage on the bracelets snapped taut. There was a scraping of metal on the table. My fingers twisted helplessly. My wrists, hurt, pulling against the steel of the bracelets. I was absolutely at their mercy. I was absolutely helpless.

"She is vital," commented a fellow.

Tupita laughed.

"How glorious that there are slaves," said another.

"Pay me," said Tupita.

"Your collar will not do, my dear," said one of the fellows, leaning over me. "We shall have to remove it."

I could not, myself, remove my collar, of course. Gorean slave collars are not made for the girl to remove. It would have to be done with tools.

"But have no fear, my dear," said the man, patting my brand, "this will stay."

I looked up at him, wildly, tears in my eyes.

"Do not fret," he said. "You will not have a naked neck for long. We do not like naked necks on kajirae. It will soon be in another collar."

Tupita pushed between the men. She stood at my right. She spit in my face. "Now," she said, "I have my vengeance on you! You think you are more beautiful than I, but you are not! You thought you would have an easy life, and be most desired among the girls of Hendow, but you will not be! I have seen to it! You thought to take Mirus from me, too, but soon I could have won him back! It is I whom he loves, not you! Because of you he is no longer in the house of Hendow! Too, it was you who undermined me with the girls and the masters, and it is because of you that Aynur, stupid Aynur, was made first girl this afternoon! I hate you all, except Sita, who alone remained loyal to me! But I will not stay in the house of Hendow without Mirus or as second girl! I have escaped, and, in one stroke, too, taken my vengeance on you."

I shook my head, no, no, no!

"You even informed on me when I was so kind as to bring you a pastry," she said, "for which I was beaten!"

I shook my head wildly, no!

"But I have made it now so that you will no longer have the protection and favor of Hendow, whom you have bewitched," she said.

I regarded her, startled.

"Now, you, too, will know the whip when men please!"

I shuddered.

"While you remain a slave, Earth slut," she said, "I will be free! And it is you, my pretty enemy, who will have bought me my freedom! Consider it, slut! Such vengeance is sweet!"

I whimpered, piteously, looking up at Tupita.

"How easily you were tricked, stupid slave," she laughed.

Tears sprang to my eyes.

She then again spit in my face, and then turned away from me.

"Pay me," she demanded of he who seemed to be the leader of the men. "I must secure tarn passage from Brundisium before morning."

He looked at her.

"Pay me," she demanded, putting out her hand. "I have fulfilled my part of the bargain. I have completed my portion of the arrangements. I have delivered the merchandise to you."

The fellow opened his wallet.

"No!" she said. "We agreed on five silver tarsks, five!"

He held a single silver tarsk.

"Our arrangement was for five," she said, "five!"

"Do you truly think she is worth five?" asked the fellow.

Tupita regarded him, angrily. Clearly she did not wish to acknowledge that I might, objectively, be of value, particularly of a value so high as five silver tarsks. She herself, perhaps, might not bring so much. "What she is truly worth, or what I might think she is truly worth," said Tupita, "is of no importance. Perhaps she is not worth even a tarsk bit. How would I know? I am not a man. But we agreed on the price of five silver tarsks, five!"

"I thought it was one," grinned a fellow.

"Perhaps you have it in writing," said another fellow, as though helpfully.

Tupita, of course, like many slaves, and like myself, could not read or write. Too, even if she could, she, a highly intelligent woman, and a slave, would never have dared to agree to anything in writing pertaining to such clandestine matters.

"Yes," she said, suddenly, with a glance at me. "I remember now. It was one." I saw that she wanted to save face, before me. Too, a silver tarsk is, after all, when all is said and done, a coin of considerable value. Although this varies from city to city, it is not unusual for a silver tarsk to be exchangeable for a hundred copper tarsks, each one of which can be worth anywhere from ten to four tarsk bits, usually eight. The only golden Gorean coins I had ever seen were the tiny ones, almost droplets, which had figured in the decorative jewelries of dancers' costumes. Brundisium was noted for its golden staters, but I had never seen one.

Tupita took the silver tarsk from the fellow, and clutched it triumphantly, tightly, in her fist. It would be more than enough to purchase her passage from Brundisium. She then came again to the side of the table. "Thank you, lovely Doreen," she said. "I am very grateful. Not only do I have my vengeance upon you, delivering you to new slaveries and degradations, as it pleased me, but you have been also the means of my own escape and freedom." She showed me the silver tarsk. "Pretty, isn't it?' she asked.

I pulled weakly against the bracelets. The men laughed.

"I am only sorry that you are not worth more," she said.

Tears welled up in my eyes.

"I will leave you now, slave, roped and braceleted, and in the power of men," she said. She turned away.

But the door was blocked by a fellow, leaning against it, his arms folded.

"Stand aside!" she said, angrily.

He did not move, nor did he respond to her.

She spun to face the leader of the men.

"What do you have there, in your hand?" he asked.

She clutched the tarsk more tightly.

"Open your hand," said the leader.

"What is the meaning of this!" she cried.

"Must a command be repeated?" he inquired.

She opened her hand, revealing the silver tarsk. He walked to her, and removed it from her hand. "Have you been permitted to touch money?" he asked.

"Please!" she said.

"We could always check with her master," suggested a fellow.

"It is mine!" said Tupita.

"Yours?" asked the leader, smiling.

"Yes!" she said.

"Surely you know that animals are not allowed to own money," he said.

Tupita turned white.

The leader dropped the coin into his wallet.

"Let me go," she said. "I will bother you no longer!"

"Remove your cloak," said the leader.

Tupita thrust it back, over her shoulders, untied the strings and let it fall to the floor, behind her.

She then stood there among them, in a brief tunic of opaque slave silk, such as might be worn during the day. She was a very lovely, and very frightened woman. The cloak removed, the collar could be seen on her neck. If he from whom she had intended to purchase tarn passage had not seen the collar, nor, of course, her brand, nor her tunic, or such, and, theoretically, at least, did not know she was a slave, he would not be held legally responsible for having sold her passage. Tupita had excellent legs.

"Remove the tunic," said the leader.

She reached to the disrobing loop, and dropped the tunic to the floor, about her ankles. Tupita was too good a slave, and too wise a slave, to dally before a Gorean male, having received such a command.

"What is the meaning of this?" she said, naked.

Her hands were then drawn behind her, and, in an instant, she was braceleted, as securely as I.

"Perhaps we are in the hire of Hendow, your master," said the leader of the men.

"No!" cried Tupita. "No!" She flung herself to her knees before the leader, and the others. "No, please, Masters!" she cried. "Take pity on me!"

"But we are not in his hire," said the leader.

Tupita sobbed with relief.

"Examine her," said the leader, curtly. I rolled to the right side of the table, and twisted about, a little. Then, frightened, I rolled again to my back.

"She had this," said one of the men, holding up a small, damp leather sack by its strings.

I turned a little and saw some of the tiny golden coins, such as adorned the dancers' costumes, spilled into the hand of the leader. I heard Tupita, on the floor, sobbing. It was a good deal more than a silver tarsk that she had thought to garner from her venture this night in Brundisium. No wonder she had been willing to leave, even without the tarsk. Had Mirus still been with the tavern, I do not think she would have been able to secure the tiny coins. He had been careful about such things.

"See if she is vital," said the leader.

I heard Tupita suddenly cry out and, startled, gasp, and then whimper.

"She is vital," said a man.

I then saw Tupita pulled to her feet. She seemed half in shock. Her hair was down about her face. A man held her from behind, keeping her from falling, by the upper arms. Her wrists were braceleted behind her. Held as she was, and with her hands braceleted behind her, the beauty of her bared bosom was accentuated. Sometimes slavers present prospective buyers with girls held in this fashion. This time, of course, it was a mere convenience that she was held so. I regarded her. Tupita was quite beautiful. There was no doubt about it.

"I would not mind owning either of them," said a fellow.

"Please!" said Tupita.

"Not in Brundisium, you wouldn't," laughed one of the men.

"Yes," said another. "They must both be sold out of Brundisium."

"Please!" begged Tupita.

"Be silent," snapped the leader. "Apparently you have not felt the whip enough."

Immediately Tupita was silent.

"You are not now with soft masters," he said. "You are not now in the house of Hendow, where, it would seem, the girls do not know the whip."

Tupita put her head down, not daring to meet his eyes.

The leader was mistaken, of course. The girls in the house of Hendow knew the whip, and knew it well. Indeed, it was not unusual for them to experience it if they had been even in the least bit displeasing. To be sure, this very understanding, in itself, knowing the discipline under which they served, its consistency and reality, encouraged them to attempt to achieve perfect pleasingness, with the result that the whip was seldom called for, unless perhaps for the amusement of the master.

"We must get these slaves out of Brundisium soon," said a man, nervously.

"Before light," said another.

"Before sleen are put on their trail," said another.

"Yes," said another.

I thought of Borko, the gray sleen. When it was discovered that we were missing, he, or other such beasts, might be set upon our trail. My blanket, of course, had been left behind in the kennel. That would suffice for any hunting sleen. Borko, of course, did not need so typical a stimulus. He, knowing my name and scent, could be set on my trail by a mere verbal command. I shuddered. Through no fault of my own I feared I might be torn to pieces. A similar fate, of course, might befall Tupita. She, had been quite anxious, I recalled, to be swiftly out of Brundisium.

"Lift your head," said the leader to Tupita.

She obeyed.

"You will not even have to pay for your tarn passage out of Brundisium," he said.

"Yes, Master," she said.

"Bring tools," said the leader.

Our collars, which identified us as the girls of Hendow, were to be removed. It is customary to change a girl's collar shortly after she has been stolen. This makes it harder to trace her.

"Where are you going to take us, Master?" asked Tupita.

The leader went to her and, with the back of his hand, lashed her across the mouth.

"Curiosity," he said, "is not becoming in a kajira."

"Yes, Master," she said. Her lip was cut.

"Gag her," he said.

I watched while a gag, not unlike mine, was fastened in

Tupita's mouth. She did not look at me, while it was being put on her. I did not think, however, that the gag was really necessary. Was she really going to cry out, and perhaps then be "rescued," only to be subsequently returned to Hendow, for his mercy? I did not think there would be even a tiny sound out of her. She would doubtless go quietly. On the other hand, the choice had not been left to her. Men had decided the matter. The gag was now packed well in her mouth, and secured tightly in place, by three sets of laces, however, rather than three straps, like mine. She looked suddenly at me, wildly, then looked away. She now was no more than me, only another slave, being stolen.

"When their collars are off," said the leader, "put the other collars on them, those we prepared for them."

Tupita looked at the leader. Two collars had been prepared. They had planned, then, from the beginning, to take her along. That was not hard to understand, of course. She was very beautiful.

"Then," said the leader, "hood them. Then put them with the others."

17 / The Square of Market of Semris

"Come along," he said.

I cried out softly, stumbling forward, barefoot on the dirt street, the steel of the collar pulled hard against the back of my neck.

"Hurry," he said.

"Yes, Master!" I said.

"We must be to the square by the tenth Ahn," he said.

"Yes, Master," I said.

I was leashed. The leash was of light chain.

The tenth Ahn was the Gorean noon. The square would be crowded at that time. To be sure, it is crowded in different ways at different times, during the day. In the morning the peasants come in from the countryside and spread out their blankets, and arrange their baskets of produce. Much shopping is done in the early morning. Later the stalls and shops around the square roll back their screens and shutters and open for business. Later men come for gossiping and the exchange of news. Some visit the temples, paying coins, buying incense and burning it, petitioning Priest-Kings for favors, such things as better crops and success in ventures, such things as luck for themselves and calamities for their enemies. Gorean petitions to the Priest-Kings seem on the whole to be very specific, and very practical. Most Goreans seem skeptical of an afterlife, or, at least, seem content to wait and see. The only Gorean caste which, as far as I know, officially believes in an afterlife is that of the Initiates, and they believe in it, it seems, only for themselves, and seem to believe it is connected with such things as the performance of secret rites, the acquisition of secret knowledges, mostly mathematical, and the avoidance of certain foods. Initiates commonly wear white and have their heads shaved. They also, supposedly, and perhaps actually, on the whole, abstain from alcohol and women. They count as one of the five high castes, the others being the Physicians, Scribes, Builders and Warriors. In some cities they are quite powerful, in others it seems they are largely peripheral to the life of the community. I have never been in one of these temples. Slaves, like other animals, are not allowed within. It is felt they would defile such places. They may wait, however, in special, small, walled areas outside the temples, usually at the back or sides, where their presence will not prove distractive or offensive to free persons. I have looked within some of these temples, from the street, through great opened doors, or through the open colonnades, such temples being roofed, but not walled, upon occasion. Some are lavishly decorated, even ornately; others seem very austere. It depends on the city, I suppose, or the tastes of the community of Initiates, those who care for the temples, in a given place. The Chief Initiate of Ar claims to be chief of all the Initiates of all the cities, but the other Chief Initiates, in the other cities, do not, it seems, at least on the whole, acknowledge this claim. I have gathered that in these temples there are no chairs or pews, or such, unless for Initiates near the altars. Goreans perform their rites, recite their prayers, and such, standing. The Gorean tends to regard Priest-Kings not so much as his masters as his potential allies, who might, if he is lucky, be flattered, wooed with gifts, and such. On the high altar in each temple there is supposedly a large golden circle, the symbol of Priest-Kings, a symbol of eternity, of a thing without beginning or end. The "sign of the Priest-Kings," similarly, is made with a closed, circular motion. The teachings of the Initiates, their recommendations, exhortations, and such, seem to be taken most seriously by the lower castes. Many men also, incidentally, enjoy sitting in on the courts, listening to the disputes and suits. Some serve on juries. Others merely enjoy the interplay and logic, often applauding an excellent point when scored by one of the advocates. Later in the afternoon, many men congregate in the baths. The baths in many Gorean towns are important social centers. Some are private, for a reserved clientele, but most are public, and their facilities, for a fee, are available to all free persons. They tend to be segregated, of course. Free persons of different sexes do not bathe together publicly. This reservation, of course, does not preclude the presence of female bath attendants in the mens' baths or of silk slaves in those for the women. In the late afternoon, after the baths, the men tend to wend their way home, looking forward to their evening meal. Sometimes rich men are followed home by their "clients." These, too, often meet them outside the house in the morning, and sometimes accompany them about, during the day. Goreans are fond of giving dinners and having parties. They are a sociable folk. If one does not own one's own slave, or enough of them, it is also possible to rent them for such occasions. The arrangements for those rentals are usually made during the day, conveniently in the square, or in its vicinity. In the neighborhood of holidays it is wise to make the arrangements days in advance. Sometimes in the evenings, and toward the end of the week there are entertainments, such as plays and concerts. Things such as races, and games, for the cities who can support them, particularly on a regular, or seasonal basis, usually occur in the afternoon, under natural light.

"Hurry!" he said.

Again I stumbled forward, drawn by the chain leash. I could not remove the leash even though my hands were free. Its snap was a lock snap, and it had been closed about the collar. It was thus secured on me. I was well leashed.

"Hurry!" he said, moving quickly before me.

"Yes, Master!" I said.

I was clad in a ta-teera, or slave rag, a brief bit of rep cloth, torn here and there, well revealing me. We were in the streets of Market of Semris. I had been sold here once. We had come from Samnium, which lies south and east of Brundisium. I had come into the possession of my current master there. I had cost him only fifty copper tarsks, half a silver tarsk. The men who had sold me had not chosen to long haggle. I had cost them nothing. They did not have to make much on me. Too, it seemed they wished to dispose of their girls, and there were several of us, brought by tarn basket to Samnium, quickly. I did not know to whom Tupita was sold, but she doubtless, too, would have gone into a cheaper slavery than she had known. On my back, tied there, was a rolled pallet, filled with straw. About my neck hung a copper bowl. It was suspended by a thong, threaded through a small hole in the bowl. My master had a double flute slung on his back. He was Gordon, an itinerant musician.

"Is she any good?" called a lad, as we hurried through the dusty street.

"Come and see," said my master.

We must now be closer to the square, as it seemed there were more people in the street. Too, the street, now, was paved. Buildings were on both sides of us. The street was about ten feet in width. It had stepping stones at the corners, for rainy weather. These stones are placed in such a way that the wheels of a cart may traverse the street. When we came to the square there would probably be barriers set up against such traffic. The square was for pedestrians. Porters there, slaves, could, for a fee, transport goods, if it was desired, within, or across the square. The gutter on the street was a long, narrow trough. It ran down the center of the street.

A free woman, throwing me a look of disgust, drew to one side, that her ornate robes not brush against me as I passed. "Oh!" I said, startled. A man had patted me as I had passed him.

"Here," said my master, with satisfaction.

I blinked against the light of the open square. Market of Semris is not a large town, and it is mostly famed, as I have earlier noted, for its markets for tarsks, "four-legged" and "two-legged," as it is said, but like most Gorean towns, its square, even as small as it was, was a matter of civic pride. It was set with flat stones, intricately fitted together. At its edges, in several places, were shops. It contained four fountains, one at each corner. The temple was impressive, a closed temple, with columns, a pediment and a frieze. The public buildings, the law court and the "house of the Administrator," the locus of public offices, were similarly structured and adorned. Commemorative columns stood here and there about the edges of the square. We entered through the vertical posts, passing the porters' station there. An open barbers' shop, with five stools, was to one side. The stools were all occupied. Three fellows were having their hair cut; one was being shaved, with a shaving knife; another was having his beard trimmed. Other folks were standing about, waiting. I followed my master, on my leash. I was incredibly thrilled to walk upon these stones. I looked about myself with wonder. I had only dreamed of such things. It was like being transported magically into the past, only here, in this place, it was the present, and I was actually here, truly, though in a collar. I knew I must obey well in such a place, among such people. I was a slave, and uncompromisingly at their mercy. Yet in spite of such things I would not have traded the beautiful world of Gor for anything, even though on such a world I was only the lowliest and most meaningless of its animals. To one side there was a sculptured group, perhaps celebrating some triumph or victory, of five heroic male figures, with shields, helmets and spears, and at their feet, amidst apparent spoils, perhaps captives, or slaves, kneeling, two nude female figures. I saw, too, about its base, an encircling, illustratory frieze. "Please, Master!" I begged. "Please, let me look. Let me look!" He glanced back, shrewdly at me. My eyes were piteous. I knew, whatever he decided, I must abide by his decision. He was not an indulgent master, but he was an intelligent one, and he could see that I was excited. I was vitally aroused in such a place. He then let me, he behind me, with the leash, look at the encircling, narrative frieze. It was in five main divisions. In the first it seemed that angry heralds or ambassadors were before a throne, on which reposed a serene Tatrix, and that perhaps an insult had been given. In the second armies were drawn up upon a plain before a city. In the third a fearful battle was in progress. In the fourth it seemed that humbled representatives of the vanquished now appeared before the camp throne of a victorious general. To him they brought, it seemed, a suit for peace, and offerings of conciliation. Among these offerings were unusual beasts, sheaves of grain, vessels and coffers filled with precious goods, and women, naked, and in chains. Too, it seemed they had brought something else. Before the throne of the victorious general, kneeling, in her tiara, fully clothed, but chained, had been placed the Tatrix. In the fifth, and last division, we saw a victory feast. Naked maidens, doubtless of the vanquished, served at the low tables, and, in the open space between these tables, and among them, danced. At the side of the victorious general, his guest, sat the Tatrix, still in her tiara, but stripped to the waist. Doubtless at the next feast her tiara would be removed from her. Slave girls have no need of such things. Doubtless, at the next feast, she, too, naked, would serve and dance, hoping then like any other slave to be found pleasing by her masters.

"Interestingly," said my master, "this monument celebrates a victory in which Market of Semris was only indirectly involved.

It tells the story of a war which took place far to the north and west, on the Olni, between Port Olni and Ti, two hundred years before the formation of the Salarian Confederation. Ti was victorious. There is a larger original of this in Ti. This is a copy. It is here because, at the time of that war, Market of Semris had been of great service to Ti as a supply ally."

"Yes, Master," I said.

"Most of what I have told you is on that plaque to the right," he said.

"Yes, Master," I said. I could not read.

"Come along," he said, with a sound of chain giving me a tug on the leash.

"That is a curvy slave," said a man, approvingly.

I did not know if he had referred to me or not. Perhaps he had. A ta-teera leaves few of a girl's charms to the imagination. I quickly followed my master, taking care not to let the leash grow taut. I may have been mistaken, but I felt that men were looking at me. Perhaps they had noticed, too, the double flute on my master's back. If so, they may have taken an additionally close look at me, more than the usual Gorean master's appraisal of delectable slave meat, deciding then whether or not it might be of interest to follow us.

"Here," said my master, stopping in a shady corner of the square.

"Yes, Master," I said.

There was a building there. In the wall of it, about a foot from the ground, there were four or five slave rings. Such things are common in Gorean public places. They provide masters with a convenience for the tethering of their slaves.

Some men gathered around.

I loosened the cords which kept the pallet on my back. I removed the pallet from my back and put it on the ground. I undid the strings which kept it rolled, and spread it. It was to the left of the nearest slave ring. I took the copper bowl from about my neck and put it beside the pallet. My master then put his end of the leash twice about the slave ring and, with a heavy padlock, passed through two leash rings, secured it there. I was now chained to the slave ring.

I knelt beside the bowl. I kept my head down.

My master removed his long double flute from his back.

I braced myself for an instant.

He played then a set of annunciatory skirls.

I think that anyone in the square must have heard those sounds. He then, for two or three minutes, played soft, full, melodious tunes, sensuous, inviting tunes. Men began to gather around, in greater numbers. There was soon a small crowd there.

I kept my head down.

My master would decide when the crowd was sufficient. I recollected the monument in the square, the heroic figures, and the women, doubtless booty, at their feet. I recollected, too, in particular, the frieze encircling the base of the monument. I recalled in particular the lofty Tatrix on her throne, in the beginning of the frieze, and later, the procession of those who came suing for peace, bearing conciliatory gifts, animals, riches, women and such. I recalled the Tatrix, fully clothed, in chains, placed on her knees before the victor. I recalled, too, the last portion of the frieze, where she had sat beside the victor, in her tiara, gracing his victory feast, half stripped, while women of her city, totally naked, served and danced. I was excited by the frieze. I was excited, too, as a slave, by the men about. In the presence of men, sometimes to my dismay and embarrassment, I would feel warm and wonderful between my legs. This was permissible, of course, for I was only a slave. Those women in the frieze had probably been free women, at least at the time. Their freedom, however, I did not doubt, would have proved fleeting, and soon they would have been distributed among the victors, or disposed of, for profit, in various slave markets. I wondered if the general would have had the Tatrix sold in a cheap market or if he would have kept her for himself, perhaps as the least of his own slaves. But I, myself, was not a free woman. I was only a slave. I loved the freedom, and liberation this gave me, to be a full woman. I then heard the soft swirl of music which I well recognized.

I rose gracefully to my feet, and stood before the men. I heard the soft intaking of breath in several of them, in anticipation. How powerful I felt then, though I was only a slave, chained at a ring.

With the music of the double flute in the background I modestly removed the Ta-Teera, putting it to the side.

"Ah!" said a man.

"Marvelous," said another.

I adjusted the chain, placing it between my breasts. It went to the ground where it lay in a coil, then moved back to the ring. By intent it was of a generous length. I pulled it down a bit, at the collar. I did this in such a way that the men could tell it was well locked there. I knew this would excite them, as it excited me. Too, of course, as a practical matter, this further assured that the draw would be at the front of the collar. I flexed my knees. I lifted my hands over my head, gracefully, their wrists back to back.

My master let me dance for four or five minutes, until the men were in a frenzy of need. I performed even what are called "floor movements" for them. I saw their eyes blazing. Such is the power of the dancer.

I then, at the finish of the music, knelt before them, submitted, as a female slave, and then, still kneeling, lifted my head. "May I speak, Masters?" I asked. "Yes," cried several of the men. "I have need of the touch of a man," I said. "I beg the touch of a man. Who will touch me?" These were words I had been taught to say, even, of course, the appropriate petition, that of a slave girl, to speak before masters. But, too, I had been excited. They were men, and I was a slave. I did want their touch, and desperately. The only sexual attention my master gave me, wanting to keep me in need for customers, was an occasional raping.

I felt myself seized by the upper arms, half lifted from my knees, and flung back on the pallet. I heard a small coin, a tarsk bit, ring in the copper bowl. I seized the lustful brute to me, desperately, thankfully! I was hot and open, and slave needful! In an instant he was finished with me. I half sat up, but was caught, and thrust back to the pallet. I heard another coin strike in the bowl. I closed my eyes, gratefully.

I served muchly that afternoon, and five times did I dance. Sometimes in my dance I made use of the chain, sometimes pretending, to the music, to fight it, a fight which I had to lose, or not to understand it, looking to the men then, as though they might explain its meaning to me; they did, with raucous cries; sometimes I used it to caress me, with the soft, lovely chain caresses of bondage, to which I, whimpering, responded; sometimes I seemed to confine myself variously, seemingly sometimes more strictly, more helplessly, more mercilessly, with it; sometimes I kissed it and caressed it, gratefully and lovingly, expressing therein the welling up within me of my joy at finding myself at last in my rightful place in nature; there is much that one can do with a chain. Once a free woman came to watch, for a moment. I dared not meet her eyes, but, too, I did not falter in my dance, or beauty; indeed, I tried to show her, lovingly, as one woman to another, what a woman could be, even a lowly slave, especially a lowly slave. She hurried away, trembling within her robes. I wondered if sometime she, too, would wear a collar, and move so before men.

I then, late in the afternoon, lay upon the pallet. I could hear, beneath its narrow, sewn canvas surface, the crinkling of the straw within. There were several coins in the copper bowl. My master had taken some out, from time to time, during the afternoon. One normally leaves enough in the bowl to act as an invitation to others, but not so much as to suggest that there is no need of more, if only to keep the others company.

"What got into you today?" asked my master.

"Master?" I asked, lying on my side on the pallet, the chain on my neck.

"I think that I have never seen you so needful and hot," he said.

"My needs grow upon me, Master," I said. It was true. But, also today I was charged with seeing the square, the buildings, and the people of Market of Semris. It was as though I had suddenly found myself marvelously transported to the past, and one in which I must helplessly meet its conditions, and obey it, and on its own terms, and perfectly, not mine. Market of Semris might have been a town in Hellas or Latium. I was thrilled to be there, if only as a slave. I would not have traded the beautiful, marvelous world of Gor, even with its perils, for anything. Too I had not forgotten the monument and the frieze. I would never forget it. It had much excited me, in its style, beauty and graphicness, and in its simple, unquestioned, unevasive public representation, albeit in a political and commemorative context, of natural biological relationships.

"Slave," said my master.

"Master?" I asked. I turned to my back. I saw that his needs were upon him. I smiled at him, eager to please him. I lifted my arms to him.

"To your stomach," he said.

I obeyed. He would keep me well in my place.

My master was Gordon, an itinerant musician. I was a street dancer.

When he had finished he stood up.

"Your slave," said a man, a tall fellow, in swirling robes, "is not without interest."

I, of course, knelt immediately, being the subject of attention, of a free man.

The fellow had been here for much of the afternoon, watching us. He had not, however, used me.

"You are an Earth slut, are you not?" he asked.

"Yes, Master," I said.

"Her ears are pierced," he observed.

"Yes," said my master.

"She is an excellent dancer, for a street dancer," said the man.

My master shrugged.

"Perhaps she did not always dance in the streets," he speculated.

"Perhaps," said my master, putting his flute again on his back.

Usually the progression is such matters, of course, is from the street to the tavern, not from the tavern to the street. When the street dancer becomes good enough, she may aspire, of course, to be purchased by a taverner. Many of the finest tavern dancers, it is said, began on the back streets, on a leash.

"Did she once dance in a tavern?" asked the fellow.

"I do not know," said my master, uneasily. He actually did not know, I supposed. He had had a good buy on me, and he had not been interested in asking questions.

"I think she was once a tavern dancer," said the man.

"Perhaps," said my master. "I do not know." He made as though to go.

"I think she is a stolen tavern dancer," said the man.

"I bought her properly," said my master.

"You have papers on her?" asked the man.

"No," said my master.

"You received stolen goods," said the man.

"Not to my knowledge," said my master.

"An investigation might nonetheless prove you have no legal hold on her."

"Are you a magistrate, or a praetor's agent?" inquired my master, narrowly.

"No," said the fellow.

My master relaxed, visibly.

"But I could always lodge a citizen's inquiry, and have the matter looked into," he said.

"What do you want?" asked my master.

"She is a hot slave, and is curvy, and beautiful," he said.

"So?" asked my master.

"Too, she dances well, and her ears are pierced," said the man.

"So?" inquired my master.

"What did you pay for her?" he asked.

"That is my business," said my master.

"Not much, I would suppose," said the man. "Stolen slaves seldom bring high prices, unless delivered to private dealers on contract, or to slavers, who know what to do with them, and where to sell them."

"She is mine," said my master. "I have held her in my collar for a sufficient time."

"I am prepared to accept that she is now yours," said the fellow. "For example, she seems clearly accomodated to your collar. The official recovery period is doubtless now passed."

"Then our conversation is at an end," said my master, angrily.

"Nonetheless it seems you might still count, officially, as a fellow who had received stolen goods," said the man.

"Not to my knowledge, if at all," said my master.

"Ignorance of the origin of the goods," said the man, "might indeed exonerate you from personal guilt in the matter."

My master shrugged.

"Still," said the man, "it might be of some interest to a praetor to hear you protest your innocence in the matter. He would be likely to be interested, too, in whom you bought the slave from, and such, and perhaps even where they obtained her."

"What do you want?" asked my master, angrily.

"I am prepared to be generous," said the man.

"She is not for sale," said my master.

"I have come from Argentum," he said. "I have come to Market of Semris looking for a certain type of slave. I think that your girl might be just what I need."

"Are you a slaver?" asked my master.

"No," he said. He looked down at me. "You are an exciting slut," he said.

I put my head down.

I did not want to be involved in this. In Gorean courts the testimony of slaves is commonly taken under torture.

"She is not for sale," said my master.

"I will give you five silver tarsks for her," said the man.

My master seemed stunned. I myself could scarcely believe what I had heard. Such prices are not paid for street dancers.

"Done!" said my master.

I looked up, startled. I had been sold.

I saw the coins, my price, change hands.

"What is your name, my dear?" inquired my new master.

"Whatever master pleases," I said.

"What were you called?" he asked me.

"Tula," I said. That was the name my former master, the itinerant musician, had given me.

"You are now Tuka," he said, naming me.

"Yes, Master," I said.

"What is your name?" he inquired.

"Tuka, Master," I said. I was now Tuka.

"Whose slave are you?" he asked.

"Your slave, Master," I said.

He pointed to his feet. I bent down and licked and kissed them.

"To all fours, Tuka," he said.

I rose up, to all fours.

Tula and Tuka are extremely common slave names on Gor. In this respect they are like Lita and Dina. Indeed, there is even a brand called the "Dina," which resembles the Dina, or slave flower, a tiny, roselike flower. Girls who bear this brand are often called Dinas, and often, too, have that name. Names such as Tula and Tuka are sometimes used for a brace of female slaves, as the names go well together. Another such pair is Sipa and Sita. Such names, too, of course, may be used individually, and often are. I did not doubt that the name Tuka may have been suggested by its resemblance to Tula, my former name. This suggested that my new master was perhaps not really much interested in what he named me. He may have just wanted something to call me. On the other hand, it was a good slave name. Too, I supposed he liked it, or he would not have given it to me. Perhaps he had once known a girl named Tuka, probably a slave, but possibly a free woman, of whom he had been fond.

My former master thrust his collar, the chain attached, higher on my neck, closer to the chin. He had its key in hand. My new master then, below the former collar, closed his own about my neck. I was now double collared. My former master then removed his collar, with the chain, from my neck. I had not been without a collar, even for an instant.

My new master then turned about, with a swirl of those long robes, and began to make his way across the square. I hurried after him, heeling him. I was naked, of course. I had removed the ta-teera for my dance, and had not put it back on. My new master had bought me, not the ta-teera. That belonged to the musician, my former master. A new girl would presumably wear it soon, as some, it seemed, had before me. I hoped that my new master would permit me clothing, at least in public. Even the tiny slave tunics and the scandalous ta-teerae are precious to a girl. Too, she is not insensible of how they show off her charms.

"May I speak, Master?" I called after him, hurrying behind him.

"Yes," he said.

"May I inquire the name of my master?" I asked.

"You will learn it soon enough," he said.

"Yes, Master," I said. It was doubtless on my collar, but,

obviously, without a mirror, I could not read the collar when it was locked on my neck. Too, even had I had a mirror, I could not read.

He walked rapidly, purposefully.

He had paid five silver tarsks for me. That was a great deal of money. My former master would have no difficulty getting another girl, or more than one, for such an amount.

"Master paid a great deal of money for me," I said.

"Yes," he said.

"Am I worth so much?" I asked.

"I think so," he said.

"May I inquire for what purpose Master has purchased me?" I asked.

"You will learn soon enough," he said.

"Yes, Master," I said.

"Curiosity is not becoming in a kajira," he reminded me.

"Yes, Master," I said, frightened. But he did not turn about to strike me, or discipline me.

I hurried along behind him. It was now late in the afternoon. The square was not crowded now. The public places and baths would soon be closed. I saw some men, some with clients in their train, leaving the square. I turned about, briefly. The square was very beautiful, even at this time of day. I did not see my former master. He had apparently left the square. I then turned about, again, and hurried even more rapidly after my new master. I did not want to lag too far behind, outside the normal heeling distance.

18 / The Grating; The Garments

"Over the grating, on the walkway," said the man.

I dreaded leaving the tavern in this fashion.

One of the men patted me on the behind. "Do not be afraid," he said. "They will soon be shipped out, to make room for others."

The sunken, iron-walled pits were below the level of the basement, in which my own cell was. They were covered with locked gratings. My cell was not a kennel, but a cell. It was very well appointed, as cells for slave girls go. I could not stand fully upright in it, and I must leave it through a small gate, on my hands and knees, or belly, but it was large enough to move about in, and it was floored with carpet. In it, too, were furs. I had water and a wastes' bucket. Cushions had been permitted me, an incredible luxury. To be sure, I was sometimes ordered to kneel upon one, or another of them, usually while receiving instructions. In this cell, too, there was a mirror. Too, there were various tiny boxes, containing jewelry and cosmetics. There was also a trunk, for silks. I might prepare myself here for the floor, or for the dance. There was even a lamp outside the cell, affording light, when the men saw fit to have it lit. Sometimes, before fellows were brought past the cell, bound or chained, thence to be incarcerated in one of the pits, I would be instructed to lie seductively on the furs and cushions. At such times I was sometimes given chocolates to eat. "Let them have something pleasant to remember," had said one of the fellows, at one of these times. "We would not want them to forget you,"had said another.

I hastened across the grating. I heard howls of rage from beneath me. A hand reached up, grasping for me, through the grating. One of the men with me kicked it away from me. Its fist clenched, helplessly, in fury. I was then over the grating.

"Your garments for the afternoon," said one of the fellows behind me, "are in the back hall, near the back entrance."

When I was ready to leave the tavern one of the men would check the alley, to make certain that my departure would be unnoticed.

19 / The Streets of Argentum; The Belly Chain and Disk

"Sir," I said, "forgive me for daring to speak to you, but only the kindness of your countenance encourages my audacity."

"Lady?" he inquired.

"I am in desperate straits," I whispered piteously.

"You are a beggar?" he asked.

I put down my head, as though in shame.

"Forgive me, Lady," he said. "These are hard times."

I looked up, my eyes over the veil. "You are understanding," I whispered.

"I was rude," he said. "I am sorry."

"One such as you could not be rude," I said, half weeping. "Clearly, too, you are kind, and noble." He was also large and strong.

"May I be of aid to you?" he asked.

I turned half away from him, as though in confusion and shame. I had been taught to do such things. The men of my master had rehearsed them muchly with me.

"Please," he said.

"I should not have bothered you," I whispered.

"Perhaps you need money," he said. "I am not a rich man, but I have a little."

"Better death in the streets, or a collar, than that I should so demean myself, and my station, as to avail myself of your generosity."

"Are you hungry?" he asked.

"Yes," I said.

"Your robes, though worn and shabby, are well kept," he said.

"I am of humble caste," I said. It made me nervous, of course, to say such things. For a slave to claim caste is a serious matter. Similarly, it would not be wise for her to be caught in the garments of a free woman. That, too, is a terribly serious offense.

"What is your caste?" he asked.

His caste, as I could see from his garments, was that of the metal workers.

"Yours," I said. "That of the metal workers."

"We share caste," he said. "Too," he laughed, "I may remind you that that is no humble caste. Where would the dwellers of cities be without us?" This was a way of saying, in the parlance of the caste, that the utilities and workings of metal were essential for a high civilization. Then he looked at me kindly, and spoke seriously, "You should not have hesitated for a moment to speak to me."

"You are kind," I said. To be sure, much charity, and fraternal organizations, and even outings, and such, are organized on caste lines. Caste is extremely important to most Goreans, even when they do not all practice the traditional crafts of their caste. It is one of the "nationalities" of the Gorean, so to speak. Other common "nationalities," so to speak, are membership in a kinship organization, such as a clan, or phratry, a group of clans, or a larger grouping yet, a tribe or analogous to a tribe, a group of phratries, and a pledged allegiance to a Home Stone, usually that of a village, town or city. It seems that in the distant past of Gor these kinship allegiances were, in effect, political allegiances, or generated political allegiances, which, later, interestingly, as life became more complex, and populations more mobile, became separated. Kinship structures do not now figure strongly in Gorean public life, although in some cities divisions of the electorate, those free citizens entitled to participate in referenda, and such, remain based on them.

"I have six tarsk bits with me," he said. "I will give you three."

I recalled my training. I recalled, too, in my training, how one of my master's men had shoved the point of a dagger a quarter of an inch into my belly, below the navel, and informed me how he could spill my guts into his hand.

"One would be more than enough," I said. "Honor could not permit me taking more."

"Take two, then," he said.

I took the two tarsk bits. I slipped them, as though thankfully, into the purse, on its two strings, dangling from my belt, hanging at my side. My master's men, of course, would gather them out later.

"I wish you well," he said, and began to turn away.

My hand stayed him.

He looked at me, puzzled.

"Please permit me to thank you," I said.

"That is not necessary," he said.

"I want to thank you," I said, "in the way of the female."

"That is not necessary," he said.

"I have been told, by others," I said, "that I am beautiful enough, even, to be a slave."

"I would not doubt it," he said.

"I am prepared to serve you," I said, "even as a slave."

"I can find that in a tavern," he said. "You are a free woman, and are of my own caste."

"Nonetheless," I said, "I am prepared to so serve you."

"Some have made you serve as much, for their coins, haven't they?" he asked.

I put my head down, as though shamed. "Yes," I whispered.

"I am sorry," he said. "I should not have asked."

I kept my head down.

"You poor thing," he said. "What beasts, what scoundrels, they were."

"They are men," I said, shrugging, "and I am a woman."

"Have no fear," he said. "I shall not so abuse you."

"But I want to so serve you," I said.

He looked at me, puzzled.

"It was not for nothing that I selected you out from the others," I said.

"Ah," he said, softly. This pleased him. Actually I had selected him out because my master's men had, when he had passed, indicated that I should do so. The choice had been theirs, not mine.

"Please," I said.

He was a Gorean male. I did not doubt but what he would want me. It was a question of overcoming his inhibitions, connected with my supposed station, that of the free woman, my caste, his own, and perhaps some reservations about seeming to take advantage of my presumed straits.

I backed a little into the alleyway, between the two buildings.

"No," he said, softly. But he did not stop me as I there, gracefully, but with a certain seeming timidity, in the shelter between the walls, brushed back my hood, and lowered my veil.

"You are beautiful," he said.

My hair was combed back, and down, over my ears. It was tied in the back.

He looked at me.

For a moment I was afraid he knew.

He lifted his hand a bit toward my throat, but then lowered it.

I sensed what he had wished to do. I then drew away the robing at my throat.

"Ah," he said, softly. There was no collar there. My throat was bare of a collar!

I stood before him. I think that he found me beautiful. I was face-stripped before him. This is very meaningful to Goreans. His eyes shone.

"Let me loosen my hair before you," I whispered.

"Not here," he whispered, suddenly, hoarsely. "Back. Further back."

I backed down the alleyway, before him, watching him. He was now excited.

Then my back was at the end of the alleyway, a closed alleyway, a *cul-de-sac*, against a building.

"No," he said, suddenly. "I must not take advantage of you."

"Let it be the tiniest of kisses then," I said, softly, "once only, and only the merest touch, my lips and yours, that, so little, or all of me, and as you want me, whatever you wish."

He placed his hands, the palms of them, fiercely on the wall, one on each side of me, at my shoulders. He put down his head for a moment, fighting with himself. He then lifted his head, and looked into my eyes.

I was small before him, and weak, and female.

I felt him loosen my belt, and then it, with the attached purse, fell to the stones of the alleyway.

He reached then to the opened collar of my robing.

Of the usual garments of the free female I wore only the outer robe, the street robe. That had been decided by my master. If I were inclined to attempt an escape, even clad merely in such a way, I presumably would not get far. I would not even have been able to disrobe, among free women, to an underrobe, or sliplike robe. Beneath the street robe there would have been only a female, and a brand.

The man's eyes blazed with the wanting of me.

To be sure, my master, even so, had taken an additional precaution with me.

Suddenly, driven in his need, impassioned, he tore open my robe.

"You wear the belly chain of a slave!" he cried.

Almost at the same time he was struck heavily from behind by my master's men. He was terribly strong. They had to strike him five times before he went down.

I stood back against the wall, frightened.

One of my master's men, from a skin, poured paga on the fallen figure. He would be transported from the alley, his arms over their shoulders. Few in the streets, given his apparent condition, and his smell, the paga souses on his garment, would think much of this. He would be taken to the back entrance of the tavern.

"Get the robe off," said the other of my master's men.

He had already picked up the belt and purse, and thrust it in a sack. I removed the robe and he thrust it, too, with its hood, and veil, into the sack.

I was then naked, except for the belly chain. Its links were heavy. Whereas it is sometimes possible for a male to slip such a chain, because of his straight hips, they stay well on females. About our waists, between the flaring of our hips and the swelling of our bosoms, they find a natural, lovely and secure mounting. This chain was locked on me with a heavy padlock, from the back. In the front, linked to the chain, and dangling down from it, over my lower belly, was a heavy, medallionlike metal disk. On this disk, so that it could be read from the front, was a large, cursive "Kef," for "Kajira," a larger version of the same letter adorning my thigh.

The fellow with the sack put it down and took the disk in his hand. He jerked on it, so that I felt the pull on the chain, and then let it drop back on my belly. He laughed.

"All fours," he said.

I went to all fours in the alley. The metal disk hung down now, swinging, below my belly.

My master's collar, taken from the sack, was put on my neck. The belly chain was then removed from me and placed in the sack. The fellow, too, held a tunic to my mouth, and I took it in my teeth. When I left the alley there would be little that would be unusual about me. I would be just another girl, well exposed in her skimpy tunic, snugly locked in her collar, nothing unusual.

20 / The Key in the Belt

"Please, Master," I said, swiftly kneeling near the entrance to the alleyway, "my master is much occupied with his business, and neglects me."

The tall, strong fellow stopped to regard me. I was the sort of woman apparently not without interest to Gorean males.

"Kind Master," I begged, "have pity on a female slave, desperate in her need."

"You are naked," he observed.

"My master punishes me," I said, "for he grew weary of my bellyings and my importunings for love."

"I do not think I would send a slave like you into the streets naked," he said.

"Master?" I asked.

"She might be molested," he said.

"Yes, Master!" I said.

He laughed.

I looked down, as though confused, and embarrassed.

"How long has it been since you have been touched?" he asked.

"Two weeks," I said.

"Incredible," he said.

"Thank you, Master," I whispered.

"Doubtless he has many women," the fellow speculated.

"No," I said, "only me."

"Then," said he, "it is indeed incredible."

"Thank you, Master," I said, shyly.

"To afford a slave such as you," he said,"he must be well off."

"He is rich," I said.

"So why would he not have many women?" asked the fellow.

"He cares more for his business than for women," I said.

"You are quite beautiful," he said, admiring me with the openness and candor of a Gorean master.

"Thank you, Master," I said, even as a slave reddening under that gaze.

"Are you truly in desperate need?" he asked.

"Yes, Master," I said. That was true. My master kept me starved for sex. It seemed to be his belief that my needs, if painful, would improve me in this sort of performance. Perhaps he was right. Surely if a Gorean master were skillful in reading a woman's body, as many are, there would be little there, now, at least in this one respect, to suggest deception. I squirmed naked before him, on my knees.

"I am sorry," he said.

I put down my head. I wished he was not truly concerned with me. Gorean masters, incidentally, almost never deprive a girl of sex, though it can, of course, be done with an end in view, for such purposes as punishment, increasing her need for a later time, or bringing her to a good, hot ready point for, say, her sale from a slave block. The deliberate starving of a woman of sex is almost unheard of on Gor. That sort of thing is, I think, more likely to be done on Earth than Gor, and, on Earth, it seems to be practiced most frequently, interestingly enough, not on slaves, but free women. Indeed, one of the major differences between the slave and her free sister is that the slave is generally far more sexually fulfilled than her free sister. This is not to say that a slave may not occasionally be made to beg for sex, or that she may not, upon occasion, have to beg for it. These things help her to understand that she has sexual needs, and that whether or not these needs are to be satisfied, is at the option of the master. A formula sometimes used is: "I acknowledge unequivocally and without reservation that I have sexual needs. Similarly I inform you that I want them satisfied. I beg you, Master, to satisfy them." It might be noted in this, of course, that a slave may beg for sexual satisfaction. She is free to do so, and it is quite acceptable for her to do so. Such a liberty, of course, would be unthinkable in the case of a free woman. Needless to say, the master commonly accedes to the pleas of the slave. When he himself desires sex, of course, he simply takes it, or imposes it on the slave. Her will is nothing. And she must strive to be fully pleasing. He is master; she is slave.

"I am lonely, I am neglected, I am in need," I said. "My master cares more for his business than for his slave."

"I am sorry," he said.

"You are strong, and a male," I said, looking up, "and I am small, and weak, and a female, and am in need."

He said nothing.

"I would tie the bondage knot in my hair for you," I said.

"Are you soliciting the touch of a man who is not your master?" he asked.

"Oh, no, Master!" I said, quickly.

He smiled.

"Do you scorn me for my helplessness?" I asked.

"No," he said.

"You are kind to a slave," I whispered.

"In any event," he said, "you wear the iron belt."

"Master," I said, quickly, quietly. "It is for such a reason that I have knelt before you. My master, in his anger, and in his preoccupation with his business, when he put the belt on me, neglected to remove the key from the lock. It is still there. I have felt it from behind my back."

"Oh?" he said, interested.

"Yes!" I whispered.

"He must, indeed, have been preoccupied," he said.

"He was angry, too," I said. "He stripped me, put the belt on me and sent me on an errand, from the house. I do not think he was much paying attention to what he was doing." This seemed to me the weakest part of the story, that a Gorean master might neglect to remove a key from a lock. Such things are commonly done by habit, if nothing else. I did have an errand capsule, a capped, narrow leather cylinder, such as may be used for carrying notes, messages, and such, on a string about my neck, the string over my collar.

"The belt then could be easily removed from you," said the fellow, "and later replaced."

"Yes," I said.

I could see that he was interested in me. I had been found desirable, apparently extremely so. To be sure, a key could be left in a lock. Such things could happen. Should a fellow question such luck?

"I do not own you," he said.

"Do so," I whispered, "for an Ahn."

"There is no place," he said.

"Take me into the alleyway," I said. "Spill garbage, or refuse, upon the stones, for I am a slave and am worth less than even it, and have no value lest it be to serve a master, and put me upon it. Make that my bed."

"My cloak, doubled, will do," he smiled.

"Enfold me then within it," I said, "as though within your arms, that I may then within its enclosing warmth, as though within the confines of a cell, tender my woman's submission to your maleness."

I then, slowly, gracefully, kneeling before him, looking up at him, tied the bondage knot in my hair, it then hanging beside my right cheek.

"Precede me into the alley," he said, kindly.

I rose, gracefully, and did so. I would rather he had not been so concerned for me. I remembered the knife of my master's man, the point entered ever so slightly into my belly, the edge of the knife turned in such a way that I knew it could open me like a larma.

He spread the cloak, doubled, on the stones of the alleyway. I knelt upon it, and put my hands, clasped, behind the back of my head. I hoped that my master's men had gone elsewhere. He reached about me, as I pressed myself against him, troubled, and I felt him turn the key in the lock. In a moment, the belt was laid aside.

"You are open," he announced.

"Yes, Master," I said.

"You are very beautiful," he said.

"Thank you, Master," I said.

"Is anything wrong?" he asked.

"No, Master," I said.

"Do we have much time?" he asked.

"I do not know, Master," I said.

"How long is your errand?" he asked.

"I do not know, Master," I said.

"What is its nature?" he asked.

"I do not know," I said.

"It is doubtless written on a paper, inside the errand capsule," he said.

"Yes, Master," I said.

"To whom were you to report, for the conduct of the errand?" he asked. "Who was to read the message?"

"He who was designated by my master's men," I said.

"Do you know his name?" he asked.

"No," I said.

"But you do know to whom you were supposed to deliver it?" he asked.

"Yes, Master," I said.

"When do you expect to deliver it?" he asked.

"I have already done so," I said.

"You are returning from your errand?" he said.

"I am in the midst of it, Master," I said.

"I do not understand," he said.

"The message is for you," I said.

He looked at me, puzzled. He then uncapped the errand capsule, and took out the bit of rolled paper. He unrolled it, and read it. He leaped to his feet, turning, but already they were upon him. They pummeled him savagely. Then he lay crumpled at their feet.

"Forgive me, Master," I said.

"Get the belt back on," said one of my master's men.

"Yes, Master," I said. The key was again left in the lock. The paper which had been extracted from the errand capsule was then rerolled, and thrust in the capsule, and the capsule again capped. The message read, I had been told, "You have been captured."

"Another for the black chain of Ionicus," said one of my master's men. Ionicus was a master of work chains. He had several, the "red chain," the "green chain," "the yellow chain," and so on, each of which boasted several hundred men. Supposedly these were free work chains, "free" in the sense of not utilizing slaves. Goreans generally do not employ slaves for such labors as road construction, siege works, raising walls, and so on. Similarly they generally would not use them for the construction of temples and public buildings. Most such work is generally done by the free labor of a given community, though this "free labor" may, upon occasion, particularly in emergencies, be "levied," the laborers then contributing their labor as a form of special tax, or, if you like, "conscripted" or "drafted," rather as if for military service. Usually, of course, the free labor is paid, and with more than provisions and shelter, either from public or private funds. Any city in which free laborers tended to be systematically robbed of their employments in virtue of imbonded competition would doubtless be inviting discontent, and perhaps, eventually, revolution. Besides, the free laborers share a Home Stone with the aristocracies of these cities, the upper castes, the higher families, the richer families, and so on. Accordingly, because of this commonality of the Home Stone, love of their city, the sharing of citizenship, and such, there is generally a harmonious set of economic compromises obtaining between the upper castes, and classes, and the lower castes, and the labor force, in general. Happily, most of these compromises are unquestioned matters of cultural tradition. They are taken for granted, usually, by all the citizens, and their remote origins, sometimes doubtless the outcome of internecine strife, of class war, of street fighting and riots, of bloody, house-to-house, determinations in the past, and such, are seldom investigated, save perhaps by historians, scribes of the past, some seeking, it seems, to know the truth, for its own sake, others seemingly seeking lessons in the rich labyrinths of history, in previous human experience, what is to be emulated, and what is to be avoided. Some think that out of such crises came the invention of the Home Stone. There are, of course, several mythical accounts of the origin of the Home Stone. One popular account has it that an ancient hero, Hesius, once performed great labors for Priest-Kings, and was promised a reward greater than gold and silver. He was given, however, only a flat pice of rock with a single character inscribed upon it, the first letter in the name of his native village. He reproached the Priest-Kings with their niggardliness, and what he regarded as their breach of faith. He was told, however, that what they gave him was indeed worth far more than gold and silver, that it was a "Home Stone." He returned to his native village, which was torn with war and strife. He told the story there, and put the stone in the market place. "If the Priest-Kings say this is worth more than gold and silver," said a wise man, "it must be true." "Yes," said the people. "Whose Home Stone is it?" asked the people, "yours or ours?" "Ours," responded Hesius. Weapons were then laid aside, and peace pledged. The name of the village was "Ar." It is generally accepted in Gorean tradition that the Home Stone of Ar is the oldest Home Stone on Gor.

"Yes," said the other of my master's men. My master was Tyrrhenius of Argentum, who owned a tavern. To be sure, I had not been allowed to dance there. He did not want me to be well known as one of his girls. He had surreptitious dealings with various masters of work chains, among them he called Ionicus. My master had once, while I was licking his feet, congratulated me on being an excellent Lure Girl. "Thank you, Master," I had said. I was a slave girl. We must obey our masters.

"Get the cart," said the first of my master's men.

"Yes, Master," I said, and hurried out to the street, where we had left the hand-drawn cart.

Whereas in the cities, where the rights of citizenship are clearest, where the sways of custom and tradition tend to be jealously guarded, where the influence of Home Stones is likely to be most keenly felt, free labor has generally held its own, the same cannot be said for all rural areas of Gor, particularly areas which fall outside the obvious jurisdiction or sphere of influence of nearby cities. Too, it is difficult to be a citizen of a city if one cannot reach it within a day's march. Citizenship, or its retention, on other than a nominal basis, in some cities, is contingent on such things as attending public ceremonies, such as an official semi-annual taking of auspices, and participating in numerous public assemblies, some of which are called on short notice. Accordingly, for various reasons, such as lack of citizenship, an inability to properly exercise it, resulting in effective disenfranchisement, or, most often, a fierce independence, repudiating allegiance to anything save one's own village, the farmers, or peasantry, are more likely to suffer from the results of cheap competition than their urban brethren. In the last several years, the institution of the "great farm," with its projected contracts, its organization and planning, its agricultural expertise, and its imbonded labor force has become more common on Gor. Some Gorean farmers own their own land, and some share in land owned by a village. It is not unknown for both sorts to receive offers from agents of the "Great Farms," sometimes owned by individuals, and sometimes by companies, whose capital has been generated by the investments of individuals who are, in effect, stockholders. Many times these offers, which are usually generous, are accepted, with the result that the amount of area under cultivation by the great farms tends to increase. Sometimes, it is said, that cruel and unfair pressure is applied to farmers, or villages, such as threats, or the burning of crops, and such, but I would think that this would surely be the exception rather than the rule. When the great farms can usually achieve their aims, statistically, by legitimate business measures there would be little point in having recourse to irregular inducements. Too, the Gorean peasant tends to be a master of the "peasant bow," a weapon of unusual accuracy, rapidity of fire, and striking force. Usually, as it is their caste policy, the farmers or villagers seek new land, usually farther away, to start again. They seldom attempt to enter the cities, where they might eventually contribute to the formation of a discontented urban proletariat. Their caste codes discourage it. Also, of course, they would generally not be citizens of the city and in the city there would be little opportunity for them to practice their caste crafts. Also, many cities, save those interested, for one reason or another, in increasing their population, for better or for worse, tend not be enthusiastic about accepting influxes of the indigent. Such have contributed, through economic hardship, or treachery, to the diminishment, and even fall, of more than one city. I think that the cities, on the whole, have mixed feelings about the great farms. Whereas they welcome currently lower prices on produce and greater assurances of its variety and quantities, they also tend to regret the withdrawal or loss of the local peasantry, which provided them not only with a plethora of individual suppliers, tending to generate a free market, complex and competitive, but also with a sphere of intelligence and even defense about the city. An organization of great farms, acting in concert, of course, could reduce competition, and eventually regulate prices rather as they pleased, particularly with regard to staples such as Sa-Tarna and Suls. Accordingly some cities have been willing to offer inducements to farmers to remain in their vicinity, such as a liberalization of the requirements for citizenship, the performance of rural sacrifices, the holding of games in rural areas, subsidizing the touring of theatrical and musical troupes in the countryside, special holidays honoring the agricultural caste, which may be celebrated in the city, and so on. In many cases, these inducements appear to have been effective. The farmer likes to be appreciated, and to have the importance and value of his work recognized. He thinks of his caste as "the ox on which the Home Stone rests." Too, of course, he generally prefers to stay where he is. He is fond of the land he knows.

I put myself between the handles of the cart and, drawing it, returned into the alleyway. The fellow was now bound and gagged. He was tied as helplessly as though he might have been a woman, and a woman who was only a slave. He was still unconscious.

"Go, watch," said one of my master's men.

I quickly turned about and ran to the end of the alleyway, where I could see the street, both ways.

Two forms of work groups not localized to individual cities are the "free gang" and the "free" chain. These differ both from the free laborers indigenous to a given city and from work groups of slaves, such as those which are commonly used on the great farms. The "free gang" consists of free men who are in the hire of a contractor who rents their services, and his own, say, to various cities, organizations, and groups. They are, in effect, something like traveling construction crews. Many of them are skilled, or semiskilled, workers, and they can come and go as they please. They travel about in wagons. Many of them are rough, but good-hearted men. They enjoy drinking, brawling and mastering slaves. I had been in the arms of some such men in Brundisium. They made me serve well. The "free" chain, on the other hand, consists usually, I had been told, of condemned criminals. Rather than bother with housing these fellows, many of whom are supposedly dangerous, putting them up at public expense, and so on, many cities, for a nominal fee, turn them over to a work master who accepts charge of them, theoretically for the duration of time remaining in their sentences. For example, if a fellow has been sentenced, say, to two years of hard labor by a praetor, he might be turned over, for a small fee, to the master of a work gang who will see to it, theoretically, that he performs these two years of hard labor. The work master, of course, profits from the services of his gang, which he rents out to various individuals, or groups, and so on, rather as the managers, or captains, of the "free" gangs can rent out their own crews. The "free" chain, of course, can be hired more cheaply. On the other hand, it usually tends to have a far more limited pool of skills than that of the "free gangs" and, accordingly, it is usually employed in ruder, less demanding labors, or even in labors which, because of their arduousness, or their onerous nature, would be distasteful to free gangs. Supposedly when the criminal's sentence has been served, he is to be released by the work master, usually then far from the city where he committed his crime or was apprehended. On the other hand,it is suspected that work masters tend to be somewhat reluctant to free the fellows on their chains. They would then, it seems, have to pay a new fee to replace him. It seems certain that more than one fellow has been kept on the chain far longer than his sentence would seem to require. For example, it seems certain that small infractions, invented or discovered, of regulations, or discipline, are utilized by work masters, at least from time to time, to "extend" the sentence, or *de-facto* servitude, of the worker in question. The hope of being freed, of course, generally keeps the chain "tame." Occasionally perhaps, a fellow is released. This is supposed to encourage docility in the others. These fellows, incidentally, are in effect under "slave discipline," which means, on Gor, that they are as much at the mercy of the work master as if they were his slaves. He may kill them, for example, if he wishes. My master, Tyrrhenius of Argentum, at whose total mercy I was, and similarly at the mercy of those whom he had appointed to supervise my work, had dealings with various work masters, prominent among them Ionicus, Ioncius of Cos. The fellow behind me, whom my master's men had bound, and whom they were doubtless placing on the cart, was destined, I had heard, for the "black chain" of Ionicus. That particular chain, I had heard, was employed in the north, currently digging siege trenches for the Cosians who had invested Torcadino. The fellow whom they had bound, of course, and the others in whose capture I had been implicated, were not, as far as I knew, criminals. My master, Tyrrhenius, spoke of his work as "recruitment." He was "recruiting" for the chains of work masters. To be sure, he must do this work surreptitiously. It would be quite unfortunate for him, I had gathered, if he were to be discovered to have been involved in such work. Judges, magistrates, and such, would not be likely to look indulgently on these activities. To be sure, he was not taking risks as great as it might seem. For example, he was not directly, personally involved in these things. The fellows captured would not know where they were being held, nor, hooded and chained, from what place they were taken forth later. Also, I supposed, later on, after he had some more use out of me, he would sell me off in some market or another. He could find himself a new lure girl. Indeed, for all I knew, he might be using others of his girls in these same cruel and delusory labors. I did not much fear another sale. I had already been sold a number of times. A girl's first sale, at least her first public one, as mine was at Market of Semris, when she is exposed on a block naked to buyers, and such, is probably the hardest for her. After that she has some sense of what it is to be vended merchandise. Indeed, I was excited at the thought of being sold again. I wanted to be beautiful, to please men, and to bring the highest price in the market. The chances of my encountering any of the fellows in whose capture I had been implicated, incidentally, were not high. They had, it seemed, all been shipped north to Torcadino. I thought of Tyrrhenius. He was not, truly, as I again thought of it, taking such great risks. Who could prove that he had been involved in these things? My own testimony, even if it were dragged out of me on the rack, would be only that of a slave; his men would presumably not betray him; and he could always claim that his tavern, the basement, and such, had been used without his knowledge. He could feign dismay. He was respected in Argentum. He did not even reside on the premises.

"Someone is coming!" I called back, softly, to my master's men. They were placing the bound, gagged fellow in the cart. They would tie him there. Then they would cover him with a tarpaulin.

"Close?" asked the first of my master's men.

I nodded.

"Delay him," called the fellow, a fierce, projected whisper.

The approaching fellow was some ten to fifteen yards away, to my left. He wore a short cloak, fastened by a large bronze pin at the right shoulder, high, bootlike sandals, and a broad-brimmed hat. A sack was slung on a stick, the stick resting over his shoulder. He carried, on a strap over his left shoulder, the strap under his cloak, a sword. I supposed that he might be able to use it. The hat, with its broad brim pulled down against the sun, with its attendant shadow, muchly concealed his features. I took him for a traveler. It is a not unusual traveling costume for males on Gor. Such a costume, too, it might be mentioned, is often worn for hunting. Head down, I hurried forth, and knelt before him, blocking his way. I put my head down to his feet. This is a suitable deference in a female slave before a free male. I tensed, for I expected, having so blocked his path, to be kicked, or struck. I must then try to seize an ankle, or knee, pleading desperate need. I knew I might risk a thrashing with his stick. But I had been ordered to delay him, and delay him I would, if I could. "A needful slave begs master to take pity upon her," I said. I trembled. But I did not feel the scorn of his foot, thrusting me to the side, toward the central gutter in the street, nor did I feel his hand in my hair, yanking my head up, to lash my face back and forth with what would undoubtedly have been a well-deserved cuffing. He did not even spit upon me, or cry out in anger, or deride me, or even order me from his path. Swiftly I began kissing, and licking, at his feet, performing appropriate obeisances before him, a male. I was puzzled. Then I was afraid. Gorean masters are often kind to needful slaves, acceding to their pleas for sex. Though I was eager to be touched, and Tyrrhenius of Argentum, my master, had, as a matter of policy, kept me in a torment of sexual deprivation, I did not want this fellow, a stranger accosted on the street, to use me. My master's men were nearby.

"You kiss and lick as well as ever, perhaps even better, Doreen," he said. "Or is it still 'Doreen'?" he asked.

I looked up, startled.

"I am now Tuka, Master," I said.

"An excellent name for a slave slut such as you," he said.

"Thank you, Master," I said.

"You know me, do you not?" he asked, smiling.

"Yes, Master," I whispered, frightened.

"It was because of you," he laughed, "curvy little she-urt, that I lost my post in Brundisium."

"Forgive me, Master," I said. I feared that he might whip me.

"I do not blame Hendow for being jealous," he said. "A man might be driven to distraction by a face and curves like yours."

"Thank you, Master," I whispered.

"But I taught you something of what it is to be a slave, did I not?" he asked.

"Yes, Master," I said. It was very true.

"You were stolen, weren't you?" he asked.

"Yes, Master," I said.

"That is what I heard in Brundisium," he said. "I did not think Hendow would have let you go."

"Perhaps not, Master," I said. I did not really know. It seemed to me implausible that Hendow could have cared for me. He had used me only once, and then ruthlessly. On Earth weaklings who wish to rid themselves of women sometimes take refuge in the comforting rationalization that they "love them enough to let them go." That position, whatever may be its moral or psychological merits, does not represent a typical Gorean response, at least where slaves are concerned. Most Goreans would regard it as absurd to let a woman go for whom one truly cared. One shows caring by keeping. And, if necessary, by fighting. What woman, I wondered, could not see through such cant? Most women, it seemed to me, would prefer a man who cared enough for her to keep her, one who was willing, even, to fight for her, rather than one who was willing to "let her go."

"Apparently Tupita was stolen at the same time," he said.

"Yes, Master," I said. It did not seem to me important to tell him that Tupita had been attempting to escape, using my sales price to purchase passage from Brundisium. "You did not come to Argentum searching for me, did you?" I asked.

"Hardly," he laughed.

"Oh," I said. I had thought he might have done so. I was a bit miffed by this.

He laughed.

"Master is far from Brundisium," I observed.

"I have come to Argentum seeking my fortune," he said. "I will seek service with some mercenary captain."

It seemed to me certainly that one might find such service closer to Brundisium.

"What happened to Tupita?" he asked. "Do you know what became of her?"

"We were both sold in Samnium," I said. "I do not know who purchased her. I do not know where she went."

"She was pretty," he said.

"Yes, Master," I agreed.

"The recovery period is passed, long ago," he said. "You are now both the full legal properties of your new masters."

"Yes, Master," I said. I heard the wheels of the cart trundling forth from the alleyway now. The fellow who had been bound and gagged was doubtless now tied down in the cart, hand and foot, belly and neck, and covered by the tarpaulin.

"What is wrong?" he asked.

"Nothing, Master," I said.

"Are your hips still loose?" he asked. "Do you still sway well?"

I cast a frightened glance back toward the opening of the alleyway. "My current master does not use me as a dancer," I said.

My master's men, with the cart, one of them drawing the cart, the other thrusting it from behind, emerged from the alleyway. "Greetings, Citizen," said the first of my master's men, he between the handles of the cart.

"Greetings," said the fellow before whom I knelt. He was not, of course, a citizen of Argentum.

"Watch out for her," grinned the first of my master's men. "She hangs out around here from time to time, begging to be touched."

"Thank you for the warning," laughed the fellow before whom I knelt.

I put my head down, so spoken of. Yet truly I was needful. It seemed my sexual needs had increased a thousand times on Gor. I could not help myself.

"Have you contented her?" asked he before whom I knelt.

"Not I," laughed the fellow. "She is in a collar. She is nothing. Let her grovel, and scream with need. It amuses us."

"I see," said the fellow before whom I knelt. He did not seem too pleased with what he had heard.

"Besides," said the first of my master's men, "as you can see, her pretty little body is snugly enclosed in the iron belt."

"So it might seem," said the fellow before whom I knelt.

They then, to my relief, seemingly continued on their way, albeit slowly, one drawing the cart, the other pushing it. Perhaps the cart was heavy.

"I must go now, Master," I said. I wished to leap up, and be on my way.

"Have I given you permission to rise?" he asked.

"No, Master," I said. "Forgive me, Master."

I could see, behind him, that the two men of my master had stopped, apparently adjusting the tarpaulin in the cart.

"The key has been left in the belt," he said. "Did you know that?" He had had no difficulty in making this determination, as I had knelt before him, earlier, my head down to his feet.

"Yes, Master," I said.

"That would seem very careless of your master," he said.

"Yes, Master," I said.

"Perhaps he does not pay as close attention to you as he might," speculated the fellow.

"Perhaps, Master," I whispered.

I looked beyond the man, to my master's men. The cart was now a few yards down the street. The first of my master's men was looking at me. The second was pretending to be inspecting the wheel of the cart.

"Doubtless Master has pressing concerns," I said. "He must doubtless soon be on his way."

"No," said the fellow. "What is the matter with you?"

"Nothing, Master," I said.

"I think you are needful," he said.

I looked beyond the fellow. I saw the first of my master's men make the sign, the signal of designation.

"Something is wrong," said the fellow before whom I knelt. "I can tell."

"No, Master," I whispered.

The first of my master's men then, unpleasantly, severely, impatiently, abruptly, as though he could not understand my dalliance, made an angry gesture across his lower belly. I put my head down, in my hands. I sobbed.

"You are in need," said the fellow before whom I knelt.

I lifted my head. I lowered my hands from before my face. "My master," I said, "is much preoccupied with his business, and neglects me."

21 / The Panels

I knelt in the alcove, naked, on the furs. A heavy metal collar, and chain, was on my neck. It fastened me to the back wall of the alcove.

I saw the leather curtains part. The fellow was drunk, and stinking of drink. He did not even close the curtains behind him. But they were closed. Perhaps by my master's men. I had not been put into the streets for the last five days. I had spent much time in my cell, in the basement. Twice I had been brought up from the basement, ostensibly to serve on the floor, but actually to interest one fellow or another in me. These were invariably strangers, and alone, in Argentum on business. Too, they were large, strong fellows. I would moan, and lick, about them, arousing their interest. If I failed, I had been told that I would be whipped or slain. My master's men would tell him, too, that I was an excellent slave lay. I hoped that this was true. I do not know, however, how they would have known this, as none of them had ever used me. Part of my master's policy with respect to me was to systematically deny my needs. When the fellow would express an interest in me I would be taken to an alcove, Alcove Two, and chained there, to await him. Meanwhile my master's men would ply him with drink, sometimes even mixed with sedating drugs. This made their work easier. Some of these fellows were very strong.

"Where is the little honey cake?" asked the fellow, looking about, squinting. He then fell forward, on his hands and knees, on the furs. He slipped to his stomach. His head lifted. His eyes were bleary with drink.

"I am here, Master," I said, shrinking back against the wall.

There were side panels on each side of the entrance to the alcove. Such panels, where they exist, are normally kept locked on the inside. These, however, were not locked. Such passages are rare in alcoves but they are not unknown. They make it possible to move between alcoves, and from alcoves to the rear of the tavern, without reentering the main floor area. Such exits have various utilities, such as making it unnecessary for a fellow on the way out to encounter another on the way in, and permitting a fellow to withdraw from the area unnoticed, perhaps thereby avoiding an enemy or enemies, and gaining time on them, perhaps two or three hours, while they wait for him to emerge. Too, as a general policy, many Goreans prefer rooms with at least two exits.

"Where?" asked the fellow, thickly.

"Here," I whispered.

The panels were well greased. They would be moved back quietly, behind the fellow on the furs.

The fellow moved himself to a sitting position, and sat there, half asleep, on the furs.

"Here," I whispered, again.

He blinked, sleepily, in my direction. He then went to all fours, to crawl toward me.

I did not know if he could reach me.

"Open your arms," he said, slowly.

I could smell his breath, heavy with drink, and garlic, and herbs, across the furs. I opened my arms, obediently, to him. Slave girls are not permitted to be fastidious. We must take what comes. What matters is that these fellows have paid their fees to our masters. Accordingly we must serve them with enthusiasm, skill and passion. They have paid their money. We must thus see to it that we are marvels to them, that we serve them with eagerness and perfection. This is not a matter, incidentally, of serving regardless of our will and possible desires, or in spite of them, but of actually adjusting our will and desires, in such a way that they now find expression and fulfillment even in such service. To be sure, some men enjoy taking a woman who hates them, and whom they hate, and reducing her to a panting, pleading slave, begging for a continuation of their touch, which they may then either grant or deny her, as it pleases them.

He crawled toward me, and then crouched, unsteadily, before me. I quickly took him in my arms, pressing myself gratefully against him. I hoped, even in this time, even in these circumstances, that I might gain from him a moment or two of relief. Perhaps my master's men would not soon enter the alcove. Perhaps, best, they would decide they did not want this man, after all. I hoped so. Then he seemed only a weight in my arms. He was too heavy to hold. I lowered him to the furs. He was asleep. The two panels slid noiselessly open.

"Back, slut," said the first of my master's men.

I crept back against the wall.

I watched the other of my master's men drag the fellow from the alcove by an arm.

"I see that your hands will have to be fastened behind you again tonight," said the first of my master's men.

I put down my head.

"Turn about, kneeling," he said.

I did so. I expected him to put a belly chain on me, padlocked in front, with slave bracelets attached, in the back. I had worn it the last eleven nights. But he did not do so. Instead I felt binding fiber cinched about my waist, and then my hands, wrists crossed, were, to this same fiber, tied behind my back. I did not understand this. He opened the heavy collar, attached to the wall chain, which had been closed about my neck. He then drew me to my feet by an arm. "The Master wants to see you," he said.

"Master?" I asked.

"Be silent," he said.

"Yes, Master," I said.

22 / Inquiries; Gagged, Hooded and Collared

"Spread your knees more widely, Tuka," said my master, Tyrrhenius of Argentum.

I obeyed.

He regarded me, not speaking.

I knelt before him on a circular scarlet rug, he in a curule chair looking down at me. My hands were tied behind my back, to a length of binding fiber cinched snugly about my waist. His men were near him, the two who had been as my masters in my work.

"You are an Earth slut, are you not?" he asked.

"Yes, Master," I said. "That is, I am a woman from Earth, who was brought here and enslaved."

"A slut," he said.

"Yes, Master," I said. "I am a slut from Earth, who was brought here and enslaved." I supposed, in a sense, I had been a slut on Earth. Certainly I had been interested in men, and in sexual experience, even then, though I had been shy, and afraid of both. Here, of course, on Gor, there was no question about the matter. I had learned that here I was a slave slut, and an exciting and attractive one.

"What is the history of your bondage?" he asked.

I did not understand his interest in this matter. On the other hand, I supposed he had his reasons. He did not seem idly curious. Besides, he was a free man, and I, a female slave, had been asked a question.

"I was captured on Earth," I said, "and brought to your beautiful world, where I was imbonded. I do not know the place to which I was brought, where I was branded and collared. It was, it seems, across a sea."

"Cos, probably," said one of my master's men.

"Perhaps," he said.

"I was sold outside Brundisium, in a sales camp," I said.

"Brundisium," said one of my master's men. "It would doubtless, them, have been Cos."

"Perhaps," said my master.

"My first public sale took place in Market of Semris," I said, "at the sales barn of Teibar, of that town. I was purchased there by Hendow, a taverner of Brundisium. I was stolen from Brundisium, and sold in Samnium. There I was purchased by Gordon, an intinerant musician. It was from him, in Market of Semris, that I was purchased by you, my master."

"What did you do in the tavern of Hendow," asked my master.

"I worked in the kitchen," I said.

"Surely one with your beauty served also in the alcoves," he said.

"Yes, Master," I said.

"Did you also dance?" he asked.

"Yes, Master," I said.

The men exchanged glances. I pulled at the binding fiber a little, confining my wrists. I was well tied. It had been done by a Gorean master.

I looked at the men. I did not understand their interest in these things.

"Would you care to be fed to sleen?" he asked.

"No, Master!" I cried. Quickly I put my head down to the floor.

"It is my understanding that six days ago, on the streets," he said, "you exhibited a momentary hesitancy in carrying out a capture."

I flung myself to my belly, my hands tied behind me, before his chair. I was terrified. "Forgive me, Master!" I cried. "Forgive me!"

"Did you know the individual?" he asked.

"Yes, Master!" I cried. "I had known him. He had been kind to me!"

"To whom does a girl own absolute and perfect obedience?" he asked.

"To her master! To her master!" I wept.

"Kick her, and beat her," he said, dispassionately.

I was then spurned and abused with the feet of his men, and I was then pulled up to my knees and cuffed several times before my master. Then they stepped back. I was then again on my knees, my lips now bleeding, before my master. I tasted blood.

"You are contrite now, are you not, Tuka?" he asked.

"Yes, Master," I said, frightened. I knew I should not have hesitated. I was a slave.

"But you have been on the whole an excellent lure girl," he said, "one of the best I have ever had."

"Thank you, Master," I whispered.

"You are extremely intelligent," he said, "as well as extremely beautiful."

"Thank you, Master," I whispered. I felt that my intelligence was small compared to that of most Gorean males, but I did not feel intellectually inferior, at least generally, to the women I had met on Gor, either girls from Earth, such as Gloria and Clarissa, who had been with me at Market of Semris, or those native to Gor, women such as Tula and Ina, and Sita and Aynur, whom I had known at the tavern of Hendow, on Dock Street, in Brundisium. I did not know if the high intelligence of Gorean men was a function of those men who had been brought to Gor in the distant past, perhaps chosen for intelligence, as well as other qualities, or if it had to do rather, for the most part, with the exhilarating, liberating Gorean cultural milieu, one alien to negativity, inhibition and frustration, one perhaps, in virtue of permitting an open, honest and freed manhood, more conducive to emotional and mental growth.

"Doubltess these qualities have contributed to your effectiveness as a lure girl," he said.

"Perhaps, Master," I said, uneasily.

"But even so," he said, "the effectiveness of a lure girl is usually limited."

"Master?" I asked, apprehensively.

"So, too," he said, "I think that your utility as such, even with your intelligence and beauty, at least in this area, may be coming to an end."

I did not say anything. I was helpless.

"Too," he said, "there is a question as to how much risk it is rational to take."

I did not respond.

"For what it is worth," he said, "you have served longer than any other lure girl I have used in this area."

I nodded, swallowing hard.

"You have made more captures than any other," he said.

"Thank you, Master," I said.

"You are now, however, I think," he said, "becoming a bit too well known in Argentum."

"As master says," I said. I had no idea, of course, as to whether or not such a thing was true. I did suppose I had been seen about the streets, here and there. This may have raised suspicions.

"Too," he said, "there have been inquiries."

I looked at him, apprehensively.

"Sometimes," he said, "I think a lure girl should be less beautiful, less striking, perhaps, than you. You are perhaps the sort who is too easily remembered."

I said nothing.

"Accordingly," he said, "I think it is now time to dispose of you."

"Master?" I asked, frightened.

"Do not fear," he said, smiling. "I have no intention of losing my investment in you."

"Then Master will sell me?" I begged.

"You have already been sold," he said.

I looked at him, astonished.

"I have received for you five silver tarsks, and one tarsk bit," he smiled. "I paid five silver tarsks for you, as you may recall. Thus I have made a profit on you."

"Yes, Master," I said.

"Hood her," he said.

One of his men then put a gag in my mouth, attached to a slave hood, fastened it in place, and then pulled the hood down over my head, and buckled it shut about my neck. I felt a collar put about my neck and locked. The collar I had originally worn then, that of Tyrrhenius of Argentum, was removed from my neck. I then knelt there, gagged and hooded, my hands bound behind me. I was trembling.

"Take her to her new master," he said.

23 / The Work Camp

"Look!" cried a fellow, elatedly. "Look!"

"The fifth slut!" cried another. "Look!"

"It is she!" cried another. "Look!"

"Do you know her?" asked another fellow.

"Yes!" said the first man.

"We know her well," said another fellow, with grim satisfaction.

I half stumbled in the chains. My feet hurt on the hot gravel. The sun was hot on my bare arms and legs. I could take only short steps for my ankles were shackled, the run of chain between them only some eight to ten inches. Iron, too, adorned my wrists. I wore manacles. With expert blows, on an anvil, these had been hammered shut, leaving only a fine line where the edges met. The manacles were joined by some seven or eight inches of chain. Another chain, some three feet in length, ran from the center of the ankle chain to the center of the chain joining the wrist rings. Standing upright, then, I could not lift my hands, even to feed myself. I was also in neck coffle, the fifth girl in the coffle. A chain ran from a ring on the back of the collar of the girl before me to a ring on the front of my collar. Similarly, a chain ran from the ring on the back of my collar to the ring on the front of the collar of the girl who followed me. Thusly we were fastened together.

"It is she," announced another fellow.

"Move, kajirae," said a fellow with a whip.

"Yes," said another man.

I looked about myself, wildly, in terror.

I heard the snap of the whip and, together, we hurried forward, within the fence, toward the square tent, the overseer's tent, on a rise in the distance.

The fellows along our route, sweating, half-stripped, in their ankle chains, paused in their labors, resting on their implements, to watch us pass.

"It is you, is it not," asked the girl before me, whispering over her shoulder, "to whom these beasts refer?"

"I fear so," I moaned.

"How is it that they know you?" asked the girl behind me.

"From Argentum," I said.

"Woe is us," said the girl before me. "These brutes are criminals, murderers, cutthroats, brigands, dangerous men, held in penal servitude. We shall be fortunate if we are not killed!"

"The guards must protect us," said the third girl.

"But how can we garner such shelter?" wept the second girl.

"If you had been a slave longer, you would know the answer to that question," said the third girl.

The second girl moaned. She was naive. Her brand had not been on her long.

We were female work slaves. Such are used among the chains largely for carrying water. Other purposes, too, as might be expected, may be found for them.

"I am afraid," said the second girl.

"Look!" cried a man, as we passed. "She! It is she, I am sure of it!"

"Yes!" said another. "You are right! I, too, am sure of it!"

I shuddered. "Not all of these men are criminals," I said to the second girl.

"How is that?" asked the girl behind me.

"Some are honest fellows," I said, "caught, impressed into labor."

"Such things are not done," said the girl before me.

"You are mistaken," I told her.

"How could it be done?" she asked.

"There are many ways," said the girl behind me. "Sometimes lure girls are used." Then she said, "Perhaps Tuka knows about that."

I was silent.

"You are very pretty, Tuka," said the girl behind me.

I was silent.

"You are probably pretty enough to be a lure girl," she added.

I was silent.

"I would not wish to be a lure girl who came within their reach," she remarked. "I might be torn to pieces. It would doubtless be far worse, of course, if I were the actual girl who had been involved in their capture."

I shuddered.

"What is wrong, Tuka?" she asked.

"Nothing," I said.

"I suppose that these fellows out here, with the digging, the labor and the whip, have little to live for," she remarked, "except perhaps vengeance."

I trembled in the chains.

"Do not be frightened, Tuka," she said. "You have nothing to fear, for you were surely never a lure girl."

Over the fence, in the distance, I could see the walls of a city. I had been told it was Venna. I had been told this by the girl who was now first on the chain. She had seen it once, long ago, when she had been a rich, spoiled, beautiful free woman, in her robes of concealment, from her palanquin. Then she had fallen to slavers. She was no longer spoiled or rich. No longer did she wear ornate robes of concealment. She wore now only the same sleeveless, brief, clinging work tunic as we. To be sure, she was doubtless much more exciting and beautiful now than she had been when she was free. This sort of thing would not be merely a matter of the brand and collar, of course, significant though they might be, but of the entire radiant transformation of her womanhood as it blossomed in bondage, she now in her place in nature.

"Master!" I called to the guard. "Master, may I speak?"

"What do you want?" he asked, walking beside me now, coiling the whip.

"Is that Venna?" I asked.

"Yes," said he.

I was confused.

"I have been sold to a chain of Ionicus," I said.

"Yes?" he said.

When I had learned, days ago, outside Argentum, that I had been sold to a chain of Ionicus, I had almost collapsed in fear. "Which chain, Masters?" I had begged. "Which chain? Please, Masters, which chain?" But my importunities had earned me then only a cuffing. It had not been until they were loading me, and four of the other girls, each of us tied within a tall, narrow leather sack, our heads exposed, the sack locked shut beneath our chins, into the cargo net, to be slung beneath a draft tarn, that I found out any specific information pertinent to my fate. "Whither are we bound, Master?" I had asked of the fellow who would fly the lead tarn, the others in a roped coffle behind him. "To the loading docks of Aristodemus," he had said, "outside the defense perimeter of Venna." "Thank you, Master!" I had cried, elated. Venna is a small, lovely city, largely a resort city, north of Ar, on the Viktel Aria. It is known for its tharlarion races. It is also a common locale, it and its vicinity, for villas of the rich, usually from Ar. I had feared that we might be bound for Torcadino, a city currently under siege by Cosians, and their allies, where, employed in the siegeworks, digging investing trenches, raising earth walls, and such, labored the "black chain of Ionicus," that chain for which I had aided in the "enlistment" or "recruitment" of several of its members. Two days ago we had arrived at the "docks of Aristodemus." Tarn traffic, because of the conditions of war, and alarms of war, was currently extremely restricted in the vicinity of Venna, as, I took it, it also was in the vicinity of Ar. The point of this was apparently to render aerial reconnaissance more difficult and to subject the environing skies to at least partial control. An unauthorized flight into the area, particularly a day flight, would thus be easier to detect. Tarnsmen, too, frequently aflight, conducted patrols. Measures of this sort not only improve the probabilities of detecting raiders, or other invaders of airspace, spies, for example, but also, of course, facilitate the deployment of defensive forces. Raiders afoot, of course, move much more slowly, and may find themselves at the mercy of the skies. At the "docks of Aristodemus" we were put in work tunics. We were also put in the chains we now wore, with the exception of the coffle chain. We were then put in slave wagons, with other girls, who had apparently been awaiting our arrival, to be taken to the work camp. In these wagons our chained ankles were threaded about the central bar, which was then locked in place. In this way we are kept in the wagon until masters might be pleased to release us. Once within the wire of the work camp we were taken from the wagon, one by one, and put in coffle. We were now making our way through the camp to the tent of the overseer, near which, for his convenience, would be our pens.

I looked about myself, and back, at the long chains of men. Some of them were still looking after our coffle. I was frightened. "What chain is this, Master?" I asked.

"It is the black chain," he said.

I cried out in fear.

"What is wrong?" he grinned. I am sure he knew.

"The black chain," I said, "is at Torcadino. It is at Torcadino!"

"It was at Torcadino," he said. "It is not there any longer. It was moved. It is here, now, at Venna."

I reeled in the chains. Things seemed suddenly to move about me, dizzily, and blackness seemed to leap about me. The chain pulling at the collar ring, in front, kept me moving.

"The siegeworks at Torcadino," he said, "or most of the heavy work there, at any rate, was completed months ago."

I felt sick, but I must move in the chains.

"Perhaps you are the slut Tuka," said the guard.

I looked at him, in misery. He had heard my name. I still bore the name which had been put on me by former master, Tyrrhenius of Argentum. It had been kept on me. I now, frightened, began to suspect why.

He looked at me.

"Yes, Master," I said, "I am the slut Tuka."

"I thought so," he said. "You have many friends on the chain."

"Protect me," I begged. "Protect me!"

"Perhaps," he smiled.

"I will serve you as abjectly as the lowest slut on Gor!" I wept.

"You must so serve anyway," he laughed. "You are a slave."

"Yes, Master," I moaned.

"The guards have heard that you were an excellent lure girl," he said. "They suspect, thusly, that you might be rather good. They are looking forward to trying you out."

"Yes, Master," I said. I would try to serve with perfection.

We were now ascending the rise toward the square tent, the overseer's tent. Behind it, and to the left, at the foot of the hill, on the low ground, in a soft area, were the pens for the female work slaves. I could see a corner of them as we climbed the hill.

"I was told, Master," I said, "that I was sold to my master, Ionicus, for five silver tarsks and a tarsk bit."

"I have heard that," he said.

"Is that not a high price to pay for a female work slave?" I asked.

"It would be quite high, under normal circumstances, for a normal work slave," he said, amused. "But my employer, Ionicus, enjoys a good joke. He is the sort of man who will pay high, to be amused."

"I see," I whispered.

"Stop here," he called to the coffle. We had now ascended the rise, and were on a flat, open space, before the tent.

"This, ladies," said he, "is the tent of the overseer. Much may depend on how you please him."

Murmurs of fear coursed through the chain.

"You will be removed from the coffle, and taken before him, one by one," he said. "It is my advice that you open your tunics."

One by one, beginning with the first girl, we were removed from the coffle. As each of us was removed from the coffle, we briefly crouched down, so that we might reach the upper part of our tunics with our chained hands, the chain joining our hands chained, in turn, to our ankle chain. We then pulled open our tunics. "Let me help you," said the guard. I stood up, before him, the collar gone now from my neck. He jerked the sides of the tunic apart, and then pulled it down, back over my shoulders. "Excellent," he said.

24 / In the Work Camp

"Let me carry water to them," she said. Her legs were excellent. She had a long mane of dark hair. It was no wonder she had once served in a tavern. The brief, clinging work tunic well revealed her. Our feet were covered to the ankles in the sand.

I stepped back. I would not dispute the labor with her. I feared to approach this group of fifty men.

"No," said the guard, grinning. "Tuka."

Ten days now I had been with the "black chain of Ionicus." Never before, however, had I been assigned to this crew. Two girls, commonly, are assigned to each crew. The "black chain," as a whole, consisted of several such groups, most of some fifty men. The other chains of Ionicus, the "red chain," the "yellow chain," and so on, were at other locations, not in the neighborhood of Venna. Ionicus was one of the major masters of work chains. He himself resided, I understood, in Telnus, the capital of Cos, where his company had its headquarters. His work chains, however, were politically neutral, understood under merchant law as hirable instruments. They might, accordingly, and sometimes did, work for both sides in given conflicts. The tarsk of gold is the symbol of such men.

I looked down into the area where the men labored. The men were bagging sand, later to be used in the making of mortar. The Vennans were concerned to repair and heighten their walls.

"Do you hesitate?" asked the guard.

"No, Master, of course not, Master!" I said.

"Beware," said the other girl.

My body, and even my legs, ached from the weight of the water bag, slung on its strap over my shoulder. I was pleased when the contents were depleted, for the weight was less, but then, soon, I must hurry back to the wooden tank, to submerge the bag again and, as the bubbles streamed up to the surface, and broke there, refill it. During the day I was not allowed to drink from the bag, but only from the tank. Usually while one girl returned to the tank, the other would remain with the crew. In this way, there was generally water available, except when the guards wished to punish the men. We might then be made to kneel or sit in the sight of them, the damp, bulging water bags beside us, which we were not permitted to bring to them. Sometimes the guards, during such times of denying the men drink, would help themselves to the water before them, sometimes spitting it out, or pouring it over their heads and bodies. Sometimes they would even empty the bag out before them, into the dirt or sand. About my neck, on a long string, threaded through the handle, hung a metal cup. This metal cup hung a few inches below my navel. It was a joke of masters. My chaining was now different from what it had been when I had been brought into the camp, that I might serve more efficiently. The vertical chain joining my wrist and ankle chains had been removed. Additional links had been interpolated into my wrist chain and my ankle chain. My ankles were now separated by some two feet of chain. There was apparently a rationale to the distance. The guards, at any rate, had taken measurements. The distance, seemingly rather small, on the one hand, and rather large, on the other, was seemingly dictated by a twofold consideration, the preclusion of my capacity to run and the convenience of the guards, particularly when I was supine, a position in which they sometimes placed me. My wrists were separated also by a similar, but somewhat shorter, length of chain. This, in its normal placement, allowed me to use my hands fairly well. This usage was restricted, of course, if the chain were thrown behind the back of my neck, or, more so, if it were looped about my neck. Sometimes, too, I was made to step over the chain, bringing it up behind me, which tends to hold the hands, as they might twist or struggle, back, near my waist or hips. These chaining arrangements were fairly normal with the female work slaves in the "black chain of Ionicus." The only differences between our chainings were usually the numbers of links separating our ankles, this being a function of the length of our legs.

"You know that he is down there, among the others," said the girl, near me, she, too, chained, standing in the sand, on the top of the small hill, her own water bag on its strap over her shoulder.

"Yes," I whispered, frightened. It was he I feared most, of all of them.

"Beware," said the girl, again.

I nodded, sick.

"Do not fear," said the guard. "It is unlikely that they will attempt to kill you while they are in their chains. How could they escape? Too, if they do attempt to kill you, I might attempt to intervene. I might even be in time."

"Yes, Master," I whispered, fearfully. If they did wish to kill me, I knew, however, they could do so quite quickly. The guard, if he remained at the top of the rise, as he apparently intended, of this low, sloping sandy hill, could never reach them in time. I could be strangled in an instant, the cartilage in my throat broken, ruptured, by strong hands. Similarly, in an instant, my neck, or my back, thrown over their knees, could be broken. I cast a frightened glance at the other girl. She, like myself, had been sold in Samnium. She, however, had been sold directly to an agent of Ionicus, and sent to the black chain, which, at that time, had been at Torcadino. She had come with the chain east to Venna. The agent in Samnium had purchased her, I had been told by another girl, one apparently sold at about the same time, and also purchased by the agent of Ionicus, for seventy copper tarsks. I had brought fifty. The other girl, she who had told me this, by her own account, had brought only forty. It seemed we had all been sold very cheaply. To be sure, we had all been stolen slaves. The recovery period having passed, of course, we were now the legal properties, fully, and in all senses, of our current master, Ionicus of Cos. I was angry that I had sold for twenty copper tarsks less than she. Surely I was as beautiful as she, or perhaps even more so. At any rate, we were both, I was sure, lovely female slaves. Perhaps much depends on the individual man, and how much we interest him? Perhaps I had been sold before the agent had come to the market? Too, my former master, Gordon, had paid fifty copper tarsks for me, and that was undoubtedly a great deal of money for him. Surely that should count for something. He was only an impoverished, itinerant musician. He was not the agent of what was, in effect, an international company, with considerable funds, those of his employer, not his own, to expend! I was sure that I was more beautiful than she, or that at least some men, nay, many men, would regard me as so! Surely I had stood higher in several of the lists at the baths than she!

I made my way slowly down the hill, through the sand. I went slowly not only because I was afraid but also because I did not want, because of the steepness, or my chains, to fall. It was shortly after the tenth Ahn, the Gorean noon. My shadow was small on the hot, sloping sand in front of me. Here and there a hardy, rough grass, or a patch of weeds, thrust up from the sand.

I looked back, once, at the guard, and the girl, another work slave, at the top of the tiny hill.

I approached the work group. It was in a shallow trough among the small hills, working at the sand in the trough. It was, by the hills about it, in its sandy valley, screened from the other groups in the area. At the time I did not give this any thought. My main concern was that the guard could see what was going on.

I was then on the level, moving through the heavy sand, it deeper, though affording better footing, than the sand on the incline.

I stopped. The men in the group, fifty of them, half-stripped, sweating, brawny, chained together in ankle coffle, turned to regard me. I had feared muchly, since coming to the chain, that I might have to serve this crew. I had not, however, been assigned to it until last night. I had hoped, on being presented, days ago, to the overseer, that he might find me of interest and keep me in his tent, as a personal slut. But it was not I who was to be chosen. When I had been put before him, kneeling in my chains, my tunic pulled back and down, behind my shoulders, already a girl was at the side of his chair. It was she who had been first in the coffle, she who had once been the spoiled, rich woman. She was on all fours, still chained. Her work tunic, however, had been removed and a narrow rectangle of silk, thrust in a leather thong knotted about her waist, hung down before her. Our eyes met. She looked down. The overseer had already made his choice. To be sure, I, too, once or twice, as had other girls, had worn the rectangle of silk in his tent. He had the call of all of us.

I would approach the men, head down. I would ask, "Water, Master?" of each. Before those who wished water, I would kneel and pour them a cup. It was appropriate that I knelt, as I was a slave, and they were free, though currently bound, justly or unjustly, in servitude. It is common, incidentally, for a slave to kneel before free men in serving them drink. "Wine, Master?" is a common expression. In it the slave usually offers the master not only drink, say, the wine in the cup, but also, implicitly, the wine of her love, body and beauty.

I had begged not to serve this chain. My pleas had been ignored, or mocked. If they had no concern for my feelings, had they, too, no concern with their employer's property, that they would subject it to such risk? Then I recalled that Ionicus of Cos had paid more for me, a great deal more, than is common for a female work slave, and that this had to do with his "amusement."

I looked at the chain, and shuddered. There were fifty men on the chain. Twenty-three of them I had helped to entrap in Argentum.

I moved slowly through the sand, toward them. Then I stopped and looked wildly back, upward, toward the top of the rise. Could I not be given a gesture of mercy, that I might turn about and flee back, scrambling up that loose sand to the comparative safety of the ridge, to seek shelter within the compass of the guard's whip and sword? The guard, however, made no motion. The girl, standing beside him, seemed very frightened. "Will I never see the last of you?" she had exclaimed, angrily, when I had first been thrust into the pen, then still wearing the chaining in which I had been brought to the camp. I had avoided her as much as possible. Now, however, I could not well do so. We were assigned to the same crew. I think she did not care for the idea any more than I. She was frightened. I think her fear, though, was not primarily for me. Perhaps she most feared what might be the action of one of the men below, an action for which he might well be punished, or even killed. Whereas I had begged not to be assigned to this group, she had, weeks ago, I had learned, begged to serve with it. To be sure she had no more to fear from it than would any other girl. I, on the other hand, had a very great deal to fear from it. The guards had acceded to her pleas. She apparently worked very hard to keep her position with this chain, carrying water, sometimes double bags, frequently and uncomplainingly, and, in the evening, zealously, and desperately, and with subtle and delicious skills, well pleasing the guards. It was whispered about in the pens, seeing the frequency with which she was summoned forth, that she had not always been a common work slave. It was speculated that she had once been a pleasure slave, that she had once been in a tavern, and had even, once, been first girl.

I was now within a few feet of the first man. I remembered him from Argentum. He had been a metal worker and I had lied, pretending to be of his own caste. He whom I most feared, however, was at the end of the chain. I considered the tools in the grip of these men. One of those shovels could with a single blow cut my head from my body. I knew I could be killed quickly, very quickly. I looked from face to face. I realized then that these men would probably not wish to kill me quickly, not at all. If they wished to kill me, they would presumably prefer to do so slowly. I did not want to serve this crew. For days I had been left free of it. Then, last night, a girl had been transferred from it, and I had been assigned to it. The matter had seemed very sudden. I suspected that the girl had been transferred from it in order to make a place for me on it. I did not know, however, why, only now, this had taken place.

"Water, Master?" I asked.

These men were chained together only by an ankle. Their hands were free. They had implements.

"Yes," he said.

I knelt down in the sand, before him, my head down. I removed the metal cup on its string from about my neck. My neck was exposed to him. I attended to the filling of the cup, and capped the spout on the bag. I feared I would be struck with the shovel, it cutting down at me. He did not raise it, however. I kissed the cup and, holding it with both hands, my arms extended toward him, my head down between them, proffered it to him. He took it, and drank, and handed the cup back to me. "Thank you, Master," I whispered. I was alive!

I then went to the next man, and the next. As I moved down the line I grew gradually more grateful, and elated. Each accepted water from me. It seemed I might have been any water girl serving them. It was impossible to describe my relief. It seemed they did not hold it against me, that I had been utilized in their entrapment. Perhaps they understood something of my helplessness, and that I, only a Gorean kajira, had had no choice but to obey. How astonishing it was that they bore me no ill will! How grateful I was to them for their understanding! Then I knelt before he who was last on the chain, he whom I most feared, and yet best knew, he who had been many times kind to me in Brundisium, and whom I had cleverly tricked in Argentum, bringing him to his current condition.

"Water, Master?" I asked.

"Yes," he said.

I poured him the water and in that same fashion in which I had served the others proffered him the cup. He took it, and then, before my eyes, he did not drink, but regarded me, with hatred, and turned the cup, pouring the contents slowly, meaningfully, into the sand. I was terrified. This action on his part seemed some sort of signal to the others. I then found myself in the midst of them, kneeling, trembling, small, in the center of that grim circle.

"Masters?" I asked, frightened. Surely the guard must come down the incline now, to threaten them, to whip them back. But, kneeling as I was, in the midst of them, I could not even see the guard. "Masters?" I asked, terrified.

They said nothing. Where was the guard!

"Please, Masters," I said, "I am only a slave. Please be kind to a slave!"

"She feigns terror well," said one of the fellows.

"She is an excellent actress," commented another.

"Please, Masters!" I pleaded.

He before whom I knelt threw the cup to the side, in the sand. The water bag was removed from me. It was put a few feet from me, by the cup.

I did not dare rise from my knees. I was a slave. I had not been given permission.

"You were an excellent lure girl," said one of the fellows.

"Thank you, Master," I whispered.

Even had I dared to rise, as I did not, I did not know if I, in my terror, could even have found the strength to do so. Too, even if I had dared to leap up, and had found the strength to do so, I could not have escaped them. They were all about me. Too, I could not run, chained as I was.

"She deceived me well," said a fellow.

"And me," said another.

"And me," said another.

"Forgive me, Masters!" I begged.

The guard did not appear.

"Help!" I screamed. "Help! Help, Master! Please, help! Help, Master!"

But only silence greeted my cries for assistance.

"Were you given permission to speak?" asked a fellow.

"No, Master," I whispered. "Forgive me, Master!"

The fellow before whom I knelt gave a sign and one of the men, a brawny fellow, lifted me up from the back, by the upper arms. Another fellow then, as I was held, cuffed me, twice. I was then dropped back into the sand, on all fours, a punished slave.

"Let her try to run," said the fellow before whom I had knelt.

I looked about, wildly. I tasted blood in my mouth.

The men behind me moved to one side, opening a place between them, leading back toward the top of the ridge.

My eyes fixed on him before whom I had knelt. I rose to my feet, half crouching, and backed warily away from him, until I was beyond the line of the chain, and then, wildly, I turned about, and tried to run. I fell, again and again, and then, clawing, and scrambling, I began to ascend the sandy slope. Again and again, I slipped back, inhibited in my chains. Then I had attained the summit of that ridge. I stood there, wildly. There, now, on the summit, was not only the guard and the other work slave, now kneeling, with her head down to the sand, but the overseer, and a palanquin, with eight bearers, and a man in silken robes, fat and bald, who reclined upon it, holding a short-stemmed lorgnon, in his right hand. Swiftly I knelt, covered with sand, in my chains, before the palanquin, doing obeisance. "Look up," said the overseer. The fellow regarded me through the lorgnon. "This," said the overseer, "is the girl, Tuka, who served your supplier, Tyrrhenius, in Argentum. We had her purchased, following your policy, for a tarsk bit over her former selling price. We had her brought here, as we thought would please you, to the black chain. We are gratified that this should have coincided with your tour of inspection." The overseer gestured to the guard and he opened my tunic, and pulled it back. I saw the lorgnon lift a little. "As you might surmise," said the overseer, "she was an excellent lure girl. She figured in the entrapment of twenty-three of the prisoners below."

I trembled, kneeling in the soft, warm sand, it up about my thighs.

"You may greet your master," said the overseer to me.

"Greetings, Master," I said.

The man in the palanquin made a small gesture with the lorgnon, hardly a movement.

The guard seized me by the upper arms, from behind, and flung me back over the ridge, and I tumbled, sprawling, rolling, sliding, down the sandy slope, until once again I was at its foot. There two of the brawny fellows seized me by the arms and, dragging me through the sand, put me again to my knees before he whom I most feared. I looked wildly up, behind me, but there I saw naught but the unmoving, observing group. I understood now why the guard had not come to my assistance. I understood now why I had suddenly been transferred to this chain. I understood, too, now, I thought, why this group was in its present place, screened by the hills from the sight of the other groups.

I flung myself to my belly in the sand before he whom I most feared, he whose shackle was the last on that chain of fifty strong men.

I would have crawled to his feet, to press my bloody lips to them, but my ankles were held.

"Master," I wept, "forgive me!"

But, looking up from my belly, covered with sand, sand in my hair, I saw no forgiveness in his eyes.

At a gesture from him, he who seemed to be their leader, I was drawn to my knees. I tried to pull together my tunic, but one of the men pulled it open again, angrily.

"Let us kill her," said one of the men.

I shuddered.

"Kill her," said another.

"Kill her," said yet another.

"Yes," said another.

"Yes!" said yet another.

But a small gesture from their leader, he before whom I knelt, silenced them.

"Are your hips still loose?" he asked. "Do you still sway well?"

I looked at him, wildly. He had asked me this in Argentum, before I had deceived him, before he had carried me, trustingly, lovingly, in his arms, back into the alleyway.

"Master?" I asked.

I tried to read his intent, but could not.

He regarded me.

"My current master does not use me as a dancer," I said. It was in this fashion, too, that I had responded in Argentum.

He gestured that I should be drawn to my feet.

"Dance," he said.

"Master?" I asked, disbelievingly.

"Need a command be repeated, slave girl?" he asked.

"No, Master!" I cried. I wound the chain a bit about my wrists, taking up its slack. I could use it, in its different lengths, later, in the dance. I lifted my hands above my head, the backs of my hands facing one another. I flexed my knees. Sometimes a woman is permitted, even a free woman, among the fires of a burning city, the glare of the flames red upon her flesh, to dance before masters as a naked slave. She must hope to be found pleasing, and that her fate will be only the brand, chains and the collar. She dances helplessly, desperately. She hopes to be found pleasing. She dances for her life. He was giving me this chance! He must still care for me! "Thank you, Master!" I cried. It had been long, I knew, since these men had had a woman, and they were Goreans. They would be half mad with desire. Too, many of them had found me exciting, and had wanted me earlier, else I could not have lured them. Too, I was a skilled dancer. Too, I was beautiful, or had been told so. Certainly many men on this world have found me attractive, and desirable, and have not hesitated to put me to their services, and fully, as may be done with a slave.

I danced.

I looked at their faces.

Many of these men, I knew, would feel they had a score to settle with me. It was my hope then that they might be persuaded to accept in settlement of these accounts, if accounts they were, not my blood but so small and innocent a thing as my mastering, my total ravishing and subjugation. That would be vengeance enough, I hoped, for such men. Certainly I had lured them. But I had not truly chosen to do so. Surely they should understand that! Of my own will I would never have dared to do such a thing! And now I danced before them, for my life, helpless, desperate to please them, in terror. What more then could they want, saving my zealous services, those commonly to be surrendered by a slave dancer to masters.

I danced.

I saw anger, and hatred, turn to desire.

I did many cunning things with the chains.

I began to sense, with timidity, and hope, and then a growing confidence, and with an increasing sense of elation, that many of them, perhaps even most, might be encouraged to find me of at least minimal interest.

"Hei!" cried one of them, smiting his thigh.

"Master!" I called to him, gratefully, then dancing back from him, in the sand. Others restrained him from following me and seizing me. Then I was too near the other side of the circle, and returned, quickly, gracefully, to its center, dancing to first one man and then another. More than one reached out for me. Their grasping hands were but a yard or two from me.

"You were surely never of the metal workers!" laughed the fellow who had been of that caste.

"No, Master," I assured him.

"No woman of my caste could move like that!" he cried.

"Do not be too sure, Master," I cautioned him.

I saw sweat upon his forehead, and his fists clench as he perhaps recalled some women he had known, of that caste. Surely the women of his caste, too, could be taught to dance, and to lick and kiss, and serve, and even superbly, such that they might drive a man wild with desire. Were they not, too, in the final analysis, only females? I had known two slaves who had once been of his caste, Corinne, in the house of my training, and Laura, in Hendow's tavern. Both had been superb slaves. To be sure, being slaves, they were no longer in his caste. Animals do not have caste.

I danced before another.

It was my desperate hope to turn their wrath, and their desire for vengeance, seemingly at the beginning so adamant, so fierce and unrelenting, to interest, and desire, and passion. "Do not kill me, Master," I begged another, "but let me live, I beg you, to serve and please you, and with all the fullness of the female!"

"Perhaps," he said, licking his lips.

I continued to dance.

There are many forms of placatory dances which are performed by female slaves. Some of these tend to have rather fixed forms, sanctioned by custom and tradition, such as the stately "Contrition Dance" of Turia. Some form of placatory dance is usually taught to the girl in slave training. There is no telling when it might be needed. Though I had had, because of the relatively advanced state of my dancing skills, for a new slave, very little instruction in dance in the house of my first training, I had been taught at least that much. The form of placatory dance taught to a girl usually depends on the girl in question. For example, I had not been taught the stately "Contrition Dance" of Turia. It had been felt that the nature of my body lent itself to a more desperate, needful, lascivious form of dance. I had been taught how to dance on my knees, for example, and, supplicatingly, on my back, and belly. Most placatory dances, however, are not fixed-form dances, but are "free" dances, in which the slave, exquisitely alert to the nuances of the situation, the particular master, the nature of his displeasure, the gravity of her offense, and such, improvises, doing her best to assuage his anger and beg his forgiveness, to reassure him of the authenticity of her contrition and the genuineness of her desire to do better.

"There is no garbage here, on which to make your bed," said one of the men, "and I have learned that, indeed, in any event, you are worth less than it."

"Yes, Master," I said.

"Nor do I have a cloak now, doubled, to soften the cruelty of the cobblestones to your back," he said.

"Hot sand will do, Master," I said, "and chains in which my limbs are enclosed."

"Yes," he said.

I saw I did not need to fear him, save in the ways any slave must fear a master.

I danced then to those whose eyes were hardest. Some of them were not even men I had trapped, but only men who knew what I had done. Some may have been as innocent as those I had lured; others might have been murderers and brigands, suitably enchained for the expiation of sentences, their custody having been legally transferred to Ionicus, my master, at the payment of a prisoner's fee, by the writ of a praetor or, in more desperate cases, by the order of a quaestor. I danced abjectly. I danced piteously. I danced beggingly. I danced as well as I could. I could not do more. They would either be pleased or not. My fate was in their hands.

"She is pretty," said one of them.

"Yes," said another.

Hope sprang again high within me. I sought then to move another, with my helplessness, and the pleas of my body.

"Are you a good slave lay?" asked a man.

"It is my hope that I am pleasing, Master," I said. "Surely I shall endeavor to be so."

He grinned.

"She has the look of a wench who would be good in the furs," laughed a man. I heard the chain move in the heavy staple on his shackle.

"There are no furs here," laughed another man.

I had not had furs touch my body since a cool evening, five nights ago, in the overseer's tent. I had then worn the rectangle of red silk, that in which he was accustomed to put his use slaves. It is such, it thrust over a leather thong knotted about the girl's belly, that it may bc easily brushed aside, or pulled away. It was my hope that I had pleased him well. Toward morning he had chained me, hand and foot, to a stake near his feet, where I could not reach him. I moaned for a time, but the kick of his foot had taught me that I must then be silent.

"She is an excellent dancer," commented a man, another whom I had lured in Argentum.

"Yes," said another fellow, another of those who owed his chaining to me.

I began to be conscious then, as I sometimes was, of the incredible power of the female slave, of how helpless men could be before her, and of what she could do to them.

"Ah," said one of the men, softly, watching.

I repeated the movement.

"Yes," said another man. "Yes!" said another.

How paradoxical I thought, that she who is branded, and collared, and owned, and is nothing, should have such power!

"Dance, slut, dance!" said a man.

And then again I danced, helplessly, piteously, suing for their favor, striving desperately to be found pleasing. In the end the power belongs to the master, totally, and not to the slave. She is his.

"Excellent," said a man. "Excellent."

I danced.

I danced in such a way that a free woman might only dream of, awakening, sweating, in the night, clutching her covers, in terror, then feeling her throat with trepidation, with the tips of frightened fingers, to ascertain that no collar has been locked on it in the night. How could she, a free woman, have such a dream? What could it mean? And what would the men do to her when they came to take her in their arms? She awakened, in terror. Perhaps she hurries to strike a light in her room. The familiar surroundings reassure her. She has had such dreams before. What could they mean? Nothing, of course. Nothing! Such dreams must be meaningless! They must be! But what if they were not? She shudders. Perhap she then, in her long silken gown, curls up, frightened, at the foot of her bed. What, too, could that mean? She does not know. Surely that, too, means nothing. But what if it did? She lies there, troubled, but somehow comforted, somehow secure, in that position. It seems to her, somehow, that that is where she belongs.

"Superb," said a man.

I saw now that they, or most of them, were pleased. I sensed now that I might be spared, at least if I pleased them, too, well enough in the sand. I had lured many of them, but now I danced before them, to please them, begging for my life, danced before them helplessly, at their mercy, submitted and dependent on their favor, for my very life, as much as though I might be their own slave. I saw to my joy, coming gradually to understand it, that they, or surely most of them, would accept this, my beauty, my submission and service, abject and total, in lieu of my blood. It would be vengeance enough for them. How mighty they were, and kind! To be sure, I would have to continue to show them perfections of slave service and total deference. How grateful I was to he whom I had most feared, he who was last upon the chain, he who had given me this eagerly embraced opportunity to save my slave's hide! But it was he, of all of them, who had refused to watch me dance. He stood with his back turned to me, his back straight, his arms folded, looking away. Many times I had danced to him, moving behind him in the sand, but he did not turn. He did not deign to glance upon me. Then, near the end of my dance, as it approached its climax, I was on my knees in the sand, writhing, bending forward until my hair was in the sand, bending back then, exposing the bow of my body, my thighs, my belly, my breasts and throat to them, my hands inviting attention to them, my hair back in the sand, and then I straightened, and then was on my back, and belly, twisting and moving, lifting my hands to them, begging for favor, piteously suing for mercy. Such things I had been taught as long ago as the house of my first training, but I think, truly, even had I not had such training, I would, in the circumstances, have done much the same. Perhaps it is instinctual in a woman. I had, when owned by Gordon, the musician, once seen a former free woman, new to her collar, in an alley in Samnium, performing so for a master, he with whip in hand, encouraging her to adequacy. She did well. She, shuddering, half in shock, learned that she would be spared, at least for the time. He then began to instruct her in how to give pleasure to a man. She attended fearfully, and well, to her lessons.

At the end of my dance, I was on my knees again, behind him. I lifted my hands to him. "Master, please!" I begged. "Look upon me!" But he did not turn.

With a cry of joy the men surged about me. I was lifted by my upper arms and flung back in the sand. My legs were lifted up, my knees bent. My wrist chain was pulled forward and thrust over and behind my feet. It was then jerked up, behind me. I could now not move my hands from my sides. I was helpless. My ankles, each in the grip of one man, were pulled apart, until my ankle chain, its links straightened, permitted no further extension. My opened tunic was thrust back on both sides. I, half submerged in the sand, put my head back, looking up, and back. I could see the figures, and the palanquin, seemingly small, seemingly far above me, seemingly far away from me on the ridge. I thought my master, Ionicus, of Cos, might be looking at me, through the lorgnon. "Oh!" I cried, suddenly, as the first of them put me to his pleasure.

"Are you all right?" asked Tupita.

"Yes," I said, lying in the sand.

"The chain is gone," she said. "It has been taken elsewhere."

I nodded, stiff, aching. I had known that it had gone. A little later Tupita had come down the slope.

"Lie on your side," she said. "Pull your legs up. Get your knees as close to your belly as you can."

She drew the chain down, from behind me, and, pushing back my ankles, I winced, put it over my feet and ankles. It was then again before me.

"Sit up," she said.

"Yes, Mistress," I said. She was not the "first girl" of the work slaves, nor even the first girl in our pen. Of the two of us assigned to this chain, however, she was surely "first girl."

"You are sure you are all right?" she asked.

"Yes, Mistress," I said.

I turned and looked up to the height of the ridge.

"They are gone," she said.

"Yes," I whispered.

"Can you walk?" she asked.

"I think so," I said.

"I think we should follow the chain now," she said.

"Mirus saved my life," I said.

She was silent.

"What is wrong?" I asked.

"I think we should follow the chain," she said.

"What is wrong?" I asked.

"It is lonely here," she said.

"I do not understand," I said.

"I heard them talking, up on the ridge," she said. "Something has happened."

"What?" I asked.

The sun was still bright. It was in the late afternoon. The sky was very blue. A soft wind moved between the dunelike hills, stirring the rough grass.

"It happened only a pasang or so from the walls of Venna," she said, "closer to Venna than our camp."

"What?" I asked, uneasily.

"A body was found, that of an official of Venna, an aedile, I think."

"I am sorry to hear that," I said. "I gather that he was robbed?"

"Apparently he was robbed," she said, "either by the assailant, or another. His purse was gone."

"I am sorry," I said.

"The body," she said, "was half eaten."

I shuddered.

"It was half torn to pieces," she said. "The visera were gone. Bones were bitten through."

I winced.

"It is frightening,' she said, "to consider the force, the power, of such jaws, which could do such things."

"There is a sleen in the vicinity," I said. I remembered Borko, the hunting sleen of my former master, Hendow, of Brundisium.

"The tracks were not those of a sleen," she said.

"There are panthers," I said, "and beasts called larls. Such animals are very dangerous."

"As far as I know, there has not been a panther or larl in the vicinity of Venna in more than a hundred years," she said.

"It could have been wandering far outside its customary range," I said, "perhaps driven by hunger, or thirst."

"They were not the tracks of a panther or larl," she said.

"Then it must have been a sleen," I said.

"Sleen have no use for gold," she said, uneasily.

"Surely someone could have found the body, and taken the purse," I said.

"Perhaps," she granted me.

"It must then have been a sleen," I said. "There is no other explanation."

"The tracks," she reminded me, "were not those of a sleen."

"Then of what beast were they the tracks?" I asked.

"That is a frightening thing," she said. "They do not know. Hunters were called in. Even they could not identify them."

I regarded her.

"They could tell very little about the tracks," she said. "One thing, however, was clear."

"What?" I asked.

"It walked upright," she said.

"That is unnatural," I said.

"Is it so surprising," she asked, "that a beast might walk upright?"

I looked at her.

"Or even that they should walk in power and pride?"

"I do not understand," I said.

"Our masters, the beasts, the brutes, those who put us in collars, and make us kneel, those from whose largesse we must hope they will grant us a rag, those whose whips we must fear, do so," she said.

"Yes," I breathed. "They do!" Our masters, the magnificent beasts, so powerful, so free, so liberated and masculine, so glorious in their untrammeled manhood, so uncompromising with us, did so.

"But this thing, I think," she said, "is not such a beast, not a human beast, not a man in the full power of his intelligence, vitality and animality, but some other sort of beast, something perhaps similar somehow, but very different, too."

"I would be afraid of it," I said.

"I doubt that you could placate it with your beauty," she said.

"Am I beautiful?" I asked.

"Yes," she said, "I who was, and perhaps am, your rival, grant you that. You are very beautiful."

"You, too, are beautiful," I said, and then I added, suddenly, "and doubtless much more beautiful than I!"

"I think that is not true," she said. "But it is kind of you to say it."

"I am sure it is true," I said.

"We are both beautiful slaves," she said. "I think we are

equivalently beautiful, in different ways. I think we would both bring a high price, stripped naked on a sales block. Beyond that it is doubtless a matter of the preferences of a given man."

"You are kind," I said.

"Did you betray me in the matter of the pastry?" she asked.

"No," I said. "Its absence was noted. Your presence in the vicinity was recalled. You were apprehended. In the licking of your fingers was revealed the taste of sugar."

"I was whipped well for that," she said, shuddering.

"I am sorry," I said.

"How I hated you," she said.

"I am sorry," I said.

"I was first girl, and you were last kennel," she said. "Now we are both mere work slaves, both of us only common sluts on the black chain of Ionicus."

"You are still first girl, of the two of us," I said.

"That is true," she smiled.

"But may I call you by your name?" I asked.

"Do not do so within the hearing of masters," she said, "for I do not wish to have to sleep on my belly for a week."

"No!" I laughed. She could not read or write, but she was a beautiful, highly intelligent woman. Too, since I had known her in Brundisium, and Samnium, I felt that a great change had come over her. I felt, too, that she had, in the last few days, come to have some concern for me. I was not altogether clear how this had come about. Perhaps it had to do with her pity for me, only a slave, one as helpless as she, but one in much greater danger here, because of her work for her former master, Tyrrhenius of Argentum. But it had to do even more, I think, with he who had been last on the chain, he who had once been second to my former master, Hendow, in Brundisium, Mirus.

"Perhaps we should rejoin the chain," I said, uneasily.

She looked about herself. "Yes," she said. "It is too lonely here."

I arose with difficulty and retrieved the cup, on its string, which I put about my neck. I would wash it at the tank. Too, I again put the water bag on its strap, on my back.

"There is something else," she said.

"What is that?" I asked.

"Two girls, too, have been stolen," she said.

"Girls such as we?" I asked.

"Yes," she said.

"Work slaves?" I asked.

"Yes," she said.

"But not eaten?" I asked.

"Not as far as I know," she said.

"Anyone could steal us," I said.

She shrugged. "I suppose so," she said, "except in so far as our masters protect their property."

"The events are doubtless not connected," I said.

"Probably not," she said.

"Let us be on our way," I said.

"Many in Venna," she said, "as I understand it, are alarmed at the killing, and the mysterious footprints. Some think it is an omen or warning. The archon is consulting augurs, to take the signs."

I stood in the sand, waiting for her.

"They will concern themselves, surely, too, with legalities, and such," she said. "For example, those in the black chain who are not criminals, and for whom Ionicus does not have prisoner papers, will presumably be at least temporarily removed from the vicinity. That would mean many of the masters on our chain."

I nodded. This seemed understandable. The archon in Venna would be interested in putting his house in order before the taking of the auspices. He would doubtless regard it as politic, at least from the point of view of soothing possible apprehensions in his constituency, to become a bit more scrupulous about proprieties, at least in so serious a situation.

"Where will we go?" I asked.

"Probably not far, and for only a week or so, until the signs are taken," she said. "Our chain will probably be used for clearing and deepening ditches at the sides of the Viktel Aria south of Venna. We can return later. Things then will doubtless be the same as before."

"How far south?" I asked.

"Probably not far," she said.

"Beyond the defense perimeter?" I asked.

"Probably not," she said. "Why? Are you afraid of being stolen?"

"Not really," I said.

"If I were you," she said, "I would want to be stolen. You do not belong in a work tunic. You should wear a string of silk and be kissing and licking at a man's feet."

I smiled. "Do you not want to be stolen?" I asked.

"No," she said. "I would prefer, at least for the time, to remain with the chain."

"I see," I smiled.

She adjusted the water bag on her shoulder. It would be a steep climb out of the trough.

"If we are outside the defense perimeter or near its edge," I said, "is there not a danger that the chain might find itself under attack?"

"For what?" she asked. "For deepening ditches?"

"I suppose it is silly," I said.

"Men seldom make war on work chains," she said.

"I am glad to hear that," I said.

"It is not like we were working on siege trenches or repairing the walls of a beleaguered city," she said.

"No, I suppose not," I said.

"I am ready," she said. "Let us go."

With difficulty, carrying the water bags, in our chains, we made our way up the sandy slope. I reached the top first and extended my hand to Tupita, who took it, and, with its help, pulled herself up, until she stood beside me.

"You are bruised," she said.

"It is nothing," I said.

"You will be stiffer, and sorer, tomorrow than today," she said.

I shrugged.

From where we were we could see men, and the tank, and the overseer's tent, on its hill, and our pens, at its foot, and the wire around the camp. I think we were both glad to see these familiar sights.

"How is your back," she asked.

"It is all right," I said.

"The sand stanched the wounds," she said.

The chain, when it had been behind me, had cut at my back a little, sawing there, when I had struggled, grasping and crying out. When I had felt the wetness of blood there, I had tried to keep my hands low at my sides, in the sand, scratching and clutching at it, but then, almost as though unable to help myself, I had again tried to reach for their bodies. This had pulled the chain tight again against me. In the throes of my submission, however, as I, a slave, gave myself from the deepest depths of my belly to masters, I think I was unaware of the pain. If I had been aware of, dimly and far off, I think I must, in my frustration and joy, trying to reach them, and yet helpless in their hands, have accepted it willingly. I could not even remember, clearly, what had happened.

"There is a little blood at the back of your tunic," she said.

I regarded her.

"Do not fear," she said. "I think it will wash out, at the tank. Besides, it is not your fault."

"I will not be permanently marked, will I?" I asked.

"No, vain slave," she smiled.

Such marks, of course, if permanent, might reduce a girl's value on the slave block.

I looked down into the sandy trough. "Do you think I will often be put to the pleasure of the chain?" I asked.

"No," she said. "Our master, Ionicus, has had his sport. You will now, presumably, be used more to frustrate them than please them. To be sure, the guard has seen you move, and dance. This will get around the camp. Do not be surprised, accordingly, if they now choose to avail themselves of you more frequently. I would not even be surprised if, say, in an evening or two, you found yourself again in the thong and silk, in the overseer's tent."

I looked over to the overseer's tent. It was about a half pasang away. He had the call of any of the slave females in the camp. Too, of course, he could assign us however he wished, and for as long as he wished, to others.

"To be sure," said Tupita, "we might be thrown to the chains, from time to time, as bonuses or rewards."

I nodded. Much as men might throw us pastries or candies, so, too, we ourselves, in turn, or our uses, might be given to others.

"Do you know anything more of the beast who slew the aedile?" I asked.

"No," she said.

"Nor anything further of the two slaves who were stolen?"

"No," said Tupita.

"Perhaps they ran away," I said. I shuddered. Even the thought of the possible penalties for such an action struck terror into my heart. Too, given the culture, her marking, the closely knit nature of the society, and such, there was, for all practical purposes, no escape for the Gorean slave girl.

"In work tunics, through the wire, laden with chains?" she asked.

I was silent.

"Too, work slaves outside the wire, not in the vicinity of a work chain, not in the keeping of a guard, they would provoke immediate suspicion."

I nodded.

"They would be in punishment yokes, on their bellies before the overseer, within an Ahn," she said.

I nodded. "Who, then, do you think stole them?" I asked.

"I do not know," said Tupita.

"The animal?" I asked.

"I would not think so," she said, "but who knows?"

"It is getting darker," I said.

"Tonight," said Tupita, "I will be glad to be locked in, behind the bars of our pen."

"I, too," I said, shuddering.

"Come along," she said.

"Tupita," I said.

"Yes?" she said.

"Call me by my name," I said.

"What is your name?" she asked.

" 'Tuka'," I said. That was the name masters had given me. It was my name, as a dog has a name, or a slave.

"Tuka," she said.

"You love Mirus," I said.

"I woud beg to lick his whip," she said.

"Does he love you?" I asked.

"I do not think he knows I exist—in that way," she said.

"He is a kindly and marvelous man," I said.

"He found you pleasing," she said.

"I caught his fancy in Brundisium, a new girl in the tavern, one not yet fully accustomed to her collar," I said. "He enjoyed teaching me, and putting me through my paces. He enjoyed using me, as have many men. He gave me great pleasure, and I hope, too, that I gave him great pleasure."

She regarded me.

"And I think he was fond of me," I said.

"Yes," she said.

"But I do not believe I was ever more to him, really," I said, "than another girl at his feet."

She did not speak.

"I am sure he never thought of me as a possible love slave," I said.

She did not speak.

"I am not even Gorean," I said. "I am only a slut who was brought here from Earth, to wear a collar and serve my betters, the masters."

"Do you truly think he is kind?" she asked.

"Yes," I said.

"And do you think he is so marvelous?" she asked.

"Of course," I said.

"And do you think he is still fond of you?" she asked.

"I know he is," I said. I looked back, down into the sandy trough. "I lured him in Argentum," I said, my voice suddenly breaking, as I considered the enormity of it, "I lured him whom I knew, he who had been kind to me, he who trusted me, and brought him to chains and servitude, and yet, this afternoon, he saved my life."

She was silent.

"I shall be forever grateful to him for that," I said. "Had it not been for him, I would have been killed."

"Beware of him," she said.

"Why?" I asked.

"Why do you think he saved your life?" she asked.

"For caring for me," I said.

"No," she said.

"Then for pity," I said.

"No," she said.

"For desire?" I asked.

"No," she said.

"I do not understand," I said.

"He did not want the others to kill you," she said.

"Of course not," I said.

"He is Gorean," she said. "I do not know if you truly understand such men. Too, he has a long memory. Too, where you are concerned, he is not himself. Where you are concerned I think he is half crazy."

"I do not understand," I whispered.

"Stay away from him," she said.

"I would not try to take him from you," I said.

"He is a determined, intelligent man," she said. "He is biding his time."

"Do not fear," I said.

"I speak to you for your own sake," she said, "not mine."

"He did not let them kill me," I said.

"Why not?" she asked.

"I do not know," I said.

"I do," she said.

"Why?" I asked.

"It is his intention to kill you himself," she said.

"Surely you are mistaken," I whispered.

"Did he accept water from you?" she asked.

"No," I said. "He poured it out, on the ground."

"Did you not see that he would not even look upon you as you danced?" she asked. "Did you not note that he, of all of them, did not put you to use?"

"Why?" I asked.

"He did not wish to risk being softened, or mollified."

I looked at her, terrified.

"That is why he did not want others to kill you," she said, "because it is his intention to do so himself."

I nearly collapsed in the sand.

"But he is in chains," she said. "I do not think you really have anything to fear. Just do not fall into his hands."

I nodded, shuddering.

"I do not really understand what you have done to him," she said, "how you have changed him so. He is very different from Brundisium."

"Yes," I said, "if what you say is true."

"I loved him in Brundisium," she said, "but I did not know how much I moved him until we were separated."

"We are slaves," I said. "We can be bought and sold, and taken, and done with, as masters please. Our dispositions need not be in accord with our own wills. Our desires, our feelings, matter not."

"Then I found he was on the black chain," she said. "How pained I was to discover his fate! Yet, too, how my heart leapt to know him near! He was so close, and yet so far! I love him so. Yet I can do little but bring him water. I cannot so much as kiss his feet without the permission of a guard. If I were to put myself within his grasp, he might be whipped, or slain. Too, I now find him to my sorrow other than he was. He is now a bitter man, one so driven with the desire for vengeance, his thirst for the blood of the girl who betrayed him, that he has little time to consider another, one who would gladly die for him."

I regarded her.

"Yes," she said. "He is my love master."

"Does he know that?" I asked.

"No," she said.

"When the guard is not looking," I said, "you must tell him. Throw yourself on your belly before him, where we belong before such men. Lick and kiss his feet, with tears in your eyes. Confess that you have acknowledged him in your heart as your love master. He can do little more than kick you from his feet."

Tears sprang to her eyes.

"Do so," I urged.

"No," she whispered. "He is now in chains. He cannot now own me. He is not now free. It is not as though he could take me in his arms, if he were so inclined, and claim me by his rape. He is a prisoner of the black chain. He might even think it a trick of the guards. Perhaps in rage he would break my neck with his foot. Perhaps he would understand the whole matter as no more than some deliberate insult or mockery."

"I would do so, if I were you," I said.

"You are not Gorean," she said.

"I would risk all, for a love master," I said.

"You are crying," she said.

"No," I said. "No."

"You have a love master!" she said.

"No," I said. "No! No!" I had recalled Teibar, who, long ago, had brought me into bondage. I had never forgotten him.

"How piteous we are, so helpless, only slaves!" wept Tupita.

"Would you be other than you are?" I asked.

She looked at me, startled. "No," she said. "And you?"

"No," I said.

"It is getting dark," said Tupita, smiling through her tears. "We do not wish to miss our gruel."

But I stood quietly on the ridge, looking down into the trough. I was barefoot. There were shackles on my ankles. They were joined by chain, the chain half submerged in the sand. There were manacles on my wrists, hammered shut about them. These, too, were joined with chain. I wore a parted work tunic. I carried a metal cup on a string about my neck, and the water bag, on its strap, over my shoulder. It was half full. I could feel the water move in it, shifting, and shaping itself to my back. I looked up into the sky, and saw the three Gorean moons.

"You are a very beautiful, and desirable, slave, Tuka," said Tupita.

I did not respond.

"Perhaps if you had been less beautiful, and desirable," she said, "you would not have been brought to this world."

"Perhaps," I said.

"Do you wish then," she asked, "that you had been less beautiful, or desirable?"

"No," I said.

"It is getting late," she said. "Let us return to the tank, and then to the pens."

"Yes," I said.

"Perhaps you should close your tunic," she said.

"No," I said. "Let the men see."

"You are a slave," she said.

"Yes," I said.

"Are all the women of your world slaves?" she asked.

"I do not know," I said.

She parted her own tunic.
"I see that you, too, are a slave," I said.
"Yes," she said.
"But you are Gorean," I said.
"I am a woman," she said.
"We are both women," I said.
"And slaves," said Tupita.
"Yes," I said, "we are both women, and slaves."

25 / In the Tent of the Overseer

It was near sunset now, some five days after I had served in the trough, between the sandy hills. That very night my chains had been removed, and I had been scrubbed clean. My hair had been washed twice, and combed with care. I had been perfumed. I had then been wrapped in a red sheet and carried to the tent of the overseer.

I heard guards calling the watch.

All was well, it seemed, in the camp of the black chain of Ionicus. Ionicus himself had left the area of the camp the same afternoon in which I had served in the trough, returning, it was said, to Cos.

It was very beautiful this time of the evening. I stood in the entrance to the overseer's tent, alone, looking out, to the southwest. I wore only my collar, that of Ionicus, and, about my waist, a knotted thong, in which was thrust a narrow rectangle of red silk. I, like Tela, it seemed, who had once been the beautiful, spoiled, rich woman, Liera Didiramache of Lydius, in the north, on the Laurius, who had been first in the coffle, when I was fifth, had been found pleasing by Aulus, overseer of the black chain of Ionicus.

The sun's light, like a soft, diaphanous, golden mantle, spread over the hills and countryside. I could not see the pens from where I stood, neither those of the women, nor those of the men. Had I gone about the tent I could have seen the walls of Venna. I looked out to the southwest, over the camp area. I could see from this rise, on which was located the overseer's tent, the low hills among which I had served chained masters. I still bore the marks of their bruisings. I did not think they had wanted to hurt me, but they had not had a woman in a long time. In their haste, and their strength, and considering I had been a lure girl, they had not chosen to be gentle. I did not much mind. I did not always want gentleness. It did not displease me to be forced to recognize, and incontrovertibly, and with my whole body, that I was in a man's arms, those of a true man, and was a slave. Sometimes, I confess, I even wanted the whip, not for its pain, which I feared, but for its proof of my domination, that I was owned, and wholly, and was going to be mastered. But, sometimes, too, I wanted gentleness, and, in a slave's helplessness, begged for it. But even when Gorean men use you with gentleness, and great gentleness, I am pleased to report that they do so with authority. There is never any doubt, even then, as to the fact that you are in their arms, and who is in command. I could see, too, though it was harder now, the posts in the distance, between which the wire was strung. The wire was slave wire, with its closely interwoven latticework of sharp, swaying strands, and, numerous and closely set, at intervals of less than a hort, its barbs and knifelike prongs. I shuddered. A slave could be cut to pieces on such wire.

I left the entrance of the tent and walked about the tent, to my left. I wanted to see Venna, and the Viktel Aria. I hoped not to be seen by one of the guards. Sometimes I was more modest than at other times. Perhaps this was a lingering reminiscence of my Earth conditioning. I do not know. Certainly slaves, officially, supposedly, are not permitted modesty. That is for free women. On the other hand, I have never known a slave who was not, at one time or another, or in one way or another, particularly in public, outside the privacy of her master's domicile, concerned about her modesty. In a slave, too, modesty has a very special nature and "feel," for she knows, of course, that she is vulnerable to men, and that she may not be permitted clothing at all, unless it pleases them. Too, it is one thing to return at dusk to the pens with one's tunic parted a bit, perhaps even by inadvertence, after one has been treated like a stormed and sacked citadel, proud in one's desirability and bondage, and quite another to be simply out in public, wearing only a collar, a thong and a bit of silk. Too, of course, there are objective reasons for permitting a bit of modesty to a slave girl from time to time. For example, her beauty can excite and stimulate men, and not just her master. Putting her naked into the streets can be an invitation to her theft. She is, after all, goods. Most importantly, however, perhaps, is the fact that she belongs to the master. Her total beauty and most intimate services, thus, are perhaps most appropriately his, and not others', to command. Too, of course, the girl sometimes tends to be sensitive to this sort of thing. This is particularly so if she has a private master. Perhaps it is connected with the female's desire to pair bond. Interestingly the girl who may be excessively modest in public may be the same girl who, without another thought, at home, naked, in her collar, gives all of herself, shamelessly, unstintingly, joyfully, to her master.

"Who is there?" called a guard, a few feet away.

I had not seen him.

"Tuka, the slave," I said, swiftly, kneeling.

"What are you doing here?" he asked.

"I came out for air," I said, "and to see the land. It is so beautiful."

"It is not only the land which is beautiful," he said.

"Thank you, Master," I said. Even in the half darkness I blushed. "I shall return instantly to the tent, if master wishes," I said.

"You may remain for a few moments," he said.

"Thank you, Master," I said.

"You may stand there," he said, "where I can see you, and stand straightly."

"Yes, Master," I said.

I went toward the back edge of the tent. I stood where the guard had indicated. I stood straight. From where I was, happily, I could see the walls of Venna, and, before them, the Viktel Aria. I think the guard had understood that I might wish to see the city, and its lights, in the distance. I was grateful to him, for letting me stand here. The beacon fires had not yet been lit on its walls. These serve as guides to tarnsmen aflight, and, too, may be used to signal their recall, and such. Between some of them tarn wire would not be stretched; between others it would; which would be known to the tarnsmen. It is changed nightly. It had been to the Viktel Aria, though not to this precise part of it, that before Venna, that, four days ago, five chains of the black chain, or "links" of it, as they are sometimes called, had been marched. Among them had been the chain on which I had served with Tupita. These chains, or "links," of some fifty men each, had left the camp to the southwest and would, by a roundabout route, join the Viktel Aria some pasangs to the south, toward Ar. In this way the exit of the links was not conspicuous. The auspices had been taken yesterday. Apparently, as the guards had conjectured, they had been adjudged "favorable." That being the case it seemed likely the links would soon be returning to the camp. The masters, incidentally, had not bothered to separate out the illicit prisoners from the genuine prisoners, rearranging the chains, as Tupita had expected, but had simply sent those links which contained any illicit prisoners from the camp. This decision was motivated, it seemed, by an understanding that the auspices were to be soon taken, and would be likely to be "favorable," as the councils in Venna were eager to get on with the repair of the walls. Shackling which is closed by hammers, as was that of most of the black chain, is not as easily changed as lock shackling, responsive to keys. Two days ago, aediles had come to the camp to inspect the chains. They found none which contained illicit prisoners. No mention was made of the fact that a third of the chains was absent. The next day the auspices had been taken, and, seemingly, all had gone well. The chains in camp were already back at work. Preceding the time of taking the auspices, of course, and until they have been taken, things are very quiet. For example, the shops and baths are closed, the courts do not hear cases, and so on. Tupita, of course, had gone with the chain, south. I had not gone with it because I had been brought to the tent of the overseer. He had seen me from the ridge, and found me of interest. Certainly I had muchly served him the last few evenings. Too, to my irritation, he made me work hard during the day, precisely as though I might have been a house slave.

"Slave," said the guard, coming up behind me.

"Yes, Master?" I whispered. His hands on my arms did not permit me to kneel. I realized then he must have been watching me stand there, Venna, and her lights, in the backgrond. I recalled he had told me to stand straightly. I had done so, of course.

"The city and the night are beautiful, are they not?" he asked.

"Yes, Master," I whispered.

"Surely you have business in the tent," he said.

"Yes," I said. "I should hurry back to polish boots. I thank master for letting me stay here for a few moments. Master has been kind."

I made as though to move away, to return to the tent, but his hands, from behind, on my upper arms, held me where I was.

"Tela can polish boots," he said.

"She is polishing the shield of Aulus," I said.

"Have you received permission to leave?" he asked.

"No, Master," I said. "Forgive me, Master."

"Do not make noise," he said.

"No, Master," I said.

He lifted me, lightly, in his arms. I felt slightly giddy for a moment, held off my feet by a man. One has no contact with the ground. One is so much in their power.

"Put your arms about my neck," he said. "Kiss me."

I obeyed. Then suddenly I kissed him again, this time as a slave.

He laughed softly.

I moaned inwardly. How had I changed? What had men done to me?

He put me gently to my back, beside the tent, perhaps not feet from Aulus, the overseer, within, working on papers.

My body leaped to his touch.

I looked up at him, wildly.

Men had done much to me on Gor. They had imperiously, for their amusement and pleasure, summoned forth from me my latent slavery, a slavery which on Earth I had hardly dared acknowledge. They had taken a woman of Earth and lit slave fires in her belly. They had taught me how to feel. They had required that I show my slavery, and yield to it, wholly and honestly. They would let me be the slave I was, lovingly and helplessly. I loved them for it! I kissed the master eagerly.

He drew aside that bit of silk, that slender mockery of a shield.

"Yes, Master," I whispered.

He then used me, as a slave.

"I must polish boots," I said, at last, frightened. "I must polish boots."

"Be about your chores, girl," he said.

"Yes, Master," I whispered. He then left me. I readjusted the bit of silk. I tried to wipe dirt from my back with my hands. I did not want Aulus to know. Perhaps I, a slave, should not have gone out of the tent, clad as I was. There were tears in my eyes. How helpless the touch of men made us!

I hurried back about the tent and reentered it. Aulus glanced up, from the small, low table, behind which he sat, cross-legged, working. I performed obeisance, and then made as though to rise, to hurry to the rear portions of the tent, where my mat was, near Tela's.

"Where have you been?" he asked.

I remained on my knees, addressed. Indeed, from performing obeisance I was on all fours. "Outside," I said. "I went out for air. The night is very beautiful."

"Do you expect Tela to do your work?" he asked.

"No!" I said. "No, Master!"

"Your nipples," he said, "are swollen. Your skin is like a field of scarlet dinas."

I did not respond. I was terrified.

"Are you well warmed?" he asked.

I flung myself, in terror, to my belly before him. I did not want to be punished.

"Tomorrow," he said, "I am going out of the camp, to the Viktel Aria, and south. There is touble with the chains. It has to do with the mercenary companies now roving the countryside. They do so with impunity. It seems they think that whatever land the tread of their tharlarion can shake, whatever soil they choose to mark with the imprint of their beasts' claws, is theirs. Venna keeps her forces in the vicinity of the city. The patrols of Ar are irregular. The forces of Ar, almost entirely, have marched north, toward Ar's Station, on the Vosk, there to meet with an expeditionary force of Cos. It seems madness, with an army of Cosians, and mercenaries, at Torcadino, but I am not a general, not the regent of Ar. In short, as Ionicus, and others, including myself, have feared there might be, there has been trouble. It is nothing, however, happily, as we are dealing with mercenaries, that some gold, some fees for their clamorous brigades, cannot straighten out. Such things have happened before."

I understood very little of what he was saying. I did know that the main body of the forces of Ar had marched north. Indeed, they had done so on the Viktel Aria itself, which, in effect, is a military road.

"Master?" I asked.

"I am going to take you with me," he said.

"Yes, Master," I said.

"Have you ever been chained by the neck to a stirrup?" he asked.

"No, Master," I said.

"You will have the experience tomorrow," he said.

"Yes, Master," I said.

"Have you finished polishing my boots?" he asked.

"No, Master," I said. "With master's permission, I will do so now."

He lifted a finger, dismissing me. Quickly I rose to my knees and performed obeisance. I then rose to my feet, and, head down, humbly, frightened, hurried to the back portions of the tent.

There I saw the shield which Tela had been polishing, a small, round shield, more of a buckler, really, than a shield. It was ornamented with bosses, and engraved with mythological scenes, the conquest, and the rape and enslavement of Amazons by satyrs. In Gorean mythology it is said that there was once a war between men and women and that the women lost, and that the Priest-Kings, not wishing the women to be killed, made them beautiful, but as the price of this gift decreed that they, and their daughters, to the end of time, would be the slaves of men. The shield, so small, so beautiful, was perhaps more for display, I think, than an implement of war. Still I did not doubt that Aulus could handle weapons. He seemed to me that sort of man. Perhaps at one time he had been in service, to some city or another. Her rag, and the polish, in its flat metal container, were near the shield. Near it, too, were the boots of Aulus, and the rags and polish I would use for them. There were many domestic labors I did not care for, but, oddly enough, I did not mind polishing the boots of men. It seemed somehow fitting for me. I knelt down and put one of the heavy boots of Aulus between my thighs. Then, carefully, bending over, in the light of a hanging lamp, doing only a tiny spot at a time, rubbing with circular motions, I addressed myself to the leather. I did not want to be punished for having been outside the tent, with the guard. I had not intended to seduce him. It was not my fault, unless it were somehow my fault to be such that men so desired me. He had taken advantage of me, even warning me to silence! Was it not my master's fault, for letting me go out of the tent in what was little more, in effect, than a collar and a G-string? To be sure, I did yield well, but what was I to have done? What did Aulus expect? I was a slave! Surely in his own tent I had given him enough evidence of that! I wished I had been given clothing. Then I might have been able to better conceal what had been done to me. I wondered if I would be punished. I wondered if Aulus would put me in close chains tonight. I hoped not. Such things, over a period of hours, build up a great deal of pain in a girl's body. But he had not seemed particularly angry with me. I did not think he intended to punish me. I hoped not. Too, if I were punished, I might not look too well at his stirrup tomorrow. I had never been chained by the neck to a man's stirrup. I wondered what it would be like. I supposed the matter had to do with the effect he hoped to achieve, perhaps like the silver shield. I gathered I would be a display slave at his stirrup, something like a golden saddle and a purple cloak, something for show. I worked hard on the boots. Too, at his stirrup he could keep his eye on me, not leaving me behind. Perhaps that would amuse him. I glanced over at the shield. It had not been finished. I hoped that Tela did not expect me to finish it. The shield was hers to do! I had been assigned, perhaps because Aulus thought it more fitting for me, to do the boots.

"Tela!" I called, softly. "Tela!"

I continued to work on the boots.

Where was lazy Tela? If she wanted to court the wrist rings and chains, to be fastened on her knees to the center post of the tent, and whipped, that was her business, not mine! To be sure, this was not like Tela. If anything, Tela was a hard worker. She was, certainly generally, at least, not the sort who would shirk her work. I wondered if she were trying to get even with me, for the time I had had her iron the tunics? But I had paid her back for that later, surely, when I, too, had done them all! I liked Tela, and she had been very kind to me, even though I think she liked Aulus, and might have preferred to be the only slave in the tent.

"Tela!" I called, somewhat more loudly. "Tela!"

I was not really angry with Tela. I did wonder where she was. It was not like her to leave off in the midst of a task. I rose up, putting to one side the boot on which I was working, and went to the side, brushing back the curtain, to where our mats were.

"Tela!" I called. She was not there.

"What is wrong?" asked Aulus, having come from the front portion of the tent.

"Nothing, Master," I said, quickly.

"Where is Tela?" he asked.

"I do not know," I said.

"The shield has not been finished," he said.

"Perhaps she is outside," I said.

He went to the front of the tent, and stepped outside, underneath the sort of awning there, over the threshold, supported on two poles.

"Tela!" he called. I heard him question guards, too.

He returned to the tent.

"I do not know where she is, Master," I said, kneeling before him.

26 / Mercenaries

"Pietro Vacchi!" exclaimed Aulus, drawing back his tharlarion, "I should have known it would have been you!" I was terrified at his stirrup, the chain on my neck. It was like being tethered at the side of a mountain of scales and muscle. These beasts are unexpectedly agile for their size. Very little I would think could stand against their charge, lest it be a terrain of pits, a forest of peeled, inclined, sharpened stakes. The handful of riders had approached us on the Viktel Aria, they moving north. Only a few yards from us had they halted, wheeling their mounts. The very earth on which we stood had shaken. It had been, I suppose, a joke, that we must wait to see if we were to be struck, trampled or impaled on their spears. Aulus had retained his composure well, I thought, considering the provocation. Actually we were not far at all from Venna, only a few pasangs. They had ridden north, it seems, to meet us.

"My old friend, Aulus!" called the fellow. He held his seat well on the gigantic, impatient, hissing beast. He had bright, dark eyes, and curly black hair. In his ears were rings. His beard, too, was curly and black, even ringleted. In it ribbons were tied. Across his back was slung a shield. Beside him, in a saddle sheath, reposed the butt of a lance. His hand was on the shaft.

"It seems you have been recruiting again," said Aulus.

"Surely recruiting is no activity unfamiliar to your employer, the good Ionicus of Cos," he said.

"What have you against Ionicus of Cos?" asked Aulus.

"Nothing," said the fellow. "Indeed, I remember him with fondness, for I once labored on one of his chains."

Aulus's tharlarion was now quiet. I therefore knelt beside it, on the stones of the Viktel Aria, the chain looping up from my neck to his stirrup. I was naked.

"Those I recruit come willingly to my service," said the fellow. "Doubtless those you recruit can say the same."

I looked up at the bearded fellow. He was a man of incredible vitality. Accordingly I spread my knees more widely before him.

"Doubtless," grinned Aulus.

"Had it not been for a captain recruiting, long ago, like myself," said the fellow, "I might still be on his chain."

"I am empowered to negotiate on behalf of my employer, Ionicus," said Aulus. "It is for that reason that I have brought coins with me, those in the wagon behind, under this guard of twenty men."

"Perhaps I will take the coins, and be on my way, keeping the chains," said the fellow.

"You may do so, of course," said Aulus, "but I think that that would not do your reputation, even such as it is, my friend, much good, nor, more importantly, would it be likely to be likely to expedite any future dealings with Ionicus of Cos, or others like him."

"You are a clever fellow, Aulus," he said. "You could ride with me."

"I have taken fee," said Aulus.

"But with Ionicus of Cos!" cried the fellow, suddenly, angrily. The knuckles of his hand were white on the shaft of the lance.

"The fee has been taken," said Aulus, quietly.

I saw the fellow's hand relax. He leaned back. He grinned, his teeth very white in the curly, ringleted blackness of that beribboned beard. "You are more of a mercenary than I," he laughed.

Aulus shrugged.

"Yes," he said, "you could have ridden with me."

"You have all five chains?" asked Aulus.

"That is a pretty slave at your stirrup," said the fellow.

I quickly put my head down.

"Look up, child," he said.

I did so.

"Kneel straight," he said. "Put your head back."

I obeyed.

"Yes," he said, "she is pretty."

"Yes," said Aulus.

"She has her knees nicely placed, too," he said.

"She is that sort of slave," said Aulus.

I blushed, but I knew that before a man such as that before me now, on the tharlarion, my knees belonged apart, widely apart.

"She is a three-tarsk girl," said the fellow.

"She cost Ionicus five, and a tarsk bit," said Aulus.

"And a tarsk bit?" asked the fellow.

"Yes," said Aulus.

"Then she was a lure girl," he said.

"Yes," said Aulus.

"Is she negotiable?" asked the fellow.

"All slaves are negotiable," said Aulus.

"Some of my men are not too fond of lure girls," he said. "I think I would let you keep her. They might kill her."

I had to keep my head back. I was very frightened.

"That would be a tragic waste of slave meat," he said.

"I would think so," said Aulus.

"What do you call her?" asked the fellow.

"Tuka," said Aulus.

"I have taken five chains," said the fellow. "I spared the guards. You may have them back, if you wish. There were two hundred and fifty men, exactly on the chains. I am recruiting one hundred and seventy-seven of them. Some I am freeing, because they are from Brundisium, whose Home Stone, before my outlawry, was mine. The rest I will sell back to you for, I think, something in the neighborhood of what you paid for them."

"You are turning back the genuine prisoners, of course," said Aulus.

"Not all of them," said the fellow. "Some of them can handle weapons. They will stay with me."

"Of what numbers are we speaking?" said Aulus.

"Five were from Brundisium," said the fellow.

"Then," said Aulus, "if you are recruiting one hundred and seventy-seven, and releasing five, from Brundisium, who may, or may not take service with you, then we are talking about less than seventy men."

"Sixty-eight, to be exact," said the fellow.

"Yes," said Aulus. "You have been very zealous in your recruiting, it seems. Can we not do a little better than that?"

"The one hundred and seventy-seven have already taken the campaign oath," he said.

"Then that is that," said Aulus. "What about the five from Brundisium."

"They are from Brundisium," he said.

"Of course," said Aulus.

"A silver tarsk apiece," said the fellow.

"That seems high," said Aulus.

"It is an average praetor's price," he said. To be sure, some, serving shorter sentences, would presumably go for less, and some, more dangerous fellows, perhaps, serving longer sentences, might go for more. "Too," he said, "I expect you pay that much, or more, for the fellows you get from illicit suppliers."

"True," said Aulus. This was the first inkling I had had of

what the fellows I had helped to entrap in Argentum might have brought Tyrrhenius. I, twice, had gone for at least five times as much. To be sure, once was because Tyrrhenius had wanted to pick up a good lure girl and once was because Ionicus, or perhaps his agent, acting on a standing policy, had wanted, as a joke, to put me at the service of men I had trapped. If it were not for such things I did not know what I would be likely to sell for, perhaps two silver tarsks. I did not know. Still I was a dancer, and we tend to bring higher prices. We are useful not only in brothels, cabarets, taverns, public pleasure gardens, and such, but wherever there are strong men, wherever there are men who enjoy seeing a woman move before them excitingly, and beautifully, and as a total female. Indeed, it is said some of the finest and most sensuous dancers are private slaves who perform in delicious secrecy, and totally, for a single master. We, and our uses, of course, may also be rented out for private dinner parties, for banquets and feasts, and such. Some of us, too, serve as imbonded camp followers, and will count as part of the loot should the camp fall into enemy hands. Some of us serve, too, in remote army posts, where we are kept to relieve the tedium of the troops. Some, too, of course, as would be expected, serve in the houses of rich men and even in the palaces of Ubars, where we commonly dance for them at their suppers, entertaining them and their guests. Dancers have many uses on Gor, both public and private. I suppose this is only to be expected, given the vitality, the masculinity, the strength of Gorean males. Any female taken to Gor, I suppose, must expect to learn at least the rudiments of slave dance.

"Very well," said Aulus, "sixty-eight silver tarsks. That is cheaper than going about, trying to replace these fellows in other ways. Too, the Vennans are eager to get on with their work."

I had not heard them say anything about the female work slaves. Surely Tupita, too, for example, would have fallen into the hands of this fellow, this mercenary captain, Pietro Vacchi. As a slave, of course, I did not dare speak. What if they saw fit to have me trampled by one of the tharlarion?

It was getting darker now. I wanted to go back to the camp. I felt very helpless, kneeling there, naked, chained to the stirrup.

"I shall return with you to your camp, to pick up the sixty-eight men," said Aulus.

"Good," said Pietro Vacchi, turning his tharlarion.

I was suddenly plunged into terror.

"You may break position, Tuka," said Aulus. "What is wrong?"

"Nothing, Master," I said, in terror.

I did not want to go to the mercenaries' camp. It was not merely that I feared such men but that Mirus, I knew, was from Brundisium. Indeed, he and Hendow, my former master, had grown up together there. They had known one another since childhood. On the last night I had seen him in the tavern Mirus had told me that he and Hendow would die for one another.

I rose to my feet. Only too clearly was Aulus going to accompany the captain to his camp.

"Master," I begged, pressing myself against the side of Aulus's thalarion, looking up at him, "please do not take me to the camp of the mercenaries, please! Please!"

"Why?" he asked.

"I fear one who may be in the camp," I said.

"Who?" he asked.

"Mirus, from Brundisium," I wept.

"If he is from Brundisium," he said, "he is probably on his way back there now."

I looked up at him, tears in my eyes. What he said, of course, might be true. I did not know.

"Do not be afraid," he said.

"Please, Master," I said. "Do not take me to the camp!"

"Was he on your chain?" he asked.

"Yes, Master," I said.

"If it were his intention to hurt you," he said, "he could have done it then."

"Please do not take me to the camp!" I begged.

"Do you really think I am going to send you back to Venna?" he asked.

"Please, please!" I begged.

"I, and many others, even Vacchi, will be there to protect you," he said.

"I leg it!" I said.

"Apparently you do not think we are capable of protecting you," he said.

"Please, Master!" I begged.

"Do not embarrass me," he said.

"Come along, Aulus!" called Pietro Vacchi, looking back over his shoulder. "Bring your men, and do not neglect, too, to bring the wagon, with the coins!"

"We are coming," called Aulus.

"Please, Master!" I wept, putting my hands up to his boot. "Please, Master!"

Then I saw him draw forth a tharlarion whip. "No," I begged, "please!" The lash cut down at me! I felt its blow. I had been whipped! I covered my head and eyes and, terrified, turning about, rushed to the end of the chain, but there, caught by the collar, pulling against the stirrup. I was brought up short, half choked, terrified. Then he reeled me in, gathering lengths of the chain in his hand. He then, as I stood there, naked, trembling, put the whip again to me, three times, and then another lash, for good measure. I was then sobbing, and weeping, wildly. He then cast loose the chain and moved his tharlarion forward, to ride with Pietro Vacchi. I hastily, whipped, stumbled after him.

"Tonight," said Pietro Vacchi, as though he might not have noted my beating, "you will be entertained as though you might be a Ubar!"

"The hospitality of Pietro Vacchi is well known," said Aulus.

I hoped, wildly, that Mirus would not be in the camp of Pietro Vacchi. I hoped he would have already set out for Brundisium. Surely he would not be expecting me to be brought to the camp.

"I have picked up a gentlewoman from Ar," said Pietro Vacchi. "Perhaps you would enjoy enlightening her on what it is to be a female."

"However I may be of service," said Aulus.

"And your little Tuka is a pretty one," said Vacchi.

"She is only a slave," said Aulus, "but she is, of course, yours for the evening."

"Excellent!" said Pietro Vacchi.

I hurried along beside the tharlarion of Aulus, his stirrup chain on my neck.

"Ho, Lad!" called Vacchi, holding in his tharlarion. "This is not the way to Brundisium!" He addressed a tall fellow in the shadows, making his way northward on the Viktel Aria.

The figure in the shadows lifted his hand.

I had quickly knelt, as soon as the progress of the tharlarion had been arrested, with my head down to the stones of the Viktel Aria. I did not want to be recognized. The figure in the shadows had been one I could not mistake.

The tharlarion began their trek again southward, toward the camp of Vacchi, the men of Aulus, and the wagon, with its box of coins, following.

There had been no mistaking the figure in the shadows. Too, it had been going north, not west, or northwest, toward Brundisium. It had been going north on the Viktel Aria, toward

Venna, in the vicinity of which lay the camp of the black chain of Ionicus.

I grasped the chain with two hands. I could not get it off my neck.

Surely in the darkness I had not been recognized. Surely I would have seemed then only another slave, only another soft, pretty thing, of no account, kneeling on the road, kneeling in the darkness, its head down, its neck chained to a master's stirrup.

I dared not look back.

How formidable the figure had seemed, so tall, so broad-shouldered, so purposeful, so menacing, in its remnants of a work tunic. But, now, too, I was sure it was armed. Over its left shoulder, there had been slung a strap, from which had hung a scabbard, the attitude of which had suggested only too clearly that it was weighted with a blade.

"Perhaps, earlier in the evening," Aulus was saying, "before you are ready for her in your tent, you might put her before your men."

"How is that?" asked Vacchi.

"She is not unskilled in the movements of slave dance," said Aulus.

"My lads could use a treat," said Vacchi. "Too, I could put ostraka in a helmet for her, with five granting her use. What think you?"

"Excellent," said Aulus. "Your men will be pleased."

I looked back. I almost cried out with fear. The fellow who had been going north was no longer going north. He had changed his direction. He had been moving toward Venna, and the camp of the black chain of Ionicus. But he was now coming south. He was behind the wagon, rather to its right, as I looked back. Indeed, he was only twenty yards, or so, now, behind me.

"Too," added Aulus, "by the time she is brought to your tent she should then be nicely ready."

"Precisely," laughed Vacchi.

I followed the men, on my chain tether. So I might dance? So soldiers might draw lots for my use? So I might serve Pietro Vacchi? But what then? Would the man following not "bide his time" as Tupita had said? Would there not come a time, sooner or later, if he were patient, and I did not doubt but what he was patient, very patient, when he could find me alone? I might even be staked out, my hands and legs widely separated. I had heard mercenaries sometimes enjoyed fastening women down in such a way. But I would be scarcely less helpless if I were in a tiny slave cage, through the bars of which he might thrust with his sword, perhaps a hundred short, sharp times, or, similarly available to him, for whatever he might choose to do to me, chained with my belly to a tree, my ankles and wrists fastened about it.

I looked back, in fear.

He was still following!

One stroke of his sword, I knew, if it were his decision to be swift with me, could remove my head.

"I am looking forward to seeing her dance," said Vacchi.

"I am sure you will not be disappointed," said Aulus.

But I did not even know if he would be swift with me.

"Have you used her?" asked Vacchi.

"Several times," said Aulus.

"How is she?" asked Vacchi.

"She is a slave," laughed Aulus.

"Do you recommend her?" asked Vacchi.

"Yes," said Aulus.

"She is a slave?" said Vacchi.

"She is a superb slave," said Aulus.

"Excellent!" said Vacchi.

I hoped that when the men were through with me, the others, and the master, Pietro Vacchi, that they would put me in a slave pen, preferably with other girls. Surely in a camp of mercenaries they would have other girls. Such should be common in such a camp. They would presumably pick them up here and there, perhaps selling some, and adding others. Perhaps some, more beautiful, or popular, might be kept more or less permanently with the troops. Perhaps some of the soldiers, officers probably, even had their own girls, taken here or there, their own property. They had spoken of a "gentlewoman," though, I suppose, if she were free, she would not be put with slaves, but might sleep chained at the feet of her captor, at least until her thigh made the acquaintance of the brand and her neck of the collar. Hopefully the bars would be sturdy, and closely set. I would want to sleep near the center of the pen. It should be safer there. Perhaps such things, the presence of other slaves, and of bars of iron, could protect me.

I looked back, again. Quietly, implacably, he was following.

I had little doubt he would await his chance.

"Well, Tuka," said Aulus, looking down at me. "You are not dallying now."

"No, Master," I said.

"One might almost think you were anxious to reach the camp," he said.

"Yes, Master," I said.

27 / The Pen; Outside the Pen

I lay in the center of the pen.

I was trembling, but here I think I was safe.

I had feared they might not have a pen here, but only a chain, perhaps stretched between trees, that we might be attached to, by the ankle or neck. Such a thing, though it might have its guard, might be more easily approached. The pen was some forty feet square, and some seven feet in height. It had an open roofing of bars, supported by hollow metal posts, and bars, too, covered now with sand, floored it. It could be assembled, fastened together with plates, bolts and chains, and similarly disassembled, and transported in wagons. Mercenaries, following the demands of their business, the exigencies of their trade, frequently move their camps. Though the wagons could doubtless be drawn by tharlarion, if speed were necessary, the harnesses I had seen on the covered harness racks, near the wagons, were not made for tharlarion. They were made for women. Girls, thus, and perhaps some stripped free women among them, would draw the wagons. Doubtless drovers would be with them on the road, with their whips, should they be tempted to lag in their zeal. There were only some twenty or so women penned with me now. Many, perhaps a hundred or more, were doubtless spending the night in the tents of soldiers, signed out to them for the night. There was one gate to our pen. It was secured with two locks, padlocks, and chains. It was guarded by two men.

I rolled over, in the soft sand, lying within the dark blanket.

How pleased I was that there was such a pen.

Here I was safe, I was sure.

I had no doubt of the menace and intent of he who had followed us back to the camp of Pietro Vacchi. He had been making his way, meaningfully, the blade in its sheath, toward Venna, and the black chain. It had been his intent, sooner or later, in one way or another, to renew his acquaintance with a certain slave, one who had once betrayed him. Then he had recognized her on the road. He had then immediately changed his route. Did they really think he had not known his way to

Brundisium, a native of Brundisium, and such a man? Did they really think he had returned to the camp only to make a fresh start in the morning? No, he had been following us for a purpose, and it had to do with a slave, one he was determined to bring within the reach of his hand, and blade. Had I had any doubt he had recognized me on the road, and that that had been responsible for his change of direction, that doubt had been dispelled in the camp. When I had knelt before a post, my hands behind me, chained back about the post, a helmet beside me, set in the sand, like a vessel, into which ostraka would be placed, men had come to look upon me. They had come to see if they thought it worth their while, in the spending of their evening, to wait about for a time, to see me dance, and then, perhaps, if they were pleased, to drop an ostrakon into the helmet. Among them came he whom I most feared. I strained forward, trying to kiss at his legs, but the chain on my wrists, pulling against the back of the post, held me back. I then realized that he had selected the place where he had stood with care. He had judged the distance with cruel exactness. It was such that I would try to reach him, desperately, to kiss him, to placate him. It was also such that I would be unable to do so. I had looked up into his eyes, and then, in terror, had put down my head. He had then left me, and another man had come to look upon me. I had danced that night between campfires, for the mercenaries. He had not chosen to watch. It seems, once again, that he would take suitable precautions against me, that the hardness of his heart, set so against me, not be softened, that the iron of his intent be neither diminished nor imperiled, that there be no possible weakening of his terrible resolve.

I turned to my back, within the blanket. It was a very dark night. I could scarcely see the bars, it was so dark.

I think the mercenaries had found me pleasing. Surely they had responded well to the dance, and the helmet had been filled with ostraka. It had not started well, for I had been hampered by terror, but soon, as I recalled my earlier beating by Aulus, and knew I might be again whipped if I did not do well, and as I reassured myself that within the camp I would presumably be safe, and as I saw the men, and I knew they wished pleasure, and that it was within my power to give it to them, and abundantly, and must do so, to the best of my power, I began to lose my terror and then, at last, I think, I danced well. "Superb!" I heard cry. Far then I was from the shy, introverted girl of the library, she who had scarcely dared to admit, even to herself, even in the concealments of her most secret heart, that in her belly lurked the dispositions and nature of a pleasure slave! But now, openly, and whether she willed it or not, she was that very slave! "Superb!" cried another man. I danced, barefoot in the sand, naked, in my collar, my body illuminated redly in the light of the fires. I was joyful, a woman! How powerful, and grand, were the men! How I wanted to please them, and knew that I must. They did not fear, or object to, masculine power. They delighted in it, they reveled in it. It ennobled and exalted them. It made them great! It made them glorious! And had they not been such men, how could I have been such a woman?

It was very dark out.

Afterwards when the five ostraka had been drawn something of my fears had returned. I had even begged two of the fellows not to take me far from the fires, but, dragged by the hair, bent over, I had followed them. Then I had served them in the darkness, between tents. Once, my hands over my head, I had felt the tent ropes. Once, when I had bent over one fellow, I had lifted my head, in terror, thinking I might have heard a sound, but, it seems, I had not. I had then again addressed myself to my labors. After I had served five men I had been conducted to the tent of Pietro Vacchi. He, among the others, had watched me dance. Indeed, I had danced my beauty particularly to him, more than once, as he was the captain of these men, and his ruggedness and strength, his entire demeanor, that of a master, stirred my belly. In his tent he put me on a rug, fastening me in a neck chain. I could not flee from him. But in a moment I would not have wanted to. He was a true master, and, in moments, licking and kissing, squirming, moaning, crying out with gratitude, I was helpless in his grasp. When he had left me I had lain on the rug, looking after him in disbelief. What a slave such men made us! I had lain on my back, the chain on my neck, my fingernails scratching at the rug. When I had seen him standing near me again I had gone to my belly and pressed my lips fervently to his feet. "Master!" I had wept. He then took me by the upper arms and, with a sound of chain, lifted me, and flung me back, again, to the rug. "Oh, yes, Master!" I had cried out, again, in gratitude.

One of the girls near me stirred in her sleep. "Let me serve you, let me serve you," she was moaning, in her dreams.

I, however, for one, was now pleased to be behind the bars of the pen. Something of my original terror had returned when Pietro Vacchi had led me to the exit of his tent and pointed the way, through the darkness, to the pen. I had bellied, and begged, for a guard. "Do you wish another whipping?" he had inquired.

"No, Master!" I said. He had, it seems, taken note of my beating on the Viktel Aria. Too, I was sure the marks on me attested to it. I rose to my feet, to creep, frightened, in the direction he had indicated. "Wait," he said, as an afterthought. "Wait." I was only too willing to dally. "You have heard of the other girl?" he asked. "Master?" I asked. "Guard," he called, "escort this young lady to her quarters." "Yes, Captain," he said. Pietro Vacchi then returned to his tent. The guard was behind me. "Lesha!" he said. Immediately, responsive to this command, I flung my wrists behind me, separated by some two inches, and lifted my chin, my head turned to the left. I felt slave bracelets flung, snapping shut, on my wrists. I was braceleted. In another moment I was leashed. "Precede me," said the guard. I went before him. In a moment we were among trees, on a path. "Oh!" I said, softly. The guard had begun to caress me. In another moment or two he stopped me with the leash, in the darkness. "May I speak, Master?" I asked. "No," he said. He was through with me quickly. Then I was dragged to my feet and conducted, again, toward the pen. I thought I saw a movement in the darkness, but was not certain. "What is it?" asked the guard, uneasily. "Nothing, Master," I said. If I had truly detected something, as perhaps I had between the tents, the tiny sound, or now, perhaps, a movement in the darkness, subtle, almost unnoticeable, I had little doubt as to what might be its source. But he had not, in either case, struck in the darkness. He had had no interest, it seemed, in killing the soldier, or the guard. It was not him he wanted. He would continue, it seemed, to bide his time. In a few moments, however, happily, I was released into the pen. "Blankets are at the side," he said. "You may take only one." "Yes, Master," I said. "May I speak?" "No," he said.

I sat up in the blanket. I thought something had been standing on the other side of the bars, toward the back of the pen, away from the guards. I strained my eyes, peering into the darkness. I could see nothing. If something had been there it was now apparently gone. I was frightened. I looked about myself. I pulled the blanket up, tightly, around my chin. I was being stalked. I was sure of it! Then I realized, with misgivings, a sinking feeling, that it was unlikely I would have heard the tiny sound, seen the movement, been aware of a presence beyond the bars, so subtle a presence, in the darkness, unless it had been intended that I, if only subliminally, take note of them. It was perhaps his intention to remind me, from time to time, particularly if I should grow too hopeful, that I had not been forgotten.

But perhaps it was all my imagination! Perhaps he had changed his mind. Perhaps he had taken his way, by now, to Brundisium! Then I was again frightened. Could an arrow, or the quarrel of a crossbow, not be sped between the bars, into my heart, even here in the pen? I lay back, frightened, holding the blanket about me. Such a missile, of course, might be as easily launched from the brush at the side of a road, as I might be walking beside a tharlarion, my neck in a chain, running to a master's stirrup. But I wondered if such things would suffice for his vengeance. Perhaps they would be too distant, too abstract, for him. I dug down a little more into the sand, until I could feel the bars of the cage floor.

I thought of Pietro Vacchi. How well he handled a woman! How well he had mastered me! I remembered that on the road a "gentlewoman," one from Ar, had been mentioned. She, as I understood it, was to have been given to Aulus for the evening, that he might help her learn what it was to be a female. Aulus, as I well knew, from when I had worn the rectangle of silk in his tent, was a strong master. I had little doubt but what the "gentlewoman," lying at his feet in the morning, wide-eyed and sleepless, would recollect in chagrin and horror her responses of the preceding night. Could she believe what she had done, and said? How she had begged and squirmed, and acted not at all like a free woman, but like a slave? How she had behaved in his arms? How could she, a free woman, have acted like that? But perhaps she was not truly, ultimately, a free woman, as she had hitherto supposed but really, truly, like so many other women, those she had pretended not to really understand, and had held in such contempt, until now, only a slave? Could that be? And could they teach her things, if she begged hard enough, that she might be more pleasing to such men, that they might find her of interest and deign again to notice her? Regardless of such considerations how could she now, after what had been done to her, and how she had acted, go back to being a free woman? Could she pretend nothing had happened? How could she hold her head up, again, now, among free women? Would she not now cringe before them, and be unable to meet their eyes, like a runaway slave, thence to be seized by them and remanded to a praetor? Now that she had known the touch of a man, such a man, how could she return, as though nothing had happened, to her former self, with its haughty, barren pretenses of freedom? What authority or right had she any longer, given what she had learned about herself last night, to claim that she was "free," except perhaps in virtue of the accident of an undeserved legal technicality?

How could she ever again, given what she now knew about herself, consider herself free? No longer had she a right to such a claim. She now knew, in her heart, that she was not truly free, but, truly, a slave. That was what she was, and right that she be. No longer could she find it in her heart to pretend to be free, to play again the role of a free woman, to enact once again what, in her case, could now be only a hollow mockery, an empty farce of freedom. Too, could she any longer even dare to do so? Suppose others came to suspect, or even to know! What if they could read it somehow in her eyes, or body? It is a great crime for a slave to pretend to be a free woman. Would they not simply take off her clothes and punish her, and then hand her over to a praetor, for her proper disposition? Too, what could such a pretence gain her but the closing of doors on the truth of her being? But even if these things were not true, as she feared they were, she did not wish to perish of shame. No longer now, knowing what she now knew about herself, could she live as a free woman. She must beg Aulus, when he awakened, for she did not dare awaken him for fear she might be whipped, for the brand and collar. No longer could she be a free woman. It was now right that she be kept as a slave, and made a slave.

As the night was cloudy, and dark, I could not see the stars, or moons.

I felt the collar on my throat. It was the collar of Ionicus. I was a work slave. Yet, tonight, I had not served as a work slave, but a pleasure slave. Too, Aulus had chained me at his stirrup. He had used me as a display slave, to enhance his appearance, to add to the effect he might make when he came into the presence of Pietro Vacchi. It is a use for slaves. I was proud that I had been put at his stirrup. In such small ways a slave may gather that she is exciting and beautiful. To be sure, he may not have wanted to leave me behind with the guards. Also, he may have had in mind that I might dance for the mercenaries and serve some of them, and their captain. Thus I might, in my humble way, like a gift, or a token of good will, make my small contribution to the success of his visit. Perhaps a tribute, or, more carefully put, a friendship fee, might even be arranged, such that the chains of Ionicus might, at least for a given time, enjoy immunity from the depredations of the mercenaries. If I had been used for such a purpose I hoped that I had done well, and that Aulus would be satisfied. I recalled Vacchi. I hoped that I had pleased him. I smiled to myself. That I had pleased him? Rather it seemed he had used me, imperiously, as a master, for his pleasure! In his arms I, helpless, moaning, crying out, sometimes even begging for mercy, had been forced to endure lengthy slave ecstasies. I squirmed in the sand, digging into it until I again felt the bars of iron, of the pen floor, beneath me, remembering what it had been to be in his arms.

Tomorrow I would presumably return to the black chain of Ionicus, though perhaps to be kept in Aulus's tent in a rectangle of silk. Surely that was preferable to wearing chains and carrying water, struggling against its bulging, shifting weight, bent over, going back and forth, back and forth, wading in sand to the ankles.

I recalled, oddly, when I had knelt before Tyrrhenius, weeks before, when I had learned that he was going to sell me, he had spoken of "inquiries." I had not much thought of it at the time, but now, in the darkness, lying in the sand of the pen, I wondered what he had meant. What sort of inquiries had he had in mind, and to whom did they pertain? Did they pertain to him? Did they pertain to me? Or perhaps he feared that they might pertain to me? Was that why he had sold me, rather abruptly, as it seemed, now that I thought of it? And who was making such inquiries? I thought that perhaps it might have been a praetor's agent, or agents, or perhaps fellows suspected of being such agents, that might have been making such inquiries in Argentum. I did not know. News of their questioning could have been brought to Tyrrhenius by his spies, or men. Whatever might be the case, it seemed that he had regarded it judicious to terminate my services as a lure girl. I had then been sold to the black chain of Ionicus.

I dismissed such thoughts from my mind.

I lay in the darkness. I wanted to return to the work camp. There, I thought, there, behind the wire, in the midst of guards, I should be safe, or at least as safe as any of the other girls. Certainly he whose vengeance quarry I might be would not wish to simply enter the camp. He might be seized and returned to the chain. Yes, I thought, I want to get back to the work camp. If I can get back to the work camp, I should be safe, at least as safe as the other girls. That is important, I thought, to get back to the camp.

"You have heard of the other girl?" had asked Pietro Vacchi of me, after I had risen to my feet, after I had bellied to him, in the entrance of his tent, begging a guard, fearing to go out into the darkness, to find my own way to the pen, there to report myself in to the guards, to be incarcerated within it. "Master?" I had asked, puzzled. He had then, in a moment, put me in the custody of a guard. I was somewhat puzzled by this. For a moment I had feared Vacchi was going to put me under the whip, for my importunities. Certainly I did not want to be whipped twice in one day. Then he had asked me that question. Then, after a moment, it seemed he had, for some reason, relented, or changed his mind. The guard had then braceleted and leashed me, and I had preceded him toward the pen. I had expected to be taken directly to the pen but the guard, once we were in the darkness, had pulled me up short by the leash, and then, I perforce keeping silent, had put me to his purposes. It was shortly after that, when we were again on our way to the pen, that I had thought I might have detected a movement among the trees. This fear, or start, had doubtless been reflected in my entire body, perhaps even in the movement of the leash. "What is it?" had asked the guard, uneasily. "Nothing, Master," I had said. It had not been difficult to detect the uneasiness, or even alarm, in the guard's voice. I did not understand his apprehension. We were in the midst of the mercenaries' camp. If there had been something there, presumably it would be only another of his fellows, perhaps relieving himself in the darkness, not wanting to seek out the latrines. If anyone had something to fear it was presumably I, and not he. Yet Vacchi had put a guard with me. It had something to do, perhaps, with the "other girl." Something, it seems, may have recently happened to another girl. I had tried, twice, to inquire about this, but, each time, had not been given permission to speak. I must then be silent. Whether or not we may speak is not at our will, but at the will of our masters. I shivered. Still, I was safe now, lying close to the ground, in the darkness, among the other girls, locked in the pen.

I thought about the morrow. Presumably I would be again at the stirrup of Aulus. I was pleased that there was not too much brush along the side of the road. I fell asleep.

I stirred, uneasily. My nose wrinkled a little. There was some sort of strong smell. I did not care for it. I did not know what it was. It seemed very close, terribly close. I opened my eyes, suddenly. I could not see anything in the darkness. Perhaps I had been asleep for only a few moments. Perhaps I had slept for an hour. I did not know. Then it seemed that I was paralyzed with fear. I had vaguely discerned, or thought I had, a deeper darkness in the darkness. Then I felt something on each side of me, like barriers, a wall, but parts of something alive. I wanted to scream, but was so terrified I could not make the least sound. I was on my back, trapped in the blanket. Its body was above my lower body, close. Its legs, or hind legs, were on either side of me. I was held in place. It seemed enormous. It leaned forward. I almost choked, from that fetid breath. A drop of liquid fell to my face, salivation from its jaws. It seemed excited. Doubtless I was meat. I felt the heat and volume of its breath on my face. Its lungs must be huge. Its oral orifice might well be as large as my head. I could not understand why it did not move. I now realize it was waiting for me to try to scream. This thing over me was not human, but, too, it was no sleen, or larl. It was a beast, and a terrible one, that much I could tell even in the terror of the darkness, but, too, I sensed, from its control, and patience, and the way it had rendered me helpless, it was in some indefinable way, some terrifying way, other than a beast, too, or more than a beast. It was a beast which, like men, I feared, could consider alternatives, envisage possible futures, choose courses of action. It could think, and plan. I lay there. It did not begin to lacerate me. It did not tear at my flesh. It did not begin to feed. It was waiting, waiting patiently. It was waiting for me to try to scream. At the time, of course, I did not know that. I moved a little. There was an almost inaudible growl. Immediately I was again perfectly still. I did not understand why it had not killed me. It was, somehow, however, within the pen. Had it been admitted? Perhaps it was uneasy in such a situation? Perhaps it wanted to carry me to its den, there to feed on me. But why, then, would it not have killed me first, and then dragged me away, like a leopard? I did not think this thing would want me as a slave. I was not of its species. Its lusts, and I did not doubt but what such a vital, powerful creature had them, would presumably be triggered by configurations and natures quite other than mine. Indeed, I shuddered to consider what might be the rituals and habits, the courtships and matings, of such a thing. Too, it was not behaving toward me, as might have a master, say, fondling me with possessive audacity or throwing my legs apart, to see how I might look with them spread, or to let me know what my relationship was to be to him. For what, then, could it want me? Doubtless food. But then why had it not killed me? Perhaps it wanted to get me somehow to its den and there make its kill, that the meat might be fresh? Or, perhaps, more plausibly, it might wish to keep me in its larder, or pantry, as it might be a rational beast, with an eye to the future, until it was hungry? It then, slowly, one by one, put the digits of its left hand, or paw, on my cheek. I suddenly shuddered. There had been five, and then, when I had thought them done, terrifying me, there had been another! The thing had six digits! It was then alien, as far as I knew, not only to Earth but Gor. It was from somewhere else! I was suddenly wild with terror, not the numbing paralyzing terror, which I now understand the thing was waiting to pass, but a different sort of terror, now a wild, helpless terror. I put back my head, wildly. I opened my mouth, widely. I took in breath to scream. But no sooner had I opened my mouth, widely, widely, and took in breath to scream, than the creature, with his right hand, or paw, from beside him, took what must have been a small bag, filled with rags, and thrust it expertly, deeply into my oral orifice. He then, as I looked up in the darkness, in disbelief, in consternation, tied it back in my mouth with cord, pulled back deeply between my teeth wrapped twice about my head, fastened under my left ear. He was apparently right-handed, or right-pawed. He then drew back the blanket from about me, and turned me to my stomach. He then drew my wrists behind my back and tied them. In another moment he had similarly fastened my ankles together. He had bound me, hand and foot. I lay there bewildered, terrified. He had handled me with the dexterity of a human slaver, surprising a woman in her bed. Not only had he seemed apprised of the human female's reflexive scream reaction, her tendency to cry out with fear, but he had taken advantage of it, exploiting it expertly, using it for the convenient opportunity it afforded for her effective gagging. I could now, the rags in my mouth, utter only tiny, helpless sounds. These were perhaps not greatly different from the small cries a woman might utter in her sleep. How expertly he had taken advantage of my female reflexes! He had also, in his way, tricked me. He had provoked my scream reflex by silently informing me, unexpectedly, and to my terror, of the alien nature of his hand, or paw. He had then gagged me, and, then, without further ado, put back the blanket, turned me to my belly and bound me, helplessly.

I lay on my stomach, on the blanket, it in the soft sand, bound and gagged. I had been quickly and efficiently rendered helpless. I suspected then that this may not have been done entirely by feel. I had the distinct feeling that the thing, even in this darkness, might be able to see. Even to me the darkness was not absolute. I could tell something of its outline in the night. There must therefore, somehow, be some light, perhaps a tiny bit of light from the moons, or even the stars, filtered through the cover of clouds. Whereas this might be so small that it was scarcely detectable by a human, it might be more than adequate for a different sort of animal, something like a tarsier, or cat, or lion, something with different, more efficient nocturnal adaptations. Humans even illuminated the streets of their cities, at least in certain areas. In venturing out into the night they were not unaccustomed to carrying lanterns with them, or torches, and that for so simple a purpose as merely to see their way. This thing near me I suspected had no need of such artifices. I heard, and felt it, its snout at my back, touching me once or twice, with its tiny intakes of air, sniffing me. Then, as I stiffened in terror, I felt digits of its hand, or paw, on my back. It was feeling some of the welts on my back. These were from my beating by Aulus, on the Viktel Aria. I had deserved that beating. I had not been pleasing to a master. Then it put its head down, close to me. I then felt its tongue, curiously, exploratory, a rough tongue, like a cat's, lick slowly at one or two of the welts. I heard a small noise from its throat. I feared it might be becoming excited. Then it straightened up. I was relieved. I was pleased that there was no blood on my back. It then turned about, its huge form crouched down. It was still for a moment, very still, perhaps looking about, perhaps reconnoitering. It then took one of my bound ankles in its paw. It then dragged me by the ankle from the blanket, between the other girls, on my side, through the sand, toward the bars. In so small a thing as this I sensed its alienness. No human, I think, would have drawn me along like this. It was more like some shambling predator pulling a four-footed animal behind it, by a leg. In a moment it was at the bars, on the far side, away from the gate. Then to my amazement it drew me between the bars which, literally, it seemed, had been bent apart. Apparently it had not been admitted. It had admitted itself. It had apparently taken the bars in its paws, those bars which might well have confined men, let alone women, and bent them apart. Outside the bars, on the dirt, it lifted me in its arms and, half crouching, carried me into some trees. There in the darkness, alone with it, I began to whimper and struggle. I did not want to be taken from the camp, not now, not this way! It then put me down, on the dirt. I struggled at its feet, bound. I feared it would now, in this isolated place, eat me. But it lifted me up, by the back of the neck, to a kneeling position. Did it know what it was doing? I was now kneeling before it, a position appropriate for a slave! It then lifted me up again, a foot or so, such that I seemed really to be neither kneeling or standing. I was held by the back of the neck again, its grip, that of only one hand or paw, easily supporting my weight. I felt the dirt on the tops of my toes, as my feet now were, their soles exposed, I having been lifted up from a kneeling position. My knees were bent. It then, with its right paw, struck me. My head was flung to the side. I lost consciousness.

28 / The Well

"Are you all right?" asked Tupita.

"Tupita!" I said.

"Yes," she whispered, touching my forehead, soothingly. "Rest. Do not try to rise. You were cruelly struck."

"Where am I?" I asked.

"Look up," she said.

I looked up, blinking against the light. Far above me, as at the end of some odd, vertical tunnel, I could see a circular opening, perhaps some seven or eight feet across, and, across this, in open sockets, there was a peeled, rounded timber, about which a rope was wound. A few feet below this timber, attached to the rope, there dangled a bucket. Over the opening, too, there were the remains, mostly a frame, of what was once apparently a small arched roof. Through the remains of this roof I could see, framed in the wreckage, the blue sky, and, interestingly, in it, like tiny points, stars. The light of the sun not obliterating them from this perspective, one could see them, even now, in the daylight.

I rose to my knees, in the dried leaves and gravel. "Tela!" I said.

"Tuka," she whispered. Tela was kneeling a few feet from me. She still wore, soiled now, the tiny, thin rectangle of red silk she had worn in the tent of Aulus. It was all that Aulus, by custom, permitted women to wear in his tent, saving their collars.

"Are you all right?" I asked.

"Yes," she whispered.

I kissed Tupita, gratefully, and Tela.

"These," said Tupita, indicating two other girls, sitting to one side, "are Mina and Cara." They wore the shreds of work tunics. On their ankles were shackles, separated by lengths of chain such that they might not run, but such that they also would constitute no inconvenience for guards. Iron, too, was hammered shut about their wrists, these bands linked by some eighteen inches of chain.

"These are the girls who were first stolen?" I said to Tupita.

"Yes," she said.

"This is Tuka," said Tupita to the two girls.

They nodded, hardly moving their heads. They were very quiet. Both seemed frightened, almost in shock.

"Greet her," said Tupita.

"Greetings, Tuka," whispered one. "Greetings, Tuka," whispered the other. They moved slightly. There was a small sound of chain.

"Mina," I said.

She looked up.

"Did you see what took you?" I asked.

She shook her head.

"Cara?" I asked.

"No," said Cara, shuddering.

"It was probably the beast, or beasts," said Tupita. "They do not know. They were struck unconscious, from behind, probably within moments of one another. I do not even know if they believe me when I tell them of the beast. Tela saw it though, in the tent of Aulus, after it had gagged her, before it put her to her belly and bound her. I, too, saw it, two days ago, but briefly in the darkness, when I was returning from the tent of Pietro Vacchi to the girl pen. It leaped out and seized me. Before I could cry out I was gagged. In another instant I was secured."

"You were used in the tent of Pietro Vacchi?" I asked.

"Two days ago," she said.

"You were freed from the chain," I said.

"The men, or most of them, were freed," she said. " I, of course, and the girls with the other chains, must simply wait to see who our new masters will be."

"Of course," I said, "we are kajirae."

"Is there a beast?" asked Mina, of me.

"Yes," I said.

"Did you see it?" she asked.

"Yes," I said.

"Our food, loaves of bread, and fruit, is thrown down to us, at night," said Tupita. "Water, too, in the darkness, is lowered in the bucket. It is then withdrawn."

"We are permitted to drink but once a day?" I said.

"Yes," she said, "so drink your fill."

"How came I here?" I asked.

"Your wrists were bound together before you," she said, "and a doubled rope put through them. When you were within our reach, and we could hold you, the other end of the rope was dropped, and it was then withdrawn. We removed your bonds."

"Of what nature was the bond?" I asked.

"Binding fiber," said Tupita.

"Is it not strange that a beast would have such fiber?" I asked.

"It would seem so," said Tupita.

"Of what nature is this place?" I asked, looking up.

"It is apparently an abandoned well," said Tupita, "but it has been changed in some respects."

"How is that?" I asked.

"The bottom of the shaft, below us, is not open to the ground, to sand, or soft dirt, but filled, apparently for several feet, with large boulders. We cannot lift them. Even if we could there is no place to put them. The floor, in effect, is made of rock."

I nodded. This place was no longer a simple well, even an abandoned one. It had now, for most practical purposes, been converted into a holding hole.

"If there is such a beast," said Mina, "what does it want of us?"

"It is such a thing, doubtless," said Tupita, "which fed upon the aedile, outside Venna."

"Then it may be saving us, to eat us," whispered Mina.

"Perhaps," said Tupita.

We shuddered. Clearly it was possible we were being kept for such a purpose. Indeed, this place might be, in effect, its larder.

"But, as far as we know," said Tupita, "no one has been taken from this place to be eaten."

"It could be saving us for later," said Mina.

"Mina and Cara were caught days ago," said Tupita. "Indeed, the recovery period is over where they are concerned. Anyone who came on them could now claim them." To be sure, they remained, even now, the slaves of Ionicus, but this proprietorship was now such that, if the case arose, it must yield to a new claimancy. This point in Gorean law is apparently motivated by the consideration that a slave always have some master. In the case of a master's death the slave, like other property, passes to the heirs, or, if there are no heirs, to the state. "They have not been eaten."

"Not yet," pointed out Mina.

"Consider," said Tupita. "All of us here are female."

"Yes," said Mina.

"That seems to me of interest," said Tupita.

"Yes!" I said. "It may well be it which, too, robbed the aedile."

"It is surely possible," said Tupita.

"It has some sense of the value of money then," I said, "and perhaps some way of utilizing it."

"Yes," said Tupita.

"And I am told I was bound with binding fiber when I was lowered into the pit."

"You were," said Tupita. "It is over there."

"What are you both saying?" asked Mina.

"We are thinking," said Tupita, "if I am not mistaken, that although this thing might eat humans, and might eat us, it may not be that we have been brought here, really, for food."

"I do not understand," said Mina.

"It may be working with men," said Tupita. "If so, they might be slavers."

"But you do not know that!" said Mina.

"No," admitted Tupita. "But look about yourself. Do you not note something else of interest here? Do you not think we might not, all, be of interest to men?"

I looked down, embarrassed. I, of all of the girls in the pit, was naked. Mina and Cara had the shreds of work tunics, and Tupita, too, still had much of her tunic, it ripped only a bit, perhaps when the beast had seized her. Tela had the soiled narrow rectangle of silk.

"It seems likely to me," said Tupita, "that we are being kept not for food, though such a thing, or things, might eat us, but to be turned over to our kind, to slavers."

"I remember now," I said, "in the darkness, before I was cuffed unconscious, it put me to my knees before it!"

"Excellent!" said Tupita. "Then I suggest we kneel before these beasts, and behave with them much as we might with men. They may well regard us, and correctly, as female slaves. Thus they may expect suitable subserviences."

We kissed one another, then, in hope.

"What is there to do now?" asked Mina.

"You wear a collar and chains," said Tupita. "You are a kajira. What do you think you will do?"

Mina looked at her.

"You will wait," said Tupita.

"How could the thing come into the work camp?" I asked.

"It dug under the fence," said Tela. "It did not strike me unconscious in the tent, perhaps for fear of the master or you hearing. I was dragged under the side of the tent and into the night. After a time it moved aside a bush, concealing a tunnel, and then dragged me after it, through it. On the other side of the wire fence, ascertaining no one was about, it struck me unconscious."

"How is it that you are here?" asked Tupita of me.

"I came with Aulus to the camp of Pietro Vacchi," I said, "where he wished to conclude negotiations pertaining to the purloined chains. I was chained at his stirrup."

"That explains why you are naked," she said.

"Yes," I said.

"You would look very beautiful chained to a stirrup," said Tupita.

"So, too, would you," I said.

"What beasts they are, to so display us for their pleasure," she said.

"They are the masters," I said.

"I wager you were proud at the stirrup," she said.

"Of course," I laughed.

"Slave," said Tupita.

"Of course, I am a slave," I said. "Are you not a slave, and a total slave?"

"Yes," she smiled. "I, too, am a slave, and, like you, my dear Tuka, a total slave."

"You said that you served in the tent of Pietro Vacchi," I said.

"Yes," she said.

"You must have been very beautiful," I said, "to have been selected for his tent."

"If you came to the camp with Aulus, at his stirrup," she said, "I wager you, too, are not unfamiliar with the neck chain of Pietro Vacchi."

I looked down. "No," I smiled. "I am not unfamiliar with it."

"He made me scream with pleasure," said Tupita.

"I, too," I smiled.

"Seldom have I been in the arms of such a man," she said.

"Nor I," I said.

"He is a soldier, and a captain," she said. "He knows well how to teach a woman her collar."

"True," I said.

"It was on my return to the girl pen that I was captured by the beast," she said.

"Doubtless it was because of you that he permitted me a guard, to conduct me to the pen," I said. "I gathered, or had intimations, that something might have happened to a girl shortly before me, perhaps within even a few days, that she might have disappeared, or have been mysteriously stolen, perhaps even on the route from his tent to the pen."

"It was probably I," she said.

"Undoubtedly," I said.

"It is interesting that both of us served in the tent of Vacchi, and that we are both here, now," she said.

"What do you mean?" I asked. "Do you think Vacchi is implicated in our abduction?"

"Certainly not," she said. "He could have put either of us in his collar, at his whim. Who is going to gainsay him with his company of mercenaries?"

"True," I said.

"But," she said, "there may be more than a coincidence here. Might it not be that the beast, not of our kind, was, in effect, utilizing the choices of Vacchi, as guaranteeing that his pickups would presumably be such that they would be attractive to human males?"

"Yes!" I said. "That is possibly it! And Tela was first on the chain, and serving in the tent of the overseer! That, too, might have convinced the beast that she was a suitable acquisition!"

"What of me, and Cara?" asked Mina.

"Were you serving near the fence?" I asked. "Was your chain there shortly before your capture?"

"Yes," said Mina.

"Perhaps you were pointed out, by men, to the beast," I said, "in effect designated as suitable quarry."

"Perhaps the aedile came on the beast unawares," said Tupita.

"Perhaps," I said. "But, too, it may have merely been hungry."

"Could it not have killed for gold?" asked Mina.

"Assuredly," I said. "But it could have killed fr both, for gold, and food."

"True," said Mina, shuddering.

"Tuka," said Tela.

"Yes," I said.

"How is the master?" she asked.

"The master?" I asked.

"Aulus," she said.

"He is all right, as far as I know," I said.

"Good," she said, relieved, kneeling back.

I looked at her, sharply, and she put down her head. I suspected then that her belly had found its love master. To be sure, we slaves must leap to the touch of any man. I did not see any need to tell her of the "gentlewoman," to whose female training Aulus had been asked to contribute.

"You know that most of the men with the chains were freed?" said Tupita.

"Yes," I said.

"He went toward Venna," she said.

"I know," I said.

"He made no attempt to negotiate for me, or secure me," she said.

"I am sorry," I said.

"Apparently your blood is of more interest to him than my love," she said.

"You think he still desires to kill me?" I asked.

"I know he does," she said.

I shuddered. I was helpless at the bottom of the shaft. Were he to come upon me here how could I escape? Perhaps he would lower the rope and bucket for the others, and not me? Perhaps he would throw great stones down upon me? Perhaps he would lower poisonous insects or snakes into the pit? Perhaps he would leave me here to starve?

Tupita then began to tear her tunic, about the hem.

"What are you doing?" I asked.

"I am going to give you some clothing," she said, "if you want it."

"Your tunic barely covers you," I said.

She had then torn a narrow strip from about the hem of the garment, and where the strip parted, tied the lengths together. "This will give you a belt," she said. She then tore down a part of her bodice.

"Tupita," I protested.

"We will both be bare-breasted slaves," she said. "Are you, former Earth woman, ashamed of the beauty of your breasts?"

"No," I said.

"Here," she said, handing me the narrow strips, knotted together, taken from the hem of her skirt. "Roll it. Twist it in your hands. It will be stronger. That is it. Good. Now tie it about your waist."

I fastened this fragile, narrow, improvised cordlike belt of twisted and rolled cloth about me, knotting it at the left hip. It was a slip knot, such that masters might remove it at a tug.

"Here," she said, handing me the strip of cloth she had torn from her bodice.

I placed it carefully, gratefully, the loose end inside, next to my belly, over the rolled cloth. I smoothed it out.

"I see that you know how to insert a slave strip in a belly cord," she said.

"Of course," I said.

"Let us see you now," she said, "in your collar and cloth." She inspected me. "I gather you are a low slave," she said, "from the exposure of your bosom and the poor quality of the belt and cloth you wear."

"Yes, Mistress," I smiled.

"Yet you are pretty," she mused.

"Thank you, Mistress," I smiled.

"And the cloth you wear, aside from questions of its quality, is suitable," she said. "It is such that it may be easily pulled aside."

"Yes, Mistress," I said. The wearing of such cloths, and tunics, that may be removed with ease, and such, serves various purposes. For example, obviously it provides her some shielding. On the other hand, because of its precarious nature, and its dependence on a man's permissions and indulgence, it also acutely increases her sense of possible exposure and vulnerability. Such clothing, then, tends to help remind her, and quite clearly, that she is a female slave. It also, of course, because of its nature, and in spite of what might be her wishes or desires in the matter, tends, on a deep psychological and physiological level, to be erotically arousing to her. It puts her more at the mercy of men. It is difficult to be dressed as a slave and not, in time, even if one is a free woman, come to feel, and desire, as a slave. Indeed, it is a not uncommon first step in the enslavement of a free woman merely to dress her as a slave.

"Am I ready to go out on the floor now?" I asked. The "first girl" in a tavern often inspects her inferiors, before she permits them on the floor.

"I think not," she smiled. "But you would perhaps do in the hay for the rough pleasures of a drover."

I laughed, and so, too, did Tupita, but then we looked about ourselves, at the sheer walls of the shaft about us, and up at the opening, doubtless wide enough, but from here, seemingly so small, seemingly so far above. I noticed again, oddly enough, yet interestingly, how one could see the stars from this place, even during the afternoon.

We then sat down in the pit, on the dried leaves, on the gravel, quiet, subdued, our backs against the sides of the shaft.

We did not know what our fate would be.

"Is there one beast, or more?" asked Tela.

"We do not know," said Tupita.

"We are kept in ignorance!" cried Tela. "They do not let us know anything! We do not know where we are! We do not know the nature of our captors, or even their number! We do not know what they intend to do with us! They treat us like—like—"

"Like slave girls?" asked Tupita.

Tela looked at her, and struck her small fists on her bared thighs in frustration.

"Yes!" she wept.

"You are no longer the free woman, Lady Liera Didiramache of Lydius," said Tupita. "You are now Tela, a slave."

"They treat us as they wish!" she cried.

"And so, too, do they with their tharlarion, their tarsks, and their other animals."

"Yes," she whispered, and I saw her draw back, frightened. But, too, in a moment, I saw her shudder, suddenly, thrilled to the quick. Then she lay down, in her collar, and her bit of silk, at the side of the shaft, trembling, not meeting our eyes.

We were then very quiet, all of us.

We did not know what our fate would be.

We were slaves. We must wait to learn.

29 / The Meadow

"Not enough! Not enough!" cried the small, twisted fellow, with the yellowish, sallow complexion, crouching down, his back to us, pointing to the blanket spread there on the ground. The entire right side of his face was a whitened mass of ancient scar tissue. The ear on the right side of his head had been half torn away. It was almost as though the right side of his face had been abraided by some terrifying, fierce passage, by some swift, lengthy, terrible friction, as of being dragged over rock. So disfigured one might doubt if he dared consort with his own kind. He seemed obviously to be held in contempt by the five men who squatted near him, on the other side of the blanket. To the right of the blanket, on the ground, there was a pack, filled, it seemed, with trinkets, a peddler's pack. The small man was, it seemed, a peddler, or one who was concerned, at least, to give that impression.

"If you disapprove of our offer," said the leader of the five men, a bearded fellow, "return to Tharna, and there mine the difference."

The small fellow sat back on his heels, angrily. "Too, there was to be meat, much meat!" he said.

"Do not be stupid," said one of the men squatting across from him. "We have brought you a quarter of a dried tarsk. That is enough for you to chew on for a month."

"It is not enough!" said the small fellow. "We need more!"

"Do you have a pen of sleen?" asked one of the men.

The small fellow did not answer. But then, after a time, he repeated, guardedly, "We need more."

"You can buy more with the silver," said the man across from him, the leader of the five men.

The small fellow had two cohorts with him, who, like the others, were squatting down, but to our left. These fellows looked uneasily at one another.

"We are offering fifteen pieces of silver, fifteen solid, sound, unclipped silver tarsks," said the leader. "That is enough."

"It was to have been twenty-five!" said the small man. "Five for each!"

"We will give you three for each," said the leader, putting his finger on his helmet, which was beside him, upturned, in the grass.

"No!" said the small fellow, and leaped up, angrily, and, limping, approached us. "See them!" he said. "There is not one there who, stripped, would not bring high bids on the block! Is there one there whom a man would not dream of marching home naked before him, to fasten her to his slave ring! See those faces, those slave curves! There is not one of them who is not worth five tarsks!"

"Three tarsks for each," said the leader. "Good tarsks."

"These two," said the small fellow, indicating Tupita and myself, "served in the tent of Pietro Vacchi. I know! I was in the camp!" He, then, I assumed, must be the human contact, or one of them, of the beasts. "And this one," he said, pointing to Tela, "was an overseer's choice, a man who could pick from almost a hundred women, all slaves!"

"Work slaves," said the leader.

Tela stiffened in her bonds. To be sure, she had been brought to the camp of the black chain as a work slave. So had we all, for that matter.

"She was a rich woman from Lydius!" said the small fellow.

"She now wears a brand," pointed out the leader.

"And this one," said the small fellow, returning his attention to me, "is a dancer!"

"Dancers are nothing," he said. "They go ten for a tarsk."

I tightened, angrily. Men in Brundisium had been willing to pay much for me. I had been, supposedly, one of the finest dancers in that city.

"And these two," said the small fellow, indicating Mina and Cara, "are obviously beauties."

"Work slaves," grinned the leader.

Tupita was to my right. Tela was to my left. Then came Mina, and Cara. We were kneeling. We had been backed on our knees to a railing, until the backs of our necks were in contact with it. This railing, in front of the remains of what had apparently once been a long low building, perhaps a stable, or bunk house, or ranch house of sorts, was a hitching device, for beasts, probably tharlarion. At one time, I supposed, this might have been a ranch for tharlarion, or perhaps a boarding or training facility for racing tharlarion. Venna was not far away. It was now abandoned. Once we were in contact with the railing, once we could feel it hard against the back of our neck, we were roped to it, by the neck. Our hands were tied behind us. That had been done as soon as we had been brought up from the pit. That had been a frightening ascent, crouching in the bucket, supported by it, swaying back and forth, clinging to the rope, while being drawn upward. We made little noise during this ascent, terrifying though it might have been, for we had coiled and placed binding fiber in our mouths, this in accordance with instructions called down to us from above. Lengths for Tela, Tupita and myself had already been in the pit, it apparently having figured, with a long rope, in our descent. Lengths had been dropped down for Mina and Cara. The long, doubled rope used in lowering us had, in their cases, apparently simply been put under their wrist chaining. In this way, at least in the case of Tela, Tupita and myself, they recovered their fiber, which would be used, in any case, again, and, in this particular mode of transporting it, prevented us from communicating, at least by explicit utterances, our terror to the others still below. By this device, too, of course, with the lengths dropped to them, Mina and Cara were kept quiet in their ascent. I was only too pleased when the hooked stick reached out and drew the bucket and rope to where a man could reach me. I was then knelt on the grass by the well. The binding fiber I must quickly force from my mouth with my tongue into a man's hand. It was then, still wet, used to secure my hands behind me. I did not mind this, though, so pleased I was to be once more on the ground. I had then been taken to the railing, knelt, backed against it, and roped to it. Then my ankles, too, had been crossed, and tied. Tupita had already been so secured. After me had come Tela, and then Mina and Cara. In the case of Mina and Cara the binding fiber had been simply threaded through links close to their manacles and shackles. These links had then, with the fiber, been drawn close to one another and then tied there, closely together. Thus, in our various ways, all of us, the five of us, had been made absolutely helpless, exactly where and as we had been placed. We had been all, in our various ways, secured with typical Gorean efficiency. From where we knelt we could see the remains of the well, about forty yards away. It seemed to rise up from a small meadow, rather at the left side of the meadow. The meadow, which was very beautiful, sloped gently down and away from us, mostly to the right, and was generally bordered by trees. There were more trees rather behind us, and to the left, trees which, from their size, had probably been there for years, antedating, and surviving, the structure, now in ruins, before which we were tied. The whole place, judging from the condition of the meadow, where the grass was sometimes very high, and the trees across from us, smaller and wilder, had probably been abandoned for years.

I noted the eyes of one of the men across the way on me. I had inadvertently, it seems, let my knees draw a bit too closely together. I immediately spread my knees much more widely, as I could, as was compatible with the binding on my ankles. This was appropriate for one such as I, a kajira, before a free male. He smiled. I put my head down.

The small fellow returned, angrily, to squat behind the blanket, across from the leader of the five men.

"Twenty-five!" he said. "And meat, much more meat!"

He had been very angry, almost from the moment these five fellows had appeared, coming through the trees, for they had not simply completed the transaction, according to the terms which, I took it, had been previously agreed upon, but, it seems, had chosen to have, or appear to have, second thoughts. They had even seen fit, as, under the circumstances, would have seemed superfluous, to conduct, or seem to conduct, critical examinations of the merchandise.

The fellow across the way grinned at me. I put my head down again. How I had squirmed, bound kneeling and helpless, the rail tight behind the back of my neck, my neck roped to it, under his touch! The work tunics of Mina and Cara had been thrust back, over their arms, and torn down. The remains of the bodices of these tunics now hung back about their wrists. The remainder of the garments, in front, torn apart, hung low on their bellies, below their navels. Their breasts were very beautiful, and the line of their waists, and the beginning of the flare of their hips. Too, their skirts, and Tupita's, too, and the slave strips, or G-strings, of Tela and myself had been lifted up, or aside, and let fall again, perhaps to see if we were depilated, or shaved, or if such cloth might conceal some defect. All in all, we had been handled intimately, and with authority. We were slaves.

"Twenty-five!" said the small fellow.

The small fellow, I had gathered, might have once been from Tharna. That is a city far to the north and east of Venna. It is well known for its silver mines. So, too, incidentally, is the city of Argentum, where I had been owned by Tyrrhenius of Argentum, and had served him as a lure girl. One can usually recognize a man of Tharna by two yellow cords, each about eighteen inches long, thrust over the belt. Such cords are suitable for binding a female, hand and foot. In seeing such cords the woman understands that it is possible for them to be used to put her at a man's mercy. The meaning of these cords has something to do, apparently, with the history of the polis of Tharna. Interestingly there are supposedly almost no free women in Tharna. Further, it is said that the slavery of a woman in Tharna is one of the strictest, most uncompromising and complete of slaveries on Gor. Similarly, interestingly enough, almost all of the female slaves in Tharna are native-born to the city. Tharnans seldom bring slaves into the city or, indeed, sell them out of the city. It is their own women, it seems, whom they keep in bondage, and a bondage of a very severe sort. Even when a slave begs to be sold out of the city, this is usually denied to her. One might almost think that the slavery of the women in Tharna was not an ordinary slavery but in some sense rather different. It is almost as though it had been imposed upon them as a punishment; it is almost as if they had been sentenced to it. Surprisingly, however, and scarcely to be expected in such a stern polity, the city itself is ruled by a Tatrix. Her name, it is said, is Lara. Also, paradoxically, Tharna's first minister, who stands second only to the Tatrix, is not of high caste but of lowly origin, only of the metal workers. His name, it is said, is Kron. Such things, I think, make Tharna an unusual city. She defends herself well, incidentally, and some, though perhaps they jest, speculate that her silver may be safer even than that of Argentum, which is an ally of Ar. One man of Tharna, it is said, is a match for ten from most cities. Whereas that is doubtless not true, it is not disputed that Tharnan warriors are among the most dangerous on Gor. It is indicative of this sort of thing that Tharnan mercenaries usually command high fees. Many mercenary companies use them as cadre and officers.

"No," said the bearded man, squatting across the blanket from the small fellow.

The small fellow, however, did not wear in his belt the two cords of Tharna. This suggested to me that if he had ever been of Tharna he now, at any rate, was no longer of Tharna. Perhaps he had been cast out of the city. Perhaps he had been banished or sent into exile. The bearded fellow had jested to him, somewhat cruelly, I thought, about the mines. Perhaps he had once served in them? If so, that suggested he might have once been a slave or criminal. In such a case then, surely he would not be anxious to return to them. Perhaps it had been in the mines that he had been injured, in them that he had been so disfigured, in them that perhaps he had acquired even the impediment in his gait.

"Yes!" cried the small fellow.

"I do not want to stay long in this vicinity," said the bearded fellow. "We were in the camp of Pietro Vacchi this morning. There is much concern there over this second disappearance of a wench from the camp. There may be a search. There is even a fellow in the camp now who has a sleen. He came in from the Viktel Aria, from around Venna, last night."

"A sleen does not exist who could follow the trail," said the small fellow.

"You are not afraid of sleen?" asked the bearded fellow, skeptically.

"No," said the small fellow.

"What is more to be feared than sleen," he asked, "saving perhaps a larl?"

"There are things," said the small fellow.

"Men," grinned the bearded fellow.

"Sometimes," said the small fellow, uneasily.

"Your girls are pot girls," said the bearded man, "kettle-and-mat girls, laundresses, stable sluts."

I heard Tupita gasp in anger, tied to my right. She had been the "first girl" in a much-frequented tavern in Brundisium. Then she shrank back, very quiet. She was afraid she might have attracted their attention. Sometimes a slave wants very much to attract the attention of a man, but sometimes, too, she does not. Sometimes she hopes that he, at least officially, will not take notice of her. It is not pleasant to be cuffed. Too, the whip hurts. I myself, too, however, though I was more restrained than Tupita, was not much pleased either. I had been first, at least for a time, on at least some of the lists at the baths in Brundisium. Too, I had been a fine dancer, one of the finest, I suspect, in Brundisium! If they could have seen me curling about a man's feet in an alcove, licking and kissing them, then inching upward, piteously, hopefully, then kneeling beside him, looking up, kissing, licking, pleading, I do not think they would have been so quick to dismiss me as a mere "pot girl." Tela, too, I am sure, was angry. After all, not only had she once been a rich free woman, of high family and significant station, of a fine city, Lydius, but even after her capture, and her prompt reduction to total and absolute bondage, she had been found so beautiful, so luscious and desirable, that she had been chosen over many women for the rectangle of red silk in the tent of Aulus. Mina and Cara, too, I think, were not too pleased. Certainly the beauty of neither was negligible, and I am sure they were both well aware of this. Both, and I am sure they understood this, would be likely to bring a high price on the slave block. Had there been originally any doubt in the minds of these fellows as to our desirability, or potential, those doubts, surely, should have been dispelled earlier, in the authoritative, intimate examinations to which we had all been helplessly subjected. What more would they have wished to do, put us to their full pleasure? Perhaps they could take us home for a week on a trial basis!

"Very well," said the little fellow. "Consider them pot girls, cleaning slaves, laundresses, what have you, it matters not to me. Put them to your lowest servile tasks. Whip them back when they would crawl pleading on their bellies to your couches! What does it matter to me!"

I think we were all startled to hear him exclaim in this fashion. Certainly we were exquisite slave flesh, all of us! I doubted that there were many slave bars on Gor to which five women such as we were fastened. To be sure, almost all female slaves on Gor must expect to be put to domestic labors, cooking, sewing, cleaning, washing, ironing, and such. We were women. Even free women, in households without slaves, perform such labors. How, then, could we expect to be exempt from them? Sometimes even high pleasure slaves in the palaces of Ubars must, if only to remind them that they are slaves, on their hands and knees, stripped and chained, scrub floors. Still, surely we were good for far more than such things. Did the beauty of our faces, and our slave curves, not suggest that? Surely the first and most essential office of the female slave, and, indeed, of any sort of female slave, is to be pleasing to the master.

"But," said the small fellow, "whatever you choose to call

them, or however you choose to think of them, we made a bargain!"

"You have no Home Stone," said the bearded man.

I shuddered. In such a fashion he had informed the small fellow that he was not such that one need keep faith with him. There is a Gorean saying that only Priest-Kings, outlaws and slaves lack Home Stones. Strictly, of course, that is an oversimplification. For example, animals of all sorts, such as tarsks and verr, as well as slaves, do not have Home Stones. Too, anyone whose citizenship, for whatever reason, is rescinded or revoked, with due process of law, is no longer entitled to the protections and rights of that polity's Home Stone. That Home Stone is then no longer his. This suggested to me, again, that the small fellow might have been cast out of Tharna, perhaps exiled or banished. He did not seem to me a likely candidate for an outlaw, at least in the fullest sense of the word. Indeed, the fellows with whom he was dealing, such rough, dangerous, unkempt brutes, seemed to me much more likely candidates for such an appellation.

"Beware," said the small fellow.

The leader of the five men regarded him, puzzled. "What then is your Home Stone?" he asked.

The small fellow looked down, angrily. He pulled up a handful of grass.

"You do not have a Home Stone," announced the leader, with a grin.

"Twenty-five silver tarsks for the women," said the small fellow. "And meat, much meat!"

"You do not have a Home Stone," grinned the leader.

"Five for each," said the small fellow, "not three!"

"Very well," said the leader.

"Good," said the small fellow.

"Not three," said the leader, "but two."

"No!" cried the small fellow.

"Then one for each," said the leader.

"Beware!" cried the small fellow.

" 'Beware'?" inquired the leader. "Are you mad? To whom will you sell these pot girls, if not to us? Will you take these two back to Vacchi, to see if he will buy them back? Will you take the other three back to Venna?"

"Deal with us fairly," said the small man.

"There are five of us here," said the leader, indicating himself with a jerk of his thumb, and then the others, behind him. "I have three more waiting with a closed slave wagon on the other side of the trees. That is eight. There are three of you."

"There was to have been more meat," said the small fellow.

The leader laughed. "Apparently you are reluctant to sell these women to us, in spite of your agreement to do so. Very well. The decision is yours. We shall not buy them. We shall simply take them with us."

Tupita and I, and the others, shrank back in our bonds, then, in terror, pushing back against the rail to which our necks were tied. If we could have we would have forced it from its posts.

The leader of the five men looked at us, and laughed. But did he think our terror was motivated by the fear of coming into the clutches of such masters, distressing though such a disposition might be? The small fellow, and his two cohorts, squatting behind him, to his left, did not move. They were all very still.

"What is wrong?" asked the leader.

Then suddenly one of his men screamed weirdly, lifted up, his legs jerking wildly. We screamed. The thing must have been eight feet tall. We had seen it lift its head, in the tall grass, some seven or eight yards behind the five men, and to their left. It had perhaps been hidden in a pit, or burrow. Its ears had been upright. It bit through the back of the neck of the man and cast the body down, with the quarter of the dried tarsk which they had brought.

Almost instantly another of the men had begun to draw his sword, but the beast, before the blade was half from the sheath, on all fours, scrambling, tearing the grass behind it, moving with incredible swiftness, not like anything on two legs, seized him and tore open his throat with a single slash of those terrible fangs.

We screamed in terror, bound, twisting at the railing, half choked.

"Do not draw your swords!" cried the small fellow. "Do not draw your swords! It is harmless. It is harmless!"

The beast then regarded the men, who shrank back from it, their hands at the hilts of their swords but not daring to draw them. The beast then took the second body and threw it with the first, together with the quarter of a dried tarsk.

"Do not run," said the small fellow, quickly. "It will pursue you then. Stay here. Do not move. Do not draw your weapons. It is friendly. It will not hurt you."

The beast now crouched near the two bodies. Its mouth was red, and the fur about its jaw and snout. It looked up at the men, balefully, and a deep growl warned them back.

"Do not approach it closely," said the small fellow.

That I surmised was the last intent of the three men.

The beast then lowered its head, but its ears remained up. I think even a tiny sound, perhaps a movement of grass, might have been audible to it, certainly the slipping of steel from a scabbard.

I looked away, sick.

"There is little to fear," said the small fellow. "It prefers tarsk."

"It is not eating tarsk," said one of the men.

"It is hungry," said the small fellow. "Do not be harsh with it. The tarsk is dried. The other is fresh. You should have brought more meat."

The beast looked up at them, feeding.

"See the hand," said one of the men.

The paw, or hand, had long, powerful, thick, multiply jointed digits. Such hands, those of this creature, or of one like it, had held the bars of the girl pen, and thrust them apart, admitting its bulk.

"There are six fingers," whispered another man.

"What is it?" asked the leader of the men.

"A beast," said the small, lame man, noncommittally. "I do not really know what it is called. I met them outside of Corcyrus, last year."

"Them?" asked the leader.

"Yes," said the small fellow. "There are two more, somewhere about."

The men looked about, frightened. Even the two cohorts of the small fellow, who had remained much in their places, seemed uneasy. This thing had arisen as though by magic from the grass. As large as these things were they were apparently not unskilled at concealment, and perhaps stalking.

"What do you mean, you 'met them outside of Corcyrus'?" said the leader.

"When Corcyrus fell to Argentum, in the Silver War," said the small fellow, "when proud Sheila, the ruthless Tatrix of Corcyrus, was deposed, they apparently fled the city."

I had heard something of the Silver War when I was in Argentum. Sheila, the Tatrix, said to be as beautiful as she was proud and ruthless, had apparently escaped for a time but, later, had been caught in Ar, actually, and amusingly, and doubtless to her shame and humiliation, by a professional slave hunter. She had been put in a golden sack and taken back to Corcyrus to stand trial. Her final disposition was as follows: she became the proprty of the man who had taken her, the professional slave hunter.

"They broke from their confinements in the confusion, in the taking of the city?" said the leader.

"I do not think they were confined," said the small fellow.

"They were kept as pets?" said the leader, awed.

"No," said the small fellow.

"I do not understand," said the leader.

"I was encamped not far from Corcyrus," said the small fellow. "I had come there hoping to make cheap purchases of valuable loot, from the soldiers. These things came to my camp. They had smelled food, I think. I threw them my food, in terror. That was where I first met them. Before that I had not even known there were such things."

"They have been with you since?" asked the leader.

"Yes," said the small fellow.

"Look!" said one of the men, pointing to the beast.

At his exclamation the beast, curious, looked up at him.

He stepped back.

The paw of the beast was wrapped about the strings of one of the fallen men's wallets. It then jerked it from the belt, breaking the thongs. Then, watching the men, it similarly relieved the second body of its wallet.

"You have trained it to steal," said the leader, startled, awed.

The beast then opened the wallets and poured the contents into its paw. There it moved the coins about, in the palm of one broad paw, by means of a digit on the other paw. It was dexterous, for so large a beast. Those were clearly sophisticated prehensile appendages.

I watched this with horror.

The beast then poured the coins back in one of the wallets, and threw it to the blanket, before the small fellow.

"They find me of value," said the small fellow. "As you can imagine it would be difficult for them to enter a town, go to the market and purchase goods."

"I do not understand," said the leader, white-faced. "These things are animals, beasts!"

"Yes," said the small fellow.

"It is hard to believe that such things were pets in Corcyrus."

"They were not pets," said the small fellow.

"I do not understand," said the man.

"They were allies," said the small fellow.

"Who is captain here?" asked the leader, frightened.

At this point the beast rose from behind the bodies. It was some eight feet, or so, in height. It must have weighed eight or nine hundred pounds. Fangs protruded from the sides of its jaw.

It had a double ring of teeth. Its mouth, jaws, now, were red with blood. It wiped them with the back of one of its long arms. It looked at the leader of the men. "I am captain," it said.

"Spare us," begged the leader. "Take our coins! Leave us our lives!" He then removed his wallet and tossed it, hastily, timidly, onto the blanket, beside the other wallet, that which contained the coins from the two fallen men. His remaining two men did so, as well.

"No, no," said the small fellow. "You do not understand. We mean you no harm. It was you who did not intend to deal fairly. We now have the meat which we needed, though I would surely have preferred another form of it. He took only what we all knew had been agreed upon. He was merely exacting his due. Similarly, we want only the five silver tarsks for each of these women."

"We do not want them," said the leader.

"Do not be silly," said the small fellow. He then, crouching down by the blanket, took the leader's wallet and removed several coins from it. He put these in small piles on the blanket. There were five such piles. Each contained five silver tarsks. He then handed the leader back the wallet. The other two men, too, retrieved their wallets. "The other money, of course, from those two fellows," said the small fellow, "is forfeit."

"Of course," said the leader.

I think they all wished to turn and run.

"Do not be afraid," said the small fellow. "He will not hurt you. He is friendly."

The beast then lifted its head, its ears erected. Too, very carefully, alertly, it sniffed the air. Such a thing then, I suspected, had unusually keen senses. I was aware of the excellence of its night vision. I had more than enough evidence of its ferocity and strength. Too, I had seen it count money. I had heard it speak. It could bend bars. It could destroy men. Such a beast, I feared, was some type of dominant life form. How small and weak humans seemed compared to such a thing. How I feared then for my species! I now wanted to be sold as quickly as possible to the brigands, and taken from this place, to be locked in the closed slave wagon. Would I be safe even there, or could such a thing tear off the plates, those bolted, iron plates which confined us so well within, in the darkness, to get at us? I had not been given permission to speak, and dared not ask it. If I had I would have begged release from the railing and submission to any bonds my captors might choose, even body cages or wire jackets, simply to be taken from this place!

"What is it?" asked the small fellow of the beast.

"Sleen," it said.

"Do you detect men with it?" asked the small fellow, anxiously.

"No," it said.

"It is then a wild sleen," he said.

"It is past noon," said the leader of the other men. "It is late in the day for a sleen to be abroad." The sleen is predominantly nocturnal.

"It is probably on the trace of tabuk, from last night," said the small man.

I pulled at the binding fiber which confined my wrists. It was still damp, from having been in my mouth, when I had been brought up from the well. I squirmed, on my knees, my neck bound at the railing. If there were a sleen about we were helpless. We could not even run. It was almost as though we were fastened on a meat rack.

"We did not even come into the area until it was light," said one of the leader's men.

From his remark I gathered that it was not likely that the animal, if there were one about, would be concerned with us. A sleen will usually follow the first scent it picks up when hunting, and then follow it tenaciously. There are stories of such beasts on the trail of something actually running between, or among, other animals, and even men, and paying them no attention.

"Too, sleen seldom attack groups," said the leader. "They prefer isolated animals."

I took some courage from these remarks.

"Let us move the women," said the leader. "We have been too long in this place."

I was pleased to hear this resolution. I would have been zealously cooperative even if I had been a free woman, holding forth my limbs to be bound, putting forth my neck for the coffle collar, and not a mere slave.

"Free their ankles," said the leader of the men.

"Look," said one of the small fellow's two cohorts, pointing across the meadow.

One of the leader's two men had scarcely bent to unknot the bonds on Tupita's crossed ankles when he stopped, given pause by this utterance. He stood up, shading his eyes.

Two beasts were approaching, doubtless the companions of the one with us. One thrust a man before it. The other was dragging behind itself, through the grass, a belt, with an attached scabbard and sword.

"No!" cried Tupita, in misery.

The fellow, pushed forward by the beast, looked at her, dully, angrily. I pulled back a little, the railing hard against the back of my neck. I saw him regard me, with frustration, with hatred.

"What are you doing here?" asked the small fellow of the prisoner.

He was silent.

There was a growl from the beast behind him.

"He came to seek me," said Tupita, boldly.

"No," said the man, looking at her.

"What then? What then?" asked the small fellow.

"I followed that thing," he said, rubbing his arm, where the beast had gripped him.

"He is from the camp of Pietro Vacchi," said the leader of the men. "I saw him there, two days ago."

"Yes!" said the small fellow. "I, too, I am sure, saw him there!"

"He is then one of Vacchi's men," said one of the small fellow's cohorts.

"There must be others about, too, then!" said the other, alarmed. "They are seeking the two women."

"I am not of the company of Pietro Vacchi," said the man.

"How came you here?" asked the small fellow.

"I followed that," he said, indicating the beast, "as I told you."

The beast growled, menacingly. I take it, it did not care to accept the fact that a man might be able to follow it.

"You are a hunter?" asked one of the leader's men.

"In a way," he said.

"You are a brave fellow," said one of the leader's men, "to pursue such a beast."

"It was not the beast in which I was interested," he said.

"How many are with you?" asked one of the small fellow's cohorts.

"I am alone," he said proudly.

"What are you doing here?" asked the small fellow. "What is it you seek?"

"I seek the blood of a slave," he said, regarding me.

I put down my head.

Tupita sobbed.

Surely he had given himself up for lost. It was hard to understand otherwise the pride, the grandeur, with which he spoke. He had risked all, and lost all. He stood there with folded arms. For my blood he had dared even to follow so terrible a beast. This was no small measure of his hatred of me and his determination. He looked about himself with scorn. He disdained to conceal his intent or objective. He had not understood, however, it seemed, in his single-minded pursuit of his bloody goal, that there might be others of that kind about. They had taken him. I did not doubt but that they, too, in their way, were hunters.

"Kill it," said the largest of the beasts, their leader.

Tupita screamed in protest, but the nearest beast to the captive struck him from the side with the back of its closed paw. There was a sickening sound, and the captive's head snapped to the side. The other beast reached down and lifted up the figure, and threw it on the store of meat beside the blanket. "No, no," wept Tupita, "no, no, no!"

"There may be others about," said the leader of the men. "Let us reconnoiter the area."

"Do you understand?" asked the small fellow of the largest beast.

The beast looked at him, and its long, dark tongue came out of the side of its mouth, and it licked at the bloody fur at the side of its jaw. Then it looked around, its ears lifted.

"He wants to look," said the small fellow, making a large, circular motion with his hand, encompassing the meadow. "He wants to look. There may be others."

The beast then again fixed its gaze on the small fellow, and he stepped back, in trepidation.

"Yes," it said. "We will look."

"Spread out," said the small fellow to his cohorts, and the others. We will return here."

I looked at Mirus, of Brundisium. The side of his head was bloody.

"It is your fault!" cried Tupita, turning her head, in her neck ropes, toward me.

"Forgive me, Tupita!" I wept.

"You are safe now!" she wept. "Rejoice! If I could get my hands on you I would kill you myself!"

"Please, Tupita!" I begged. "I, too, am in sorrow! He was kind to me!"

"This is what you wanted!" she cried.

"No," I said. "Never, never!"

"It is you who have killed him!" she wept. "It was you who drove him to madness! It was you who changed him, who made him some crazed beast, who made him thirst for blood! It is you who are responsible! It was you who did this to him!"

"No!" I wept. "No!"

Then she began to weep uncontrollably, her head back.

"Forgive me, Tupita," I said. "Forgive me!"

"You killed him!" she sobbed.

"No! No!" I said. Then, I, too, in my sorrow, wept. We could not, as men had put us, wipe our tears. They coursed down our cheeks. Their salty flow fell even upon, and ran down, our bodies. I looked upon the bloody, still figure, cast upon the bodies and the quarter of a tarsk. "Tupita!" I said.

She did not respond, so lost in her grief she was.

"Tupita," I whispered. "I do not think he is dead."

"What?" cried Tupita.

"Look," I said. "He is still bleeding."

"Oh, Master!" she cried, suddenly, frightened.

"He is very strong," I said. "I do not think he is dead."

"No!" she said. "He is alive! My master is alive! He lives!" She looked at me, wildly, in her neck ropes. She laughed, sobbing. Her tears now were tears of joy. Then suddenly she looked at me. She was very frightened. "Oh, Tuka," she said. "You are in terrible danger!"

I tightened in the binding fiber, shuddering. "He may not recover consciousness before we are taken away," I said. "Perhaps the beasts may not notice he is alive. Perhaps he can make good his escape."

Suddenly Tela, to my left, made a frightened noise. "There!" she said, suddenly. "There, beside the well!"

"What is it?" asked Mina.

I could not see anything. I tried to lift my head but, bound as I was, kneeling, tied by the neck at the rail, I could do very little. I sobbed with frustration.

"What is it!" said Mina, insistently.

"You cannot see it now," said Tela. "I think it is behind the well."

"What was it?" asked Mina.

"There!" said Tela, frightened. "A sleen!"

Terror coursed through us.

"It is probably not on our scent" said Tupita. "Do not move!"

We could see it now, by the well, its head lifted above the grass.

It was looking at us.

"Do not move," said Tupita.

I did not know if we could move, we were so frightened even had we desired to do so.

The head of the sleen remained immobile for more than twenty seconds. Had we not seen it, had we not known where it was, we might not have noticed it, even though it was only a matter of yards away. It is incredible how still such things can hold themselves. Then, suddenly, it moved. It circled the well. Then, oddly enough, it put its front paws, of its six legs, up on the well, and thrust its head over the upper wall of the well, and then lowered its head, apparently peering within. It then withdrew its head from the opening of the well, and slipped back into the grass.

Mirus stirred, lying on the two bodies. He groaned.

"Oh, Master," moaned Tupita, almost silently, "do not awaken now. Do not make noise!"

"He has blood on him," said Cara. "It will come this way!"

"It must not come this way," said Tupita. "It might hurt the master."

"What of us!" said Cara. There was a small sound from her wrist chains, where the links near the manacles had been bound together by the binding fiber.

Surely the animal could hear that!

"We do not matter," said Tupita. "We are only slaves."

Cara moaned.

"Do not awaken, Master," whispered Tupita to Mirus. "Lie still."

He, I think, though, could not hear her, or could not understand her.

Interestingly, though I think such a beast might easily detect the small sounds, even the whispers, we made, it did not seem to notice them. It seemed, rather, intent upon some other business.

Mirus groaned, and lifted his head. He lifted his body, too, a little. He was a very strong man.

"Lie still, Master," whispered Tupita. "There is a sleen about."

"It is on a scent," whispered Tela. "Look at it!"

The animal now seemed to be very excited. It was near the well, its snout to the ground. It circled the well twice, and then circled it again, increasing the size of the circle. I heard it making small, eager noises. Then it hurried in our direction for a moment, and then stopped, and then, again, began to move toward us.

Groggily Mirus, blood running down the side of his head, crawled toward the scabbard and blade, taken from him by one of the beasts, which lay near him. The blades, too, for that matter, of the two slain fellows were also in the vicinity, one still in its sheath, the other half drawn.

"Go away! Go away!" cried Tela to the sleen.

Its eyes were now very bright. It was a gray hunting sleen.

Mirus staggered unsteadily to his feet, discarding the scabbard. He nearly fell, but regained his feet. He held the hilt with two hands.

He came toward me, reeling, bleeding. I then realized it was his intention to strike me.

"There is a sleen behind you!" cried Tupita. "Turn around! Turn around!"

"That is not a wild sleen!" cried Mina.

It wore a collar, a large, heavy, spiked collar.

Mirus reeled about. He stood then, sword drawn, between the beast and us.

Tela put her head back and screamed, wildly, shrilly, helplessly.

The beast regarded us.

"It is Borko, the sleen of Hendow!" cried Tupita. "It has come to kill us!"

It had come after us, pursuing us, doubtless, as runaway slaves!

I suddenly recalled the reference to an inquiry, or inquiries, in Argentum, that on the part of my former master, Tyrrhenius. I had been sold shortly thereafter. I also remembered that I had walked barefoot on the Viktel Aria, at the stirrup of Aulus, and, too, had so trod the camp of Pietro Vacchi.

"No," said Mirus. "It is on one scent. It is after only one quarry."

I saw the sleen view me.

"Master," I called out to Mirus. "Defend me!"

But he, both hands on the hilt of his sword, holding it at rest now, pointed downward, backed away. He stood between the beast and Tupita.

Borko looked at him. He remembered him, doubtless, from Brundisium.

Without taking his eyes off the sleen, by feel, Mirus cut the ropes that tied Tupita to the railing, and then cut free the binding fiber on her ankles, and wrists.

"Do not mind me," wept Tupita. "Do not let him kill Tuka!"

But Mirus held her by one arm, and backed away.

"I find this," he said to me, "an acceptable and suitable vengeance, superior even to the sword, or to the thousand cuts, that you, my dear Doreen, or Tuka, or whatever masters now choose to call you, you stinking, worthless, curvaceous, treacherous slave slut, should be torn to pieces by a sleen!"

"No!" screamed Tupita.

"Kill, Borko, kill!" he cried, indicating me with the point of his sword.

I closed my eyes, sobbing.

I felt then, however, the huge, cold snout of the beast thrusting itself under my left arm. I gasped, and cried out, softly. But there had been little, if anything, of menace in the gesture. Perhaps it was confirming my scent, prior to its attack. Then, again it rubbed its snout on my body. This seemed clearly an act of affection. I had seen it act so with Hendow himself. It was nuzzling me. Then I felt its large tongue lick across my body.

"Good Borko! Good Borko!" cried Tupita.

"Kill!" cried Mirus. "Kill her!"

Borko looked at him, quizzically.

"Very well, then, stupid beast," he said, "I shall do so myself!" He then raised his blade. Immediately the entire attitude of the sleen altered. It suddenly became alive with menace and hate. Its fur erected, its eyes blazed, it snarled viciously.

Mirus, startled, stepped back.

I think perhaps if the sleen had not known him from Brundisium, and as the friend of his master, he might have attacked him. Certainly, it seemed, as it was, he had no intention of letting him approach me.

"It is protecting her!" cried Tupita, delightedly. "See! It will kill you if you try to hurt her! Come away! Let her go! Why fuss with a slave?"

Mirus then, in fury, held the blade with one hand. If he raised it, even a little, Borko growled, watching him.

"Free the other girls, Master," said Tupita. "Then let us away, before the beasts return!"

Mirus regarded her in rage.

"At one time you used to muchly pleasure yourself with me," said Tupita. "Am I not still of interest to you? Have I become so unattractive? Have you forgotten? Is it so long ago?"

Mirus made a noise, almost like an animal.

"See Tela there," she said. "She was an overseer's girl. See Mina, and Cara! Both are beautiful! You can put sword claim on us all!"

Mirus, in fury, lashed back with his hand, striking Tupita from him. She fell back, her mouth bloody, by the post to my right, that supporting the rail on that side.

He wavered. Fresh blood shone then at the side of his head. He staggered.

"Look!" cried Tupita, pointing across the meadow.

Mirus sank to one knee. He was weak from the loss of blood. It seemed he could scarcely hold his sword.

We looked where Tupita had pointed. Another figure was treading the meadow now, toward us. I could not mistake him, though he now seemed much different from when I had remembered him.

"It is Hendow!" cried Tupita.

"Yes!" I said.

But it was not the Hendow I remembered from Brundisium. It had the same stature, and shoulders, and mighty arms, but it was now a bronzed, leaner Hendow, one even more terrible and fierce than I had known, one who held now in his hand a bloodied sword.

"Mirus!" he cried. "Old friend! What are you doing here!"

"Hendow!" said Mirus, tears in his eyes. "Beloved friend!"

"You are hurt," said Hendow.

"You are welcome here," said Mirus, weakly.

"Forgive me, old friend, for thrusting you aside in Brundisium," said Hendow. "I was a fool."

"How did you find us here?" asked Mirus.

"I was following Borko," said Hendow. "Then I heard a scream." That would have been Tela's scream. Others, too, of course, might have heard that scream.

"Masters, let us away!" said Tupita.

"Your sword is bloody," observed Mirus.

"I met one who disputed my passage," said Hendow.

"Let us away, please, Masters!" said Tupita.

"Kneel," said Hendow to her, with terrible, savage authority.

Immediately Tupita knelt, and was silent.

Hendow came toward me, and crouched down before me. "Good Borko," he said. "Good Borko!" The sleen pushed his snout against him, and licked his bared arm. Hendow touched me on the side of the head, with extreme gentleness. "Are you all right?" he asked.

"Yes, Master," I said.

"They have you well secured," he smiled.

"As befits a slave, Master," I said.

"There are others about," said Mirus. "There were six men here, and three strange beasts, not sleen."

"Somewhere," said Tupita, "there is a slave wagon. Another three men are said to be there."

"I saw no slave wagon," said Hendow.

"You finished a man?" said Mirus.

"It would seem so," said Hendow. "His head is gone."

"Then there are still five about, at least," said Mirus, "and the beasts, they are most dangerous."

"There are said to be three at a slave wagon, Master," said Tupita.

"That would be at least eight then," he said, "and the beasts."

"Can you fight?" asked Hendow. "It would be like old times, before the tavern."

"I can be of no help to you," said Mirus. "It is hard to see. I am weak. I think I have lost much blood. I can hardly hold my sword. I fight to retain consciousness."

"I have no intention of leaving you here to die," said Hendow. "Better that we would perish together."

"No," said Mirus. "Better that only one die."

"I will not leave you," said Hendow.

"Do but one thing for me, before your departure," said Mirus.

"I am not leaving you," said Hendow.

"Put the fangs of Borko to that slave," said Mirus, indicating me, "or, if you wish, slay her for me, with your sword."

"Beloved Mirus!" said Hendow.

"She betrayed me to the chains of Ionicus!" said Mirus.

"False! False!" cried Hendow in fury.

"It is true," said Mirus. "I swear it by our love."

"Is this true?" asked Hendow of me, incredulously.

"Yes, Master," I wept.

"She was a lure girl!" cried Tupita. "Must we not obey, as we are slaves!"

"It seems," said Hendow, "that there is one here whose neck might well be consigned to the sword."

"Yes," said Mirus.

"Have you the strength to strike?" asked Hendow.

"I think so," said Mirus.

"You would prefer, surely, to do this deed yourself," said Hendow.

"Yes," said Mirus, rising unsteadily to his feet. He gripped the sword again with two hands. I did not know if he could stand for more than another moment.

"Very well," said Hendow. "Strike Tupita."

"Tupita?" asked Mirus.

Tupita shrank back, small, where she was kneeling in the grass.

"Yes," said Hendow. "I caught a thief, to whose lair I was led by Borko. He spoke quickly, after only his legs were broken. Tupita stole Doreen, duping her into leaving the house, she thinking she was still first girl, and intended to sell her, using her price to secure tarn passage from Brundisium in the guise of a free woman. She is, thus, a runaway slave. Moreover, I now put sword claim upon them both. Dispute it with me, if you will. I further learned from the thief they were both sold in Samnium. I spared his life, as he was cooperative. He is now doubtless, with his fellows, stealing other women. It was in Samnium I again picked up the trail. Borko and I have followed it for weeks. We lost it many times, but, each time, managed to find it again. Most recently we found it on the Viktel Aria, south of Venna. Thus, you see, had it not been for Tupita, for her running away, for her betrayal of a sister in bondage, for her willingness to assume the habiliments of a free woman, in itself a great crime, this slave would not have been in Argentum, to lure you. If one is covered with guilt here, surely it is Tupita. Accordingly, I now give you my permission to strike her."

"No!" cried Mirus.

"Perhaps both should have their necks to the sword," said Hendow.

"No!" cried Mirus. He put himself between Hendow and Tupita. "Run!" he said to Tupita. "Run!"

"Remain on your knees, slave," said Hendow, in a terrible voice. "Before you could run two steps I would put Borko on you."

Tupita remained where she was.

"Why did you flee Hendow?" cried Mirus to Tupita.

"You were no longer there!" she wept. "You had been sent away. You were gone! I was consumed by hatred for Doreen, because of whom Hendow dismissed you. I decided to sell her, and show you all, escaping from Brundisium."

"But you did not escape, did you?" asked Hendow.

"No, Master!" she wept.

"You are now obviously a slave, collared, half naked, kneeling in the grass, fearing for your life!"

"Yes, Master," she said.

"Even had you made your way from Brundisium, where would you have gone?" he asked. "In what city or village would you expect your antecedents not to be inquired into? Where would you get your collar off? Would you still not wear a brand?"

She sobbed.

"Is there escape for such as you?" he asked.

"No, Master," she wept. "There is no escape for such as I."

"Why would you have done such a thing?" asked Mirus, not taking his eyes off Hendow. I did not think Mirus could long remain on his feet.

"Do you not understand?" she wept. "I did it because of you!"

"Absurd," said Mirus.

"I did not want to be without you," she wept.

"Little fool," he said.

"Too, I was jealous of Doreen. I thought you cared for her!"

"Certainly I found of her of interest," said Mirus, "as I have many slaves, but she, though perhaps more beautiful than most, was never more to me, really, and I know that now, and have for a long time, than another wench whom I might, from time to time, for an Ahn or so, to the tune of my whip, if I pleased, put to my pleasure in an alcove."

"Oh, Master!" she breathed.

"But what are such things to you?" he asked.

"Do you not understand, Master?" she sobbed. "Though you scarcely know I exist, though you may despise or hate me, though you might scorn me or laugh at me, I am your love slave!"

He seemed startled.

"Yes," she cried. "I am your love slave! I have known this from the first time you put me to your feet! If you weighted and wrapped me with a thousand chains and a thousand locks they could not hold me more helplessly than the love I bear you! Alas, I have confessed! Kill me now, if you will!" She put down her head, sobbing.

"If you will not put her to the sword," said Hendow, "it seems, then, I must do so."

"No!" cried Mirus.

"Do you think, in your condition, you can adequately defend her?" asked Hendow.

"I will defend her to the death!" cried Mirus.

"Do you think she is a free woman?" asked Hendow. "She is only a slave."

"She is worth more to me than ten thousand free women!" cried Mirus.

"A slave slut?" asked Hendow, scornfully. "A woman who may be purchased from a slave block?"

"Yes!" cried Mirus.

"Stand aside," said Hendow.

"Have pity on her!" said Mirus. He could barely hold the sword. I feared he might collapse at any moment.

"Show mercy, Master!" I begged Hendow.

"You are losing blood, old friend," said Hendow. "I do not think you will long be able to stand. Perhaps then, while you have the strength, you will wish to attack."

"By the love you bear me," said Mirus, weakly, "do not kill her."

"You would kill this slave, would you not?" inquired Hendow.

"Yes," said Mirus.

"But you do not wish Tupita to die?" he asked.

"No," said Mirus.

"Perhaps then," said Hendow, smiling, "we might negotiate."

Mirus looked at him, unsteadily, wildly.

"It is too late!" wept Tupita. "Look!"

We looked up, to see, encircling us now, some yards away, men. There were five of them. With them, too, were the beasts.

Borko growled, menacingly.

"There is a sleen," said the bearded man, he who was the leader of the men who had come to pick us up. "It is unfortunate we do not have spears with us."

The small fellow, he who had been dealing with the leader, hung back. His two cohorts were somewhat in advance of him. Both were rough, grim-looking men, armed with blades. I thought them, though, perhaps less to be feared than the leader and the man with him. He had left, I recalled, with two. Two of the beasts came forward. They snarled, as Borko snarled. I realized, suddenly, they did not fear even a thing as terrible as a sleen. Armed only with their own teeth and jaws they regarded themselves as superior to it.

"What are those things?" asked Hendow.

"Where is Licinius?" asked the bearded man.

"They are certainly big fellows," said Hendow. "I, too, would not mind having a spear."

"Your sword is bloody," said the bearded man.

"Perhaps then I met Licinius," said Hendow.

"You should have fled," said Mirus.

"No," said Hendow.

"Beware of him," said the bearded man. "I think he may be skilled."

"Come closer," said Hendow. "Examine the blood on the blade. Perhaps you will recognize it."

Borko crouched low, his front shoulders a bit higher than his head. He growled.

"I free you, Borko, old friend," said Hendow. "Go. Return to the wild. Go. You are free!"

But the beast remained where it was, beside its master.

"As you will," said Hendow. "The choice is yours, my friend."

"We are lost," said Mirus. "I cannot help you."

"Stand near to me, behind me," said Hendow.

But Mirus sank to one knee, where he was. I did not understand how it was that he could remain even so. He must have been a man of incredible strength.

"You are surely ugly fellows," said Hendow to the two beasts. They were coming forward very warily. "Ho, lads," called Hendow. "Do not send your pet urts before you. Come forth boldly yourselves. Show that you are men!"

"Do not respond to his taunts!" said the bearded men. "The blood of Licinius warns you to caution!"

"Clever lads!" laughed Hendow.

"Watch out for the sleen!" called the small fellow to the beasts. "They are dangerous!"

The lips of one of the beasts, it very near now, only some fifteen feet away, drew back, about its fangs. It seemed an expression, oddly enough, of amusement. Then I recollected these things were rational.

"Run, Master!" I said. "Flee!"

But Hendow did not move. His whole body seemed as alert, as alive, as ready and as vital as that of Borko. He would not, of course, leave Mirus. Too, of course, he could not outrun the beasts. I had seen them move. I sobbed.

"Beware the beasts, Master," I said. "They are rational. They can think. They can speak!"

"So," said Hendow, "you still have a lying tongue in that pretty little head of yours. Perhap you remember the last time you lied to me?"

I moaned. I had been whipped. Then I must perforce kiss the whip. Then I had been put to my knees, my head down, my hands clasped behind the back of my neck, and, in that common slave position, raped. "I am not lying, Master," I said.

"You there, you big ugly brute," called Hendow to the leader of the beasts, which stood back a bit. "She is lying, isn't she?"

Its lips drew back. "Of course," it said.

"I thought so," said Hendow.

I felt confused, and frightened, but, too, elated, for I thought I understood then, by his response to the beast, that he had believed me, even when I had made what must have seemed so strange a claim. But then, in a moment, I realized that their capacity at least to understand human speech had surely been suggested by the small fellow's admonition, and by the one beast's response. I realized then that Hendow had used me, in his way, to distract the beasts, and to play with them. He had used me, a slave girl, in his strategy. How superior he was to me! How right it was that I should in the order of nature be only the slave of such a man!

"You fellows are some sort of urts, are you not?" asked Hendow.

The leader of the beasts rose up to his full height. The fur seemed to leap up about its head and shoulders, crackling. Its eyes blazed. Tela screamed. Its ears, oddly, then, lay back, flattened against the sides of its head. So, too, were Borko's. This, I supposed, was a readiness response, making them less vulnerable, less likely to be torn or bitten.

"I have never seen urts so large!" called Hendow.

"We are of the People!" said the leader of the beasts.

"Amazing," said Hendow to the small fellow, whom, he took it, rightly, was in association with the beasts. "How do you make them talk?"

"Do not let him anger you!" called the small fellow to the beasts. "Can you not see? He is tricking you!"

But I think they were not prepared to listen to him. Their attention was on Hendow. I moaned, bound at the rail, helpless. I moved my wrists. How helplessly they were held in place, so perfectly behind me, by the binding fiber! I could not begin to free myself!

"It is a marvelous trick," called Hendow to the small fellow. "Do it again! Make them seem to speak!"

The leader of the beasts, then, in fury, and in some inhuman, snarling, barbarous, fierce tongue, something like the roar of a lion, the hiss of a sleen, the snarl of a panther, yet clearly, frighteningly, an articulated stream of sound, some form of modulated utterance, communicated with its fellows. He then pointed to Hendow. In these moments, of course, the sleen was forgotten. It, however, had never taken its eyes off the nearest of the beasts. The first beast charged at Hendow but never reached him. Borko sprang for its throat, seized it in his jaws, and clung to that great body, his back four legs tearing and ripping at its belly. The other beast leaped to the aid of its fellow, but Hendow struck it on the back of its neck with his sword. It did not penetrate. It was stopped by the thick vertebrae, but blood drenched its back. It spun about to seize Hendow, but he thrust at it with his sword. The blade entered its body by six inches, but the beast stood there, then, slowed, stopped, regarding him. It did not fall. Hendow stepped back. I think only then did he fully comprehend the nature of the beasts, their power, strength, their energy, how difficult it might be to kill or disable such a thing. The two fellows of the small man rushed forward. Hendow stepped back to meet their charge. Mirus tried to rise, but could not. I felt Tupita's hands at my bonds. She was trying to untie them. The beast Hendow had struck returned to the fray with Borko. The leader of the beasts crouched near them, on all fours, circling them, wild-eyed, waiting its chance. Borko and the two beasts rolled in the grass, snarling, turning and rolling, tearing, biting in a savage blur. It was hard even to tell them apart, or where one might be, so swiftly did their positions change. "Sword! Sword!" said the leader of the beasts, near the fighting animals, beckoning to the bearded man, pointing to the fighting beasts. He himself perhaps knew the danger of entering such a violent, unpredictable tangle of teeth and claws. With a sword one might perhaps strike from the outside. The fellow who had been with the bearded man, at the instigation of his commander, hurried to the fighting animals, to try and strike the sleen. To be sure, there is not inconsiderable danger even there. Suppose the sleen, struck, suddenly turns on you. Tupita freed my neck from the railing. Hendow felled one of the cohorts of the small fellow. Then he turned to engage the bearded fellow who, after urging his man to the fray of beasts, not caring to join it himself, had come cautiously forward. He preferred, it seemed, a human antagonist. But he had, too, as I realized in a moment, a plan. The other cohort of the small fellow, frightened, backed away. The bearded fellow defended himself desperately. He, too, was very skilled. He was protecting himself. It is difficult to strike a man, I gather, who is primarily concerned to defend himself. "Fight!" cried Hendow to him. "Strike the other fellow!" called the bearded man to the cohort of the small fellow. "Kill him!" Mirus could not defend himself. Tupita screamed in misery, leaving off in her labor to free me. The cohort of the small fellow raised his blade and rushed on Mirus. Hendow turned to defend Mirus, and did so, stopping the assailant, spitting him on his blade, but, in doing this, of course, as the bearded man had doubtless hoped, he had opened his own guard. I screamed, and saw Hendow stiffen, thrust through by the bearded man's weapon. The bearded fellow then drew it back. "He is finished," he said. Hendow sank to his knees, beside Mirus, then went to all fours. The bearded man kicked away his weapon. Hendow, of course, had realized that in defending Mirus he would have exposed himself to the blow of the antagonist on his left. But he had not hesitated. Tupita had fled from behind the railing, where she had been attempting to free me and ran to cover the body of Mirus with her own. The bearded man, however, was not interested in Mirus. Perhaps, even, he thought him already dead. His sword, still clutched in his hand, was down. He wiped it on his leg. He then went to where the animals were, but not too closely. There, too, but not too near them either, was the small fellow. The other man, too, who was the last of those who had come forward with the leader to acquire slaves earlier, now stood back. He was white-faced. He held his arm. It was lacerated. His sword was bloodied. I did not even know if he had managed to strike the sleen. I had been concerned with Hendow and Mirus. One of the beasts in the tangle, oddly, seemed inert, trapped, dragged about. Its head was loose on its shoulders, almost like a toy on a string. Then the bulk of the beast, freed, fell to the side, lifeless in the grass. It had been the first of the beasts to approach Borko and Hendow, the one which had seemed amused upon hearing the warning of the small fellow. It had learned, however, and its fellows, as well, now, I think, the dangerousness of the sleen. The second beast grappled with Borko, thrusting his head up and back. Such beasts had not only the teeth and claws of predators, but prehensile appendages of a sort not unlike those selected for in arboreal or climbing forms of life. Both it and Borko were covered with blood. I thought it might want to break Borko's neck, but then I realized it was only trying to expose the throat. Meanwhile Borko's hind legs, the four of them, were tearing at its abdomen. The beast bit at Borko's throat but there it encountered the heavy, spiked collar. The spikes cut through the sides of its face and tongue. Blood gushed from its mouth. It howled in rage. In this moment the leader of the beasts, which at times had been sitting back, almost catlike, observing, and at other times had been crouching, and moving about the fighting animals, waiting to strike, seeing its opportunity, leapt to the fray, seizing Borko's collar from the back, but, I think to its astonishment, it might as well have tried to grasp an exploding bomb, for the sleen spun about, twisting in the collar, biting and tearing. The leader of the beasts, astonished, fell back. He put his paw to his breast and wiped blood from his fur. He looked at it, disbelievingly. It was his own blood. Borko tried to leap at him but one of his hind legs was caught in gut. The other beast screamed in pain. It seized Borko then by the hind leg, dragging him back, back from attacking his leader. The leader crouched growling on the grass, warning Borko away. But he did not seem eager to again enter the range of the sleen's jaws. "Kill it!" screamed the small fellow to the engaged beast. "Kill it!" he screamed to the bearded man, and to the other fellow, with the torn arm. "Use your sword!" said the bearded man to his cohort. "Use yours," said the fellow, bitterly. Tupita wept over Mirus, who had fallen, who was unconscious. With her hands and hair she tried to stanch the flow of his blood. Hendow, on all fours, lifted his head. The grass was drenched with blood at his side. His sword was gone. The engaged beast, now that it was behind Borko, holding him, began to inch up his body, clinging to the fur with its claws and teeth. Borko's attention was still focused on the leader of the beasts, who, warily, bleeding, was beyond his reach. Hendow groped for the knife at his belt. I saw the huge, balled fist of the engaged beast lift and then come down like a hammer on the back of Borko, again and again. I think such a blow might have shattered railings. It then loosened the collar from behind, and cast it aside, and lifting the sleen into the air, bit through the back of its neck, then dropped it to its feet. The leader of the beasts leaped in its place, up and down, howling, lifting and raising its arms. The victorious beast, itself a mass of blood and wounds, stood over Borko. It then, curiously, observed its abdomen. With one paw it thrust back into its belly the exposed gut. Hendow staggered to his feet, his knife raised. The victorious beast turned to look at us. Its lips drew back, over the fangs. Then Hendow drove his knife into its breast, to the hilt. The bearded man rushed forward and struck Hendow from behind, twice. Then Hendow fell to the grass, dead. The beast, too, a moment later, fell dead. The men were white-faced, and trembling. Even the leader of the beasts, I think, was shaken.

There had been five men who had come to acquire slaves. Of these two survived, including the bearded man, who had been their leader. The other fellow, not the bearded man, had been lacerated, probably in an attempt to interfere in the tangle of fighting beasts. Indeed, he may even have struck, perhaps with an uncertain blow, not Borko, but the other beast, who had perhaps then, or the leader, turned on him, biting at him, forcing him back. He had not cared, it seemed, the unwisdom of such a project perhaps now clearer to him, to approach the beasts a second time. Three men had been in league with the beasts. Of these only one survived, the small fellow. There had been three beasts. Of these two were dead, one by Borko, the other by Hendow. The leader of the beasts, too, was bloody, but I think his wounds were not grievous. He had been probably protected by the width of his body, affording little place for the closing of jaws, and the sturdiness of his ribs.

"It is a bloody afternoon," said the bearded man.

"My beautiful friends are dead," said the small man, looking at the beasts.

The leader of the beasts growled at him.

"Who were these two?" asked the fellow with the torn arm, indicating Hendow and Mirus.

"That one," said the bearded man, indicating Hendow," was a fine swordsman."

"But what was he doing here?" asked the small man.

"He had a sleen," said the bearded man. "He was doubtless a slave hunter."

"The other one may still be alive," said the fellow with the injured arm. The blood was slow on it now, as he had his hand clasped over the wound. Blood, as he held the wound, was between his fingers, and was visible also in rivulets, running to his wrist and the back of his hand.

Tupita looked up, frightened, from where she crouched over Mirus. His eyes were now open. Her hair and hands were covered with blood. She had stopped the bleeding. I did not think, however, he could rise.

"Kill him," said the bearded man to his cohort.

"No!" protested Tupita.

"No," said the man.

"He is helpless," said the bearded fellow.

"Do it yourself, if you wish," said the wounded man.

"Very well," said the bearded man.

"No, please!" begged Tupita.

The bearded man regarded her, amused.

"Please, no," she wept.

"And what is he to you?" he inquired.

"I am his love slave!" she wept.

"Ah, yes," he said, amused.

"Do not hurt him," she wept. "I will do anything for you!"

"Do you think you are a free woman," he asked, "bargaining

for the life of her lover, willing to surrender all her fortune that he might live, willing perhaps even to strip herself and make herself my slave, to serve me thenceforth with all perfections, if I will but spare him?"

"No, Master," she wept. "I am not a free woman."

"Do you bargain?" he inquired.

"No, Master," she said.

"Do you have anything with which to bargain?" he asked.

"No, Master," she wept. "But I beg you to spare him!"

"Do you really think I am going to leave an enemy behind me?" he asked.

"Please, Master!" she begged.

Mirus regarded him, dully, half conscious. He could not rise.

"He came here," said the bearded man, amused, "it seems, for the blood of a slave, and if I recall the intent of his glance, for that slave." He indicated me. "Is that not so, my dear?" he asked.

"Yes, Master," I said.

"We have saved your life, then," he said.

I nodded. I supposed they had, or the beasts.

"If we leave this fellow behind us, and he recovers, as he seems a very determined fellow," he said, "I would expect he would resume your pursuit."

"Yes, Master," I said. That seemed quite probable.

"You untied her neck from the railing," said the bearded fellow to Tupita. "Apparently you wanted her free. Very well, free her, then. Finish freeing her."

"Please, no," said Tupita.

"Do not fear," he said. "She will not be free long."

"Please," wept Tupita.

"Now," said the bearded man.

Tupita, weeping, came to where I was, before the railing. Sobbing, fumbling, with difficulty she freed my ankles. It seemed she was loath to free my hands.

"Callisthenes approaches," said the fellow holding his arm. He was looking back over the meadow.

"He will be concerned with the delay," said the bearded man to the small fellow. "We left him with the slave wagon, with Alcinous and Portus."

The approaching fellow hesitated, understandably enough, in seeing the beast. Yet, noting that his fellows stood with it, and that they beckoned him forward, he continued to advance, though with some caution.

"What has happened?" asked the newcomer. "What is that?"

"Do not mind it," said the bearded fellow, lightly. "It is friendly."

"There has been war here," said the other man.

"Alcinous and Portus are anxious to be on their way," said the newcomer. "It will soon be dark." He looked at the body of Borko, in the grass. The collar had been removed by the second beast. "There may be sleen about," he said.

"That is a domestic sleen," said the small fellow.

"It was killed by our friend here," said the wounded man, ironically, indicating the beast that had slain Borko.

"These have been well worth waiting for, have they not?" asked the bearded man.

The newcomer's eyes glistened. "An excellent bag of slaves," he said.

"And surely they are worth at least five silver tarsks apiece," said the small fellow.

"Surely, at least," agreed the newcomer.

"Solid, unclipped silver tarsks," said the small fellow.

"Surely," said the newcomer.

The small fellow looked at the bearded man.

"We had some trouble with these two," said the bearded man, indicating Hendow, and the prostrate Mirus, "but there is nothing to fear now."

The newcomer looked around, apprehensively.

"Are things all right at the wagon?" asked the bearded man.

"Yes," said the newcomer. "There was a traveler on the road a few Ehn ago, but he is gone now."

"Go back to the wagon," said the bearded man. "Tell Alcinous and Portus we will be along in a moment."

He turned about, and retraced his steps across the meadow. The wagon, I supposed, was hidden somewhere in the woods, away from the level area, away from the road.

It had been the good fortune of Callisthenes, Alcinous and Portus, it seemed, not to have been in the meadow earlier.

The wounded man's arm had apparently stopped bleeding, or nearly so. With one hand, and his teeth, he tore his tunic, and bound cloth about his arm. Some blood came through the cloth, but very little, little more than a sudden, fresh stain, then nothing.

He looked down at me. I was still on my knees. Tupita had stopped working at the bonds on my wrists when the newcomer had appeared. My wrists were still bound behind my back. He was the fellow who had looked at me, before, during the dealing. Again, frightened, as before, I opened my knees more widely. My relationship to him was very clearly defined.

He grinned, and I, again, put my head down.

I recalled how the eyes of the other man, too, he who had come from the wagon, had looked upon us, all.

"Have you not finished untying her?" asked the bearded man.

"Forgive me, Master," said Tupita, and bent again swiftly, to her task. It was hard for her, for the knots had been tied by a man.

"Stupid, slow slave," said the bearded man, and came behind me. He thrust Tupita to the side. He then put his blade beside him, on the grass. He then undid the knots. From the fact that he had not cut the fiber I gathered that I was to be again confined in it. He retrieved his blade. He then stepped back from me, and motioned that I should get up. I did so, unsteadily, for I had been closely bound, hand and foot.

I stood before the rail. Tupita was back of me, and half under the rail, where she had been thrust. She, frightened, was partly on her side, and partly on her elbow. She was very beautiful there, bare-breasted, her neck in the slave collar of Ionicus, about her hips and thighs the brief shreds of the skirt of her work tunic, that tunic sacrificed that I might have at least the little I wore, a slave strip thrust in a narrow belt of rolled cloth. Tela, incredibly luscious, in the rectangle of red silk, which she had had to wear on the orders of Aulus, and Mina and Cara, half-stripped, scarcely less beautiful, bound in that order, still neck-roped to the rail, were to my left.

"Step forward, my half-naked beauty," said the bearded man, coaxingly, gesturing with his hand.

I came out a little from the rail.

"There," he said, pointing, grinning, "is the fellow who followed you, who would have your blood."

I looked at Mirus.

"What a fortunate slave you are, to have him so at your mercy," said the fellow.

I looked at him. I did not really, completely, understand him. Surely they were not going to let me run away. He had told Tupita I would not be free for long. Too, they would surely not be concerned for me. Too, they had paid five tarsks for me, silver tarsks.

"Should you recover, you would follow her again, would you not?" he asked Mirus, crouching down by him, eagerly.

Mirus looked at him weakly, but in fury and pride. "Yes," he said. "I would."

"There," said the bearded fellow, "is the sword of the slave hunter in the grass. We give you our permission to go to it, to pick it up. Yes, you may touch it. You may hold it for a moment or two. Yes, even though you are a slave. You may use it to finish this fellow now. Then you will be finished with him. No longer then do you need to live in terror, shrinking back at every strange sound, every shadow in the darkness."

"Do not, Tuka, I beg you!" cried Tupita. "He cannot move. He is helpless. Do not hurt him!"

"Doubtless she will not make a clean job of it, with her girl's strength," said the bearded man to Mirus, "but I am sure, in time, she will get the job done."

Tupita burst into tears.

I did not even want to go near the sword. It was almost as though it radiated out warnings, and alarms and terrors, and invisible flames that might burn me. It was a weapon! I dared not even approach it.

"Do not be afraid," said the bearded man.

Too, I did not want to touch it because it had been the sword of Hendow. Too, he had used it to save the life of his beloved friend, Mirus, though in doing the deed he must have understood, opening himself to the blade of his enemy as he had, that he had made his own life forfeit. How ironic then, how unthinkable, that I should use that same blade now to kill Mirus.

Mirus turned his head toward me. Even in his weakness, his eyes blazed with hatred. "Pick up the sword," he said. "Use it, while you can!"

I looked at him, sick.

"Do it!" he said.

I looked at him, in misery.

"Expect no mercy from me," he said. "If ever I should be able, I shall seek you out. I shall hunt you. I shall pursue you with the relentlessness of a sleen."

"Go ahead," urged the bearded man, eagerly. "Do not be afraid! Show that you are brave! Show that you are strong! Show what you are made of! Do it! We will admire you! We will praise you!"

I fell to my knees in the grass.

"I may not touch a weapon," I said.

"You have our permission!" said the bearded man.

I shook my head, frightened.

"You are afraid," he said.

"Yes, Master," I said.

"You are a weakling," he said.

"Yes, Master," I said. "But even if I were not a coward and a weakling, I would not do it."

"Brave Tuka!" cried Tupita.

"I am a female slave," I said. "I exist for the pleasure, service and love of men. I may not hurt them. Too, I do not wish to do so. Kill me if you must."

"We will give you your freedom, if you do so," said the bearded man.

"Forgive me, Master. No, Master," I said.

"Put your head down to the grass," he said. "Throw your hair forward, exposing the back of your neck."

I obeyed.

"Please, no, Master!" cried Tupita.

I felt the edge of the sword at the back of my neck. I felt it above the collar, move against the small hairs on the back of my neck. The blade seemed very sharp, for the sturdiness of the weapon.

"Please, Master, do not!" cried Tupita.

"Perhaps you have changed your mind," said the bearded man.

"No, Master. Forgive me, Master," I said.

I felt the blade lift from my neck. I closed my eyes. Then I heard him laugh.

I opened my eyes, startled.

I heard the sword thrust into its sheath, its guard halting its further progress.

"Bara!" he snapped.

I flung myself to my belly in the grass, putting my hands behind me, wrists crossed, and crossing my ankles, too.

I lay there in confusion, in obedience.

He went to pick up the binding fiber which had been removed from my ankles by Tupita, from my wrists, a bit before, by himself.

I had been spared!

He returned to crouch over me. Tightly then were my wrists and ankles tied. He knew well how to tie women. "Oh!" I said, as my ankles were pulled up and fastened to my wrists. He then pulled me to my knees and I knelt helplessly, closely and perfectly bound, before him. He seemed amused.

"Master?" I asked.

"You are an excellent slave," he said.

"Master?" I said.

"It is to that that you owe your life," he said.

"I do not understand," I said.

"And your slave intuitions are excellent," he said.

"My slave intuitions?" I asked.

"Yes," he said.

"I do not understand, Master," I said.

"Do you truly think we would have let you live, if you had slain a free man?" he asked.

"You promised me my freedom," I whispered.

"Once you had done the deed," he said, "we would have cut off your hands. Then we would have cut off your head."

"You promised me my freedom," I said.

"And we would have given it to you after the deed, have no fear, for a moment, for our amusement," he said. "Then we would have returned you to bondage for your punishment."

"Yes, Master," I said, trembling.

"Thus we would have seen to it that you were punished as a slave, and died as a slave."

"Yes, Master," I said.

"See that you continue to serve men well," he said.

"Yes, Master," I said.

"Oh, Tuka, Tuka!" cried Tupita, softly, in joy.

The bearded man turned to look upon her, and she shrank back. "See that you, too," he said, "continue to serve men well."

"Yes, Master!" she said.

He then looked at Tela.

"Yes, Master!" she said.

His gaze then fell upon Mina, and Cara.

"Yes, Master!" said Mina.

"Yes, Master!" said Cara.

"What of him?" asked the man with the bandage on his arm, indicating Mirus.

"I will kill him," said the bearded man. He drew the sword from his sheath.

"No!" cried Tupita, running to Mirus, covering his body with her own.

"I will kill, her, too," said the bearded man.

"No, please, Master!" I cried.

"I keep the five tarsks!" cried the small fellow.

"Ho, Fulvius! Fulvius!" we heard, a man running toward us, across the meadow. It was Callisthenes, he who had come earlier, from the wagon, who had been ordered to return to it.

The huge beast, that which had survived, who had been the leader of the others, rose up from where it had been sitting, resting back on its haunches, in the grass, half crouching now, to look. It was no longer bleeding but its entire chest was matted with dried blood.

"I told you to go back to the wagon," said the bearded man, apparently Fulvius. "You were to wait with Alcinous and Portus."

"They are dead!" gasped the man. "I found them dead!"

Fulvius and the man with the bandaged arm exchanged glances.

I saw Tupita draw back from Mirus. He rose up, painfully, on one elbow.

"How did they die?" demanded Fulvius. "What was the nature of their wounds?"

"By the sword," said Callisthenes, breathing heavily. "The sword!"

"They were set upon in stealth?"

"From the nature of their wounds it would seem they were attacked frontally," said Callisthenes. "And both their swords were drawn."

"How many assailed them?" asked Fulvius.

"I think, one," said Callisthenes.

"There must be more," said Fulvius. "Alcinous and Portus were not unskilled."

"I do not know," said Callisthenes. "Perhaps."

"What of tracks?" asked Fulvius.

"I saw those of Alcinous and Portus, and detected only those of one other," he said.

"What was the nature of their wounds?" asked Fulvius.

"The wound of Alcinous was deft, lateral and to the heart," said Callisthenes. "Portus was run through."

"Portus died second," said Fulvius. "In Alcinous the fellow did not wish to risk the jamming of his blade."

The fellow with the bandaged arm opened and closed his hand, testing its grip.

"The wagon is gone, the tharlarion?" asked Fulvius.

"No," said Callisthenes.

"What of the purses of Alcinous and Portus?" asked Fulvius.

"Gone," said Callisthenes.

"Good," said Fulvius. "Then we are dealing with a brigand."

"He has probably fled by now," said the small fellow, eagerly.

"The wounds of Alcinous and Portus were frontal wounds," said Callisthenes.

"Why would he not flee?" asked the small fellow.

"Perhaps he has fled," said Fulvius. "We do not know."

"He may linger in the vicinity," said the fellow with the bandaged arm. "He may be hungry for more gold."

"And there may be several of them, a band!" said the small fellow.

"Perhaps," said Fulvius. "But I do not think so."

"What shall we do?" asked the fellow with the bandaged arm.

"Can you handle your sword?" asked Fulvius.

"I think so," he said.

"Callisthenes?" asked Fulvius.

"Yes," he said.

"The beast is gone," said the man with the bandaged arm, suddenly.

Its departure had been unnoticed.

"Where is it?" demanded Fulvius of the small fellow.

"I do not know," he said.

"It is wounded," said Fulvius. "Too, I suspect it has had its fill of blood for the day."

The small fellow looked about, anxiously.

"Are you with us?" asked Fulvius.

"I am not a fighter," said the small fellow. "I am going to go away, too!"

"Your beast has deserted you," said Fulvius.

"I did without them before, and can do so again," he said. He hastened to his pack, near the blanket.

"Leave the blanket, and the coins upon it," said Fulvius.

"No!" cried the small fellow.

"Throw your purse upon it, too," advised Fulvius.

"No!" he cried.

"Do so, quickly," said Fulvius, "unless you prefer to put your pack and clothes upon it as well and take your leave with no more than a length of binding to your name, that fastening your hands behind you."

Angrily the small fellow hurled his purse to the blanket, shouldered his pack, and hurried from the meadow, going in the direction opposite to that from which Callisthenes had come.

"What if the beast returns?" asked the fellow with the bandaged arm.

"I do not think it will," said Fulvius. "If it does, I do not know where our small friend went, do you?"

"No," laughed the fellow with the bandaged arm.

"If it is angry, presumably it will be angry with him. Perhaps it will even think it has been deserted. Perhaps it will even track him down."

"In such a case, I would not care to be him," said the man with the bandaged arm.

"And if it does return here," said Fulvius, "we may pretend to deal with it, as he did."

"You may deal with it," said the man with the bandaged arm. "I want nothing to do with it."

"We need only watch our chance, and kill it. It is wounded. There are three of us."

"Perhaps," shrugged the man with the bandaged arm.

"But I do not think it will return," said Fulvius.

"I hope not," said the fellow with the bandaged arm.

"I did not know there were such things," said Callisthenes.

"I did not either," said the fellow with the bandaged arm.

"I will kill this fellow," said Fulvius. "Then we will go to the wagon, and see if we can find the other."

Tupita again put her body between those of Fulvius and Mirus. Mirus was now sitting up, his head in his hands.

"Kill him later," said the fellow with the bandaged arm. "It will soon be dark."

"Very well," said Fulvius.

They then set out in the direction from which Callisthenes had come.

It would have taken but a moment to thrust Tupita aside and kill Mirus, but I sensed that the man with the injured arm, again, had little taste for dispatching a helpless foe. Fulvius, perhaps more ruthless or practical in such matters, but a judicious tactician, had, I think, not wished to proceed at that time with an action which might bring about a disagreement or confrontation with his subordinate, one of whose sword he might shortly have need. Too, he could always kill Mirus later. He did not care, as I recalled, to leave enemies behind him.

"Can you walk, Master?" begged Tupita, crouching near Mirus. "Can you run? They are gone! They will be coming back! Get up! Run! Flee!"

Mirus looked over at me, his eyes glazed with pain.

"Get up, Master!" begged Tupita. "I will help you!"

She helped him to his feet. He stood, unsteadily. He looked at me.

"Good, Master!" cried Tupita. "Lean on me! I will try to help you!"

How strong Mirus must be, I thought, that he could even stand.

"Hurry, Master," said Tupita. "Hurry!"

But suddenly he moved his arm and flung her to the side.

"Master!" she cried.

He bent down, nearly fell, and picked up the blade which had fallen from the hand of the man who had been urged earlier by Fulvius to kill him, he whom Hendow had dropped, the blade with which he himself had been threatened.

His eyes wild he staggered toward me, the blade lifted over his head, in two hands.

I screamed.

Tupita leaped to her feet and flung herself between us, shielding me with her own body.

"Stupid slave!" cried Mirus. "Withdraw! Get out of the way!"

"You are out of your head, Mirus!" she cried. "You are not the master I know. She is only a slave. Do not hurt her!"

"She betrayed me!" he cried, the blade poised.

"Hendow, your friend, loved her!" she cried. "He cared for her. He sought her! He saved your life! Will you now kill her with the very blade from which he saved you?"

"She betrayed me!" he snarled.

I was startled to hear her asserveration of Hendow's affection for me. He was so terrible, so fierce. Yet it seemed he had not in truth followed me to recapture me and punish me, visiting upon me the terrible severities to be suitably visited upon a runaway slave. I remembered how gently he had touched me on the side of the head. I wept, confused, startled, astonished, in wonder, considering his love. Had I been so blind to it? Yet I do not doubt that he would have kept me always, even in his love, as a helpless slave. He was that sort of man. Indeed, how could I, a woman, truly, fully, love any other sort?

I saw he did not want to strike Tupita. Her beauty, so wild and pathetic, bare-breasted, in its collar and shreds of skirt, was between us.

"I tried to warn you, Master," I wept. "I tried to withdraw! You would not let me. You would not listen! Masters were watching!"

"What would you have had her do?" cried Tupita. "Do you not understand? We are slaves, slaves! What do you think her life would have been worth if she had not been successful in her work? If she had even been suspected in her work would this, too, not have been dangerous for her masters?"

"Get out of the way!" he cried.

"You are not yourself," she cried. "Do not kill her!"

"Get out of the way," he cried, "or you will die first!"

"Go, Tupita!" I wept. "Go, run!"

"Move!" cried Mirus.

"No," said Tupita, firmly. "If it is your will, so be it. I will die first."

I saw the blade waver.

"It is my desire to be pleasing to my master," she said.

I saw the blade lower. Mirus stepped back.

"By the love I bear you, if not the love you bear me," she said, "spare her."

I saw Mirus look at me, with hatred. But he crouched down then, the point of the blade in the dirt, his hands on the guard, steadying himself with the weapon, almost as with a staff. "She may live," he said. Then he sobbed.

"Oh, my master, I love you!" wept Tupita, rushing to him. "I love you! I love you!"

"I have followed you, hunting for you, even from Brundisium," said Mirus. "I traveled from city to city. I took service here and there. But always I searched for you. I did not wish to live without you. I sought you even in Argentum."

I recalled I had asked Mirus if he had been looking for me in Argentum. He had not been.He had claimed he was seeking service, and his fortune. I had been somewhat chagrined by this answer, that he had not been looking for me. I now realized that he had been seeking Tupita. Many Gorean men, in their vanity, will not admit to caring for slaves. Even the thought of it, it seems, would embarrass them. Who could care for a meaningless slut in a collar? Yet too often, for just such women, luscious and helpless, and in bondage, men are prepared to kill. Indeed, more than one war on Gor has been fought to recover a single slave. I should have realized that Mirus was after Tupita. Indeed, had I not still found him so attractive, and had I not, in my own vanity, been so concerned with my own possible beauty and desirability, rather than that of others, too, I might have understood that immediately. Certainly he had inquired closely after her. I had not been able to help him. Then he had fallen to the men of Tyrrhenius, later to be sold to the black chain of Ionicus.

"Oh," cried Tupita, "I love you so! I love you so, my master!"

Slave girls must address all free men as "Master." Commonly, however, the expression "my Master," when it is used, is reserved for the actual master of the girl, he who is her literal master, he who literally owns her. For example, when I was in Argentum it was proper for me to use the expression "Master" to the men of Tyrrhenius, and indeed, to all free men, but the expression, "my Master," if used, would have been appropriately, suitably, addressed only to Tyrrhenius. To be sure, sometimes a girl will use the expression "my Master" to a man who is not her literal master, to suggest to him that he is to her even as would be her literal owner. Sometimes that is done in an attempt to wheedle with the male, or flatter him. It can be dangerous, however, as it might, say, earn her a cuffing. He knows, of course, he is not her literal owner. As Tupita used the expression, though, in such a spontaneous, and heartfelt way, it expressed in its way, I think, a truth of her heart, that she in her heart belonged to him, that she in her heart was his slave.

"Try to stand, Master," urged Tupita.

But he crouched where he had, his hands on the guard of the sword, keeping himself upright with its aid.

"Get up, Master," said Tupita. "Try to stand. Try! Please, Master! We must hurry away, before the men come back!"

"It is too late!" cried Tela, fastened at the rail. I squirmed in my bonds, on the grass. I, too, like Tela, Mina and Cara, though I was not bound at the rail, was helpless.

"We could not find him," said Fulvius.

"Perhaps it is just as well," said Callisthenes.

"Coffle the sluts," said Fulvius to Callisthenes. "We will take them to the wagon. I will finish this fellow off."

"No!" cried Tupita.

"He is on his feet," said the fellow with the bandaged arm.

Mirus had struggled to his feet, holding the sword. "Get behind me," he said to Tupita.

"Master!" she said.

"Now," he said.

She obeyed.

"Ah, Sempronius," said Fulvius to the fellow with the bandaged arm, "look at this!" This was the first time I had heard the name of the man with the bandaged arm.

"I see," said Sempronius.

"There is no point now in your squeamishness," said Fulvius. "You see? There he is! He is up and ready, prepared for a fair and proper fight."

"He can scarcely stand, he can scarcely hold his sword," said Sempronius.

"Such upon occasion are the fortunes of war," said Fulvius.

"Take the women, and let him go," said Sempronius.

"You may not have this woman," said Mirus, indicating Tupita.

"Let them take me away!" she begged.

"No," he said.

"I choose not to leave an enemy behind me," said Fulvius. "Do you gainsay me in this?"

Fulvius, I suppose, if nothing else, understood that Mirus, if he survived, would be likely, sometime, to pursue them, perhaps for his honor, perhaps to recover Tupita, or me, perhaps to avenge Hendow.

Sempronius shrugged. "You are first here," he said. "Your sword, if nothing else, makes you so."

"On guard, my friend," said Fulvius to Mirus.

"No!" wept Tupita.

"Back, slave!" said Sempronius. "Let him have at least the dignity of dying on his feet, with a sword in his hand."

Mirus struggled to lift the blade. He held the hilt with both hands.

"Look!" cried Tupita, pointing out, over the meadow, behind Fulvius and Sempronius. Callisthenes was to one side. He had delayed in releasing the girls from the rail, to coffle them, apparently choosing to postpone his work until the resolution of the pending affray with Mirus.

Fulvius stepped back a few steps, and turned to look. Sempronius, half turned, was watching something. He removed his blade from his sheath. I heard, too, to my left, and behind me, the blade of Callisthenes leave its sheath.

I tried to rise up a bit on my knees, but, tied as I was, wrists to ankles, I could not do so. I could see little more than the high grass from where I was.

"You could not find him," said Mirus. "But it seems he has found you."

I could then see, approaching over the grass, a solitary figure.

"It is a brigand," said Fulvius. "He is masked."

I gasped. I feared for a moment I might die. My heart began to beat wildly. I did not wish to faint. I suddenly felt great heat, helpless heat in my belly. It seemed my thighs flamed. I was bound helplessly. My responses were suitable for a slave. I hoped the men could not smell me. Then I was terrified.

"His features are well concealed,"said Callisthenes.

"Fan out," said Fulvius. "Callisthenes to my left, Sempronius on the right."

Suddenly the stranger moved toward Fulvius with great speed. The suddeness of this attack took Fulvius by surprise. He had barely time to lift his sword. I could not even follow the movements of the steel, so swift they were! Both Callisthenes and Sempronius, after having been arrested for a moment, startled, almost in shock, at the speed of stranger's rush, hurried toward the swordsmen, but then they stopped. The stranger had moved swiftly back, warily. Before him Fulvius had fallen. He was on all fours, with his head down. He trembled. He spat and coughed blood. Then he sank to the grass. He slowly rolled to his back. The sword left his hand. Then he stared upward, at the sky, but did not see it.

Tela screamed, only now seeming to comprehend what had been done.

The stranger had not permitted them to take him between them, Fulvius engaging him, Callisthenes and Sempronius seeking their openings from the sides. He had moved too quickly, before they could close their simple formation, before they could join their forces. Even Fulvius, whom I knew from before was a master of defense, had not been able to stand before him. I do not think steel had crossed more than three or four times before the stranger had leapt back, and then backed away.

I shuddered.

I felt terror before this man, this swordsman, this fighter. I had not known one could handle steel like that. It had been an awesome exhibition of prowess. I was shaken, even at the thought of it. For a brief moment I wanted desperately to run away. But I was bound.

The stranger motioned with his sword that Callisthenes and Sempronius should move together. Reluctantly they did so, carefully keeping blade room between them. Their leader was gone. They could form no plan, it seemed, between them as to who should hold, who should seek an opening. Neither cared, it seemed, to advance. It there was an initiative here, or some advantage, oddly enough it seemed to lie on the side of the stranger, not the pair of them. They kept their eyes on him. Fulvius, I suspect, had been a very fine swordsman. Certainly Sempronius, earlier, had acknowledged his supremacy among them, with the blade. Yet Fulvius had lasted hardly an exchange with the stranger. This could not fail but weigh with them. Too, I did not doubt but what in their minds were the fates of their fellows, Alcinous and Portus, back at the wagon.

I looked about.

The other girls, too, were dumbfounded. I think they, even Gorean girls, in a culture where the knife and sword were familiar, common weapons, had never seen anything like this. Mirus, even, seemed stunned. He had lowered his own sword. Tupita, near him, white-faced, held him, supporting him.

I regarded the stranger. He was tall, very tall. He was broad-shouldered and narrow-waisted. He had long, bronzed arms. His hands were very large. I trembled. He held a steel sword, where such things made law. He was tall, fierce and hard. I was very small, and soft and weak. It was only the swords of Callisthenes and Sempronius which separated him from me. I saw myself then, noting his eyes in the mask, the subject of his gaze. I saw the point of his sword. He, looking at me, moved it, slightly. Inwardly I laughed with joy. I swiftly, in response to his gesture, as I could, spread my knees before him. Callisthenes, first, then Sempronius, hurled their swords, blade first, into the earth at their feet. The handles, upright, were visible in the grass. We belonged to the stranger! I looked wildly at him.

He motioned Callisthenes and Sempronius away from their weapons.

Callisthenes, I suspect, was not a fine swordsman. He had expressed some relief or satisfaction at their earlier inability to locate the stranger. I think he had not really wanted to meet up with him, he who had slain his fellows, Alcinous and Portus. Sempronius, probably more skilled, had been wounded.

He ordered Callisthenes and Sempronius to stand to the side. He then approached Mirus. Mirus thrust Tupita behind him, and held his sword, ready to defend himself and his slave. The stranger then, with a decisive movement, sheathed his sword. It cracked into the sheath. Mirus grinned, and lowered his sword. Then, overcome with his exhaustion, his weakness, the loss of blood, he sat down in the grass.

The stranger came to the rail and examined Cara, and then Mina, and then Tela. "You are well curved," he said to Tela. "Thank you, Master," she said. Instantly I hated Tela. Then he came to stand before me. "You, too, are well curved," he said. "Thank you, Master!" I said. I cast a glance at Tela. "And you look well, tied so helplessly," he said. "Thank you, Msater!" I said. I cast another glance at Tela. He had said two things to me, and only one to her! But when I looked back he had turned away from me! I squirmed in my bonds. I wanted to cry out "Master!" to him, but I did not dare. I did not want to be whipped. Did he think I could not recognize him in his mask? Did he not remember me?

We remained bound for several Ahn, until well after dark. In this time he had walked Callisthenes and Sempronius before him, back toward the trees, in which direction, it seemed, lay the slave wagon. There they had apparently buried three bodies, those of Licinius, who had been slain by Hendow, and Alcinous and Portus, victims, it seems, of his own blade. Too, from the wagon, or its vicinity, they retrieved supplies. These, however, were not immediately fed to us. Sempronius and Callisthenes first busied themselves, under the stranger's supervision, with burying what humans lay about. The strange beasts were left for jards. Borko, however, was buried beside Hendow. The graves of the men had swords thrust in the earth, that they might thus be marked. Mirus scratched a board, taken from the ruins of the buildings about, which he fixed on the common grave of Borko and Hendow. I cannot read Gorean. Mirus told Tupita it said, "Borko and Hendow. Hendow was of Brundisium. He was my friend." Most Gorean graves, incidentally, are not marked even in so simple a fashion. Most Goreans do not care for such things. They believe that it is a man's deeds which truly live after him, and that the difference, great or small, which they make in the world, the difference which he made, for having been there, is what is important. No matter how insignificant or tiny one is, in the Gorean belief, one is an ineradicable part of history. That can never be taken from anyone. That is better, they believe, than scratched wood or marked stone. There would be no pyres. Such might attract the attention of men about, or perhaps of tarnsmen aflight, even as far away as Venna.

"Shall we now dig two more?" saked Sempronius.

"For whom?" asked the stranger.

"For ourselves," said Sempronius, indicating himself and Callisthenes.

"No," said the stranger. "Wash. Perform the customary purifications."

Sempronius and Callisthenes looked at one another. "Very well," said Sempronius.

After they had washed and performed the rites we were fed. Of slaves only Tupita was permitted to feed herself. She also fed Mina and Cara. I was fed by Sempronius, Tela by Callisthenes. The stranger did this perhaps to torture them, I supposed, that they might be so close to half-naked female slaves and yet be forbidden to so much as touch them.

After we had been fed, and Callisthenes and Sempronius, too, had partaken of food, the stranger directed them to put us in coffle, with the exception of Tupita. He also specified the exact positions we would occupy in this coffle. Accordingly, in a given order, we were roped together by the neck. Mina, Cara and Tela were then freed of the rail, and all our ankles were untied. Mina and Cara, of course, still wore their shackles. Though it was with joyful relief that I felt my ankles at last freed from my wrists and could get up, though in pain, and stretch my legs, my hands still bound behind me, it was with chagrin that I considered my position on the coffle. I was last! Last! Did he think I did not recognize him in the mask? Did he not remember me? Did he not even know who I was, he of all men! To be sure, Tela was before me, and she had led a much larger coffle entering the work camp of Ionicus near Venna, that of the black chain. Mina and Cara were ahead of us. And Mina was first on the coffle! How proud she seemed! Look at her, so beautiful, so proud to be first!

Callisthenes and Sempronius supported Mirus between them, and helped him toward the woods. Tupita followed, closely. After them came the stranger. He paused, on his way, to pick up the swords of Callisthenes and Sempronius. He had also taken the blanket and the silver, and purses, which had been on it. The bodies, too, I gathered, of those who had been about had been relieved of what coins or valuables they might have carried. The coins of Hendow the stranger had given to Mirus. He was, then, truly a brigand! A masked brigand! 8ut how he could handle a sword! How he had fought!

The group now made its way toward the woods. We, Mina, Cara, Tela and I, in coffle, followed it. It did not even seem that they were paying any attention, to see if we came or not. We followed them, of course, docilely, like tethered animals! But, of course, we were tethered animals. We were slaves.

I looked back in the moonlight once, at the grave of Borko and Hendow. I could see the hilt of Hendow's sword there, and, behind it, the narrow board fixed in the earth by Mirus, that simple, crude marker, not bearing much of a message, really, little more than the data that Hendow had been of Brundisium, and had had a friend.

I cried on the way to the woods.

30 / The Slave Wagon

I sat up.

I could not believe what he apparently intended to do to me. Yet I suppose it was not anything that unusual for a slave.

The three moons were full. It was late. We were now in the

woods. The slave wagon was not far away. The tharlarion, unhitched, but tethered, browsed among the trees, pulling at herbs in the grass, lifting its neck to nibble at wide leaves.

Cords encircled my ankles. I could not bring my legs together. My ankles were tied at the insides of two saplings, about a yard apart. My hands were no longer tied behind me. They were braceleted there. This was far more comfortable. On the other hand whereas before I had had only to contend helplessly with simple binding fiber I was now the prisoner of clasping steel.

Surely he did not intend to put me through this! Did he not recognize me!

Was I to be treated only as another slave?

I, sitting up in this awkward position, jerked at the bracelets, sensed the sudden straightening of the linkage, heard the small metal noise, and felt the occasioned cruelty of the bands on my wrists. In struggling I could only hurt myself. The choice was mine. In the end, whether I struggled or not, whether I hurt myself or not, I would still be held, and perfectly. I cried out with frustration.

"What is wrong, Tuka?" asked Tela.

She was secured identically as I was, a few feet to my right, her ankles fastened with cords, on the insides of two saplings, about a yard apart, her wrists braceleted behind her. She had risen up on her elbows, her head turned, to look at me, in the moonlight.

"Oh, be quiet!" I said.

"Very well," she said.

"I am sorry, Tela!" I said.

"It is all right," she said. "What is wrong?"

"Nothing," I said. "Nothing!"

Tela, undoubtedly puzzled by what she must take to be my strange behavior, lay back on the leaves.

I, sitting up, jerked at the bracelets again. Again I felt pain. Again I had hurt myself. I sobbed with frustration. Was that all I was to him, only another slave?

I could see the small campfire by the wagon. Back from it a bit, to the left, Tupita was tending Mirus. About the fire, were the stranger, still masked, and, unarmed, Callisthenes and Sempronius. Their blades were hung on the side of the closed slave wagon. They were talking, and passing a bota about, which probably contained paga.

Mira and Cara, still in their shackles and manacles, from the chain of Ionicus, had been put in the slave wagon, which was locked. The slave wagon was little more in effect than a large iron box, secured on a wagon frame. Its door, in the back, was reached by a short flight of broad, wooden stairs. In the upper portion of the door there was a small aperture, about a half inch in height and six inches long, which was fitted with a sliding panel. It was now shut, latched. It could not be opened from the inside. In the bottom of the door there was a larger opening, about three inches in height and a foot in width, through which pans of water or food could be slipped into the wagon, without opening the main door. That, too, had its panel which, too, was now latched. It, too, could not be opened from the inside.

The stranger had now screwed shut the lid on the bota.

He had showed them hospitality. They had, so to speak, "shared his kettle."

They rose to their feet.

Earlier in the evening, in the frontward portion of the meadow, near the ruins of the long, low building, indeed, only a few feet in front of the rail, to which at that time Tela, Mina and Cara had still been fastened, Sempronius had fed me. Callisthenes had similarly put nourishment in the mouth of Tela, even as she was at the rail, neck-roped there. I had wondered if the stranger had permitted Callisthenes and Sempronius to feed us, half-naked slaves, in order to have them in proximity to us, whom they might not touch, as a torture for them, Gorean males.

The men were coming in this direction.

Now it seemed, however, that I had misread his intent.

Sempronius crouched before me. "Lie down," he said.

I obeyed.

How tightly my ankles were bound with cord! How closely my wrists were enclosed in steel!

He removed the belt and cloth I wore.

He then began, kneeling beside me, to caress me. I regarded him with dismay, twisting. It was his intention that I should be hot, and open, to him! I must resist! I must try to resist! What if the stranger should see! But men had changed my body. I now needed their touch, more so than I had ever dreamed could be possible, even in my moments of most frustrated passion on Earth. Let it be acknowledged straightforwardly and honestly. I had been made a slave.

"What is wrong?" asked Sempronius, puzzled.

"Nothing, Master," I said, firmly.

Sempronius had been permitted earlier in the evening to feed the slave Tuka, as Callisthenes had Tela. Tuka had knelt before him, clad only in a slave strip and belt of rolled cloth, her wrists crossed and bound behind her back, fastened closely to her crossed, bound ankles. He had put food in her mouth, and she must eat. But, as Tuka understood now, this had not been to torture him. Rather, if anything, it had been to bring him into her proximity, to excite him, to whet his appetite, to give him a foretaste of the delights which might, if he wished, await him. And, too, from the woman's point of view, she so helpless, so close to him, so much at his mercy, unable to defend herself, or even to feed herself, dependent on him for her very food, this produced a sense of distinct unease, and arousal.

I heard Tela, under the touch of Callisthenes, cry out, softly, to my right.

Sempronius knew what he was doing. I tried to steel myself, and think of other things. I turned my head to the side.

I heard Tela gasp with pleasure.

I suddenly hated being a slave! Was this possible? That I should be so casually put, so cordially put, in the liberality of a Gorean host, at the disposal of guests? But of course it was possible! I was only a slave! But why would he do this to me, to me? Was I truly to him only this, only another salve, to be put without a second thought to the purposes of guests, merely another amenity or convenience to them, as might be a napkin or finger bowl, or a comfort, such as a blanket, or an extra cushion for his couch?

I must not let Tela's cries arouse me. I must try not to hear them! What pleasure she must be enduring!

Perhaps the stranger did not recognize me?

"Oh!" I said, suddenly, softly.

Sempronius chuckled.

I knew then, and so did he, that he would conquer me.

"Is she satisfactory?" asked the stranger, standing behind Sempronius.

I looked up, wildly, at the stranger.

"It seems she will prove so," said Sempronius.

The stranger held, coiled in his right hand, a slave whip. "If you are not fully satisfied," he said, "let me know."

"Very well," said Sempronius.

I knew then that the stranger would whip me if I were not pleasing.

But I began, unable to help myself, to squirm beneath the touch of Sempronius.

"You are a hot slave," said Sempronius to me.

"Oh, oh," I moaned, softly.

"Are you not pleased?" he asked.

"Yes, Master," I sobbed. "Thank you, Master."

I heard Tela, in a moment, begging to be freed of the bracelets, that she might hold Callisthenes. He released her from one of the bracelets. Callisthenes and Sempronius apparently held the keys to our bracelets! How gracious of the stranger!

I was frightened, for I sensed that my responses were beginning to become uncontrollable.

I reared up a little, and saw, to my relief, that the stranger was back with Mirus and Tupita.

I closed my eyes.

I lay back on the leaves, gasping, my head turning from side to side.

"I cannot stand it, Master!" I said. "I cannot stand it! Do not stop! Do not stop! Oh, please, Master, do not stop!"

I loved being a slave! I loved it!

I begged Sempronius to free my hands that I might hold him, clutching my softness to him.

He twisted me a bit to one side and removed one of the bracelets. I then clutched him eagerly.

"Oh! Oh, oh, ohhhhh, ohhhh!" I said. "Ohhhhh."

"You yield well, slave," he said.

I looked up. Tears sprang to my eyes. The stranger had returned. He had been watching. In his hand was still the slave whip. Then he turned away, again. I gathered then it would not be necessary to whip me.

I responded to Sempronius' lips, and kissed him, too, softly, about the neck and chest.

Twice more that night he used me, and twice more was I reminded of my slavery, and how total it was.

The stranger did not return later to ascertain again for himself the adequacy of my yieldings. Apparently, on the basis of what he had seen, he assumed they would be acceptable. Too, of course, if Sempronius had not been satisfied, I could have been put beneath the whip.

Late that evening Sempronius and Callisthenes were permitted to leave the camp. Before they left they replaced the bracelets on the hands of two slaves, Tela and Tuka, so that their hands were again confined behind their backs. The keys to these bracelets were given to the stranger. They, too, reclothed us, if, given the nature of our scanty garmenture, such an expression is appropriate. They then had their swords returned to them. They were permitted to keep their purses.

Tela and I watched them withdraw, disappearing into the darkness.

After Callisthenes and Sempronius had left the camp, Mina

and Cara were brought forth from the slave wagon and knelt down near the fire. They were still in their chains. Tela was then freed of the cords on her ankles, holding her between the trees. She was then pulled to her feet, drawn along, and then knelt down, in a line, with Mina and Cara. I was then freed of the ankle cords which had kept me in place, between the trees. I was then knelt before the sapling to which my right ankle had been fastened. One of the bracelets I wore was then removed, and my wrists dragged back, about the sapling. It was then replaced in such a way that my hands were now confined behind me, and braceleted about the sapling.

"In that direction," said the stranger, addressing himself to Mina, Cara and Tela, Mina and Cara in their chains, Tela with her wrists braceleted behind her, "lies the Viktel Aria, and beyond it, continuing in the same direction, the camp of Pietro Vacchi. If you wish to return to Venna, and the camp of Ionicus, go right when you come to Viktel Aria."

Mina, Cara and Tela looked at one another.

He then removed the bracelets from Tela.

"Stand," he said.

They all stood.

"Whence?" he inquired.

"I do not wish to return to the black chain," said Mina. "I shall attempt to fall into the hands of the men of Pietro Vacchi."

"I, too," said Cara.

"I am sure," said the stranger, "that you will both make lovely camp slaves."

"It will be done with us as masters please," said Mina.

"And what of you, my dear?" inquired he of Tela.

"I, too," she said, "shall attempt to venture to the camp of Pietro Vacchi, in the hope that one into whose hands I hope to fall will still be there. If he is not, I shall beg, then, to be returned to the camp of Ionicus."

"You have the look of a love slave," he said.

"Perhaps, Master," she said, putting down her head in confusion.

How much I thought must she love Aulus, to be willing to return to the black chain of Ionicus, if only to carry water in the work pits, her limbs chained, where from time to time she might look up to the hill, to the overseer's tent atop it, or perhaps even to serve in the tent itself, in a rectangle of silk, as before.

"You do not know what became of the rest of us," said the stranger, warningly.

"No, Master," they said.

"Go," he said.

"May I kiss Tuka?" asked Tela.

"Very well," he said.

Tela came to kneel beside me. "I wish you well, Tuka," she said. She kissed me.

"I wish you well, too," I said to her, and kissed her.

She then, following Mina and Cara, left the camp.

The stranger then stood before me.

I looked up at him, frightened.

He went to the slave wagon, climbed the steps and swung open the iron door. He then returned to where I was secured and removed my bracelets. He then put me to all fours.

"In the slave wagon," he said, "on the right, as you enter, there is a water bag, which is full, and a food pan, in which there are two rolls. In the front of the slave wagon, on the left, as you face forward, there is a wastes bucket."

"Yes, Master," I said.

"Go," he said.

"Yes, Master," I said. He had put me to all fours. I had not been given permission to rise. It was thus clear to me how I was to enter the slave wagon. When I was inside he shut the door and I heard it secured, with heavy locks. Then the tiny aperture in the upper part of the door, through which I could see one of the moons, was slid shut, and latched. I was then in total darkness. I felt about and discovered that there were some blankets on the iron flooring. I would be warm tonight. I also felt about the wagon and detected that it contained various rings and chains, such that girls within it, if masters wished, could be separately secured. There was also a small water bag, filled with water, and a pan, with two rolls in it. These were where he had said. The wastes bucket, too, was where he had said, at the other end of the wagon, near the front, in the corner opposite the food and water. What luxury, I thought to myself. What more could a slave girl want, other than perhaps the heat of a master's body? I felt about the inside of the slave wagon. The plates were solid. I was well confined within, in the darkness. My escape would be impossible, even if I had dared to think of such a thing. He had seen to that. I wondered if the tharlarion would be hitched up in the morning, and the wagon would move, or, if, for some reason, he preferred to stay here. I spread two blankets in the center of the wagon, and put another, loosely, over my shoulders. I then crawled to the food pan and took one of the rolls. It was stale, but suitable for a slave. I knelt there, the blanket over my shoulders, and ate it in the darkness. I then took some water. I then returned to the center of the wagon, to the place I had spread the blankets, and knelt there, the blanket clutched about my shoulders. It would be easy for him to keep me indefinitely in such a place, I realized, as there was a wastes bucket, and food and water could easily be thrust through the narrow, now-closed aperture at the bottom of the door. He would not even have to take me out on a leash to relieve myself. Indeed, as he could feed me through the aperture, he did not even have to look at me. I looked about, in the darkness. It was his will which would determine how long I stayed here. It was up to him. He was a master, I was a slave. I supposed, however, that his needs might be upon him sometime and then I might be summoned forth, as the property I was, to serve them. Or perhaps he thought to keep me here, for his amusement, until my own needs began to work on me. Perhaps he wanted to hear me begging and pleading, scratching and whining, sobbing behind the iron door? I resolved I would not give him such satisfaction. But I realized that, as I was a Gorean slave girl, if that was what he wanted, he would probably not have to wait long. I laughed to myself. He must remember me! Or could it be only that he found me of interest, as he might have any woman? That was possible, I supposed. Certainly he had given no sign of knowing me. In any event, he had sent Mina, Cara, and Tela away. It was I who was in the slave wagon! He must remember me! I lay down then on the blankets, wrapped in another blanket. I wondered if he were going to leave with the slave wagon in the morning, and I would be transported helplessly in it, or if he was going to stay here for a time, in the woods, and, if so, for how long? I wondered, too, for how long, whether it left the woods or not, I would be kept in the slave wagon. I must wait to learn the answers to these things. I was a slave girl.

31 / Placation; In The Slave Wagon

The iron door opened. "Come out," he said.

I think I had been in the slave wagon for two days. It was again evening outside. I hastily adjusted the rolled cloth belt and the slave strip, tucking it in. I touched my hair, worried about it. Then I rose to my feet and hurried to the door. There he took me by the arm and conducted me down the stairs. I was pleased he did this, as I had not walked for a time, and was a little unsteady, and might have stumbled. A campfire was lit and near it were Mirus, and Tupita. She seemed radiant. I was startled to look upon Mirus. He seemed much recovered. When the man, who still wore a mask, removed his hand from my arm, I went timidly to Mirus, and knelt before him. "A slave is pleased," I whispered. "Master looks much stronger." Then I put down my head, frightened. He still looked upon me with severity. It had been only because of the intercession of Tupita, as I recalled, that I had been spared.

"Cook," said the man with the mask.

"Yes, Master," said Tupita, happily. "Come, Tuka, help me!"

"Yes, Mistress!" I said. I called her "Mistress," because I assumed she must be first girl. The men did not correct this impression, so she must be first girl. When not in their presence, whether I called her "Tupita," or whatever her name might now be, would be up to her. I did not doubt, however, but what she would let me use her name to her, whatever it might now be, when we were alone. As she had called me "Tuka," and had not been corrected, I assumed I still was, for the time being at least, or until Masters wished otherwise, "Tuka." Together we prepared a meal, cooked over the campfire. There were supplies and utensils in the wagonbox. I think it gave both Tupita and myself much pleasure to cook for the men. This simple domestic pleasure, preparing a small amount of food for particular masters, and hoping to please them by it, is not one paga slaves, or work slaves, often enjoyed. It is a different matter altogether to labor in a tavern kitchen, at a narrow task, or to stir the cooking pots in a work camp, which must feed perhaps a thousand slaves. Indeed I had never cooked in the work camp or even in the tavern, though in the latter place I had labored from time to time with Ina, usually naked, on my knees, at the washing tubs. Happily, Tupita did most of the real cooking, while I mostly watched and fetched. I wished I knew more about cooking. I was eager to please masters in this way, too. Too, I thought it was something I should know how to do. What if it were to be required of me? I was afraid then that if I did not do well I might be punished.

While Tupita and I busied ourselves in this fashion the men spoke of politics, of tharlarion, of war, and arms.

When we were ready we put the food on plates and proffered it to the men, kneeling before them, lifting the plates to them. Tupita lifted the plate to Mirus. I lifted the plate to the man who wore the mask. I hoped Tupita had cooked the food well! "Good," said Mirus, congratulating Tupita. "Excellent," said the stranger to Tupita. Tupita knelt back, muchly pleased. I, too, knelt back, pleased, though to be sure little of the credit was due to me. Tupita and I would wait to see if, and when, we would be fed. But after the free persons had taken a few bites, eating first, thus ritualistically in the Gorean fashion expressing the difference between themselves and us, and their precedence, Mirus shoved a bit of food to one side of his plate, from which Tupita, happily, helped herself. The stranger then picked up a tiny piece of food from his plate and indicated that I should lean forward. He then put it in my mouth. He did this at various times throughout the meal. I was being fed by hand. Once I tried to catch at, and suck and lick at his fingers, eagerly, surreptitiously, but his eyes warned me to desist. Later he let me finish the food on his plate. I was famished. He had not chosen to fatten me in the confinements of the slave wagon. I had had only some more bread, and a raw vegetable. From time to time during the meal Tupita had cast a glance at me, smiling, as though she had some secret. I did not understand what she might have in mind, if anything. Once or twice I glanced at Mirus, but his eyes were severe.

I wiped my hands on my thighs.

Tupita was a good cook, indeed!

Then, while the men continued to talk, we attended to domestic tasks, suitable for us, consequent upon the completion of the meal. I found a kind of fulfillment, and reassurance, and confirmation of what I was, in doing these things. I was particularly pleased to do them before the stranger. I wanted him to see me performing these tasks. Too, I would have loved to do small tasks for him, even if he did not see me do them, such things as sewing his tunic or, as I had for Aulus, polishing his boots.

We were then finished with the work and came and knelt by the fire, Tupita and I, slaves.

I would soon, I suspected, now that the work was done, be returned to the slave wagon.

I wanted to hurry about the fire, and throw myself on my belly before the stranger, tears in my eyes, covering his feet and ankles with kisses, his helpless slave, begging his touch. Surely he knew me! My belly burned, my thighs flamed. I put down my head. I hoped he could not smell me.

"My friend," said the stranger to Mirus.

Tupita drew back a little. Only in a moment or two did I understand her action.

"Yes," said Mirus.

"She is pretty, isn't she?" asked the stranger.

"She is beautiful," said Mirus, regarding Tupita.

"I mean the other one," said the stranger.

I suddenly knelt very straight, back on my heels. I did not understand what was going on.

"She?" asked Mirus.

"Put your shoulders back, thrust out your breasts, girl," said the stranger.

I obeyed.

"Yes, she," said the stranger.

Mirus regarded me. I felt very much a slave. "She is acceptable," he said. His voice was dry, and cold.

The stranger then took a length of binding fiber from his wallet and walked about the fire. I assumed he was going to bind me for some purpose or other. Perhaps he was not pleased that I had tried to suck and lick at his fingers when he had fed me. Perhaps I was to be put back bound, as a punishment, in the slave wagon. I hoped he did not intend to strangle me, or give the fiber to Mirus, that he might do so. Certainly it had been a small thing, and I could hardly have helped myself, with the feelings I had toward him, and being a slave. I might even have done so if I had been a free woman, in a mute, slave-like plea for attention! Surely a girl would never be punished for such a thing, or with little more than an angry, impatient cuff.

But he went not to me but to Tupita.

"What are you doing?" asked Mirus.

"Binding a slave," he said.

He, as she knelt, pulled her wrists behind her, crossed them, and bound them together. He then crossed her ankles and, with the same length of fiber, bound them to her wrists. Fulvius had earlier tied me in much the same manner. It is a common slave tie. In it the female is fastened in a position of subservience, cannot rise to her feet, is well displayed, cannot defend herself, and is utterly helpless.

I suddenly feared they wanted to tie Tupita in this way so that she would be unable to interfere in whatever they planned to do to me.

"Why have you bound her?" asked Mirus, puzzled.

His puzzlement reassured me. If this were some plan on the part of the stranger and him presumably he would not have asked this question. Mirus, then, I was relieved to note, seemed as much in the dark on this matter as I.

"Master, may I speak?" I asked the stranger.

"No," he said.

Tupita was smiling.

I then realized that this must be some scheme into which she had entered with the stranger. She and he seemed to understand what was transpiring, even if Mirus and I did not.

"I am well bound, Master," said Tupita to Mirus.

"Obviously," said Mirus. He had watched the stranger place, pull tight and knot the cords. I, too, had watched. He had worked unhurriedly, even, I suppose, casually, but efficiently. I shuddered. He was clearly no stranger to the binding of women.

The stranger then returned to his place on the other side of the fire, where he sat down, cross-legged. He picked up a bota, which I had learned contained paga, took a swig, and passed it to Mirus. Mirus drank, too, and returned the bota to him. The stranger closed it.

Mirus looked at the stranger.

"Perhaps we should be entertained," he said.

"Perhaps," said Mirus, puzzled.

"I can do little, Master," said Tupita. "I am bound!"

"Do not underestimate yourself," he said.

"True, Master," she laughed, delightedly. There are many things, of course which a woman, bound, can do for a man, and, indeed, if she is bound she knows, if anything, she must strive even more desperately to be pleasing to him.

"Please him," said the stranger to me, indicating Mirus.

"No," said Mirus, coldly.

The stranger looked at me.

"Please, Master," I said to him. "I think he would prefer to kill me."

"Please him," urged Tupita.

I looked at her, wildly. Surely she, of all people, would not desire that!

"Must a command be repeated?" inquired the stranger.

"No, Master!" I said. The tone of such a voice is unmistakable to a slave girl. She knows she must obey unquestioningly, perfectly, immediately. I hastily crawled to Mirus.

"Do not touch me, slave," he said, with unmistakable menace in his voice.

"Master!" protested Tupita.

I looked back, at the stranger, frightened.

"Very well," said the stranger, to Mirus. I knelt back on my heels.

I realized now what the plan of Tupita and the stranger must have been. In the two days or so since he had been with Mirus and her he had doubtless been informed, or had gathered, what the situation was amongst us. The specific suggestion I suppose had been Tupita's. I looked at Mirus. I did not think, really, now, he still wanted to kill me. I think that had gone from him. On the other hand he was still, obviously, consumed with hatred for me. Too, undoubtedly somehow, on some deep level, perhaps something far beneath the level of discourse, of excuses, of considerations, of reason, he may have felt that he had been denied or thwarted, that he had been deprived of some due satisfaction. Surely his decision to spare me had not come from deeply within him, spurred my his own misunderstandings, and acceptable to him, but had been the result of yielding to the unwelcome, perhaps resented intercession of Tupita. His hand had been stayed not by the merits of my case, if it had them, or even by a master's decision to spare a contrite, errant slave, but by his love for a woman, and, indeed, one who was only a slave. In this he may even have felt that he had lost honor. The plan, then, of Tupita and the stranger had been a simple one, involving the utilization of a common biological universal, the placatory behaviors of the errant female before the dominant male. In this way, it seemed, they hoped that his wrath might be diverted to desire, and that in place of my blood he might be persuaded to accept in substitution something as simple as my beauty, and my total subjugation and conquest. This sort of thing is not unknown. Many times in conquered cities women kneel before invading warriors, baring their breasts and bodies, begging not to be put to the sword but rather to be permitted to please them, and then be kept as slaves. It is a well-known fact, too, that it is not easy for a man to remain angry with a beautiful, contrite female who strips herself before him, kneels, kisses his feet, begs his forgiveness, and pleads to be ordered to the furs, that she may there await him in trepidation, and, when he chooses, attempt to assuage the harshness of his wrath with the softness of her beauty and love.

"You do not mind, do you?" asked the stranger, "if she performs for the rest of us?"

"Of course not," said Mirus.

"I understand, girl," he said, "that you are a dancer."

"Yes, Master," I said. "I have danced."

"Are you a dancer?" he asked.

"Yes, Master," I said. "I am a dancer."

"And have you danced before men?" he asked.

"Yes, Master," I said. Surely he knew this. I gathered then that he did not wish it known that he knew me. This, like his features concealed in the mask, it seemed, he wished to keep secret, at least from Mirus and Tupita. It was possible, of course, I suppose, that he really did not remember me from before. But I knew him, even with the mask. Surely he most know me. I was not even masked. Indeed, I was hardly clothed. If he did not remember me, then, I supposed, it was because there had been little about me of interest to him, or to make me worth remembering. But if he gave me a chance I would try, and desperately, through sedulous service and unstinting love, to make myself well worth remembering to him! Perhaps he had known many women, and really did not remember me?

"Do you feel," he asked, "that you truly know how to dance—*before men*."

"I think so, Master," I said, reddening.

"There are no free women present," He said. "Therefore your performance need not be inhibited."

"I understand, Master," I said. Too, to my pleasure, I gathered that he himself was not disinterested in seeing me dance, and that I was to dance as what I was, a slave.

"You may begin," he said.

"Dance, dance, Tuka," urged Tupita.

I rose to my feet. I rubbed my hands on my thighs. I touched myself about the waist, lifting my hands slightly, calling attention to my bosom. Such things are subtle. I wanted so to please the stranger. I wanted to show him what I could do, and now was.

"Your legs are short," said the stranger.

"Forgive me, Master," I said.

"It is not a criticism," he said.

"Thank you, Master," I said. Such legs, I knew, were splendid for this form of dance, in which, from time to time, the woman becomes a writhing, cuddly love animal, made for a man's hands and arms.

I saw from the stranger's eyes that I was to particularly dance myself to Mirus. I turned to face him. I lifted my left hand, holding my right low, at my hip. My head was down, humbly, and turned to the left.

I knew Mirus would try not to watch me. He would nurse his fury. He would attempt to resist me. He did not wish to permit me to placate him.

I knew I must attract his attention.

"Ai!" I cried suddenly, as though in pain, and reacted as though I had been, from his quarter, struck with a whip.

Mirus looked at me, startled, and I looked at him, reproachfully, and frightned, and then, as though he had whipped me, and commanded me, I began to dance. There was no music, of course, and so the dance must content itself largely with the expression, as it were, of my servitude, and my subjection to his will. I moved as beautifully as I could, and as though in fear before him, trying to please him, begging to placate him. From time to time in the dance I reacted again as though I had felt the whip, crying out in pain, looking at him in terror, sometimes struck even to my knees. Sometimes, too, I tried to dance before the stranger, but his eyes would inform me that it was before Mirus that I was to dance slave beauty.

"Look at her, Master!" cried Tupita. "See how beautiful she is!"

"Master," I wept to Mirus, "I beg forgiveness!"

Then I reacted, again and again, as though he might have been angered by my plea, as though I were struck with the whip. Then I was on my back, and stomach, even, reacting as though I was struck, turning, twisting, as though in terror and pain to fend blows. It was as though he were punishing me.

"She dances well," said Mirus.

"Forgive her, Master," begged Tupita. "She is sorry! She begs forgiveness!"

I looked to the stranger, in his mask, from where I lay. His eyes shone. I almost cried out with pleasure. Had he thought that he had known me? Well, perhaps now he was wondering if he had really, at all, known me!

I leaped to my feet and moved sensuously but, too, as though prodded and shoved, as though driven, herded, to the slave wagon. Tupita gasped. I seized the slave whip and thrust it between my teeth, harshly, as might have a man, and then I flung myself to the dirt. Then, bit by bit, sometimes on my knees, sometimes as though I had tried to rise, and had then again been thrust to my knees, sometimes on all fours, sometimes as though trying to rise to my knees, and being forced again to all fours, I made my way to Mirus. As I approached him it seemed I became more and more terrified, and contrite, and then, at the conclusion of my dance, I put my head down and placed the whip humbly before him. I then put my head down again licked and kissed it, and then I put myself on my belly, prostrate before him, a slave at his mercy. "Forgive me, Master," I begged..

"You have placed a whip before me," he observed.

"That it may be used to punish a slave, Master," I said. How naturally I thought of myself as a slave! I was a slave.

"It would seem in your dance," he said, "that you were already much punished."

I said nothing. In the dance, of course, not a blow had fallen upon me.

"But it is not my whip to which you are subject," he said. I was startled, and my heart leapt to hear this. Could he mean that the stranger had put claim upon me, and that it was to his whip that I was now subject? But, of course, he may have meant only that I belonged to Ionicus of Cos. That could be read upon my collar.

"I am at your mercy," I said. "I am yours to punish."

"And for what," he asked, "would I punish you?"

"Master?" I asked, lifting my head.

"For having obeyed your master, or your master's men?" he asked.

"Master!" I said, tears in my eyes.

"Surely such was your duty," he said.

"She might have been terribly punished, even slain otherwise!" interpolated Tupita.

"Did you choose to be a lure girl?" he asked.

"No, Master!" I said.

"I am sure now," he said, "as I reflect on these things, not in anger, that you were indeed reluctant to entice me, and might have preferred to be permitted to withdraw."

"Yes, Master," I said.

"But in my pleasure at seeing you again," he said, "such signs, obvious as they might have been, I overlooked. It did not even occur to me that you might then be a lure girl. Any other girl, one unknown, of course, I might have immediately suspected, particularly under the circumstances, the loneliness of the street, the absurdity of a key in your belt, and such."

I said nothing.

"I was a fool," he said.

"It is my fault," I said. "You were beguiled by your affection for me, by your trust in me."

"No," he said. "I was stupid."

"Forgive me, Master," I said.

"You are not stupid, Master," said Tupita. "Look at Tuka. See how well curved she is, how desirable she is! She could have lured a general!"

"Slave," said Mirus to me.

"Yes, Master," I said.

"What do you think should be the punishment for a free woman who did what you did?"

"Whatever masters please," I said, "once she was branded, and put in a collar."

"Kneel," he said.

"Yes, Master," I said.

"Are you not somewhat overdressed?" he asked.

"Yes, Master," I said. I removed the bit of clothing I wore, the belt, the narrow strip of cloth.

"Approach," he said, "on your knees."

"Yes, Master," I said.

He rose to a crouching position. He put his hands on my upper arms. He was very strong.

"You are a well-curved slave," he said.

"Thank you, Master," I said.

"What do you think should be the punishment for a slave who did what you did?" he asked.

"Whatever masters please," I said.

"The whip?" he asked.

"If masters please," I said. I would be more than happy to settle for the whip!

"Perhaps," he said, "for the whip of the furs."

"Oh, yes, Master!" cried Tupita. "Yes! Yes!"

"My anger with you," said Mirus, "I think was in part motivated by anger with myself, that I so easily succumbed to your charms."

"Yes, Master," I said. I had never doubted that.

"Do not entirely blame yourself, Master," called Tupita. "I

am sure she was a very clever lure girl, a brilliantly lovely and skillful lure girl!''

I did not think this contribution by Tupita was really necessary.

''Yes,'' said Mirus, looking at me, ''that is true.''

He then lifted me up, and carried me back, away from the fire, into the darkness.

''Use her well!'' cried Tupita! ''Make her pay! Teach her who is master!''

He then threw me to my side in the leaves, in the darkness. I lay there, my legs pulled up, frightened.

''I am somewhat angry,'' Mirus informed me.

''Yes, Master,'' I said. That was only too obvious.

''I am first girl, slave,'' called Tupita to me. ''See that you serve him well! If you do not serve him well, I will beat a bucket of slave oil out of you!''

''Yes, Mistress,'' I called to her.

Mirus crouched beside me. He thrust me to my back. He unceremoniously flung my legs apart. I, serve him well? It seemed clearly his intention, at least at first, to help himself. I did not expect to be given much more consideration than a free woman taken in the streets of a burning city, subjected to hasty loot use, thence to be dragged away stripped after her captor, her hands bound behind her, a rope on her neck.

''Yes, you did well,'' said Mirus, almost a growl.

''Forgive me, Master!'' I said.

I was then, helpless in his angry grasp, put to his pleasure. It was only when he was done with me, so abruptly, and I looked up into his eyes that I saw them, to my relief, cleared of anger. It had not been necessary to slay me. The thing was done now. Mirus was now again himself, the Mirus I remembered from Brundisium. The debt, if debt it were, on some deep level, had been paid. Once again I was only another slave.

''You may touch me,'' he said.

I bent over him.

''Do not use your hands,'' he said.

''Yes, Master,'' I whispered.

Once again, later, he put me to his use.

''Did she serve well?'' called Tupita.

''Yes,'' said Mirus. ''She served well.''

I was relieved to hear his asservation. I did not doubt but what Tupita, love me though she might, would as first girl have put me well and lengthily under the whip if he had not been satisfied.

Mirus looked down at me. "And in the end," he asked, "who is master, who is salve?"

"You are the master," I said. "I am the slave."

"And who is victorious?" he asked.

"You are, Master," I said, "and totally, and I am nothing." I did not tell him that, truly, we were both victorious, that he was victorious in his victory, and I, a woman, was victorious in my utter defeat.

"Please, Master," I begged, "touch me more." Mirus was a master in the handling of women. He well knew how to subdue us, and make us beg for further subjugation.

"There is another whom I would touch," he said. "You may crawl back to the fire."

Head down, still muchly aroused, I crawled back to the fire. He followed me and began to untie Tupita. "Is Tuka not beautiful?" asked Tupita. "Yes," he said, "but you are a thousand times more beautiful." I did not think that was really true. Certainly at any rate not a thousand times! "I love you, Master!" she exclaimed, being unbound. "Perhaps you care for me, a little?" "Yes," he smiled, "a little." "A slave is pleased," she said. She was now unbound. She knelt on the backs of her heels, her hands on her thighs, looking up, happily, at Mirus. "Kneel higher," he said, "off your heels." "Master?" she asked. This had brought her into suitable cuffing position. "Did you not speak at various times during the evening," he asked, "without having requested permission?" "Yes, Master," she said. "Forgive me, Master." She then was flung to the side, cuffed, and lay on the dirt, to the side. "Return to your former position," he said.

She returned, apprehensively, to the high kneeling position, before him. The left side of her face was a flaming red. He then took up the slave whip which was there, where I had dropped it before him, earlier, and looped it about her neck. He then, by this means, pulled her up straighter, and holding her head up, looked down into her eyes. "Did you think that in my love for you," he asked, "I would cease to be your master?"

"No, Master," she said, happily, looking up at him.

Even in the greatness of his love for her he would not cease to be her master. Indeed, had he done so, how could she have loved him so much?

He then cast aside the whip and lifted her gently in his arms, and carried her back into the shadows, away from the fire.

I was on all fours, by the fire.I looked to the stranger. I was still muchly aroused.

"Get dressed," he said.

In chagrin I found my "garments," the slave strip and belt. I knelt back, and put them on.

"On all fours," he said, "return to the slave wagon."

I looked at him in protest, but did as I was bade. I crawled across the ground to the slave wagon, and up the steps. I paused at the threshold. "May I speak?" I asked.

"No," he said.

I then entered the slave wagon. The door was shut behind me. Inside, in the darkness, I turned and knelt by the door, putting my fingers against it. I heard the door being locked, and then heard his steps descending the stairs. I had apparently served my purpose for the evening! I had now been "kenneled." He had not even permitted me to speak! He treated me as a slave! Then I drew back from the door, and found a bit of bread in the pan. I also felt a slice of raw vegetable. I ate these, and then took some water. I then relieved myself at the bucket in the other part of the wagon, and then lay down in the center of the wagon, on the blankets. The wagon was dark, and a firm prison, but it was not uncomfortable.

I awakened once in the middle of the night. He had treated me as a slave! But then, of course, that was what I was. I was a slave. Then I returned to sleep.

32 / The Camp

"You are dressed suitably as a slave," he said.

"Yes, Master," I said. I was in the belt and cloth. On my neck was still the collar of Ionicus. I knelt in the camp, at his feet. I was tied much as Fulvius had tied me earlier, and as he had tied Tupita last night, wrists crossed and bound behind me, fastened closely to my crossed, bound ankles.

He then looked after the slave wagon. I could not see it now, but I could hear it, in the distance, descending toward the road. I could see the narrow print of its wheels in the leaves. A moment or two ago, drawn by its tharlarion, it had left camp. Mirus had been on the wagon box, Tupita beside him, in a tunic fashioned of one of the blankets which had been inside the wagon. My eyes were still moist from their departure. Tupita, her hands braceleted behind her, had knelt and kissed me. "I wish you well, Tuka," she had said. "I wish you well, too, Tupita," I had said. Mirus had then crouched near me and kissed me. "I wish you well, slave," he had said. "I wish you well, Master," I had said. They had then left. Tupita and I could not wave to one another as our restraints did not permit it, but we exchanged a common slave girls' farewell, kissing to one another, tears in our eyes. Most of the coins and valuables which had fallen to the stranger as sword loot he had divided with Mirus. The wagon and tharlarion, too, would surely have value. Such things should give Mirus more than enough means to make Brundisium. Too, it was good for Mirus to have the wagon, at least for a few days, until his strength might be fully recovered. "They are gone now," he said. The wagon, then, I gathered, must be out of sight, even from his vantage, standing. Doubtless it would soon be on the road.

There was a soft wind, rustling the leaves.

I looked up at him. We were alone.

He reached to his mask. He removed it. Sempronius and Callisthenes had left three days ago. Mirus and Tupita had now gone. None of these, I supposed, would be able to recognize him again, unless perhaps by his skill with the sword. He had concealed his features, and his identity. It would be difficult for anyone, in the future, if they were so inclined, to connect him with the transactions in the meadow. To be sure, he might be a simple brigand. If so, he was an extremely dangerous one.

He looked down at me, the mask in his hand. "Perhaps you remember," he said, "that I once told you that there was a world where women like you were bought and sold."

"Yes, Master," I said. He had spoken in English. It had taken me a moment, a frightened moment, to realize that. Then I had made the transition from Gorean to English.

"And have you been bought and sold?" he asked.

"Yes, Master," I said.

"And how is my modern woman?" he asked.

"Only as much is left in me of the modern woman as you might wish," I said, "only as much as you might wish to recollect, and then, if it pleases you, to humble or hurt me."

He smiled. "I see that you have learned to be concerned to please men," he said.

"Yes, Master," I said.

"You look well, tied helplessly," he said.

"Thank you, Master," I said.

"Have you been taught much on Gor?" he asked.

"Yes, Master," I said.

"And have you been taught to throw your legs apart quickly?" he asked.

"Yes, Master," I said.

"You danced well last night," he said.

"Thank you, Master," I said. I was so pleased that he was pleased!

"What do you call that sort of dance?" he asked.

" 'Slave dance,' " I said, in Gorean.

"In English," he said. "We are speaking English."

" 'Ethnic dance,' " I said.

He smiled.

" 'Belly dance,' " I said.

"Are you a belly dancer?" he asked.

"Yes," I said.

"Say so," he said.

"I am a belly dancer," I said.

"And do you love to belly dance?" he asked.

"Yes," I said.

"Say so," he said.

"I love to belly dance," I said, reddening. But then I looked at him, gratefully. I was a belly dancer! I was! And I did love to belly dance! How free I suddenly felt, and happy, that I had now said these things, that I had confessed them to myself, honestly, openly, in my native language.

"Perhaps, sometimes," he said, "I will permit you to dance for me."

"A slave would be pleased," I said, "if she might so please her master."

"How naturally you speak of yourself as a slave," he said.

"I am a slave, Master," I said.

"Yes," he said. "You are. I knew that the first moment I laid my eyes on you."

I looked down, shyly. I remembered the first moment I had seen him, looking up from the desk, seeing him there, before me, I in the dark sweater and the long-sleeved blouse, he in that dark suit, with a tie, such things seemingly so ungainly on him. He had looked at me in a Gorean fashion. I had felt I might have been stripped naked before him. If I had known then what I knew now I would have felt slave naked before him, as though I had just been stripped for slave assessment, that masters might decide what I might realistically be expected to bring them on the block. It was shortly after this experience that I had fearfully enrolled myself in a class in belly dancing. Somehow, probably in the depths of my subconscious, I wanted to do almost anything I could, to learn how to please such a man, and surely dancing beautifully before him, vital and half-clad, might contribute to such an end.

When I looked up he was still looking down at me. He was looking at me, musingly, studying me.

I was silent. I had not been spoken to.

He tossed the mask he had worn to the side, among his things. He then crouched down before me.

"Master," I whispered, begging, pulling against the ropes.

He removed the cloth belt and slave strip from me and tossed them, too, to the side, among his things. He owned them, even such small things, not I.

He then moved back a little, and looked at me.

"You have become very beautiful," he said.

"Thank you, Master," I said.

"Apparently the Gorean diet, the movements of slave dance, the attentions of masters, and such, have much improved you," he said.

"It is my hope that I have been improved," I said.

"Your ears have been pierced," he said.

"As befits me, Master," I said.

He smiled.

I saw that he was pleased that my ears had been pierced. I rejoiced in his pleasure.

"Greetings, Miss Williamson," he said.

"I am no longer Miss Williamson," I said, frightened, shrinking back, "unless master wishes to put such a name on me."

"Your response is acceptable," he said. "What is your name?"

"Whatever master pleases," I said.

"What have you most recently been called?" he asked.

" 'Tuka,' " I said. He knew that, of course. He wanted to hear the slave name from my own lips.

"That will do," he said.

"Yes, Master," I said. In a sense, then, I had the same name, 'Tuka,' but, in another sense, it was a new name, put on me afresh. I now wore it not by the will of another, but by his own will. Once I had been Miss Doreen Williamson. Now, again, by a man's decision, I, an animal, was simply "Tuka." It was an exciting name.It made me flame between my thighs. I squirmed a little.

"Do you know what this is," he asked. He had picked up the slave whip.

"A slave whip," I said.

He held it before me and I eagerly licked and kissed it.

"You do that well, slave," he said.

"Thank you, Master," I said.

"Can you speak Gorean?" he asked.

"A little, Master," I said. He knew, of course, I could speak at least a little Gorean. For example, he had heard me speak with Mirus and Tupita. "Master would know more of such matters," I said, "had he, when I requested it upon occasion, given me permission to speak."

He toyed with the whip. I hoped I had not been too bold.

"A girl can understand simple commands," I whispered.

"Perhaps, by now, she should be better than that," he said.

"I can speak Gorean," I said, "at least well, I think, for my time here. I have had to learn it rapidly and efficiently. It is the language of my masters."

He nodded. Slave girls from Earth learn Gorean quickly. We are encouraged, of course, by the switch and whip. They are useful pedagogical devices.

"May I speak?" I asked. It seemed strange to request permission to speak, in English. Yet it was fully proper, for I was a slave. That was what was important, that I was a slave, not the language in which I spoke.

"Yes," he said.

"Is it to your whip that I am subject?" I asked.

"Yes," he said.

"I am yours?" I asked.

"Yes," he said. "I put sword claim upon you. Let he who will dispute it with me."

I twisted in the bonds. I was his, then, girl loot, kajira spoils, as much as a tharlarion or a crate of jewels, by the right of the sword.

"Did you search for me?" I asked.

"Yes," he said, "for months, from Market of Semris, to Brundisium, to Samnium, to Argentum, to Venna."

I recalled Tyrrhenius had spoken of "inquiries." I had thought they might be inquiries being made by praetors' agents, or something. It had not been clear, even, whether the "inquiries" were related, or were being made by one or more parties. It now seemed that at least two parties, separately, doubtless unknown to one another, each with its individual motivation, had been searching for me. No wonder Tyrrhenius had wanted to sell me out of Argentum as quickly he could!

"Why?" I asked. "To free me?"

"Do you think you should be a free woman?" he asked.

"No," I said.

"Do you really think, too," he said, "I picked you out from hundreds on Earth, and selected you, screening you according to my own tastes and criteria, as my final and most exquisite Earth capture merely to bring you here to be a free woman?"

"No, Master!" I said.

He looked at me, and he seemed angry, and I was afraid of him.

"I realized, after I had let you go, that I had really brought you here for myself."

"Oh, Master!" I cried, joyfully.

"So I followed you," he said, "fool that I was ever to have let you go."

"Why did you not buy me from your employers, and put me in your collar, and keep me, and train me to please you, according to your dictates?"

"I feared you would drive me mad with passion," he said. "But there is a way to handle such women, to keep them in collars, and under strict control."

"Yes, Master!" I said. "Yes!" He had searched for me! He had found me!

He looked down at me.

"Master has labored long to find me," I said. "He has risked much for a mere girl."

He shrugged.

"It is my hope that master is not disappointed, now that he has me in his bonds," I said.

He smiled.

"I gather that master is not disappointed," I said.

"I shall let you know later," he said.

I laughed. But how tightly I was bound! How helpless I was! "It is surprising, is it not," I asked, "that you should search so long for a mere slave?"

"I suppose so," he said.

"May I not inquire more closely then into master's motivation?" I said. I so wanted him to tell me that he found me of interest, that he found me pleasing!

"You are a not unattractive slave," he said, drily.

"But surely there are many attractive slaves," I said.

"That is true," he said.

"Might a slave hope that master might care for her, just a little?" I asked.

"Rather let her hope that such an improper, impertinent question does not earn her a meeting with the whip," he said.

"Yes, Master!" I said.

"You were desired," he said.

"Yes, Master," I said. I must then put aside all thoughts of love or affection. I was unworthy of such, from such a man. I was inutterably beneath him, worth less than the dust beneath his sandals. How absurd was my question! How shamed I was at my pride! How bold I had been! How could I even think of such a thing? Did I not know I was from Earth, and only a slave! But I loved him, and with the whole heart and body of me! I tendered to him the wholeness of my helpless slave's love, worthless though it might have been. I had love enough in my small, marvelous body for a thousand of us, a thousand times over! So I was not loved! What did it matter! I was desired, and this would be enough. Too, I myself felt desire, and profound, raging slave desire, as he on his part must have felt the passions of the master. I was inflamed with need and heat before him, my master. Unworthy though I might be he had clearly wanted me! He had picked me out on Earth, he had fought with himself on Gor, then he had pursued me like a sleen, threading patiently through the harrows of time, disregarding the perils of both men and beasts. Loved or not, I had been for months, unknown to myself, an indisputable object of Gorean passion. I had been woman prey, a hunter's curvaceous quarry. Now the hunt was done and the lovely beast was taken, and tied naked at the hunter's feet. She desired muchly to serve him.

I tried desperately to conceal my passion. "May I inquire," I asked, as unconcernedly, as lightly, as I could, "what may be your intentions with respect to me?"

"It is my intention," he said, "at least for a time, to keep you as a slave if you endeavor to prove satisfactory."

"As an imbonded girl," I said, "I shall, of course, endeavor to prove satisfactory."

He smiled.

"Never let me go again," I wept, suddenly. "Keep me forever!"

He looked at me.

Swiftly I spread my knees further apart. I did not wish to be whipped.

"You smell like an aroused slave," he commented.

"I am an aroused slave!" I wept.

"Are you not a highly intelligent modern woman?" he inquired.

"I beg permission to kiss the feet of my master," I said.

"You have come a long way from your library, librarian," he said.

I looked up at him, tears in my eyes.

"They have put slave fires in your belly, haven't they?" he asked.

"Yes, Master!" I said.

"How cruel of them," he said.

I squirmed helplessly.

"Perhaps a girl wishes to serve her master?" he asked.

"Yes, Master!" I said. "Yes, Master! Please, Master!"

He then went behind me and untied my ankles. He then put his hands gently on my flanks, and waist, and body, and I pressed back against him, sobbing, my eyes closed, moaning, begging to be touched. Then he whipped loose the fiber on my wrists and, rolling it and putting it in his pouch, went to stand before me. I put my head down and began to lick and kiss his feet, sobbing.

"Yes, you are obviously a highly intelligent woman," he said. "You do that very well."

I sobbed.

"You look well, modern woman," he said, "at my feet."

"Please, Master," I begged. "I am not a modern woman. There is nothing left in me of the modern woman, really, as you, of all men, must know and recognize, even if ever there was anything of that sort in me to begin with! I am now only a Gorean slave girl at the feet of her master!"

"And what is the name of your master?" he inquired.

"My master is Teibar," I said.

"And of what city is he?" he asked.

"I do not know, Master," I said.

"He is of Ar," he said.

"Yes, Master," I said.

"Whose slave are you, then?" he asked.

"I am the slave of Teibar of Ar," I said. This was the first time I had ever spoken these words. I was thrilled to speak them. They gave the name and city of my master. If a guardsman or any free person, or even a male slave, or a female slave in a position of authority, were to inquire as to the identity of my master, that was the information that I would be expected to give them. To be sure, such things may be read on collars. At this time, however, I still wore the collar of Ionicus. The recovery period, germane to that collar, expired at midnight tonight.

Sword claim, however, if uncontested, took priority. I knew little of Ar, but I did know it was a large and powerful city.

"You are lovely, slave of Teibar of Ar," he said, looking down at me.

"Thank you, Master," I said.

"I think," he said, looking down at me, "that indeed, truly, there is little of the modern woman left in you."

"There is nothing of that hateful tragedy, of that barreness and lovelessness, left in me, Master," I said, "if ever there was anything of it in me to begin with. And I love you. I love you! I love you!"

"Interesting," he said.

"Do not whip me, Master," I said, "I beg you, but I do love you, and from the depths of my heart! I loved you and wanted to please you, and be yours, from the first moment I saw you!"

He looked upon me.

"Forgive me, Master," I said. I seized up the slave whip and handed it to him. "Let an impertinent slave be whipped!"

But he only held the whip to my lips and I kissed it, fervently, gratefully, and then looked up at him.

He looked at me, and I squirmed in need.

He touched the whip to my shoulder and I moaned, and put my head to the side, and kissed it.

"You seem to be in need," he said.

"Yes, Master!" I said.

"Indeed, you seem to be an extremely aroused, excited slave," he said.

"Yes, Master!" I said.

"Do you wish to serve your master?" he asked.

"Yes, Master!" I said.

"Perhaps I shall permit you to do so," he said.

"Thank you, Master!" I said. He was the most exciting man I had ever known. His least touch made me want to cry out with passion and surrender myself, totally.

"You may do so," he said.

"Thank you, Master!" I breathed, looking up at him, with tears in my eyes. I was more than eager to serve him in a thousand intimate and delicious modalities. I would try to be more marvelous than the most marvelous slave he might ever have dreampt of. "Command me, Master!"

"But first," he said, "as it is still light, we are going for a short walk. You will be taken on a leash. We will then return to the camp."

"Yes, Master," I said, puzzled.

In a few minutes we had returned to the camp, I on my leash. Though he had waited for me, once, to relieve myself, I do not think that that was the purpose of the walk. That I could have done anywhere outside the camp, chained to a tree, if necessary. We had gone down by the long building, beyond the well, in the meadow, where the beasts lay. He unsnapped the leash and I knelt before him, then, waiting to be commanded.

"Yes, Master?" I said, eagerly.

"Cook," he said.

33 / Dust

I knelt down, across the fire from him, in our small camp in the woods, not far from the meadow. It was dark now. There was a space of some fifty feet of cleared ground behind him. Closer to me there were some trees and brush.

I was naked. He had not given me clothing, even the belt of rolled cloth and the slave strip, which he had earlier removed, when I had been bound, after the departure of Mirus and Tupita, they with the tharlarion and wagon.

"Is the camp in order? Is your work finished?" he asked.

"Yes, Master," I said. I had tried to do my best to cook well for him. I hoped he had not been dissatisfied. He had eaten in silence, but well. I hoped I had not done too badly. I had not been whipped. The whip is a very tangible symbol of the relationship between the master and the slave, and if the master is not satisfied, it can quickly become, as the slave knows well, more than a symbol. After he had begun to eat he had given me a piece of bread, thrusting it in my mouth as I was, by his command, on all fours near him. After that he had, from time to time, thrown me scraps, tossing them to the crushed leaves. These I must eat without the use of my hands.

As a female I looked across at him, such a master. To no weaker man would I have cared to belong. He would command; I would obey. I was his.

"Perhaps Master will now bind his slave," I said.

He regarded me.

I could not deny that I loved bonds, both of a physical and social sort, those tangible evidences of my womanhood, and my place in nature. He might bind me, I supposed, merely to secure me for the night. On the other hand, I hoped that he might now bind me not for the night but rather for the evening, either in such a way as merely to make clear to me that I was a slave, little more than a symbolic binding, or even in such a way that I should be utterly helpless to resist his attentions, whatever they might be.

"You are a woman made for bonds," he said.

But he made no move to secure a neck chain, or physical bonds of any sort, nor did he order me to fetch such, hurrying to him, say, with chains, responsive to his command, that would be placed on my own body.

"And love, Master," I said, boldly. "And love!"

He frowned.

"Forgive me, Master," I said.

To be sure I already wore the most marvelous and joyous bonds of all, those of my womanhood, identical with myself, those of my slavery, natural and legal, and those of my love.

When I saw his eyes upon me I moved my knees a tiny bit further apart. I was a subtle thing. He was not supposed, really, to notice it, or much notice it, at least on a conscious level.

"You are a sly slave," he said.

"Forgive me, Master," I said. I considerably narrowed the gap between my knees.

"No," he said. "Open your knees even more widely than they were before."

"Yes, Master," I said. Now, of course, I was merely a slave, obeying the orders of her master. How far away then seemed Earth, and the library.

"May I speak, Master?" I asked.

"Yes," he said.

"Fulvius," I said, "who was one of the brigands, did not care, it seems, to leave an enemy behind him."

My master nodded.

"I do not care to do so either," he said.

"But you released Sempronius and Callisthenes," I said. "You even showed them hospitality. You even put Tela and myself to their pleasure."

"They were not enemies," he said.

"I see," I said.

"One must beware of enemies," he said, "and the nobler they are, the more dangerous they are."

"I am surprised that you have kept this camp as long as you have," I said. "I gather this was in deference to Mirus, who was recovering his strength."

"Perhaps," he said.

"But you did not leave with him this afternoon," I said.

"No," he said.

"Perhaps you intend to leave the camp in the morning?" I asked.

"Perhaps," he said.

I looked at my master. He had never used me. On Earth, and in the first house of my bondage, my virginity, it seemed, had protected me. Such was supposed to improve my price on the slave block, at least for certain buyers. Certainly it must have appealed to Hendow, for he had made good money on me, in the selling of chances, in raffling it off. Then I had been lost to him for a long time. Then, in the meadow, he had found me. I had come again into his power. He had put sword claim upon me. I was his, his slave! But he had still not used me. He had put me to the pleasure of Sempronius. Later, by another simple exercise of the rights of his mastery, I must serve Mirus. Yet he had sought me for months. Surely that had not been done merely to put me to the purposes of others. I looked at him. Surely he must desire me. He had said as much. I shuddered. I was afraid, a little, but terribly excited, to be the object of such desire, Gorean desire. It was so powerful, so ruthless, so absolutely uncompromising. Yet, too, I thought, he must care for me. Surely he must! Indeed, he must care very much for me! Perhaps he even loves me, I thought, absurd though that might seem. Was that really so impossible? He must love me, I thought. He must!

"What is wrong with you?" he asked.

"Nothing, Master," I said.

I looked at him. I was sure he loved me!

"Are you sure there is nothing wrong?" he asked.

"Yes, Master," I said. "Master," I said.

"Yes," he said.

"You own me," I said. "I am your slave."

"Yes?" he said.

"But I am curious to know what my status is, Master," I said. I would try, slyly, to determine his feelings toward me.

"Your status?" he asked.

"Yes," I said. "What sort of slave am I?"

"What do you mean?" he asked.

"Am I a high slave?" I asked.

"Do you wish to be whipped?" he asked.

"No, Master!" I said.

"Turn about," he said. "Kneel down. Put your head to the ground, clasp your hands together, behind the back of your neck."

"Yes, Master!" I wept. I hastened to obey. This is a common position for slave rape.

"Oh!" I cried. Then I shuddered and gasped, and cried out. Then I gasped, again and again. Then he spurned me to the dirt, by the fire, with his foot. I turned about, from my belly, shuddering, to look at him.

"That is your status," he said. "That is the sort of slave you are."

"Yes, Master," I said.

"Speak your status, the sort of slave you are," he said.

"I am a low slave!" I said.

"And you are the lowest of the lowest!" he said.

"Yes, Master!" I said. There were tears in my eyes. Obviously I was a full slave to this man. No intention in the least had he of weakening or compromising my bondage. He had not picked me out on Earth to be a half slave. My feelings were very mixed. I was wildly grateful to have been taken, but yet he had given me little time or pleasure. His attentions, and his domination, had done little more than teach me that I was a slave, and further arouse me. It had been little more than an instructional and disciplinary taking, but still I had wept and reveled in it. It was the first such touch, even so arrogant and contemptuous, which my master had granted me. Too, I knew that even though I might be a low slave, as I had little doubt that I was now, and even among the lowest of low slaves, I was not disheartened, or, indeed, even disappointed. First, I knew that women who are kept as low slaves, and even strictly so, are often among those most loved. Many love masters keep their love slaves, for example, as low slaves. I had little doubt that Mirus would keep Tupita as such. She was even braceleted when she left the camp. I knew, too, that even high slaves are occasionally subjected to such imperious uses, which in their way are delicious, just as they might, to their shame, frustration and pleasure, find themselves occasionally clad in rags and put to disagreeable tasks. Such things remind them that they are slaves, and must obey their masters. Such enforcements, too, tend to be reassuring, and arousing, to a woman. Even if I were not loved, I now had no doubt that I was keenly desired, and that I need not fear that I might not be put to my master's pleasure and as a slave. The ruthlessness of his use only doubled my desire, that of a slave, to serve and love him. It was clear he had known what he was doing when he had picked me out on Earth.

"You may resume your position," he said.

"Thank you, Master," I said, returning to my place, kneelig across the fire from him. I was still shaken and heated from my rape. To some extent I was ashamed and chagrined, for had I not once been a free woman of Earth, but mostly I was very pleased, and grateful, and loving. Too, I was in awe of him. He had wanted me; he had taken me. He would do what he wanted with me. I would be treated as he pleased. There would be no compromising with me. I was his slave.

"May I speak?" I asked.

"Yes," he said.

"How did you know that you might trust Callisthenes and Sempronius?" I asked.

"I think I have some skill in reading men," he said.

"Can you read women, as well?" I asked.

"Yes," he said.

"And what do you read in me?" I asked.

"Straighten your body, and spread your knees more widely," he said.

I complied.

"I read that you are an exquisite female slave," he said, "who needs only a strong master to achieve the total perfections of her femininity."

"It is true, Master," I said, reddening, putting down my head. I was sorry I had asked. I was so embarrassed! It was as though he could read my innermost thoughts and needs. Was I truly so open to him? It seemed that my thoughts and needs were as naked to him as now, by his will, was my body.

He then fetched a bit of oil and a sharpening stone from his things and, returning to his place, removed his sword from its scabbard. He then, slowly, patiently, with great care, addressed himself to the blade. Gorean men usually sharpen their own swords. They tend to trust the edge on the weapon to no one but themselves. I regarded the blade with uneasiness, but fascination. I had seen such things at work.

"Be certain that we speak in English," he said, not looking up.

"Very well, Master," I said. We had been speaking in English. I did not understand why he should say that now.

"We must make do, as we can," he said.

"Master?" I asked.

"Had you oil to pour upon the fire, causing it to blaze up

suddenly, from the darkness of embers, that might make it difficult to see, for a moment, the light."

"Yes, Master?" I said.

"But it is too early for the fire to have died down as yet," he said.

"Yes, Master," I said, puzzled.

I watched the sharpening stone move on the blade, so slowly, so smoothly, so evenly.

"If someone were to approach," he said, "from behind me, you would undoubtedly see him almost immediately."

"Yes, Master," I said. "There is a clearing behind you, for perhaps fifty feet or more."

His head was down. He worked with the stone.

"Accordingly," he said, "if someone did not wish to be observed in approaching the camp, he might come from that direction which lies more behind you, where there are trees and brush."

"I suppose so, Master," I said.

"Do not look around," he said.

"Very well, Master," I said.

"Such an individual," he said, "might await his opportunity, for example, for a time when he might approach, unobserved."

"Master?" I said, frightened.

"For example," he said, "when someone might be intent upon some other task, not paying attention to that avenue of approach."

"Master?" I asked.

"Do you recall this afternoon," he asked, "when we went for our walk?"

"Of course," I said.

"Do you recall the bodies of the two beasts in the meadow," he asked.

"Yes," I said. I had not cared to much look at them, but he had drawn me to them, by the leash, and had had me do so. They had lain contorted in death. The sight was not pretty. He had then, mercifully, had us return to the camp.

"Do you recall anything unusual about them?" he asked.

"No," I said.

"Do you not recall," he asked, "that on each there was a sprinkling of dust?"

"Yes," I said, puzzled.

"How do you suppose it got there?" he asked.

"Blown by the wind," I said.

"No," he said. "not in the meadow."

"I do not understand," I said.

"You do not understand the significance of that dust?" he said.

"No," I said.

"They, too, have their ceremonies, and rites," he said.

" 'They,'?" I asked.

"Yes," he said. "The dust is ceremonial."

I said nothing.

"It counts as a burial," he said.

The tiny hairs on the back of my neck rose.

"It would seem," he said, "I am now nearly finished with sharpening the sword. Shortly, then, I might be expected to look up."

"Oh, Master," I said, terrified.

"Do you detect anything?" he asked.

"No," I said.

"He will approach from downwind," he said.

"Yes, Master," I said.

"If you have time," he said, "you are not to rise to your feet, but to throw yourself to the side. You may then rise up and flee." He spoke with an unnatural calmness. His movements with the stone on the blade were smooth and unhurried, but I sensed that every nerve and cell in his body was tense and alive. "I will have the opportunity for only one thrust," he said. The blade was now oriented toward me. Almost directly toward me. "Do you remember the direction in which I sent Tela, and Mina and Cara, from the camp?"

"Yes," I said.

"In that direction lies the camp of Pietro Vacchi," he said. "It will also, of course, bring you to the Viktel Aria."

"Master!" I said.

"Do you understand?" he asked.

"Yes," I whispered.

"Remember that there is no freedom or escape for you on this world. You are merely a collared slave. It is my advice, accordingly, that you submit yourself as soon as possible to the first man, or men, you think are capable of defending you. If you are caught, on the other hand, you might be considered a runaway, and be forced to bear the grievous consequences of such a foolish indiscretion."

"I am a slave," I said. "I do not want to be free."

"You will not be," he said.

"I am afraid," I said, "terribly afraid."

"Do not be afraid," he said. "He is not coming."

"Oh, Master," I breathed, joyously, "Master!" I felt incredible relief. My entire body relaxed. I leaned forward, toward him, toward my master.

Almost at the same instant I heard a sudden, bestial, deafening, screaming roar behind me and the movement of a huge body and my master was leaping to his feet lunging over the fire thrusting his sword into the darkness behind me over my head and I twisted and saw two great, hairy arms outstretched reaching for him, which closed about him, and I screamed, the body and jaws of the thing over me, I between it and my master, and I threw myself to the side.

In an instant I turned, wildly, on all fours, and, in the half darkness, the fire muchly struck and scattered, tiny flames about, from fiery brands and flaring leaves, saw two shapes, a gigantic bestial shape, and that of a human being, a man, locked together, swaying, clawed feet and sandals moving in the dirt, struggling for leverage and position.

My master had said it was not coming, but how could he have known that, I now realized, at that particular time, without even looking up? No, he had known it was coming. When he had said that it had seemed, in my relief, that the entire physiology and tone of my body had changed. Perhaps this had suggested to the beast, by sight, and perhaps even by smell, that its presence was undetected, unsuspected, that we were unready, that we thought ourselves safe, that that was the moment to attack. Naturally it would wish to dispose of the man first. I, a female, unarmed and naked, if it were interested in me at all, could be left for later. I had even leaned forward, happily, clearing the path to him.

The two forms seemed very still now, near the remains of the fire, standing, hardly moving.

"Tuka," called my master, throatedly.

"Yes, Master!" I cried.

"Your permission to flee," he said, speaking the words one at a time, slowly, "is revoked."

"Yes, Master!" I cried elatedly.

I saw the long, hairy arms of the gigantic beast slowly relaxing their grasp on my master's body. The tunic was torn from his back. I did not know if he could stand without the support of the beast.

"Build up the fire," he said. His voice seemed strangely full and resonant. But, too, it seemed he could hardly speak.

I hurried to gather the scattered brands, and other wood, and thrust them to the fire. I attended also to the few remaining tiny flares of flame about, those left from the scattering of the fire. It was not difficult to extinguish these.I scattered some and heaped dirt on others. Some I stamped out.

Approaching the fire with an armful of sticks, from the pile to one side, gathered earlier in the woods by Tupita and myself, I saw the eyes of the beast turned upon me. I do not know if it understood what it saw. They seemed expressionless. It was still on its feet. From its chest there protruded the handle of a sword. It had been halted from further penetration by its guard. It had been, the force compounded by its own charge, driven through the body. My master stood back a bit, his tunic in shreds upon his back. His arms were bloody. His chest was bloody, too, though I think from the blood of the beast. He was trembling. The beast then sat down, back on its haunches, by the now built-up fire. It shook its head and bit at the fur on its arm, as though grooming itself. It then, slowly, lay down. The handle of the sword rose an inch or so, then, showing the blade, as the beast lay back. The point had apparently entered the dirt behind it, but, too, in virtue of this resistance, the blade itself, pressed up, emerged slightly from the body. The beast reached to the handle of the sword with its large hands, or paws, with those six, tentaclelike digits. They touched the handle but could not close about it. It then put its arms down, to the sides. Blood was at its mouth, and chest, from around the blade.

My master looked at me. He was breathing heavily. He was visibly shaken.

"Lie across it," he said, "on your back, with your head down."

Swiftly I put the sticks on the fire and lay across the beast, on my back, my head down. I was terrified. It was still alive. I could feel the heat of its body, its breathing, its blood on my back. My master's weapon was still in the beast. It was near my waist, as I lay, on my left. He was breathing heavily. He looked down at me. He then suddenly, rudely, fiercely, not sparing me, thrust apart my knees. We were alive, the two of us! We had survived! "Master!" I cried, impaled by, and submitting to, the beauty, the glory, the surgency of his eager, claimant, merciless, rejoicing manhood. And it was thus he took the slave, who was his, putting her to his pleasure on the body of the beast. This act, in its emotional power, its significance and complexity, was indescribable. It was an act of assertive aggressiveness, of vitality, of joy, of significance. It was a release from the fear of death, it was a thanksgiving for fate and fortune, it was an affirmation of life, it was the cry of a wild verr in the mountains, the leaping of a fish in the sea, the roar of the larl, the hiss of the sleen, the scream of a tarn in the sky. Only to those who have been closest to death is the value of life most clear.

He then, gently, drew me from the beast. He kissed me, and held me to him.

"Tomorrow we will leave the camp," he said.

"It was for this that you were waiting?" I asked.

"Yes," he said.

"It is dead," I said.

"Yes," he said.

He then drew his sword from the body of the beast, and cleaned it on its fur.

"You did not choose to leave an enemy behind you," I said.

"Nor did he," he said.

"Would it have followed you?" I asked.

"Yes," he said.

"You knew that it was about," I said, "because of the dust on the others, those in the meadow, their burial."

"I thought it would linger," he said. "The dust, of course, convinced me that my conjecture was correct."

"You seem to know something of these things," I said, shuddering.

"A little," he said.

"What is to be done now?" I asked.

"I shall take it to the meadow, and put it with the others," he said, "burying it, as it did them, with a handful of dust. After that there is the matter of the rites, of suitable purifications."

"It is only a beast," I said to him.

"No," he said, "it is more than a beast."

I looked at him.

"It was of the People," he said.

"Yes, Master," I said.

"Remain here," he said.

"Yes, Master," I said.

34 / Love

"Master well knows how to use a slave," I gasped. "Will he not be merciful with me? What does he want of me? I am only a slave! Must he drive me mad with passion?"

"Be silent," he grumbled.

I twisted helplessly in the love chains. I jerked helplessly against them, the rings cutting into my ankles, pulling against my wrists. There are many varieties of such chains. These were simple and had been earlier taken from the wagon box of the slave wagon, the lid of which forms the wagoner's bench, part of the loot which my master had divided between himself and Mirus. Each consisted of a wrist ring and an ankle ring, joined by about ten inches of chain. My left wrist had been attached to my left ankle, my right wrist to my right ankle. I was on my back. A chain was also on my neck. It fastened me to a nearby tree, a yard or so from our blankets.

"You danced well, earlier," he said.

"Master!" I gasped. "Master!"

His tongue was incredible, so gentle, so subtle and yet so persuasive, so forceful, so irresistible.

"You are a hot slave," he commented.

Hot! I was flaming, and helpless!

He drew back a bit, amused.

Quickly I lifted myself piteously, suppliantly, to him.

"Is this how the women of Earth behave?" he asked.

"I am no longer of Earth," I said. "I am of Gor, and a slave! Be merciful, I beg it, to a helplessly aroused slave!"

He chuckled, the beast, at my discomfiture, and helplessness, and need!

"Please, please!" I begged.

"You are far from Earth now, and your library, slave," he said.

"Yes, Master! Yes, Master!" I said. "Please, please, Master!" I lifted myself to him in mute petition.

How he relished the power he held over me!

"Oh, yes!" I cried, as his tongue again touched me. It had been a tiny, subtle touch, and yet, as he doubtless knew, from my distraught condition, it had brought me to the point where my response was totally within his power and I must beg. "Please, Master!" I whimpered.

"Do you beg?" he asked.

"Yes, Master!" I said.

"Who begs?" he asked.

"Tuka, the slave of Teibar of Ar, begs!" I moaned.

Again his tongue touched me and I threw back my head and screamed with joy jerking against the chains. "Oh!" I cried. "Oh!" I shuddered, and thrashed and gasped. Then I lay quiet in his chains, looking up at him in wonder, in gratitude. I was his. My entire body was rich in the memory of what he had done to me, in one sense what he had made me beg for, in another sense what he had forced me to endure.

"I am yours," I said.

"That is known to me," he said. He then touched me again, this time gently, with his hand.

Again I looked up at him, helplessly.

"You are mine to caress," he said.

"Yes, my master," I whispered. Then he made me cry out, softly, and then turned me to my belly on the blankets, and lifted me to him. Then he permitted me to lie on my side, and I tried to kiss at his body.

"You are a grateful slave," he said.

"Yes, Master," I said.

"And a passionate one," he said.

"Yes, Master!" I said.

"Where are the severe garments of the librarian?" he asked. He referred doubtless to the long-sleeved blouse, the dark sweater, the severe skirt, the low-heeled shoes, such things.

"I do not know, Master," I said.

"And where, too, now, is that librarian?" he asked.

"She who was that librarian," I said, "is here, but she is now only a naked slave, and she begs to kiss her master."

"She may do so," he informed me.

In a time, then, again, he aroused, he seized me and rose to his knees, and held me, he kneeling, I kneeling, and then he thrust me back, and my head was down, and he lifted me up, to him, he kneeling, and he then again, I so helpless, hanging back and down, put me imperiously to his pleasure.

"I did well to pick you out on Earth," he cried.

"Yes, Master!" I wept, loving and ravished, helpless and yielding, a slave, in his hands.

He then put me gently to my back and I looked up at him, in awe and love.

"You are a treasure," he said.

"A treasure," I laughed, "that may be purchased for something in the neighborhood of five silver tarsks!"

"Not from me," he said. "I would not sell you for a thousand."

"Mirus thought that Tupita was a thousand times more beautiful than I," I said.

"He was wrong," said my master.

"Thank you, Master," I said, pleased.

"She is no more than nine hundred times more beautiful than you," he said.

"Master!" I protested.

"To me," he said, "you are a thousand, thousand times more beautiful than she."

"Thank you, Master!" I purred.

"Kneel," he said.

I struggled to my knees.

"Do you know what time it is?" he asked.

"Late," I said.

"Are you chained?" he asked.

"Of course, Master," I said. I wore his love chains, and the chain on my neck fastening me to the nearby tree.

"Whose chains are they?" he asked.

"Yours, of course, Master," I said.

"It is past midnight," he said.

"Ah!" I said. When the recovery period pertinent to the collar of Ionicus had expired, I had been in the power of Teibar of Ar. Indeed, I had been literally wearing his chains. The legalities of simple slave claim, based on active proprietorship, had now superseded, with respect to that collar, the rights contestable by the sword under which I had hitherto been held, those of sword claim.

"Perhaps I will put love chains on you again," he said. "You serve well in them."

"Thank you, Master," I said. It was indeed my hope that he would do so again, and, indeed, put me in many different bonds, which, in their various ways, for various reasons, both physical and psychological, influence and condition the responses of the female.

He then removed the love chains from me, and tossed them to the side, among his things. He then, too, freed the neck chain from the tree, and then, in a moment, from my neck as well. He tossed the chain to the side, so that it lay with the love chains, among his things. He then lay back on the blankets, with his hands under his head. He looked up, at the moons. I knelt beside him.

"I am not chained," I said.

He was silent.

"Are you not afraid I will escape?" I asked.

"No," he said.

"Do you want me to promise that I will not run away?" I asked.

"No," he said.

"A slave may not lie," I said. "She is not a free woman." Interestingly, on Gor, as on Earth, morality, for the most part, was not required of free women. They might do much what they pleased. On the other hand, slaves had no such liberties at their disposal. As they are owned, such things as honesty and truthfulness are required of them. Indeed, it is commonly expected of the Gorean master that he will take steps to significantly improve the moral character of his slave.

"Enter the blankets," he said. "Pull them up about us. The evening is cool."

"Perhaps I will try to escape," I said.

"Do you think it would be wise to attempt to escape from a Gorean master?" he asked.

"No, Master," I said, frightened.

"And do you think it would be wise to attempt to escape from Teibar of Ar?"

"No, Master!" I said.

"Lie down, here," he said.

"There?" I asked. "Beside you?"

"Yes," he said. "Why?"

"I thought you might chain me at your feet, sleeping me there, like a sleen," I said.

"Perhaps later," he said.

I snuggled up, against him. How huge and mighty seemed his body, that of this magnificent, primitive male, on this barbaric, beautiful world, and how small and soft I seemed next to it.

"Master," I said.

"Yes," he said.

"You told me earlier, at the fire, that 'he' was not coming," I said. "This relieved my anxieties. It assuaged my fear. I relaxed. I even bent forward."

"Yes," he said.

"You used me to lure the beast in, to the attack," I said. "You tricked me. You used me without my knowledge. You used me without taking me into your confidence. You used me as a slave!"

"Yes," he said.

But, of course, I thought to myself, he had used me as a slave. I was a slave!

"Master," I said.

"Yes," he said.

"Tela would seek out Aulus, overseer of the work camp of Ionicus, near Venna. She is his love slave. Do you think she found him?"

"It is possible," he said. "I do not know."

"But Ionicus owns her," I said.

"If the fellow Aulus is the overseer," said my master, "he is doubtless empowered to buy and sell slaves from the chain. Thus, if he wants her, it would not be difficult for him to purchase her. Probably no more would be required than the transfer of a sum between accounts."

"But what if she did not come into his power?" I asked.

"Then," he said, "she has presumably been transported elsewhere, carried away in the chains of another, to a different fate, presumably never to see him again. She is, after all, only a slave."

"Yes, Master," I said. I was frightened. How much we were at the mercy of our masters! We were only slaves!

"Master," I said.

"Yes," he said.

"I am your slave," I said. "I am owned by you. You have total power over me."

"Yes?" he said.

"Will you be gentle with me, and kind to me?" I asked.

"You are a slave," he said. "You will be treated precisely as it pleases me to treat you."

"Am I to be permitted clothing?" I asked.

"Only if it pleases me," he said.

"Am I to be often whipped?" I asked.

"When may a slave be whipped?" he asked.

"Whenever a master pleases," I said.

"That, then," he said, "is when you will be whipped, whenever a master pleases."

"Yes, Master," I said. "Forgive me, Master."

"You are a cuddly slut," he said.

"Thank you, Master," I said.

"You are very female," he said.

"Thank you, Master," I said.

"Are there many women like you on Earth?" he asked.

"I suppose so, Master," I said. "I do not know."

"It is incredible that there should be any," he said, "given the depth and extensiveness of the masculinist conditioning programs to which they are subjected, the values they are trained to accept, the seeking of which is reinforced, the models they are encouraged to emulate, the images which are held forth for them to fulfill, the manifold enticements and rewards offered for male surrogation, the contempt in which love and service, and biological womanhood, are held. It is as though all the forces of communication, education and law had gone insane, with no better objective than to bring the sexes to ruin, destroy the human gene pool and doom the species."

"Only there, Master," I said. "Not here."

"How is it that a woman like you should have come from such a place?" he asked.

"I am sure there are thousands, perhaps millions, like me," I said. "I think it must be the case that all women, at least when they are alone, know the truth, if only in their bellies."

"Perhaps," he said.

"You have done slaving on Earth," I said. "Apparently you find us not unattractive."

"True," he said.

"Once collared, do we not prove satisfactory?" I asked.

"You would be well whipped, did you not," he said.

"Even so!" I said.

"Yes," he said. "It is true."

"Freed, we will destroy you, and then ourselves," I said. "Kept in collars, we will worship you, and serve you well."

"Perhaps I will have you write your story, in English," he said.

"But who could read it, here?" I asked.

"I have been to Earth," he said. "I have seen works there dealing with my world."

I looked at him, startled.

"Yes," he said.

"But how could they know?" I asked. "How could such things get to Earth?"

"I am not sure," he said. "I think perhaps they are put on the platforms outside the palisade of the Sardar Mountains, for Priest-Kings. Then perhaps the Priest-Kings see that they reach Earth."

"I do not think there are such things as Priest-kings," I said.

"Some people," he said, "do not believe the beasts exist."

"Do such exist on Earth?" I asked.

"I think some," he said, "probably exiles, and the offspring of exiles, marooned criminals, beached on a foreign world, degenerate scions of the People, and such."

"Where?" I asked.

"In lonely areas," he said, "the mountains of Asia, the forests of the Pacific Northwest, and such."

"If such works exist," I said, "then some women must know that there is such a world as Gor."

"Or that there might be such a world," he said. "Did you know of it?"

"No!" I said. "Do they know that such slaving occurs?"

"Some, perhaps," he said. "On the other hand, such books are generally regarded as fiction. It is better that way, don't you think?"

"I don't know," I said, frightened. I touched my right hand to my breasts, so soft, and my left hand to my collar. I was now a Gorean slave. Would it have been better on Earth if I had known such things were possible, or had it been better if, as in my case, I had not even suspected their possibility? I did not know. But, in any event, I was now here, and in a collar.

"We will leave in the morning," he said.

I wondered what sort of man he was, this magnificent, formidable brute to whom I now belonged.

He had not even given me clothing!

"Master keeps his girl naked," I pouted.

"Sometimes a bit of clothing looks well on a female," he said, "if it is sufficiently revealing, and can be swiftly removed, or torn away."

"Master?" I asked.

"For example," he said, "some of the lingerie, as you call it, with which you Earth females delight to secretly bedeck yourselves, concealing it beneath the camouflage of your prescribed habiliments."

"I am no longer an Earth female," I said, kissing him.

"Such garments," he said, "though perhaps too indecent for the streets or market place a Gorean master might require of his slave in the privacy of his own quarters."

"Yes, Master," I said.

"—if he permitted her clothing, at all," he added.

"You took away my slave strip, and my belt of rolled cloth,"

I said. "They were almost nothing, but they were all I had to cover myself."

"That was in accord with my decision," he said, "that for the time being, at least, you will be kept naked."

"I shall be proud to walk naked behind you, on the road," I said.

"My pack is not heavy," he said.

"I shall carry it?" I asked.

"Yes," he said. "Of course."

"May I ask where we are going?" I asked.

"I am going to my small villa, deserted now, in the hills northeast of Ar," he said. "You will simply follow, as my draft animal."

"Does master have other slaves?" I asked, apprehensively.

"You will learn," he said.

I moaned.

"No," he laughed.

I cried out with pleasure, and kissed him, happily, in relief. "I will be a thousand slaves to you!" I said.

"Yes," he said. "You will. I will see to it."

"Yes, Master," I said, happily. I kissed him, again, delightedly.

"At my villa, too," he said, "I will decide whether I will keep you or sell you."

"Master!" I protested.

"Perhaps you will endeavor to be such that I will decide to keep you," he said.

"Master may be assured that I will do my best," I said. "I shall earnestly endeavor to be pleasing to him in all respects!"

"I think you will like the villa," he said. "It is not large, but it is, I think, quite lovely. It is white, with a small court, and stuccoed walls. There is a porch which overlooks a little valley. It is quiet and secluded. It has a lovely setting, hidden in the hills. I withdraw there, from time to time."

"I shall endeavor to serve master well there," I said.

"In such a place, too," he said, "it might not be inappropriate to have a slave write her story."

"Do you wish to have me do so, Master?" I asked.

"I have not decided," he said.

"In the first house of my slavery," I said, "I was given a series of injections. I am curious about them. Were they innoculations against diseases?"

"I know those you mean," he said. "No, they were the stabilization serums. We give them even to slaves."

"What are they?" I asked.

"You do not know?" he asked.

"No," I said.

"They are a discovery of the caste of physicians," he said. "They work their effects on the body."

"What is their purpose?" I asked.

"Is there anything in particular which strikes you generally, statistically, about the population of Gor?" he asked.

"Their vitality, their health, their youth," I said.

"Those are consequences of the stabilization serums," he said.

"I do not understand," I said.

"You will retain your youth and beauty, curvaceous slave," he said. "That is the will of masters."

"I do not understand," I said, frightened.

"Ageing," he said, "is a physical process, like any other. It is, accordingly, accessible to physical influences. To be sure, it is a subtle and complex process. It took a thousand years to develop the stabilization serums. Our physicians regarded ageing as a disease, the drying, withering disease, and so attacked it as a disease. They did not regard it as, say, a curse, or a punishment, or something inalterable or inexplicable, say, as some sort of destined, implacable fatality. No. They regarded it as a physical problem, susceptible to physical approaches. Some five hundred years ago, they developed the first stabilization serums."

"How could I ever pay for such a thing!" I gasped.

"There is no question of payment," he said. "They are given to you as an animal, a slave."

"Master," I whispered, awed.

"Do not fret," he said. "In the case of a woman from Earth, like yourself, they are not free."

"Master?" I asked.

He took my collar in both hands, and moved it in such a way that I could feel how sturdily, and obdurately, it was locked on my neck. "For a woman such as you," he said, "their price is the collar."

"Yes, Master," I said. The serums, in that sense, did indeed have their price. We paid for them with the collar. It was with a strange feeling that I realized that even if I did not wish it so, even if I vehemently desired otherwise, my youth and beauty would continue to remain fresh and lovely for Gorean masters. Not even for it was there an escape! It, too, was "collared."

I shuddered, considering the effects of the stabilization serums.

"What is wrong?" he asked.

"Nothing, Master," I said. I scarcely dared to cope with even the thought of the serums. I had not understood their effects. Perhaps my master was mistaken! I must think of other things!

"Master," I said.

"Yes," he said.

"You seemed to be familiar with the beasts," I said. "Were you once associated with them?"

"Yes," he said.

"Are you associated with them any longer?" I asked.

"No," he said.

"Are the beasts," I asked, "involved in the slaving?"

"In a way, yes," he said. "They provide, for the most part, the means for conducting the trade."

"The trade?" I asked.

"The slave trade," he said.

"Of course, Master," I said.

"Do not grow arrogant at the thought of the stabilization serums," he said.

"Arrogant?" I asked.

"Yes," he said. "Keep clearly in mind that regardless of their value or benefits from your point of view, they have other consequences as well. For example, you will continue to be of interest to masters, you will continue to excite them, you will continue to be the sort of woman they want for their collars and chains. As you remain as you are, so soft, so lovely, so attractive and desirable, you must expect to continue to face the risks and perils attendant on your beauty, on a world such as this, where it is a common mode of currency, a familiar means of exchange, where it may be used to bribe traitors, and be given to heroes as a reward, where it is a prize for courage and audacity, where it may count as tribute to conquerors, where it can be used to bargain for cities and states, and where it is bought and sold in markets."

"Yes, Master," I whispered. Perhaps I was a terrible person, but I did not mind the thought of being exciting and beautiful. Perhaps it was fitting then that I be punished with bondage.

"You are a beautiful slave," he said.

"Thank you, Master," I said.

I wondered if my master was weak. Some men are very strong with men, and yet weak with their women. He had just said I was beautiful. That was surely a compliment. Surely it indicated some interest in me, or approval of me, surely in at least one respect. He had said I was beautiful. Could I not then, though it was I who was in a collar, make use of his feelings to own him?

Too, he had followed me for months, over thousands of pasangs. He must like me then, at least a little. That seemed likely. Indeed, he must care for me. I suspected that perhaps he even loved me. Perhaps I could make use of that. I wondered if he was weak. It would not hurt to test him. I knew that some girls twisted their masters about their little fingers. I wondered if I could do that. "Master," I said.

"Yes," he said.

"I am not a common Gorean girl," I said. "You know that I am from Earth."

He was silent.

"We are going to leave the camp tomorrow," I said. "I would like to have some clothing. I could make a tunic from a blanket, as Tupita did."

"Had you not heard my decision, announced to you earlier," he inquired, "that you were to be kept naked?"

"Yes, Master," I said. "But I do not wish to be kept so. I would like some clothing. Perhaps you could change your mind."

He was silent.

"I would kiss you very well," I said, "if you would give me some clothing."

"For a highly intelligent woman," he said, "you are inutterably stupid."

"Master?" I asked.

"Perhaps it is your femaleness," he said.

"Master?" I asked.

"Kiss me now, with perfection, or die," he said.

"Yes, Master!" I said.

"Swallow," he said.

I did so, terrified.

"I wondered how you might behave," he said, "if I gave you even a hort of room, even an Ihn of indulgence."

"Master!" I wept.

But he had then seized my wrists and, with a thong, bound them together, before my body. He then dragged me toward a low-hanging branch and tied my hands, so bound, over my head to the branch. "No, Master!" I cried. "Please, Master!" He then whipped me. He then, angrily, released me from the branch, I blubbering and weeping, half in shock, and dragged me back to the blankets. There he threw me to the foot of the blankets and chained me there, hand and foot. I looked up at him, in terror. Then, angrily, he lay down on the blankets, drawing them about himself, to sleep. "Master," I begged, "may I speak!"

"No," he said.

I lay there in misery until morning. He was my master. I loved him! I loved him more than anything! But I had failed my first test with him! I had only wanted to know, foolishly, the nature of my power with him, if any, and the nature of the discipline to which I might be subject. I had only wanted to know if, truly, I was his slave or not. Then he had made me serve him, uncompromisingly. Then he had whipped me and put me chained, at his feet. The library was indeed faraway, and I was indeed his slave! I had asked earlier if I was not to be slept at his feet, as might be a sleen, and he had said, "Perhaps later." Why had I not understood then that my behavior was under scrutiny, that he was even then inquiring into the qualities and nature of me? I was in misery, and overcome with contrition. How badly I had behaved! I had failed my first test with my master, whom I loved! Yet, too, I felt grandly and warmly reassured as to his strength and dominance. I knew then my master was master, that he would never relinquish his sovereignty, that he was a true man. I was content now, and eager, a female, to be his perfect slave. If I had failed his test, he had passed mine. To be sure, I was aware that there might be continuing penalties attached to my having displeased him. I wanted so to sleep next to him, or at his thigh, but instead, now, I might indefinitely be slept at his feet, as a sleen or dog, or as less, as a female slave. But I would rejoice to be even so near to him! Too, perhaps I might be often whipped. I did not know. Too, perhaps, now, I would be indefinitely denied clothing. All such things, of course were within the will of Teibar of Ar, my master. A little before morning, I fell asleep. When I awakened I discovered that a blanket had been put over me.

"Master," I said. "I beg forgiveness."

He bent over me and removed the chains. Swiftly, tears in my eyes, I knelt before him. I then, unbidden, contritely, timidly, lovingly, kneeling before him, kissed him, serving him with all the sweetness, delicacy and perfections I could. I then swallowed, and looked up at him, hoping to find some particle of forgiveness or kindness in his eyes.

"Cook," he said.

"Yes, Master," I said.

In less than an Ahn I knelt beside his pack. He looked about the camp, and extinguished the fire. He kicked dirt over its remains. He then turned about, and looked at me. To my surprise, he seemed amused. "Did you satisfy your curiosity last night, Tuka?" he asked.

"Yes, Master," I said.

He had realized then, well enough, what I had been doing! Could I have no secrets from such a man? Was I so open to him then, in my mind, as well as, by his decision, in my beauty?

"And have you learned your lesson?" he asked.

"Yes, Master," I said.

"Speak," he said.

"I have learned my lesson, Master," I said.

"Well," he said, "your ears are pierced, so you are not all bad."

"I am pleased," I said, "if even by such a small thing I may please my master."

"We shall get you some earrings," he said, "but they will not be valuable ones, for you are a low slave."

"Yes, Master," I said.

"Too," he said, "we would not want you stolen for the value of your earrings."

"No, Master," I said, smiling.

"You are dangerous," he said. "One might grow fond of you."

"Master!" I breathed.

He then walked over to where I knelt, crouched down, opened his pack and reached within it. He took out a tiny handful of scarlet silk, and opened it.

"Master!" I cried.

It was the tiny garment, fit for a muchly displayed slave, which I had made for myself on Earth, long before I had known there was a Gor, or a Teibar, or the possibility of a collar.

"It is perhaps a bit too lengthy," he said, looking at it, "and it could be slit at the sides, and the neckline could be cut more deeply, and it is not diaphanous, or is insufficiently diaphanous, but still it is a not unattractive garment. Perhaps, sometime, if I decide to permit you clothing, at least for an Ahn or so, I will see again how it looks on you." He had seen me in it once before, of course, at the library, when I had knelt before captors. The existence of that tiny garment among my things, in my apartment, of course, had shown them that I was a slave, though at that time one not yet fittingly imbonded.

"You brought it from Earth!" I said. "You did not destroy it there!"

"Perhaps from time to time in the villa," he said, "I will let you wear it, or less, when you serve me."

"I love you," I said. "I love you!"

He put the silk away.

"I love you!" I said.

"There is something else, too," he said.

"Master?" I asked.

He reached again into the pack. "Do you recognize these?" he asked.

"Oh, Master!" I said, softly, delightedly.

"They are the thong and bells which you wore at the library, when you danced," he said.

"Yes, Master!" I said.

"Perhaps you remember, too," he said, "that we kept them on you when you were naked there, in the darkness, to help us keep track of you."

"Yes, Master!" I said.

"Such things make useful adornments to a female slave," he said, "and help to mark her movements."

"Yes, Master!" I said. I remembered that when I had been placed on the library table, long ago, prior to having the rubberized mask placed over my face, through which the chemicals had been put which had forced me to unconsciousness, the silk, which had been being used as a gag, a mnemonic device reminding me I must be silent, had been drawn from my mouth and put to the side. The bells, too, I recalled, had been placed upon it. He had kept them both, both the silk and the bells!

"Perhaps, from time to time, you shall wear them, too, at the villa," he said.

"Yes, Master!" I said, delightedly. How rightful it seemed that I should serve him in such things, here on Gor, even from Earth.

He put the bells away.

He then removed the whip from his pack, and held it to my lips, and I kissed it.

He then put the whip away, inserting it into the pack. He then rose to his feet and walked a few feet away, to the edge of the camp, and then turned and regarded me.

I stood up, and shouldered his pack. It was not heavy. In it I could feel some chains. Some of them I had worn. In it, too, was the whip, his, to which I was subject. I heard, too, within the pack, the tiny sound of the bells, here, on Gor, slave bells.

"I love you, Master!" I said. "I love you, my Master!"

He shrugged.

"Master," I said.

"Yes," he said.

"Am I to be permitted to tell what has happened to me?" I asked. "Am I to write my story?"

"I do not know," he said. "I do not know if it is good for the women of Earth to know of these things or not."

I was silent. I did not know either.

"What would you like to do?" he asked.

"I?" I asked, startled.

"Yes," he said.

"I think I would like to tell my sisters on Earth," I said.

"Do you think they will believe you?" he asked.

"No," I said.

"Would you, before you learned what you now know, have believed it?"

"No," I said.

"They will not believe you, certainly not most of them," he said.

"That is all right," I said. "I do not care. I do not even think that is really important. Perhaps that is best. I do not know. But what is important, I think, is to say these things."

"Perhaps," he said.

"And so, Master," I asked, "am I to be permitted to write my story?"

"Perhaps," he said. "I am not sure. I have, as yet, no firm thoughts on the matter."

"Yes, Master," I said.

"I have not yet decided," he said.

"Yes, Master," I said.

He then turned about and walked a few paces from the camp. I stood there, naked, a brand on my thigh, a collar on my neck, bearing his pack. I wondered if the women of Earth would believe my story. I supposed not. But then, too, what did it matter? Perhaps it was better that they not believe it. Their life, then, would surely be easier, knowing that there was no world such as Gor, no collars for them, no masters such that they must be uncompromisingly served. But in any event, dear sisters, whether you long for the collar, or fear it, it is real.

He turned about. "Follow me," he said, in Gorean. It took me a moment to make the transition from English to Gorean. Then I said, "Yes, my Master," in Gorean, and, at a suitable distance, naked, bearing his pack, followed him from the woods. We would go to the Viktel Aria and travel south. He had a villa, northeast of Ar, in the hills.